North Side Story

A Novel

Randee Mack

This is a work of fiction. Names, characters, places, and incidents either are the product of the author's imagination or are used fictitiously. Any resemblance to actual persons, living or dead, events, or locales is entirely coincidental.

Copyright © 2023 by Randee Mack

All rights reserved. No part of this book may be reproduced or used in any manner without written permission of the copyright owner except for the use of quotations in a book review.

First paperback edition May 2023

ISBN 979-8-3949-4680-6

To all whose dreams go on forever…

CONTENTS

Chapter 1.	We Gotta Get You a Woman	1
Chapter 2.	Halloween Party	7
Chapter 3.	The Devils	17
Chapter 4.	The Victims Commiserate	22
Chapter 5.	The Alley Cats	28
Chapter 6.	Discontent	32
Chapter 7.	The Breakup	38
Chapter 8.	The Girl in White	45
Chapter 9.	Thank You For…	48
Chapter 10.	Getting to Know You	57
Chapter 11.	Back to Reality	68
Chapter 12.	Balancing Act	76
Chapter 13.	The Plan	80
Chapter 14.	Sorting It Out	82
Chapter 15.	The Jewelry Store	85
Chapter 16.	The Heist	92
Chapter 17.	Preparing to Meet the Enemy	97
Chapter 18.	Shannon's Bad Day	101
Chapter 19.	Mandey's Friday Night	112
Chapter 20.	Shannon's Friday Night	120
Chapter 21.	First Date	123
Chapter 22.	Happy Birthday	128
Chapter 23.	The Honor Society	141
Chapter 24.	A Huge Disappointment	151
Chapter 25.	Looking for Trouble	154
Chapter 26.	Party Prep	164
Chapter 27.	Brotherly Love	170
Chapter 28.	Jackie's Party	175
Chapter 29.	The Devils' Party	187

Chapter 30.	A Risk and a Warning	194
Chapter 31.	Regret	202
Chapter 32.	Double Date	204
Chapter 33.	Project Partners	212
Chapter 34.	Family Dinner	217
Chapter 35.	Thanksgiving	219
Chapter 36.	The Lovers Quarrel	228
Chapter 37.	Watch 'Em Burn	236
Chapter 38.	Burning Again	248
Chapter 39.	Just in Case	251
Chapter 40.	Rules of Engagement	255
Chapter 41.	Too Much All at Once	260
Chapter 42.	The Rumble	264
Chapter 43.	Reconciliation	279
Chapter 44.	Avoidance Strategy	283
Chapter 45.	Introductions	297
Chapter 46.	Reckoning	304
Chapter 47.	A Little Good News	315
Chapter 48.	Christmas Concert	317
Chapter 49.	The Christmas Dance	322
Chapter 50.	Shannon's Doubts	331
Chapter 51.	Confrontation	340
Chapter 52.	A Visit with the Parole Officer	347
Chapter 53.	Christmas Party	353
Chapter 54.	Almost	362
Chapter 55.	Christmas	369
Chapter 56.	Sick	385
Chapter 57.	New Year's Eve	390
Chapter 58.	Annette's Announcement	394

Chapter 59.	A Visit to the Principal's Office	399
Chapter 60.	Mid-Term Tension	405
Chapter 61.	The Unthinkable	410
Chapter 62.	A Waking Nightmare	419
Chapter 63.	Jail	426
Chapter 64.	The News	428
Chapter 65.	Another Visit with the Parole Officer	437
Chapter 66.	Valentine's Day	439
Chapter 67.	Worried and Discouraged	442
Chapter 68.	The Truth Will Set You Free	444
Chapter 69.	Taking the Initiative	448
Chapter 70.	Mandey and Annette	452
Chapter 71.	SS, DD	458
Chapter 72.	Mandey and Annette, Part II	461
Chapter 73.	Powerless	466
Chapter 74.	Spring Break	469
Chapter 75.	Girls Night In	474
Chapter 76.	Brunch and a Breakthrough	477
Chapter 77.	Patience for the Process	487
Chapter 78.	Reunion	491
Chapter 79.	Adjusting to the New Normal	495
Chapter 80.	The Dress	501
Chapter 81.	Prom	504
Chapter 82.	After the Prom	517
Chapter 83.	Two Weeks	524
Chapter 84.	Number 18	526
Chapter 85.	Meet the Parents	541
Chapter 86.	Graduation	547
Chapter 87.	The End of Their Beginning	554

1

We Gotta Get You a Woman

It was a warm day on Memorial Day weekend. The sky was clear blue with the occasional fluffy white cloud drifting by. Shannon was out on the stairs that led up to the second floor of his apartment building, listening to "Fly like an Eagle" by the Steve Miller Band, loud, on his portable radio, feeling unapologetic about the fact that it wasn't the type of music the people in this neighborhood liked. It was a good day to be outside. It would have been a nice day for a bike ride, if Leon hadn't been drunk and driven over it where it was parked in the yard back at the old house. It would have been nice to go somewhere on picnic, or to the beach, but he was stuck there.

He was sixteen-and-a-half that day, could pass for twenty, felt a hundred, and he was still a virgin. He was dwelling on what happened between him and Kerri, or more accurately, what didn't happen. It was nerve-wracking, trying to do it for the first time with a girl who had a lot of experience. When he became flustered, she laughed at him. As he continued his clumsy overtures, she yelled at him. It had killed his hard-on, as well as the courage he had been trying to build up for the last month.

He wasn't prepared to embarrass himself again, so the following night, when she tried to initiate sex, he had pretended he was tired. That had enraged her. He blew up at her in return and kicked her out of his room.

Then he saw her yesterday with Raff, who was doing what Shannon hadn't. They saw him standing there, looking at them, and they hadn't stopped. He turned and forced himself to walk, not run, away, although the humiliation was almost more than he could bear. He wondered what Kerri was telling everybody about him. Shannon thought that maybe that would be too humiliating for her to admit that a guy wouldn't (or couldn't) do her. She was probably saying he was awful in bed.

His eyes were opened. She was beautiful, but she was ugly. He wanted nothing more to do with her. He had wasted three weeks thinking she wanted to be his girl, thinking she was worth having as his girl. He thought maybe it was good Kerri wasn't the type who could stick to one guy; she was so mean, she probably couldn't hold on to one for longer than a couple weeks, anyway.

Shannon was so lost in his thoughts that he did not see John approaching until he was right in front of him.

"Yo, Shannon," John greeted him, sitting down on the stairs next to him.

Shannon turned down the radio. "Hey, John," he replied half-heartedly.

"Man, you look down," John said. "What the hell could be wrong on a day like this?"

Plenty, Shannon thought.

"It's Kerri, ain't it?" John asked. "I heard you caught her and Raff doing the nasty. Man, I tried to warn you; she ain't cut out to stick to one guy. She stayed with you for three weeks. I think that's a record for her."

Shannon didn't say anything. This was not a subject he wanted to discuss with John or anyone else.

"To, be honest, Kerri ain't that great," John said. "Sometimes you've got to force her to do it the way you like it. Of course, forcing it on a girl's exciting, but damn, sometimes you just want to say, 'Get on your knees and suck it, bitch,' without her bitching and moaning."

I don't want to hear this, Shannon thought.

"I tell you, if I was a rich man, you know what I'd do? I'd get myself a whole harem of whores," John said.

"Why would you do that?" Shannon asked.

"Because," John said, "with a whore, you can get anything you want for the right price. Sure, there's ones that have their limits, but if you look hard enough, you can always find one who'll give you whatever you want, if you're willing to pay. It's a business deal. Everyone comes away happy, and no one complains that they didn't get what they wanted."

"You've been to a lot of wh--them?" Shannon asked John, his curiosity piqued. "You're only nineteen."

"They don't care, as long as you look like you've reached puberty. My dad took me to get my cherry popped when I was fifteen. I didn't tell him he was about two years too late."

Shannon looked at John, his eyebrows raised. "Damn," he said.

"Have you ever been with a whore?" John asked him.

Shannon shook his head.

"You want to?"

Shannon shook his head again, but then he shrugged.

"You got twenty bucks on you?"

"Yeah." It was all he had.

"Then come on. I know someone you should meet."

Shannon rode with John to another apartment complex about ten minutes away. Shannon couldn't tell what the place was called because the sign out front looked as if someone had pitched rocks through it.

"I thought they worked at night," Shannon said nervously.

"They do," John said, opening his door, "but they work during the day, too. But this gal ain't a streetwalker. She just turns a few tricks for a little extra money. Are you going to sit here all afternoon, or do you want to get laid?"

Shannon got out of the car. *I don't want to be here,* he thought. *Being a virgin isn't so bad.*

But he couldn't wimp out in front of John unless he wanted to be labeled a limp dick. He followed John over to Apartment 110.

"You stand here and let me do the talking," John said.

John knocked on the door. A short, chubby blonde in denim cut-offs and an overflowing white tube top opened it almost immediately.

"What?" she yelled, then she saw who was there. "Oh, John, I thought you was someone else."

"Tammy, I've got a favor to ask you," John said.

"Oh, Lord," she said, rolling her eyes. "I don't like that word, 'favor.'"

"Just listen," John said, taking her by the arm and going inside. He looked over his shoulder at Shannon. "We'll be right back."

They shut the door. Shannon stood outside, shuffling his feet self-consciously, wondering what John was telling Tammy. Tammy didn't look too bad, he guessed. She looked to be about nineteen or twenty, and she was sort of a short, chubby, not-as-pretty version of Kerri. He supposed it wouldn't matter whether she was a hag or a beauty queen, because he was convinced that he wasn't going to be able to do it. Then Tammy would tell John that his friend was a limp dick who had wasted twenty dollars.

He was sick to his stomach. He decided he would go sit in the car and wait for John, and when John came out, he would tell him he didn't feel good and wanted to do this some other time. But before he even left the doorstep, the door to Apartment 110 opened again.

"Hey, Shannon," Tammy said with a smile.

"For twenty bucks, she's all yours for the next thirty minutes," John said. "I'm going to go get a coke. I'll be back in half an hour. Have fun."

As John walked off, Shannon tried to find the words to tell him to stop and wait for him. Then he felt a hand on his arm, and he looked down at Tammy. Damn, she was short. She didn't even look to be five feet tall. He wondered how in the hell someone his size was supposed to do it with such a short person.

"Come on in," she said, and he allowed himself to be led inside.

She shut the door, and the room became very dim because the curtains were all drawn. She led him through the living room into her bedroom.

"I need the money first," she said.

"Oh. Okay," Shannon said, and reached into his pocket to give her the twenty-dollar bill.

She took the money and put it in a small slot in the top of a locked strongbox on her nightstand. Then she stripped, taking off her tube top, shorts, and string bikini panties.

Shannon stared. Her tits were huge, hanging down almost to her navel. She had stretch marks on her stomach and her hips. She didn't look like Kerri, but he still felt his cock rising.

"Like what you see?" she asked him with a smile.

Shannon nodded.

"Are you going to take your clothes off, or do you need some help?"

"I'm fine," Shannon said quickly, taking off his T-shirt.

Tammy got into bed, laid back, and watched him undress. He wished she wouldn't look at him.

"John said you was kind of a shy one," Tammy said. "I know we just met, but you don't got to be shy. What you look like, whatever kind of sex you like--easy, rough, whatever--it don't make no difference to me."

She reached up and fondled her breasts for him to see, then one hand sneaked under the sheet. She threw back the covers so he could see her playing with herself. All the time she continued to brazenly stare at him, and he found himself compelled to stare back.

When he took his pants off, he was hard. He realized he didn't feel quite as nervous as before. When he got into bed with her, she immediately reached under the covers to grab his cock.

"Mmm, you've got a big dick," she said. "I love tricks with big dicks."

He wondered how the hell he was going to maneuver around without accidentally hurting her. Those tits were everywhere. She had said it didn't matter if he was rough. He didn't intend to be, but if he was, by accident, she probably wouldn't mind.

She sucked on his nipples as she fondled him down below. He closed his eyes and felt the blood pounding in his organ. Shannon reached down to touch those incredibly big breasts of hers.

"Want to suck on them?" she asked him.

He nodded, and she moved up so that he could take her breasts in his hands and bring them up to his mouth. He sucked one nipple, then the other, and they grew large and hard on his tongue. Kerri had small ones; they were nice, but not that big. Tammy's breasts even seemed to taste different.

He put Kerri out of his mind. Tammy eased on top of him and straddled him.

"I think it will be easier this way," she told him.

It was an amazing feeling, the heat, the wetness, the pressure of her pussy. She bounced up and down, her big tits bouncing along with her. He reached up to hold them in his hands.

"Like it?" she asked him. "You like my big tits? You like my hot pussy on your big stiff cock?"

He managed to nod, but that was all. "Auhhhhnn!" he cried out suddenly as he exploded inside her.

She rocked more slowly then stopped. Without a word she got off him and left the bedroom. Shannon lay there, pulling himself together, watching his hard-on slowly collapse. It had been incredible, but it was over so fast. When he whacked off, it took him at least a couple minutes, even if he was really horny. He hadn't even lasted a minute with Tammy. He finally had first-hand experience with why pussy was so powerful.

Tammy came back, still naked, and stared at him. "You ain't getting another go at it," she told him. "I know John said thirty minutes, but if you want to go again, I'll need another twenty bucks."

Shannon quickly got up and got dressed. It hadn't been on his mind to "go again," as she had put it, although he would have liked to—later, after he recovered.

"Look, if you don't mind, I'd rather you wait outside for John to get back," Tammy said, pulling on her panties. "They baby's getting up from his nap, and he's hungry."

"You've got a baby?" Shannon asked, surprised. That explained the stretch marks.

"Yeah. I moved him into the bathroom while we were busy," she said.

Then he heard a wail, and Tammy went back to the bathroom. When she came out, she was holding the baby to one huge breast.

Shannon was mortified. He finished dressing as fast as he could.

"Thanks," he said, almost running for the door.

"Sure," Tammy said. "Come back again."

He shut the door behind him. John wasn't back yet. Shannon sat down on the concrete step outside Tammy's apartment. He wasn't bothered by the fact that she had a baby. It was seeing the baby sucking on his mother's breast.

I was doing that, he thought, shuddering. *No wonder it tasted different. Yuck. Gross.*

He spat twice on the ground and shuddered again. The rest of it had been fine, but he wished it had lasted longer. He shut his eyes and replayed the experience, and he felt himself getting hard again. He stopped thinking about it, because he didn't want John to come back and see that he had a hard-on again.

Ten minutes later John returned. Shannon got up and got into the car with him.

"So, how was it?" John asked.

"Why didn't you tell me she has a baby?" Shannon demanded.

"What difference does that make?" John asked.

"I was sucking on the tits of a nursing mother!" Shannon said.

"So?"

"So? That's disgusting!"

"Really? Some guys think it's a turn-on."

"Not me," Shannon said emphatically.

"Well, besides that, how was it?"

"Fine."

"Fine? Is that all you have to say about it?" John asked.

"Yes, fine, great, terrific, whatever!" Shannon said.

"What did you do?"

Shannon looked at John. "We fucked, John."

"Well, duh, Shannon. I mean, how did you do it?"

"She was on top of me."

"Yeah? And?"

"And we screwed."

"That's it?" John asked.

"What do you mean, 'That's it?'"

"You could have had anything you wanted, and that's all you did?"

"That's all I wanted. Is that okay with you?"

"Man, you're just plain vanilla," John said. "You'll make some boring, innocent, young girl real happy one day."

Twenty minutes later he was back on the steps of the apartments again, listening to Boston's "Don't Look Back" on the radio. He was still sixteen-and-a-half, he still looked twenty, and he still felt a hundred years old, but at least he wasn't a virgin anymore.

2

Halloween Party

Mandey Rowan's '77 blue Ford Econoline van pulled into the driveway at eight o'clock on the dot. She blasted the horn once, and through the white brick house's glass sliding doors came a figure with lots of sandy blonde hair wearing a red satin party dress and black spike-heeled pumps. Mandey's jaw dropped.

"What do you think?" she was asked as the passenger side door opened and a duffel bag was tossed into the back.

She laughed. "I don't usually date guys who are prettier than I am, James," she told him.

James grinned as he hoisted himself into the passenger seat and adjusted the dress to sit. An expert make-up job, dangling gold earrings, suntan-colored pantyhose, and a well-padded bra underneath his outfit completed his look.

"Do you like it?" he asked her.

"You look great," Mandey replied. "Isn't that Gayla's dress?"

"Yeah, she helped me. This is all her stuff."

"I would have helped you."

"I know," James said, "but I wanted to surprise you."

"Well, you certainly did that."

"You've got to let me change at your house before you bring me home," James told her. "My parents would kill me if they saw me like this."

"No problem," Mandey said, turning up the radio. "Out of Touch", the newest single by Daryl Hall and John Oates, was playing. They were her favorite band. She backed out of the driveway.

"You look nice tonight," James said.

Mandey smiled. "Thanks," she said, a little surprised by the compliment.

She was dressed up as a flapper. Browsing at the thrift store, she had become enthralled by the beaded, fringed, 20's style flapper dress. It was even in her size, so she knew she had been meant to have it. Her best friend, Georgia, had been with her, and she had flipped out over it, too.

"You look so cute in it!" she had exclaimed when Mandey had tried it on. "You've got to get it. You know it must look good if I'm telling you to buy a green dress."

It cost a little more than she wanted to spend at a second-hand store for a costume, but after a few minutes of indecision, she bought it. She could wear the dress for a night out, not just as a costume. She might even wear it to the prom. Tonight, however, she was on her way to a Halloween party at Liaisons in the green dress with the iridescent beads and the matching flapper cap.

"Why did you have to choose green, though?" James asked her. "We look like Christmas."

Mandey sighed inwardly. "James, you knew two weeks ago that I was wearing green. Why didn't you choose another color?"

"Red is my favorite," he said with a shrug.

"Well, green is mine, and besides, there weren't any other colors to choose from."

"Then I guess they can call us 'Stop and Go'. I'm 'Stop' and you're 'Go'. Go, Mandey, please go." He started laughing.

Mandey gave him a withering glance, but he didn't notice. Lately, she was spending a lot of her time feeling hurt by one thing or another he had said or done to her. Still, she stood by him. She was afraid of what might happen to him if she didn't. Her mind went back to what had happened last summer.

Mandey picked up the phone on the second ring. "Hello?"

"Mandey?" a whispery voice asked.

"Yes?"

"I'm tired of it all. I'm tired of everyone in my family, everyone at school, everyone in my life."

"James?"

"My life isn't worth living."

"James? What are you saying?"

"I just wanted to say goodbye to you. You're the only real friend I have."

"James, don't talk like that!" Mandey cried, tears coming to her eyes. She felt like her heart had frozen and settled in the pit of her stomach.

"I'm tired of the pressure," he said. "My parents never leave me alone. Nothing I do is ever right."

"James," Mandey said, trying to keep herself under control, "a year from now you'll be away at college on your way to becoming a doctor. You've got everything to look forward to. You can't throw it all away!"

She heard him mumble something. She thought it sounded like, "Maybe I don't want to be a doctor."

"What?" she asked.

"My life isn't my own," James said, speaking louder. "My life is my parents'; I do what they want. If I don't, I suffer the consequences. It doesn't matter if I'm here or ten thousand miles away. The only way I'll get away from them is if I take my whole life away."

"Please, James—" Mandey began.

"It's okay," he said, and uttered a weird chuckle that sent icy prickles down Mandey's spine. "I'm a Buddhist. We believe in reincarnation. I hope I come back as a pig." There was a click and silence.

She frantically dialed the phone to call him back. The phone rang three times and was picked up by James's youngest brother, David.

"Is James there?" she asked.

"No, he's at the park playing tennis."

Mandey ran out to her van and sped over to the park as fast as she dared, hoping that was where James had been when he had called. When she got there, she scanned the park as she drove over to the tennis courts. There were a lot of children and teenagers around, playing basketball and using the playground equipment, but she didn't see James. The tennis courts were empty. She parked by them and got out of the van.

"James, are you here?" she called.

No one answered. She wondered if she should have looked over by the ball diamond, since that was where the phones were. She walked around the courts, which were at the far end of the park near the woods, and caught a glimpse of white through the underbrush among the trees.

"James?" she called again, walking toward the woods.

She found James about twenty feet away, sitting at the foot of a large fir tree, wearing tennis whites and with his gym bag on the ground next to him. In one had he held a nearly empty bottle of Bartle's and Jayme's, and in the other there was a bottle of pills. Mandey reached down and snatched the pills from him.

"Did you take any?" she asked him.

"A couple," James replied, his speech slightly slurred.

The bottle's label said that it contained Valium, and that it belonged to "Betty Maxwell". The dosage said to take one twice daily.

"How did you get these?" Mandey asked, shaking the bottle in his face.

"I took them out of Gayla's purse yesterday at the beach," he said. "They're her mother's."

"Yeah, I noticed," Mandey said, sinking down onto the ground next to him. "You can't do this."

She took the wine cooler out of his other hand with no resistance. "You've got so many people who care about you, and you have so much to offer the world. Things may seem hard right now, but it's going to get better. Don't you realize that you are so much better off than so many people are? You can't throw it all away."

"Who cares about me?" James asked sullenly. "No one at school likes me. The principal even has a vendetta against me. I'm a disappointment to my family. If I go away, everyone will be happy. There'll be one less person to compete for valedictorian, too."

"Damn it, James, you are stronger than this!" Mandey exclaimed. "I've looked at you as the one person in this class who could rise above all the others and succeed. You can make it through one more year of high school. College is going to be different."

James sighed and gazed at the canopy of trees, his eyes unfocused. Mandey hoped that he had only taken a couple of those Valiums, and that part of a wine cooler was all he'd had.

"James, you are so special," she said. "You are so smart and talented at so many things. You've got so much to give." Mandey took his hand in hers. It was slightly bigger than hers, a smooth, cool brown hand with long, slender fingers. "These fingers play the piano, create fascinating works of art, and will someday save lives, if you don't waste them. All I've heard you talk about for the last year is how you are going to be a famous cardiovascular surgeon
one day, and if you kill yourself now, you're killing all those patients whose lives you might have saved."

James closed his eyes. "I don't know, Mandey," he murmured. "I don't know if I can take this much longer."

"You can," Mandey said. "You will. You're going to make it. You're too valuable to me and to others not to." She brought his hand to her mouth and kissed the back of it. "I love you, James."

"I want to go to sleep now. I'm tired," James said, rolling over onto his side away from her.

"No!" Mandey said, protesting. She was afraid that if he did, he might not wake up.

"Just go, Mandey," he said. "You took the pills away from me, so I guess I get to go on living for another day."

"James—"

"Go," he said again.

"I'm not leaving you here in the woods, James. Get up."

"I'll walk home later."

"No, you won't. Get up."

Mandey pulled his arm as she stood. Reluctantly, he got up as well. She picked up his tennis bag and led him over to her van, tossing the wine cooler bottle in a garbage can on the way.

"Do you have anything else in this bag I should know about?" Mandey asked.

"No," James said petulantly.

She opened the door for him. "Get in," she told him. Then she looked through the bag as she walked around to her side. She found only tennis gear.

"Didn't believe me?" James asked sourly as Mandey slid into the driver's seat.

"It's better to be safe than sorry. I'm only doing it because I care about you." She tossed the bag into the back.

During the five-minute ride to James's house, he said nothing, sitting back in the seat with his eyes closed.

"James, we're here. James?" Mandey said as they pulled into his driveway. "James!"

"What?" he asked, opening his eyes.

"James, are you going to be okay? Are you sure you only took two?" Mandey asked

"I'm fine," James said, irritated, slowly reaching behind the seat to get his gym bag. "I'm going to go sleep it off."

"I feel like I need to call someone to help you."

"Don't you dare!" James said, suddenly emerging from his stupor. "I'm fine! Now go home and forget this ever happened!"

He got out of the van with his bag and headed into the house. Mandey sighed and sat there for a moment. She got the Valium bottle out of her shirt pocket and examined it. The label said that it had originally contained sixty tablets, and the directed dosage was to take one twice a day. It had been dispensed over three weeks ago. She dumped the contents into her hand and counted seven. Gayla's mother had probably taken most of them before Gayla swiped it, and she supposed Gayla had already had a few, as well. Mandey felt fairly confident that James hadn't had more than the two he had admitted to taking. She funneled the pills back into the bottle and decided to take them back to the Maxwells' house. When she got there, she wasn't sure if she wanted to knock on the door, so she left the bottle in the mailbox.

Mandey guessed she had gotten through to James, because when she called him the next day, he had acted if nothing ever happened. Their relationship, however, was taking a turn for the worse. The trip to the beach the day before the incident with the pills had been a disaster. James had always had emotions that ran torrid and frigid, but after that day, frigid was more the norm of what he displayed toward Mandey. Still, Mandey stayed with him. Good old "Stand by Your Man" Mandey.

The parking lot was nearly full when they arrived at the club. Mandey pulled into a spot in a dim corner in the back, between a white Toyota Cressida and a black Turismo Duster.

"I'm glad we didn't come any later or we would have had to park on the street," Mandey commented.

The parking lot was rough and full of mud puddles from Thursday night's rain. James held on to Mandey's arm as they walked.

"I should have worn lower heels," he said, wobbling. "And I've got to adjust these pantyhose. How do women stand these things?"

They got in line at the door. The doorman, Tony, who sported a shaved head except for a long purple topknot, was passing out masks.

"Oh, shit," James said. "My wallet's in my bag. Mandey, can you go get it?"

"Come with me," Mandey said.

"I can't," James said. "I don't want to walk back through that parking lot in these heels."

Mandey sighed. She had brought some money with her, so she could pay. However, she paid James's way often, and she didn't know why, as he was as able to pay his own way as she was. He had offered to pay this time, and she was going to let him. She got her keys out of her purse and set off toward the back of the building.

She picked her way around rough spots and puddles, weaving through the cars. As she approached the far edge of the parking lot, she noticed two dark figures by her van. One was trying to pop the lock of the Cressida with a slim jim. Her stomach turned inside out. Mandey looked around for help, but saw no one else in the dark, deserted corner of the lot.

Silently, she moved closer, hiding behind the next row of cars. The guy with the slim jim had succeeded in getting into the Cressida, and Mandey assumed he was trying to hotwire it. The other figure was standing behind the car, apparently acting as a lookout, but hadn't spotted Mandey yet.

A strange buzzing sensation was coursing through Mandey's whole body, and she realized that she was shaking. It wasn't only fear making her feel that way, because she found herself wishing for a giant two-by-four that she could bash some heads with. As she didn't have one, she decided the best course of action to take would be to go into the club as fast as she could to get help.

She tried to sneak away without being seen, but suddenly she heard footsteps in the gravel and turned to see the lookout coming straight for her. There was no use in trying to run across that parking lot in high heels, so Mandey whirled around where she was, held onto the nearest car for support, raised her leg and kicked as hard as she could, hitting the black-clad figure in the stomach.

"Help!" Mandey screamed.

The figure recovered from the blow and stood up straight. The person wore jeans, a black T-shirt, black gloves, and a black ski mask. Long brown hair flowed over the shoulders, and Mandey realized with surprise that it was a female.

"Help me! They're stealing a car!" Mandey yelled.

The girl came at Mandey, grabbed her by the arm, and smashed her fist into Mandey's mouth. Mandey grabbed a handful of that long brown hair and made a fist around the car keys she held in her right hand. She only had three keys, but several key chains, despite being told the weight could break her ignition. Now she was glad she hadn't pared down her collection. The punch she threw at the girl hit her in the jaw with a resounding smack.

"Bitch," the girl muttered as she grabbed at Mandey's hair, knocking her cap to the ground. The girl grasped Mandey's wrist and tried to wrench the keys away. Mandey fought back by digging the fingers of her left hand into the girl's neck and kicking her in the shin. The girl let go of her wrist, but she hit Mandey hard across her left temple. For a moment Mandey's vision blurred.

"Go away!" Mandey screamed, feeling something inside her break. She swung back her fist full of keys and hit the girl squarely in the face.

"Bitch!" the girl screeched, holding her nose.

"Hey!" said a male voice from across the parking lot. Mandey heard people running in her direction.

"Let's go!" the girl shouted, turning to run.

The other person was out of the Cressida, and they fled into the dark street. Mandey heard a car start and roar away. A couple guys ran to the road to try to catch them, but the car was already out of sight.

"Are you okay?" James asked Mandey, walking gingerly toward her around the puddles.

"Yeah," she said, her voice wavering. She bent down to pick her cap up off the ground. It wasn't too dirty. She brushed it off. At least it hadn't fallen in the mud.

"What happened?" Tony asked.

Mandey took a deep breath. "I came to get something out of my van. There were two people in dark clothes and masks trying to steal the car next to it. The lookout saw me and jumped me."

"Can you describe them?" asked Rick, the security guard.

Mandey frowned. She wanted to give him a piece of her mind. He was paid to keep people safe, not to hang out at the bar and flirt with every attractive girl he saw.

She held her tongue. "No, not really. The girl was wearing jeans, a black T-shirt, and a black ski mask. She had long brown hair. She was about my height and slender. The other one, all I know is he had on dark clothes, and he was big. I'm pretty sure that one was a guy."

Rick went over to look at the Cressida. "Maybe they left some fingerprints."

"I doubt it. The girl had on gloves," Mandey told him.

"Well, let's call the cops to report it, anyway," Rick said.

The police were called, and Mandey spent ten minutes on the telephone answering a set of rudimentary questions. Afterward she sat down at the bar.

"Are the police on their way?" James asked her.

"No," she said.

"No?" James asked.

"No, they said they could get all the information they needed over the phone," Mandey said.

"No fingerprint check or anything?" James asked.

"Nope. I mentioned the gloves the girl wore, and they said it would be pointless to do a fingerprint check."

"They never come out here," Rick said. "I think someone could get murdered and they wouldn't come out here."

James looked disappointed. "Well, I like this song. I want to go dance," he said.

Mandey sighed. She wasn't much in the partying mood anymore, and now she noticed her ankle was hurting. It must have happened when she kicked that girl. "You go ahead," she told him. "I don't feel like it right now."

James sashayed away to the dance floor. Mandey stayed at the bar, holding ice cubes wrapped in a clean bar rag to her lip, The establishment was nice enough to serve her free drinks to make up for being assaulted in their parking lot, and she was feeling ornery enough to order the expensive ones. She was on her second virgin Almond Joy, which appeared to be flavored with almond extract, and was wishing she had a real one with Amaretto liqueur.

"Thank you! Oh my God, thank you!" she heard someone say.

A tall blonde girl dressed like Madonna stood next to her, very wound up. "That Cressida is my car! Are you the one who stopped them from stealing it?"

"Uh, yeah," Mandey said.

"Thank you so much!" the girl said, wrapping her arms around Mandey and hugging her. "My name's Tina. Did they hurt you? Oh my God! If there is ever anything I can do for you, let me know!"

Then she was gone, disappearing into the crowd as quickly as she had appeared.

"Okay," Mandey muttered.

As she looked to where Tina had gone, she saw Danny Sanchez and Jeremy Matthews standing behind her. Despite the theme of the evening, neither one wore a costume. Jeremy was short, with thick, wavy brown hair and sapphire blue eyes. Mandey thought he looked like he belonged on one of those sickly-cute sitcoms on television, with articles and glossy pin-ups of him in *Tiger Beat*. Danny was a bit taller than Mandey was, slightly on the heavy-set side, and had shiny black hair, dark brown bedroom eyes, and a sensual mouth. From seventh grade to the beginning of ninth grade, Mandey had had an immense crush on him.

She knew that he knew that she liked him, and she also knew that although he liked her, it wasn't in the same way.

Now, however, even if Danny professed his undying eternal love for her, she wouldn't have him. Not because of James, but because Danny dealt drugs. He had been selling since the beginning of junior year, but Mandey hadn't realized it until the past summer, when Gayla showed her some uppers she had gotten from him. He dealt different drugs, but his main staple was one called "Ecstasy" or "X", which was popular with the Liaisons crowd. That made Mandey a bit nervous to be around him.

"Hi, guys," she said as Danny sat down next to her and Jeremy on the one beyond him.

"I heard what happened to you tonight. Goddamn gang. I'd like to stomp all over those mother-fuckers," Danny said.

"You and me both," Mandey said. "I wished I had a two-by-four so I could whack them over their heads."

Danny gaped at her, then grinned. "That doesn't sound like the sweet little Mandey I know."

"I don't feel too sweet right now," Mandey grumbled.

"Man, I'm starting to get nervous," Jeremy said. "Danny and I got jumped two weeks ago in the parking lot."

"Yeah, I heard about that," Mandey said. "Did they ever get caught?"

"Hell, no," Danny said. "Did the cops even try? I doubt it. I think they're scared, too." He peered at Mandey's swollen lips. "You got smashed pretty good, huh?"

Mandey smiled, although it hurt her mouth. "Yeah, this and a couple broken fingernails. You should have seen the other girl, though. I think I broke her nose."

"All right!" Jeremy said, and reached across to give her a high-five.

"Damn, I guess I better not mess with you then," Danny said.

"That's right," Mandey said, standing up to stretch and smooth out her dress. She gingerly tested out her ankle. It seemed a little better.

"That's a cool dress," Danny told her. "You look nice tonight, even if you did get in a fight."

"Thanks," Mandey said, blushing.

"You want to dance?" he asked her.

Mandey looked out on the dance floor at James. He had never come back to see how she was doing, and he was out there dancing with several people of both sexes.

"I thought I was supposed to be here with James, but I guess not," she said. The look that passed between Danny and Jeremy did not go unnoticed by her. "Sure, Danny."

The opening notes to Michael Jackson's "Thriller" played as Danny took her by the hand out to the dance floor, and Mandey couldn't stop her heart from fluttering a tiny bit. If Danny weren't into drugs, she could become infatuated all over again. Although she still cared about James, she knew deep inside that he didn't truly care about her, and she wanted something different. Something more.

James was undisturbed when he saw her dancing with Danny. He grinned and danced over to them.

"Loosen up and feel the music!" he exclaimed. He grabbed Mandey's and Danny's hands and put them together. "Get down!" Then he danced away.

"Freak," Danny muttered.

Mandey stared at James and then at Danny. "Did you sell him something?" she asked him.

Danny looked at her incredulously. "Are you kidding? Like he needs anything to make him a weirdo?"

As "Thriller" was ending, a guy dressed like Prince tapped Danny on the shoulder and mumbled something to him that Mandey couldn't hear.

"Duty calls," Danny told her.

Mandey sighed. "Whatever."

"Oh, don't look at me like that," Danny said.

Mandey shook her head and walked off. She had no desire to be around Danny anymore; his "extracurricular" activities made her too nervous. She wanted to dance, but James didn't come over to see what she was doing; he was too busy running around visiting and dancing with other people. Mandey knew that if she felt like it, she could go out on the dance floor by herself and dance with James or with anyone she pleased, but she didn't feel like it. She went back to her bar stool and sat there, surveying the crowd, searching for a certain person she always looked for when she was there, but hadn't seen in over a year.

James didn't come back to her until it was time for them to leave. The club closed at 1 a.m., but he had to be home by midnight. Mandey didn't say much on the way home, but if James noticed her quiet mood, he didn't mention it. He was too busy babbling on about what a great time he had had, and how so many people thought he actually was a female, and how that was so hilarious. Mandey just nodded and agreed with him at the appropriate moments.

They stopped at her house so he could transform himself back into the model-handsome high-school senior that he was, then she drove him home. He didn't bother kissing her goodnight as he got out of the car and headed into his house. It hadn't turned out to be the kind of night she had hoped for, but then, most nights she spent with James never did.

3

The Devils

The tires of the white '74 Oldsmobile screeched as the car lurched around the corner into the parking lot of a crumbling apartment complex. It came to an abrupt halt in front of one of the buildings, and a young man of nineteen and a girl of seventeen jumped out.

"God damn it, Trick, why did you have to be so fucking slow?" the girl complained, holding her nose gingerly with a bloody hand. Tears were in her eyes, and she did not cry easily. "I think my nose is broke."

"Aw, quit it, Annette," Trick said. "That girl didn't hit you that hard."

"Yes, she did," Annette said. "Feel it. It's swollen."

"For God's sake, don't start bawling," Trick said. "Let me see."

He reached over and touched her nose. Annette yelped.

"Don't touch it! It hurts!" she cried.

"Damn, I guess it is broke," Trick said, surprised.

"I told you!" Annette wailed. "What am I gonna do?"

They reached the door of a first-floor apartment in a building that had been half-destroyed in a fire two years before. Subsequently, the building had been abandoned and condemned. The apartment they were entering was the only one left wholly intact, and it was where the rest of the Devils were waiting for them.

"Get some ice on it," Trick told her as they walked inside.

"But what if it mends all crooked like Lenny's finger did last year when he broke it?" Annette asked.

Trick was losing his patience. "If you want to go sit in the emergency room at Ben Taub until four A.M., fine, go ahead. They can't set a broken nose, and about all they'll do for you is maybe give you some pain pills. Just don't expect me to take you."

"You ought to! It's your fault!"

"Quit bitching about it."

"Quit bitching about it?" Annette screeched. "My nose is broke because of you and you tell me to quit bitching about it?"

She lunged at Trick and punched him in the mouth. Trick stared at her for a moment and put his hand to his bleeding lip. Annette moved toward him to hit him again, but Trick grabbed her by the shoulders and slammed her up against the wall.

"Don't you ever do that again!" he said savagely, shaking her as hard as he could.

She pushed him away, then spat in his face. He grabbed a handful of her long brown hair as she tried to flee and yanked it.

"I hate you, you son-of-a-bitch!" she screamed, holding the back of her head.

Trick didn't respond to her last comment. He followed her into the living room.

A sharp-featured Hispanic teen was sitting on a third-hand ottoman. A long, thin scar wound its way from his left ear down his jaw line almost to his chin. He stood up as the two came in.

"What happened?" he asked.

Annette slammed herself down onto a folding chair in one corner. "Stupid Trick couldn't hotwire the car he picked out and the bitch who was driving it came out and caught us. She broke my nose and then security came along, so we had to split. If the fucking pigs turn up here, Raff, you'll know why."

Raff turned to look at Trick. "Shit, that's real good, Trick."

"Fuck you," Trick muttered under his breath and turned to leave.

Raff grabbed the tail of Trick's jacket and jerked him around.

"You make me sick," he sneered.

Trick looked down at Raff's smirking face. "At least the feeling's mutual," he replied, pulling his jacket out of Raff's grasp. He stormed out of the apartment and slammed the door behind him, making the walls shake.

Raff stood in front of the others, a look of disgust on his face. "Why the hell do you want him as our leader?" he demanded of the group. "Since he got back it's been one fuck-up after another. He's lost his edge."

"Well, go ahead and challenge him," said a short, scrawny boy named Marco.

Raff scowled. "You know I can't beat him in a fair fight. He's probably got 75 pounds on me."

"Aw, he ain't doing such a bad job," Lenny said.

"Man, he's a wimp," said Checkmate, who stood up to join Raff in his campaign against Trick. "He's got us doing all this penny-ante bullshit. If Raff took over, we'd all be rolling in dough."

"Before he got busted, he was okay. I didn't like him, but he had some guts," Raff said. "Now he's just gone soft. I thought jail was supposed to make you tough and hard, not turn you into a pussy."

"Well, what do you want?" Lenny asked. "Should we kick him out?"

"Kick him out?" Raff asked sarcastically. "What good would that do? He'd still be in our faces all the time. He'd probably start informing his parole officer about us. He don't want us to do nothing no more." A thoughtful, vaguely sinister expression crept across his face.

"Then what the fuck do you want to do? Kill him?" Lenny asked.

A wicked grin spread across Raff's face.

"Over my dead body!" shrieked a girl with long honey-blonde hair and big blue eyes, springing up from the dilapidated couch to confront Raff. She pointed a finger in his face.

"Oh, give it up, Kerri," said Annette. "What do you care? He's never given you a second look since you broke up. Hell, I don't even much give a shit what happens to him, and he's my own brother."

"She's right, Kerri," Raff said, grinning lasciviously at her. He took her pointing hand by the wrist, sat down on the couch, and pulled her down onto his lap. "What do you want with that *pendejo,* anyway? If you need a real leader, a real man, you know I'm right here for you."

Juanita, Raff's girlfriend, glared at him from across the room.

"No abras la boca," Raff warned her.

"No me digas que hacer! Si quieras a esa puta, vale, pero no vengas más a mi alcoba."

"Bitch!" Raff said, pushing Kerri off his lap.

Juanita was storming out of the apartment. Raff ran out after her. As they left, the others could hear them screaming at each other in Spanish until they went into their building.

Kerri sat on the couch, elbows on knees, chin cupped in her hands. "Why don't Trick like me, Annette? I'm always here for him, but all he wants to do is go out and fuck some whore. I got my pride. I don't sell my body."

Marco cracked up. "Yeah, you just let any guy who wants it have it for free."

"Shut up," Kerri said, reaching across Lenny to hit Marco, who was sitting on the arm of the couch.

"Come on, baby, let me make you feel better," said Curt, a portly fellow with frizzy red-blond hair and dark blue tinted glasses. He sat down next to Kerri on the couch and reached over to grab her. She slapped his hands away.

"Leave me alone, Curt," she said. "I'm not in the mood."

"Give us a break," said John, with a short laugh. "You're a bitch in eternal heat."

"Fuck you, John," Kerri said crossly as he walked up behind her. He slipped his hands over her shoulders and down the front of her blouse. He bent over and kissed her neck. Kerri closed her eyes, and winced in a combination of desire and dread. She knew she would end up with him again tonight. John was extremely attractive, with long blond hair and gray eyes, but he tended to be very rough. She had attempted to resist his advances in the past, but each time found herself regretting it. When he was in the right mood, sex with John was great. It was better to give in and take her chances.

John took her by the arm and she stood. She walked with him to a small house on the next street where John lived with his father. The rest of the group dispersed, as well.

Annette and Checkmate made their way up to an apartment on the second floor of the building where Raff and Juanita lived on the first floor. Checkmate shared a small two-bedroom apartment with his mother, who was working her second job as an office cleaner that night, and his little brother Sonny, who was in bed, asleep. Checkmate wrapped some ice in a dishtowel and Annette held it on her swollen nose as they watched television. After a while they went into his mother's bedroom and shut the door behind them.

Trick lay on his bed. His mother and Leon were fighting in their bedroom, but he wasn't paying attention. He was hoping that Annette wouldn't bring Checkmate over again tonight. For the past three nights he had tried to fall asleep despite the noises of them screwing on the other side of the room. It was impossible.

He yawned and his thoughts turned to the most recent visit he had had with his parole officer. That prick had a holier-than-thou attitude that made Trick want to puke. He kept telling him to cut his ties with the Devils, as though he could cut himself off from people he had to see every day. And his sister. How the hell could he ignore someone he was unfortunate enough to have to share a bedroom with, for God's sake?

"If you would stop running around with that bunch of heathens, you might be able to make something out of yourself someday," the prick had said.

"Ain't I already something?" Trick had asked sourly.

"Yeah, you're something all right," the prick replied, sarcastically. "But if you tried, you could become a contributor to society instead of a threat to it. You could become a real leader."

Trick had chuckled sourly. "You tell every sorry case that comes in here, 'Straighten up and you could be a leader, you could even be President one day!' That's bullshit."

The prick's face turned red. "One of these days you're going to end up in jail again, and I'm not going to pity you one single bit. The judge who had your case was far too lenient with you. You obviously haven't learned a damn thing!"

"Aw, c'mon," Trick said. "All I did was knock over a lousy liquor store. It was my first offense!"

"It was an armed robbery and you pistol-whipped the clerk!" the prick replied angrily.

Trick sat back in his chair, silent.

"You're proud of your record, aren't you?" the prick had asked him. Not waiting for an answer, he continued. "You're a lazy punk who wants attention, but won't do anything decent and responsible to get it. You—"

"Hey, my time is up," Trick said, getting up out of the chair.

"I'm not finished with you yet," the prick said, looking at his watch and realizing what Trick said was true.

"It sure was good talking to you," Trick said with an annoying grin as he backed toward the door. "Can't wait to do it again." With that, he walked out.

Trick lay there on his bed, staring into the dark, wondering if he really was bright and if he could be President of the United States one day.

No, he decided. *I wouldn't want to be, either. I don't even like being the leader of this gang, much less leader of a whole damn country.*

4

The Victims Commiserate

Mandey looked over her music. She had it almost memorized already, and the choir concert was still over a month away. They were going to perform quite a variety this year: A Christmas cantata in Latin, another Christmas song in German, and a selection old standards.

"I heard about what happened to you Saturday night."

Mandey turned around. Jesse Galindo was talking to her.

"It's getting really bad," Jesse said. "Every week someone else I know becomes another one of their victims."

"You talking about those bastards?" asked Zachary Stewart, sitting down in the chair next to Jesse's. "They still haven't found my car, and it's been six weeks. It's gone for good."

"They have almost no security," Mandey said. "They need to hire about six more people."

"Yeah, but that would cost money," Jesse said. "So far, none of this shit has stopped the crowds from coming. They ain't going to do nothing unless business starts dropping off, and if it hasn't started by now, it ain't going to happen. So maybe it's time we take things into our own hands."

"How?" Mandey asked. She was thinking they could stage a major boycott.

Mr. Donovan stepped up to the piano as the tardy bell rang.

"Meet us after school at my car," Jesse told Mandey. He got up and moved to his seat in the baritone section.

Mr. Donovan began playing chords on the piano. "Everyone up," he said. "Sing the scale on 'la'."

As she did her warm-ups, Mandey looked back at Zack and at Jesse on the other end of the room. She didn't think they had a boycott in mind.

Mandey didn't tell James what Jesse had said about meeting after school.

Fortunately, James had a French club meeting, so he wouldn't be around to see her, anyway. After the last bell, she got her books for her homework assignments out of her locker and went directly out to the parking lot.

Jesse drove a sharp-looking maroon '82 Thunderbird. When she got there, a small crowd was already congregated around it. There was Jesse and his girlfriend, Angelina Longoria; Zack and his buddies, Jim Corbett and Brad Davidson; Danny Sanchez, Jeremy Matthews, and Dina Diaz. As Mandey approached, so did one other person—Terry Owens.

"Let's go over to Jack in the Box and talk," Jesse suggested. "I think it's going to start raining any minute."

They piled into their cars and drove down the street to the popular hangout. Fifteen minutes later they were all seated, taking up most of the restaurant's tiny dining area, eating burgers and fries and drinking Cokes and Dr Peppers.

"Okay, so what are we talking about here?" Danny asked, his mouth full of bacon cheeseburger.

Jesse put down his Dr Pepper. "Okay. The reason we're all here is because we've all had bad experiences with those assholes calling themselves the Devils. Maybe even more people at school have had problems, but I haven't heard about them--yet." He paused. "What I figure we ought to do first is share our experiences, so we all know what we're dealing with here."

Zack immediately piped up with his story. "They stole my car!" he said. "I worked three summers for and saved all my Christmas and birthday money for that car! It's been six weeks now and there's been no word on it. It's probably gone through a chop shop by now."

"They almost stole Mandey's van, too," Jesse said. "Tell us about it, Mandey."

Mandey felt nervous as all their eyes focused on her. "No, no, it wasn't my van, it was the car next to it they tried to steal. Saturday night I was going to my van to get something and I saw two people, a guy and a girl, trying to steal the Cressida parked next to it. When they saw me, the girl attacked me. We fought for a minute, but people heard me screaming, so they ran away."

"That's nothing," Terry said. "They knocked me fucking unconscious. My brother has a wrecker service and storage lot about a half a mile away from there. They kept breaking in and stealing cars, so we started taking turns sleeping down there. It was my turn one weekend, and two of them broke in the office. I came out of the back room with my brother's shotgun, but one big guy, the leader, I guess, got me. I barely saw him out of the corner of my eye when he slammed me over the head with a chair. They got $600 that night, plus my brother's CB radio and the shotgun and another car! I didn't come to until 6:30 the next morning."

Danny chimed in next. "There's one guy, Ralph, or Raff, or whatever-the-hell he's called, who's the thorn in my side. I know he's the asshole who slashed my tires two weeks ago. I was parked right up next to the front of the building, too. Security sucks!"

"Then we got jumped the next week!" Jeremy said. "It was Raff and a black guy. We went in my car since they couldn't identify it, but we were late and had to park on the street. When we were leaving, they jumped out of a car and mugged us! Danny had a lot of cash on him, too!"

There was a pause as everyone absorbed this information. Brad swallowed a mouthful of French fries and said, "Well, my story isn't as bad as some of yours. There's one guy who shows up at the club once in a while. He gets really aggressive with the girls sometimes. I guess some of them seem to like it, but most I've seen seem to get scared of him. Anyway, one night he started harassing this girl I'd met. Kept coming over to the table and trying to cut in when we were dancing and being a real asshole. I got fed up with it and told him to step outside. Jim and Zack were there, too, and when we got outside, the dude had two friends with him. We all got into it out back of the club, and no one came to break it up until someone came out to dump some trash. He yelled at us and said he was going to call the cops, and they took off. At least my car didn't get stolen."

"Yeah, but they stole my bike!" Jim exclaimed. "It was tied to the top of Brad's car because he had just picked me up from a show. Had it chained and everything and they still got it!"

"That's not as bad as a car," Zack said.

"My bike is how I make my money!" Jim said.

"What's your stake in this?" Terry asked Jesse.

Angelina spoke up. "We went in my car to the club Friday night, Jesse, Dina, and me," she began. "You know how creepy it is on some of those streets around there. We were leaving and another car rammed us from behind. We stopped and got out to check out the damage and five people got out of the car, two girls and three guys. They had masks on, so we couldn't get a good look at any of them."

"They knocked Jesse out cold," Dina said, "and they robbed all three of us."

"Did you see what they did to Angie's hair?" Jesse asked. "Show them."

Angelina took the pins from her hair and let it down. A hunk of her long, black hair had been cut off near the scalp in back.

"Just for kicks," she said, and pinned it back up.

"How many of you have talked to the cops?" Jesse asked.

Everyone said they had.

"How many of you have gotten any results?" he asked.

"Shit," Zack said. "It's been six weeks now and they ain't got a clue. I've written it off as a lost cause."

"When was the last time you saw a patrol car in that area?" Jesse asked everyone.

"I saw one back in August," Mandey said.

"What I'm saying is, the cops don't care, the club management doesn't care. Unless we do something, we are going to have to continue putting up with that shit, or quit going there. I personally don't like the idea of going back to hanging out here at Jack every Friday and Saturday night. We ain't doing nothing to them. We mind our own business. We've got to do something to make them leave us the hell alone."

By now, Mandey knew that a boycott was not on anyone's mind.

"Let's fight back," Jesse said. "Let's form our own gang."

There was silence, then Brad said, "Aw, Jesse, this isn't *West Side Story*."

"You got a better idea, short of not going there anymore? You're one of the most popular guys in the regular crowd, Brad. The girls love you. I don't think you want to do that."

Mandey surveyed the other nine people sitting there with her. She didn't think any of them was what anyone would consider your everyday gang material.

There was Danny. He was popular, friendly, and taking college-track classes. He was vice-president of both the Latin club and the psychology club, and he also happened to deal recreational drugs.

Jeremy was also popular and very cute. At five-foot-two, Jeremy was the object of desire of nearly every short girl in school, as well as quite a few of the taller ones. He was president of the drama club, and acted outside of school. He had even appeared in a commercial for a local waterbed dealership.

Jesse was handsome, with short black hair, fine features, and a perfect smile. He was vice-president of the drama club and had a great baritone voice. He was a sharp dresser and was notorious for having gone steady with a long list of girls, but Angelina seemed to have strong hold on him; they had been together almost six months.

Angelina was pretty, headstrong, and had a good sense of humor. She was also a member of the drama club, DECA, and sang soprano in the choir. She had been voted best dressed girl in their class for the past two years.

Zack was a tenor in choir and a drama club member. He had adopted the "surfer chic" made popular by Sean Penn's character in *Fast Times at Ridgemont High*.

Jim had been a baritone in the choir, but had to drop out because he had failed junior English and had to take it over again as an elective so he could graduate on time. He did freestyle shows with his bicycle and sang with a band outside of school. Like Zack, he wore a spiky hairdo and had adopted the surfer style.

Brad shared his friends' surfer aesthetic, but he was on the college track and was the star pitcher on the varsity baseball team. He was tall, blond, and a bit of a flirt, but in a nice way. Mandey couldn't think of a girl who knew him who didn't like Brad, herself included. He was open and ingenuous, which made him charming.

Dina was what Mandey thought teachers referred to as a "chronic discipline case." She had fought her way through school, and frankly, Mandey was amazed she hadn't dropped out. She should have been a senior, but Dina had repeated ninth grade, so she was only a junior. She was not quite as warlike as she had been as a freshman and sophomore, but she was still pretty scrappy. She and Angelina were cousins.

Terry was a bona fide redneck. He wore T-shirts or western shirts; jeans with the telltale faded round circle on the back pocket, indicating where he carried a can of Skoal; and cowboy boots. He was about six feet tall, burly, and had sandy blond hair, which was already developing a receding hairline. He took Auto Mechanics in the afternoons.

And then there was Mandey. She was secretary of the National Honor Society, vice-president of the Spanish club, a member of the gifted program, and she sang alto in the choir.

The others were examining the other members of the group with doubtful expressions on their faces. Apparently, they had the same misgivings Mandey had.

"What would we do as a gang?" Danny asked, looking skeptical.

"Oh, we wouldn't do the kind of stuff they do. Not to innocent people, anyway," Jesse said. He grinned, malice creeping into his smile. "I suppose we could slash a few tires."

The grin spread to Terry's face. "Smash a few windshields."

"We could think up all kinds of stuff to do if we needed to," Jesse said, "but I think we just need to stick together and try to protect each other and the rest of the Liaisons crowd. But if they get too nasty, then so will we."

No one said anything. Mandey coughed.

"Oh, come on. I'm thinking that just the image of being a gang and standing up to them will be enough to get them to back off."

"Maybe," Danny said reluctantly.

"Or it might antagonize them even more," Mandey muttered.

"What?" Jesse asked.

"Nothing," Mandey replied, shaking her head.

"Well, think about it," Jesse said. "Let's meet at Taco Bell after school tomorrow. But listen, don't talk about this to anyone else, okay?"

"Okay," the rest agreed.

"I'm serious," Jesse said, looking at Danny. "Not a word. We could get in deep shit."

"Why are you looking at me?" Danny asked defensively.

"Just keep a lid on it, all right?"

"Yes. Fine."

After the meeting broke up, Mandey got into her van and headed home. Despite her doubts about the whole idea of forming a gang to combat the Devils, it still fascinated her. Inspired by the book and the movie *The Outsiders*, she had done her psychology class term paper last year on gangs. During her research she had learned that most gangs were comprised of teenagers with self-esteem issues. She didn't think that was a problem that affected any members of the group beyond what was supposed to be normal for teenagers. She supposed it wasn't a real gang they were forming, anyway; it was more along the line of the Guardian Angels in New York City. At least, she hoped that was the idea.

5

The Alley Cats

On Tuesday, Mandey told James she had to go to a dentist appointment immediately after school, so not to expect to find her waiting at her locker for him. At 3:30, she was seated in Taco Bell with the rest of her prospective gang members.

"Does this mean we're together on this?" Zack asked.

"I guess so," Terry said, as others nodded.

"Something has to be done. We'd might as well give it a shot," Danny said.

"Good," Jesse said. "Now we need to come up with an identity for us. A name and some colors. The Devils are black and red. I think we ought to have black and another color. Any suggestions?"

"Blue," Jeremy suggested.

"Uh-uh," Angelina said. "Black and blue don't look good together. I don't want to walk around looking like a giant bruise. I think that since the Devils use the color red, we should take the opposite color, green. It's our school color, anyway. Black, green, gold, and silver would look really sharp."

"I second that," Jesse said. "Let's vote. All for black, green, gold, and silver?"

Everyone but Jeremy and Terry raised their hands.

"Majority rules," Jesse said. "Those are our colors. Now to choose a name."

"The Jets," Jeremy said, and laughed. "Get it? The Jets, like in *West Side Story*, and like the New York Jets, who are green and white?"

"If we're going for football names, why not make it obvious and call ourselves the Green Bay Packers?" Terry suggested sarcastically.

"The Renegades," Danny said.

"That was a TV show," Mandey said.

"Nuh-uh. When?" Danny said.

"Last summer," Mandey said. "It didn't last very long."

"Was it any good?" Danny asked.

"I never watched it," Mandey said. "I guess not, or it would still be on."

"How about the Avengers?" Jesse suggested.

"Another TV show," Mandey said.

"The Panthers," Jim said.

"No, I don't think we should use the school mascot," Jesse said.

"The Alley Cats!" Angelina cried. "Our colors are black and green, like a big black cat with green eyes."

"Oh, that sounds fierce," Terry said, rolling his eyes. "Who would you be more afraid of, Devils or Alley Cats?"

"I like it," Dina said.

"I do, too," Mandey agreed.

"Females," Terry said in disgust.

"Well, we've got a second and a third on this one. Let's vote on it," Jesse said.

"Wait a goddamn minute here, Jesse," Terry said. "Just how the hell did you become the leader of this outfit?"

"Yeah, we need to vote for officers," Danny agreed.

"Okay, we will," Jesse said impatiently, "but I'm conducting this meeting for right now until that happens. Vote. All in favor of our social club being known as the Alley Cats?"

The vote passed seven to three in favor.

"Now for the leadership question," Jesse said. "Who's going to run this operation, and how do we decide?"

"We've got to consider that we might have to take them on one day, face-to-face. Their leader is big, about six feet, probably 250 pounds or so," Terry said. "We'll need to have our biggest guy to meet him. That's me."

"Yeah, but I've organized and planned this whole thing up 'til now," Jesse objected. "Besides, it's possible we'll never be in that kind of a situation."

"But what if we are?" Terry asked. "You couldn't fight that guy!"

"Couldn't we divide the leadership duties?" Mandey asked cautiously. "Jesse could be in charge of organization and Terry could be in charge of execution?"

"Yeah," Angelina said. "Come on, y'all. We've got to be together on this, not fighting. Let's vote. Who's in favor of co-presidents?"

Eight hands raised.

"Against?"

No hands.

"I abstain," Jesse said.

"Me, too," Terry said.

"It doesn't matter," Angelina said. "It's passed. You're co-leaders."

Mandey wondered if it wasn't Angelina who was actually in charge.

"We ain't gonna be able to get nothing done if you two can't get along," Dina said. "You've got to be together on this."

"She's right, you know," Jesse said to Terry.

Terry sighed. "I know, damn it. Okay."

"All right co-leaders, lead us. What are we going to do?" Danny asked.

"That's the first order of business," Jesse said. "Now that we are the Alley Cats, what do we do? Ideas?"

"Well, we know the two problem areas that affect us are Liaisons and Terry's brother's storage lot," Zack said. "I suppose we need to show up in those two places and try to act as a deterrent."

"Terry, when have there been problems at the lot? During the week or on weekends?" Jesse asked.

"Both," Terry said.

"You said people are staying overnight down there now?"

"Yeah. My brother and this guy that works for him take turns. I usually take a turn over the weekend, either Friday or Saturday night."

"Okay, so it's weekends we'll concentrate on," Jesse said.

"Yeah, but what are we going to do?" Danny repeated.

"To start, I think we just need to show up," Jesse said. "Make our presence known. We should wear something to identify us, like matching jackets or T-shirts. If we go to Liaisons and go check out the storage lot, they will see us, and they'll know we're there to challenge them. How they react will tell us what our next move should be."

"And when are we going to do this?" Jeremy asked. "Remember, the Westview game is Friday night, and then you and I and Zack will be at the speech tourney all day Saturday."

"Yeah," Jesse said slowly, thinking. "I was going to say we could go Saturday after the contest, but it's out in College Station, and it'll probably be late when we get back. Let's sit on it for this weekend and agree to meet here on Monday again. Is that okay with everyone?"

Everyone nodded, but Terry looked unhappy. "We've got to do something soon. It's hurting my brother's business. At this rate, there won't be anything for me to buy into once I get out of school," he said.

"I know. Terry, you and I should probably get together and talk some more before Monday," Jesse said. "Do you have 'D' lunch?"

"No, I have 'C', Terry said, "but I can skip study hall."

"Yeah, we'll figure out when to meet," Jesse said.

"Are we through here?" Brad asked. "I've got basketball try-outs to get to."

"Yeah," Jesse said. "Let's all be thinking about what we can do to get the Devils off our backs and meet here after school on Monday."

Mandey followed Danny and Jeremy outside. The guys had ridden in Jeremy's lime-green Nova, which was parked next to her van.

"What do you think?" she asked them. "Is this going to work?"

"I don't know," Danny said. "I guess we won't know until we give it a try."

"Until the Devils turned up, I didn't even know we had gangs in Houston," Jeremy said.

"We aren't exactly your typical gang members, are we?" Mandey said.

"Are you referring to us postponing our activities because of a speech tournament?" Jeremy asked, grinning.

"That, among other things," Mandey said.

"Are you having second thoughts?" Danny asked Mandey.

"No," she said. "I'm still mad enough to fight. See you tomorrow."

They got into their vehicles. Mandey started the van, cranked up the stereo, and pulled out into the street. *I'm an Alley Cat*, she thought. *I dig it.*

Maybe we can do it, she thought. *We can't let them walk all over us, and if no one else is going to look out for us, we'll have to stand up to them ourselves. We've got to try, anyway.*

On the way home, she stopped at Western Auto and came out with a black padded steering wheel cover. She was slowly fixing up her van to reflect her tastes and personality. The interior of the van wasn't in bad shape, but it was very utilitarian, and she wanted it to be a little funkier. On Sunday she had finally finished a "curtain" of jewel-toned beads which she had hung directly behind the front seats. She had a lot of ideas of what she wanted to do, but it could only be done bit by bit. The exterior was going to have to remain blue with a few rusty patches (the van's original owner was from Michigan) for a while longer until she had the time and money to get it painted black the way she wanted.

Mandey had a suspicion that part of the reason she had been asked to join the Alley Cats was because she had a van that could haul around ten passengers. Well, if that was the case, she should decorate the interior accordingly. Therefore, after she finished her homework, she brought out her craft box. While listening to *Along the Red Ledge*, the album which contained the song "Alley Katz," she set to work embellishing the plain steering wheel cover in gold, green, and silver studs, stones, and sequins. It was a true Alley Cat steering wheel cover. By the time it was bedtime, Mandey felt herself getting into the spirit of things

6

Discontent

The apartment was quiet when Trick returned home after the early shift at the service station Wednesday. No one appeared to be around. He peered cautiously into his mother and Leon's room. The television, a portable black and white model, was on the dresser, tuned to a rerun of *Petticoat Junction*, but no one was watching. His mother was asleep on the bed. The room had been torn apart in the violent argument they had had the night before, and no one had straightened it up. There were empty Coors cans littering the floor.

Trick looked at his mother with a mixture of pity and disgust. Every time Leon and his mother had a fight, Leon would leave, sometime for a few hours, sometimes for a few days, leaving Trick and Annette to cope with their drunken fool of a mother. Or rather, Trick was left to cope; Annette didn't care, and most of the time she was so drunk or stoned herself she didn't know what was going on, anyway.

He went to his room and slammed the door behind him. He searched through his nightstand drawer and found a joint hidden far in the back. Trick flopped down on the bed, lit up, and stared at the cracks in the ceiling. The walls were cracked, too, and the paint was peeling. The floor had cheap orange shag carpet that was almost worn through in spots. The worst part of it was the fact that he had to share the room with his sister. A curtain divided their halves, but that wasn't enough, especially when she had her boyfriend there with her.

He hated that room. He hated that cramped, ugly apartment. He hated his family—they didn't give a damn about him, and he sure as hell wasn't going to spend any time giving a shit about any of them. He hated that neighborhood and everybody in it, especially Raff. He hated the whole wide fucking world, in fact.

Reaching back into his nightstand drawer, he pulled out a worn issue of *Hustler* magazine and thumbed through it. Suddenly he tore it into pieces and threw them on the floor. He extinguished the joint, hid what remained of it in the nightstand, and then headed out to his car.

The Starlite Motel was an L-shaped structure in dire need of repairs. The olive-green paint was peeling, the roof was sagging in some places, and the stairway to the second-floor rooms was so rickety that with each step it seemed as though the whole thing was about to come crashing down. Trick was familiar enough with the stairs to know to be extra-careful on step eleven, which was on the verge of breaking in two.

He knocked on the door to Room 12. He waited a couple minutes and was about to knock again when the door opened by a tall, tired-looking brunette woman in denim cut-offs and a black velvet blouse, holding a cigarette in her right hand.

"Hi," she said to him.

"Hi, Arlene," he replied as he entered the room. Arlene shut the door behind them. Shannon handed her two twenties.

He sat down on the bed and looked around. He was used to this kind of room, this one in particular, but today he really noticed it for the first time. The walls were as dirty and cracked as the ones in his own bedroom. There had been an attempt to cover up the squalor with a big mirror on one wall and a tapestry on the ceiling over the bed, but it only served to make the room look sleazier. Worst of all was the bed, which was made up with a worn red bedspread and an even more worn set of red fake satin sheets.

He looked at Arlene, who was already undressing. He had never seen her outside the confines of this room. In the dimness, she looked to be about thirty to him, but in the light of day that hit her face when she opened the door, it was clear she was closer to forty. He had tried out a few different ones at first, girls closer to his age. With them, it was always quick and dirty—get hard, get off, and get out. John had hooked him up with Arlene after he got out of jail, and she was the one he kept coming back to. She let him take his time; they would smoke a cigarette together afterward; they even made a little small talk. There was no mistaking that their relationship was anything but business, but he felt comfortable with her.

Arlene, now naked, turned off the television set and sat down next to Trick. She reached over to him and began unbuttoning his flannel shirt. Trick finished undressing, and slipped between the sheets with her. Arlene used her hands and her mouth, but it took him a long time to get hard. She was helping him slip on a condom when his erection went soft. Trick sighed, then got out of bed and began redressing in silence.

"What's wrong?" Arlene asked him, propping herself up on one elbow.

"Nothing," he replied, pulling on his jeans, his back to her.

"You never had this problem with me before," Arlene told him.

He didn't answer. He sat down on the edge of the bed to pull on his socks.

"Did I do something wrong?" Arlene asked him. "God, I almost feel like I ought to give you your money back."

"It wasn't you. Just keep the money," Trick said.

"I don't understand—"

"Let me be, will you?" Trick shouted, turning to face her. "There ain't nothing the matter! Get off my back!"

Arlene studied him silently for a moment.

"I never understood why a good-looking, nice-seeming kid like you was coming around so much, anyway. I understand young fellas coming around to see what it's like, but regulars are usually middle-aged men with wives. Why ain't you got a girlfriend?"

Trick turned away and put on his shirt, pretending to be deaf.

"That's it. You want a relationship. You want something deeper."

He finished buttoning his shirt, then stood and turned to glare at her. "My life is deep enough already. I'm just having a bad day." He headed for the door.

"'Bye," Arlene said.

Trick ignored her and slammed the door behind him. He stomped down the stairs and nearly tumbled down them as step number eleven finally broke. He grabbed the handrail for dear life to keep himself from falling.

"God damn it!" he roared after he caught his balance.

A cleaning woman was coming out of one of the downstairs rooms. "You need to fix those goddamn stairs!" he yelled at her. "I nearly broke my fucking neck!"

She looked at him blankly and unlocked the next room to be cleaned. He knew she probably didn't know a word of English. He limped down the stairs and got in his car. Gravel sprayed as he peeled out of the parking lot.

You want a relationship. You want something deeper. Arlene's words repeated in his mind.

He sighed. "I wish I knew what I was looking for," he whispered to himself.

Nothing had changed at the apartment in the two hours Trick had been gone. The place was still a mess, and his mother was still out cold on her bed. Trick started to straighten up the living room, but then he stopped himself.

If they don't care, why the hell should I? he asked himself. *They'll probably tear the place up again tonight, anyway.*

He went to the kitchen and opened the refrigerator to see what he could fix himself for supper. A bottle of ketchup, a jar of mustard, the small remainder of a large block of government cheese, and a six pack of Lone Star were all that was left. There was half a loaf of white bread on the counter. He made himself a cheese sandwich and took it and the six pack to his room. He shut the door behind him.

He sat down on the bed and popped open a can. *Forty bucks and I couldn't even get it up,* he thought bitterly. *What a goddamn waste.* He gulped down half the can of beer.

"I've got such a great life," he said aloud to himself, the bitterness hanging on. "I've got a police record. I live in this shitty neighborhood full of shitty people in this shitty apartment with my shitty excuse for a family. I pump gas for minimum wage for a guy who's got me by the short hairs, I lead a gang that would just as soon kill me as listen to me, and I spend my money on fucking whores. It's a wonderful fucking life."

He simmered in his discontent, eating his sandwich and drinking beer, drinking more than he was eating. Suddenly, he looked at the half-empty can in his hand, as if seeing it for the first time. It was the last one of the six-pack. He crushed it in his hand and threw it as hard as he could across the room. It hit the bedroom door with a dull thwack. Beer splashed out of it, and it fell to the floor where the remaining contents flowed out.

Goddamn it! You whine because you hate this fucking place and everyone in it, but all you do is lay there and get drunk! You're just like everyone else around here! You ain't no better than the rest of them! he raged at himself.

He flopped back onto his pillow, feeling like he wanted to cry, but he couldn't. The last time he had cried he had been eight years old. Leon had cured him of that. Trick didn't want to remember, but the memory resurfaced before he could stop it.

Trick and Annette were playing tag in the yard of the small house where they were living in El Campo. Trick was "it". Trick was a slightly chubby kid who couldn't run very fast, so he spent quite a bit of time being "it". Momma was at work. Their new stepfather, Leon, was in the house watching television. He kept yelling at them through the window to keep quiet, even though they weren't being that noisy.

"You can't catch me!" Annette squealed, peering at Trick across the hood of Leon's car.

"Can too!" Trick retorted.

He raced around to tag his sister. She turned to run away and ran into the driver's side mirror.

"OWWWWIEEE!" she screamed.

"Are you okay?" Trick cried, concerned.

She was holding her mouth. There was a long silence, and then she let out another long howl. She staggered toward the house, with Trick close behind.

Leon got up from the couch as they burst in the door. "What the hell happened?" he shouted.

"My tooth!" Annette wailed.

She took her hand away from her mouth. Both were bloody, and one of her front teeth was in her palm.

Leon glowered at Trick. Trick backed up against the wall, not liking how Leon was looking at him.

"We were just playing tag. She ran into the mirror on the car. It was an accident," he said in a small voice.

"Quit crying!" Leon yelled at Annette, then turned his attention back to Trick.

"How many times have I told you brats to stay away from my car?" Leon asked him.

"I'm sorry," Trick said, and he started to cry, too.

Leon took Annette by the arm and led her to the kitchen. Trick followed. Leon got two dishtowels out of a drawer and wet down one under the tap and gave it to Annette. Then he got the ice cube tray out of the freezer, popped some of the cubes out onto the other towel, wrapped them up, and handed that to Annette, too.

"Quit crying, the both of you!" Leon yelled, then said to Trick, "Especially you. "You ain't even the one who got hurt!"

Trick tried to stifle his tears, but it must not have been quickly enough to suit Leon. He grabbed Trick by the arm and dragged him into the bedroom that Leon shared with Trick's mother. Leon picked up the black leather belt hanging over the back of the chair in the corner and pulled down Trick's shorts.

Trick didn't think Leon was ever going to stop, but finally he did. Leon grabbed the boy by the scruff of his neck and locked him in the hall closet. Trick was terrified. He hurt, and the closet was hot, stuffy, and dark. He cried and begged and pounded on the door to be let out. He heard Leon yelling and cursing at Annette and then locking her in the bedroom she and Trick shared. Next, Leon was cursing and yelling over the phone at his wife, telling her to come home and take care of her goddamn kids. He heard his mother when she arrived home and thought she would make Leon let him out. He heard her try, but then he heard the fighting start: screaming, shouting, swearing, things breaking.

Trick eventually fell asleep on the floor of the closet, totally exhausted. When he woke up sometime the next morning, the house was quiet and the closet door wasn't locked anymore. He went into his mother's room. He didn't see Leon anywhere, but his mother was asleep, a nasty cut over her right eye, lips swollen.

He had never cried since that day. He had cried and gotten whipped for it, then Momma had gotten hurt, too. It was much later before he realized it wasn't his fault, but by then he had been restraining himself for too long.

"Where's the goddamn beer?"

Trick's stomach tightened into a knot.

"Where's the GODDAMN BEER?"

The bedroom door burst open and Leon stormed in. He glared at the beer cans strewn on the floor. Trick sat up straight and felt the room sway back and forth. All that beer so fast on a mostly empty stomach hadn't done him much good.

"You bastard!" Leon said. He grabbed Trick by the collar, pulled him off the bed, and slammed him against the wall. Trick hit his head hard and was dazed. He tried to fight back, but Leon caught him by the throat and pinned him against the wall, choking him. He punched Trick in the face and the stomach with his free hand, then kneed him in the groin and shoved him to the floor.

"Stupid goddamn kid," Leon said, kicking Trick in the ribs before walking out of the room.

Trick lay there for a few minutes, catching his breath. His mouth and nose were bleeding. His stomach hurt. He scrambled to his feet and made it to the toilet just in time. Beer and bile and the cheese sandwich came up. He vomited and vomited and then dry-retched for a few minutes more. At last, his stomach calmed down. He sat on the floor of the bathroom, sweating.

"Oh, God, I've got to get out of here," he moaned.

7

The Breakup

The 3:15 bell rang, signifying the end of the school day and the school week. It was Friday at last, and tonight was the big game between Rogers and their arch rival, Westview High. Mandey, her friend Andrea, Andrea's boyfriend Martin, and James were going out for pizza and then on to the game. It might be the last game of the season, depending on the outcome. The team that won would be district champion and would go on to the Class 5A playoffs in the Astrodome. Rogers had won district two years ago and the choir had gotten to sing the national anthem before the game at the Dome. Mandey hoped that they would win tonight so they could make a repeat trip.

James was slow in meeting Mandey at her locker that afternoon. Mandey saw him approaching with his overloaded backpack slung over one shoulder.

"Good Lord, it looks like you're going to be studying this weekend," Mandey said as they began walking down the hall. "When are you going to find time? Are you going to get that all done on Sunday?"

"I guess," James said.

"Good luck," Mandey said. "All I've got is a little bit of Spanish, and I need to catch up on my English journal before next week."

"I don't have much homework; I just need to study," James said.

"Bound and determined to be valedictorian, huh?" Mandey said.

"Yes, I am."

"More power to you. I don't want any part of it. The idea of getting up and making a speech to five hundred classmates, the faculty, and the families does not appeal to me."

"I *need* to be valedictorian. I need to get into a university with a good med school. If that means I have to get up and give some insincere bullshit speech edited by Mr. Tichner, so be it."

They made got into her van, and Mandey started it up. The radio came on, blaring "Wake Me Up Before You Go-Go."

"Oh God, George Michael is so gay," James said, rolling his eyes.

"Huh?" Mandey said, turning the radio down a tad. "Nuh-uh."

"Trust me," James said. "It's obvious."

"Whatever," Mandey said, shifting the van into reverse.

She drove out of the parking lot and up to the stoplight at the intersection. "Anyway, I'll pick you up at 5:00 and we'll meet Andie and Mart at Pizza Inn. We have to be at the stadium by seven if we want to be in the GSL ceremony." The light turned green and Mandey turned out onto the main drag.

"Mandey, you have to go without me," James said.

"Go without you?" Mandey asked. "Why?"

"I'm not going tonight."

"Why not? You can't have that much studying. What about our trip to Galveston tomorrow?"

"I don't want to go."

Mandey gave a loud sigh. "What changed your mind?"

"It's going to be cold tomorrow, and…I don't want to go anywhere with you anymore. This relationship we have is doing nothing for me. I want to end it."

They were sitting at the stop light at the intersection of the street that led down to James's subdivision. Mandey sat there, frozen and stunned, until the light turned green and the car behind her blasted its horn.

"Do you want to tell me what made you come to this decision?" she asked him, trying to keep tears back.

"You're too serious, Mandey. I feel suffocated, like I'm gasping for air. I have to get away from you."

"Me? Too serious? You're the one who was begging me to go to the same university as you. You're the one who said you wanted to marry me after you got out of med school."

"Well, I take back the offer. Anyway, I want a woman who can bear me blue-eyed children."

That was James, driving her to tears one minute, then making some off-the-wall remark to boggle her mind the next.

"You aren't my type," James added.

"Not your type?" Mandey asked. "We've been dating since April. It took you six months to figure that out?"

"You've changed," he told her.

"I've changed? How have I changed?" Mandey demanded.

"I can't explain it," James said. "All I know is you drive me crazy."

"Well, I can say the same thing about you."

"I can't take it anymore," he said. "You want too much from me."

"How do I want too much?" Mandey asked weakly, tears threatening to fall again.

"You expect me to be this perfect boyfriend, and I can't do it."

"I don't expect you to be perfect, James. Nobody is perfect."

"Well, you want me to love you and accept you the way you are, and I can't. I don't love you."

Trying to force the tears back, she almost missed the turn onto his street. She saw it at the last second, and the van took the corner almost on two wheels.

"And you're too dangerous!" James exclaimed.

Mandey sped down his street and pulled into the driveway, tears silently coursing down her face. James got out of the van with his backpack and headed to the house without another word to her.

Mandey pulled out and left, driving more slowly now. She cried all the way home with James's words echoing in her mind. They had spent six months together, and he didn't love her. When she got to the house, she went to her room and put on some music to cry by.

After lying on her bed and sobbing her heart out for about ten minutes, she tried putting James out of her mind. As she lay there, clutching her pillow in her arms, wetting it with teardrops, thoughts of someone else crept into her mind.

Liaisons had recently opened its doors for business. She and her friends Georgia and Andrea had gone together to check it out. It had been bedlam. They had to wait half an hour to get in. A lot of people she knew were there, including some old classmates she hadn't seen since junior high. She had danced with Stephen Harrison, whom she hadn't talked to since the summer after eighth grade. He was finally taller than she was. She had also danced with Keith Saunders, whom she also hadn't seen since eighth grade. He was planning on joining the Marines, he told Mandey, which surprised her. He had always been such a precocious wise-ass in junior high. He hadn't seemed the military type to her at all.

It was while she was dancing with Keith that she caught a glimpse of a familiar face in the crowd, a guy she hadn't seen in well over a year. She tried to keep track of him without seeming rude and inattentive to Keith. When the song was over, she excused herself from Keith, but didn't immediately rejoin Georgia and Andrea. Instead, she wandered into the crowd and found him and another guy, who appeared to be an albino, standing along the second level railing around the dance floor. Mandey stood about ten feet away and made a positive I.D. It was Shannon! Then the albino guy saw her looking in their direction. Shannon turned around to see what his friend was looking at, and he locked eyes with Mandey. After a moment, she quickly turned and returned to her friends.

"Where'd you go?" Georgia demanded.

"There's a guy here that I used to like," Mandey said. "He moved away when we were freshmen."

"Where?" Andrea and Georgia asked at the same time, scanning the crowd.

"He's on the second level, near the pool tables."

"Let's check him out," Georgia said.

"You're not going to do something to embarrass me, are you?" Mandey asked.

"Would I do that?" Georgia asked innocently. "I just want to look at him."

They had gone over to where he and his friend were standing and stopped where Mandey had stood before, about ten feet away.

"It's the dark-haired one in the beige shirt, standing next to the albino guy," Mandey said.

"Ooh, he's nice-looking," Georgia said, looking appreciatively at him.

"What's his name?" Andrea asked.

"Shannon."

"Go talk to him," Georgia said.

"And say what?" Mandey asked.

"Say, 'Hey, baby, you come here often?'" Georgia said, and laughed.

"I'm so sure!" Mandey replied.

"Well, you've got to talk to him," Andrea said. "Ask him to dance."

"I can't do that," Mandey said, turning to look toward Shannon. Her face flamed when she saw him looking back at her. They locked eyes again, then she quickly looked away.

Georgia elbowed her in the ribs. "He's looking at you!" she exclaimed. "You've got to talk to him! If you don't, I will!"

"No, Georgia! Don't!" Mandey exclaimed.

Andrea was looking toward the door. "Julia is here," she announced.

Mandey was thankful for the distraction, but not very happy to leave her spot so close to Shannon. She reluctantly followed Georgia and Andrea to the other side of the dance floor, where Julia Garza was standing near the bar. She was a year ahead of the three of them, and in band with Georgia and Andrea, so she was more their friend than Mandey's. A moment later, two more of their classmates, Charlene Sager and Jackie Seymore, found them. After the initial greetings, Mandey only half-listened to the other girls' chatter. Some guy asked Andie to dance. Mandey figured Andie was glad about that, as she and Jackie weren't too fond of each other. Mandey stood at the railing, looking out across the sunken dance floor to the other side, where Shannon and his friend were standing. They were talking, but she noticed that Shannon kept meeting her gaze. Suddenly Shannon walked one way and his friend went the other.

Andrea came off the dance floor and nudged her. "You want to get a Coke?"

"Sure," Mandey said, and they walked to the bar.

While they were in line, someone tapped Mandey on the shoulder. Her heart jumped into her throat.

She turned around. It was Shannon's friend.

"I know this guy who likes you," he said. "He's a tall, white boy with dark hair. His name's Shannon. You know who I mean?"

Mandey couldn't speak. She nodded dumbly.

"Well, he likes you." And then he left.

Mandey had been thunderstruck. Andrea told her later that she had looked as though she had gone into shock. Mandey supposed that maybe she did, a little.

"I've got to find him," she told Andrea, and tore off into the crowd.

She was so dazed she could barely see straight. She searched through the entire club, but there was no trace of him. His friend had disappeared, as well. She got her hand stamped and ventured into the parking lot. He wasn't out there, either.

She returned to her friends, her heart feeling like a lump of lead in her chest. He was gone. The whole evening was ruined for her. She had come so close, and she had royally screwed up her chance.

Why do I have to be so shy? she asked herself, tears welling in her eyes. *Why couldn't I have just said 'hi'?*

She was able to control herself until she got home that night, then she broke down and ended up crying herself to sleep.

Mandey broke into a fresh flood of tears thinking about Shannon. She had finally found in him someone who was mutually attracted to her, and she let him get away. She had returned to Liaisons often, and even when she was with James, she always hoped to she Shannon. But he had never appeared again.

Mandey pulled herself together and called Andrea to tell her she wasn't going to the game.

"Why not?" Andrea asked.

"James broke up with me," Mandey said.

"He did?"

"Yeah. He said I was suffocating him and I expected too much of him and that he doesn't love me."

"Expected too much? All you wanted was for him to treat you decently, and he couldn't even do that most of the time. You're better off without him."

"I know. I guess..."

"You are better off without him. Someone better will come along soon, wait and see."

"Somehow I doubt that."

"Don't be so negative. Are you sure you don't want to go to the game?"

"I don't know. I might change my mind, but I really don't know right now."

"Well, come and find us if you do."

Once off the phone, Mandey dragged herself out to the kitchen to find something to eat. There was a box of Kraft macaroni and cheese in the cupboard, and twenty minutes later she was eating tube-shaped pasta in reconstituted powdered cheese sauce. It tasted delicious.

Marcia came in while Mandey was cleaning up her dishes.

"I thought you'd be long gone by now—what's wrong?" Marcia asked when she saw Mandey's face.

Although she didn't want to, Mandey broke down crying again. Sobbing there by the sink, the whole sad story came pouring out.

"Oh, what a jerk," Marcia said, disgusted. "Mandey, I know you don't want to hear this, but it's probably a good thing. You don't deserve to be treated that way. What a little ass."

Mandey giggled at the remark, in spite of herself.

"I know, I know, I know. Things haven't been right between us for a while now, but I just kept hoping it would go back to the way it was in the beginning." Mandey drew a deep, if shaky, breath and exhaled. "Oh, well. On to bigger and better things, right?"

"Exactly," Marcia said. "Are you still going to the football game?"

"I haven't decided," Mandey said. "I'm not exactly in the mood."

"I think you ought to go," Marcia told her. "It's your last high school football game. Go have fun with your friends. It will make you feel better."

In the end, Mandey decided to go. Because she waited to make up her mind, she didn't leave until late and got caught up in the heavy traffic heading to the stadium. She made it inside as the seniors were meeting down on the field. All the seniors present from Rogers and Westview were going to participate in the customary Good Sportsmanship League ceremony before the game.

She didn't see Andrea or Martin, but she found Gayla Maxwell and Charlie Murrill. They, along with James and Mandey, comprised the top four ranking students in the class. When the semester ended in January, their graduation rankings would be final.

"Hey!" Gayla said, pleased to see Mandey. "I thought you were coming to the game with James."

"James and I aren't going anywhere together anymore," Mandey said, and relayed the story of her break-up once more. It was getting easier; this time she only got a little misty-eyed.

"You're better off without him," Gayla and Charlie chorused.

Mandey laughed. "How many times have I heard that in the last couple hours?" she said.

"You know you've always got me," Charlie said, putting one arm around her shoulders and one around Gayla's.

"Please," Gayla said, rolling her eyes and shrugging his arm off her.

In the end, Mandey was glad she went to the game. During the GSL ceremony, she saw several people from Westview who had been her junior high classmates before they were split up and sent off to four different high schools. Afterward, Georgia, Charlene, and several others came over and sat behind Mandey, Charlie, and Gayla in the stands. Danny, Jeremy, and Mark Ruggeri joined them, as well, and at halftime Andrea and Mart found Mandey. She was surrounded by a throng of friends and classmates, cheering the football team, and laughing their asses off at the horrible drill team dance routine at halftime, where half the girls pretended to "shoot" the other half, and the ones who were "shot" fell over backwards and laid on the field with their legs spread in the air. Charlie laughed so hard he turned red and started coughing, and Mandey thought Danny was going to fall out of his seat, both of which made her laugh even harder.

"Oh, man, I'm going to give Jackie so much shit when I see her," Danny gasped.

She had a blast, even though Rogers lost the game, 24-12. For a while, she didn't miss James at all, but on the way home, driving alone, the passenger seat seemed terribly empty. She went home and cried, but only a little bit. Worn out, she fell asleep quickly.

8

The Girl in White

Trick sat in the sand, staring out to sea. It was peaceful here, with no one around to make him miserable. He knew his troubles still existed, but he shoved them behind a curtain in the back of his mind and tried to think about something pleasant. He let his mind wander. Whenever he did, he often found his thoughts going to the same place.

He and his friend Curt had gone to Liaisons when it opened. It wasn't the kind of scene either of them was into, but it was in the neighborhood, and they wanted to check out the joint. Curt had wanted to scope out the chicks, too. Trick wasn't as eager. He had had a bad experience with a girl, and had decided it might be better not getting too personal with any of them.

He and Curt had been standing near the dance floor, talking, while Curt ogled the girls in short skirts. Despite telling himself that he wasn't interested, Trick had been looking at the girls on the dance floor, too. There was one who caught his eye. She had brown hair, wore a white shirt and pants, and was dancing with a thin blond guy with glasses. He liked the way she danced, and she had a cute smile. He couldn't articulate exactly why, but to Trick, she was the only girl in the whole place worth a second look. She disappeared from the dance floor for a few minutes, but then reappeared with a different guy, one with acne scars and limp brown hair. A buxom blonde girl was dancing next to her now with the blond guy, and she and the girl in white appeared to be friends. He didn't get the impression the girl in white was there on a date with either of those two guys.

After that song ended, the girl and her partner left the floor and vanished into the crowd. The blonde girl and guy did, also. A few minutes later, he noticed Curt look past him, over his shoulder. He turned around and noticed the brown-haired girl in white looking at him. Their eyes met for a long moment, then she turned quickly and walked in the opposite direction.

"That chick in white was checking you out," Curt said.

"No way," Trick said.

"She was, man. She was acting like maybe she knew you or something," Curt said.

"You're hallucinating," Trick told him. "If I knew her, I wouldn't forget."

"I'm serious," Curt said.

A few minutes after that, the girl, the blonde, and another girl were standing ten feet away.

"She's showing you to her friends," Curt said.

Trick had to admit that Curt might be right. He looked at the three girls, but paid special attention to the girl who seemed interested in him. She had on white pleated slacks, a low-cut white blouse with silver threads through it, and dangling earrings with stars on them. Her hair was shoulder-length and brown; her skin was fair; she had a dimple in her left cheek.

Suddenly, she looked over at him, and their eyes locked again. It lasted only a few seconds, but it was enough to tell him she was interested. A funny feeling shot through him, all the way to his toes. Trick felt his face getting warm. He saw her friend elbowing her as she looked away. Then the girls turned around and went over to the other side of the club, but he saw her glance back at him.

"Man, go talk to her," Curt said. "It's obvious she wants you. Free pussy tonight."

"Aw, Curt," Trick said. "I wouldn't know what to say to a girl like that."

"What do you mean, 'a girl like that'? A chick is a chick," Curt said.

"What the hell would she want with me, anyway?" Trick asked.

"Fucked if I know," Curt said, "but it's clear that she does, for some reason."

Trick watched the girl, now on the other side of the club. Her friends were talking. She was watching the dancers…and him. He couldn't help returning her gaze. She was so pretty, and she looked so nice. If he could just work up the courage…

"Man, it's time for us to leave," Curt announced. Victor wanted to meet with all the Devils at ten. "I've got to use the can. I'll meet you outside."

Trick gave her one last look before he left. He wanted so much to go over and say hello, at least, but he had run out of time. He was scared to talk to her, anyhow. She would probably laugh at him, and at the way he would be stumbling over his words.

He walked outside and waited for Curt. They were in Trick's car, heading out of the parking lot, when Curt said, "I told her your name and that you like her."

"You what?" Trick exclaimed. "What did she say?"

"Nothing. She looked shocked, like she couldn't believe it. She went running off into the crowd to look for you, I think."

Trick sighed loudly and looked at his watch. He wanted to go back, but he didn't have time, unless he wanted to get his ass busted.

"Man, go back again. I'll bet she'll be coming back, looking for you," Curt said.

Trick had intended to go back. The only problem was that five days later he had been arrested. He had never gone back inside the club after that. What would she want with him now, anyway? She had been a chance for him to maybe have something good in his life, and he had let her slip away. It was just as well, he supposed, considering what had happened to him.

I should quit torturing himself with that memory and forget about her, he told himself. But she didn't want to leave his mind.

9

Thank You For...

Mandey parked the van and lugged the bag of food and the blanket out of the back. It was about sixty degrees, and the wind was blowing off the ocean. The sky was overcast, and the water was rife with whitecaps. Mandey couldn't see a single living thing on the beach.

Where are the seagulls? she wondered.

She also pondered why she had driven 70 miles to have a picnic all by herself on a chilly, deserted beach. To wallow in self-pity and savor the solitude, she supposed.

She walked over to three picnic tables under a covered shelter. It had only a roof, no sides, so there was no shield from the wind. Mandey put the bag and blanket on one of the tables. Several feet away, a slope led down to a sandy, if not very pretty, beach. She glanced down and noticed a lone figure sitting on the sand, apparently gazing out to sea. He had dark hair and wore a pair of faded blue jeans and a red plaid flannel shirt.

Is that...? she thought, her heart fluttering. She didn't want to get her hopes up.

Mandey made her way down the slope of rocks, sand, and weeds to the beach. He didn't seem to have heard her. As she approached him, she saw him in profile, and she was almost positive.

"Shannon?"

He looked up at her, startled. It *was* him, and he looked just the same to her—husky; dark, slightly wavy hair; golden brown eyes--except for a bruise on his left cheek.

"Hi," Mandey said, feeling her shyness trying to choke her. "I don't know if you remember me—"

"I remember you, but I don't know your name," he said. "I saw you at Liaisons last year." He pronounced it "lay-zahns".

Mandey smiled but felt her face flaming, as well. "You remembered. I didn't think you would."

Shannon looked down, focusing on the hole in the left knee of his jeans. He picked at the loose threads that ringed it. "I've got my reasons for remembering."

He remembered, he remembered! Mandey's brain shrieked in excitement.

"My name is Mandey Rowan," she said.

He looked up at her again. "Shannon Douglass."

"Douglass," Mandey repeated. "Now I know your last name. Pleased to finally meet you."

She held out her hand to him. Shannon looked at it for a moment, then reached out to take it. His hand was big, strong, and cold.

"Are you cold?" Mandey asked. "Wait a minute. I'll be right back."

Her heart was pounding as she ran up to the van and got an old but warm blue jacket that she loved to wear, but it was about two sizes too big for her. She ran back as fast as she could, afraid that he might disappear before she returned. He didn't; he was still sitting there on the sand, watching her approach. She handed him the jacket, and he slipped it on. It was a bit snug, but it served the purpose.

"Thanks," he mumbled.

"What are you doing here on a day like this?" she asked, sitting down on the sand next to him.

"I could ask you the same thing," he replied, looking back out to sea. "I had to get away to clear my head. Life's been kind of rough lately."

Mandey nodded her head. "Life's a bitch."

"And then you die," Shannon finished, and chuckled humorlessly.

He turned toward her again, and they looked at each other for a few moments.

"Are you hungry?" she asked. "I came down here to have a picnic. I brought enough food for two, but I ended up coming alone."

Shannon smiled. It was the first time Mandey had ever seen him smile. He was adorable.

"I am kind of hungry," he admitted.

"Good," she said, getting up. "Come on."

Mandey reached out to him. Shannon took her hands and she helped him up. They walked up the hill without a word.

At the table, Shannon sat down and watched Mandey unpack the bag. His mouth watered as she pulled out fixings for roast beef and turkey sandwiches, a big bag of sour cream and onion potato chips, hard boiled eggs, and a box of homemade chocolate chip cookies. She brought a Thermos bottle and Styrofoam cups out of the van.

"Do you like coffee?" she asked him, as she poured some into a cup. "It's got cream and sugar in it."

"I do, but anything hot would taste good right now," he said, taking the cup from her.

"Do you want roast beef or turkey?" she asked him, using a knife to slice open a kaiser roll on a paper plate.

"Roast beef," he said.

"A man after my own heart," Mandey said, smiling. "Cheese, tomatoes, onions, pickles, mustard, mayo?"

"Everything," Shannon said.

When she finished with the sandwich, Mandey added an egg and a couple handfuls of potato chips to the plate and set it in front of him. He dug in immediately, eating voraciously.

As Mandey fixed her own lunch, she mustered up the courage to ask Shannon the one question she wanted most to know the answer to. Before taking a bite of her sandwich, she drew a deep breath and said, "Your friend told me that night at Liaisons that you were interested in me. Was that true?"

Shannon put down what was left of his sandwich, which wasn't much, and swallowed. He looked at Mandey. She was looking back at him expectantly, her face pink. He liked the way she looked.

"Yes," he said, looking at her seriously.

Her heart started pounding again. She smiled. "I was interested in you, too," she said. "Are you still interested?"

Shannon nodded. "Are you?" he asked.

Mandey's smile grew. "Yes," she said, then her face turned serious. "That night—oh my gosh. When your friend told me you liked me, I nearly freaked out. I almost started hyperventilating. Once I pulled myself together, I went to find you. I looked everywhere, but you and your friend had disappeared. I was heartbroken."

"Seriously?" Shannon asked, smiling but incredulous.

"Yes!" Mandey said emphatically, hoping he didn't notice that a few tears had sprung to her eyes. "I've known you longer than you think. From before that night at Liaisons."

"You do?" Shannon asked, remembering what Curt had said. "From where?"

She pointed at the big *R* on her letterman's jacket. "You can't tell me you don't know where I go to school. You went there, too, for a little while. You lived up the street from me. We rode the same school bus! I've had a crush on you since ninth grade!"

Mandey saw Shannon's face turning red. He smiled, looking embarrassed. "Really?" he asked.

"I looked a little different then. Had my hair permed, wore glasses. That's probably why you don't recognize me."

He continued to smile that same smile.

"What?" Mandey asked.

He shook his head, his smile becoming more furtive. He finished his sandwich. He was through before Mandey was halfway finished. She poured him another cup of coffee and pushed the sandwich fixings toward him.

"Make another sandwich," she urged. "You act like you're starving."

"I am," Shannon said, slicing a roll and stacking both kinds of meat on it. "This is my first meal in three days."

"What?" Mandey asked, shocked. "Why?"

"Long story," he said.

"I'm a good listener," Mandey said.

Shannon scowled slightly.

"I mean, you don't have to tell me anything, and I don't expect you to," Mandey said quickly, "but if you want to talk, I'll listen."

Shannon finished putting his sandwich together and began intently peeling a hard-boiled egg. Mandey didn't think he was going to respond.

"My life has sucked the last few years," he said, still concentrating on the egg. "I'm trying to change things, but it ain't easy."

Mandey nodded sympathetically.

"I live with my mother, sister, and stepfather. It's a fucking hellhole, if you'll excuse my language. My stepfather is a total bastard. We got into it a few days ago and I came down here to get away."

"I'm sorry," Mandey said. After a pause she added, "I remember when your sister got in that fight after school, and your mother came up and got into it."

"You saw that?" Shannon asked in despair.

Mandey nodded. "Yeah. And I saw you. You'd dropped out a couple months before. You came up there with your mom. I felt so sad for you, standing there by the car when the police came and took Annette and your mother away. Did your mother really have a gun? That's what I heard, anyway."

"No, she didn't, although she threatened to shoot that chick. We came up there to pick up my sister because she said she was afraid someone was going to jump her after school and she didn't want to wait for the bus. When we got there, she was already starting to get into it with a couple girls. My mom got out of the car and got in the middle of it."

"What ended up happening? I never saw Annette again after that, and you moved away a couple months later."

"Momma got booked for assault and making threats against that girl. My—my mom's got some problems, so they took that into consideration. They put her on probation as long as she went to therapy. She did, and it helped some, for a while, I guess. Annette got sent back to the alternative school. She'd just gotten out, too."

Mandey reached across the table and took Shannon's hand in hers. "I saw you standing there, looking so lost when the police had Annette and your mother in the police car. I wished I could have gone up to you and hugged you and made it all better," she said.

Shannon was surprised by what he saw in her eyes. When was the last time anyone touched him that way, or looked at him that way? He couldn't remember. Probably never.

"Anyway, I had to get away from all the bullshit for a while, so I took off and came here for a few days. But I left in such a hurry, I forgot I didn't bring much money with me. I've been sleeping in my car and eating Doritos and Dr Pepper."

"You must be so cold and hungry," Mandey said sympathetically.

"Kind of," he said. "To be honest, I haven't noticed it all that much. I've been doing a lot of thinking, and it's been good to be out here, alone, where it's peaceful. But I'm glad you came along."

"So am I," Mandey said. "So, what are your plans for today?"

"Umm, nothing," Shannon said.

"Would you—do you want to spend the day with me?"

"Sure," Shannon replied. "What do you want to do?"

"Oh, I don't know. We'll figure it out."

They finished eating, then cleaned up their mess and got into Mandey's van. Shannon looked around. It was a cargo van, with no real seats in it besides the ones he and Mandey sat in, but it was far from utilitarian.

"I like this," he said, admiring how she had decorated it with cloth curtains and beads. She also had two black bean bag chairs in the back.

"Thanks," Mandey said. "I'm working on fixing it up. One of these days I'd love to customize it with plush seats and carpeting, a cool stereo system, TV, waterbed, you name it. . .but first I've got to get rich." She chuckled.

"That's different," Shannon said. "Most people want little red sports cars."

"That's me—different," Mandey said.

She started the van and slipped a cassette into the player as they pulled out onto the road.

"Lobotomy! Lobotomy!" Mandey chanted, pounding on the steering wheel. "Do you like the Ramones?" she asked Shannon.

"Sure," Shannon said, grinning. He didn't really know any of their songs, but he liked Mandey's enthusiasm.

She returned the grin. "But, God, Joey Ramone has got to be the homeliest human being on God's green earth," she said. "That's probably why he wears the sunglasses and the hair in his face. He's totally cool, though, and that's what counts."

"Do you mind if I smoke?" Shannon asked her, as he pulled a pack of cigarettes out of his shirt pocket.

Mandey looked over at him. "No. Just crack the window a little."

He did and lit up. He took a long drag, then asked. "Okay, now it's your turn. What are you doing here in Galveston, having a picnic all alone?"

Mandey sighed, and looked a bit sheepish. "Same basic reason you're here, to try to get my head on straight," she said. "My boyfriend broke up with me."

"You want to talk about it?"

Mandey smiled bitterly. "Not really."

"That bad?"

"I don't know. But I feel bad." She changed the subject. "Let's go to the Strand and look around for a while," she said.

"Fine with me," Shannon said.

She parked the van and they walked down the old wooden sidewalks of the Strand, the historical district of Galveston, which was full of shops, restaurants, and historic sites. It was a big tourist attraction, but on this day, it was not very crowded. Tourists weren't thinking about Galveston in early November.

Mandey liked the cool air, a welcome relief from the stifling, steamy heat of the summer, which seemed to last forever. They spent a couple hours poking around the shops and looking at the historical landmarks. Several times Mandey was startled to see Shannon out of the corner of her eye. She was used to seeing James by her side, but she was glad it wasn't.

Around three they took a break and went to McDonald's. Mandey wasn't all that hungry, but she figured that Shannon probably was.

Shannon was concerned because he had no money.

"Don't worry about it," she told him. "When you have money, you can treat me sometime. It's no big deal."

Shannon ordered a Big Mac, a six-piece Chicken McNuggets, fries, and a large Dr Pepper. Mandey had a six-piece Chicken McNuggets, fries, and a small Dr Pepper. They sat in a booth in a secluded corner of the restaurant, which was nearly empty.

Mandey sighed as she dipped one of her McNuggets into the sweet and sour sauce.

"Maybe we should have gone to Burger King," she said.

"What makes you say that?" Shannon asked, his mouth full of hamburger.

She was quiet for a minute, debating whether she wanted to get into this. "My boyfriend—ex-boyfriend--and I ate at McDonald's a lot. We always ordered Chicken McNuggets. I don't know why. They're not even that good. They're more like Gristle McNuggets." Mandey tossed her half-eaten chicken nugget into the box. "We ate at this very McDonald's this summer when we came to Galveston with some friends. That day was the beginning of the end for us."

"What happened?" Shannon asked. "He must be really dumb."

Mandey chuckled and took a sip of her soda. "He's very handsome and very smart, but he's also a first-class jerk. All I know is that at first, everything was great, but as time went on, it seemed like there was nothing about me and nothing I could do that was right." She couldn't stop two big tears from forming and rolling down her cheeks.

"Don't cry," Shannon said softly, and awkwardly he reached out and took her hand in his, as she had taken his before.

"He's not worth it," Mandey said, wiping her eyes with the back of her other hand. Her mascara smeared. He offered her a napkin and she used it to dab at her eyes. "I know I'm being stupid."

He must be an idiot, Shannon thought. *If I had her, I'd be so happy.*

"I know I'm better off without him," Mandey said. "I'm mad that I wasted so much time on him, and I got nothing in return. Not that I wanted that much—just to be appreciated."

I'd appreciate her, Shannon thought. *I'd thank God every day for her.*

"I don't want to talk about this anymore. I want to know more about you and your life," Mandey said.

"My life?" Shannon echoed. "All I know is I can't go on living the way I'm living. It's gonna kill me." He paused long enough to finish his Big Mac, then wiped his mouth with a napkin. "No one wants to give me a break. I've got a stupid part-time job at a service station making minimum wage, so basically, I don't make diddly-squat. No one else wants to give me a job because of—"

"My record" he was about to say, but he didn't want Mandey to know about his time in jail yet.

"—me being a dropout, so I'm stuck that way. My stepfather beats the hell out of me sometimes, but no one cares. All ever hear from anybody is that I ain't gonna amount to nothing, and I'm starting to believe them. I wonder sometimes if there's any use in going on."

He noticed Mandey's alarmed expression. "I ain't suicidal, if that's what you're thinking."

"That's good," Mandey said. "Don't listen to those people. You know, I think you're pretty special just the way you are."

Shannon felt his face burning as he smiled. "Thanks," he said. "I don't know the last time anyone said something that nice to me. I don't think anyone ever did."

"Well, remember it, it's the truth," Mandey said. "So, what do you want to do now?"

He shrugged.

"I was planning on coming down here with James today," Mandey said. "It was in the 80s a couple days ago, and we were going to hang out on the beach and maybe rent skates and skate along the seawall, but it's a little chilly for that. What about going to see a movie?"

Shannon shrugged again. "Sure."

Revenge of the Nerds was the only comedy out of the five movies showing, so although Mandey had already seen it twice, that's what they chose. Mandey wanted to see it again, anyway.

"This is the greatest movie," Mandey said as she purchased the tickets. "Maybe you won't agree, but I loved it. I'm a nerd."

Shannon carefully surveyed her in her jeans, Pony high-tops, sweatshirt, big silver hoop earrings, and letter jacket. She didn't look like any nerd he'd ever seen.

Noticing the look, she said, "I am. Omega Mu all the way. I used to look more like it, too. I'm trying to revamp my image, but it isn't easy."

Shannon didn't know what "Omega Moo" meant, but the part about changing her image, he did.

She bought refreshments, too. "Popcorn and Raisinets," she said happily as they took their drinks and treats into the theater, "are depression cure-alls."

Mandey enjoyed the movie just as much the third time around as the first two times she had seen it—even more, because she enjoyed gauging Shannon's reaction to it. He obviously found it funny, too, from the way he was laughing. She had never heard him laugh before. It was deep and rich, like his voice, and she loved it.

When the popcorn and candy were gone, Mandey found herself holding hands with Shannon. James had never held her hand at the movies. In fact, James had never been a particularly physically affectionate person. At least, not with Mandey. Shannon seemed the opposite, and that made her happy.

After the movie, it was getting dark, and Mandey took Shannon to where he had left his car.

"What are you going to do now?" she asked him.

He heaved a sigh. "I've gotta get home. I've gotta work tomorrow, and if I don't show up, the shit's gonna hit the fan. But I can't go on living there much longer. I've got to figure out my next move."

"You will," Mandey said, reaching over to give his knee a reassuring squeeze. "It's going to work out somehow."

He stared at her intently, silently, and then finally he said, "When I met you this morning, I thought you were so far out of my league, we wouldn't have anything in common. But I was wrong."

"I'm glad you were wrong," Mandey said.

"Me, too."

He started to open the door to get out, then hesitated and turned to look at Mandey again. He was tangled up in his emotions, and he wasn't sure what he should do.

Go for it, said a voice in his head.

They gazed at each other for a moment, then Shannon gave in to his impulse by slipping his arm around her, gently tipping her face up to look into her eyes, then he kissed her. He wondered if he should have asked her first, but she kissed back so willingly that he decided that he hadn't offended her. He kissed her softly, sweetly, but with much emotion. God knew he was feeling a lot of emotion.

When their lips parted, Mandey felt herself blushing furiously. "I've never been kissed like that before," she said softly.

"Me, neither," Shannon replied.

Mandey pulled him closer, and they kissed again, longer and deeper this time, holding each other close.

"Aggressive, aren't you?" Shannon remarked with a chuckle.

Mandey giggled. "Not usually. I guess I'm afraid you're going to get away again."

"Not this time," Shannon declared. He kissed her cheek and got out of the van. "I'll call you tomorrow," he said, as he felt his pants pocket to make sure the piece of paper with her number on it was still there. He shut the door and went to his car.

Mandey blew a kiss to him as he pulled out onto the road. He pretended to catch it. He followed her all the way back to the city to where I-45 crossed U. S. 59. He continued up 45, while Mandey took the 59 exit.

He felt numb, but it was a nice numb. *Comfortably numb,* he thought, as a snatch of the Pink Floyd song flashed through his mind. For once in his life, things didn't look quite so bad. His instincts had been right. When he had seen her at that club over a year ago, he'd been instantly attracted to her. Maybe it had been love at first sight. Well, second sight, since he had overlooked her before.

The thought of sleeping with her entered his mind, and he groaned out loud. He was nervous enough without having to think about that yet, but he couldn't help it. When he kissed her—hell, then when <u>she</u> kissed <u>him</u>—there was that <u>heat</u>…He wondered if she could be a virgin. He doubted it, because he didn't know any 17-year-old virgins. She had probably slept with her ex-boyfriend, but she was no slut, he could tell. He thought about her crying in McDonald's. That guy had to be a total asshole not to appreciate a girl like her. Shannon was determined to make her forget all about him.

He decided that as far as trying to sleep with her, he wasn't going to rush it, for his sake as well as hers. She didn't seem like the type who wanted to jump in the sack the first thing, anyway, and that was a relief to him. She was a nice girl. Shannon knew he would have to be very careful not to mess this up, and he was scared. He was terrified he was going to make a mistake with her, and he didn't want to screw up the one thing he finally seemed to have going for him.

Mandey replayed those kisses over and over in her mind on the way home. Just thinking about them gave her goosebumps. She had found Shannon, and she had his phone number in her purse. She almost could not believe it. He was <u>not</u> going to get away again.

She put a new cassette in the player and queued up a song. John Oates began to sing, "Thank you for..." She was thankful for the day she had spent with Shannon. She had sung along with the radio on the way to Galveston that morning to channel her grief. Tonight, she was singing again, with just as much emotion, but this time it was pure joy.

10

Getting to Know You

"Hello?"

"Uh, hi, Mandey?"

A smile came to her face as she recognized his voice. "Hi, Shannon."

"Hi." He felt a flash of relief. Despite how well things had gone the day before, a small part of him had feared she had given him a fake phone number.

"What's up?" Mandey asked, sitting down on her bed.

"Not much. What about you?"

"Nothing here either. Are you at home?"

"No, I'm at work. I get off in an hour."

"Great! You want to come over?"

"Sure."

"I'll see you in about an hour and a half?"

"Give me two hours. I want to take a shower and change clothes first."

"Okay. I'll see you then."

That gave her two hours to get ready. She showered, did her hair and makeup, then tried to decide on the right outfit to wear. Something not too fancy but nicer than the jeans and sweatshirt she had on the day before. She ended up choosing a newer pair of jeans and a tight, scoop-necked, short-sleeved marled rainbow sweater, along with gold jewelry. She liked what she saw in the mirror. She hoped Shannon would, too.

Two hours later Shannon drove into the driveway. Mandey was waiting anxiously at the front door and invited him in.

"This is Shannon," Mandey said to Marcia, who was sitting on the couch doing bills. "Shannon, this is Marcia."

Marcia looked up and smiled at him. "Hi," she said.

"Hi," Shannon replied, smiling nervously.

"Mandey has talked about you non-stop since she got home last night," Marcia said.

Shannon blushed. "Well, I've been thinking about her non-stop since last night," he said.

"Do you want something to drink?" Mandey asked Shannon. "We have Pepsi, Tab, and lemonade. Or water."

"Uh, no thanks."

"Sure?"

"I'm okay."

Mandey led him down the hallway to her bedroom. "Have a seat," she said, sitting down on her double bed.

Shannon sat down next to her, looking around the room. It sure wasn't like his own. This room had a stereo and a stereo cabinet with lots of albums and tapes, a TV and a VCR in one corner, a desk, a nightstand, and a chest of drawers. The most striking thing about the room was that nearly every inch of available wall and ceiling space was covered in magazine poster pin-ups. She had Daryl Hall and John Oates, Duran Duran, the Police, the Stray Cats, the Cars, Wham!, Blondie, Culture Club, the Ramones, the B-52's, the Fixx, ABC, the Go-Go's, Human League, Billy Idol, Talking Heads, the Pretenders, Prince, the Eurythmics, Queen, Cyndi Lauper, Tina Turner, David Bowie, Def Leppard, and more. Shannon wondered why he'd never thought of doing something like that to his room. Then he thought again and decided it wasn't such a great idea. They would just get ripped down.

"I like your room," he said.

"Thanks," she replied.

"I like that sweater you're wearing, too."

"Thanks," she said again, smiling.

"It seems weird being out here in this neighborhood again," Shannon said. "I liked living out here better than anywhere else."

"I was so depressed after you moved," Mandey said, moving closer to him.

"Really?" Shannon asked, smiling slightly, not quite believing her.

"Devastated," she replied. "You know what? You have a gorgeous smile."

He smiled even bigger and looked down at his lap.

"Thanks," he said, embarrassed.

They were silent for a few moments. "Are you sure you don't want something to drink?" Mandey asked him again.

He thought it over. "Well, yeah, a Pepsi, I guess."

"Okay, I'll be right back." She left the room.

Shannon stood up and walked around. He looked at the bookshelves on one wall of the room. Shannon thought most girls read romance books, but from what she had on her shelves, it was obvious that Mandey's tastes ran more toward science fiction and Stephen King.

He picked up what appeared to be a photo album of some kind and opened it. It was full of pictures and ribbons and awards. He jumped guiltily when Mandey re-entered the room.

"I was just looking at your books," he said lamely.

Mandey smiled. "Look all you like. It there's anything I don't want anyone to see, I don't put it on my shelves," she said, offering him a glass of Pepsi with ice.

"Thanks," he said, taking it and sitting down on the edge of the bed again. He laid the scrapbook next to him.

She sat down on the bed with a can of Tab in her hand. "Get comfortable. Kick your shoes off. Have a pillow." She tossed him one, then opened the book Shannon had been looking at. "Most of these things are junior high awards." Mandey flipped over those pages.

"Wait," Shannon protested. "Show me. I want to see."

"Okay," Mandey said, flipping back to the beginning. "National Junior Honor Society membership cards. Honor roll awards. Outstanding social studies student award in seventh and eighth grade. Ribbons from academic meets. Science fair ribbons, history fair ribbon, choir award, perfect attendance. . ."

"Wow," Shannon said in admiration. "You're smart."

"Yeah. I guess so."

"That's great!" Shannon said.

"I hope you aren't intimidated by that."

"No!"

"Are you sure? Lots of guys are. They can't handle intelligent women. They feel threatened by them. I'm more than a brainy goody-two-shoes!" Mandey said, frustrated.

"I know you're not," Shannon assured her, "and I've only known you since yesterday."

They went back to looking at the book. "Here are some of my friends when we were in junior high. This is my best friend, Georgia. She's the most popular girl in school. We don't seem like candidates to be best friends, but we have been since I moved here seven years ago. This is another good friend, Andrea. Oh, God, don't look at these." She put her hands over the next page.

"Aw, come on," Shannon said, pulling her hands away.

"Ugh," Mandey said. "Me in eighth grade. Yuck."

"You don't look so bad," Shannon said.

"But I look much better now."

"Everybody looks dorky in junior high," Shannon said, making Mandey laugh.

"Let's get off this page," she continued. "Here's Georgie and I when we were eleven, and here I am on the night of the eighth-grade prom. I went dateless, but then, most of us did. A pink dress, yuck. All they had for prom dresses that year were pastel colors in about five different styles. And here are my elementary school class pictures. That's me," she said, pointing herself out in the pictures. "Same face, just a different hairstyle."

"You were a cute little girl."

"I was a fat little girl. Now I'm a fat big girl."

"You aren't fat," Shannon said.

"Some people seem to think I am." Mandey said, thinking of James.

"Well, I don't. Now me, I'm fat," Shannon said.

"No, you aren't," Mandey said. "Big, strong, husky, yes. Fat, no."

Mandey closed that book and took another off her shelf. This one had more recent photographs. Mandey turned the page, and Shannon saw her expression change. He looked down at the book and knew why.

"Is this you and James?" he asked.

"Yeah," she said softly.

Shannon studied the pictures. Mandey looked fantastic. In one picture, she was gorgeous in a black sleeveless dress with a silver sash. Shannon paid even more attention to James. James was a bit shorter and much slimmer than Shannon, with black hair, brown eyes, light brown skin, and wire rimmed glasses.

"He's…Chinese?" Shannon said in surprise.

"Vietnamese," Mandey said.

He studied the picture again. James was wearing black pants, a white shirt with sleeves rolled up to the elbows, a black vest with a fancy silver pattern on it, and a black string tie with a silver clasp. He looked very slick. Mandey looked so happy in those pictures. He wondered if she could look that way again, but with him instead of James.

Shannon glanced at Mandey and saw tears in her eyes. He slipped his arm around her.

"I don't love him anymore," Mandey said, impatiently wiping away the tears. She got off the bed to check herself in the mirror on the wall. She continued talking as she got rid of the smeared mascara. "In fact, there were times I think I absolutely hated him. If I only understood why he acted the way he did toward me, I'd feel so much better, but it's like talking to that cliched brick wall." She took a deep breath to pull herself together.

She sat back down next to Shannon and turned the page. "Let's go on to something with better memories," she said.

Shannon put his arm around her again. "Why did you stay with him when he treated you so bad?"

Mandey thought for a moment. "A lot of reasons, I guess, but mostly it comes down to the fact that he needed me. At least, I thought he did. James is good-looking, smart, athletic, and so on, but a lot of people don't like him. He needed a friend, and I was there for him. I guess somewhere along the line I grew to love him, and I think he felt the same way about me, too, in the beginning. But then he changed. I kept hoping things would be like they were before. I couldn't turn my back on him. So instead, he turned his back on me." She paused. "I'd like to think it's not all my fault. I'd like to think he has a deeper problem that's made him push me away. Lord knows he's got all kinds of problems. But still. . ."

Shannon gave her a comforting squeeze. "Don't blame yourself. It sounds like you tried to be there for him, and he told you to go to hell. That's his problem, not yours."

"I know," Mandey said. She smiled a genuine smile at him and leaned over to kiss him on the cheek. "Thanks."

They perused Mandey's scrapbooks for a while longer, then Mandey looked at the clock.

"We're going to have supper soon. I hope you'll stay and eat with us."

"I, uh, well, I don't want to barge in. . ."

"It's okay. I already told Marcia I was going to ask you."

"Well, okay."

"Good," Mandey said, pleased.

Shannon was somewhat apprehensive about sharing a meal with Mandey and Marcia. He was concerned about making a good impression and was convinced that he probably couldn't.

As it was, he had little to worry about. Marcia was very jovial and quick to make jokes, and she made Shannon feel at ease. She was also a smoker, so he felt comfortable enough to light up with her after they ate. The only time he felt nervous was when Marcia asked him what he did. He felt stupid saying that he worked at a gas station. Marcia was an accountant at a law office, and Mandey surely was going on to college, and here he was, a dumb grease monkey. But then Marcia asked if he would look at her car sometime; it was making a strange noise, and she could never get it to make the noise for the people at the garage. He told her he would be happy to, and breathed an inward sigh of relief.

After dinner, Mandey and Shannon returned to her bedroom, and she closed the door behind them.

"Marcia doesn't mind that we're alone in here?" Shannon asked as they sat down on the bed.

"Nah," Mandey said. "For one thing, she knows I'm a heck of a lot straighter than she was at my age. And she said that when the time comes that I do have sex, she'd rather have me here under my own roof than out God-knows-where with God-knows-who." Then she stopped and turned red, realizing what she had just said. "Not that I am talking about having sex right now," she added hastily.

"She's pretty cool," Shannon remarked. "When you told me you lived with your older sister, I wasn't expecting her to be that much older."

"That's because she's actually my mother."

Shannon looked at Mandey blankly.

"Marcia had me when she was nineteen. My father ran off before I was born, and my grandparents adopted me. I was raised as her sister," Mandey explained.

"Wow," Shannon said. "Where are your grandparents?"

"My father had a heart attack last spring and had to retire from his job. They moved back to Connecticut over the summer. I would have gone, too, but I had this last year of school. Marcia came when our father got sick last spring, then she got a job and moved in permanently."

"Do y'all get along okay?" Shannon asked.

"Oh, yeah. But it isn't a mother-daughter relationship. I was raised as her sister, and that's how I feel about her. I never knew her very well until she moved in. She didn't live close by, so she wasn't around much," Mandey said.

Shannon noticed the sad expression that spread across her face.

"I miss my parents," she said with a sigh. "I don't know yet what I'll do when I graduate. I've been trying to decide if I'll stay here or if I'll move up there to be near them. I'll have to wait and see, I guess."

He slipped his arm around her, and she looked at him. "I guess I shouldn't complain. My family life is light-years removed from yours," she told him.

"I didn't get to know my father very well, either," Shannon said. "He died when I was seven, almost eight. I remember he was big and strong. He laughed a lot, and played the guitar. And he never beat on me. I wish he hadn't died and left us."

"What happened?" Mandey asked softly.

"He was in a convenience store when it got held up, and he got shot."

Mandey gave a little gasp. "I'm sorry," she said.

"Nowhere near as sorry as I've been for the last eleven years."

Mandey gave his knee a gentle squeeze. Shannon kissed her forehead. Mandey slipped her arms around him and kissed him on the mouth. Shannon embraced her and kissed back.

"Let's have some music," Mandey suggested, turning the stereo on her favorite station, and setting the volume low.

She laid down on the bed and motioned for Shannon to join her. He laid down next to her, feeling slightly nervous. They cuddled close.

"Hi," she said, smiling at him.

"Hi," he replied, and smiled back, feeling less nervous now.

"I have spent so many hours daydreaming about having you here next to me, in my arms," Mandey said. "I can hardly believe it's not a dream anymore."

Shannon smiled. "I've thought a lot about you in the last year, too," he said, then his smile dimmed.

"I've gone to Liaisons pretty often over the past year," Mandey said. "Every time I went, I hoped I would see you again, but I was always disappointed. I thought maybe if what your friend said was true, that you would have been there looking for me..."

Shannon noticed Mandey's smile dimmed, as well. He <u>would</u> have been there that very next weekend, and he <u>would</u> have mustered the courage to find her and talk to her, if he hadn't screwed up. He hesitated for a moment, but then decided she deserved an explanation, although he was nervous about what her reaction would be.

"Mandey, if I tell you why I never showed up there again, you may not want me around no more," he told her.

"Why?" Mandey asked. "What happened?"

He looked directly into her green eyes. He was scared, but he figured she was going to find out eventually. "Would it scare you if I said I've been in trouble with the law?"

"I guess it depends on what you did," Mandey said. "You didn't murder or rape anybody, did you?"

"Good Lord, no," Shannon said, looking genuinely shocked.

"Then it probably won't scare me."

Shannon sighed. "I did something stupid, I'm ashamed of it, and I paid the price. I was in jail for eight months. I was lucky. They put me in a youthful offender program because it was my first offense. I was seventeen, so they could have treated me as an adult. I've been out about five months now."

Mandey was quiet for a minute. "Why did you get arrested?" she asked finally.

Shannon paused. Although he had known that question was eventually going to come up, he still didn't want to answer it. But, he figured, if she was willing to be with him knowing that he had been arrested, she probably could handle the reason why. He might as well tell her. Lying would probably get him in bigger trouble with her.

"Armed robbery," he said in a low voice. "I was running with a rough crowd and got mixed up in a lot of shit I had no business being in. I was with a couple other guys, but I was the one they caught."

Silently Mandey absorbed this information. "From what I always observed of you, you were kind of a quiet, gentle person. It's hard for me to believe you would do something like that," she said, "especially considering what happened to your father."

A wave of guilt swept over Shannon. He had thought about his father when he committed the crime, but, in the end, his reasons for going along with the robbery had been much more persuasive than the guilt he felt.

"I know," he said quietly. "I know it was wrong, and I was really stupid. I've regretted doing it ever since. I used to lay in my bunk at night when I was in jail, and sometimes I'd think about you. Then I would remember where I was, and I doubted you'd want to have anything to do with me if I ever did see you again."

He was silent for a moment, then looked at Mandey. "Do you hate me now?"

She smiled. "Of course not. But I'm glad you're not doing stuff like that anymore."

"Yeah. Me, too."

Shannon knew he couldn't tell her the truth right now. He hoped that soon he would finally have his own place to live, far away from the people who were presently in his life, and then it would be the truth. He wouldn't be doing stuff like that anymore.

Mandey hugged him and kissed his cheek. "Why do you look so sad?" she asked him. "You were always so sober. I never heard you laugh before yesterday. I want to be able to bring a smile to your face."

Shannon smiled at her. "Oh, girl, you do, believe me."

"Oh?" Mandey asked, grinning. "And what happens when I do this?"

She pressed her lips to his and kissed him passionately, her tongue meeting his. When their lips parted, Shannon said seriously, "I feel like this has to be happening to somebody else."

Mandey shook her head. "Wrong. It's happening to you," she told him, gently poking him in the chest.

"You're only the second girl who's ever liked me," Shannon said. "I guess you were the first, if you liked me back three years ago."

"Really. Who's the other one?"

"Oh, this chick who lives in my neighborhood. I went with her for a couple weeks when I first moved there. She's pretty, but I found out fast what she's really like, and since then I ain't had nothing to do with her."

"Hmmm," Mandey said. "I think I know someone else who liked you."

"Who?" Shannon asked, curious.

"You remember Denise Wharton?"

"Denise?" he asked, his face getting warm.

He remembered Denise, a heavy-set girl who chain-smoked, swore, and picked fights. Although she was his own age, she had been two grades behind him. Denise had been friends with his sister.

"Mmm-hmm," Mandey said. "I heard this a couple years ago on the bus at the beginning of tenth grade. Denise had finally made it to the freshman class, and she said she wished you hadn't moved away. She said that you had always liked her, and she should have gone steady with you."

"She did not," Shannon said, grimacing.

"Yes, she did," Mandey insisted.

He thought about it. Maybe he had acted sort of interested in her, but he really hadn't been. Well, maybe a little. It was only because she tried to flirt with him.

"Well, I-I don't know," he stammered. "Maybe I gave her the wrong impression. I mean, she used to hang around with Annette, and she used to kind of flirt with me. I don't know."

Mandey chuckled, trying to imagine Denise flirting. Mandey thought that to flirt, a person had to employ a certain amount of reserve, of coyness. Denise was pretty blunt. Her idea of flirting was probably, "You want to go fuck, or what?"

Then she became serious. "I felt bad when I heard that, because I figured if you'd like a girl like her, you'd never be interested in someone like me," she told him. "You never noticed me on the school bus, and I sat right across the aisle from you."

Shannon noticed the forlorn look on her face, and it made him sad. All that time, there had been someone so special who had wanted him, and he had never known it.

"I remember you now, though," he said. "You sat with that girl, Theresa, and you always had school books with you."

Mandey looked up at him, encouraged, then looked sad again. "But you didn't notice me then. The guys I liked never did. I wasn't much to look at, and I didn't talk much, so I faded into the background."

"I'm sorry," Shannon said. "If I had known. . .but I didn't."

Mandey looked at him. "You had lots of girls who liked you, I think. What about Verna Carlisle?"

Shannon drew a blank for a moment, then recalled a husky girl, nice-looking, who was almost as tall as he was. They had been in Algebra I together.

"I remember watching you after school one day, before the bus picked us up. You were horsing around with her, picking her up and carrying her around on your back. She was laughing," Mandey said, frowning. "I was jealous."

Shannon drew Mandey close and hugged her tightly. "Mandey, I just didn't know. I didn't know you. I wish I had."

Mandey hugged him back. "It's not your fault," she said. "I guess I could have tried to come up and talk to you, but I was too shy. What's important is that we're together now. Having had to wait so long makes this all that much sweeter."

Shannon kissed her. "You are sweet--and beautiful," he said. "You were definitely worth the wait."

He kissed her again, and tried to ease himself on top of her. As he did, he accidentally rammed his elbow into her left breast.

"Ouch!" Mandey winced, holding her breast with her right hand.

Shannon froze. He remembered a similar occurrence, and how his girlfriend at the time had screamed and ranted at him.

"I-I'm so sorry," he stammered, lying back down next to her.

Mandey noticed that Shannon looked like he expected her to start yelling at him.

"It's okay," she said. She took his hand in hers and kissed his cheek. Shannon turned his head to look into her eyes. To his surprise, she wasn't angry.

"I'm sorry," he repeated. "It's just—"

"Just what?"

It was just that he was nervous, like he had been with Kerri. He could hear Kerri's voice in his head, berating him. He didn't tell Mandey that. Instead, he shook his head and said, "I'm a fucking klutz. I'll try to be more careful."

Mandey smiled. "You're not a klutz. Maybe you just need some practice," she said, teasing.

Shannon chuckled. She was closer to the truth than she knew. "I guess so."

They began making out again. Mandey let Shannon touch her breasts over her sweater. Gently squeezing them made Shannon hard, but he felt himself getting nervous, as well. He decided not to try to go any further with her right then. He wouldn't even have gone as far as he did, had she not encouraged it. Her hand unintentionally brushed lightly over his hard crotch. He would have loved to feel her touch it, but didn't pursue it.

There will be lots of time, he thought. *Lots of time for us to spend together, to hold each other, to get to know each other.*

At seven Mandey went to the kitchen and brought back a tray of homemade chocolate chip cookies and two glasses of milk, and they watched *Murder, She Wrote* on her bedroom television. At eight, when the show was over, Mandey had to get ready for school the next day, and it was time for Shannon to leave.

"This has been the best weekend ever," Shannon said, as he lingered with Mandey on the front steps. "When can I see you again?"

"Whenever you're free and I'm not at school," Mandey said. "Next weekend, for sure."

"I'll give you a call tomorrow night," he said. "When's the best time?"

"Before ten is probably the best," Mandey told him.

"Okay," Shannon said, but made no move to leave. He sighed. "You know I don't want to go."

"I don't want you to, either," Mandey said, sliding her arms around his waist.

Shannon put his arms around her and squeezed her tightly. "You feel so good in my arms," he told her.

"So do you," she replied, laying her head against his shoulder.

They kissed again, then reluctantly let go of one another.

"Thanks for the meal. It was great," Shannon said.

"You're welcome. Anytime."

"Goodnight," he said, kissing her lips quickly.

"Goodnight."

She watched as he got in his car, started it, and pulled out into the street. She didn't go back inside until he was out of sight.

"He seems very sweet. Did you have a nice visit?" Marcia asked as Mandey came back into the house.

"Very," Mandey said, a huge smile on her face.

She felt slightly dazed. The feeling stuck with her as she took a shower then chose a cute outfit for school the next day. She repainted her fingernails to match. All the while, she thought about Shannon being there with her, on her bed, kissing her, and her kissing him back. She had dreamed about that for three long years. The same thoughts were running through her head when she finally got in bed, but there was also something else. His confession about what he had done to get thrown in jail was unsettling. She knew from the incident with Shannon's sister and mother at school that Shannon's family was a bit wilder than her own, but somehow, she didn't think that was Shannon's character. He hadn't been up there getting into the fight; he had stood there alone, looking defeated and sad. She had never seen anything from him that indicated violent tendencies. When she questioned him about his arrest, he seemed truly sorry it had ever happened. She had to believe the person who tried to rob a liquor store was not the real Shannon. The real Shannon was the one who kissed her so sweetly (and also passionately), who touched her so softly, who talked with her and laughed with her for hours, who made her feel like she was the most special person in the whole world. That thought lulled her to sleep.

11

Back to Reality

When Shannon walked into the apartment Monday afternoon after work, his mother was lying on the sofa, wrapped in a ratty old housecoat, watching the noon news. She didn't say anything to him; she didn't even look up. Her eyes were glassy. Shannon knew she had been drinking. Then he heard a loud, snorting snore from the other bedroom.

"Shit," he muttered under his breath.

Leon had moved in when Shannon was eight, and eventually became Shannon's stepfather when he married his mother the following year. Over the last eleven years, Leon had come and gone many times. For a few years he was a long-haul trucker that kept him on the road much of the time, but Shannon always dreaded the days when he was back, as Leon spent most of that time drunk and mean. He lost his job when it was discovered he was stealing from shipments and selling the merchandise, and occasionally transporting illicit goods. That had also gotten him the all-expenses paid vacation to Huntsville. They had had to move to this God-forsaken place when he had returned after a two-and-a-half-year stint in prison and began drinking up Shannon's and Annette's social security checks again.

Shannon's mother received SSI checks, too; she had been diagnosed with manic depression and was able to get disability payments. Her check along with his and Annette's were enough for rent and utilities and groceries and gas, when Leon wasn't around.

"They should never have let that fucker out," Shannon muttered.

Shannon showered and changed into jeans and a flannel shirt, then went to the kitchen to scrounge up some lunch. He found some bread that wasn't too stale and made a peanut butter sandwich. He needed something to drink to wash down the peanut butter. There was a six pack of beer in the refrigerator, but he wasn't going to touch that, no way, no thanks. There was also a pitcher of purple Kool-Aid, which Annette loved. Shannon thought the stuff was kind of sickening, but it was better than the tap water. He picked a plastic tumbler out of the sink, rinsed it out, and filled it with the sweet purple liquid.

He took his sandwich and Kool-Aid to the living room and sat down in the armchair.

His mother was still staring listlessly at the television, which was now in the middle of *As the World Turns.*

Shannon thought back to the time Leon was in prison. It was a couple of the best years of his life. It hadn't been perfect, for damn sure, but he was going to school and liking it all right, and he had made a few friends. His mother was getting psychiatric help and wasn't in a boozed-up stupor all the time. She talked to him about school and his friends, and would even share her beer with him. She wasn't exactly Mrs. Brady, but she was his mother.

Then Leon was released, and his mother took him back. Why, he did not understand, but she was vulnerable, and Leon found a way to worm himself back into their lives.

He didn't want to think about it any longer. He watched Steve and Betsy arguing about Craig on the soap opera as he finished his sandwich. He gulped down the Kool-Aid to get the stickiness out of his mouth, then went out to the kitchen and put his tumbler back in the sink again. His hunger and thirst were abated, but he felt slightly queasy.

Guess I'm not used to such fine cuisine, he thought sourly.

It was a letdown from the delicious dinner he had had at Mandey's the day before, and from the picnic lunch they had shared on Saturday. He could get used to eating that way very quickly.

Shannon headed toward the front door. He looked at his mother again. She hadn't moved. It was creepy. If he didn't see that she was still breathing, he could have mistaken her for dead.

Although he was not in the mood for it, he headed over to see what the gang was doing. He hadn't been in contact with any of them for almost a week, and he knew they would be wondering where the hell he had been. He figured it was his duty as fearless leader to check in. He didn't want to see any of their faces at all. He knew exactly what he wanted—to be with Mandey again, in her room, in her arms, kissing her and holding her.

The thought of her both cheered him up and depressed him at the same time. He knew even if he wasn't here where he was now, he couldn't be with Mandey until after school let out, anyway. He had a sinking feeling that he wasn't going to be able to get away to see her tonight because he was going to be tied up with Devils' business for a while. As soon as he could, though, he was going to lock himself in his room with the telephone, call Mandey, and enjoy the little piece of heaven for as long as he could.

In the meantime, he had matters to attend to here. He made his way into the crumbling building, and the first person he saw was Kerri sitting on the raggedy couch, looking in a compact mirror and applying lipstick in the weak gray light coming through one of the partially-boarded up windows.

Damn, he groaned inwardly.

"You're back!" she squealed, and jumped up off the couch. She threw her arms around him. Shannon pushed her away, not gently.

"Where have you been?" Kerri asked, unabashed.

"Around," he said shortly. "Anybody else here?"

"Lenny, Curt, and John are playing cards in the other room," she told him, stepping in back of him and reaching up to massage his shoulders. "You seem tired and tense. Why don't you let me make you feel better?"

He brushed her off and walked into the next room without a word, without even looking at her. Kerri stared after him for a moment, then dropped back down onto the couch. An hour earlier she had been making Lenny, Curtis, and John all feel better. Most guys would get horny watching a girl giving a guy (or three) head, but not Trick. If he had come upon the scene, he would have walked away.

Kerri thought back to when Trick and Annette moved into the apartments. Trick had been so fine--tall, dark, strong, and handsome. She could hardly wait to get her hands on him; the other guys in the gang had become boring. Kerri could see the way he looked at her, but realized he was too shy to make the first move. That made him all the more attractive to her, for she didn't often get the opportunity to initiate the action.

Once she began showing her interest in him, he had asked her to go steady. Kerri hadn't gone steady with anyone since she was thirteen, and she almost laughed at him. Still, she decided to give it another try, so she had agreed.

To her dismay, Kerri realized that even though Trick wanted her to be his girlfriend, he was a little slow when it came to having sex with her. They had gotten close, even as far as getting naked in her bed. They had been fondling each other, and his cock was huge and hard in her hand. She had spread her legs to invite him in, but as he rolled on top of her, he acted like he didn't know what the hell he was doing, accidentally pulling her hair and ramming an elbow into her breast.

"You clumsy ox!" she yelled at him.

Trick scrambled off her. "Sorry. I'm sorry," he said, concerned. "Are you okay?"

"That hurt, you fucking klutz!" Kerri snapped, rubbing her breast. "Do you even know what you're doing?"

He had looked at her for a moment, then got out of bed. "Sorry," he said again, and started putting on his clothes.

"Where are you going? Don't you leave me! I swear to God, I'll go find somebody else!"

Trick hadn't replied. He left.

What the hell? she thought. She had expected him to get angry and passionate and fuck her brains out. Instead, he left.

Although Kerri had been furious, she didn't follow through on her threat. She still wanted Trick, so she decided to give him another chance. The next night they had been together in his bedroom, and she began unbuttoning his shirt. He pulled away, saying he'd had a rough day and was tired.

She exploded. "What the fuck is your problem?" she shouted.

"Aw, Kerri, don't start."

"No! Why won't you fuck me? Huh? Are you a faggot or something?"

"Shut up!"

"Cocksucker! Faggot! You ain't man enough to fuck me!"

"I said SHUT UP!"

At that point Trick had pulled her up off the bed, picked her up, and dumped her out of the bedroom window. "Get the fuck out of here!" he told her, and then shut and locked the window. Then he pulled the shade.

Kerri had been dumbfounded. She had said those things to goad him into proving her wrong, and fully expected him to grab her, force her down, and screw the hell out of her. She screamed and pounded on the window until it cracked, but got no response. She finally left, seething. On the way back to her house, she ran into Victor, who was then leader of the Devils. She went with him, and he didn't disappoint.

The next day she had been all alone at the hideout, still furious and humiliated by Trick's rejection. It wasn't fair, asking her to go steady and then not sleeping with her, and expecting her not to sleep with anybody else. She barely noticed when Raff walked in. He came over to where she was sprawled on the ratty sofa and without asking, he started pulling at her clothes. She didn't resist. Raff unbuckled his belt and pulled down his pants. A minute later they were fucking, doggy-style, on the couch. They were still busy when Trick walked in.

Trick had stood there with a shocked look on his face. Kerri looked at him, then back at Raff, and she and Raff began laughing.

"Sorry, man, I guess you weren't getting the job done," Raff said to Trick.

Trick, true to form, didn't say anything. He just slowly turned around and walked back out.

That ended Kerri's stint as Trick's girlfriend, but it didn't end her yearning to bed him. If anything, her desire for him was intensified. She knew he wasn't gay, not the way his cock had stood at attention for her. Kerri wanted him, desperately, and wanted him to want her, too. But he didn't, and she couldn't figure out why.

"Trick, you bastard. Where have you been keeping your ass?" John asked as Shannon walked into the room where John was slaughtering Lenny and Curtis at poker.

"Had to leave town for a few days. Personal business," Shannon said, in a tone that made it clear that he wanted no more discussion about the topic. He pulled up a chair and sat down. "Where's Raff and Checkmate?"

"Don't know," John said, laying down a full house.

"Fuck," Curtis said, as he and Lenny threw down their losing hands. John raked the money on the table to his already considerable pile.

"They went some place with 'Nette and 'Nita," Lenny said.

"Anything happen while I was gone?" Shannon asked.

"Nope," Curt replied.

However, the glances exchanged by the three card players did not escape Shannon.

John dealt another hand to himself, Lenny, and Curtis. He didn't deal Shannon in or ask if he wanted to play. They began playing the next hand in silence.

Shannon didn't want to play cards, anyway, not after he caught a glimpse of the way they had looked at each other when Curt said nothing important had happened. He took his chair and set it in a dim corner. He knew something was wrong; something had happened in his absence that he needed to know about. Whatever it was, he was positive Raff was in the middle of it.

Regardless of whatever else might have gone on, he knew that Raff had probably bitched and raved the entire time he was away. He didn't need dissension spreading through the ranks, not if he wanted to hold on to his position as leader. He shouldn't have had to, but he knew he was going to have to prove himself again, to redeem himself in the eyes of the rest of the gang.

He closed his eyes to think. His mind came up with several possibilities that he promptly dismissed. He was going to have to plan something that would make everyone some money. A burglary or robbery of some sort, but not a liquor store. He'd learned his lesson about that.

Mentally he drove through the streets of what they considered their gang territory until he came upon a shopping center. One shop in the corner stood out in his mind, which was sandwiched between the Wild Style Hair Den and Angel Donuts. It was a small jewelry store with a name he couldn't remember. Although the shopping center was on a busy street, the property behind the stores was underdeveloped and separated from the stores by a solid wooden fence, so that could work to their advantage. He could send someone in to scope out the place, to locate any weak spots or things they needed to avoid. After a couple days of observations, a heist would likely be no problem. He supposed that it might happen that they would have to rob the place during store hours, but only as a last resort. He would prefer to break in after closing, when there would be no witnesses.

A wave of guilt broke over him as Mandey suddenly came to mind. What would she think of him if she knew what he was planning? She wouldn't want anything to do with him; she thought he was reformed.

I am reformed, he thought determinedly. *I'm only doing this to save my ass.*

Mandey wouldn't understand, though. She couldn't. She had no idea what his life was like, even though he had told her a lot (but far from everything) about it. Shannon knew that Raff was becoming more discontented because he felt Shannon didn't take enough risks, or organize jobs they could get rich from. Shannon also was not oblivious to the fact that Raff would not mind it if Shannon turned up dead.

If he had a majority of the gang on his side, Shannon knew he would be okay. In fact, as long as a majority wasn't on Raff's side, he would probably be all right. Some of the members of the gang were on the fence and could be swayed. Right now, Raff had Checkmate, Juanita, and Annette for moral support. Shannon knew he had Marco and Kerri, but Lenny and Curtis were now up for grabs. And John was never on anyone's side except his own. He had started up the gang with Victor years ago, but John was never interested in being the leader. Since Victor died, John was content to go along with the one who came up with the best schemes.

If he wanted any chance of keeping control, Shannon was going to have to plan and participate in a successful heist. Otherwise, he would soon lose what support he had left, and he would be forced out. Then, if Shannon couldn't get the hell out of Dodge, Raff would have him doing dangerous, stupid shit to make sure that he would end up back in jail, if not worse.

Shannon shuddered at the thought of going to prison. Those eight months in the youthful offender program had been no picnic, but he knew it was a cakewalk compared to prison. If he got sent to Huntsville, it would probably be for eight years, not eight months, and he'd probably end up as some ogre's bitch.

And to lose Mandey, now that he had finally found her? Never to feel her arms around him, to feel her soft kisses, to feel the soft curves of her body pressed against him? The idea was more than he could stand to think about. Somehow, he had to pull off this job, then keep himself as far from trouble as possible until he could find a way out.

It was only two-fifteen. Mandey wouldn't be home from school for over an hour. He didn't feel like hanging around with his gang mates, so Shannon decided to take a ride by the shopping center where the jewelry store was. He would see if his idea could possibly work. He got up and walked back through the living room to the door.

"Where are you going?" asked Kerri, who was again seated on the ratty sofa.

"Out," he said shortly. He knew it was rude, but he didn't care. If he acted any nicer toward her, Kerri would get the idea he wanted her again.

He was thinking about Mandey and Kerri as he got into his car and pulled out of the parking lot. There was no comparison. Kerri had long, fluffy, blonde hair, clear blue eyes, and a perfect figure (size 5, according to the tag he saw in one of her blouses once). Shannon knew she was physically beautiful, but he also knew that on the inside she wasn't beautiful at all.

Mandey, on the other hand…with her slightly wavy brown hair, those green eyes, that cute little nose, the dimpled smile—she was beautiful, too. Plus, on top of that, Mandey was sweet, smart, and funny.

"Good Lord, what did I ever do to deserve her?" he asked aloud, half to himself, half to God above.

His thoughts turned to the wonderful weekend he had spent with Mandey. *If only every day could be that great,* he thought. *Maybe one day they will be.*

His mind replayed how it felt to hold her and kiss her, and how it felt to touch her breasts through her tight, low-cut sweater.

Stop, he told himself. *You're going to give yourself a boner.*

He had a tremendous urge to turn around, go home, lock himself in the bathroom, and fantasize about Mandey.

Later, he told himself. *Down, boy. Think about Kerri. That will kill it.*

He did, and it did. It was odd how thinking about a knockout blonde could deflate him so fast.

The shopping center was a large, shallow block U-shaped set of buildings. Besides the jewelry store, which was tucked in one of the corners, the donut shop, and the hair salon, there was a grocery store, a health and fitness center, and a few other small shops and businesses.

Shannon liked the jewelry store's location. It was set back as far from the road as possible, and there was a breezeway right next to it that led to the back of the building. There were trees planted every thirty feet or so in the sidewalk that ran in front of all the stores, and one tree was right in front of the jewelry store. It wasn't a very big tree, but enough to provide a little camouflage, anyway.

It looked like it could be done. Someone would have to go inside the store before they tried to do anything, though, to check out the inventory, see what security was like, and identify the weak spots. Then they could break in, grab handfuls of jewelry and be gone in a flash. They would have to get the loot to a fence ASAP. He knew the person they would use, too, and it wasn't Leon, that was for sure. The guy's name was Rogelio Dupree, and the Devils had utilized his services in the past. Shannon thought back to the first time he had met Rogelio, after the Devils had ripped off a Radio Shack. Rogelio had done a good job; he had gotten rid of the stuff fast and got good money for it. Since the time Shannon had been released from jail and taken over leadership of the gang about five months ago, he had chosen not to have the Devils do anything that required Rogelio's services. He had enough to do stealing cars to keep his boss at the garage happy.

But discontent was brewing in the ranks. He couldn't blame them much. The only payoff from stealing those cars was keeping his ass out of jail; there was no monetary gain in it for anyone. He had only come up with a couple good schemes since taking over as leader: There was the time they had broken into a laundromat and run off with sacks full of quarters.

It was kind of hard to pass a lot of quarters without making anyone suspicious, so they had all played a lot of video games for a couple weeks. Once they had gotten a hold of a Schwan's truck, and they and their families had eaten well off all that fancy frozen food for a week or so. Neither one of those netted a load of cash. Victor, when he was leader, planned a lot of robberies. Besides the Radio Shack rip-off, there had been several others. But then there was the liquor store robbery, which was Shannon's downfall. After that, he never wanted to steal anything ever again—not that he had ever wanted to in the first place. Then he had gotten out of jail and he had nowhere to go but back to the Northview Apartments, and soon he was in deeper than ever.

Now he was planning this jewelry store burglary to prove himself as leader. He was overcompensating—at the same time he was so desperate to get away, he felt the need to do something impressive to try to make everyone believe he was more committed than ever.

Shannon would have to round up the gang later and tell them about his plan. He thought they would be excited about it; it could mean a nice chunk of change for each of them. If it went well, he might even get Raff off his back for a little while, too.

As he drove back home, his thoughts drifted back to Mandey again. Yes, he was definitely going to have to spend a little private time in the bathroom.

12

Balancing Act

The after-school meeting of the Alley Cats that Monday was short. The plan was to meet up and together in Mandey's van to Liaisons on Friday night. Five of them would go inside and see what was happening, while the other five would keep an eye out in the parking lot for suspicious activity. Later they would go over to Owens Towing and Storage to check out that area.

The girls were given the task of coming up with a club "uniform" to have ready by Friday. Dina begged off; her boyfriend Eduardo was a long-haul truck driver and he was coming in the next morning for a three-day layover. She hadn't seen him in three weeks and wanted to be free to be with him. Angelina and Mandey collected ten dollars from each of the Alley Cats who had it on them and took IOUs from those who didn't, to cover the clothing expense.

She was about thirty minutes later getting home. The answering machine light was blinking.

"Mandey, it's Shannon. Are you home?...Guess not. I've been calling your other phone. I'll call back later."

Mandey smiled at the disappointment she heard in his voice as she erased the message. It was nice to be missed.

She went to change out of her school clothes and was in her bra and panties when the phone in her room rang. She picked it up and said hello.

"Hi, it's Shannon."

"Hi. I got your message. I'm glad you called back. I was going to call you, but I'm kind of nervous about who I might end up talking to."

"Yeah, you never know who—or what—might answer here," Shannon said. Mandey giggled.

"Can you hold on a second?" Mandey asked him. "You caught me in the middle of changing my clothes."

"I did?" Shannon said. His tone told Mandey that he found this fact interesting.

She giggled again. "Yep. I'm here in just my bra and panties."

"Oh my God," Shannon said with a little moan in his voice.

"Hold on."

Mandey giggled to herself as she slipped on her jeans and a T-shirt. When she got back on the phone Shannon asked, "Are you dressed now?"

"Yes, I am. Jeans and a T-shirt."

"Damn," Shannon said ruefully. "I've got a great picture in my head, though."

Mandey laughed. "Okay. Enjoy," she said. "How was your day?"

"Same old thing as usual, except I got to come home and hear you tell me you're wearing nothing but a bra and panties."

"The highlight of your day, huh?"

"Oh, yeah," he said emphatically. "What color?"

"What color?" Mandey repeated, laughing. "A white lace bra. White lace panties with pink roses."

"Ahhhh, thank you," Shannon said. Mandey could tell he was adding those details to the picture in his head. Then his mind came back to their conversation and he asked, "How was your day?"

"Fine," she said. "Finer now that I'm talking to you. I've got a ton of homework tonight, though—Spanish, government, and chemistry."

"Bummer," Shannon said. "Probably not a good night for me to come over."

Mandey sighed. "You know I want you here, but no, probably not. I'd want you to stay, and stay a little longer, and then a little longer, and my homework wouldn't get done."

"Talking on the phone is pretty good, too, though," Shannon said.

"'Reach out, reach out and touch someone,'" Mandey sang.

They talked for over an hour, then Mandey said, "Marcia will be home soon. I should go start something for supper."

"All right," Shannon said. "I've got a few things I should do, too."

"Call me tomorrow night? Or maybe I'll call you," Mandey said.

"Either way," Shannon said. "One of us will call the other."

"Okay. Enjoy the rest of your evening."

"Oh, I will. I'm going to be thinking about you in your underwear."

"Will you stop?" Mandey said, laughing.

"Can't," Shannon said.

"Talk to you tomorrow," Mandey said.

When Shannon got off the phone, he went into the bathroom again, this time with the image of Mandey wearing nothing but a white lace bra and panties with pink roses in his head. He jacked off slowly, savoring the picture in his mind.

Someone banged on the door. "What are you doing in there, beating off or taking a dump?" Annette demanded.

He bit back a groan of frustration. "Give me a minute, will ya?" he said as he zipped up his pants. He flushed the toilet, washed his hands, and opened the door to see Annette standing there, leaning against the wall.

"Can't a guy even use the john in peace?" he asked, annoyed.

"Yeah, right," Annette said, entering the bathroom. "Remember, beating off makes hair grow on your palms."

Shannon sighed and went to his room, his balls aching. It had been a while since he had suffered a case of blue nuts. Usually when he got in a horny mood and wanted more than a do-it-yourself job, he went and rented himself a honey. He couldn't imagine doing that now. Mandey was the only one he wanted.

Annette came into the bedroom a minute later. "Man, if Kerri knew you was in there whacking off instead of doing her, she'd throw a hissy fit." She closed the curtain to separate their halves of the room. "Damn, I wish you'd move out. It was nice having the room to myself when you were gone."

"I'm working on it," Shannon muttered. "Annette, I've got to talk to all the Devils tonight. I've got something I want to run past y'all. I need you to help me round up everyone later."

"I suppose," Annette said with an exaggerated sigh.

Shannon lay there on his bed, thinking. He would much rather be spending the evening with Mandey instead of skulking around in the dark with the Devils, but he didn't have much choice in the matter. Duty called, for both him and her.

He considered his finances and his living situation. He made $3.35 an hour at his job and worked an average of thirty hours a week. That was about $400 a month before taxes, about $340 after taxes. He could probably get a decent one-bedroom apartment for about $200 a month, if he was lucky. That would leave $140 a month for utilities, gas, and groceries. Electricity would be about forty or fifty dollars, more in the summer if he ran the air conditioning. Gas for his car usually set him back about fifty or sixty a month. That would leave between $30 and $50 for food each month. He might be able to get by if he ate a lot of ramen noodles, cheap bologna, and off-brand macaroni and cheese.

He didn't have much in the way of furnishings for an apartment, only his bed and nightstand. He did have some money stashed away (money from the Devils' activities) so he could probably find some decent second-hand furniture with that, but once that extra money was gone, what would he have to fall back on in an emergency? His car occasionally needed repairs, and he had to have enough money to buy the parts so he could fix it. What about buying items like razors, shaving cream, soap, and deodorant? What about other utilities, like a telephone? And spending money, so he could take Mandey out?

It wouldn't work, with his present paycheck. He would have to find a better job, with more hours and higher pay. He couldn't be assured of getting a better job, though. With his police record, no one would want to hire him, and his parole officer had been dragging his feet about helping him get different employment.

Shannon sighed. His head was beginning to ache. He wanted to get in bed, pull the covers up over his head, and sleep for about sixteen hours. Instead, he was going to have to get the Devils together that evening and begin plotting a jewelry store robbery with them. This was going to be the last time doing something like that. He hated all the stupid gang bullshit.

I just want to live a normal life, is that too much to ask? he thought.

13

The Plan

The Devils assembled in the living room of the Den. Shannon stood with the weary, skeptical eyes of the others all on him as he described his idea to rob the jewelry store. He told them how he had briefly scoped out the place, and thought it would be a safe bet for them. Surprisingly, everyone seemed to be on board with the idea, even Raff. Shannon began assigning roles to each of the members.

"No, I don't think so," Raff said.

"Don't think what?" Shannon asked, his temper flaring.

"You ain't driving the getaway car this time, Trick," Raff said.

"Why the hell not?"

"'Cause you ain't been doing shit for us lately," Raff said flatly.

John chimed in, "All we do is watch your back while you steal cars for your boss, and we don't even get a cut of that, it's just to keep your ass out of the can."

"You know I don't think you have the cojones to be our leader. I ain't the only one who thinks that, either," Raff said. "Am I right?"

The rest of the gang looked like they didn't want to be put on the spot. However, there were some nods in agreement, and a tense silence from everyone else. He didn't hear anyone rushing to defend him, not even Kerri.

"Fine," Shannon said impatiently. "I'll go in with the rest of y'all. We don't need a getaway driver in the middle of the night, anyway."

This is bullshit, he thought as he outlined what he wanted each of the other gang members to do.

"When's this all goin' down?" Checkmate asked.

"Wednesday night," Shannon replied.

"Why are we waiting?" Raff asked. "Why don't we do it right now?"

"Because I said so," Shannon snapped, then in a calmer tone said, "I want to scout the place out a little better before we jump into this. Raff and Juanita, I want you two to go over there tomorrow. Go inside, pretend you are interested in buying something. Check out the security they've got and stuff and report back. Then I want Kerri and John to go over the next afternoon and do the same thing. Act like you're a couple looking at rings or something."

"Is that necessary?" John asked. "What do you need two sets of us going over there for?"

"Do I need to knock some heads together?" Shannon asked, rapidly losing patience. "Because I fucking said so. That's all the reason you need."

"Okay, okay. Jesus, calm down," John said.

"This has the potential to be low-risk, high-payoff—if we play it right. That means we gotta be careful about it. No going off the plan, no taking stupid risks, no making dumb mistakes. Understand?"

A murmur of agreement came from the others.

"Okay," Shannon said, satisfied with the response. "Once I hear back from Raff and 'Nita and then John and Kerri, we'll plan to go ahead."

When he left a short time later to go back to the apartment, he was full of mixed emotions. His head and his insides felt like a whirlpool. He didn't want to rob a jewelry store. The only thing he wanted, the only thing that had been consuming his mind since Saturday, was Mandey. If Mandey knew about this, she would never want to see him again. But the Devils were restless. Raff and John were both openly challenging his authority now. Everyone else had been uncharacteristically quiet. He knew they had doubts about his dedication to the gang, and he knew full well that those doubts were justified. His heart had never been in it, and now more than ever, he wanted to be done with it. But he had to do his best to hide it. They were like a pack of vicious dogs, and if they could start sensing his weakness, smelling his fear, they would tear him apart.

14

Sorting It Out

Mandey's clock radio began blaring Def Leppard's "Photograph" at six A.M. It felt too early; she had trouble falling asleep the night before. Reading a chapter from her American Government textbook had finally fixed the problem around one A.M.
Despite the second cup of coffee Mandey brought in the van with her, she yawned almost continually as she drove to school. She hoped her classes would be halfway stimulating so she wouldn't nod off.

As she pulled into the school parking lot, she realized what had been in the back of her mind, keeping her awake. Why would she never consider dating someone like Danny, who was smart, funny, and popular, but dealt recreational drugs, but she had no reservations about having a relationship with a high school drop-out convicted of armed robbery?

Well, Shannon had been reformed. Danny, on the other hand, enjoyed what he was doing and had no intention of stopping. But was that all there was to it?

The journal topic in English was free choice that morning. Mandey opened her notebook and got out her purple pen.

"James and I dated for several months, but that came to an end on Friday. I could say I was devastated, but in truth, I wasn't. I'd been expecting the demise of our relationship since before this school year began, but that didn't make the reality that much easier. It upset me, but I was not 'devastated.'

"I went to the beach Saturday, all by myself. It was a cold, gray day, perfect for mooning, moaning, meditating, and general wallowing in self-pity. I kind of relished the idea of sitting on a deserted beach, pondering what went wrong. However, that's not what happened.

"I met someone at the beach, someone who used to live close to me and used to go to this school. He was someone I had a crush on. Now I have a new boyfriend. I, Amanda Rowan, who before James came along had never had a date in my entire life, acquired a new love interest just as easy as that. I'm still stunned.

"He's not at all like James. He's not the kind of guy anyone would expect me to be with. It's almost a bad movie cliché, the good girl falling for the bad boy with the heart of gold, only the bad boys in those movies always drove motorcycles. My guy drives a beat-up '74 Oldsmobile.

"Something about this relationship was bothering me last night, but I didn't know what it was until now. My new boyfriend isn't totally unlike James. At least, my feelings for him aren't totally unlike what I felt for James. One emotion I have I'm a little worried about. I always felt that James needed me. He has a lot of problems, and I wanted so much to help him. My new boyfriend has a whole different set of problems, and I want to help him, too. That's okay, but I don't want to feel taken for granted, like the way James made me feel. I don't want to get in over my head trying to solve someone's problems that are beyond my help.

"I like to help those who help themselves. And from now on, God help those who think it's okay to help themselves to me and give nothing in return."

That afternoon after choir practice, Angelina and Mandey went shopping. Although they had a basic idea of what they were looking for, they were going to shop around to see what was available and where they might get the best deals.

The first place they went was the T-shirt shop down the street from the school, where most of the school-sponsored clubs had their shirts made. After talking to the clerk, they decided that having the shirts done there would be too expensive. Mandey and Angie were sure they could get shirts for less.

On the way out of the store, Angie noticed a bargain bin filled mostly with Halloween iron-on decals. She and Mandey pawed through it and found ten iron-ons of a fierce-looking black cat with its hackles up, fangs bared, and glaring green eyes, all marked down to fifty cents. They purchased those and left.

"Let's try K-Mart for the shirts," Angelina suggested. "They're usually pretty cheap."

At K-Mart they struck pay dirt—black T-shirts in all different sizes for $4.99 apiece. In the notions department they found embroidered initials in emerald green with gold trim, marked down to 35 cents each, and were lucky enough to find ten *A*'s and ten *C*'s. On the way to check out, they stopped by the men's department again and spotted a rack of black denim jackets marked, "Just reduced--$11.99."

"Oh, these would be so cool!" Mandey said, pawing through the rack to check sizes.

"I definitely want one," Angelina declared, taking one jacket off its hanger and trying it on.

"Me, too," Mandey agreed. "It looks like they have one to fit everyone."

"I'm going to call Jesse and tell him. If the others want them, we can come back tomorrow and get them. You go check out," Angelina said. "I'll meet you up front."

Mandey got in line and dug the envelope with the money out of her purse. She was checking out when Angelina came back from using the pay phone.

"Jesse said he's going to call everyone and see what they think. He'll tell them to bring money tomorrow if they want one," Angelina said. "I'm going to get one for sure, and so is he."

"So am I," Mandey said. "We can make them look really cool."

"I'm going to start making a design for them tonight when I get home," Angelina said.

Mandey's homework assignment for that night included watching the election results for government class. Politics was not one of her favorite things. She wouldn't be old enough to vote until May, but if she had been old enough to vote, she probably would have voted to re-elect Reagan. She did think, though, that if Mondale won, it would be a terrific thing to have Geraldine Ferraro as vice-president. As it was, the election results were not exciting. By the time she went to bed, they were still tallying votes on the West Coast, but Mondale had only won Minnesota and Washington, D.C. Four more years of Reagan it was going to be.

In bed, she thought about the phone conversation she had had with her mother after she got home from school. Mandey had been excited to tell her all about Shannon. Her mother sounded happy for her, but then had asked about getting Mandey a plane ticket so she could spend the two weeks of Christmas vacation with her parents in Connecticut. Mandey had been looking forward to going and spending the holidays with her parents and extended family, but now there was Shannon. Her very first Christmas with a boyfriend. Her mother noticed Mandey's hesitation.

"Mandey, I understand if you want to stay down there for Christmas," her mother said.

"I want to come see you and Daddy and everyone else, but…I'd like to be here to have Christmas with Shannon," Mandey admitted.

"Then stay there," her mother said, not unkindly.

"You don't mind?"

"We'll miss you, but I want you two to have a happy Christmas together."

It was a load off Mandey's mind. She truly did want to go back home to see her family, but even more than that, she wanted to make Christmas a happy one for Shannon (and herself). Marcia wasn't going home for the holiday, either, so it wasn't going to be a problem staying in Houston for Christmas. She could hardly wait. She fell asleep that night planning how to make this Christmas the most special one ever for Shannon.

15

The Jewelry Store

Wednesday was a cold, gray, rainy day, much the same as the previous three days. Shannon left work at three o'clock, his stomach churning in anticipation of that evening's planned activities. He got in his car and lit a cigarette to calm his nerves. After a few drags, he felt calmer and headed for home.

No one was home when he got to the apartment, which was unusual. Shannon didn't complain. He picked up the phone and dialed John's number. He wanted to see what he and Kerri had found out during their visit to the jewelry store that afternoon.

John's father answered the phone.

"John ain't here," he told Shannon. "I ain't seen him all day. I ain't even sure he was here last night."

"All right. Thanks," Shannon said and hung up the phone. He figured John had to be over at the Den, so he left the apartment and walked across the parking lot.

There he found only Marco, who was sitting on the old sofa doing his homework in the dim gray light. He was chewing on the end of a pen, reading a textbook. Shannon admired Marco's determination to stay in school. Raff often tried to bully Marco out of going to school or doing his homework, but Shannon took up for Marco whenever he could. He was only a freshman, but it looked like Marco might be the first of their group to graduate high school. Shannon knew Marco was as desperate as he was to get out of that hellhole, and he wasn't about to begrudge the kid any method that might help him.

"How was school today?" Shannon asked him.

"Pretty good," Marco said, looking up at him. "I found out I got an 'A' on my English test."

"Cool," Shannon said. "What are you studying now?"

"This?" Marco asked, holding up his book. "Physical science. Got to study. Big test tomorrow."

"Well, I won't bug you," Shannon said. "I was looking for John. Have you seen him?"

"Nope," Marco said. "But Kerri was here about fifteen minutes ago. She was looking for him, too."

"Did she say anything about them going to check out that place?"

"No, but she acted like she was real anxious to find him."

"Hmmm," Shannon said. That didn't sound good. "I guess I'll have to go talk to Kerri. Thanks, Marco. Study hard."

"I will," Marco replied, looking back to his homework.

Shannon went back out into the gray drizzle. He didn't want to go see Kerri, but it looked like he didn't have much choice.

Kerri and her mother lived down the block from the apartments in a two-bedroom house that, like many of the other houses in the neighborhood, needed a new roof and a paint job. He trudged up the creaky steps to the front door. Kerri must have seen him coming, because she opened the door before he knocked.

"Trick!" she said, surprised. He hadn't been to her house since before they broke up. "Come in."

"Uh, that's okay," he declined. "I wanted to see if you and John checked out the jewelry store today, like I said."

"Oh, Trick, don't be mad," Kerri said, pleading. "I couldn't find John nowhere. Nobody's seen him since yesterday."

"Shit," Shannon muttered under his breath. He wasn't going to feel comfortable until he'd sent another scouting party to the store. He reconsidered sending Annette and Checkmate, but decided against it. Besides, he didn't know where they were, either.

He looked at Kerri, who was standing there looking up at him with those big cornflower blue eyes. He sighed.

"Okay," he said. "I'll be back in half an hour. You and I will go check out the jewelry store."

"Okay!" Kerri agreed eagerly. "I'll be ready."

Shannon turned and walked down off the steps, stuffing his hands in his jacket pockets as he headed back to the apartments. He didn't want to go to the jewelry store, particularly not with Kerri, as she was likely to get crazy ideas in her head that he was taking an interest in her. He was only doing this because he didn't have any other choice. He couldn't send her with Lenny or Marco, because they were too young. And he couldn't send her with Curt, because, well, no one would believe Kerri was supposed to be in love with him. Raff and Juanita had said they didn't see any surveillance cameras, but Shannon didn't trust Raff, which is why he wanted John and Kerri to go and get a second opinion. Now Shannon was stuck having to scout out the place. He hoped Raff and Juanita's report had been accurate, because the last thing he needed was to be caught on video in the jewelry store the afternoon before it was burglarized.

The apartment was still deserted when he got back. He regretted the fact that he wasn't going to be there long enough to enjoy it. He took a quick shower and changed out of his work uniform. He checked his wallet to see how much cash he had. He figured a good way to throw off suspicion would be to buy something. Maybe there would be silver-plated lighters.

Shannon supposed it was a good thing that he was going to see the place before the heist went down; it was better for him to have firsthand information regarding the store, rather than relying on what Raff had to report.

He drove up in front of Kerri's and honked the horn. Kerri came out of the house wearing a royal blue dress and black high-heeled shoes.

"How do I look?" Kerri asked him as she got into the car. Shannon noticed the way she hitched up her skirt to show her thighs.

"Conspicuous," Shannon said.

"Well, do you want me to change?" she asked, annoyed.

"No," Shannon said. "You're all right. Let's get this over with."

As he pulled out into the street, he glanced sidewise at Kerri. He was tempted to tell her she looked nice, because she did, but she would take the comment the wrong way, and he didn't want to encourage her.

They pulled into the parking lot of the shopping center where the jewelry store was located. Shannon parked in a space two stores down. He didn't want anyone at the jewelry store to have too clear a view of his car.

"So, what do we do?" Kerri asked him.

"Come inside with me and look around. Act interested in the jewelry, but look at the rest of the store, too. Just don't be too obvious about it. See if you can see any cameras or alarm systems. Anything that we'll need to know about."

They got out of the car and made their way toward the store. Kerri took Shannon's hand in hers.

"What are you doing?" he asked, trying to pull loose.

She squeezed his hand hard. "We're supposed to be getting married, remember, darling?" she said, smiling sweetly.

Shannon sighed and let her keep holding on. As the approached the store, he noticed it had burglar bars on the windows and door, but they were spaced rather far apart. He was sure that if they broke the glass, Marco could fit through them. He opened the door, and he and Kerri stepped inside. The store was longer than it was wide, and had two displays in the front windows, a long display case on each side, and a shorter one in the back. A Vietnamese man of maybe fifty was sitting behind the right-hand display counter, watching a black-and-white television. There were no other customers in the store.

"Good afternoon. Can I help you?" the man asked Shannon and Kerri in a thick accent, but he made no move to leave his stool.

"Oh, we want to look at engagement rings," Kerri said excitedly. "We're gonna get married."

"Oh. They over here," the man said, getting up and going around to the opposite side. "In this case. Wedding ring are here, too. Let me know if you want to see." He went back to his stool.

Kerri began examining the rings. "Oh, Sugar, look how pretty!" she exclaimed.

Shannon groaned inwardly. She was useless. "I'm going to look around," he told her pointedly, and moved to the display case opposite the front door. His eyes moved over the walls and ceiling. There was no evidence of a security camera anywhere. The store hadn't been open that long, so maybe they hadn't gotten around to installing one yet. There wasn't even a mirror that might have hidden a camera. Lots of stores had them to make you think you were being filmed.

The ceiling panels looked flimsy. He bet if they had to and if there was a way, it would be easy to get in through the roof. He would make sure they brought a rope with them tonight.

He shifted his attention to the merchandise in the case before him. There were several gold- and silver-plated cigarette lighters. They also had 14-karat gold charms. One caught his eye. It said, "I Love You" in a heart and had a pink gold rose on either side of the "I" and one under the "You." He looked at the price tag. He could afford it. Mandey had a thin gold chain she could wear it on. She had been wearing a gold "M" on it the other day. He had planned on buying something, anyway, and he could think of no better way to spend his money than this.

"Ooh, baby, look at this one!" Kerri breathed. She motioned for him to come back over to her.

Shannon knew they had to appear like a couple looking at engagement rings, so he reluctantly rejoined her. He looked at the ring Kerri was pointing at. It was an oval diamond about as big as a robin's egg.

"Isn't it gorgeous?" Kerri raved.

"Beautiful," Shannon said flatly. He thought it was a little too flashy, but maybe good if you were lost at sea and needed to signal for help.

He scanned the diamond rings until his eyes stopped on the perfect one. It was a heart-shaped diamond solitaire.

Kerri looked at what Shannon was staring at so intently. "Oh, the heart," she said. "That's the best one."

It certainly was, and Shannon knew exactly whose finger he wanted to slip it onto.

"Would you like to see?" the man asked from across the room.

Before Kerri could reply, Shannon said, "Yes, please. The heart-shaped one."

The man shuffled over, unlocked the case, reached in, and removed the ring from its black velvet nest. He handed it to Shannon.

Shannon held the ring up to the light. Rainbows of color spilled from it. It was perfect. It even looked like it was the right size.

"Let me see," Kerri begged.

Reluctantly, Shannon handed to ring to Kerri. She slipped it onto her left ring finger.

"It's so beautiful!" she gasped.

Shannon had to suppress the urge to slap the ring off Kerri's hand. Instead, he gently took her hand in his and carefully removed it. "It sure is, but unfortunately, we can't afford it right now," he said, and handed it back to the man.

"Would you like to see another?" the man asked.

"I don't think so," Shannon said. "I think Janie here has her heart set on that one, but it's going to be a few more months before I'll have enough saved up for it."

Kerri glared at him. Shannon pretended not to notice.

"But I want to see this over here," Shannon said, going back over to the other display case. Kerri remained looking at the rings for a few moments, then followed Shannon. He wished she would stay over where she was. He didn't want to answer her questions.

"Why don't you go over and look at that case over there?" he suggested to Kerri.

She pouted. "I don't want to," she said petulantly.

Shannon sighed. "I want to buy this," he said, pointing at the "I Love You" charm.

The man took the charm out of the display case and held it out for Shannon to look at. "Very pretty charm for very pretty girl," he said to Shannon while smiling at Kerri.

Shannon winced. He didn't dare look at Kerri. "That's fine. Just put it in a box, please," he said.

"You need chain, too? We have chains over here," the man said, starting toward the display case Shannon had urged Kerri to go look at.

"Not today," Shannon said. "I've got to save the rest of my money toward that ring."

Shannon followed the man over to the cash register and paid for the charm. He now got a good look at the third wall of the store. He still saw no evidence of any video cameras.

"Come back when you want the heart ring," the man said. "If I sell that one, I can get another like it."

"We will," Shannon said.

Shannon noticed an alarm on the door. However, it looked as though it would be easy enough to disarm. They could break the glass, reach around, and cut the wires in less than 10 seconds. He half wondered if maybe the owner didn't hope to get robbed in order to collect insurance money.

When he and Kerri got outside, Kerri asked him, "Can I have the charm?"

Shannon stopped and stared at her. "What makes you think I'm giving it to you?"

"Well, who is it for?" Kerri asked. "You didn't buy it for some prostitute, did you?"

"No, and it ain't for you, either," Shannon replied. He got in the car and slammed the door.

"Then who the fuck did you buy it for?" Kerri asked again, getting in on the passenger side.

"Nobody," Shannon said impatiently. "I just bought it to help throw off any suspicion."

"Then why the hell didn't you buy a fucking lighter or something you could use?" Kerri asked. "What the fuck are you going to do with an 'I Love You' charm? Why can't I have it?"

"Because it's not for you!" Shannon exclaimed. "It says, 'I love you.' If I give it to anyone, it will be someone I love. I don't love you!"

"What the fuck do you even know about love, Trick?" Kerri asked with a sneer. "All you know how to do is fuck whores."

"What, and because you'll fuck anyone anytime for nothing you know more about love than I do?" Shannon asked.

"Fuck you," Kerri said, turning toward the window.

Shannon sighed but didn't say anything. Talking to Kerri gave him a headache. He knew his language could stand to be cleaned up, but he definitely wasn't the garbage mouth Kerri was. He wished she would just shut up.

"I don't understand why you'll go out and pay some hooker when I'm always here for you."

Because I can't stand you, Shannon was tempted to say. *Because when I did try to make love to you, you made me feel like shit.* But he kept his mouth shut.

"Ain't you even going to answer me?"

Shannon remained quiet. He didn't care about sparing her feelings, but he didn't want to listen to her rant and rave anymore. He hoped if he didn't say anything, she would give up and shut up.

"I don't know what the fuck is wrong with you," Kerri said, still looking out the window.

My God, would you please shut up? Shannon begged in his mind.

"Come on, Trick," Kerri said, her voice taking on a high-pitched whine. "You wanted me." Then her voice got low and husky. "I remember how big and hard your cock was. God, it was huge! Wouldn't you like to be naked with me in my bed again? I remember how your hands squeezed my tits, then ran down over my stomach, down to my pussy. Remember how hot and wet I was for you?"

Shannon vividly remembered that night, and how nervous and excited he had been, getting ready to make love for the very first time. But mostly he recalled how in his nervousness he had accidentally pulled her hair and slammed his elbow into her chest. When she began swearing at him, he had gone soft. It had been horrible.

Then he thought about Mandey, and how she had been when he had done practically the same thing when they were making out on Sunday.

"It's okay," she had said, holding her left breast. Then she had kissed him.

He stopped in front of Kerri's house to drop her off.

"I see a smile on your face," Kerri said, moving closer to him. "Come inside. Let me make you feel good." Her hand went down to his crotch and squeezed.

"Hey!" Shannon shouted, pushing her hand away. "Stop that!'

"What's your problem?" Kerri shouted back. "You wanted it!"

"I did not," Shannon said. "I was thinking about something that had nothing to do with you."

"Fucking goddamn liar!" Kerri said, and slapped him across the face.

Shannon stared at her for a second, then grabbed her by the arms and pulled her so close they were nose to nose.

"You're hurting me," Kerri whined, struggling. He held her tighter.

"Kerri, I want this to get through your thick skull. I do not like you, much less love you, and I wouldn't fuck you if you were the last woman on Earth. I'd be afraid my dick would fall off. Now leave me the fuck alone!"

He let go of her with a little push. She scrambled out of the car and slammed the door.

"I hate you, you fucking asshole!" she screamed, and slammed her fist down on the hood of the car.

Shannon flipped her the bird and peeled out. He shook his head in disgust. It had been a total waste of time taking her with him. If John had just done what he was supposed to do, he could have avoided this shit.

16

The Heist

The alarm clock went off at 2:15 A.M. Shannon awoke, startled, and fumbled around in the pitch black to shut it off before it woke Leon in the other room. He didn't need to be waking up his grumpy ass in the middle of the night. He sat up, groggy. The divider curtain was open; Annette wasn't there. After a minute, Shannon got out of bed and quickly dressed in his darkest-colored clothes. He stopped by his car to get his gloves and mask and headed to the Devils' Den.

He was the first one there. Slowly the others trickled in—first Annette and Checkmate; then Raff with Juanita and Marco; Kerri, Curt, and Lenny came in one right after another; and John dragged in last. Raff seemed sharp enough, but everyone else looked as groggy as Shannon felt. He hoped their heads would all clear in a hurry. This was no night for slackers.

"Okay, let's get this straight. Do it right, and we should each be looking at a minimum of a thousand apiece. But that means no fuck-ups," Shannon told them.

"Practice what you preach," John said, "and it'll all be cool."

Shannon glared at him. He would deal with John later for blowing off his assignment with Kerri. They went over the plan one last time. The girls and Curt were going to take Shannon's car. Kerri, Juanita, and Annette would serve as perimeter guards around the shopping center while Curt circled the area in the car, making sure they were okay. Shannon and the rest would go in Raff's car to the jewelry store. They would break the glass, and then Marco would slip through the burglar bars, cut the alarm wires, and let them all in. Next, they would quickly smash the display cases, grab all they could, and head out the back door to where Raff's car would be parked. In and out in less than two minutes is what Shannon wanted. Then they would meet up with Curt, have him pick up the girls, and then back to the Den.

"I want the heart ring," Kerri declared. "I don't care about anything else, but I want that ring."

Like hell, Shannon thought. *That's the first thing I'm grabbing. That's Mandey's ring.*

"You never let me do nothing!" Annette whined. "I hate being lookout!"

Annette could not understand that it was for her own good that he kept her out of the thick of things. She had been in trouble with the law more often than Shannon had, but her offenses were not as serious—things like shoplifting and fifth degree assault. She had been on probation twice, and she was still only seventeen. Another arrest would almost surely net her jail time, and he did not want that to happen to her. As much as he despised her at times, she was still his little sister, and he felt obligated to protect her.

"When we get back here, we'll check out the loot all together," Shannon said. "I know you're going to be tempted to keep some of it, but I don't recommend it. There's always a chance the cops may be by to ask us a few questions, and we don't want to be caught with any of it. First thing in the morning, Raff and I will take it all to the fence. He guaranteed us top dollar, minus a twenty percent commission."

"Twenty percent!" John objected. "That means he gets more than any one of us."

"That's his fee," Shannon said. "If you want to keep your share and try pawning it yourself, that's your business."

"I might just do that," John said, disgruntled.

"Let's get to it," Shannon said.

Ten minutes later their "security forces" were at their assigned posts, and Raff parked his car in the alley behind the jewelry store. A large wooden fence separated the shopping center from the few residences behind it, so there wasn't much chance of being seen.

Dressed in their dark clothes, gloves, and masks and armed with hammers and a large pair of wire cutters, the six of them stealthily got out of the car. A breezeway connected two parts of the shopping center next to the jewelry store's corner space. Shannon sent Lenny out to the front to see if the coast was clear.

"Not a soul in sight," Lenny said when he came back a couple minutes later.

Shannon took a deep breath. He wished this was going down under normal circumstances, and all he would have had to do is drive. But his position was in jeopardy, and he had to prove himself by putting himself into the thick of things.

"Fast, guys. Marco, we're relying on you to cut those wires in five seconds. Run in, smash the cases, fill your bags. Don't take the black display things the jewelry sits on—merchandise only. When I say the word, we're out the back door and gone."

They crept around front. There was no traffic on the street, and the parking lot was deserted.

"Go," Shannon said.

Raff took a hammer and smashed the glass of the door, setting off the alarm. Marco slipped partway through the burglar bars and cut the wires, silencing the ringing almost before it began. He struggled through the narrow bars and opened the door for the others. They ran in, hammering the glass display cases to smithereens.

Shannon went to the case where he and Kerri had seen the heart-shaped diamond. He obliterated the glass and reached in to find the ring first. He dropped it into his shirt pocket, then filled his black bag with whatever he could grab. They had been in the store perhaps 45 seconds, but Shannon was anxious to leave.

"Go!" he told them, and they all followed him through the store and stampeded out the back door.

"Drive like normal," Shannon told Raff. "We don't want to attract attention.".

They passed Curt and gave him the okay signal and headed back to the Devil Den. Curt and the girls arrived about five minutes later. Annette and Kerri lit some candles and they all sat in a circle as the guys emptied their loot bags in the middle. There was an array of rings, pendants, earrings, bracelets, and chains, and even in the dim light, the jewels sparkled.

"Where's the heart ring?" Kerri asked, pawing through the pile.

"Hands off," Raff told her, slapping her hands.

"Ow! Stop it, Raff," she said, withdrawing. "Trick, where's the heart ring?"

"I don't know, Kerri. I didn't see it," Shannon said.

"Liar," Kerri said, pouting. "You left it there on purpose because I wanted it."

"Kerri, get over it," Shannon told her.

"You're an asshole," Kerri said to him.

"Why do you let her talk like that to you?" Curt asked him. "If it were me, I'd slap the shit out of her."

"Shut up, Curt," Kerri said petulantly.

Curt reached over and slapped her upside the head. Kerri lunged at him, punching his fat stomach.

"Knock it off!" Shannon roared, pushing the two apart. "Let's finish this up so we can all go back to bed."

Some of the pieces had price tags attached, and after going through the items, they estimated they had about 100,000 dollars-worth of jewelry. Of course, that was the retail price, but if the fence could get them even twenty percent, they would each net close to $1600 apiece.

"Okay, John said he might want to take his share and sell it himself," Shannon said. "Does anyone else feel that way?"

The rest of the Devils looked at each other and shook their heads.

"You might as well keep mine, too," John said. "Too hard to divide it up equally when not everything has a price on it."

"There's nothing there I want, anyway," Kerri said sulkily.

At 4:30 in the morning Shannon was back in bed with half the jewelry in a bag tucked under his pillow. Raff had the other half. Shannon dozed fitfully for two hours, then got up and showered and dressed. He retrieved the heart ring from his other shirt pocket and held it up to the light coming from the bathroom. Regretfully he added it to the bag of jewelry. The ring was perfect for Mandey, but he couldn't give her stolen merchandise. She deserved better than that.

He met Raff at his car at eight. A half-hour later, they met their intermediary, Rogelio, at his place. Rogelio was from a Caribbean island Shannon couldn't recall. He had large Afro, a small mustache, and a gaudy gold tooth, which shone through the smile on his face.

"Come in and let's see what you've got," he said.

They walked into his dim apartment. The living room was decorated with low sofas and chairs large abstract art prints. Fragrant incense permeated the air, but it didn't quite cover up the scent of ganja or the spicy smell of last night's evening meal.

Shannon and Raff produced the bags and dumped them out on the coffee table. "We estimated the retail value to be close to a hundred grand," Shannon said. "I told the gang you were going to get us top dollar for this. I estimated we could net about ten thousand, but if you can walk the walk and not just talk the talk, I think we should get twice that."

Rogelio sifted through the jewelry carelessly. "Yes. Twenty, no problem," he said confidently.

"How long will it take you to sell it all and get us the money?" Shannon asked.

"A week. Ten days, tops," Rogelio replied.

Shannon and Raff looked at each other.

"You can do it that fast and get a good price?" Raff asked.

"No problem. Trust Rogelio. The more I can get for you, the more I can keep for myself. It's in my best interest," Rogelio said with a glinting gold grin.

"What do you think?" Raff asked Shannon.

"Sounds okay to me."

"Just remember what you told us," Raff said. "Top dollar in ten days."

"Less than that. Come back a week from Friday and you'll be all set," Rogelio promised.

"We'll be here," Shannon said. "Don't you worry."

"I don't trust him," Raff said on their way back to their apartments. "He's going to sell all that in a week and not give it away? I don't see how he can do it."

"He's got to get rid of the stuff quick. No fence wants to keep hot merchandise too long," Shannon said.

"Well, I don't doubt he can get it off his hands fast. I just hope he can get a good price, too."

"He said he could. He's come through for us before. It's what he does, so he should know."

"Let's hope so."

When Shannon got home, he went back to bed. He didn't have to go to work until three, so he could sleep for four or five hours, if the rest of his family would let him. Surprisingly, they did.

17

Preparing to Meet the Enemy

As it was, all the Alley Cats wanted a jacket, and on Wednesday Mandey and Angelina checked out of K-Mart with ten black denim jackets in various sizes and several packages of silver and gold studs, green rhinestones, and assorted green, silver, and gold spangles.

The Alley Cats met Thursday after school and received their shirts, which had the embroidered initials on the front left breast surrounded by silver studs. Silver studs also encircled the hem of each sleeve. The unanimous opinion was that the shirts looked sharp, which pleased Mandey. The gang wanted their jackets, too, but they weren't done yet. Angelina had ironed on all the cat decals, and Angelina and Mandey had come up with a pattern for embellishing the guys' jackets and another for the girls'. They were each going to take five jackets and finish them that night. Mandey was glad she had finished her homework in study hall, because those jackets were going to take a while.

It was after eight before she could even start on them. She had to wait for Marcia to go take her shower so she could sneak the jackets out of her van and into her room. She was busy with her rhinestone setter when Shannon called her at nine.

"Hi," Mandey said. "I didn't hear from you yesterday."

"Things were kind of crazy," Shannon said, "but you were definitely on my mind."

"Was it Leon again?" Mandey asked, concerned.

"No, nothing like that," Shannon said. "Just some shit going on. What are you up to?"

"Not too much," Mandey said. "Contemplating taking a bath and going to bed."

They talked for about thirty minutes, during which time Mandey fervently hoped Shannon wouldn't suggest that they go out the next night. She was relieved and excited when he asked her to go out to eat with him on Saturday evening, instead.

She was left with a happy, warm feeling inside after talking with him, and then she did go take a bath. But when she finished, she still had a lot of work left ahead of her. It was almost one A.M. before she went to bed.

The next day the Alley Cats met at Mr. Gatti's to receive their jackets and talk last minute details about the evening's planned activities. They took up most of a corner section, scarfing down pizza and watching *Jeopardy!* on the projection television. They played along, trying to blurt out the questions to the answers before the contestants. When the show ended and *Divorce Court* came on, Jesse mercifully started the meeting.

"All right, here's the game plan," Jesse began. "Tonight, we're going to Liaisons. Our purpose is to present ourselves so the Devils see us and wonder who we are and what we're up to. What we don't want is to get into some kind of confrontation with them unless they give us a good reason.

"Terry and I decided we should split into two groups. Me, Angie, Dina, Danny, and Mandey will scope out what's going on inside. The rest of you guys will be out in the parking lot with Terry, seeing if anyone is causing any shit out there."

The others murmured and nodded their assent. Mandey noticed that they had planned it so all the females would be inside the club, where it was probably less dangerous. That was fine with her. She had had enough of that parking lot.

"Whatever we do, no one goes off by themselves," Terry said to Zack, Jim, Brad, and Jeremy. "We don't want to let our guard down even for a minute. When it hits them that we could be a threat to them, they're going to get ugly. Maybe not tonight, but then again, maybe they will. We've got to be prepared. They ain't just going to take a look at us and give up and go away."

Mandey raised her hand to interrupt and immediately wished she hadn't. The gesture made her look like such a schoolgirl.

"I have a question," she said.

"Go ahead," Jesse said.

"How exactly do we know what we're up against?" she asked. "Aside from the two people I encountered, whom we're assuming are Devils, the only evidence of a gang I've seen is a few guys lurking around wearing black jackets. What I want to know is how many of them there are, what they look like, and how we're supposed to identify them."

"Yeah," Dina agreed. "It's hard to tell what we're up against when a lot of the time they're wearing masks."

Jesse looked at Terry, then said, "You've got a good point. I'm hoping that after tonight we'll know more about what we're dealing with here, but let's put together all the information we have so far and see what we've got. Let's see. . . there's Raff. Danny, you know the most about him, so describe him to us."

"He's a typical greasy Mexican," Danny said, with a look of distaste on his face. "He's about my height, but skinny, has black hair, brown eyes, dark. He's got a long scar along his left jaw line. Wears a couple of flashy rings."

"There's a black guy, too," Jeremy added.

"What does he look like?" Jesse asked.

Jeremy looked stumped. "Like a black guy," he said with a shrug.

"You know they all look alike," Terry said.

Mandey's mouth dropped open. Everyone stared at him.

"What?" Terry asked defensively. "It was a joke."

"Yeah, like them white bed sheets you got in your truck," Angelina said.

"I ain't got no god damn sheets in my truck!" Terry sputtered. "Man, I've got friends that are black. It was a joke! Jeez, you didn't get pissy when Danny mentioned a greasy wetback!"

"I said 'Mexican', not 'wetback'," Danny said.

"Let's keep going," Jesse said, trying to gloss it over. "We've got Raff and a black guy. Who else can we identify? There's someone named John, right?"

"Yeah, the blond dude," Brad said.

"Anyone else?" Jesse asked.

"Man, who was that with John that one time?" Jim asked Brad, then said to the group, "I don't know his name, but there's this fat weird-looking dude with this frizzy reddish hair and Marvin Zindler glasses."

At the same time Jim was giving this description, a hysterical woman on the television screeched, "You emptied our bank account and ran off with my best friend!" The outburst was enough to distract them for a few seconds. Angelina and Dina turned around to see what was happening. Mandey, although she hated *Divorce Court* with a passion, had her attention diverted long enough that she didn't hear all of Jim's description of the 'weird-looking dude,' only catching the part about the Marvin Zindler glasses.

"Oh, man, he's weird-looking," Zack said. "I know who you mean."

"All right, we've got Raff, John, the black guy and the ugly guy," Jesse said. "Terry, what about the guy you said you thought was their leader?"

"He's big," Terry said. "About my size, but a little heavier. That's about all I can say about what he looks like, because they were all wearing masks that night. Although, I've been thinking about it, the night they broke into the lot, and maybe I'm wrong about this, but I could almost swear that before I got smashed over the head with that chair, I heard someone say 'trick.' I thought they were talking about someone playing a trick, but now that I've thought more about it, I think they might have been calling this guy 'Trick,' like it was his name."

"I wonder if it's a reference to his sex life?" Danny mused with a malicious grin.

"Yeah, him and John," Brad said.

The guys all snorted with laughter.

Angelina took this opportunity to add her two cents. "And there are females in the gang," she said. "There were two girls in the group that mugged us, and Mandey said it was a girl that attacked her."

"So, there's five guys and two girls at least," Jesse said. "I'm sure that's not all of them, though. Anyone else have something to add?"

They all looked at each other and shook their heads. "Guess not," Danny said.

"Well, with any luck, after tonight our image of the Devils should be a lot clearer," Jesse said. "And they'll have gotten a good look at us, too."

18

Shannon's Bad Day

Ed Grubbs was a sharp-looking man in his fifties. Everything about him was pointed and angular—a square jaw; a long, pointed nose; blocky shoulders; and a high square forehead. His iron gray hair was buzz cut, and you could almost believe that if you touched it, the short, spiky hair could slice open a finger. But the sharpest aspect of Ed Grubbs's appearance was his eyes, which were pale gray many shades lighter than his hair. When angered, those eyes narrowed to slits, and some who were the object of his anger swore they could feel those eyes burning into them like lasers.

On this Friday afternoon, Shannon was in Ed Grubbs' tiny office—a windowless, cluttered room in which there was barely enough space for a desk, file cabinet, and "the victim's chair," which was where Shannon was seated, enduring a thorough ass-chewing from his boss.

"Boy, when I hired you, we had an understanding, didn't we?" Grubbs asked him.

"Yes, sir," Shannon replied.

"Would you mind telling me what that understanding was?"

Shannon sighed inwardly. "You would keep giving good reports to my parole officer if I kept delivering cars to your nephew's chop shop."

"That's right," Grubbs said. "And I've kept up my end of the deal, haven't I?"

"Yes, sir."

"Then why did Gary call me this morning and tell me he hasn't gotten a car from you for almost two weeks?"

Shannon didn't answer.

"Answer me, god damn it!" Grubbs shouted. His coffee mug sailed by Shannon's head. Shannon squeezed his eyes shut as the mug exploded against the wall, spraying him with ceramic fragments.

He paused a moment before replying. "I don't know, sir," Shannon said quietly.

Grubbs got up and came around the desk. He grabbed Shannon by the collar of his coveralls.

"You don't know?" he spat.

Grubbs was obviously ready to strangle him, but Shannon didn't feel particularly physically threatened by him. It was his ability to hurt Shannon in much worse ways that worried him.

"I don't know how I fell behind. Things have been kind of busy lately."

Grubbs' grip on his collar did not loosen any. "I don't know what the fuck has been keeping you busy, but it's not what you're supposed to be doing," he said, giving Shannon a shake, then letting him go.

He went back around his desk to the file cabinet and pulled out a file with Shannon's name on it. He tossed it on his desk.

"Do you see this?" Grubbs asked him, tapping his index finger on the folder. He didn't wait for an answer. "This is your personnel file. In it are receipts and records, undated for the moment, which can show you have been stealing money from me. All I have to do is date them according to the nights when you've closed, and you'll be on your way to the state pen. Comprende?"

Shannon nodded. "Yes, sir."

"Then listen, and listen good. Gary wants two cars by tomorrow morning. He wants a new '85 Mustang for a re-VIN, and a pre-1980 Firebird. If he doesn't get those from you, I'm putting in a phone call to the police department and to your parole officer and your ass will be back in the can so fast your head will spin. Now get out of here."

Shannon wanted to tell Ed Grubbs to go fuck himself, but that wasn't an option. Instead, he silently got up out of the chair and walked out. God, he didn't need this today. A raging headache was coming on, and now he had to go see his parole officer and get his ass chewed again. Shannon wanted to be with the one person who didn't rag on him, but Grubbs had just made sure that wasn't going to be an option tonight. Shannon was glad he hadn't made plans with Mandey for tonight, so he wouldn't have to cancel. He would call her later, though. He had to have something to brighten up his day.

He got in his car, lit a cigarette, and headed for home to shower and change clothes before his appointment downtown with Kevin Holtz. These dreaded standing appointments occurred every other Friday at 3:30 P.M. Of all the probation officers he could have been assigned to, he got the one who resembled a constipated weasel and had the disposition to match. He was still going to be pissed about the way Shannon had walked out on him last time, so it wasn't going to be a pleasant visit, not that they ever were.

When he walked into the apartment, he found his mother and Leon in the living room, watching Judge Wapner.

"Home early, ain'tcha?" his mother asked.

"Yeah," Shannon said. "Have to go see Ass Holtz."

Leon snorted. "Can't have much of a paycheck, leaving work early and running off to God-knows-where like you did last week."

"I don't ever have much of a paycheck," Shannon mumbled as he went to the refrigerator to see what he could grab to eat. There was leftover meatloaf from the night before, so he could make a sandwich.

"You got enough to pay your rent?" Leon asked him.

"Yeah, Leon, I've got my damn rent money," Shannon said, annoyed.

"Don't swear at me, boy, or I'll take you out," Leon said, getting up off the couch. "Give it to me."

"I haven't cashed it yet," Shannon said.

"Don't lie to me, boy," Leon said threateningly.

Shannon whipped his paycheck out of his pants pocket and waved it at Leon. "It's not cashed yet," he said, very deliberately. "What do you need it for now, anyhow? The rent's already <u>supposed</u> to have been paid for the month."

"Look, son, if you're going to live here, you pay your rent whenever you're told," Leon said, grabbing Shannon's wrist.

"I ain't your son," Shannon said angrily, jerking out of Leon's grasp. He put the check back in his pocket. "I'll get it cashed on the way home and you can have the fucking money, but you'd better remember at the end of the month that I already paid it, and don't ask me for it again."

He turned back to making his sandwich, and suddenly felt Leon's large hand swat the back of his head so hard that he pitched forward and smacked his forehead on the kitchen cabinet.

Shannon put his hand to his head and swung around. Leon was on his way back into the living room. Shannon was ready to lay into Leon, with words and with his fists, but he knew it wouldn't solve anything. The only thing it would accomplish would be the demolition of the apartment, and probably of Shannon's face. It wasn't worth it. They had had the same fight many times before, and there was no sense in rehashing it when the result would be the same.

He took a deep breath and finished making his sandwich, then poured a glass of milk and sat down at the kitchen table. The headache that had started at work was now going full-throttle thanks to Leon's double-whammy. He kept repeating Mandey's name in his mind, trying to keep bad thoughts at bay. He was going to call her as soon as he got home from his appointment.

He looked at the clock and quickly finished his sandwich, then went to take his shower. He changed into jeans and a T-shirt, and although it wasn't cold out, he wore his black leather jacket, the one that gave Holtz fits.

The traffic was heavy; schools were dismissing classes and a lot of people were taking off early from work. By the time he got downtown to the building and found a parking spot, it was already 3:30. He considered running so he wouldn't be late, but decided against it. He didn't want to look like a dork, like he cared about whether he was late. He was going to be happy when it was finally December and he would only have to check in once a month instead of every two weeks.

He strolled into the building and took an elevator to the third floor. When he reached Holtz's office, he went to open the door, but the doorknob was jerked from his hand as the door was pulled open.

"You're late," Holtz snapped at Shannon. "My time is valuable, and you're wasting it. You aren't my only case, you know."

Shannon sighed but didn't apologize, and followed Holtz into his office. Any other time he would have smarted off to Holtz; after all, he knew he was Holtz's last appointment of the week. He was pissed because he probably wanted to go home early, and Shannon wasn't being cooperative. Too damn bad.

He sat down in the brown swivel chair in front of Holtz's desk. Holtz's office wasn't much bigger than Grubbs', but the big difference was that Holtz's office was extremely neat. There was a place for everything, and everything was in its place. Holtz, however, believed there was something in his office that was not in its place, and that something was Shannon.

"These visits with you are a waste of time and taxpayers' money," Holtz said, sitting down in his chair behind the desk.

"I agree with you totally," Shannon said. "Any time you want to tell the judge these visits ain't necessary is fine with me."

"Son, if I had my way, I'd tell the judge to send you to the pen and just get it over with."

"I ain't your son," Shannon said.

Holtz ignored the remark. "Work reports?" he asked, and Shannon handed over a sealed envelope from Grubbs.

Holtz opened the envelope and scanned over the contents. "You didn't work from Wednesday through Saturday last week. Where were you?"

"The only day I was scheduled to work was Friday. I was sick. I called in. You know, it would be nice if I could get more than thirty hours—"

"Mmmm," Holtz said, still perusing the report and ignoring Shannon.

Shannon persisted. "I'd like to work a full forty-hour week, but Grubbs won't give me full-time hours. I need to get a different job. If I could earn more money, I could finally get ahead."

"What have you been doing the last two weeks?" Holtz said, putting the report into Shannon's file and setting it aside.

Holtz asked the question in a manner as if he expected Shannon to confess all his sins.

Shannon knew he had a right to be suspicious, but he was nuts if he thought Shannon was going to spill his guts about how he had violated his parole, first by leaving the county without permission, and then by burglarizing a jewelry store.

"Nothing," Shannon said.

"Somehow I doubt that," Holtz said. "You work twenty-five or thirty hours a week. What do you do with the rest of your time? I'll tell you what you do. You and that bunch of heathens cause trouble. Do you know that the area within a five-mile radius of where you live is second in the Houston metro area in auto thefts?"

That comment unnerved Shannon. Did Holtz suspect something? He couldn't let Holtz think he had rattled him.

"Gee, only second?" Shannon asked sarcastically.

"I don't like your attitude."

Shannon didn't reply. He just gave Holtz a weary "fuck you" look.

"What, no more smart remarks? It's because you know I'm right."

Shannon sat back and crossed his arms in front of himself. "Well, if I told you I spent last weekend with my new girlfriend, who's a high school honor student, you wouldn't believe me."

"Oh, that's a good one," Holtz said with a look of sour amusement on his face.

Shannon shook his head and looked up to the ceiling. "It doesn't matter what I say to you. You don't ever take anything I say seriously."

"That's because you don't take any of this seriously."

"Wrong!" Shannon said vehemently, sitting up straight. "I take this <u>very</u> seriously. I don't take <u>you</u> seriously because you don't ever listen to me!"

"Why should I listen to you when you don't ever tell me the truth?" Holtz replied.

"You wouldn't know the truth if it bit you on the ass!" Shannon said. "You don't believe a word I say, so this is a waste of time. Can I go now?"

"No, you can't go now, although I'm surprised you bothered to ask instead of waltzing out like you did last time."

"Look, I don't know what you want from me. I thought you were supposed to be helping me. It seems like all you want is for me to screw up so I can get sent back to jail and you won't have to deal with me no more."

Holtz nodded. "Yes, I'm supposed to aid in your readjustment and rehabilitation, but you don't want to be rehabilitated," he said. "When you show me you want to walk the straight and narrow, I'll help you. Otherwise, I'd rather send you to prison and let them straighten you out there."

"Jesus!" Shannon swore. "What the hell do you want from me? How do you get off telling me whether or not I want to be rehabilitated?"

"Because I know you're out there breaking the law even now!" Holtz shouted, slamming his fist down on his desk. "You haven't gotten caught yet, but it's only a matter of time. If you were even halfway serious about living a straight life, you'd listen to me and separate yourself from that element you choose to associate with!"

"If you'd bother to listen to me, you'd realize that I've been telling you for three months that I don't make enough money at that stupid job I have to be able to afford to move and get the hell out of there!"

"If you were serious enough about it, you could find a way."

"You tell me what to do, but you don't give me a clue about how I'm supposed to go about doing it!" Shannon shouted, getting to his feet. He was ready to walk out, the same way he had last time, but he paused a second to calm down. He slowly sat down again, and in a composed voice he asked, "Isn't there a form I can fill out to request help in finding a new job placement?"

"Yes, but I don't have any of them right now," Holtz told him.

"Shit!" Shannon said, standing up again.

"Sit down."

"Forget it. I'm out of here. See you in two weeks."

"No, you won't. That's the day after Thanksgiving, and the office will be closed," Holtz said, looking at his appointment calendar. "I have you down to come in at 1:30 on the 21st. That's a Wednesday."

"Whatever," Shannon said. "It's all bullshit, anyway. It ain't worth wasting the gas to come down here."

"I'm just waiting for you to miss an appointment so I can get a warrant issued for your arrest."

"You'd love that, wouldn't you?" Shannon muttered and walked out the door, slamming it behind him.

Once outside the office, he stood there for a moment. He closed his eyes and took several deep breaths until he felt a little calmer, but his nerves were shot to hell. Only a week ago, he would have tried to unwind by going to see Arlene, maybe smoke a little weed, and he'd feel a little better. But today he was going to go home and do something much safer, cheaper, and more satisfying—talk to Mandey on the phone. It wasn't as good as talking to her while holding her body against his, feeling her soft kisses on his face and neck, but it would have to do.

Shannon smoked a cigarette in his car in the parking lot before leaving, then fought the rush hour traffic on I-45 to get home. He stopped at a Fiesta grocery store to cash his check at the courtesy booth. He bought a bottle of Tylenol before leaving the store, and bought a Coke from the vending machine on his way out. He took a big swallow to wash down four of the pills, then headed home to give Leon the damn money.

He considered returning to the apartment via his bedroom window to avoid Leon, but decided he would only be postponing the inevitable. He walked into the apartment and found his mother in the kitchen, cooking spaghetti. It surprised him, because it was a rarity for his mother to cook two nights in a row.

"Where's Leon?" he asked her.

"Oh, he went somewheres. Didn't say where, but said he wouldn't be gone long," his mother replied. "You want some spaghetti? It'll be ready in about ten minutes."

"Sure," he said. He decided to wait to call Mandey until after he ate. He wanted to talk to her longer than ten minutes.

Shannon turned on the news and sat down on the couch. The news was boring, just more talk about Reagan's landslide re-election. Politics meant nothing to him. He didn't think it mattered who was president; it had no effect on his life. It had been shit during the last four years of Reagan, it had been shit when Carter had been in office, and it had been shit when whoever was president before that.

"How was your visit with your parole officer?" his mother asked as they sat down at the kitchen table to eat.

Shannon shrugged. "Same as ever. The guy hates me. He's just waiting for me to screw up so he can throw me back in jail."

"Why does he want to do that?" his mother asked.

"I don't know, Momma," Shannon said, a sudden wave of weariness washing over him. "He doesn't think I've learned my lesson. He thinks I need to suffer more."

"What? Suffer more?" his mother exclaimed. "The nerve. I'll tell him what I think of him. What's his number?"

"Calm down, Momma," Shannon said.

"*Mi hijo* spent eight months in jail and he says you need to suffer more?" she asked angrily.

"Momma, it's okay. Just drop it," Shannon said, and changed the subject. "Did Leon tell you why he wanted the rent money now?"

"No, but I imagine it's because he spent the checks already."

"On what?"

His mother shrugged. "He didn't say."

"Damn it!" Shannon said, throwing his fork down in disgust. "I wish I'd been here last Friday when the checks came. I hate it when he gets a hold of them. What about your food stamps?"

"He kept some of them," his mother replied.

"Damn it!" Shannon cursed again. "Talk about someone who belongs back in jail. He's got no business taking your money and Annette's money and your food stamps, and doing God-knows-what with it! Then he demands money from me to replace what he's spent. I'm sick of it!"

"But we get by," his mother said, shrugging.

"Barely. What happens when Annette turns eighteen and her social security checks stop? Her share of the food stamps will stop, too. What happens when I'm not here anymore, handing over my paycheck for rent? I don't just pay half the rent, either, Momma. Since I got out of detention, I've been paying the phone bill and the light bill and helping with extra groceries. I'm not always going to be here. Someday it's just going to be you and Leon, living on your disability and food stamps. You can get by, but not if Leon spends your check on drugs and booze before he pays the bills!"

"Why are you talking about leaving?" his mother asked him, alarmed. "Where are you going?"

"Nowhere yet, Momma," Shannon said. "But, I'm nineteen years old—well, I will be on Sunday, anyway. There's going to come a time, not too long from now, when I'll be leaving home for good."

"Oh, no!" his mother exclaimed, her hands flying to her face. Shannon thought she was objecting to the idea of him leaving, but then she said, "Your birthday! I forgot about your birthday!"

"Don't worry about it, Momma."

The front door opened with a loud bang, making Shannon jump. He expected to see Leon's bulk filling up the doorway, but instead Annette was entering the apartment, stumbling and laughing, obviously stoned.

"Hey, y'all," Annette said, giggling. "What's cooking?"

"Spaghetti. Grab yourself a plate and sit down," said their mother.

Shannon wasn't very hungry anymore. His plate was nearly empty, so he got up and scraped the remainder of his dinner into the trash and put the plate in the sink.

"What, you're too good to sit down at the table with us?" Annette demanded.

"I've got a phone call to make," Shannon said curtly. "Don't run off after you eat. We've got stuff to do."

He took the phone and went into the bedroom, locking the door behind him. He dialed Mandey's number and stretched out on the bed.

"Hello?"

Her voice was music to his ears. "Hi, Mandey, it's me," he said.

"Hi! What's up?"

"Not much," he said, trying to be nonchalant. "I've got to go back to work and fill in for someone until closing."

"Bummer."

"Yeah, I'd rather be with you."

"Me, too."

"What are you doing tonight?"

"Oh, going out with some friends. We might go see a movie or hang around the mall."

"That sounds fun."

"What's the matter?"

He smiled to himself. She already knew him that well. "It hasn't been a good day," he told her.

"What happened?"

"Well, first I got my ass chewed out at work by my boss. He and I don't see eye-to-eye on how he runs his business, 'cause he's a liar and a cheat, but he let me know that either I do things his way, or he'll send a bad report to my parole officer. After that, I had to go for my appointment with my parole officer, and I got into it with him. He told me that he doesn't think I learned my lesson in jail, and he's itching for any excuse to send me back. I was yelling at him because he never listens to me and he refuses to help me get a new job. In between, I came home, and Leon demanded my rent money three weeks early. I know he's going to go out and blow it on something, and then at the end of the month he's going to want the money from me again."

"Oh, Shannon," Mandey said, sounding dismayed. "You poor thing. I wish I could be with you tonight. It sounds like you could use a little TLC."

"Yeah, I do," Shannon said heavily. "My nerves are about shot."

"If I were with you, I'd give you a nice, long back massage."

"Oh, don't torture me that way!" Shannon protested, burying his face in his pillow.

"What?"

"Don't go describing massages to me when I'm here suffering and can't be with you."

"I'm sorry."

"I wanted to come by and see you all week, but there was always something going on. But I'm looking forward to tomorrow night."

"So am I," Mandey said. "I've missed you."

"I've missed you, too," Shannon said. "I have to work until three, so is it okay if I pick you up around five?"

"Perfect."

"Good. I want this to be a special weekend. I'm going to be nineteen Sunday, and I want to start the next year of my life off right."

"Do you have anything specific you want to do to celebrate?"

"I don't," he said. "All I want to do is spend the day with you, and I'll be happy."

"Your wish is my command," she told him. "I take it your family doesn't make a big deal about birthdays?"

"Oh, when 'Nette and I were little, it was different, but now no one pays attention. Momma forgot all about it until I said something a little while ago. I don't care. What makes me mad is Leon, and the way he takes everyone's money and blows it. I ain't never going to get ahead, living here and working that dumb job. I mean, this apartment rents for $300 a month. I'm only one of four people living here, but I pay half the rent. Sometimes I end up paying all of it. A couple months ago the landlord came knocking on our door one day saying he was going to evict us because our rent was overdue. Momma wasn't feeling good, so I was glad I was around or who knows what she would have done to the guy. But we were both real confused, because I had given Leon my half of the rent the week before. He went out and spent it, so I had to scrape up enough money to pay it. I ended up paying $450 in rent that month."

"Did you confront him about it?"

"Sure I did. He said he paid the rent, and that the landlord was a liar and I shouldn't have paid him any more. I called Leon a liar and we got in a fight. I don't know why I even bother. It don't do any good, and I got my ass kicked. I get so damned frustrated, Mandey. Practically every time I open my head, we get into it, and nothing ever changes."

"What does Leon look like?" Mandey asked. "He must be huge if he can take you in a fight."

"He is," Shannon said glumly. "It's bad enough that my mother had to hook up with a sleazebag like him, but why did she have to find somebody so goddamned big? When I was a kid, I dreamed of growing up to be big enough to beat him. I got big, but not that big. I mean, I'm about six-foot, 250 pounds, but Leon's about six-three and weighs over 300."

"Good Lord," Mandey said faintly.

"I was terrified of him when I was little. I swear, sometimes I wonder how I ever made it this far without him killing me."

"Poor baby," Mandey said. "I get these visions in my head of you as a little boy, being abused and hurt, and it makes me want to cry."

Shannon could hear her voice getting teary. "Don't cry, Mandey. It's okay. I got through it."

"Are you any closer to being able to move out of there?"

"No...I'm more desperate than ever, but I'm never getting out of here if I can't get a better job."

Someone banged on the bedroom door.

"Go away, Annette. I'm on the phone," Shannon said.

"Boy, I want that money now," he heard Leon say.

"Aw, shit. Hold on a second, Mandey," Shannon said to her and put down the receiver.

He stood up, got the money out of his wallet, and opened the door. Leon's hulking figure stood before him.

"Here," Shannon said shortly, holding out the money.

Leon snatched it away and began counting it.

"It's all there, damn it," Shannon said, and shut the door and locked it again.

He picked up the phone again and lay back down. "That was Leon demanding the rent," he told Mandey.

"Did you get a receipt?" she asked dryly.

"Like that would make a difference," Shannon said in derision.

"I can hardly wait to see you tomorrow night," she told him, changing the subject.

"Me, too" he said. "I've been dreaming about holding you and kissing you."

"Same here. I want to hold you in my arms and feel your big, strong arms around me. Do you know how good I feel when I'm with you?"

"Well, it can't be as good as I feel when I'm with you."

There was banging on the door again, and this time it was Annette. "Hey, if you don't get off the phone now and tell me what's up, I'm leaving," he heard her say.

"Aw, shit," he muttered again. "Mandey, I've got to go."

"Okay. I'll see you tomorrow, then."

"Looking forward to it."

"So am I. 'Bye."

Shannon hung up the phone. Damn, he didn't want to be here; he didn't want to go steal cars. He wanted to be in his own place, with his own life, and to be with Mandey whenever he wanted. He sighed heavily and went out into the living room to tell Annette what had to be done that night.

19

Mandey's Friday Night

The Alley Cats had agreed to meet in the Forest Creek Shopping Center parking lot at 9:45. Although all the other stores, including a Safeway, closed at ten P.M., there was a movie theater there that had midnight movies on the weekends. The parking lot was the place where Rogers High students came to hang out and hook up. Their vehicles could be parked there and not raise suspicion.

Mandey arrived a few minutes early. Terry was the only other one there, sitting in his truck in the northwestern corner of the lot. He was drinking out of a can nestled in a small paper bag that concealed the label, as if that wouldn't attract a cop's attention just as much as the beer can itself.

"Luckenbach, Texas" was blaring from Terry's truck's stereo. Mandey's own stereo was blaring back XTC's "No Thugs in Our House," which she found to be an ironically appropriate song. She was sitting there, enjoying her music, and thinking about her phone conversation with Shannon earlier in the evening when Jeremy's car pulled into the space between her and Terry. Jeremy and Danny got out and came over to get in the van.

"I've got shotgun," Danny declared, hopping into the front passenger seat.

That had been James's seat for a long time. Now it belonged to Shannon. Mandey had never dreamed that Danny would ever be sitting there.

"Fine," Jeremy said, opening the sliding door and getting in the back. "Hey, I've never been in your van before. This is cool." He plopped down in one of the two beanbag chairs.

"Yeah, it is," Danny agreed.

"Thanks. I'm trying to make it how I want it," Mandey said.

The others arrived shortly thereafter, and everyone piled into the van. The drive to Liaisons took about twenty-five minutes.

"What if they see us all dressed alike and don't let us in?" Mandey asked nervously as she, Dina, Danny, Angelina, and Jesse got in line.

"They'll let us in; we're regulars," Jesse said. "They let the Devils in with their jackets. There won't be a problem."

"I hope not," Mandey said.

"Relax," Dina said.

It was awkward for Mandey to walk into Liaisons with Danny; she was worried that people might make the wrong assumption about her. She had never used drugs or even been in the presence of anyone in the process of using them, save for the concerts she had been to where the smell of burning joints permeated the air as soon as the lights went down.

Danny had promised, although reluctantly, not to conduct business that night. Jesse and Terry wanted everyone's attention focused on the business at hand, and Mandey was adamant that anyone she transported in her vehicle leave any illegal substances at home or in their car. Naturally, she couldn't be sure her passengers adhered to the rule, but if they did break it, at least they were very discreet about it and were unlikely to attract unwanted attention.

No one had contested her policy. Mandey supposed they accepted it because of her goody-two-shoes reputation. Even though she was part of this outfit, this <u>gang</u>, her cohorts still thought of her that way. Despite all her efforts, her image hadn't changed. She was beginning to accept that fact and hope that people would like her anyway.

"Don't take this the wrong way, but I hope that people don't get the wrong impression," Danny said to her as they stood in line to get in. "Here I am with the straightest person on Earth, and I'm not conducting business tonight. People might think I've turned over a new leaf."

Mandey boggled at him. "<u>You're</u> worried about <u>your</u> reputation?" she asked, then dropped her voice to a hissing whisper. "<u>I'm</u> the one who needs to worry about her reputation. I try to forget about what you do. When I remember, it hurts my head and makes me want to run away from you, screaming."

Danny laughed. "Sounds like you dropped some bad acid."

"You are something else," Mandey said, turning away in disgust. She crossed her arms in front of her and tapped her foot impatiently.

"Are you two fighting?" Angelina asked.

"No," they both replied.

"His audacity just amazes me sometimes," Mandey said.

"What'd you do to her?" Angelina demanded of Danny. "Mandey never gets mad."

"Nothing!" Danny cried defensively.

"I'm not mad," Mandey said, turning around to face them. "'Flabbergasted' is a better word. Or 'exasperated'."

"Danny?" Angelina asked ominously.

"What?" he replied, still acting innocent.

They had arrived at the head of the line, so they paid the cover charge and walked inside. The club was full, as it usually was. The crowd was mostly high school aged. With the drinking age being nineteen (although there was talk of it being raised to 21 soon), there had been a lot of skepticism as to whether a nightclub geared toward underage patrons could succeed, but it had. Only a few years before, the same crowd had jammed the roller rinks on Friday and Saturday nights, Mandey included. Now that the skating craze had waned, Liaisons was the cool place on the north side for the underage crowd to hang out.

Mandey remembered the night she had seen Shannon there. It was nice to be able to recall that night without tears. She remembered clearly how he had been dressed—a long-sleeved light beige shirt tucked into black corduroy pants with a black belt, and black chukka boots. The most striking thing about his outfit—to Mandey, anyway—had been his wallet chain, the long silver chain that looped from the front left belt loop to his back left pocket, hanging down two-thirds of the way to his knee. Usually, Shannon's wardrobe, as she remembered it, was jeans, cords, or even worse, *polyester pants*, with plaid flannel shirts and T-shirts. She had a soft spot in her heart for corduroys and plaid flannel herself, and Shannon just wouldn't be Shannon without his flannel shirts.

"You look like you're a million miles away."

Mandey snapped out of her thoughts and looked at Danny.

"I'm back," she said. "I wonder when our Devil counterparts will show up."

"With any luck, they won't," Danny said.

"Well, I'm hoping they do," Jesse said. "I'm ready to start sending them the message that we aren't going to take it anymore."

"I'm still unclear on exactly how we're going to do that," Danny said. "I mean, we aren't going to confront them, are we?"

"That would be resorting to their kind of behavior, and we don't want to do that, do we?" Mandey asked. The Alley Cats hadn't exactly worked out the logistics of their endeavor, and Mandey was rightfully worried about what might happen.

"Man, don't sweat it," Jesse said. Mandey wasn't sure if he meant "man" or "Man," short for her name.

"I'm ready to kick someone's ass, myself," Dina declared. "Let one of them look at me the wrong way, and they'll know something all right."

The drum machine beat of the extended remix of "She Blinded Me with Science" came over the sound system. Jesse and Angelina got took off toward the dance floor. Mandey got antsy; she loved dancing to this song. She and Dina looked at each other.

"Let's go dance," Dina said to her. "Are you coming, Danny?"

"No, you go," he said, shaking his head.

Mandey followed Dina and they worked their way through the crowded dance floor to join Jesse and Angelina.

Mandey lost herself in the song, which wasn't hard for her to do. When she danced, she could make herself oblivious to everything but the music. When she got into that mode, she could dance on and on, not caring if it was a song she liked, as long as the beat was good. That was one thing she liked about Liaisons; the deejay would get on a roll and play stuff you could move to, unlike the deejays they had at their school dances, who had to break it up with slow dances and country songs. Not that that was so bad, but they never played anything long enough for Mandey to get into that extended state of involvement with the music.

"She Blinded Me with Science" segued into "Fascination" by Human League, and Angelina, Jesse and Dina left the floor. Mandey continued alone, engrossed in the music. She did remain mindful of the reason she was there, however, and scanned the crowd to see if she could identify any rival gang members. When she felt a heavy hand come down on her shoulder, she jumped, startled.

"Hey," Danny said.

She moved closer to him so they could hear each other.

"You scared me," Mandey told him. "What's going on?"

"Nothing," Danny said. "Just thought I'd join you. Have you seen anything?"

"Nada," Mandey said.

"Me, neither. It can stay that way for all I care."

"Don't you want to get the Devils out of our hair?"

"Of course, I do. I just hope we can do it with as little conflict as possible," Danny said.

"Well, I don't like conflict, either, but the sooner we get this done, the better."

The music flowed into "One Thing Leads to Another" by The Fixx. The deejay was on fire, in Mandey's opinion. She couldn't enjoy it long, though, as she caught a glimpse of Jesse and Angelina dancing on the other side of the floor. A dark-haired girl in tight black pants and a black satin jacket danced near them; in fact, she appeared to be attempting to wedge herself in between Jesse and Angelina.

Danny saw it too. "Uh-oh, it's starting," he said.

"What do you mean?" Mandey asked.

"That girl there, trying to piss Angie off, is Raff's girlfriend."

Suddenly there appeared next to them a Hispanic male about the same age as Mandey and Danny. He had on black pants, a white T-shirt, and a black satin jacket with a small red devil on the left breast.

It's the Underwood devil, Mandey thought crazily when she saw the icon on the jacket.

Then she noticed the scar on his jaw and knew who he was.

"Raff," Danny said flatly.

"What is this? I hear you're not dealing tonight?" Raff said.

"No, not tonight," Danny replied.

"Too bad for you. Terrific for me. I'm raking in the bucks. Getting all kinds of new customers. I plan on keeping them, too."

"Yeah, well, think what you want," Danny said sourly.

"In fact, the word tonight is you've quit dealing for good," Raff said.

"Don't believe everything you hear," Danny said.

"No?"

"No."

"What's with the jackets?" Raff asked, plucking at the fabric of Danny's sleeve.

Danny pulled away. "Hands off."

"What? You think I'm going to get your pretty kitty jacket dirty?" Raff asked mockingly.

"Fuck off," Danny said.

"Are we in a bad mood tonight?" Raff asked.

"Raff, go bug somebody else," Danny said. Raff reached out to tug at the hem of Danny's jacket, but Danny pushed his hand away. "And quit touching the fucking jacket!"

"You don't like me touching your little pussy?" Raff asked. "You're nothing but a big pussy with a little pussy on your jacket."

Danny made a lunge at Raff, but Mandey threw herself between them. "You'd better get out of here or you're gonna be sorry," she warned Raff.

Raff turned his attention to her. *His eyes*, she thought, *are like cold, black marbles.*

"Are you threatening me?" he asked her.

"Yes," Danny said, getting in between Mandey and Raff again. "Look, I don't know why you want to provoke us, but we're sick and tired of your gang bullshit."

At that moment there was a screech, and the three of them turned to see what was happening. Angelina and Raff's girlfriend were engaged in a catfight in the middle of the dance floor. Jesse was trying to restrain Angelina, but the other girl was swinging, unhindered.

"Do you want to go do something about your girlfriend?" Danny asked, pushing by Raff and into the crowd to try to put a stop to the scuffle.

Raff grabbed Danny's arm. "Don't you dare think about touching my woman," Raff told him threateningly.

"Let go!" Danny said, shoving Raff.

"Danny, don't!" Mandey cried.

"You want a piece of me, pussy?" Raff asked Danny, shoving him back.

Mandey stepped back to avoid being rammed by Danny. When she did, she bumped into someone.

"Ow! Watch where you're going, you fat cow!"

Mandey whirled around. "Sorry," she said, then stopped and stared at whom she was speaking to—a girl with long, fluffy blonde hair and cornflower blue eyes. She wore black spandex pants and a black satin jacket with a red devil on the front.

"What are you looking at?" the girl demanded.

"N-nothing," Mandey stammered.

"Clumsy bitch," the girl said.

The girl was pretty, but her face was hard and her blue eyes cold, like light glinting off polished steel. Mandey realized she was purposely trying to start something with her. The Devils must have noticed the Alley Cats' jackets and decided to try to intimidate the competition.

Mandey turned back around to see what was happening. Danny had succeeded in getting past Raff and over to where Jesse and Angelina were. A crowd had formed around the altercation, but from what Mandey could see, Dina had joined the fray and was now engaged in combat with Raff's girlfriend. Angelina had a hank of the girl's long, black hair in her hand as Jesse tried to pull her away. Danny had his arms around Dina's waist, attempting to pull her off the other girl, while Rick the security guard tried to extract Raff's girlfriend out of the middle of it all.

The blonde girl grabbed the back of Mandey's jacket and yanked her backward.

"Hey! I was talking to you!" she said.

"What do you want?" Mandey asked frustrated.

"You have a lot of nerve coming in here acting like you're some kind of gang or something," the girl said.

"Well, we're pretty nervy people," Mandey said, brushing her off and edging her way closer to the melee.

"I want you out of here, <u>now</u>, all three of you girls and whoever came with you," Rick was saying. "You've got five minutes to clear out before I call the cops."

"I want to kill that bitch!" Angelina shouted, still fuming.

"Later," Jesse said firmly, taking her by the arm. "Where's Mandey?"

"Right here."

"We're out of here. Let's find the others and go."

Mandey followed Danny, who was dragging Dina by the arm toward the door. She turned around and saw Raff talking to his girlfriend, the blonde girl, and a blond male. She hoped they wouldn't follow them outside. She didn't want this to continue out in the parking lot.

When they got to the door, they met Jeremy running in.

"We've had kind of a scuffle out here," he said breathlessly.

"What happened?" Jesse asked. "Where are the others?"

Jeremy started to reply, but then Jesse said, "Never mind. Go get them. We're leaving."

"Can we hurry?" Mandey asked anxiously. "I'm afraid they might follow us."

"Step on it," Jesse said to Jeremy. "Get them to the van ASAP."

They all started running the second they stepped outside. Terry, Zack, Jim, and Brad were already waiting by the van. Mandey unlocked it, and they all scrambled to get in. She pulled out of the parking space and spun her wheels on the gravel as they left the lot through the northeast corner.

"Tell me if you see someone following us," Mandey told them. Raff and the others had appeared around the corner of the building as they were leaving the parking lot.

"Don't see anyone yet," Terry said.

"Let's hope it stays that way," Mandey said.

When they were sure no one was following them, Mandey drove to Denny's. They sat at two tables pushed together and discussed the night's events over burgers and breakfast.

The guys assigned to the parking lot had separated into two groups—Terry and Brad, and Jeremy, Jim, and Zack. They had circled the club, looking for suspicious activity. Jeremy, Jim, and Zack had come upon two of the Devils, the big ugly one and a skinny Latino boy, wandering through the parking lot. The Devils had been belligerent, demanding to know what the hell they were doing there. There had been an exchange of words, and then the ugly one took a swing at Jim, and then they all got into it. When Terry and Brad had circled around, they saw the fray and joined in. They ended up chasing the guys out of the parking lot and down the street.

Meanwhile, inside the club, Raff's girlfriend, whose name was Juanita, had instigated the trouble by flirting with Jesse and calling Angelina some uncomplimentary names in Spanish. Danny told about how Raff had tried to rile him up, and Mandey mentioned her encounter with the blonde girl.

"They must have seen our jackets and decided to target us," Angelina said.

"I think there was something bigger going on, though," Jesse asked. "It seemed like they wanted to create a scene."

"Like as a distraction," Jim said.

"Maybe," Jesse said.

"I know those guys in the parking lot were up to no good," Zack said. "They were probably going to steal a car."

"Actually, we saw a car leaving around the time we saw you guys fighting," Brad said. "It was a nice black Mustang."

"Could have been getting stolen," Terry said. "Maybe those guys were the lookouts."

"Well, if it did get stolen, we didn't do a very good job of stopping it," Zack said.

"Hey, we're new at this," Jesse said. "But now they know we're here. Let's tally up who we've got. There's the ugly guy, the skinny kid, Raff, his girlfriend—"

"The blond guy," Brad said.

"The blonde girl," Mandey added.

"And the black guy and the leader," Terry said, "but we didn't see them tonight, did you?"

"No," Jesse said. "So that's eight, at least."

"Maybe nine," Mandey said. "I think it was another girl who jumped me that night. Her hair was long and brown and curly-ish. Not black or blonde like the other two."

"Okay, it seems like we're pretty evenly matched," Jesse said.

"If that's all there are," Danny said.

"Well, we'll find out. Let's meet again next week and go back to Liaisons. We'll switch off. Terry's group will go inside, and we'll stay outside next time. Do we want to do it Friday or Saturday?"

"Friday," Danny said. "Jackie Seymore is having her belated birthday bash on Saturday night."

"Okay, Friday it is."

20

Shannon's Friday Night

"What is so all-fired important?" John demanded as Shannon walked in.

The entire gang was congregated in the Devils' den, none of them looking particularly enthusiastic. He hadn't needed or even wanted all of them to be in on what he had planned, but here they all were. If it had been important for them all to be there, he wouldn't have been able to find half of them.

"The chop shop has put in an order for a couple of cars. They want them tonight. I need y'all to cover for me."

Annette sneered. "I hope you're going to do a better job than you did last time," she said.

"Like you ain't never had a bad day," Shannon said sourly.

"You been having a bad month," Checkmate said.

"Month? Try year," Raff said with a mean-spirited grin.

"Anyway," Shannon said, ignoring the snide remarks, "I want to hit the club first. What I need is for some of y'all to go inside and cause just enough ruckus to distract that doofus rent-a-cop and get him out of the parking lot."

He assigned John, Kerri, Juanita, and Raff to go into the club. When Shannon was ready, he would send Marco inside, and that would be their cue to do something to divert the security guard's attention. Meanwhile, Lenny and Curt would be staking out the parking lot for potential witnesses, and it would be their job to keep them from seeing anything they weren't supposed to.

"Checkmate, you and Annette stay in my car and watch the street, and be prepared to take off if anything goes wrong," Shannon said. He didn't want a repeat of what had happened the last time he had tried to steal a car at Liaisons.

"Man, you never let me do nothing!" Annette cried petulantly, slamming herself down on the couch.

"Get over it," Shannon told her.

"You're a prick, Trick," she said.

"Yeah, I am, and I'm a mighty big prick, too, so don't you forget it."

"At least you admit it," Annette grumbled.

The Devils drove to Liaisons in two separate cars, with John, Kerri, Juanita, and Raff departing a half-hour earlier than the rest. When Shannon arrived at the club with the others in his car, he drove around the lot, pretending to search for a parking space, but he was checking out the cars. He didn't check the cars parked on the east side of the building closest to the entrance. If he had, he would have seen Mandey's van parked there.

He found what he wanted parked in the second row from the street—a black Ford Mustang. It was a fine-looking car, a new '85 with dark tinted windows and a spoiler on the back, and the paper temporary plate was still in the back window, although the permanent plates were now on the car. He also set his sights on a gold '79 Trans Am in the third row, near the end. He drove out of the lot and down the street, then parked on the side of the road, out of sight from Liaisons.

"You know the routine," he said tersely, getting out of the car. "Let's go."

He let Marco, Lenny, and Curt get a head start. When Shannon made his way into Liaisons' parking lot, Marco was up near the entrance and Lenny and Curt were on the east side of the lot, smoking cigarettes and trying to look aloof. Shannon didn't even see Rick, the rent-a-cop.

He sauntered up to the Mustang, looked it over, then gave Marco the signal. Marco disappeared inside.

With professional swiftness, Shannon pulled a slim jim from under his jacket and slid it down between the window and door frame. With a pop he opened the lock. Inside, he made a cursory check of the car for the keys, looking in the glove compartment, over the visor, and under the seat, but came up empty, so he set to work. Within a minute he had hot-wired the car to life. He slid into the driver's seat and shut the door. Slowly and casually, he backed the car out of the space. When he did, he saw Lenny and Curt, still on the east side of the lot, but they were being confronted by three guys in black denim jackets, and it looked like the confrontation was on its way to becoming violent.

"Shit," Shannon muttered. Stealing from the Liaisons lot was getting to be more trouble than it was worth.

He didn't let it rattle him, though, and drove out of the parking lot. He pulled up to Checkmate and Annette in his car and rolled down the passenger window.

"Give Lenny and Curt about five minutes. If they aren't back here by then, you'd better check on them. They looked like they were about to get into it with three guys. I'll see you over at the chop shop."

Shannon rolled up the window and drove away before there was any more discussion.

He turned on the radio and relaxed slightly. Damn, this was one fine car. Fancy control panel all lit up in green and red, power windows, just 479 miles on the odometer, that new car smell filling his nostrils. The stereo wasn't that cheap factory shit, either; it was a Pioneer stereo/cassette player with a cassette in it. Shannon pushed it into the player, and Huey Lewis and the News started to blare over the speakers. He punched the button to pop the cassette back out. How could someone with such good taste in cars listen to such sucky music? He rolled down the passenger side window and threw the tape out onto the street, then turned on the stereo. He fiddled with the dial and found Sammy Hagar singing, "I Can't Drive 55." Shannon was more than a little tempted to leadfoot the accelerator and see what this baby could do, but the last thing he needed to do was attract any attention.

    He wondered what the hell was happening back at the club with Lenny and Curt. He hoped it wasn't serious. He didn't need any stupid shit going on tonight. He didn't dare go back to Liaisons to try to nick another car. The Owens impound lot was another place he was able to snag some decent rides from, but the last time he had been there, he had gotten into a fight with the guy on overnight watch. Normally, he would have picked the lock on the gate, gone in and hotwired a car, and driven out, but on this night, Raff insisted on going, too, and burglarizing the place. They hadn't known there was someone sleeping in the office. Shannon had picked up a chair and hit the guy upside the head with it, not a dead-on hit, but enough to knock him out. He wanted to lay low from there for a while. After he dropped of the Mustang at Grubbs' nephew's place (the night guy there let him in when Shannon drove up to the gate and blinked the car headlights three times), Checkmate and Annette picked him up, and off they went to find another car. He didn't like to go too far out of the area, because he didn't want to get caught driving a car that had been reported stolen. There was a movie theater a few miles away with a midnight showing of *The Rocky Horror Picture Show*. There, he was able to find a silver '77 Firebird Trans AM parked in a secluded spot. Soon he was on his way back to the chop shop. He hoped this would shut Grubbs up for a while.

21

First Date

Mandey bounced down the front steps as soon as she saw the white Oldsmobile pulling into the driveway, right on time on Saturday. "Back in Black" by AC/DC blasted out of the half-open windows.

"Hi," she greeted Shannon as she got into the car.

"Hi," he replied, turning down the radio volume and leaning over to kiss her. "You look cute tonight."

She had on a pair of skin-tight teal parachute pants, a white shirt with lots of zippers on it, and a faded blue denim jacket with several buttons. A couple of them had pictures of Duran Duran and Hall & Oates. On the jacket's collar was a white button that declared in red letters, "In Russia I couldn't wear this button." Another one, pink with black letters, said, "shy".

"Thanks," Mandey said, smiling. "You look as handsome as ever."

Shannon looked down at his jeans, white T-shirt, and blue plaid flannel shirt and gave a short laugh. "Thanks," he said, backing the car out into the street. "Where do you want to eat?"

"I don't know. Where do you want to eat?" Mandey asked.

"I asked you first," Shannon said.

"I don't know," Mandey said again. "I don't care. I'm not picky."

"Do you like Mexican food?" Shannon asked her.

"I love it," Mandey said enthusiastically.

"Good. All day all I've been able to think about is Monterey House," he said.

"Mmmm," Mandey said, dreamily. "Cheese enchiladas."

"That's settled then," Shannon said. "You eat those with or without onions?"

"Well, usually with, but maybe not tonight," Mandey said. "Why?"

"Well, I was going to say that I like onions, so don't go onionless because of me."

"Okay, good," she said. "We'll both have onion breath and cancel each other out." She giggled and laid her head on his shoulder.

Shannon slid an 8-track tape into the player. In a moment they heard the opening piano to Meatloaf's "Two Out of Three Ain't Bad."

"Is this *Bat Out of Hell?*" Mandey asked.

"Yeah," Shannon replied.

"Cool," Mandey said. "I used to have an 8-track of this, too, but it broke. I need to get it on cassette."

"Yeah, someday if I get a little money saved up, I should get a cassette player for the car," Shannon said.

When Meat Loaf began singing, Mandey did, too. After a few moments, Shannon joined in. Mandey watched Shannon as he sang. He looked like he enjoyed singing, and he had a nice baritone voice and could carry a tune.

Shannon noticed Mandey watching him. He wondered what she was thinking, but didn't feel too self-conscious. She was smiling, holding his hand, and singing along with him. This was great.

When the next song, "Paradise by the Dashboard Light" came on, Mandey and Shannon sang along so enthusiastically that people in passing cars were giving them odd looks. Neither one of them cared.

"I never imagined you had such a nice singing voice," Mandey said when they were seated in the restaurant.

"You think so?"

"Yes, I do," Mandey said, crunching a tortilla chip with salsa.

"Thanks," Shannon said. He reached for a chip and doused it in the bowl of chili con queso they had ordered.

"I always loved your speaking voice, though. It's so deep and sexy."

Shannon laughed. "You make me sound like Barry White."

They were both laughing as the waitress brought their food. Mandey had ordered the cheese enchilada dinner, while Shannon had the Monterey dinner.

"That's a lot of food," Mandey commented, looking at the two plates the waitress had set before him.

"Are you trying to say I'm a pig?" Shannon asked with mock indignance, taking a mouthful.

Mandey giggled. "No, I like a man with a big appetite," she said.

"Then you're gonna love me," Shannon said. "What do you want to do after we eat?"

"I don't know," Mandey said. "What do you want to do?"

Shannon shook his head. "You don't like making decisions, do you?"

Mandey shook her head, shrugged, and smiled.

"Well, what did you and James used to do?"

Mandey thought for a moment. "We used to go dancing at Liaisons, like every other weekend, almost. To be honest, a lot of the excitement of going there was thinking that I might see you again. Now that I've found you, that part is gone."

Mandey didn't want to go there with Shannon. It would be her unfortunate luck to run into someone who had seen her there the night before with the Alley Cats, and she didn't want Shannon to know about that yet.

Shannon was relieved that Mandey didn't sound as if she cared about going to Liaisons. They might run into some of the Devils, and he didn't want to have to explain that to Mandey.

"We used to go to the movies once in a while, or we'd go to the mall," Mandey continued. "I asked him once if he wanted to go bowling or to play miniature golf, but he said he didn't like to."

Shannon's ears pricked up. "You want to go bowling?"

"Sure," Mandey said. "I haven't been a lot, so I'm not very good, but I like to bowl."

"I haven't been bowling in about two years. Me and my friend Phillip used to go sometimes. There's a bowling alley close to here, isn't there?"

"Yeah, over on 525."

"That's where we used to go. All right, we're going bowling."

After dinner they drove to the bowling alley, where they had to wait fifteen minutes for a lane. They played three games, all of which Shannon won. He was a fairly good bowler. He showed Mandey how to hold the ball so she wouldn't throw so many gutter balls, and it helped her to get four strikes and three spares in the three games. She was pleased.

When they finished bowling, they went over to a pool table and Shannon taught her how to play. She nearly won a game. They decided that she might have more talent for pool than for bowling. Before they left, they played video games, and Mandey showed Shannon her skill in playing Centipede. She did well, but not her best because the track ball was filthy and kept sticking.

As they walked hand-in-hand out to Shannon's car, Mandey said, "I have made a decision."

"A decision?" Shannon asked. "About what?"

"I have decided that I am in the mood for ice cream," Mandey declared.

They found a Baskin Robbins open out on 1960. No one was in the store but them. They ordered a banana split to share. Mandey wanted to pay for the ice cream, but Shannon wouldn't let her.

"You paid last weekend at the beach," he said. "I told you I'd treat you when I had some money."

"All right," she conceded.

After a few minutes of deliberation, they chose chocolate almond, vanilla, and butter pecan ice cream for the sundae. A few minutes later they were seated with their treat.

"This is terrible," Mandey said.

"I think it's good," Shannon said, inspecting the spoonful on the way to his mouth, then popping it in.

"No," Mandey said. "It tastes wonderful, but I'm afraid of splitting the seams of these pants."

Shannon grinned. "I wouldn't mind seeing that."

Mandey grinned back. "You're bad," she told him.

"I know," he replied. "What time can I come over to your house tomorrow?"

"Whatever time you want," Mandey replied.

"Is noon too early?" he asked.

"Not at all," she said.

"I just want to have a happy birthday. The less time I have to spend at home, the better."

"I hope I can make it a very happy birthday for you," Mandey said.

"As long as I can spend the day with you, I'll be happy."

"Well, you can," Mandey said. "We're going to have a nice dinner and a birthday cake, and we'll spend the day doing whatever you like."

"Whatever I like, huh?" Shannon said, grinning.

"Within reason," Mandey amended quickly, with a smile.

"How about more of what we were doing last Sunday?" Shannon asked. "Is that 'within reason'?"

Mandey smiled bigger, remembering the wonderful make-out session they had had. "That's definitely within reason."

"Then I'll be very happy," Shannon said.

It was going on midnight when they drove into the driveway of Mandey's house. The porch light was on, but all the other lights in the house were out. Marcia, unlike their mother, didn't wait up for Mandey to get home. Shannon shut off the ignition.

"I had a wonderful time tonight," Mandey said. "This was the best date I've ever been on."

"Really?" Shannon asked.

"Really."

Shannon reached over, opened the glove compartment, and pulled out a small white box. He handed it to Mandey.

"It's your birthday and you're giving me a present?" Mandey asked, pleased.

"Sorry it isn't wrapped," he said, turning on the dome light.

She opened it. There, on a bed of white batting, was a heart-shaped Black Hills gold charm that said, "I Love You." She looked up at Shannon.

"I love you," he said.

Mandey felt goose bumps break out all over her body. No guy had ever told her that.

"I love you," she replied. "Oh, Shannon."

She hugged him, and then they kissed a long, slow kiss.

"Thank you," Mandey said. "I love it. And you."

"Thank you," Shannon said. "Hearing you say you love me is the best present."

They hugged again and held each other for a long time. When they finally let go, Mandey sighed and said, "I guess I'd better go in."

Shannon kissed her. "I guess," he said. "I'll walk you to the door."

They walked with their arms around each other up to the steps.

"I hate saying goodnight," Mandey complained.

"Me, too," Shannon said, "but I'll be back tomorrow."

"I know," Mandey said, "but this evening has been so wonderful, I hate for it to end."

"The end of tonight only means we're that much closer to more wonderful times together," Shannon reminded her.

Mandey smiled at him. "I do declare, it sounds as if there's a poetic soul underneath that rough exterior."

Shannon grinned sheepishly. Mandey put her arms around him again, and they kissed.

"I love you," she said. She liked how the words sounded rolling off her tongue.

"I love you, too," he said, giving her a squeeze. "See you tomorrow."

Mandey unlocked the front door and went inside. Shannon went back to his car. He saw Mandey looking out the window at him. He waved. She watched him until he left. Feeling giddy, she practically skipped to her bedroom to get ready for bed.

22

Happy Birthday

On the morning of his 19th birthday, Shannon awoke to the sounds of Annette and Checkmate having intercourse on the other side of the bedroom.

"Jee-zus Christ, you two are like fucking rabbits," Shannon grumbled loudly, getting out of bed.

"Fuck you," Annette and Checkmate chorused, and then resumed their groaning and moaning.

Shannon dragged himself to the bathroom, half asleep, and stood in front of the toilet. His cock was stiff. He wondered what it would be like to have regular sexual relationship with a girl. He hoped that with Mandey, he would find out before too long. He held his cock in his hand and stroked it, imagining Mandey naked, her legs spread wide, and plunging into her tight, hot, wet depths. He came quickly, his teeth clenched to keep back the moans of pleasure that threatened to escape his lips.

He sighed, urinated, and quickly cleaned up. He went back into the bedroom, but Checkmate and Annette were still at it. As it was obvious he wasn't going to get to go back to sleep, Shannon got his clothes and went back into the bathroom to shower, shave, brush his teeth, and get dressed. When he was done, he went back to the bedroom one more time to put on his socks and shoes. The happy couple had finally finished. He heard them talking in low voices beyond the curtain but couldn't make out what they were saying, not that he cared.

He decided to call Mandey to see it he could come over. It was 9:30, so he supposed she was probably awake. He went into the kitchen to use the phone.

"Hello?" he heard her say.

"Hi, Mandey."

"Hi! Happy birthday!"

"Thanks," he said. "I was wondering if it's okay if I come over to your house now instead of at noon. I'm just hanging around here with nothing to do."

"Sure! The more time we can spend together, the better," Mandey said.

"Great. I'll be there in a half an hour or so."

"I'll be here. See you soon."

As he hung up the phone, Leon staggered out of the other bedroom, hungover and wearing nothing but a pair of stained boxer shorts, and headed for the bathroom. At the same time, Checkmate walked out into the hall. He saw Leon and ducked back into the bedroom, but it was too late; Leon had seen him, too.

"God damn it, Annette, how many times have I told you I don't want that nigger in my house!" Leon shouted, storming toward the bedroom.

Shit, I thought I was going to avoid this today, Shannon thought.

He followed Leon into the bedroom. Fortunately, Checkmate and Annette had made a hasty exit out the window.

"Annette, you little slut!" Leon yelled.

He slammed the window shut and turned around to see his stepson watching him.

"What the hell are you looking at?" Leon snarled, and pushed past Shannon to go to the bathroom.

Shannon was relieved that Annette and Checkmate had made it out in time, although by the looks of what was strewn on the floor, neither one of them had been fully clothed when they went out the window. Annette would stay over at Checkmate's for a few days, and when she came back home, Leon would more than likely have forgotten about the incident. He hoped so, anyway. Leon had a quirk; sometimes he would remember some transgression (either real or imagined) of Shannon's or Annette's that had gone unpunished, even if it had happened weeks before, and then a beating would follow, seemingly out of the blue. Life with Leon meant never, ever letting your guard down. Shannon decided that this would be an excellent time to leave, before Leon had a chance to come out of the bathroom and take out his frustrations on him.

Something smelled good when he walked into Mandey's house. Mandey met him with a hug and a kiss.

"Happy birthday, sweetie," she said.

He hugged her. "Thanks," he said. "What smells so good?"

"It's a special Sunday dinner in honor of your birthday," Marcia said, coming from the kitchen into the living room.

"Wow, thanks," he said.

"We're having roast beef, mashed potatoes and gravy, corn-on-the-cob, and rolls," Mandey told him.

"Don't forget birthday cake," Marcia said.

"That, too. And ice cream," Mandey added.

Shannon's stomach gave an audible growl. Mandey and Marcia both laughed.

"Dinner will be ready around noon. I hope you can wait that long," Marcia said, teasing.

"Yeah, I think so," he replied, grinning.

"Let's go in my room for a while," Mandey said, leading him down the hallway.

"Oh, I see she wants you all to herself again," Marcia said as they walked away.

"Always," Mandey said.

Mandey turned on the stereo, and they got comfortable on her bed.

"I've been dreaming about this all week," Shannon said as Mandey cuddled up to him.

"So have I," Mandey said, smiling.

"I had a great time with you last night," he said.

"I hope you'll have a great time with me today, too," Mandey said.

"I already am."

"I have a question," Mandey said. "What are you doing Tuesday night?"

Shannon thought for a minute. "Nothing," he replied. "I work day shift that day. Why?"

"Well, I was thinking that, if you want to, you can come with me to the Honor Society induction at school. We're inducting new members, and since I'm Honor Society secretary, I have to light a candle and recite a little speech during the ceremony. It's no big deal, but it would be something for us to do together. If you'd want to."

Shannon nodded slowly. "Sure, I'll go with you, if you want," he said, then frowned and added, "If it won't embarrass you too much to show up with a tenth-grade drop-out."

"Of course you won't embarrass me. I'm not that shallow," Mandey told him, then asked. "Why did you quit school, anyway? You didn't like it?"

He shook his head. "No, I liked school okay. My mother wasn't doing so great, and I felt like I needed to be home more to keep an eye on her. Then Leon came back and added to the chaos. I figured that since I was finally sixteen, I'd might as well quit."

"Do you ever think about going back to school?" she asked. "Maybe getting your G.E.D.?"

Shannon knew Mandey would be starting college in the fall. Of course, she wanted to know what he planned to do with himself. The only thing was, he didn't know what to tell her because he had no idea.

"When I was in jail, they made us take prep classes for the G.E.D. test, but I never took it. I got out, then I didn't think about it no more." He looked down into her green eyes. "The truth is, Mandey, I don't know what I'm doing," he admitted. "I know a few things about fixing cars and operating a gas station. That's it. I haven't been able to think too far into the future. All I've been thinking about is finding ways to get by." He paused for a moment. "What do you think I ought to do?"

Mandey thought for a moment before answering. "I think the first thing you should do is get your G.E.D. I know there are prep classes for the exam on Monday nights at Rogers. You could register to start those in January, when the spring semester starts. If you've already done the prep for it, a little review might be all you need before you take the test. Once you get your G.E.D., you can take classes at North Harris. I think they have a certification program in Auto Mechanics, if that's what you're really interested in, or you might have something else you'd rather go into."

She paused and surveyed Shannon's face. He looked to be deep in thought.

"It's just a suggestion," she said. "I'm not trying to tell you what to do."

"Oh, I know," Shannon said. "I'm thinking about trying to study at home."

"You could come over here to do your studying," Mandey said. "We'll do our homework together."

"Do you know how much those prep classes cost?" he asked.

Mandey shook her head. "I don't think they cost too much, though. They might even be free. We can find out."

He nodded. "All I know is, I've got to do something to start getting myself out of the position I'm in now."

It was a bright, warm day, so after a leisurely make-out session, a satisfying dinner, and watching the Houston Oilers get their first win of the season over Kansas City, which Shannon thought was a great birthday present, Shannon and Mandey decided to take a walk up the street. They held hands as they made their way from Mandey's end of Foxwood Lane, across Northwood Road, and to the end of Foxwood Lane where Shannon once lived in a single-story off-white brick house with blue trim. Once they crossed Northwood Road, the houses on Foxwood became smaller and closer together. Some were neat and well kept, and others had fallen into disrepair. Shannon's old house was one of the larger ones, and it was located next to the new middle school. The neighborhood guys used to play football in the vacant field where the new school now stood. Now there was a real football field with bleachers for them to use, and it looked like a game was forming.

Shannon and Mandey stood in front of 542 Foxwood Lane and looked at the house where Shannon used to live.

"I remember driving by with my mother and seeing you out here, sitting on a car in the driveway with Phillip Forbes. It was winter, and although it was kind of warm, it wasn't <u>that</u> warm, and there you sat with a Dr Pepper in hand, wearing blue jeans but no shoes and no shirt. Were you showing off for the girls or something?"

Mandey's eyes were twinkling. Shannon was slightly embarrassed for a moment, then said, "Well, it got your attention, now, didn't it?"

Mandey laughed. "Yes, it did. The thrill of my life, to that point."

Shannon snorted. "Oh, yeah. Right."

Still holding hands, they walked over to the middle school athletic field, where a dozen or so of the neighborhood's adolescent denizens were milling about, trying to get organized.

"There's Phillip. Damn, I haven't seen him since a few months after I moved," Shannon said, his face brightening, then darkening. "Man, I hope he isn't too pissed that I haven't stayed in touch with him."

Phillip Forbes was tall and heavy-set, with blond hair now approaching his shoulders, and glasses. Mandey had always thought he wasn't half-bad looking for a blond. He had graduated last year, but was still living at home, working as a dispatcher for an ambulance service, and going to school to become a paramedic. Right now, though, he was attempting to get the guys divided into two teams when he spotted Shannon.

"Shannon Douglass, you son-of-a-bitch!" Phillip boomed, plowing through the crowd to greet him. "Where the hell have you been? I thought you fell off the face of the earth!"

"Man, not quite, but close," Shannon said, a smile coming to his face as he shook hands with his friend.

"Come on and join us. We're getting a game together. It'll be like old times. Except look what we have now—a real field and bleachers," Phillip said, making a sweeping motion with his arm. "Not like when this was an overgrown cow pasture and we had to go hunting for the ball in the grass every time someone missed a pass."

Shannon looked at Mandey. "You mind if I play for a while?"

Mandey smiled. "Of course not. Besides, it's your birthday. Do whatever your heart desires."

"It's your birthday?" Phillip asked.

"Yeah. Nineteen and legal today," Shannon replied.

"Like being underage ever stopped you before," Phillip said, grinning. "After the game's over, I've got a beer in my fridge with your name on it."

"Sounds good," Shannon said.

"Where's Charlene today?" Mandey asked Phillip as they walked toward the bleachers. Phillip had been going out with Charlene Sager for a couple of months, but she didn't appear to be around, not that Mandey minded. Charlene had something of a temper. Some people said (behind her back, of course) that she had a chronic case of P.M.S. Because of this, Mandey was surprised Phillip was still seeing her. Phil was easygoing, but he didn't have a reputation for taking bullshit off anybody.

Phillip shrugged. "Your guess is as good as mine. When I talked to her this morning and told her I was planning on playing football with the guys, she got pissed and hung up on me, and then she wouldn't pick up the phone when I called back."

"Come on, we want to get this started!" shouted a guy Mandey knew as Craig, but didn't know his last name. She was surprised he was there, as she couldn't recall having seen him since she was in sixth grade and he was in eighth.

Maybe he just got out of jail, she thought with a mental giggle, then quickly became sober. That was Shannon's situation, and it wasn't funny at all. She had to admit that, for this neighborhood at least, it wasn't unheard of.

Mandey climbed the metal bleachers and sat three rows from the bottom. Some elementary school boys were climbing up and down the bleachers, apparently playing some sort of game of their own fashioning. On the other end of the bleachers, she noticed two girls, Janice Frye and Debbie Purvis. Neither one of them had made it past tenth grade, which seemed to be the norm for that neighborhood. Mandey had little more than a nodding acquaintance with either of them, so she gave them a wave and left it at that, hoping they wouldn't get it in their heads to come over and keep her company. She recalled mornings at the bus stop, standing there with Janice and Debbie, among others, and watching them smoke their cigarettes and listening to them talking about whose asses they were going to kick. Mandey wasn't afraid of them, but she had nothing in common with them, so she kept her own mouth shut, as usual, and stayed out of their way.

On the field, Phillip had succeeded in getting the group split up into two teams. They were going to play shirts against skins, and had flipped a coin to see which team had to take off their shirts. It turned out to be the team Phillip and Shannon were on.

"How did you two end up together?" Phillip asked Shannon, referring to Mandey, as they stripped off their shirts.

"Met her in Galveston last weekend," Shannon said. "It's kind of a long story."

"She used to sit across the aisle from us on the school bus, remember? You never noticed her then?"

Shannon shook his head. "That was my mistake."

"What's she doing with a clown like you, anyhow?" Phillip said, teasing.

"Damned if I've been able to figure it out," Shannon admitted.

Mandey watched with amusement as Shannon took off his T-shirt. History was repeating itself, in a sense. She thought he was physically perfect for her. Everything about him was perfect for her; she had felt that the moment she had laid eyes on him.

The game got underway, and Mandey cringed at the guys' roughness. She wished they were playing touch football instead of full contact. She watched Shannon take a couple particularly hard hits that scared her, but he had gotten up, a bit slowly, but not any worse for the wear. It pleased her on a certain level that she had such a strong, tough boyfriend.

The game had been going on for about a half-hour when she noticed two girls approaching the bleachers. One was Phillip's younger sister, Patty, who was a freshman. Patty was short and had blue eyes and curly blonde hair, but possessed a large girth and an attitude that was a carbon copy of Janice's and Debbie's. One interesting note about Patty was the fact that she had a hopeless crush on Danny Sanchez.

With Patty was, of all people, Denise Wharton. *What is this, Old Home Weekend on*

Foxwood Lane? Mandey wondered. She, like Janice and Debbie, never made it past tenth grade, and Mandey hadn't seen her around in so long, she thought she had moved. But here she was, and she looked to be pregnant, as well.

Patty and Denise joined Janice and Debbie on the other end of the bleachers. Mandey went back to watching the game. Shannon's team was in possession of the ball. The teams got into formation, and Phillip, as quarterback, called the play. Eli Quintero hiked the ball to him. Shannon was blocking Eli's older brother, George, who was a bear of a guy, bigger than Shannon. They wrestled with each other, and then Shannon lost his balance and ended up flat on his back with George falling squarely on top of him. Mandey leapt to her feet, a gasp catching in her throat.

To Shannon, it felt as though an elephant had plopped down on top of him. George got up and brushed himself off, unfazed. Shannon, however, lay on the ground, trying to get his wind back.

"Hey, man, are you okay?" George asked, looking down at him and offering a hand to help him up.

"Yeah," Shannon said, grasping George's wrist and getting to his feet. "Damn, you knocked me down like fucking freight train."

"Get in my way and I'll do it again, too," George said, with a good-natured grin.

"Not if I can help it," Shannon replied, grinning back.

He glanced over to the bleachers and saw Mandey looking concernedly at him and gave her the "okay" signal. It was different having someone to worry about him.

While Mandey was engrossed in what was happening on the field, she didn't notice that the little coffee klatch had moved to absorb her into their group.

"Hey, we saw you walk up with Shannon," Debbie said. "Are y'all going together?"

Mandey's head snapped around to see the four girls. "Uh, yeah," she said. On a whim, she slipped her finger underneath her collar and pulled out her gold chain that held the "I Love You" charm. "He gave me this last night."

Denise sat down on one side of Mandey, Patty on the other, and Janice and Debbie on the row behind them. They took turns fondling the charm and exclaiming over it.

"Where'd you find him?" Denise asked. "He hasn't been around here for a couple years."

"I ran into him down in Galveston," Mandey said.

"Does he live down there now?" Denise asked.

Mandey shook her head. "No, we just happened to be in the same place at the same time."

"He's still as cute as ever," Patty said. "Cuter, even. He's almost as cute as Danny."

Although most of the girls Mandey associated with rolled their eyes at the mention of Patty Forbes's name, Mandey couldn't come to treat her with quite such derision. After all, if her taste in men so closely resembled Mandey's, she couldn't be all bad. Of course, maybe behind Mandey's back, girls rolled their eyes at the mention of her name, as well.

"Danny, Danny, Danny, that's all you ever talk about," Janice said, rolling her eyes.

Mandey guessed it wasn't just her friends who did it.

"Yeah, Patty, the way you talk about him, you'd think you were actually going with him," Denise said.

"Well, I will be soon, if I have my way about it," Patty said, scowling.

Denise lit a cigarette. Janice and Debbie were already smoking. Denise gave one to Patty and offered one to Mandey.

"No thanks," Mandey said, shaking her head.

"Aw, come on," Denise urged her.

Mandey continued to shake her head. "I'd turn green and get sick and that would be really uncool."

"Yeah, Denise, we don't want anyone to start puking," Janice said.

"Oh, man, talk about puking," Denise said. "I had the worst morning sickness when I first got pregnant. Damn, it was worse than some of the hangovers I've had. I was sick as a dog. Thank God that's over with. If I'd been gonna be that sick through my pregnancy, I woulda had an abortion."

Mandey spotted a cream-colored Toyota Corolla driving into the school parking lot and saw Charlene get out. Suddenly, Mandey was rather glad to see her. At least she was used to socializing occasionally with Charlene, and now they had something in common: Their boyfriends were good friends with each other.

Charlene came striding over to the field, her denim-clad over-sized hips swaying and her big strawberry blonde hair bouncing in the wind. She stood on the sidelines with her hands on her hips, glaring at Phillip, and then she turned to face Mandey and the other girls.

"Christ, he didn't want to spend the day with me so he could play grab-ass with a bunch of sweaty guys?" she demanded. "Mandey, is your boyfriend out there too? What is wrong with men?"

Mandey shrugged indifferently. "Boys will be boys?" she offered.

"What have you got against guys getting together and having some fun?" Debbie asked. "I don't mind Steve playing. At least I can keep an eye on him."

"Yeah, I wish my old man had spent his spare time playing football with the guys instead of cheating on me with some slut," Denise said. "Wasn't no fun having to kick her ass when I was having that morning sickness."

Charlene was not mollified. "Phillip! Phillip Forbes!" she yelled.

"Jesus, leave it to her to pitch a hissy fit," Janice said, disgusted.

Charlene whirled around to face her. "Phillip and I had plans today, and he blew them off so he could go out and play with his friends. Damn straight I'm pissed. You want to make an issue out of it?"

Janice stood up. She was about the same height as Charlene but so thin she was almost scrawny. "I can kick your fat ass," she said, starting down the steps toward Charlene.

"Come on down here and do it, then," Charlene said defiantly.

"You asked for it," Janice replied, smiling.

Oh, no, not a fight, Mandey groaned inwardly.

Fortunately, Phillip and Shannon were on their way toward the sidelines. They broke into a run when they saw Janice grab Charlene by the arm and Charlene grab a handful of Janice's long platinum hair. They didn't get much further than that before Shannon got Janice in an arm lock. Phillip somehow pried Charlene's hand open to release Janice's hair and was pulling her away by her arms.

"Would you let go of me?" Charlene protested, trying to wrest herself out of his grasp.

"Not 'til I know you're not going to go back after her," Phillip said.

"I couldn't care less about that white trash bitch. You're the one I'm pissed at."

"You've got one high and mighty old lady there, Phil," Janice shouted, trying to escape Shannon's hold on her. "She's gonna pussy-whip you good if you ain't careful."

"Oh, shut up and mind your own business," Charlene snapped.

"I'm gonna—" Janice began, but Shannon clapped a hand over her mouth.

"Enough," he said quietly in her ear. "She's pissed enough. Don't piss her off anymore or there'll be nothing left of Phil when she's through with him."

Janice relented and relaxed. "All right for now. She'll be back around, though. This isn't the end of it," she said.

Shannon finally let go of her, and she went back up into the bleachers with the other girls. Phillip and Charlene were walking away down the sidelines, involved in a heated discussion.

"Shannon!" Denise called out.

He looked up at her. She was smiling and waving, then she stood up and headed down toward him. It was then that he noticed her belly. He thought about the conversation he and Mandey had had about Denise the weekend before, and he felt his face get hot for some reason.

"Denise. You're. . .pregnant," he said as she stood before him.

"Yeah, and wouldn't you know my old man took off with another woman two months ago," she said. Then she lowered her voice to a stage whisper. "I'd ask you how you'd feel about instant fatherhood, but I guess you've already got yourself an old lady."

Shannon knew for sure he was blushing now, and then Denise changed the subject. "Where's Annette?"

"At home," he said. "Probably out with her old man right now."

"You should tell her to come out here and party with us. I moved back home last month after my old man left. It'll be like old times."

Phillip and Charlene looked to be headed toward Phillip's house, still arguing. The rest of the guys had re-aligned themselves to balance out the teams and had resumed playing. Shannon looked at Mandey. "You ready to go?" he asked her.

Mandey stood up and made her way down to his side.

"Going so soon?" Patty asked.

Shannon went over to pick up his shirt. "Yeah."

"Well, you and Mandey are together now, so you don't have no excuse not to come and see your old friends," Denise said.

"Guess not," Shannon said, buttoning his shirt.

Mandey took his hand in hers and smiled up at him.

"See you later," she said, giving Janice, Debbie, Denise, and Patty a parting wave as she and Shannon walked away.

"That was weird," Shannon said when they were a safe distance away. "Like I never left, in a way. And Denise—jeez, it was like you conjured her up when you brought up her name last week."

"Don't blame that on me," Mandey said. "I didn't even know she was living around here anymore."

"I guess I'm not going to get that beer today, thanks to his old lady," Shannon said, a bit mournfully, as they walked past Phillip's house.

"Shannon, would you promise me something?"

"What?"

"Don't start referring to me as your 'old lady.' Not until I'm a senior citizen, anyway."

He grinned at her. "You're thinking of keeping me around that long?"

"Maybe," she said, "unless you start calling me 'old lady' before I'm sixty-five."

"How about I call you my young, beautiful girlfriend? Is that okay?"

"I can accept that."

"Good," he said. "Can I kiss my young, beautiful girlfriend?"

Mandey didn't give him a verbal answer. She stopped and put her arms around him. He bowed his head to touch his lips to hers. Kissing this big, handsome, sweaty guy in the middle of the street for God and everyone to see was different from what she had experienced with James, who was furtive in his occasional expressions of affection, and whom she had never seen break a sweat. It was a welcome difference.

Back at her house, Mandey told Shannon to take a shower if he felt like it, and he took her up on the offer. Mandey waited for him in her room, listening to Hall & Oates' *X-Static* album, singing along and dancing about a little. She felt peppy and hyper, and the music matched her mood.

"Oh, man," Shannon groaned, stretching out on Mandey's bed when he came out of the bathroom. "I'm beat. I haven't had a workout like that in a long time."

"I'll be you're going to be sore tomorrow," Mandey replied.

"I'm sore now," he said, "but it was worth it."

Mandey sat down next to him on the bed. "Hey, why don't you let me give you that back rub I was telling you about on the phone the other night?"

Shannon smiled. "You don't have to ask me twice," he said, rolling over onto his stomach.

Mandey put her mouth against his ear. "Take your shirt off. It'll feel better," she told him.

He looked at her a bit curiously, but then obliged.

"Why are you giving me that look? I watched you run around shirtless all afternoon," Mandey said.

"Yeah, but that was on a football field. This is in your bedroom."

"Yeah, so?" Mandey asked with a saucy grin.

Shannon shrugged and lay back down without saying anything.

"Are you afraid I've got you in a compromising position here and I'm going to try to take advantage of you?" she asked him jokingly, as she rubbed her hands together to warm them and set to work on his back.

"What? No," Shannon said, then asked, "Are you?"

Mandey laughed.

Those soft hands of hers with those perfectly shaped fingernails were doing wonders. Mandey massaged his arms, then his shoulders, working up to his neck and the back of his head, then down his back to the waistband of his jeans. He felt his spine crack in a couple of places, and knew that when he stood up again and stretched, his back would sound like a bowl of Rice Krispies. That was, if he stood up again; when Mandey finally stopped, he didn't want to move. His muscles felt soft as butter, his eyes were nearly closed, and he realized with some embarrassment that he had drooled on Mandey's pillow.

Slowly he turned over on his back and looked at her. "Where did you learn to do that?" he asked her.

"I don't know," she replied with a shrug. "I just did what I figured would feel good to you."

"Oh, man, 'good' doesn't begin to describe it. I could get down on my knees and worship you."

Mandey laughed. "Now I see how to get my way with you. Give you a back rub, and you're putty in my hands, both literally and figuratively."

He held out his arms, and she fell into his embrace, and with his lips pressed to hers they rolled over until he was on top of her. She ran her hands all over his bare torso; for a long time she had wondered what it would feel like, and now she knew.

Shannon gazed down at her with those hazel eyes of his, and she was overwhelmed by what she saw in them. No one had ever looked at her that way before. In his eyes was a mixture of love, admiration, and a little disbelief—a reflection of all the things she was feeling herself.

"Oh, Shannon," was all she managed to say, and then her mouth was against his again, and their tongues met enthusiastically.

She liked how it felt to have his weight on top of her, with his body pressing down against hers. She wondered what it would be like to let him make love to her. Actually, she knew it would be absolutely wonderful. But she wondered how it would feel to let go and lose herself in coupling with him.

His mouth traveled from her mouth down to her neck, and she felt him biting her. She started to giggle.

"What?" Shannon asked, stopping to look at her.

She shook her head, still giggling. "No one's ever given me a hickey before," she told him.

"Well, it's about time," he replied. "Do you want me to stop?"

Mandey shook her head again. Shannon smiled.

"Good, 'cause I don't want to stop."

His mouth returned to her neck and completed its mission to leave a conspicuous red mark. Then he eased off Mandey and lay next to her again.

Mandey touched the spot, tender and saliva-covered, and then she grinned at Shannon. "If I've got to have one of these, you're going to wear one to match," she told him

"I am, am I?" Shannon asked, amused.

"Yes, you are," Mandey said. "Which side would you like to have it?"

"Right here," he answered, pointing at a spot on the left side of his neck.

"Remember, I've never done this before. I hope I don't hit your jugular or something," she said.

Shannon chortled and put his arms around her. "Just take it easy."

She put her lips against his neck and began to kiss him, then to suck gently. After a minute, she stopped and admired her work.

He put his hand up to his neck. "I will wear it proudly," he told her.

Mandey got up off the bed and went over to her desk. She opened the bottom drawer and pulled out an envelope and a box wrapped in birthday paper.

"You got me a present?" Shannon asked as she handed them to him.

"Of course," Mandey replied, sitting next to him. "What kind of girlfriend would I be if I didn't get you something for your birthday?"

"You made a great dinner and a cake and we've been having a great day together. That would have been enough," Shannon said, opening the card. As he read it, his face flushed. "Geez, I never had a card that said anything like that before."

"I hope I didn't get too carried away."

"No! No, I like it. I like it a lot. I'm just not used to people talking to me, or writing to me, that way."

They kissed, then he turned his attention to the box. "I didn't know what to get you," Mandey said shyly as he opened it and revealed a Houston Oilers T-shirt with a 34 on it, Earl Campbell's number.

"This is great!" Shannon said enthusiastically. "You know they're my team!" He leaned over and kissed her cheek. "Thank you, sweetie."

"You're welcome," Mandey replied, pleased with his reaction. "Happy birthday, hon."

"Wow, if anyone had said ten days ago that this is how I'd be spending my birthday, I would have told them they were nuts," Shannon said.

"It's crazy how fast things can change. I'm just glad it was a good change," Mandey said.

"Amen," Shannon agreed.

Shannon left Mandey's house at nine. It was not quite as difficult to leave as it had been the Sunday before, because he knew he was going to be back over to see her in two days, but there were still long kisses and longing glances before he was able to tear himself away.

His mind was reeling as he drove home. What an amazing weekend it had been. Last weekend, too, for that matter. Mandey—oh, Mandey. That mushy Barry Manilow song popped into his brain, but he didn't mind. Part of the words said something about sending her away. He had no intention of doing that. This girl was actually in love with him—what the hell? He felt like his heart was going to burst. Finally, he had something good in his life, that made it feel worthwhile. He was going to hold onto it with all his strength.

Mandey got her books together and picked out an outfit to wear to school the next day. It had been the best weekend ever. She still could hardly believe that she had found Shannon again after all this time, and he was as crazy for her as she was for him. This kind of thing never happened to her—until now. Finally, she had gotten something she truly wanted.

23

The Honor Society

On the evening of the Honor Society induction ceremony, Shannon arrived at Mandey's house at 6:45 P.M. Mandey came out of the house wearing a navy-blue dress with a large white floral pattern on it. She looked so pretty and mature, Shannon thought. He felt a little shabby in his tan corduroy pants and brown plaid flannel shirt. He wondered if it mattered that he wasn't dressed up.

"You look nice tonight," Shannon told her as she got into the car.

"Thank you," Mandey said. "So do you. The brown in that shirt matches your eyes."

Shannon laughed to himself. He guessed he was dressed okay.

Mandey slid next to him and put on the lap belt. He put his arm around her shoulders and backed out of the driveway.

"The first thing I have to do when we get there is go onstage in the auditorium to get our Honor Society group picture taken for the yearbook. Then I'll come out and sit with you for a while until I have to go sit onstage for the ceremony. There will be refreshments in the cafeteria afterward."

"I'm kind of nervous about meeting your friends," Shannon said. "What are they going to think about you being with someone like me?"

Mandey laughed. "What, do you think we Honor Society students only date other Honor Society members?" she asked.

"Do you?"

Mandey laughed again. "Obviously not," she said. "There are no current members dating each other. James and I were the exception. I know that in past years some of the members, especially the officers, have gotten flak about their choices of boyfriends and girlfriends because they were dating non-members. That hasn't been going on this year, because we're all dating non-members. And I'm not even the first to date a drop-out, either, so this is no big deal."

"Is James going to be there?" Shannon asked.

"He said today he was coming," Mandey said.

"I'm curious to meet him," Shannon said.

Mandey looked at him in surprise. "You are? Why?"

"I want to see what kind of idiot he has to be to have dumped you," Shannon said.

Mandey chuckled. "Well, if he makes the first move to talk to me, I'll introduce you. I'm not going to be obnoxious and go over to him if he's trying to ignore me and say, 'Here's my new boyfriend.' That would be the kind of thing he would do to me."

They walked into the school through the entrance to the music wing. Mandey spied Andrea and her boyfriend, Martin.

"Hi, Andie. Hi, Mart," she greeted them, pulling Shannon along behind her.

"Hi," they greeted her in unison.

Mart was as tall as Shannon, but nearly a hundred pounds thinner. He had brown hair, blue eyes, and a slightly goofy smile that matched his slightly offbeat sense of humor. He was wearing jeans, a plaid dress shirt, and a gray sweater vest. Andie had on a beige skirt, a matching suit jacket, and a white blouse.

"Andie, Mart, this is Shannon Douglass," Mandey introduced him. "Shannon, these are Andrea Lawrence and Martin Patterson."

"Honor Society members and inductees, we are taking our group pictures in the choir room, not the auditorium," they heard Mrs. Cloessner, the Honor Society sponsor, say in a loud voice. "Senior members, your picture will be taken first. All senior members, come into the choir room, now!"

"Let's go," Andrea said to Mandey, then to Martin and Shannon, "We'll see you in a few minutes."

Mandey smiled at Shannon, then turned and followed Andrea down the hall.

"Come on," Martin said to Shannon. "Let's go watch."

Shannon followed Martin down to the choir room, and they stood against the wall by the door to watch. The Honor Society members were congregating and arranging themselves on the risers. Mandey and the other officers were sitting on chairs in front of the risers.

Jackie Seymore, the vice-president, was sitting next to Mandey. She leaned over and asked Mandey, "I saw you walk in with that guy. Is he your new boyfriend?"

Mandey nodded. "That's him."

"He's kind of cute," Jackie said, looking over at him. "What's his name?"

"Shannon," Mandey replied, looking toward him as well. She smiled and waved at him.

"You know, I'm having a party Saturday night," Jackie said. "Why don't y'all come?"

Mandey was surprised. She hadn't been invited to a party, except for small ones given by Georgia and Andrea, since elementary school. She thought that perhaps her attempt at an image change was finally working. That, and being rid of James.

"Sure," Mandey said. "Thanks."

Mandey and Jackie saw James walk in. He was dressed in black pleated slacks, a white dress shirt, and a tie. He was laughing at something, or someone.

Jackie grimaced. "What did you ever see in him?"

Mandey shrugged. "He has his good points. I guess I didn't want to see the bad ones."

To Mandey's surprise, most of the senior members had shown up. Many of them had said they weren't going to dress up and make a special trip to the school just to have a group photo taken for the yearbook, but she only noticed the absence of about four of the members. Then she saw Brad come in, and it was down to three missing.

Shannon watched as all the members lined up on the risers for their picture, but he paid particular attention to James, whom he had recognized from the photos he had seen at Mandey's. He watched as James chatted with a couple of teachers. He looked very smart, very sure of himself, and very much like an asshole, in Shannon's opinion. He wondered what it would be like to be that kind of person, with money and brains and a plan for the future.

The photographer took three shots of the group to make sure he got a good one, then they dispersed so that the junior inductees could take their picture.

A teacher came up to Martin and Shannon and asked, "Are you two inductees?"

Martin grinned. "No, we're the rejectees," he answered.

Shannon laughed. This guy was sharp.

Mandey and Andrea were coming through the crowd to rejoin them.

"What's so funny?" Mandey asked.

"Mrs. Furlong asked me if we were inductees," Martin said. "I told her we're the rejectees."

Andrea and Mandey laughed. "Come on, rejectees," Andrea said. "Let's go to the auditorium."

The four of them walked together out of the choir room and around to the front entrance of the auditorium, where they each received a program for the ceremony. They walked down and took seats in the fifth row on the left side.

"How does it feel to be back in this school after three years?" Mandey asked Shannon.

Shannon had been looking around at the people. He stopped and looked at Mandey. "It's kind of weird."

"'Weird' is a good description of this place," Martin said.

"Oh, Shannon," Mandey said, "we've been invited to a party this Saturday."

"We have?" Shannon asked, surprised.

"Yep. Jackie Seymore, that blonde girl I was sitting next to for the picture, invited us to her party."

"Us? Or you?" Shannon asked.

"Both of us, silly," Mandey said. "She noticed you. She thinks you're cute."

Shannon was embarrassed, but also a little flattered. "Okay," he said. "I have to make sure I don't have to work that night, though."

Mandey noticed some of the officers taking their seats onstage. "I guess I'd better get up there," she said. "See you in a little while."

Shannon felt awkward being left there alone with Andrea and Martin. They both moved over a seat to take up the seat vacated by Mandey.

"I was telling Mandey the other day that the four of us should double date sometime," Andrea said to Shannon.

"She and James used to go out with us once in a while," Martin said. "He was a wack-a-doodle."

"He was such a jerk," Andrea said. "He'd insult her to her face. He'd act nice to her one day and the next he'd be a total ass."

"Sometimes when we'd go out together, he would practically ignore her. He'd go off on his merry way and leave her alone with us," Martin said. "He's just a real dickhead."

"Everyone is glad they broke up," Andrea said, then stopped, her eyes focusing on a point behind and beyond Shannon.

Shannon turned around. James and a dark-haired girl were seating themselves in the row behind him, Andrea, and Martin.

"Hi, Andrea. Hi, Mart," James said brightly.

"Hi," they replied together, and then turned around to face forward again.

"Anyway," Andrea continued, going back to the original subject, "let's plan on all going out somewhere together soon."

"Okay. Sounds good to me," Shannon agreed.

Wow, he thought to himself. *I've been here half an hour, and already I've been invited to a party and out on a double date. This isn't my life, is it?*

The induction ceremony lasted a little over half an hour. Shannon watched proudly as Mandey walked over to the table on stage, lit a candle, and then went to the podium to recite a speech about "service." He had never imagined having a girlfriend who would be participating in such a ceremony.

After the induction, Mandey met Shannon, Andrea, and Mart in the foyer outside the auditorium.

"You did good," Shannon told her, putting his arm around her waist.

"Thanks," Mandey said, smiling up at him. "Let's go get some cake."

"I told Shannon that you have to double date with us sometime soon," Andrea told Mandey as they walked down to the cafeteria.

"That would be fun. Don't you think so, Shannon?" Mandey asked him.

"Sure," he said. "I'm game."

In the cafeteria, punch, cake, cookies, and mints were being served. The four of them each got a cup of punch and a plate of refreshments and sat down at one of the tables. They were conversing and eating when Mandey got a pained look on her face. Mr. Tichner, the principal, was walking toward them.

"Well, hello, Mandey," the principal said, putting his hand on her shoulder.

"Hello, Mr. Tichner," Mandey replied sweetly, wishing that he would go away.

"You look nice this evening," he told her. "You did a good job during the induction ceremony." He smiled down at her squeezing her shoulder.

"Thank you," Mandey said, managing to smile brightly up at him.

"Hey, come over here," Mr. Tichner said, motioning to Johnny Oakes, who was taking pictures for the yearbook. He stood behind Mandey with his hands on her shoulders. "You look so pretty tonight, I want to have my picture taken with you. Smile," he told her.

Mandey managed a small, tight smile, and Johnny took a photo.

"Well, you all enjoy your refreshments now," he said, mercifully moving on to his next victim.

Andrea and Martin snickered. Shannon sat there, frowning.

"That wasn't too bad," Mandey said, making a face. "At least I was sitting down so he couldn't hug me."

"He had no business putting his hands on you," Shannon said indignantly.

"That's how he is, all touchy-feely," Mandey said, squirming slightly in distaste.

"I'm lucky," Andrea said. "He doesn't like me."

"You are lucky," Mandey agreed.

Gayla and Charlie came over to the table and sat down next to Mandey.

"We saw old Touchy-Tichner go by. We figured we'd be safe coming over now that he's made his rounds past here," Charlie said.

"Is this him?" Gayla asked Mandey, looking past her at Shannon.

"Yes, this is Shannon Douglass. Shannon, these are Gayla Maxwell and Charlie Murrill."

"So, you're the guy who has Mandey all hot and bothered," Gayla said, smirking.

Mandey giggled, embarrassed. Shannon felt his face get warm.

"Your reputation has preceded you," Charlie told him.

Shannon turned to Mandey. "What have you been saying about me?"

Mandey shook her head and kept giggling.

"Oh, she told us how wonderful and handsome and sexy you are," Gayla said.

"And how horny she is for you," Charlie added.

"I did not say that!" Mandey objected, laughing.

Shannon turned red. Mandey, still laughing, slid her arm around him and kissed his cheek.

"I didn't mean to embarrass y'all," Gayla said.

"I did," Charlie said.

"Well, at least she's saying good things about me," Shannon said.

"Nothing but," Andrea said.

"I'm just glad Mandey has someone making her happy now," Gayla said. "James is such a dickhead."

"Yeah, and not your ordinary, run-of-the-mill dickhead. He's king of the dickheads," Charlie added.

"King of the dickheads? Thank you. What a nice compliment."

The six at the table turned to see James a short distance away, looking at them with a humorless smile on his face.

"You're welcome," Charlie replied, not at all embarrassed that his comment had been overheard. In the past he had said worse to James to his face.

"Well, you know what they say, 'It takes one to know one,'" James said, walking by Gayla and Charlie over to Mandey and Shannon.

"I'm James Huynh," he said to Shannon, extending his hand. "I presume you are Mandey's new boyfriend."

Shannon stood. "Shannon Douglass," he said, shaking hands with James.

"Nice to meet you," James said, looking Shannon over. Although Shannon was three inches taller than James, the way James scrutinized him made him feel about three feet tall.

"I must say, you two certainly make an _interesting_ couple," James said in a voice dripping with sarcasm. "I'm sure you'll make each other very happy."

He dropped Shannon's hand and walked off. Shannon stood there, his mouth slightly open, trying to figure out how to react. He felt like socking James in the mouth, but he realized he couldn't do that. Confused, he sat down.

"He _is_ a dickhead," he said.

"It's unanimous!" Martin declared, throwing his hands in the air.

Gayla's chair crashed to the floor as she jumped up and stormed after James.

"What the hell is your problem?" they heard her say. "Can't you even try to be nice?"

"I _was_ being nice," James said innocently. "What did I do wrong?"

"Oh, screw you, James," Gayla said disgustedly. "There's no point in even trying to talk to you."

She stomped back to the table, picked up her chair, slammed it down upright, and sat down.

"I hate him," she said.

"Join the club," Charlie said. "You should have flattened him, Shannon. Everyone would have applauded, including Mr. Tichner."

"I wanted to," Shannon said, "but I couldn't say, 'I hit him after he told me that me and my girlfriend should be happy together.'"

"Lie!" Martin said, grinning.

"Yeah!" Charlie agreed. "We'd back you up. We'd say that he called you a fucking bastard and took a swing at you, so you nailed him."

"Oh, he's not even worth the effort," Mandey said, reaching over to take Shannon's hand in hers.

At nine Mandey and Shannon were on their way back to her house.

"This was an interesting night," Shannon said. "It was not quite what I expected."

"Is that good or bad?"

"Good, actually," he said. "I always thought honor students were really strait-laced and stuff. I guess that's not the case."

"No, we aren't all a bunch of goody-two-shoes bookworms. In fact, some of us are downright screwed-up. And sometimes the smartest ones are in dire need of a little common sense."

Shannon looked at her. "What about you? Would you say you're 'screwed-up'?"

Mandey smiled. "No, I'm fairly normal, I suppose. I sort of feel abnormal because I'm not abnormal. Does that make sense?"

"Not at all," Shannon said. Mandey laughed.

"I mean, for example, I've never tried drugs. I've never even tried a cigarette," Mandey said.

"Not even a puff?" Shannon asked.

"Nope," Mandey said, shaking her head. "I've never even had an urge to try a cigarette. I can't see what's so cool about sucking smoke into your lungs."

"Want to try one now?" Shannon asked, reaching into his shirt pocket and pulling out a pack of Marlboros.

"No, thanks," Mandey said.

"I've been cutting back," Shannon said, stuffing the pack back into the pocket. "I was up to a pack a day at one time. Now I go through a pack every two days."

"That's good," Mandey said. "What inspired you to cut down?"

"The cost, for one thing. And coughing. I sounded ninety instead of nineteen."

Mandey yawned.

"Am I that boring?" Shannon asked.

She smiled. "No, I'm just a sleepyhead. It's getting close to my bedtime." She tried to stifle another yawn, then said, "I was happy to have you with me tonight."

"I think your friends seemed to like me okay," Shannon said.

"Of course, they did. What's not to like?"

"Well, except for James."

Mandey sniffed scornfully. "James doesn't count. He doesn't like anyone unless they are as perfect as he seems to think he is."

"You weren't perfect enough for him?" Shannon asked.

"I guess not," Mandey said, gazing out the window.

"Can I ask you a personal question?" he asked her.

"Sure," Mandey said, turning to face him.

"You don't have to answer it if you don't want to, but I was wondering if you and James ever slept together."

Mandey didn't hesitate with her answer. "No, we didn't. Why?"

"Why?" Shannon repeated. "Well. . .I wasn't sure. I couldn't tell."

"I never slept with him, and I've never slept with anyone. Does that make a difference to you?"

"No."

"I realize now that if I had slept with him, it would have been a mistake," Mandey said. "I would only have been trying to get him to love me, and I don't think he's capable of loving anyone. As it was, he never expressed any real interest in going to bed with me, anyway, so it all worked out for the best."

"Would you, if he had asked you to?"

Mandey paused and said, "Maybe. Like I said, I wanted him to love me back. If I thought that doing that would make him love me, I probably would have. I was attracted to him; I can't deny that. I can remember wanting to make love to him, but it wouldn't have meant anything to him. Anyway, I didn't look perfect enough. I was too heavy; my hair was the wrong color, and so on and so forth. He was never physically attracted to me. He pretended to be because he wanted to use me."

"I'll never use you," Shannon said seriously. "I think you're beautiful and sexy just the way you are."

Mandey laughed and blushed. "Is that your way of trying to seduce me?"

Shannon felt his face flush. "No," he said, and meant it, but he didn't know what to say next. He didn't mean for Mandey to think he was hinting around at that.

There was an awkward silence, then Mandey reached over and squeezed his leg affectionately. "I'm sorry, Shannon. I didn't mean to make you mad."

"I'm not mad," he replied, but was still at a loss for words. "I just. . .I wasn't trying to. . ."

"I know, Shannon," she said, kissing his cheek. "You paid me a compliment and I was too self-conscious to accept it graciously. I'm sorry."

"I probably shouldn't have even asked that question in the first place," Shannon said.

"That's okay," Mandey said. "We should be honest with each other about those things.

But, really, why did you want to know?"

He smiled a strange smile that Mandey couldn't quite decipher. "I thought you might be a virgin, but I was getting mixed signals," he said. "You're probably the only virgin I know."

"Is that bad or good?"

"Good."

"As for you, I am assuming you are not a virgin," Mandey said.

Shannon paused. He didn't want to go into the details of his sordid sex life, but he couldn't lie to her. "You assume right."

He volunteered no further information, and was relieved when she didn't press him for more.

In the driveway of Mandey's house, he put the car in park and shut off the motor.

"You really think I'm beautiful and sexy?" Mandey asked timidly.

He smiled. "Yes, I do."

She smiled back. "Thank you."

He walked her up to the door. On the porch they stopped and kissed.

"I'm glad you came with me tonight," Mandey told him.

"I was glad to," he replied, and he kissed her again. "I love you."

"I love you, too," Mandey answered.

"I'll call you tomorrow night," he said.

"Okay," she said, and quickly kissed his mouth once more before going inside.

Shannon was deep in thought on his way home, as he usually was after spending time with Mandey. She was a virgin. He had thought she might be, but hadn't been sure. Now he knew.

He had never slept with a real girl, just hookers. They were simple and uncomplicated. You paid them for what you wanted, and they gave it to you. He never asked for too much, usually a plain old screw or a blowjob. But he realized that he had no idea how to turn a girl on or how to please her in bed. He had never had to think that much about it before.

He wondered what Mandey was going to think of him when he finally told her the truth about his sex life. He thought about lying to her, and found that he <u>wanted</u> to lie about it, but he didn't think he would be able to. There was something about Mandey that was so honest; he didn't think she would be very happy if he lied. He figured that it might be better to be up front about everything and then work through the problems if they had to. He decided, though, that he wasn't going to volunteer any information. If she asked, then he would tell her, and he would tell her the truth.

The only thing he knew he wouldn't tell her about was the gang. She thought he was straight, and he would be as soon as he could get out of that damned place. He didn't think she would be very understanding if he told her that some of those nights when he wasn't able to be with her, he was out burglarizing jewelry stores and stealing cars.

Next month, damn it, he thought. *By the end of next month, I'm out of there. I can't go on like this if I want to have a chance with Mandey. Somehow, some way, I don't care how, I'm getting the hell out of there.*

24

A Huge Disappointment

Shannon and Raff went to Rogelio's apartment midmorning on the 16th. He had told them to come back a week from Friday, and they took him at his word. It took three rounds of knocking before Rogelio finally answered the door, wearing only a pair of black shorts.

"You two," he said when he saw Shannon and Raff standing there in the doorway.

"You said to come back a week from Friday, Rogelio. So, where's our money?" Raff demanded.

"You're expecting money?" Rogelio asked, sounding disbelieving. "That shit you brought me was almost worthless."

Shannon and Raff looked at each other. "What are you talking about?" Shannon asked.

"I mean it was worthless. All those diamonds were fakes set in about the cheapest gold you can get. Every place I took them looked them over and laughed. The gold jewelry, the chains and stuff, that was okay, but it don't bring much when it's just gonna get melted down." He shut the door partway for a minute, then reopened it. "I got a thousand bucks out of what you gave me. I took my twenty percent, so here you go." He held out a wad of bills.

"Eight hundred bucks? Are you fucking kidding me?" Raff asked in disbelief.

"The stuff was shit. Nobody's paying for shit," Rogelio replied.

Shannon was stunned. It had all looked real enough to him. "How can that be?" he asked. "A jewelry store can't be selling fake stuff like that."

"Yeah, I don't know, man," Rogelio said. "Mighta been keepin' fakes on display and the real stuff locked up in back. Maybe hoping it would get stolen so they could collect insurance. Maybe it was a front for a money laundering outfit. I don't know. All I know is it ain't real."

Raff was on the verge of exploding. "You're fucking liar, man! Where the hell is the rest of our money?" He tried to muscle past Rogelio to get into the apartment.

"There ain't no other money! This is all you got! You ain't comin' inside!" Rogelio shouted, pushing back.

Raff reached into his back pocket, whipped out his switchblade, grabbed Rogelio by the throat and held the knife about two inches from Rogelio's nose. "I want that fucking money," he said grimly.

Jesus, that's all we need, to have Raff stab this guy, Shannon thought.

"Raff, put the knife away," he ordered.

"I ain't doin' nothin' until we get our money," Raff said, not taking his grip or eyes off Rogelio.

Shannon was a little scared of that switchblade, but he had to stop this from escalating. As he started to reach for Raff's arm, Rogelio suddenly brought his knee up sharply, landing squarely in Raff's groin. Shannon caught his arm as he doubled over in pain and wrested away the knife.

"We'll take the eight hundred," Shannon said to Rogelio, holding out his hand.

Rogelio threw it at him, and it fell to the floor. "Take it and don't come back. Ever. I don't want nothin' to do with either of you again." He slammed the door, and Shannon heard him lock it.

Shannon bent down to pick up the money. Eight hundred bucks. A lousy eighty bucks apiece. Everyone was going to be pissed.

"Why the fuck did you do that?" Raff asked angrily, slowly standing up straight.

"Because I didn't want you to do something stupid. I don't think he's cheating us. He's always done right by us before, and I don't think he was lying."

"Well, if he's not cheating us, then this is all on you, Trick. You picked some fucked-up version of a jewelry store. You're as worthless as all that shit we stole," Raff said.

Shannon did not know where he got the restraint not to punch Raff in the face. He silently turned and started to make his way down the stairs.

"What, nothing to say? Not gonna clean my clock?" Raff taunted, following him down to where Shannon's car was parked. "You're nothin' but a pussy, Trick. A big, fat pussy."

"Shut the hell up, Raff," Shannon said tiredly. "You sound like a broken record."

"You ain't shit anymore, Trick," Raff said. "You're never around, and when you are, you're just a fuck-up. Victor would roll over in his grave if he knew what kind of leader you've been for the Devils."

Shannon didn't particularly care if Victor was rolling around down there or doing the goddamn hokey-pokey. He was more worried about going back to the Devils and doing damage control. Eighty bucks apiece when they were thinking 1600 was not going to sit well with any of them. He was going to have to put on his gang leader bravado and not let anyone give him crap over it.

Back at the apartments, Shannon sent Raff to round up the rest of the gang while he sat in the Devils' Den, stewing. No, he hadn't been a great leader for the Devils in the few months since he had taken over. That was mostly by design. He didn't want them doing anything too risky. The cops seemed to have a *laissez-faire* attitude toward a lot of what went down in the 'hood, but he didn't want to push their limits. Now, when he tried to do something big, it had backfired. He tried to understand what was going on with the fake merchandise at the jewelry store and couldn't figure it out. Maybe Rogelio had double-crossed them and kept most of the cash, like Raff said? He didn't think that was the case, though. At any rate, the rest of the Devils were going to be pissed off when they heard the news. Shannon was sure that Raff was telling them what happened as he told them to come to the Den. He had to psych himself up to behave like badass gang leader before they arrived.

The Devils began trickling in, silent and sullen. Soon nine faces, ranging from disappointed to furious, were all looking at him.

"Rogelio said the jewelry was fake and he only got a thousand bucks for the lot," Shannon said, peeling four twenties off the roll and giving it to Marco, then repeating the action for each of the others. "I don't know what was going on there at the jewelry store, why they had fake jewelry. It looked real to me, and I think it did to Raff and Juanita when they scoped it out." He saw Raff glaring at him when he said that, but he wasn't going to let Raff get away with complaining that Shannon had picked out a "fucked-up version of a jewelry store" without reminding everyone that Raff hadn't seen anything wrong with it, either.

"You all did a good job. The plan went perfect. It sucks that we didn't get the payout we thought we would. But eighty bucks apiece isn't that bad for about 15 minutes of work. You got some money to party with, at least."

"That's fucked up, man," John said. "Couldn't even tell junk jewelry from the real thing, Trick? Jesus."

Shannon had thought he had himself under control. That's why he surprised himself when his fist shot out and cracked John in the jaw.

"You've got no room to talk," Shannon said heatedly, as John looked at him, also surprised, holding his face. "You were supposed to go with Kerri to check things out. If you're such an expert, you could have done your part and saved us from wasting our time." Shannon looked around at the others. "Anyone else got somethin' to say? You wanna lead this outfit and make the decisions? Bring it on! Raff? I know you'd like nothing better. Don't wanna see if you can beat my ass and take over?"

He could see Raff seething, but he didn't open his head. Neither did anyone else. For that, Shannon was thankful. He was a little surprised that they didn't say to hell with what was supposed to be gang protocol and band together to get rid of him. So far, they hadn't, but Shannon was becoming increasingly worried that whatever thread he was hanging by was going to break before he could cut it himself. He turned and headed out of their Den. As much as he hated working for Ed Grubbs, he was glad he had an excuse to leave.

25

Looking for Trouble

Mandey's heart wasn't in it as she drove to Liaisons that Friday night with her fellow Alley Cats in tow. She had lied to Shannon about what she was doing that night—she had told him she was sleeping over at Georgia's house. Then he had told her his work schedule had changed so he would not be able to go with her to Jackie's party the next night. They would have to wait until Sunday to see each other.

"I wonder what we're going to find tonight?" Danny asked.

Mandey glanced over at him where he was riding shotgun once again.

"Well, we're looking for trouble, and I have a feeling it won't be hard to find," Mandey replied.

"Man, I'll be glad when this is over with. Not being able to sell while we're out doing this is hurting me."

Mandey shot him a look that he didn't seem to notice. "You can quit whenever you want to, Danny," she told him. "No one's forcing you to do this."

"I know, I know," he admitted, "but getting jumped and having my money stolen by those bastards doesn't help me, either."

"That bothers me a little," Mandey said, frowning.

"What?"

"That one of the reasons we're trying to get rid of the Devils is so that you can sell illegal drugs unimpeded. That's not right," Mandey said.

"Mandey, if they don't get it from me, they'll get it somewhere else," Danny said.

"Rationalize it all you want; it's still not right," Mandey said.

"Oh, don't get all self-righteous on me," Danny said, disgusted.

"Don't worry. I'm shutting up now," Mandey said.

"Thank you."

"It's not like you'd listen to me, anyway," she added.

As they had discussed, Terry's group went into the nightclub and Jesse's stayed outside. Jesse took off with Dina and Angelina, leaving Mandey to wander the parking lot with Danny. It did not make her feel safe.

Walking around and around the parking lot was boring. Danny didn't say much to her; he seemed lost in his own thoughts. Each time they circled around front, someone wanting to buy some X approached Danny, but he regretfully had to turn them down. Mandey continued walking on alone each time he was accosted. She wanted nothing to do with his business, even if he wasn't actually doing any.

There was no sign of the Devils anywhere. Mandey and Danny were getting their share of funny looks from people who likely thought that they were the ones up to no good. After about an hour of making slow circuits around the club, Mandey got three dollars out of her pocket and got in line to go inside.

"I've got to use the restroom," she told Danny. She probably could have held it, but she needed a break from the monotony.

"That sucks, having to pay three bucks to go pee," Danny said. "You should just duck into the woods over there."

"No, thanks."

"I'll wait out here for you."

"I won't be long," she said.

The line to get in was not too long as it was getting later. She gave her money to Tony at the door and headed inside toward the restrooms. There was a short line in the ladies' room, so that took a few minutes. Once she came back out, Mandey glanced around to see if she could spot any of the guys. She didn't see anyone until she was almost at the door. At a small table near the bar, she spotted Terry. He was talking to a girl with long blonde hair. Mandey recognized her, even without the black satin jacket. The girl was flirting shamelessly with Terry, and he was eating it up. Mandey didn't think Terry had a clue about who she was.

Mandey eased up to them. "Terry, can I talk to you for a minute?" she asked him, not daring to look at the blonde girl.

"Sure," he said, getting up from the table, and said to the girl, "I'll be right back."

He followed Mandey to a spot a few feet away. "What's up?" he asked.

"That girl you're talking to—do you know her?" Mandey asked.

"Naw. We just met. Her name is Kerri. We rhyme, Terry and Kerri," Terry said, with a goofy grin on his face. "She is one hot babe."

"I hate to tell you this, Terry, but she's one of the Devils," Mandey said.

Terry's eyes got wide. "No way."

"I'm serious," Mandey said.

"You're just messing with my head."

"Terry, I saw her here last week," Mandey insisted. "She tried to start something with me."

"I don't believe it," Terry said, and looked past Mandey at Kerri. "Hey, she's gone."

Mandey turned to see Kerri's chair, now empty.

"Terry, believe me, she's one of them," Mandey said.

"Damn," Terry said mournfully, "and I was about to get lucky."

"Be glad I saved you," Mandey said. "See you later."

She hurried back out to the parking lot to meet Danny. He was talking to Tony the doorman.

"You were gone awhile. Had to do more than pee, huh?" Danny said when he saw her.

"Oh, stop being gross," she said. They fell into step together and began trudging around in circles again. "That blonde girl who was harassing me last week was in there trying to seduce Terry."

"Seriously?" Danny asked, laughing.

"Yeah. I took Terry aside and told him. He didn't want to believe me, but then we turned around and she was gone," Mandey said. "Did Jesse and the others go by while I was inside?"

"Yeah. They haven't seen much of anything going on either."

"God, this is boring," Mandey said as they shuffled on.

They were coming around the back and up the west side of the building when Jesse came running toward them.

"Hey," he said. "Some of the Devils just came out. I want to follow them. I want to know where they hang out besides here. Hurry."

Mandey and Danny trotted behind Jesse over to Mandey's van, where Angelina and Dina were already waiting.

"They got into a black car over there," Angelina said, pointing to a car halfway down the next row.

Mandey opened the van and they all quickly piled in.

"Wait," Jesse said to Mandey. "We don't want them to see us."

They watched the car pull out and head toward the parking lot's south exit. Mandey pulled out and followed at what she hoped was an unobtrusive distance.

"That's Raff's car," Danny said. "Who's with him?"

"Juanita and a couple of younger guys," Dina said.

"Good, we outnumber them," Jesse said.

In less than ten minutes they found themselves at Raff's destination—a small, run-down, U-shaped apartment complex called The Northview. Mandey slowed down as the black car turned into the apartments' parking lot. She drove the van almost at a crawl past the entrance. Raff's car was parked at the far end, by a building that had been partially gutted by a fire.

"Did you see the graffiti as we were driving up?" Jesse asked excitedly. "I think we've found the Devils' home base. Circle around the block."

It was a shabby neighborhood, with tiny houses in disrepair and a few vacant lots overgrown with weeds. An old wooden fence with many missing planks surrounded the apartments. It was covered with red and black graffiti, marking the territory as belonging to the Devils.

When they came back to the apartment entrance, Jesse said, "Let's drive in there."

"No," Mandey said. "There's no outlet and I don't think I could turn around fast enough if I had to."

"Aw, come on," Jesse said.

"Jesse, she's right," Angelina said. Mandey was glad Angelina took her side. Jesse wouldn't listen to her, but he would listen to his girlfriend. "We don't want to get caught in there."

"All right," he relented. "Let's circle around and head back to the club."

They made one more circuit and drove back to Liaisons. The lot was full, so Mandey had to park on the street this time.

Once again they began walking around the club. Jesse, Angelina, and Dina took off first, with Mandey and Danny a couple minutes behind them. Mandey looked at her watch. It was almost midnight. Another hour to walk in circles. Her feet were hurting. Mandey sighed.

About fifteen minutes later, Mandey and Danny heard shouting and running footsteps as they approached the corner from the north side of Liaisons to the west. They both broke into a run, and as they rounded the corner, they nearly collided with two black-clad people in ski masks. Being dragged by the arm by one of them was Kerri.

"Stop them!" they heard Jesse yell.

Mandey made a lunge at Kerri while Danny tried to grab one of the guys by the tail of his jacket. The guys in black and Kerri dodged by Mandey and Danny and ran into the wooded lot behind the club. Mandey and Danny darted into the woods behind them, with Jesse and Dina on their heels.

The three fugitives separated, each running in a different direction. "Split up!" Jesse bellowed, taking off after one of the men in black. Danny took after the other, leaving Dina and Mandey to pursue Kerri.

Mandey was about three steps ahead of Dina when she stepped in a rut and stumbled. That didn't cause her to fall, but Dina ran into her from behind, knocking Mandey down. Dina tripped over her, but stayed on her feet.

"You okay?" she asked, stopping.

Mandey waved her on. "I'm okay. Keep after her."

Dina didn't hesitate; she turned and sped off.

Mandey carefully stood up. She wasn't going to be doing any more running that night. She hobbled out of the woods and back to the Liaisons parking lot. Angelina was standing by a silver Ford Fairmont. The driver's side door was open, and a figure was sitting hunched over with his head in his hands.

"What happened?" Angelina asked when she saw Mandey limping toward her.

"I twisted my ankle," Mandey said. "The others are still chasing those guys. They ran off in the woods and onto the next street. What happened here?"

The person sitting in the car looked up. "Mandey?"

"Keith?" Mandey said, surprised. "What happened?"

"You know him?" Angelina asked.

"We went to junior high together," Mandey replied.

"I met this girl inside," Keith said. "We came out here to my car, and she started getting friendly with me. Suddenly, these two guys in ski masks came up. One grabbed her and pulled her out of the car, and the other pulled me out and socked me in the stomach. Then they ran off, taking Kerri with them. I thought they were kidnapping her."

"We saw them running off, and Keith started yelling, so Jesse and Dina took off after them," Angelina said.

"After they ran off, I noticed my wallet was gone. Is it true Kerri was a part of it?" Keith asked.

"I'm afraid so," Mandey said.

"Son-of-a-bitch," Keith said, shaking his head. "I thought I dropped it inside, but she must have filched it. I just got paid and had a lot of cash with me, and she must have seen it."

Mandey leaned against the car so she could take the weight off her foot. "I wonder if I should go drive around to see if I can spot any of them?" she asked Angelina.

Angelina shrugged. "It wouldn't hurt, I guess. I'll go with you. Are you okay, Keith?"

"I've been better," he said, getting up out of the car. "Go ahead. I'm going inside to call the cops."

"Good luck," Mandey said.

"What makes you say that?" Keith asked.

"We haven't had a lot of luck getting any results from the cops in these kinds of situations," Mandey said.

"Is that what's up with the jackets and stuff?" Keith asked, surveying Mandey in her gang garb.

"Yeah," Angelina said. "We got tired of being pushed around, so we decided to push back."

"Well, push a little harder, willya?" Keith said.

"We're trying," Angelina said.

A few minutes later Mandey and Angelina were in the van, making a right turn out of the parking lot and heading in the direction where the others had run. As they slowly cruised down the dark road, peering carefully into yards and vacant lots, Mandey cursed the fact that Houston didn't provide more streetlights.

Six blocks from the club, they made a right turn and caught sight of a figure in the headlights. He whirled around when the lights hit him.

"That's Jesse!" Angelina exclaimed, rolling down her window. She shouted out to him, "Jesse, it's us!"

He jogged over to the van, opened the sliding door, and hopped in.

"Shit. I lost him," he said breathlessly. "Have you seen anyone else?"

"Just you so far," Angelina said.

"Dammit. I probably would have caught him, but a dog started chasing me. I had to jump a fence into someone's yard to get away. That's when I lost him."

"We'll get them eventually, Jesse, don't you worry," Angelina said, consoling him.

The van continued trawling through the area and about five minutes later they came upon Dina and Danny walking together, hurrying in the direction of the club.

"Hey!" Angelina yelled out the window as the van pulled up behind them.

"Did you lose them, too?" Jesse asked as Dina and Danny got in.

"The girl and the guy Danny was chasing hooked up and this red car came by and picked them up," Dina said.

"Which way did they go?" Jesse asked.

Dina pointed in the direction the van was headed. "But they might have turned off."

"They came from Liaisons' way?" Jesse asked.

"Yep."

"Shit," Jesse said. "I bet one of the guys circled around and went back to the club to get their car. What kind of car was it? Did you get a plate number?"

Danny, who was still a little out of breath, shook his head. "I didn't see anything but the taillights speeding away," he said. "I got there too late. Dina saw more than I did."

"It was a little red car. A Datsun, maybe," Dina said. "I didn't catch the plate number."

"We ought to take a ride by those apartments and see if there's a red car there," Jesse said. "Let's go collect the others first, though."

Fifteen minutes later all ten of the Alley Cats were in the van as they carefully approached the Northview Apartments.

"Okay, Dina, everybody, look and see if you see a little red car parked out there anywhere," Jesse said.

Everyone except Mandey, who had slowed the van down just short of a complete halt, craned their necks and peered out the windows. Raff's car was still there. Many other cars were parked there, as well, but only two weak floodlights lighted the lot, and it was difficult to see from their vantage point if a small red Datsun was tucked among them.

"Mandey, we can't see anything," Jesse said. "Nobody's around. Drive in there."

Mandey stopped the van and looked into the dimly lit parking lot. It was deserted. No lights were on in any of the visible apartment windows. She sighed. Although she didn't want to, she went against her better judgment, shut off the headlights, and turned into the apartment parking lot. The van crept the length of the parking lot, all the way down to the crumbling building at the end, the one that had been gutted by a fire sometime in the past. She pulled into a parking space and turned around.

"See anything?" she asked, looking at the others in the rearview mirror.

"Uh-uh," Dina said.

"I ought to get out and let the air out of his tires," Danny said, glaring at Raff's car.

Terry whipped out a pocketknife and held it out to Danny. "What's stopping you? Have at it."

Danny stared at the pocketknife for a moment, then looked back out at the car. "That's okay."

"Give it to me. I'll do it," Jesse said, grabbing it from Terry's hand.

"No!" Mandey protested.

The van was still moving as Jesse opened the sliding door and jumped out.

"Jesse!" Mandey and Angelina yelled in unison, as Mandey slammed on the brakes, pitching everyone forward.

"Watch it!" Terry exclaimed.

"Sorry."

Jesse had run over to Raff's car and was burying the three-inch blade of Terry's knife to the hilt in each of the four sidewalls. Then he ran the blade over the body of the car, scratching the paint.

A light came on in a second-floor window.

"Jesse, come on!" Zack yelled out the door.

"Hush!" Angelina said.

"Jesse!" Zack yelled again, this time in a stage whisper.

Jesse jumped back in. Mandey stepped on the gas before the door was shut.

"Are you nuts?" Jeremy asked.

"Go!" Jesse said.

Mandey stomped on the gas and the van roared out of the parking lot and made a left turn onto the street. She flipped the headlights back on. She was glad to get out of there. The place was giving her the creeps.

Shannon was glad to be getting home. After getting up early to meet the fence, working until nine, and finding out he had to go steal another car for Gary Grubbs' operation, he was exhausted. The pitcher of beer probably didn't help any. The flashing arrow sign in front of Tandy's, offering "BEER WINE SET-UP POO," had beckoned, and Shannon had followed. The exterior was wooden, with peeling gray paint. The inside was dingy as well, with utility tables flanked by a variety of chairs, some of the metal folding type, others wooden with worn finish. The jukebox was filled with old country music and rock like Bob Seger. A pool table was in one corner, and a small area devoid of tables served as a dance floor. Men with beer guts and dusty cowboy boots with worn heels and blue jeans with worn white rings on the back pockets from the cans of Skoal shuffled around with plain women who weighed about 300 pounds, or tiny, hard women with dye-jobs and too much make-up. Both types wore jeans they were close to popping out of. There were candles on the tables, in different glass holders of red, blue, or green. The merry flickering did much toward masking the dim dinginess.

Shannon sat alone at a small corner table with a candle in a green candle holder. Green, Mandey's favorite color. He had a pitcher of beer in front of him as he watched the action. He wished Mandey were with him. These kinds of places always let underage people in, and she didn't look underage, anyway. He didn't think Mandey belonged in a place like that, though. She deserved better than a date at Tandy's Ice House.

A couple women, big tough women, like Denise or Charlene might turn out in twenty years, had tried to talk to him, to get him to dance with them, but Shannon declined.

"I'm seeing someone," he said.

One of the women, with bleached blonde hair with black roots, glanced at the empty chairs around his table. "You must be seeing things, 'cause these chairs is empty. You look like you're on your own tonight. Come on and shake a leg with me, sugar."

Shannon shook his head. "Sorry, I only dance with my girlfriend, and if she ain't here, I ain't dancing."

It was great to be able to say that— "my girlfriend." It was nice to have Mandey as an excuse, too. Otherwise, he'd be hemming and hawing and trying to come up with a logical-sounding reason why he wasn't interested.

When he finished nursing his pitcher, leaving about a third of it, he headed for home. He was glad he didn't have far to drive, because the beer had made him sleepy. He was jerked back into the moment as he approached the apartments and a vehicle tore out of the parking lot and sped down the street away from him.

"What the--?" he said out loud.

It was large, a truck or van. As it sped away, Shannon considered following it, but he was too drowsy and he decided against it.

"Shit!" Terry screamed. "Shit, shit, shit!"

At the impound lot, a sad sight greeted them. The two Rottweilers were lying still on the ground by the fence. The padlock on the gate had been snapped open by a pair of bolt cutters.

"I can't believe this! We spent all night at that stupid fucking club, and we couldn't even keep some guy from getting mugged, and in the meantime, they were <u>here,</u> and they broke in and killed my dogs! Fuck!"

Terry continued ranting, waving his arms, and stomping around like a madman. The rest of the Alley Cats stood next to the van, dismayed.

Jim went over to take a closer look at the two dogs. He backed away slowly.

"Uh, Terry, they ain't dead," Jim said.

"What do you mean, 'they ain't dead'?" Terry demanded. "They are mean junkyard dogs. If they wasn't dead, they'd be gnawing on your sorry ass right now."

"Well, they're <u>breathing</u>," Jim said. "I think one of them's even snoring."

Terry hurried over to the two dogs and knelt down. "Hot damn. You're right."

"I think somebody drugged them," Danny said.

"And you'd be the one to know," Mandey muttered.

"Damn it," Terry said. "I thought when we got them dogs we could quit sleeping down here. I'd better call my brother and get him down here so we can figure out what's missing." He rose and headed toward the office. "Y'all can leave if you want. My brother will be here in about fifteen minutes."

"We'll stay until he gets here, just in case someone comes back," Jesse said.

The night air was damp and cold, so the other Alley Cats got back into the van.

"Well, I'm not impressed," Mandey muttered.

"What?" Danny asked, reclaiming shotgun from Angelina.

"This sucks," Zack said from the back. "We sure didn't do a hell of a lot of good tonight. This place got broken into, Keith got his wallet stolen, and everyone got away."

"The Devils are probably laughing their asses off at us," Jim said, disgusted.

"We can't get discouraged," Jesse said. "None of us has ever done this kind of thing before. We're still learning."

"We'd better learn fast, then, or just forget it," Brad said.

"Don't be so pessimistic," Jesse said. "We'll try again next week, and we'll show them we mean business."

Mandey started the van, turned the radio on 93Q, and watched Terry try to rouse the two unconscious dogs without much success. He came over to the van.

"Go ahead and take off. I don't think they're gonna come back. I'm sure they got what they wanted already. Besides, I'm going in and getting the shotgun. They'll be dead meat if they come near here again," Terry said.

"You sure?"

"Yeah. Go home. Go to bed."

Mandey was glad to do just that. It was about 2:15 A.M. when she crawled into bed, exhausted, her tired feet and left ankle throbbing, glad that the night was over.

26

Party Prep

Although she had hoped to sleep in after the late night she had, Mandey woke up at 8:30 on Saturday morning. She tried to go back to sleep, especially since she had been in the middle of an intensely sexual dream concerning Shannon--they were just about to do it--but it was no use. She got out of bed, but figured she would have to take a nap in the afternoon if she wanted to keep from yawning all evening at Jackie's party.

It was still a surprise to her that she had been invited. She was both excited and nervous about it. The fact that this was the first time she was going to attend a party with a lot of the popular crowd didn't faze her. Although she wasn't really a part of that social circle, that didn't make her nervous. She was edgy because she knew there would be alcohol and drugs and people getting crazy, and she was fervently hoping the cops weren't going to show up and bust everyone.

After a breakfast of cherry Pop-tarts while reading the newspaper, she spent a half an hour trying to figure out what to wear to the party. She decided on a tight, sleeveless, black and silver turtleneck sweater, black fishnet hose, and her black leather-look skirt with zippers up the sides. James used to call it her "easy access skirt", not that he had ever made much of an indication that he would like to take advantage of it. But that was just as well, considering how things had turned out.

She put on a pair of jeans and a sweatshirt and headed for the grocery store to buy ingredients for two batches of chocolate chip cookies. Jackie had asked some of the girls she invited to bring food, and some of the guys were going to bring booze to supplement what Jackie had. There would be plenty of others who would get to eat and drink for nothing, but Mandey didn't mind. To help with the refreshments meant she was helping to "hostess" the party, which was more of an honor than just being invited.

She was halfway through baking the cookies when Marcia came home from spending the night with Michael.

"What's all this?" Marcia asked, surveying Mandey's mess in the kitchen.

"Cookies for the party tonight," Mandey replied.

Marcia laughed and sat down at the kitchen table. "You're taking cookies to this party?"

"Yeah. Jackie asked some of us to bring something. Why?"

"Oh, I don't know. I'm thinking back to the parties I used to go to. They were more 'pot' than 'potluck.'"

"Well, I know nothing about party protocol, so I'm just doing what I was told," Mandey said. "Georgia said she's making hors d'oeurves."

"What?" Marcia asked, laughing harder.

"Hors d'oeuvres. Don't ask me what she means by that."

"All I can say is I can't worry about you too much if you're going to a party where they're serving hors d'oeuvres."

"I don't know about that. We could all come down with food poisoning from Georgia's cooking."

"Well, I'm going to have a nap," Marcia said. "I'm meeting Barbara and Maxine for an early dinner, and then we're going out."

"I'm going to take a nap myself once I finish with these cookies."

"If I don't see you before I leave, have fun and be careful."

"I will. I always am."

Around three o'clock, Mandey laid down on her bed under the patchwork quilt her grandmother had made for her and slept until she heard the phone ringing around five.

"Hello?"

"Hi, Mandey, it's me."

"Hi, Shannon."

"Is something wrong? Are you sick?"

"No. Why?"

"You sound funny."

"No, I'm all right. I was taking a nap and I just woke up."

"I hate not being able to go with you tonight," Shannon said. "I miss you."

"I miss you, too," Mandey said. "Are we still on for tomorrow?"

"You bet," Shannon said.

"Good. I need a kiss and a big hug."

"Don't worry. I'll give you all the kisses and hugs you need," Shannon told her. "I've got to go. I'll call you in the morning. Have fun at your party, but not too much fun."

"I won't," Mandey said. "I love you."

"Love you, too."

Mandey had mixed feelings about Shannon having to work late that evening. On one hand, she wanted to bring him to the party and show off her new beau to everyone. On the other hand, most of the gang was going to be there, and she didn't want to expose Shannon to that situation when he was trying to turn his life around. She guessed it was just as well he had to work.

She went into the living room and looked outside. Marcia's car was already gone. Mandey decided to order in a pizza all for herself. She dialed up Domino's and ordered a medium pizza with extra cheese, mushrooms, and onion. Then she painted her nails. She had to decide between the scarlet and the silver, and she chose the red. She painted her toenails, too, even though no one would see them, because it made her feel sexy.

The pizza arrived at about the same time her polish was dry. She got a Pepsi out of the refrigerator, grabbed some napkins and the salt and pepper, and then sat down on the couch with the pizza in front of her on the coffee table. She flipped on MTV and dug in. As she ate, she wondered if it had been prudent of her to order pizza with onion, considering she was going to a social event, but she decided to throw caution to the wind. She would brush her teeth and use mouthwash before she left, and she had breath mints if she needed them. Besides, she wasn't going to be kissing anybody, anyway.

The pizza was cut into eight pieces. She ate four and considered a fifth, but ended up leaving the remaining half for lunch or for Marcia, whichever came first. She put the leftovers in the refrigerator and went to get ready.

Mandey showered, washed her hair, and shaved her legs. She used the blow dryer and curling iron on her hair, which she didn't do very often. For the most part, Mandey didn't like to fuss with her hair, preferring to wash it and go, but that wouldn't do tonight. In fact, since meeting Shannon, she had been spending a lot more time on her hair, and it didn't seem like such a chore anymore.

She was putting on her make up when Georgia called.

"Are you getting ready?" Georgia asked her.

"I'm doing my face, then all I have to do is get dressed."

"What are you wearing?"

"A black and silver sweater and a black skirt," Mandey replied.

"Oh, you'll look cute," Georgia said. "Well, I'm going to jump in the shower. Come down whenever you're ready."

"Okay."

Since Georgia had asked Mandey what she was wearing, Mandey knew that Georgia hadn't even picked out an outfit yet. Typical Georgia, always running late. Mandey looked at the clock. It was almost eight. Georgia probably wouldn't be ready until 9:30. Mandey hoped that she at least had the hors d'oeuvres ready.

Mandey did her face up more than usual. She only wore foundation make up on special occasions, which this was, but she didn't want to look painted. A lot of girls at school had this bad habit of wearing blush that stood out in bright, unnatural blotches on their cheekbones, often on top of make-up that didn't match their skin tones.

She used a light foundation that closely matched her complexion. She used eyebrow pencil to add some definition to her brows. Her top eyelids she lined with black eyeliner. She also lined the outer half of her bottom lids with black liner, but softened it up with a silvery brown liner. She used similar colors of eye shadow, highlighted with a frosty white on her brow bones. The blush she used was more reddish than pink, and she blended it in well, then finished with face powder. Her one flashy feature was red lipstick.

She pulled on her hose, her sweater and skirt, and her black lace-up jelly shoes. Black and silver earrings, black and silver beads, black and silver bracelets, and black and silver rings completed her look. She also wore her silver watch; she felt lost without it. Mandey lived by the clock, unlike her best friend.

The reflection that greeted Mandey in the full-length mirror was a complete contradiction of her image as a nerd, a bookworm, and a goody-two-shoes. If only Shannon were there to appreciate it.

She threw on a sweater and went to the kitchen for her foil-wrapped tray of cookies. She picked up her purse and keys and headed out to the van, locking the door behind her, to drive down the street to Georgia's.

As expected, Georgia was not ready. She was wrapped in a towel with her hair fixed, at least, trying to decide what to wear. Mandey sat on the edge of Georgia's bed and watched her go through her closet, piece by piece. Georgia continuously asked Mandey's opinion about each outfit, but didn't seem to listen, holding each piece up to herself and looking in the mirror, then pitching each article on the bed.

Thirty minutes later Georgia was putting on hose, a tight black skirt, a white form-fitting blouse with a low-cut scoop neckline, and a bright red jacket. While Georgia made up her face, Mandey sat on the toilet seat, watching.

"So, your new beau had to work tonight," Georgia said as she applied her eyeshadow.

"Yeah," Mandey sighed.

"When do I get to meet him?" Georgia asked.

"Soon," Mandey said.

"You're sure he's nothing like James, right?" Georgia said. "I'm sorry, but you know how I feel about him."

Mandey laughed. "Yes, you and everyone else."

"He's just so arrogant," Georgia said.

Mandey nodded. "Shannon's nothing like that."

"I love that name for a guy," Georgia said.

"I've got a picture of him now," Mandey said, going into Georgia's bedroom and returning with her purse. She pulled out a snapshot Marcia had taken of her and Shannon on his birthday and handed it to Georgia.

"Mmm-mmm-mmm, honey, he is fine," Georgia said, studying it.

"Are you being serious?" Mandey asked.

"Yes!" Georgia said emphatically. "Why? Don't you think he's good looking? Honey, I'll take him. Especially if he has a hairy chest."

"It's not that hairy. And, of course I think he's good-looking. You just sounded fake when you said that."

"What? You think I'm lying?" Georgia asked.

"Georgia, last week I was with you when Charlene was going on about how fine Phillip is. You agreed with her, but when she wasn't looking, you rolled your eyes at me and mouthed, 'He's a dog.' You lie and you know it," Mandey said, smiling.

"Well, you're my best friend, and I wouldn't lie to you. He is fine," Georgia said, inspecting the photo again. "Tall, dark hair, brown eyes, nice nose, nice build. If you get tired of him, send him my way."

"Won't happen," Mandey said.

"Shucks," Georgia said, handing the picture back to Mandey. "Does he have a brother?"

"Nope, only a sister. Sorry," Mandey said, putting the photo back into her purse.

"Anyway, you know who's supposed to be coming tonight? Kirby McLendon. I haven't seen him in a year. I wonder what he's been up to?"

Kirby McLendon had been a football star for the Rogers High team and had graduated in '83. Mandey had no idea what he was doing now, either, but she knew Georgia had had a crush on him from the time they were freshmen. Georgia had lots of male admirers, all of which she could take or leave. Kirby was the only guy Mandey had ever seen her go a little loopy over. Naturally, he had barely acknowledged her existence.

Georgia finished her make up, retouched her hair, and put on her jewelry and shoes. Mandey looked at her watch. It was only 9:15.

"Not bad, huh?" Georgia said. "Ready in almost record time. And guess what? The hors d'oeurves are all ready."

She pulled plastic-wrapped tray out of the refrigerator. On it were toothpicks, which skewered little squares of cheese, green olives, maraschino cherries, and mini-marshmallows. Not cherries and marshmallows together on some toothpicks and cheese and olives together on the others. All on one toothpick.

"Cheese, olives, cherries, and marshmallows?" Mandey asked doubtfully.

"Yes," Georgia said, in a "What planet have you been living on?" tone of voice. "The recipe is in all the good cookbooks."

Mandey thought Georgia might have made a mistake. Oh, well, the crowd would be so drunk that they wouldn't notice.

"I'll drive," Georgia said.

"Okay," Mandey said. "I'll drop the van back at my house."

27

Brotherly Love

Shannon sighed when he hung up the phone with Mandey that Saturday afternoon. He hated lying to her, but he couldn't very well tell her he couldn't go to Jackie's party because he had to show up at a gang party. He thought about the party Mandey was going to and realized there might not be all that many differences between her party and his. Basically, the same shit was going to go on—drinking, drugging, and fucking.

He hoped Mandey would be okay. She had said that this was going to be her first "real" party, so he figured she might not know exactly what to expect. She was going to be out of her element. He wanted so much to be with her that night. Part of it, he supposed, was possessiveness on his part. He didn't want some guy trying to get her drunk so he could molest her. He wanted to be with her, to protect her, and to make sure she got home safely.

His mood was glum as he took a shower, thinking about being separated from Mandey, but his mind was also on the Devils.

"Damn it, are you going to take all night? I need to use the bathroom!" he heard Annette say, banging on the bathroom door.

He was convinced that she did that not because she had to go but because she loved to annoy him, but Shannon was in no mood to argue. "Just a second," he said, and quickly finished dressing. He opened the bathroom door and walked out past his sister, silent.

Annette stared at him as he exited the bathroom. She had been prepared for an argument; instead, he hadn't said a word.

She had noticed he had been acting differently since the time he had disappeared for a few days. He was even quieter than usual, much more secretive, and, even though he tried to hide it, less interested in the gang than ever. Annette had an idea that Trick was going to announce any day that he wanted to quit, but if he did, he was going to have to get the hell out of the neighborhood.

Shannon went into the bedroom, shut the door, turned his radio on loud, and rocked along with Ozzy doing "Crazy Train." He finished buttoning his blue plaid flannel shirt and combed his wet hair. He looked at himself in the small mirror hanging on his wall. He wouldn't look good enough to go to a party with Mandey, anyway, not with these old jeans and old shirt. He thought about buying some new clothes, and wondered why he hadn't bothered before. Well, what would have been the point? He didn't need a fancy wardrobe to sit in a condemned building and try to keep control of a bunch of destructive freaks.

He finished dressing and was ready to go to the store to buy booze for the party. He decided to ask Annette if she wanted to go, too. He realized he missed the days when he and Annette used to get along. He didn't know if he could change anything back to the way it used to be, but he supposed trying wouldn't hurt.

He waited by the bathroom door. The toilet flushed, and a moment later she came out.

"What are you standing there for?" Annette snapped.

Shannon felt his temper flare but controlled it. "I'm going to the liquor store. Do you want to come with me?"

Annette stared at him as though he were speaking in tongues. She was about to ask him who the hell he was and what did he do with her brother, but she decided it would be better to keep her mouth shut.

"You buying?" she asked.

"Didn't I just give you eighty dollars?" Shannon replied.

Annette snorted. She was about to make a sarcastic remark about that pissant amount of money from the jewelry store robbery, but then she changed her mind. "I have other things I need to spend it on."

Shannon was startled by her reasonable tone. "Yeah, I'm buying," he told her. "Let's go."

She followed Trick out to his car, stunned by this turn of events. He hadn't asked her to go anywhere with him (except to steal cars) since before they moved there to the apartments, and he had never offered to buy her anything.

He turned on the radio in the car, but didn't talk. That wasn't unusual; he never talked much. Annette didn't say anything to him, either; she didn't know what to say, and she didn't want to say something that might change his mind. She and Trick hadn't gotten along at all since they moved into the apartments. Part of it was because they had to share a room. He got mad whenever she brought Checkmate over for the night, and they argued about that a lot. She couldn't help it; she couldn't always stay at his place, and at this time of year the hideout was too cold. Mostly, though, she resented Trick because he was leader of the Devils. She thrived in the gang environment, while Trick was only involved because he had to be. It wasn't fair for him to lead when she knew he hated it, while he treated her as a second-rate citizen and never let her in on the dangerous stuff.

The liquor store they went to was not the one Shannon and Raff had tried to rob; that one had burned down about three months after Shannon was convicted and sent to the detention center. It had been arson, but no one ever proved who was responsible. Nonetheless, Shannon had a good idea about who might have set the fire.

Annette followed her brother inside. "I can pick out anything I want?" she asked him.

"Yeah," Shannon said, "within reason. I've only got so much money."

"What kind of beer are you getting?" Annette asked.

"I don't know. It don't matter to me," Shannon said.

"Get Bud," Annette said. "That Old Milwaukee we had last time gave me a hell of a hangover."

Shannon picked out a case of Budweiser, a bottle of Jack Daniels, and a bottle of tequila.

"Damn," Annette said when she saw the liquor he had chosen. "You going to drink all that?"

"Yeah, right," Trick said sarcastically. "I'm going to have to hide anything I don't want the others to get into."

Annette picked out a bottle of peach Schnapps and a bottle of Fireball Cinnamon Whiskey.

"Check this out. This is something new," Annette said, showing him the bottle of Fireball.

Shannon took it from her and examined the label. It sounded pretty good.

"You gonna share?" Shannon asked her, fully expecting her response to be, "Fuck you."

Annette paused. "I will if you share the tequila with me."

"Deal," Shannon said.

Shannon also picked up a 12-pack of Coke and checked out with their selections. The clerk didn't ask for any identification. Even though he had barely turned nineteen, the legal drinking age, no one ever carded him.

Getting into the car, he asked Annette, "Do you want to go to Taco Bell and get something to eat?"

"Sure," Annette said, ever more astonished at her brother's generosity.

Fifteen minutes later they were sitting in Taco Bell with a tray laden with food and two Dr Peppers. Annette had ordered a Taco Bell Grande, and Enchirito, and a Burrito Supreme. Shannon hadn't even minded that she had chosen some of the most expensive items on the menu. Shannon himself was eating two Tacos Bell Grande, a Bell Beefer, and a combination burrito.

They ate in silence until Annette couldn't stand it any longer. She had to know what was going on.

"Why are you being so nice to me?" she asked him.

Shannon took a swig of his Dr Pepper. "Why are you so suspicious?"

"Well, you ain't asked me to go nowhere with you, much less bought me something, since I don't know when."

Shannon finished chewing and swallowing a bite of his burrito. "Well, you're the only sister I've got. It ain't right that we don't get along. I know I can be a son-of-a-bitch sometimes, and you ain't exactly easy to live with, either, but we are family."

Annette sat back and stared at him skeptically. "And what got you thinking about all this family stuff?" she asked.

"Annette, do I have to have a reason to think?" he asked her.

"It's just I've noticed you've been acting weird lately, Shannon," she said.

Shannon stared at her for a moment. It was the first time he remembered her addressing him by his real name since he had gotten stuck with that stupid nickname.

"What do you mean by 'weird'?" he asked her.

"Weird. Strange. Like you're off in another world half the time," Annette said.

Shannon rubbed his temples wearily. "Maybe I am," he said.

"Huh?"

He paused, thinking about what he should tell her. He decided to tell her the truth—some of it, anyway.

"You're going to be eighteen in two months," he said to her. "Have you been thinking at all about the future? Where you'll be and what you'll be doing a year from now? Or five years from now?"

"Sure," Annette said. "Soon as we can afford it, me and Dewayne are going to get an apartment together."

"How are you going to afford an apartment?" Shannon asked her.

"We'll find a way," Annette said. "I thought we were talking about you."

Shannon sighed. "Yeah. Well, I've been thinking a lot about my future. I'm thinking about going back to school to get my G.E.D."

"Why? What do you need a G.E.D. for working at a gas station?"

"That's just it," Shannon said. "I don't want to work at a gas station the rest of my life. I want to go to college."

"College?" Annette asked. She seemed confused and surprised, but she didn't laugh, Shannon noticed. "Where did you get that idea?"

"A friend of mine suggested it," Shannon said.

"What friend?" Annette asked suspiciously.

"Just a friend," Shannon replied firmly.

"What does that mean for the gang?" Annette asked.

For a moment he didn't say anything, because he dared not say anything disloyal. He and Annette might be getting along for the moment, but that didn't mean that two hours later he might not do something to piss her off and that would send her blabbing to Raff.

"I don't know," he said finally.

"You don't really want to be a part of the gang any more, do you?"

He thought about denying it, but Shannon couldn't find the emotion to do so. Carefully he said, "I don't want to be twenty-five years old leading a bunch of kids around painting graffiti and stealing cars. Can you understand that?"

"It beats working at Safeway for three bucks an hour," Annette said with a shrug.

"Maybe it does and maybe it doesn't," Shannon said. "At least you don't get arrested working at Safeway. The point is, I want to do something with myself. I don't want to turn forty and find out I've turned into Leon."

"Well, amen to that, brother," Annette said.

Shannon crumpled up his food wrappers and drank down the last of his Dr Pepper. "Let's get our asses over to the party," he said heavily.

"Try not to be so enthusiastic," Annette said sarcastically.

"I had an invite to another party, but I had to turn it down for this bullshit," he said, grumbling.

"A party at your 'friend's' house?"

"Friend of a friend."

"Who is this friend of yours?" Annette said, pressing for information.

"Drop it, Annette. Forget I said anything."

"Fuck, Trick, what's the big deal?"

"I don't want to talk about it. Let's go." He got up and took his tray over to the trashcan, ending the conversation.

28

Jackie's Party

As Mandey and Georgia drove into the subdivision, "1999" by Prince could be heard from a block away. The street in front of the house where Jackie Seymore lived with her father (who was out of town on business) was jammed. Georgia had to park on the next cross street.

Georgia and Mandey walked through the front door, which was open to provide ventilation, and into the foyer. The place was packed. Everyone who was anyone at Rogers was there, from people who had graduated two years before down to popular freshmen. A group of guys was congregated around a table, playing poker. Another table was set up next to a keg, and there a co-ed group was playing quarters. Between them, people were milling around, talking. In the living room beyond, people were dancing. People greeted Georgia and Mandey as they worked their way through the crowd toward the kitchen. Georgia reciprocated with a big smile for everyone. Mandey was not as at ease, but she smiled, too.

Jackie, Charlene, and several other girls were in the kitchen. A giant cooler of what Mandey thought was Kool-Aid was sitting by the refrigerator, with several bags of melting ice on the floor next to it. Everyone's dirty shoes were tracking around the water from the ice, making the floor a wet, filthy mess.

Georgia and Mandey put their food on the counter, where there were open bags of several varieties of chips, bowls of dip and salsa, a raw vegetable platter, a tray of sandwiches, two-liter bottles of assorted soft drinks, and several bottles of various hard liquors.

"Hey!" Jackie said. She had a plastic cup of the Kool-Aid in her hand. Her eyes were red. Mandey thought that must be some potent Kool-Aid. "What'd you bring?"

"I made hors d'oeuvres," Georgia said, unwrapping her tray. "Mandey made homemade chocolate chip cookies."

"Cookies?" said Amber Vernon, a cheerleader who looked to be even more wasted than Jackie. She was holding onto the counter with one hand, as if to keep her balance. "Cool."

Mandey unwrapped her tray and put the foil in an overflowing paper bag that was serving as a trash receptacle. Amber, Jackie, and Charlene each grabbed one.

"Hey, everybody, there's cookies!" Amber yelled.

Jackie clapped her hand over Amber's mouth. "Don't tell everybody or they'll eat them all."

"Man," Georgia said, peering out of the kitchen into the living room, "everyone and their brother showed up."

"Yeah," Jackie said. "Hey, try the jungle juice Danny and Mark made. It's great."

So that's what they call the Kool-Aid stuff, Mandey thought.

"Is it strong?" Georgia asked. "I mean, can you taste the alcohol?"

"Uh-uh," Charlene said. "It's good."

"I heard someone say my name," Mark Ruggeri said as he walked into the kitchen. "What were you saying about me?"

"We were speculating about the size of your wang," Charlene said. "My guess was three inches."

"Oh. You don't have to guess. I'll be glad to show you," Mark said, starting to unbutton his jeans.

"No, no, no!" Georgia and Jackie screamed, covering their eyes. Mandey stared at him, her face turning red.

Mark pulled his jeans down and reached inside his underwear. "Wanna see?" he asked Mandey, grinning drunkenly.

"No!" all the girls screamed.

"Aw, shit, y'all are no fun," Mark complained, and pulled up his jeans again.

Mandey sighed in relief. Thank God Mark wasn't quite that drunk yet.

"Anyway, if you really want to know, just ask Georgia," he said.

"You lie!" Georgia exclaimed, acting shocked but laughing.

Danny had also appeared in the kitchen. "Who made these?" he asked through a mouthful of cookie.

"I did," Mandey said.

"They're great," he said, and then picked up one of Georgia's toothpicks.

"What the fuck is this?" he asked with a laugh, holding it up so everyone could see.

"Don't you know?" Georgia asked haughtily. "It's an hors d'oeuvre."

Danny inspected it and set it back down on the tray. "If you say so, George."

He grabbed another cookie and went over to the cooler. He dunked the plastic cup he held into the jungle juice and chugged half of it.

"Let me try some of that," Georgia said, getting a cup of her own and filling it. "Mandey, get you some."

"No thanks," Mandey said.

"Yeah, you need some," Danny said, getting another cup. He filled it and held it out to Mandey. She didn't offer to take it from him.

"Oh, come on," Georgia said. "You don't have to get drunk. Just sip it."

"I'll take it," Mark said, grabbing the cup out of Danny's hand. Half of the drink spilled out onto the floor and Danny's shoes.

"Shit, Mark, you idiot!" Danny said, looking down at his shoes.

"Well, hell, you know she's not going to drink it!" Mark said, and drank down the rest of the contents of the cup.

"I'll drink if I feel like it," Mandey said coldly. "I'm just not crazy about drinking spiked Kool-Aid that everyone's had their hands in."

"Amber, hand me some paper towels," Danny said.

"Where?" Amber asked, looking around disoriented.

"I'll get them," Georgia said, squeezing past Danny, Mark, and Mandey to get them from the counter next to where Amber stood.

"I'd love to see you get drunk," Mark said, moving in closer to Mandey, so he was almost nose-to-nose with her. "I wonder what you'd be like."

Danny laughed. "Knock it off, Mark."

Mark stayed in her face, swaying slightly. He smelled of after-shave, sickly sweet Kool-Aid, and beer.

"I hope I wouldn't be like you," Mandey said, and made her way out of the kitchen.

She saw Jesse and Angie making out on the couch. Jesse nearly had Angie's shirt off. Mandey thought they ought to move it to a bedroom. The living room was jammed with people dancing to "Strut" by Sheena Easton. Jason Barnes, who had graduated the previous year, was the deejay, and one end of the living room was set up with his equipment. The music was so loud it drowned out all other noise more than a foot and a half away.

"Hey, Mandey."

Mandey whirled around to see Ken Sherman behind her, beer in hand. He had been the valedictorian of the class of '83. She had been friendly with him during her sophomore year, when advanced Biology I and II were being taught in a combined class. They had been in the same lab group. Nothing bonds people like dissecting a fetal pig together.

"Hi, Ken," she said, delighted, and they hugged.

"Look at you," Ken said grinning. "Where'd you park your motorcycle?"

Mandey blushed and smiled. "Oh, Ken. What have you been up to? Still going to University of Houston?"

"Yeah. Second year. I haven't made up my mind on a major yet, but I've got another semester before I've got to cross that bridge. Have you decided where you're going yet?"

"Probably U of H. I like the city of Austin a lot, but the University of Texas is too much of a party school for me."

"Not true," Ken said. "That would be just the thing for you. But I'm still living at home, so if you do go to U of H next year, maybe we could carpool."

"That's a thought," Mandey said.

Jason put on "No Parking on the Dance Floor."

"You want to dance?" Ken asked her.

"Sure," Mandey said.

The squeezed their way into the dancing crowd and joined in. Mandey was facing the foyer. She noticed Georgia, Charlene, and Jackie talking to the guys playing quarters, Alex Vargas, Max Williams, and Claude Hamilton, all of whom had played high school football for Rogers before they graduated last spring. They apparently hadn't continued their football careers in college, if they were even in college, or else they would have been playing ball that day. She saw Kirby McLendon walk in. Georgia immediately lit up and began to flutter nervously, which was so unlike her normal calm, confident manner.

Fortunately, Ken wasn't trying to talk to her much while they danced; she wouldn't have been able to hear him over the music. She surveyed everyone while she danced. Jesse and Angie had vacated the couch; she hadn't seen where they had gone. Another couple had taken their place. Danny was over in a corner, plying his trade. Terry was at the poker table with three other guys. She saw Jeremy dancing with a cute little blonde junior named Valerie. Zack, Brad, and Jim were in a corner talking to three girls, two of whom Mandey recognized from school, and one she didn't know at all. Dina had been around when she came in, but she was nowhere in sight now.

After dancing to a few songs, Mandey and Ken parted ways, leaving Mandey at loose ends. She shuffled through the crowd, trying to get to a spot where there might be a little more breathing room. She made her way over to Georgia, who was still with Kirby at the Quarters table, but she was only watching the action. Mandey pulled up a chair to be a spectator, as well.

"Why don't you play?" Georgia asked her. "It's fun."

Mandey shook her head.

"Come on. I'll play if you will," Georgia said.

"No, thanks," Mandey said.

"You should play, anyway," Kirby told Georgia, offering her a quarter. "Here."

"No, no, no," Georgia protested, laughing, but then she gave in and joined the game.

After forty-five minutes or so, it became boring, so Mandey wandered through the throng once more. Besides Georgia, she didn't have anyone to hang out with. None of her other friends were there. Neither Gayla nor Charlie had come, and Andie and Mart were not invited. The Alley Cats had all shown, but they weren't really what she considered to be friends.

Eventually she worked her way into the kitchen. Her cookies were long gone. She poured herself some Coke in a plastic cup and nibbled on some chips with ranch dip. She sipped her Coke and surveyed the liquor bottles on the counter. There was a Bacardi bottle with a little more than a finger of rum left. She poured the remnants into her cup with the Coke, ate a few more chips and a couple of Georgia's hors d'oeuvres, then headed back out into the action.

The loveseat in the corner of the living room had become vacant, so Mandey sank down into it. She was running out of steam. She took a sip of her drink and looked at her watch. It was five until midnight. She was ready to go home, but she doubted Georgia would be ready to leave so soon.

"What are you drinking?" Danny asked Mandey, sitting next to her on the arm of the loveseat.

"Rum and Coke," Mandey replied.

"Uh-uh," Danny said, disbelieving. "Really?"

"Yeah."

"Need another?" he asked.

"No."

"Sure you do," Danny said, taking her nearly empty cup from her hand. "I'll be right back."

Mandey sat back in the loveseat. She was getting sleepy, and that drink hadn't helped any.

In the other corner of the living room, Georgia and Kirby had left the quarters table and were sitting and talking. Georgia looked to be having a great time. Kirby had his arm around her, and Mandey deduced that he had something more than conversation on his mind. Mandey wondered what was going to happen. Georgia, despite all her racy and flirtatious ways, was very adamant about <u>no sex</u>. Perhaps that was because she hadn't met anyone she truly wanted. She wondered if Kirby was turning out to be all that Georgia had thought he was cracked up to be, or if he was going to be another disappointment.

Her thoughts turned to Shannon, and she wondered what he was doing at that moment. She wished he were there with her. She wanted him to take her home to her house so she could fall asleep in his arms in her bed.

Danny returned and sat down in the loveseat with Mandey. He had a drink in each hand, and gave one to her.

"It's a double," he told her. "You look like you need a strong drink."

"Oh, Danny," Mandey said. "Thanks, but it'll make me giggly for about twenty minutes and then I'll get so sleepy I'll be miserable." She took a sip. It was strong, but not so strong that she couldn't drink it.

"Are you having fun?" Danny asked her.

"Sure," Mandey said. "Why do you ask? Don't I look like it?"

"No, actually, you don't," he said, laughing.

Mandey smiled. "I'm getting sleepy. The alcohol is depressing my nervous system." She took a drink.

"People are wrong about you," Danny said. "You like to party, but you just aren't that used to it."

Mandey shrugged, drinking some more until it was almost gone. She could feel the alcohol warming her stomach and then rushing straight to her head. It wasn't an unpleasant feeling.

"There's a lot more to me than an oversized brain," Mandey said. "People might be surprised."

Danny glanced down at Mandey's cup. "Damn, you downed that fast. We might make a drunk out of you yet."

He finished up his drink. "I'll be right back," he said to Mandey, grabbing her cup and getting up again.

Mandey sat there, watching everyone dance, feeling the alcohol doing its job. She felt warm all over and much more inclined to talk and say things she usually wouldn't. She realized that alcohol, in small doses, could be an effective social tool for someone as inhibited as herself.

She smiled at people stumbling past her. She could get up and begin talking to anyone there and not be shy about, and she would be able to keep up her end of the conversation, provided that whomever she talked to wasn't too drunk to converse.

Then she laughed at herself. *Only a nerd would sit here analyzing the effects of the alcohol instead of just enjoying it.*

She stretched, yawned, lay back and closed her eyes. Despite the loud music, she felt like she could drift off to sleep right there. A few moments later she felt someone sit down next to her. She sat up and opened her eyes. Danny was back.

"Here," he said, handing her a jumbo-sized plastic cup.

"Are you trying to get me drunk?" Mandey asked, taking the drink from him.

"You bet," Danny said with a smirk.

Mandey laughed. "Well, this is about as drunk as I'm going to let myself get. Otherwise, my judgment will become impaired, and I'll probably get sick."

"Just drink it," Danny said impatiently, but smiling.

Mandey took a sip. She would nurse this one for a while. She didn't want to get any tipsier, but she figured drinking this slowly would prolong her buzz.

"I hear you're going out with someone new," Danny said. "Why isn't he here?"

"He had to work," Mandey replied.

"Does he know you're here?"

Mandey nodded. "He was invited to come, but he couldn't."

"He doesn't know what he's missing," Danny said.

Mandey turned her head slowly to look him in the eye. "What do you mean by that?"

"I mean if I were here with a drunk chick in a miniskirt, I'd be getting her out of this place about now and taking her somewhere nice and private."

Mandey smiled. "You certainly don't mince words, do you?" she asked.

"Have you slept with him yet?" Danny asked her.

Mandey blinked. "What?"

"Are you banging your boyfriend?"

That made Mandey laugh. "What business is it of yours?" she asked. She wasn't offended. In fact, she was kind of glad that Danny had asked, as bizarre as that might have seemed. It made her happy to think that someone thought of her as normal enough, human enough, and desirable enough to have sex.

"None at all," Danny said cheerfully, "but inquiring minds want to know. I mean, everyone knows you and James never did anything."

"How would everyone know that?"

"Well, you didn't, did you?"

"No," Mandey admitted.

"You know, there are a lot of guys at school who want to get in your pants."

Mandey gave a derisive snort of laughter. "Yeah, right."

"You know what they say about the quiet ones—they're always the wildest," Danny said.

Mandey managed to stifle her giggles. Her face was growing warm, but she wasn't sure if it was from the alcohol or Danny's remarks or a combination of both.

"I'd expect to hear something like this out of Mark's mouth, not from you," she said.

"He's one of those guys who wants to get in your pants."

She couldn't stop herself from laughing again. "You're being ridiculous. No one except James has ever shown even a glitter—glimmer—of interest in me. Well, except Charlie, but he's just oversexed."

"Guys are scared of you," Danny said.

"Oh, please," Mandey said, rolling her eyes. "They think I'm a boring goody-two-shoes."

"Sure, there are some guys who wouldn't ask you out because they think you're too tough a nut to crack, but there are others who are afraid to ask you out because they think you'd reject them."

Mandey thought about that for a moment. "Do I come across as that stuck-up?" she asked.

"No," Danny said. "Everyone thinks you're real sweet, and they all know you're just quiet, but some of them think you might think they're stupid. And they know you've got high moral standards."

"How the heck do they know that?" Mandey asked.

"It's obvious, Mandey. You don't run around with guys, you don't party a lot, you don't do drugs—although you know I can help you out in that department, if you want," Danny said, grinning.

"Are you crazy?" Mandey asked. "No thank you."

"Anyway," Danny continued, "you don't spread gossip, you don't cuss—"

"I do too cuss," Mandey said in mock indignation. "I say 'damn' and 'hell' every once in awhile."

"Well, excuse the fuck out of me," Danny said teasingly. "But seriously, there are a lot of guys at school wondering what you'd be like in bed. Girls like you, the ones no one knows about, are the best kind to speculate about."

"I'm not even going to ask what gets said. I don't want to know," Mandey said.

"Let me tell you that more than one guy has observed the way you tease Charlie at lunch. You know, that very provocative way you eat your ice cream?"

Mandey threw her head back and giggled. "Well, I have to practice, and sometimes I need feedback."

She took Danny's hand in hers, brought it to face level, and then took his index finger in her mouth. She sucked it, licking it in the manner she intended to use someday on a certain part of Shannon's anatomy.

"Jesus!" Danny cried, taking her finger from her mouth. Mandey grinned at the wide-eyed expression on his face.

"What's wrong?" she asked him playfully.

"That tongue of yours could make a lot of men happy," Danny said, swallowing hard and shaking his head.

"Sorry. There's only one I want to make happy," Mandey said with a big smile.

"Well, you never answered my question. Have you fucked him yet?"

"No, I haven't," Mandey said, exasperated.

"Why not?"

"We've only been seeing each other for two weeks!" Mandey exclaimed. "Do you want him to submit a report to you once it happens?"

"Would he do that?" Danny asked, grinning. "Maybe we could print it in the school paper."

Mandey socked him in the upper arm. "Why all the nosy questions?" she asked him. "Were you sent here on behalf of all these poor, love-starved young men who are pining away for me?"

Danny took the drink out of Mandey's hand and set it on the floor, and then he put his arm around her, pulled her to him, and kissed her. In a second, he was lying on top of her in the loveseat, kissing her neck. The alcohol gave it a dreamlike quality, as though it were happening in slow motion. For a moment Mandey responded, then she resisted.

"Danny!" she protested as he tried to give her a hickey on her neck. "Danny! Quit it!" She beat him on his back with her fists.

Although she struggled beneath him, she couldn't get him off her. A minute later he stopped and sat up of his own accord.

"Danny!" Mandey said, sitting up and straightening her rumpled outfit.

"Sorry," he said with an unrepentant grin. "I couldn't help myself. I'm drunk. I'm not responsible for my actions."

Mandey stared at him long and hard. He certainly didn't look sorry. If that had happened a couple of years earlier, she would have been ecstatic. She couldn't help it; she still found Danny attractive, but it wasn't Danny she wanted anymore.

"Well, I'm not so drunk that I'm not," Mandey said. She wasn't angry with Danny, but she was a little confused.

"You want to dance?" he asked her.

Mandey figured that was a good idea. "Okay."

They stood and merged with the crowd. They had to dance close, and Danny put his arms around her waist even though it was not a slow dance. Mandey was mystified by the way he was acting. It had to be the alcohol. He obviously had no idea what he was doing, and he would be mortified the next day, if he was able to remember what happened. From the looks of the rest of the crowd, they were so far gone that they wouldn't remember what they did, either, much less what anyone else did, so Danny had that in his favor. Most likely no one would recall seeing him groping Miss Goody-Two-Shoes.

Danny pulled her close and kissed her neck again. She pushed him away.

"Stop it, Danny!" she exclaimed.

"I'm sorry," Danny said, grabbing her and pulling her to him again. "I'll be good."

Suddenly Jesse and Angelina were standing next to them.

"Are you up to taking a ride?" Jesse asked them.

"Where are we going?" Danny asked.

"We thought we might pay the Devils a visit," Jesse said. "Mandey, did you drive?"

She shook her head. "No, I rode with Georgia. I'm in no condition to drive right now, anyway."

"You've been drinking?" Angelina asked her, as though this was an impossibility.

"A little," Mandey said.

"We'll go in my car, then," Jesse said.

"Are you sober enough to drive?" Danny asked him.

"Yeah. I purposely didn't drink much. I'm okay," he replied. "Terry's going, too. Have you seen anyone else?"

"Jeremy left," Danny said. "I haven't seen the Three Musketeers around lately, either."

"I know I saw Dina somewhere," Angelina said, glancing around. Mandey could tell by looking at her that Angie was further gone than she herself was.

"Well, we aren't searching for her. Let's get Terry and go," Jesse said.

"Let me tell Georgia I'm leaving," Mandey said.

She wove through the crowd to where Georgia and Kirby were continuing to get acquainted.

"Mandey, Kirby wants to go get breakfast. Do you want to go with us?" Georgia asked Mandey as she approached them.

"Um, I don't think so," Mandey said.

"Oh, come on," Georgia said. "I saw you sitting over there with Danny. Tell him to come, too."

Mandey blushed. She wondered how much Georgia saw, but didn't want to ask her right then. Georgia wasn't giving her a knowing smirk, so Mandey didn't think she'd seen much. "Well, I was coming to tell you that I'm going somewhere with him, Jesse, and Angelina."

"Where are you going?" Georgia asked.

"We're going to get something to eat."

"Well, we're going to Champ's. Why don't you meet us there?"

"I'll see if they want to," Mandey said. "Are you going to be okay?"

"Oh, yeah," Georgia said with a careless wave of her hand. "Go on. Charlene is coming with us. Have fun."

Charlene? Mandey thought, suddenly remembering that she was there at the party. She hadn't seen Charlene around when Danny was trying to get too familiar with her, so she hoped Charlene hadn't seen them, either.

She hurried outside and met the others outside the house. The air was chilly compared to the stuffy, jam-packed house, and her sweater was in Georgia's car.

"Brrrrr," she said, hugging herself.

Danny put his arm around her. "I'll keep you warm."

They piled into Jesse's car, with Angelina riding shotgun and Mandey wedged between Danny and Terry in back.

"What exactly do you have in mind?" Danny asked Jesse.

"I've got some spray paint in the trunk. I thought we might paint some graffiti in their territory. That will piss them off," Jesse said.

"Let's take a swing by my brother's place, too," Terry suggested.

"Will do," Jesse said.

Mandey laid her head against the back of the seat. Now that she was snug and warm between two bodies, she was getting sleepy again. She wished she were at home, in bed, with Shannon. That would be nice.

She opened her eyes when she felt a hand undoing one of her skirt's zippers.

"Danny!" she protested.

He grinned at her. "Nice skirt."

"Please stop."

He put his hand on her left knee. "Can I keep your legs warm?"

"I'll help," Terry offered, putting his hand on her right leg and rubbing it.

"You guys need to find yourselves girlfriends," Mandey told them.

"Nah," Terry said. "They're too much trouble. You ask one to start going steady, and suddenly, she's showing you pictures of wedding gowns and invitation designs. I ain't ready to settle down with one woman yet. I've got wild oats to sow."

"Yeah, well, make sure the fields you plow aren't too fertile," Jesse said, joking.

"Damn, ain't that the truth," Terry said. "I know I learned my lesson. This girl I was seeing told me she was pregnant and said that the baby was mine. Well, maybe it was and maybe it wasn't. I couldn't be sure, you know. Anyway, it turned out to be a false alarm, but ever since then, I don't go nowhere without a rubber. You can't trust women for shit."

Angelina turned around in her seat to look at Terry. "My, aren't you charming," she said, sarcastically.

"Hey, I'm just telling the truth," Terry said.

"Not all women are like that, Terry, just the way not all men are like you," Angelina said.

"What the hell do you mean by that?" Terry asked.

"Never mind," Angelina said, starting to face front again.

"No, I want to know," Terry insisted.

She turned around to face him once more. "I meant there are women who can be trusted, just like there are men who aren't afraid of having a relationship with a woman."

"I ain't afraid of having a relationship," Terry said. "I'd just rather not. Women are too treacherous."

"You just haven't found the right one yet," Mandey told him.

"I've found a few right ones," Terry said. "The ones who'll go out with me, go for a roll in the hay, and then go away."

Mandey blinked. "I agree with Angelina. My, aren't you charming."

"You're disgusting, Terry," Angelina said.

"You two don't have anything to worry about. I ain't about to ask either of you out," Terry said.

"Then why the hell is your hand slowly creeping up my thigh?" Mandey asked him.

Terry took his hand away. "Well, excuuuuse me."

He pulled a can of Skoal out of his shirt pocket. Mandey grimaced but kept quiet as he took a pinch of the stuff and put it in his mouth. She was glad she had nothing to worry about, as Terry had put it.

"What about you, Dan?" Mandey asked, turning to him.

"What about me?"

"Well, we just heard Terry's perspective of women, sex, and relationships. You were asking me a bunch of personal questions earlier. Now it's your turn."

"Women are the root of all evil," Danny said solemnly. "If I didn't learn anything else in Mr. Murphy's class, I learned that."

Mandey laughed, remembering their eighth-grade science teacher. He had told that to their class on more than one occasion. He had been going through a divorce at the time.

"So, you agree with Terry, that women aren't to be trusted?" Mandey asked him.

"I just haven't found the right one yet," Danny replied, grinning.

"What about Patty?" Mandey asked, teasing.

"Oh, God, don't even mention her," Danny begged, rolling his eyes. "You know what she's done now? She invited me to her house for Thanksgiving! She wants me to meet her parents! I swear, I don't encourage her, I barely even talk to her, but she thinks I like her!"

Mandey laughed. "I wasn't that bad," she said.

"'That bad'? You were nothing like her," Danny agreed. "You were sweet. She's psycho!"

"You weren't 'that bad'?" Angelina asked.

"In junior high," Mandey explained to Angelina and Jesse, who had gone to another junior high school, "I had a huge crush on Danny."

"No way!" Angelina said, turning around to look at them.

"Jeez, Angie, you act like it's impossible to imagine someone liking me," Danny complained.

"I did," Mandey said, "and it was hard being a thirteen-year-old girl who was desperately in love with a boy who hadn't even reached puberty yet."

"Hey!" Danny protested. "I resent that! I'll have you know I had my first wet dream when I was twelve."

"Ewwwww!" Angelina exclaimed, grimacing. Mandey burst into laughter.

"Thank you for that bit of information. I'm not sure I could have lived without knowing that," Mandey said, covering her eyes in embarrassment.

"Jesus Christ," Terry said, rolling his eyes.

"You're sick, Danny," Jesse told him, laughing.

29

The Devils' Party

By ten-thirty the Devils' soiree was in full swing. It had been intended to be a celebration of their jewelry store robbery and all the money they made from it, but even though the whole thing had been a failure, the party didn't reflect that. Checkmate had brought his boombox, which was blasting funky grooves from Majic 102 FM. The wiring of the apartment had been destroyed in the fire along with most of the rest of the building, so electricity was not an option. Instead, there were candles lit in all the rooms, giving the place the lighting ambiance of an expensive, romantic restaurant. That was the only thing the least bit refined about the party.

All the Devils were in attendance plus some invited guests. John had brought a couple girls who Shannon thought looked like he dragged in off a corner. Checkmate had invited his cousin, Charles, and Charles's girlfriend, Schae, both of whom lived over in Sharpstown. There were also three boys of fifteen or sixteen, all of whom lived within a few blocks of the apartments and went to school with Marco. There were a few other people floating around, as well, but Shannon wasn't sure who they were, or who had invited them.

He was watching the chaos going on around him from where he sat in a corner with his bottle of Jack, but he wasn't really seeing it. His mind, as usual, was occupied with one thing—Mandey. If he had any idea where that girl Jackie lived, he'd be on his way in a second. He had put in an appearance and done his duty here. But, since there was nowhere to go but back to the apartment, he stayed. He figured that Mandey was at a party, and he was at a party, so they were both partying, even if it wasn't together. He knew his reasoning made no sense, but it kept him from leaving just the same.

Marco came over and sat on the couch next to the chair where Shannon sat. He had a beer in hand and looked miserable.

"Why so glum, Marco? It's a party, not a funeral," Shannon asked dryly.

"Yeah, you look like you're having the time of your life," Marco retorted.

Shannon grinned in spite of himself. "There ain't nothing I'd rather be doing than sitting here, drinking myself blind, watching people making idiots of themselves. What about you?"

Marco shook his head.

"Who are the dudes you brought?" he asked Marco.

"Guys from school," Marco said. "It wasn't my idea. Raff's wanting to recruit more guys into the gang."

Shannon snorted. "Who died and made him King Shit?"

Marco ignored the comment. "He told me to get them to come or he'd beat my head in. It wasn't too hard. They were falling all over themselves, they were so excited. They think we're cool."

"Dumb asses," Shannon muttered.

"Marco! What are you doing?" one of the boys yelled from across the room.

"I'd better go over there," Marco said, slowly getting up.

About two minutes later Marco's place on the couch was taken by Kerri, who had a joint in one hand and a drink in a plastic cup in the other.

"This is some good shit. Here," she said, holding out the joint in a roach clip to him.

Wordlessly he took it from her and took a hit. She was right; it was some good shit. He handed it back to her.

"What do you think about those girls John brought?" Kerri asked him.

"Dogs," he replied.

"Really? I thought they were just your type," Kerri said. "They ain't working tonight, but I'm sure if you want to pay them, they won't mind, since that's the only thing that seems to get your dick stiff."

Shannon gave her a black look. "Shut the fuck up, Kerri."

"I swear to God that's all you know how to say. 'Shut the fuck up. Shut the fuck up.' You sound like a fucking parrot," Kerri said, deeply inhaling smoke from the joint.

Shannon put the bottle of Jack Daniels to his lips and took two long swallows. He had already made a good dent in it. He glanced over to where one of John's girls, a brunette, was sitting on another old sofa with Curtis. Her hand was in his pants and they were kissing. Shannon remembered making out with Mandey when she had put her hand on the hard crotch of his jeans.

"It's plain to see what you want," he heard Kerri say. "If you want a whore that bad, I'll swallow my pride and take money from you, seeing as that's the only way you can get excited."

He turned to look at Kerri again. "You don't have any idea what it takes to satisfy me. Not a clue," he told her.

"I could satisfy you better than any whore ever could, if you'd let me," Kerri said.

"They don't satisfy me. They're just a quick fix. And you, you just make me sick."

"Then you must be a fucking faggot," Kerri said angrily.

"Get out of my face and go find someone who wants your nasty pussy," Shannon said, losing his patience.

"You sorry mother-fucker!" Kerri shouted, and threw her drink in his face.

Shannon jumped to his feet. "Get the fuck away from me before I slap the shit out of you!" he roared.

Kerri stood up. "Fuck you!" she shouted back at him as she walked away.

Shannon sat down again, wiping his face on his sleeve. He was shaking a little. Kerri was out of sight, and it was a good thing. As much as he had been tempted to hit her, he was glad he didn't. He wished he hadn't even given her the satisfaction of seeing him get angry. It seemed that if Kerri couldn't get him to sleep with her, pissing him off was the next best thing.

It scared him a little, the violent way she could make him react. Sometimes he wanted to snatch her long blonde hair and slap her silly, and it was a feat of great self-restraint that he had never given in to that urge. He didn't want to be the kind of guy who beat on women. Well, he had hit Annette before, but she was his sister, so that was different. He wasn't proud of himself for hitting her, either, though.

He tilted his head back and took another swig of whiskey. It was going to be a long night.

"I hate Trick, that stupid son-of-a-bitch!" Kerri screamed when she found Annette in the next room, sitting on the floor with Checkmate, Charles, and Schae, passing around a bong.

"Aw, Kerri, why do you even bother?" Annette asked, reaching up and pulling her down by the arm.

"He said whores don't satisfy him and he said I don't know how. He probably likes it up the ass or something."

Annette slapped her.

"Ow! What'd you do that for?" Kerri whined, holding her cheek.

"My brother ain't no faggot. He don't want nothing to do with you because he's got a girlfriend."

"No shit?" Checkmate asked. "Why ain't he brung the woman around?"

"He's got a girlfriend?" Kerri repeated, stunned. "Are you sure?"

"Sure, I'm sure," Annette said. "He's gone all the time. When he is home, he shuts himself up in the bedroom with the phone and talks forever. Last weekend he brought home part of a birthday cake someone made for him. I saw a birthday card he got, too. I didn't see the inside, but the outside was all lovey-dovey."

"You ain't seen her?" Checkmate asked.

"Nah. He don't bring her around, not that I blame him. He ain't told nobody about it, either. I'm just going by what I've seen. Tonight we were talking about stuff and he kept talking about his 'friend.' I know he means 'girlfriend.'"

"Well, if he's got a girlfriend, why the hell ain't she here?" Kerri demanded.

"Jesus, Kerri, I don't know, and I don't care, either. She's probably too good for us or something."

Kerri sat there, seething, hating whoever this girl was who Trick was with now. She wondered what was so great about her. What Annette had said about the birthday cake and card went in one ear and out the other. It didn't occur to Kerri that things like that could mean more to Trick than sex.

One of the guys Marco had brought to the party was tall and skinny with a long, curly germ tail and a "La Mafia" T-shirt. He had invaded the sofa next to Shannon along with the other of John's two girls, this one a redhead.

"Dammit, can't you do that someplace else?" Shannon said.

In way of a reply, the girl's bra came flying and landed at Shannon's feet.

"Jesus," he muttered, picking up the bra and throwing it back at them.

He decided to get up and see what was going on elsewhere and maybe they would be finished by the time he got back.

In the first room he walked into, which was the bedroom closest to the living room, he found Checkmate's cousin and his girlfriend getting busy on a mattress on the floor, and some chick he didn't recognize at all was in a corner with Lenny, giving him head. A ragged old loveseat held Kerri and another of Marco's friends. It looked like she had taken Shannon's advice and found someone who wanted her. She saw Shannon looking at her and gave him the finger. Shannon turned around quickly and went down the hallway to the next bedroom. Sitting in a circle on the floor around a low coffee table playing quarters with a shot glass and a bottle of Wild Turkey were Checkmate, Annette, Raff, Juanita, John, Curt, and the dark-haired girl who had been making out with him.

"Yo, Trick, come join the game," Checkmate said.

Shannon shook his head. "I'm okay," he said, holding up his whiskey bottle. "I'll just watch."

"No, man, come on," Curt said, getting up and pushing Shannon over to the table. "You been sitting over there in that corner like a bump on a log. This is a party, dude. Start acting like it."

Reluctantly Shannon sat down and joined the game, but soon he became engrossed in it. He was good at bouncing the quarters into the shot glass, usually making at least one of his two shots. Twice he made both of his shots, and so he was allowed to make up two new rules for the game. The first one was that no one could use the words "drink," "drank," or "drunk." When he made the second double shot, he made up another rule that would be impossible for this group not to break—no cussing.

"No cussing!" John exclaimed as everyone groaned.

"We'd might as well drink up now and get it over with," Annette said.

"Hey, what did you say?" Shannon asked her.

"Shit," Annette said, and clapped her hand to her mouth.

Everyone laughed. Shannon took the bottle of Wild Turkey, which was getting low, and poured her a shot.

"Here's your first one," he said, sliding it over to her.

She picked it up, threw her head back, drank it down, and then pushed the glass back across the table at her brother for her second.

The game went on, but now it was much more difficult. Everyone, Shannon included, ended up having to down shots for breaking the rules. As people were getting drunker, fewer shots were being made, and more drinks were being taken for missing both shots than for being picked to drink by someone who had made a shot.

It was Raff's turn again, and this time he made both of his shots. Shannon knew he was going to be picked to drink; Raff had been singling him out throughout the entire game.

"First, I want to make a new rule," Raff said. "Instead of a shot, I want Trick to do something else."

With that, Raff placed a mirror, razor blade, a rolled-up dollar bill, and a small baggie of white powder on the table. "Do two lines," he told Shannon, pushing the paraphernalia toward him.

"Aw, man, why d'you want to go and have me do that?" Shannon complained drunkenly.

"It's time for something new. We're almost at the end of the bottle," Raff said.

"Man, I hate doing coke," Shannon said, looking down at the mirror.

"Will you quit fucking whining and play the game?" Raff shouted.

"Uh! You swore!" Shannon said, pointing at Raff. "Okay, I'll do two lines if you do two lines for cussing."

"Fine," Raff said, taking back the drug paraphernalia.

He poured the cocaine onto the mirror and cut it with the razor blade, and then separated it into four thin lines. He passed it back to Shannon with the rolled-up bill. "Go ahead."

Shannon took the dollar bill and placed it to his right nostril. He snorted one line into it, then switched and snorted the second line into his left.

"Satisfied?" he asked, pushing the mirror back to Raff.

"Yeah," Raff said, and he snorted the remaining two lines.

Shannon immediately felt the coke's effects. He nostrils and throat burned, his head and heart pounded, and his mouth was filled with the bitter aftertaste of the white powder.

Why the hell he had gone and done that, he didn't know. He had never liked doing cocaine and hadn't done it over three or four times. If it was something he could puke up, he would go vomit now, but he knew of no way to take back cocaine once it had been snorted. He had once blown his nose repeatedly, trying to blow it back out, but he had only succeeded in giving himself a nosebleed.

"Man, I've had enough. I quit," Shannon said, staggering to his feet.

The room spun around him, but somehow he managed to stay upright. He made his way back to the living room to his safe corner with his bottle of Jack still with him. The loud music felt like it was physically pressing in on him, and the candles all burned like little suns, with rainbows of color streaming from them.

Damn, that was a dumb thing to do, he cursed himself as he sat down.

Cocaine was not a drug that agreed with him. Pot put him in a good, mellow mood. Coke was the opposite. It usually gave him a quick rush, and then it made him hyper and touchy, in addition to the unpleasant physical effects.

He sat in the corner and waited for the rush to end. Mandey came to mind, but this was one time he tried to get her out of his thoughts. He didn't think she'd be very thrilled to see him in the state he was in right now. Sitting back in his chair with his eyes closed, he tried to relax.

"Hey, baby, what are you doing over here all by yourself?"

Shannon's eyes opened. The girl who had been playing quarters, and who was supposedly working for John, plopped down on his lap. He stared at her. She had long dark hair and big dark eyes, and was wearing a white tank top with a black net blouse over it, along with a black skirt that was so short that Shannon didn't know why she had even bothered wearing it. He thought she might be kind of pretty somewhere underneath the five layers of makeup she wore.

When Shannon didn't reply, the girl said, "I guess you ain't the talkative type." She put her arm around his neck. "It's a party, babe. You're supposed to socialize and have a good time."

She planted her lips upon his and kissed him hard, her tongue pushing its way into his mouth. Shannon sat there for a moment, dazed. He set his whiskey bottle down on the floor next to his chair and stood up, carrying the girl in his arms. She kissed his mouth, worked her way down to his neck, and then nibbled on his earlobe.

Shannon carried the girl into the room where he had seen couples fucking earlier. John was sitting on the dilapidated loveseat, watching Curt and the redhead doing it on the mattress where Charles and Schae had been.

"Here," Shannon said, dropping the brunette on top of John. "Take your two-bit whore."

"Son-of-a-bitch!" the girl screeched and kicked Shannon in the shin.

"Ow!" he yelped, reaching down to rub his leg.

"Hey!" John exclaimed, pushing the girl off and standing up. "Since when do you have anything against whores, Trick?" he asked, emphasizing Shannon's nickname.

Shannon stood up straight, grabbed John by the collar and shook him. "Just keep them out of my face," he said, and then pushed John away and walked off.

He decided he had had enough abuse for one night and limped back to his chair to get his whiskey bottle. It was gone. It was just as well, he supposed. He took his black satin jacket from where he had laid it over the chair, put it on, and was on his way toward the front door when Raff stepped in front of him.

"Where the hell are you going?" Raff asked.

"Home," Shannon said shortly, trying to step around Raff.

"What do you want to leave now for? They party's just beginning," Raff said.

"Raff, I'm tired and I've had enough. Get out of my way."

"No. No, man," Raff said, pushing Shannon back. "You're supposed to be our fucking leader, and now you're always running out on us. You ain't even around half the time no more."

"Where do you get off giving me orders?" Shannon demanded, irritated.

"Somebody around here needs to be giving orders, because you're doing a piss-poor job of it yourself."

Any other time Shannon would have blown him off, but tonight the cocaine made him belligerent. He drew back his fist and punched Raff squarely in the mouth. Raff fell back against the wall, his lips bloody.

"I'm the fucking leader of this outfit, you arrogant fuck!" Shannon shouted, grabbing the front of Raff's shirt with both hands and pulling him so close their noses were nearly touching. "Don't you ever fucking forget it!"

Then Shannon turned and threw Raff halfway across the room and onto the floor. As he walked away from the party, he heard Juanita yelling out the door, cursing him out in Spanish. He turned around and gave her the finger and then headed toward his apartment.

30

A Risk and a Warning

A light was on in the office at Owens Towing and Storage, and a blue wrecker was parked in front. The two Rottweilers ran to the fence and began barking ferociously as Jesse's car slowed up. They apparently were none the worse for wear for eating tainted meat night before.

A guy who looked like an older, heavier version of Terry wearing jeans, a Chevrolet T-shirt, and a baseball cap came out of the office. Terry rolled down his window as Jesse stopped in front of the gate.

"Jerry, it's me," Terry called.

Jerry and Terry, Mandey thought, amused.

"What are you doing?" Jerry asked, coming up to the gate. The dogs came up behind him, still barking.

"Everything going okay?" Terry asked him.

"So far so good. Ain't seen or heard nothin'—Starsky, Hutch, will you two shut up?" Jerry yelled at the dogs. "Here, go get it!"

He pulled some dog treats out of his pocket and tossed them across the parking lot. The dogs ran off to get them.

"We're cruising, checking things out," Terry said.

"Well, I doubt they'd come back tonight," Jerry said. "They usually leave us alone for a while after they hit us. But dang, this is getting old. We shouldn't have to spend the night here all the time. It's costing me big time, having to pay overtime when Pat or Jace stay, plus the business it's making me lose."

"We'll get it to stop, don't you worry," Terry said.

Jerry stooped to look in the car. "I don't know what y'all are doing, but I would advise you to be careful," he said.

"Don't worry," Terry said again. "We are."

"Are you still going to stay here next weekend?" Jerry asked. "Me n' Darla and the kids will be back from Killeen on Sunday."

"Yep, I'll be here," Terry said.

"Good deal."

"We're going to get going. I'll talk to you later," Terry said.

"Be careful," Jerry repeated.

The thumping beat of music could be heard out in the street as they approached the rear of the Northview Apartments.

"Sounds like they're having a party of their own," Jesse remarked as he parked his car.

"Is this such a good idea?" Mandey asked, nervous. "If they're here, do we want to risk them catching us?"

"Stay away from that end where they are. It looks like the windows are mostly boarded up. That music's so loud they won't have any idea we're even out here. They're probably so stoned they don't know their asses from a hole in the ground, anyway," Jesse said.

Still, the five of them were quiet getting out of the car. Jesse opened the trunk. In it was a box containing several cans of green, black, silver, and gold spray paint. Each of them grabbed a can or two and slipped through the broken wooden fence to the alleyway running behind Devil headquarters. The fence and back wall of the fire-ruined building were covered in Devil graffiti in red, black, and silver.

"They'll shit when they see this," Angelina said, spraying black paint to cover a spot where "Devils" was written in fat, blood red letters a foot high.

"Where'd Dan go?" Jesse asked, looking around.

"I'm right here," Danny said, coming through the fence.

They spread out over the wall, each taking a portion. Mandey began obliterating the graffiti from her section with silver paint. Her heart was beating rapidly. She tried to concentrate on the task at hand. She wrote "Alley Cats" in green letters over the silver patch she had made, then added an inverted v over each word and three lines on either side of the phrase to resemble the ears and whiskers of a cat. Then she borrowed the black paint from Terry and painted a cat face. She gave it big green eyes with gold pupils, and long silver fangs and whiskers.

The others were busy with their own artistic endeavors. No one noticed that Danny was no longer with them.

Danny had stayed behind at the car for a minute, long enough to take a hit of Ecstasy. He needed to take something to build up his nerve, and didn't want the others to know his bravado was artificially induced. The exhilarating rush of the drug not only gave him a shot of courage, but it totally distorted his judgment; Danny felt invincible. He thought it would be a good idea to leave the Alley Cats' mark on every building of this sad excuse for an apartment complex. The thought of running into one of the Devils didn't faze him in the least. He had a can of spray paint, and to him that was as good as having a can of mace. The prospect of meeting up with several members of the gang didn't even enter his mind.

He left the others painting on the back wall of the building where the party was going on and turned the corner. He walked along the alley in back of the next building, spraying green paint in swirls on the wall, the fence, the windows, and the ground. The X made it look psychedelic, like the green was fighting with the red and black graffiti, and the green was winning.

He finished decorating the back wall of that building and was walking back toward where the other Alley Cats were when he heard someone shout, "Hey!"

Almost on top of him was a tall, heavy-set guy with dark hair who was wearing a black satin jacket with a tiny red devil embroidered on the front. Apparently, he had come out of the party and spotted Danny between buildings.

Everything seemed in slow motion. They guy made a lunge for Danny, and Danny raised his arm to aim the paint can at the guy's face. The action, which took place in a second, seemed to take ten times as long to Danny. He pressed the button and watched the paint spray out. He could make out the tiny individual droplets as they journeyed out into the air.

The high may have magnified his senses, but it caused his aim to suffer. Instead of squirting the guy in the face, he hit him squarely in the chest.

"Mother fucker!" the guy swore, and grabbed the paint can out of Danny's hand. He threw it over Danny's head, and it went over the fence. Then he grabbed Danny by the collar with both hands and shook him.

"What the fuck are you doing?" he asked, slamming Danny against the wall.

Danny looked into the Devil's eyes. In the dim light from a security lamp on the building, he could see that they were hazel and bloodshot. He was messed up, drunk or stoned or both. The guy was also angry and bigger than Danny was. It wasn't a good combination.

"I—" Danny began.

"Shut up!" the guy said ferociously, slamming Danny against the wall again. "I don't like punks like you coming around here, sticking your nose where it don't belong."

He pulled Danny away from the wall, jerked him around, and took his wallet out of his back pocket.

"Give that back, you asshole!" Danny said, and pulled out of the guy's hold on him, trying to snatch at the wallet.

The guy grabbed Danny by the back of the neck and with one easy movement he smashed Danny's face against the wall.

"Shut the fuck up or you'll wish you had," the guy said, holding Danny against the bricks with one hand and putting the wallet in his shirt pocket with the other.

Danny regretted taking that hit of Ecstasy. The euphoric high was gone, but the drug still magnified and intensified his surroundings. The cold bricks were burning an imprint in his cheek, and he could taste their dusty grit. He was most aware of the pressure of the guy's hand on the back of his head. Danny remembered the part of the brain back there was the medulla oblongata, which controlled a lot of basic, involuntary functions such as respiration. He wondered if this guy could kill him by squeezing it until he quit breathing.

Christ, Danny thought. *I'm being mugged and I'm thinking about biology class.*

"Listen to me," the guy said in his ear. Danny could smell alcohol on his hot breath. He supposed the guy could smell the same on him. The guy jerked Danny around to face him again. Danny saw a long, thin silver knife blade in front of him, his face reflected minutely in it, distorted like a funhouse mirror.

"For your own good, stay out of our way," the guy told him. "Go back to your rich dopehead clients at Liaisons, or you're gonna get hurt bad."

The guy put the knife away, but grabbed Danny by the throat, and pressed him against the wall once more. Danny wanted to scream, but the guy was choking him. His lungs burned, his heart pounded, and he was convinced something inside him was about to explode. The guy punched him twice in the face, twice in the stomach, then there was a burst of pain in his groin, and the next thing he knew he was on the ground. His instinct was to get up and run, but his legs didn't listen to him, so he lay there, curled up in pain, relieved to be able to breathe again. Through his loud, gasping, greedy breaths he heard the guy talking to him.

"I know you got friends you're running with," the guy said. "You go back to them and let them know Trick did this. Tell them this ain't nothing compared to what's going to happen if they keep fucking around with us."

An object fell on the ground in front of Danny's face—his wallet, he realized, with all of the night's profits removed. He looked up, but the guy had already disappeared.

Danny picked up his wallet and struggled to his feet. Something warm dripped from his nose. He looked down at his fifty-dollar Polo shirt. It was covered in red blood and green paint. This time, he thought the red had won. Since the shirt was ruined anyway, he wiped his nose on his sleeve, leaving a long red streak on the blue fabric.

He was shuffling down the back alley when he saw Mandey and Terry running toward him.

"Holy shit!" Terry exclaimed. "What the fuck happened?"

"Guy jumped me," Danny croaked.

"Where is he, damn it? Where'd he go?" Terry demanded.

"I don't know," Danny said. "He jumped me, took my money, beat the hell out of me, pushed me down, and when I looked up, he was gone."

"Come on, let's get out of here," Mandey said anxiously.

"I want to find that mother fucker," Terry said, his blue eyes practically giving off sparks.

"Terry, we've got to get out of here!" Mandey insisted. "Do what you want. I'm taking Danny back to the car."

She put her arm around Danny and started back down the alley. Terry stayed behind, looking for clues as to where the guy might have gone, but he knew it was hopeless. He followed them back to the car.

When they got back to the car, Jesse and Angelina weren't there.

"I'll go find Jesse and Angie and tell them we found him," Terry said, and ran off.

Mandey helped Danny into the car and got in next to him.

"Oh, Danny," she said, dismayed, looking at his bruised and bloodied face. "We'll have Jesse stop at a convenience store for some napkins and water."

"My parents are gonna freak," Danny said unhappily. "What the hell am I gonna tell them?"

Mandey thought for a moment. "Say we went out for breakfast and you got jumped in the parking lot." She looked at his shirt. "I'm not sure how you're going to explain the green paint."

Danny sighed and closed his eyes.

Out the window Mandey saw the other three coming through the fence and running to the car.

"Someone saw us," Angie said breathlessly, as she dived into the front passenger seat and slammed the door behind her.

Jesse and Terry jumped in. Jesse was peeling out before Terry even had both feet in the car. Mandey looked out the rear window. No one else had come through the broken fence yet.

"Some guy came out of the party and saw us between buildings. He went back inside to tell someone, I think," Jesse said, looking in his rearview mirror. "Jesus, Danny, what happened?"

"One of the Devils mugged me," Danny said. "He said his name was Trick, and this was nothing compared to what they'll do if we keep coming around."

"Shit," Jesse said. "What did he look like?"

"He was tall, big, had dark hair," Danny said.

"I'll bet that's the same guy who knocked me out," Terry said.

"Danny, why the hell did you wander off? You could have gotten killed!" Jesse said.

"Jesse, lay off. You're not my father," Danny said, sighing.

"Man, if those drugs you deal make you do stupid shit like that, you won't have any customers left," Jesse said. "They'll go do stupid shit, too, and get themselves killed."

Danny didn't respond. He closed his eyes again with a pained expression on his face.

"Jesse, can you stop at a convenience store?" Mandey asked. "We need to get some water, ice, and napkins for Danny."

"Sure," Jesse replied.

A Stop-n-Go was on the corner at the next light, and Jesse pulled into the lot. He parked, but left the motor running.

"What do you need?" Angelina asked.

"A cup of ice, a cup of water, and a handful of napkins," Mandey said. "I don't have my purse with me, otherwise I'd give you some money for Band-Aids and some Bactine."

Jesse got his wallet out and handed Angelina a ten-dollar bill. He glanced at Danny in the rearview. "You owe me."

Danny didn't respond. Angelina got out of the car and went into the store.

"So now what?" Terry asked. "We've got to get that bastard. We've got to get all those bastards." He pounded his fist against the door.

"We will," Jesse said confidently. "We'll have a meeting Monday after school and we'll make some plans." The look of confident determination left his face as he glanced into the rearview mirror.

"A cop. Shit!" Jesse said. Two spaces away, a blue Houston Police cruiser pulled in.

"Danny, look alive. We don't want him to think you're passed out. Shit! He can't see your face like that! Mandey, kiss him, quick," Jesse said, frantic.

"What?" Mandey said.

"Kiss him. Don't stop until I tell you to."

Mandey hesitated a second, then Danny's hand was on the back of her head, pushing her face toward his. Their lips met, his arms went around her, and then she felt his hands making their way up her back, underneath her sweater.

"Christ, Danny, don't undress her!" Terry said.

"There's two of them," Jesse said. "Be cool."

Mandey wanted to see what was happening, but Danny wouldn't let her pull away. In her peripheral vision, she saw two blue-clad police officers walking in front of the car on their way into the store.

"Evening," she heard Jesse say, and saw him give a short wave of greeting toward the officers.

"Okay, they've gone inside," Jesse said.

Suddenly Danny's hands were up to her bra, trying to unhook it.

"For God's sake, Danny, the cops are gonna bust you two for indecent exposure!" Terry exclaimed.

Mandey jerked away from Danny. He grinned at her. "Mouth-to-mouth resuscitation. I feel much better now," he said.

"God, you're a lech!" Mandey said, slapping Danny on the leg.

"Here comes Angie," Jesse said.

Angelina got in the car and passed the water, ice, napkins, and a plastic bag with Bactine and Band-Aids to Mandey.

"Man, those cops were looking at me funny," Angelina said. "Do I look wasted or something?"

"I don't know, but we're getting out of here," Jesse said, putting the car into reverse.

Mandey dipped a napkin into the cup of water and began dabbing at Danny's cut face.

"I've always had fantasies about women playing nurse with me," Danny told her, grinning again.

"You'd better watch out, or I'll give you a cold shower," Mandey said, showing him the cup of water threateningly.

She cleaned the blood from his face as best as she could with the water, then sprayed Bactine on his scrapes and cuts, making him wince. She dried his face and put Band-Aids on cuts, one over his left eye and one on his chin.

"You know, he kneed me in the groin, too. Maybe you ought to check that to make sure it's okay," Danny suggested.

"You've had the crap beaten out of you and you're still horny! Good God!" Angelina exclaimed. "I wouldn't make any more fuss over him if I were you, Mandey."

"Did that beating make you horny, Danny? You pervert," Jesse said, teasing.

"You didn't know I was into that?" Danny asked innocently. "I bet you didn't know Mandey's into whips and chains, either. At least, that's what I've heard."

Mandey blushed. She hadn't been aware that Danny knew about that joke. Her friends teased her that because she seemed so sweet and innocent, she had to be very kinky in the bedroom.

"What?" Angelina asked, her eyes wide. Jesse was laughing.

"Jesus, that's sick," Terry said. He was taking the remark as seriously as Angelina. "Ain't no woman going to use a whip on me. Not unless she wants to wind up in the hospital."

"It's true," Danny said. "She's got this leather bustier she wears, and has this long black whip, and she handcuffs men to her bedposts and flogs them until they get a hard-on, and then—"

"Stop it, Danny!" Mandey said, horrified, hiding her face in her hands. She didn't want him to see her laughing.

"Danny, you're such a liar," Angelina said, disgusted.

"You're sick, man," Terry said. Jesse was still laughing.

"Here," Mandey said, shoving the remaining napkins at Danny.

"Aww," Danny said, ruffling her hair with his hand. "You know I love you."

It was around two-thirty when Jesse dropped her off. Marcia was home, but the house was dark. Mandey got the house key out of the pocket in her skirt and let herself in. She quickly got ready for bed. She felt wiped out, both physically and emotionally, and once she got under the covers, she was asleep within minutes.

A disturbing thought woke her up abruptly about an hour later.

What was I thinking letting Danny bring me drinks? He could have spiked them, especially with the way he was acting.

Normally she wouldn't have worried about Danny doing such a thing, but tonight was the first time she had ever seen him messed up, and she had no way of knowing what he could have done in that state. She had some very limited experience with alcohol, but enough to know how it made her feel. She didn't feel anything out of the ordinary, so she was fairly sure he hadn't given her anything but rum. Still, she had taken a huge risk, and it was one she didn't intend to take again.

I make a really lousy bad girl was her last thought before going back to sleep.

31

Regret

Shannon lay in bed, unconsciously chewing his thumbnail. The clock on his nightstand read 2:15 A.M. He wondered if Mandey was home yet. He wanted to call her, but decided against it. She was probably at home and fast asleep in her bed. Although she would never show it, Shannon didn't think Mandey would appreciate being awakened by the phone in the wee hours of the morning just because he wanted to talk. The phone ringing in the middle of the night might scare her, too.

Besides, he was in bad shape. His heart was racing, his head throbbed, and everything in his sight had a wavery appearance, like he was underwater. It was difficult to think straight, much less talk straight. Mandey would know he was wasted the second he started talking.

How stupid was he, anyway, to snort coke on demand from Raff? There was no telling what he could have cut that coke with—rat poison, maybe.

As bad as he felt, he knew from experience that he would feel even worse in the morning. However, the physical effects of the substances he had ingested weren't the worst of it. Shannon was angry with himself for what he had done to that punk, Danny. Taking his money was no big deal; the guy was a dope dealer, and stealing drug money didn't count, as far as Shannon was concerned. What bothered him was what he had done to Danny and how he had done it because it was the same way Leon liked to beat on people.

To make matters even worse, while he was mugging Danny, Shannon had seen something in his wallet that disturbed him—a Rogers High School ID card. Danny Sanchez went to the same high school as Mandey, and if he did, it was more than likely that some of those other Alley Cats did, too.

He wondered if Mandey knew Danny, and if so, how well. He figured that even if they didn't go to the same school, she would still likely be acquainted with him. She had gone to Liaisons frequently, from what she had told Shannon, and all the regulars probably knew who Danny was, even if they didn't utilize his services. Shannon himself hadn't set foot inside the club in well over a year, but he knew who Danny was because he was Raff's competition.

He turned over on his side and faced the clock. The red numbers blurred and swam before his eyes, so he closed them. The face of John's dark-haired slut came into his mind. Shannon was ashamed of himself, because for a moment he had been tempted by her, and it made him sick. A month had gone by since the last time he had sex, and was he already that desperate, that he would want to cheat on the girl who was the best thing that ever happened to him?

Shannon shook his head violently, trying to dispel the thought. Even with his eyes shut, the action made him feel dizzy and a little sick to his stomach. He smothered his face in his pillow and moaned.

He wanted to go to sleep and forget that this whole night had ever happened. If he had it to do over again, he would have blown off the Devils and gone with Mandey to Jackie's party, and he wouldn't have gotten so drunk or done those stupid lines like some peer-pressured dork.

It was a long time, after four, before Shannon finally slept, but his sleep was broken and full of nightmares. He dreamed of Leon beating up his mother, something he had seen too many times to count during the last ten years. Then suddenly it was Shannon that was doing the beating, and it wasn't his mother cowering and crying, it was Mandey, and he was shaking her and hitting her and she was begging him to stop, but he wouldn't listen. Her eyes were black and her nose was bloody, and he kept hitting her and punching her and choking her, over and over. . .

32

Double Date

Shannon showed up at Mandey's house the next day at 1:30. He would have been there much earlier, but he hadn't fallen asleep until 4 A.M., and then he woke up with a severe hangover. He had taken a long shower and had downed most of a pot of coffee along with four Tylenol to try to come alive. He was feeling about 75 percent himself again as he drove to her house, but he still had a slight headache, and he couldn't hide the dark circles under his eyes. Mandey did not comment on it. She looked a little worn out from her Saturday night, too.

Now he was sitting on her bed, watching Mandey rummage through her closet as she searched for a particular item of clothing.

"Where is that skirt?" she asked herself aloud, and with a frustrated growl began pulling hangers off the rack, tossing blouses, skirts, dresses, pants, and sweaters onto the bed next to Shannon.

"Girl, you've got way too many clothes. No wonder you can't find anything," Shannon said, teasing.

"A girl can never have too many clothes. It's more a matter of not enough closet space," she said pawing through the clothes that remained hanging. Then she stopped and put her hands on her hips. "I would have sworn that skirt was in here. Maybe I put it in the guest room closet."

She left to search through the part of her wardrobe that she kept in the next room. While she was gone, Shannon casually looked through the stack of clothes she had thrown on the bed. He liked all of her outfits, but the sheer number she had was a little overwhelming.

His attention was caught by a clear plastic garment bag. Inside was a beaded emerald green dress. He stared intently at it, wondering why it seemed familiar to him. He knew

Mandey had never worn it when they had gone out.

A smaller bag was attached to the larger one. It contained some type of hat, made from the same material as the dress.

Then it hit him.

While he was trying to steal that Toyota at Liaisons before Halloween, Annette had fought with a girl in the parking lot who had been wearing an outfit like this one. The Toyota had been parked next to. . .a blue Ford van. It wasn't the driver of the car Annette had fought with; it was Mandey.

The realization brought out goose bumps all over his body. "Jesus," he muttered aloud.

Part of him tried to deny it. After all, she had never mentioned that anyone had attacked her. That struck him as strange, that she had never said anything about it, even if it had happened before they met down in Galveston. Obviously, she hadn't recognized Annette under her ski mask or he would have heard about it.

Things were going from bad to worse. He had been worried enough by the fact that the guy he had beaten up last night, Danny Sanchez, went to the same high school as Mandey did. Now he found out that he had hurt Mandey, too, without knowing it. This was not good at all.

Mandey came back into the bedroom holding up a colorful long paisley skirt.

"I found it," she announced, then asked, "Is something wrong?"

Shannon gave his head a quick shake. "Uh, no," he replied. "I was looking at your clothes. That green dress there is nice."

Mandey glanced at the outfit. "Oh, my flapper dress. It was a Halloween costume."

"Oh, yeah?" Shannon said, feeling the slight bit of hope he had remaining evaporate.

"Yeah. It's nice enough to wear for a special occasion, though," she said, and didn't offer any further information. She began hanging up the clothes in the closet again.

"Uh, did you go to a Halloween party or something?" Shannon asked casually. He wasn't asking because he needed the information; he already knew it was Mandey that Annette had been fighting with. He just wanted to see if she would tell him about it and what she would say about the experience.

"I went to Liaisons with James. It was kind of a lousy night."

Why did I have to go and mention Halloween? she thought. She hadn't told Shannon about what had happened that night because of how it led to her involvement with the Alley Cats, and that was the last thing she wanted him to know about. But she supposed it wouldn't hurt to tell him about it. She wasn't going to say anything about the Alley Cats, though. Shannon was trying to walk the straight and narrow; he didn't need to be involved in anything that could get him into trouble.

"I had a run-in with a couple of thugs that night," Mandey continued. "They were trying to steal the car parked next to mine. They would have gotten away with it, too, except James forgot his wallet in the van, and I went back to go get it. As I got closer to the van, I could see someone lurking around. I guess there was a guy inside the car, trying to hotwire it, and this girl in a ski mask was standing outside keeping watch, and she spotted me. I wanted to run away, but I was wearing high heels, and she was nearly on top of me. I started screaming at the top of my lungs, and she and I got into it. I was scared, but I was mad, too. I wanted to knock her head off. I had to settle for giving her a bloody nose." Mandey grinned at that. Shannon was a little unsettled by how pleased she looked with herself.

"Anyway, people heard me screaming and came running, and the girl and her partner took off. I talked to the police on the phone, but no one even came out to the scene. I haven't heard anything more about it, so nothing's come of it, I guess, not that that surprises me."

Mandey looked at Shannon. He said nothing, and his face wasn't telling her anything, either. Then he stood up, walked over to her, and took her in his arms.

"I would die if anything ever happened to you," he said, holding her tightly. "Why didn't you tell me about this before?"

Mandey put her arms around him and embraced him just as tightly. She felt so safe in his arms, held against his strong, solid body.

"I guess I didn't want you to worry about me," she said.

They kissed, then Mandey said, "Let me change clothes and we can take off."

He let her go, and she took her skirt and sweater into the bathroom to change. Shannon sat down on the bed again. He felt bad about what he and Annette had done to Mandey that night. Another part of him was relieved that Mandey seemed to have withstood the experience so well. Still another part was stunned by just how well she had withstood it. Mandey—sweet, gentle, quiet Mandey—had broken his sister's nose. Once he absorbed this fact, he found he was okay with it. Annette deserved it, and he deserved one himself, for what they had tried to do. But that fact aside, Shannon realized he liked seeing that Mandey had a tough streak inside her. He was finding out that Mandey had as many sides to her personality as she had styles of dressing.

When she came out of the bathroom, however, the way she was dressed did not belie the tough side she had revealed to him. She was wearing the paisley skirt along with a soft lilac purple sweater with elbow-length sleeves and a low round neckline. She looked soft and sweet, and Shannon had a flash of desire to lay her down on her bed and wallow in her softness and sweetness. But if they didn't get on their way, they would be late.

They were meeting Andrea and Martin for a movie and dinner afterward. As they drove to Greenspoint Mall in Shannon's car, they listened to the Oilers game on the radio. They were playing against the Jets in the Astrodome that day, but the game did not sell out, so it could not be televised in Houston. It was late in the fourth quarter, and the Oilers were ahead, 31-20. That was the score as the game ended.

"Yeah, buddy!" Shannon shouted happily. "Two in a row!"

"Too bad it's only the second game they've won this season," Mandey said.

"They're turning around," Shannon said defensively. "I bet they'll beat Cleveland next week."

The mall parking lot was deserted except for near the theater entrance. Texas blue laws dictated that the malls be closed on Sundays. Only the movie theater and a few of the mall restaurants were open.

Hand-in-hand they walked through the parking lot. Mandey squeezed Shannon's hand, hugged his arm, and smiled up at him. Shannon looked down at this lovely girl who was gazing up at him so adoringly. He could see down the front of her sweater a little bit, too, which was a nice view. It was almost unreal that the night before he was with his gang, drinking Jack Daniels, snorting coke, and beating up people, and today he was with his honor student girlfriend on a double date with a total preppie couple.

Andrea and Martin were waiting inside the mall entrance. The couples greeted each other and went to stand in line for tickets, having previously decided to see *Give My Regards to Broad Street*.

"How was Jackie's party?" Andrea asked Mandey.

"It was okay," Mandey said. "It would have been more fun if Shannon had been there."

"You didn't go?" Mart asked Shannon.

"I had to work," Shannon said. "Didn't you and Andrea go?"

"No," Mart said. "We weren't invited."

"Jackie doesn't like me," Andrea said. "But that's okay, because I don't like her, either."

"You didn't miss much," Mandey said. "It was a bunch of people dancing and getting drunk."

"Did you dance and get drunk?" Andrea asked, smiling.

"No," Mandey said. "I danced and got slightly tipsy."

"Shame," Mart said, teasing.

"You were drinking last night?" Shannon asked Mandey, surprised.

"A little," Mandey said. "I had a couple rum and Cokes."

Going solo to Jackie's party hadn't been much fun, but in the end, she was glad Shannon hadn't been there. He was better off not knowing about the Alley Cats or the Devils. She pushed that out of her mind. She didn't want to think about gangs, or graffiti, or Danny getting mugged, or Danny kissing her. Shannon was with her today, and all was right with the world.

They bought their tickets, then proceeded over to the line for the concession stand. Shannon and Mandey each got a drink and shared a medium popcorn during the movie, which was enjoyable, and when it was over the four of them walked to the other end of the mostly-closed mall to Dalt's to have dinner.

They sat in a booth by a window and ordered fried cheese for an appetizer and each had one of the various kinds of burgers on the menu.

"We should all come here for brunch sometime," Andrea said. "They've got the best Belgian waffles."

"They're huge and they cover them with strawberries," Mart said.

"I love brunch," Mandey said dreamily.

"What are you doing for Thanksgiving?" Andrea asked Mandey.

"We're having dinner at my house," Mandey said. "At least, I think that's the plan, isn't it, Shannon?"

"Well, we're definitely not having it at mine," Shannon said.

"It will be Marcia, Michael, Shannon, and me," Mandey said.

"Your parents aren't coming down?"

"No," Mandey said, sounding disappointed. "They're not coming for Christmas, either. They wanted me to come up there for Christmas, but I didn't want to miss Christmas with Shannon." She slipped her hand under the table to take his hand in hers. "I don't think I'll be seeing my parents until graduation."

"Your day sounds pretty low-key. We're doing two dinners," Andrea said. "Mart's family is having dinner at one and we're having dinner at six. There's going to be a houseful of relatives at both places."

"My house is always chaos at holiday time," Mart said. "My two older sisters each have three kids, so it's screaming brats and crying babies all day long. I just go to my room, shut the door, and play with my computer."

"You've got a computer?" Shannon asked, impressed.

"Yep. A Commodore 64," Mart said proudly.

"He's got some cool games on it," Andrea said.

"I've never used a computer before," Shannon said.

"I'm scared of them," Mandey said.

"Why?" Mart asked. "They don't bite. They can crash, but they don't bite."

"When I took Algebra II my freshman year, Mrs. Royal gave us a book about Basic, told us to read it, took us to use the computers in the library a few times, and expected us to be able to write whole programs. It was my first experience using a computer. There are only five computers, so we had to work in groups of three or four. I think I only touched it once."

"That sucks," Martin said. "But you shouldn't be afraid. They're fun. You're not afraid of video games, are you?"

"No," Mandey admitted.

"Well, think of a computer like you think of video games."

"He has this one game that's a parody of *Star Trek* that's a riot," Andrea said.

"'Dammit, Jim.'"

"But it gets worse than that," Mart said, grinning. "Computers are good for more than games, though. They're the wave of the future. You'd better quit being scared of them, because they're going to be everywhere."

On the way back to Mandey's house, Shannon asked her, "Do they have computer classes at North Harris?"

"I don't know," Mandey said. "Why?"

"Well, if Martin's right, it sounds like knowing how to use a computer is going to be a good thing to know."

"I didn't know you were interested in computers," Mandey said.

Shannon shrugged. "I don't know if I am or not. I hadn't thought about it much 'til Mart brought it up. Phil used to have a friend who had a computer, and he said they'd play games on it. He used to talk about getting a computer of his own, but I don't know if he ever did. I ought to call him."

"I hope they do have computer classes," Mandey said. "Then you can teach me."

Shannon chuckled dryly. "Yeah, right."

"I'm serious," Mandey said.

"Okay," Shannon said, "but I can't imagine teaching you anything."

"Why not?" Mandey asked. "You taught me how to throw a bowling ball and how to play pool. I'm sure there's a lot of stuff you could teach me."

"But not much of it is worth learning," Shannon said.

"Stop it," Mandey said. "Have a little faith in yourself. I do."

He chuckled again and patted Mandey on the leg. Coyly, Mandey pulled her skirt up above her knees. Shannon glanced down. Mandey had nice legs, and he squeezed her left leg just above the knee. He thought of the day he had gone with Kerri to the jewelry store, and how she, too, had hitched up her skirt for him in an obvious attempt to arouse him. Mandey's gesture was just as obvious, but yet totally different. He looked at Mandey, who returned it with a knowing look of her own and a grin. Then she laughed out loud.

That was one of the sexiest things about her. She had such a sense of humor and didn't take everything too seriously. He tried to think of a time when he had seen Kerri laughing. All he could remember were times when she was laughing at somebody.

"I want to see some more of that when we get back to your house," Shannon said, challenging Mandey.

She grinned wider. "If you're a good boy, who knows what you might see?"

Back in her bedroom, they turned on the stereo and laid down on her bed. Shannon's torso was bare; Mandey's skirt was hiked up high around her thighs. She had no stockings on; underneath was a pair of pale purple panties. They kissed passionately with their bodies pressed together and their legs entwined.

This is better than I ever dreamed, Mandey thought. *I'm going to make love to him one of these days. He's the one who's going to take my virginity.*

"Oh, Mandey," Shannon gasped, suddenly pulling away. He was getting overheated.

He knows I'm not ready, she thought. *Maybe he's not ready, either. It's only been two weeks.*

They settled down and held each other quietly. Mandey kissed the base of his throat. Shannon's arms tightened around her and he kissed the top of her head.

"I could stay this way all night," Mandey said.

"Me, too," Shannon replied.

"I had fun today," Mandey said. "I hope it wasn't too hard for you to keep from smoking around Andrea."

"Nah," he said. "Like I told you--" he paused, snapped his fingers, and made a hand gesture "--I'm trying to cut down."

Mandey laughed. "Did you used to watch that show, too?" she asked.

"Yeah," Shannon admitted. "Me and my sister, every week."

"I had such a crush on Brett Hudson," Mandey said. "I used to imagine he was my boyfriend, although he was like, 21, and I was seven."

Shannon chuckled. "You know who I had a crush on when I was a kid?"

"Farrah Fawcett," Mandey replied promptly.

"No," Shannon said.

"Who?"

"Marie Osmond."

"Marie Osmond?" Mandey asked, laughing.

"What's so funny about Marie Osmond?" Shannon asked indignantly.

"Nothing. She just so very…sweet."

"I kind of like sweet. That's why I like you."

Mandey smiled and kissed his chin. "Well, you can be kind of sweet yourself."

Shannon snorted. "Sweet, my ass."

Mandey laughed. "You are, and don't try to deny it. I promise I won't tell anyone," she said. Her hand slid down to the seat of his jeans. "And you're right—you do have a sweet ass."

Shannon looked at her, eyes agog. "I can't believe you said that!"

"Maybe I'm not as sweet as you think I am," Mandey said saucily.

"You're sweet enough for me," Shannon said, "and I like this other part of you I'm getting to know."

"I'm enjoying getting to know you, too," Mandey said. "For so long you were my quiet, MIA mystery man in plaid flannel shirts. Now when I wake up each morning, I remember that you really are a part of my life, and I practically bounce through my day."

"Wow," Shannon said. "I never knew I could have that kind of an effect on anyone."

"You do," Mandey said, smiling up at him. "I've never been so happy in my entire life as I have been the last two weeks."

When Shannon left for home around nine-thirty, he felt like Superman. He couldn't believe how Mandey felt about him, and he thought he loved her even more, if that was possible. He agreed whole-heartedly with Mandey—he had never been so happy in his life as he had been since he met her that day at the beach. He was already convinced that she was the only person he wanted to be with for the rest of his life.

It had been hard for him to pull away from her when they were making out. He had been getting so damned excited, but it wasn't right yet. There were parts of his life he wasn't being honest about. He hadn't even told her exactly where he lived yet, because he didn't want her showing up there one day and running into any of the Devils. He would never be as close to Mandey as he wanted to be until he was straight with her about everything.

Depression slowly oozed through him like a leaking septic tank. He was on his way back to his other life. Every time he was with Mandey made it that much harder to go back there. More than anything else, he wanted it all to go away. He had to make it all go away, or he would never have what he wanted more than anything—a life with Mandey.

33

Project Partners

What had happened to Danny's face was the topic of the day at school on Monday. When Mandey stopped by Georgia's locker between second and third period, the first thing Georgia asked her was if she had seen Danny yet.

"No," Mandey said. "Does he look terrible?"

"Girl, I almost didn't recognize him when he came into Latin class," Georgia said. "He said y'all were leaving Denny's and some guy tried to grab your purse and they got in a fight."

So that's the story he's telling, Mandey thought. *I'm glad somebody told me.*

"Yeah," she agreed quickly. "I'm surprised he even came to school today."

"Mandey, you didn't take your purse to the party, unless you went home and got it after," Georgia said, closing her locker.

Georgia could be pretty sharp sometimes. Leave it to her to be sharp at the wrong time.

"Um, well," Mandey said, lowering her voice to a level of confidentiality, "you know Danny. He wanted it to sound better. It sounds better to say he saved me than to admit that he got stomped on and his wallet stolen. But you didn't hear that from me."

"My God, I heard about what happened to you after you left Saturday night! Danny looks like a Mack truck hit him! Are you okay?" Jackie greeted Mandey as she walked into English class.

"What happened?" Gayla asked.

"I'm okay. I think I should let Danny tell you about it. It's really his story," Mandey said.

"There's been a lot of crap like that going on lately, hasn't there?" asked Thad Hurley. "That's the second time in three weeks somebody's jumped you, isn't it? And Danny's third?"

"Something like that," Mandey said.

"Danny said some big ugly guy grabbed you and tried to pull you into a car," Jackie said.

I thought it was a purse snatching, Mandey thought.

"To be honest, the whole thing's a blur in my mind," Mandey said.

"My family's going to Monterrey over Thanksgiving. Want me to bring you back a Mexican switchblade so you can defend yourself?" Trish asked, joking.

More questions were coming, but the tardy bell rang, and Mr. Crenshaw came in to begin class. Mandey was relieved to be left alone. She wondered exactly what Danny was telling everyone.

Danny was in Mrs. Silverman's classroom already when Mandey arrived for fourth period. He had a crowd around him, but she could see his black eye, swollen mouth, and cut and bruised face. He was too busy recounting his version of early Sunday morning to notice Mandey's inquiring glance.

Halfway through class, Mrs. Silverman brought up a dreaded subject, as she had promised last week—research papers or projects, to be due a week before the end of the semester, after Christmas vacation. She handed out a list of suggested topics.

"You may use one of these topics or choose one of your own, but if you choose your own, it will need my approval. You may write research papers individually, or you may work individually or in groups no larger than four to do a project. If you do a group project, I want to know exactly what contribution each person in the group made. I don't want one or two people doing all the work and the others in the group taking credit they don't deserve. I'm going to give you the rest of the period to look over the list of topics and get into project groups if that's what you want to do. By the end of class, I want everyone to hand in a sheet of paper telling me your topic, whether you plan a project or a paper, who you'll be working with if you're in a project group, and a thesis statement."

There was a smattering of moans and protests, and several people raised their hands to ask questions. People began moving about the room, forming project groups. Mandey looked over at James. He had a piece of paper in front of him on which he had written "Research paper—thesis." A month ago, they would have been project partners. She looked back at Charlie, Gayla, and Trish, who beckoned her to come back and join them. She started to get up, but then Danny sat down in the desk behind her.

"You want to be my partner?" he asked her.

Although she and Danny had become closer due to their involvement with the Alley Cats, and despite what had happened to them over the weekend, Mandey was stunned. She glanced over at Jackie, Thad, and Mark, who were puzzled because they had expected Danny to join their group.

"Um, sure," Mandey said, sitting down again.

They moved their desks together. "So, what are we doing for our project?" Danny asked her.

"Oh, I see, you ask me to be your partner and then expect me to make the decisions and do all the work and put your name on half of it," Mandey said, teasing.

"Nice to know you think so highly of me," Danny said sourly.

"I'm kidding. Actually, I'm more concerned about what you're telling people happened the other night."

"Why?" Danny asked.

"I don't care what you tell them, but I just want to know exactly what you're saying. I've been hearing different stories, and I need to know what I'm supposed to be telling people. I don't want to sound like I'm trying to make you out to be a liar."

"Well, you know how stories get exaggerated," Danny said. "If anyone asks, tell them some guy tried to snatch your purse, and he and I got into a fight. And I saved your purse."

"Okay. I just wanted us to have our story straight," Mandey said. "You look terrible. Does it hurt a lot?"

"Not much, but I've got some help," Danny said nonchalantly, opening a notebook. Mandey took that to mean he had taken something for the pain, which might or might not be legal.

"Did your parents freak out?"

"Mom did. She wanted me to go to the emergency room, but I didn't want to. They might run tests on me that might—well, you know," Danny said. "Once she realized I wasn't about to die, she ragged on me all day yesterday about how my choice of friends is leading me to trouble, and I'm going to end up like Tío Alberto."

"What happened to Tío Alberto?"

"He's rotting in a Mexican prison."

"Nice prospect."

"My dad said he was proud of me for defending you. Of course, that made me feel like shit," Danny said.

"I'm glad you're okay. I didn't expect to see you here today. I was going to call you yesterday to see how you were, but I got sidetracked," Mandey said.

"I see. I got half-beaten to a pulp and you were too busy playing kissy-face with your boyfriend to care," Danny said.

The remark unsettled Mandey a bit, because she wasn't sure Danny had made it solely in jest. She waved her list of topics at him and changed the subject.

"You tell me, what looks good to you?" she asked him.

"None of them," Danny said promptly. He looked at his own list and rattled off some of the suggestions. "'The Evolution of the Platform of the Democratic Party.' 'The Women's Suffrage Movement.' 'Pros and Cons of the System of Checks and Balances.' Old, tired stuff." He raised his hand and began talking to Mrs. Silverman before she addressed him. "Why do we have to do this, anyway? None of the other classes are doing projects."

"It's because you're such special students, Danny," Mrs. Silverman replied sweetly. "You're so wonderful, I wanted you to show off how smart and talented you all are."

"Meaning, we're the only advanced class, so we have to do this while the regular classes don't," Danny said.

"Exactly," Mrs. Silverman said.

"Is it too late to transfer into another class?"

"Much too late for that," Mrs. Silverman replied.

Danny sighed, then asked Mandey, "What do you want to do?"

"I don't know," she said. "Give me a few minutes to think."

She wracked her brain while Danny flipped through his textbook. When she had six possible topics scribbled down, she looked them over and saw one that stood out.

"How about McCarthyism?" she asked Danny.

"You mean that guy in the Beatles?" Danny asked with a grin.

"No, Danny."

"No, I know who you mean. That senator in the Fifties who was afraid of the Commies."

"What do you think? That could be interesting."

"Yeah," Danny said thoughtfully. "That could make a good project. That was when they started blacklisting a bunch of Hollywood people and stuff, right? Maybe we could do a video presentation of clips of people who were blacklisted."

"Yeah! That would be cool!" Mandey agreed enthusiastically. "Let's hope Mrs. Silverman will approve the topic."

"And what would that be?" Mrs. Silverman asked, stopping by Mandey and Danny's desks.

"Joseph McCarthy and the House Un-American Activities Committee," Mandey said. "A biography of the senator, his views on Communism, how his attitudes were able to infect the government."

"Yeah, and we might make a montage of film clips of people who were blacklisted," Danny added.

"Oh, a multimedia project," Mrs. Silverman said. "That sounds like a topic you could delve into and make into an interesting presentation. I don't think I'll have any problems approving it. Now, Danny, make sure you don't let Mandey do all the work."

"Jeez!" Danny exclaimed, rolling his eyes. "Everyone's against me!"

"This is going to be a lot of work, but I think it will be worth it," Mandey said. "Let's figure out what we have to do and when we're going to find time to get together to do it."

Danny smirked at her.

"Oh, get your mind out of the gutter," Mandey said, rolling her eyes.

They agreed to meet after school at the school library, which stayed open until four-thirty, to start doing research. Another afternoon they would go to the public library next door to work. They also decided to meet at Mandey's house on Friday to screen videos to get clips for their presentation.

"This is going to be cool," Danny said as the bell rang. "See you later." He got up and joined Thad, Jackie, Mark, and some others on the way to the cafeteria.

"Danny hijacked you from us!" Charlie exclaimed as Mandey joined him and Gayla on the way to lunch.

"Yeah, what's up with that?" Gayla asked.

"I don't know," Mandey said.

"You're getting kind of friendly with him, aren't you?" Charlie asked. "You went out together after the party Saturday night, and now you're doing your project with him."

"We didn't go out together," Mandey said. "A bunch of us went to get something to eat. He just happened to be one of them."

"Yeah, sure," Charlie said, leering at her. "Mandey's got a man, plus a man on the side."

"I do not, Charlie!" Mandey said. "You'd better not go around saying stuff like that." Danny would be mortified. Shannon would be none too happy if it ever got back to him, as well.

"Whatever," Charlie said. "Have it your way." Then that evil leer spread across his face again. "With two, I'm sure you do."

He ran into the cafeteria before Mandey could smack him.

"He's just jealous," Gayla said as they went to join Charlie in the ala carte line. "You know he wishes you and I were his own personal harem. Which reminds me, I need to find myself a new boyfriend before people start thinking Charlie and I are a couple."

Mandey was quiet as she waited in line with Gayla and Charlie. She watched Danny over at his table with Georgia and the rest of the popular crowd. His attention was flattering, to be sure, but what she didn't need was Danny taking any interest in her now, stirring up leftover feelings from her silly adolescent crush on him. She had Shannon now, and Shannon was everything she ever wanted. Then she realized that maybe she was reading too much into Danny's actions. After all, he'd been wasted when he kissed her. Picking her for a project partner was probably his own self-interest in making sure he got a good grade. Besides, as he had acknowledged, hanging around with Mandey too much would ruin his reputation.

Mandey laughed to herself and put Danny out of her mind. She thought instead about making out with Shannon the day before. That sent a thrill through her, and decided that maybe she shouldn't think about that until later. She loved having someone who could make her feel that way just by thinking about him. She wouldn't trade that for anything.

34

Family Dinner

Shannon worked the 7 A.M. to 3 P.M. shift at the service station that Monday. When he got back to the apartment, he changed clothes, found a bag of chips and a cold Dr Pepper, and went to his bedroom. He shut the door, turned on the radio, and settled down on his bed. The Eagles were singing "The Long Run". Don Henley was right; all the debutantes in Houston couldn't hold a candle to Mandey. Once he finished his snack he laid down. His mother was the only other one home, watching television in the living room, so it was mostly quiet. He would call Mandey in a few minutes, while things were peaceful…

Suddenly he was being shaken awake by Annette. "Wake up!" she said.

He looked at his clock. Six P.M. He hadn't meant to fall asleep.

"Momma wants to know if you want to eat," Annette said.

"Sure," he said, a bit groggily. No one needed to ask him that question twice.

He followed Annette to the living room. Their mother was in the kitchen, cooking. Leon was sitting in the armchair, smoking a cigarette and watching the news.

"Dinner is ready. Come fix you a plate," their mother said to them.

She had made charro beans and rice, and there were warm tortillas to go with it. Shannon and Annette went to the stove and started filling their plates.

"Deb, did you make that Mexican shit again?" Leon asked from the living room.

"Yes, I did, and if you don't like it, why did you marry a Spanish lady?" Deb said.

"'Spanish lady'?" Leon scoffed. "Your maiden name was Farrell."

"Well, Mr. Farrell ran off on us when I was six. My mama was a Rodriguez and my stepdad was a Ballesteros. I'd say I qualify," Deb replied.

Leon didn't argue the point. "Well, I'd like it more if we didn't have to eat it for a week when you make it," he grumbled.

"Anytime you want get in the kitchen and make dinner, you're welcome to do it," Deb replied.

Shannon listened warily to this exchange. Leon was being his natural asshole self, but he wasn't drunk, so the picking probably wouldn't turn into an argument and then into a full-blown knock-down drag-out.

Leon snorted, then got up to get his dinner. Shannon and Annette sat down on the couch with their plates. Deb sat at the kitchen table.

"What's all that green shit all over the walls outside?" Leon asked Shannon and Annette. "Did y'all get tired of the black and red shit you painted all over the place?"

"No," Shannon said shortly, thinking back to very early the previous morning.

"Some bunch of assholes are trying to start something with us," Annette said.

"What, a turf war or something?" Leon asked.

"Something like that," Shannon replied.

"You gonna go trash their territory?" Leon asked.

"Don't know where they're from," Annette said. "They go to that Liaisons club a few blocks over. They might live in a lot of different places."

"One of them goes to Rogers High," Shannon said.

Annette stared at him. "How do you know that?"

"Saw his ID when I took his money."

"When was this?"

"After the party. I caught one of them."

"You caught one of them?" Annette exploded. "Why didn't you tell us?"

"I beat his ass and told him to go warn his friends to stay away," Shannon said.

"God damn it, Trick, if you'd let us know, we could have caught the rest of them! What the hell were you thinking?"

"I was messed up and all I wanted to do was go to bed. I don't even know if anyone else was with him."

"Lenny heard something and went outside, and he said he saw a couple of people, but they saw him, too, and by the time we got outside, we could only hear a car racing away."

"Maybe they'll get the message and stay the hell away," Shannon said.

"Now I got an extra reason to hate them," Annette said. "I went to school there less than two weeks and made nothing but enemies. Momma and I ended up getting arrested, and I got sent back to that fucking alternative school. And it was those bitches' fault. If I ever see any of them again, especially Dina Diaz, there is gonna be hell to pay."

35

Thanksgiving

It was nine-thirty before Shannon stumbled out of bed on Thanksgiving morning. He had slept almost eleven hours and wished he hadn't, because now he felt groggy, almost hungover. He showered and dressed, then went to the kitchen. The coffee pot was almost empty, but there was enough for half a cup.

In the living room, Annette was on the couch with a cigarette and a Dr Pepper. Leon was sitting in the armchair, also smoking a cigarette, and the television was tuned to the Foley's Thanksgiving Day Parade. Shannon's mother was at the kitchen table staring into space with a cup of coffee in front of her and a cigarette between her fingers, the cigarette turning into a long gray ash. It had all the makings of another memorable family holiday.

As he headed toward the door, Leon growled at him, "Where the hell are you off to?"

"Why the hell do you care?" Shannon retorted, opening the door.

This exchange brought his mother out of her trance. "It's Thanksgiving, Shannon. Are you coming home for dinner?" she asked, putting out her cigarette. "We went to the food shelf, and they gave us a little turkey. I just put it in the oven. We got some sweet 'taters and cranberry sauce, too."

Shannon went back to the kitchen to peek in the oven at the turkey. His mother was right when she said they had been given a little turkey. It looked like it could feed four people, but not very well.

"I've been invited to dinner at a friend's house," Shannon explained, closing the oven door.

"You mean your girlfriend's house," Annette said.

Shannon looked across the counter into the living room at his sister.

"What's it to you?" he asked, wondering how she knew about Mandey.

She shrugged and tapped the ash off the end of her cigarette into the ashtray on her lap.

"What girlfriend?" their mother asked. "It ain't that trashy little girl, is it?"

Shannon sighed. "God, no, Momma. Don't worry."

Leon snorted. "I can't believe you found someone who'll have you," he said.

Shannon glared at him. "Why not? You did."

"Boy, if it wasn't Thanksgiving, I'd take you out for that one," Leon said, "but your Momma wants it to be a nice family holiday, and I ain't going to ruin it for her. But it looks like you are, running off to eat somewhere else."

Shannon grabbed his coffee cup and headed toward the door again, desperate to leave before things got out of hand. "Leon, you're full of shit," he said, and slammed the door behind him.

He hurried to his car. He knew it was just as well he wasn't having dinner with them, because now they could all have more to eat. And as far as his mother wanting a "nice family holiday," well, it would probably be nice if he weren't around to spar with Leon, anyway. With any luck, the turkey would actually get eaten, and not go flying out the window, as it had once before.

Mandey was at the door waiting for him when he got to her house. She was a bright spot in the gray day, in jeans and an oversized pumpkin-orange sweater with a long string of golden beads around her neck.

"Hi, honey," she said, letting him in. She put her arms around him and gave him a kiss.

"Hey, beautiful," he replied. "Mmmmm, something smells good."

"We're going to eat around one, one-thirty or so, at the half of the first game. I hope that's okay."

"That's fine with me."

They went into the living room and sat down on the couch. The football pre-game show was on. The house was warm and the windows were steamed from the food cooking in the kitchen. Shannon's stomach gave an audible growl, making Mandey laugh.

"Sorry," he said. "It smells so good. What are we having?"

"Let's see," Mandey said. "Turkey, dressing, mashed potatoes, gravy, squash, mixed vegetables, rolls, cranberry sauce, and pumpkin pie. How does that grab you?"

"Grabs me just fine," Shannon replied.

"What's going on at your house this morning?" Mandey asked him.

"My mom's actually making dinner. They got a turkey from the food shelf. Leon was trying to lay a guilt trip on me for leaving, saying I was going to disappoint Momma if I didn't have dinner with them. Mandey, I looked at that turkey before I left, and it's going to be doing good to feed the three of them."

Mandey sniffed. "What's with the 'family togetherness' trip?"

"Damned if I know. I guess if I had been going to stay, Leon would be ragging on me because I didn't help buy the dinner. Leon ain't happy unless he's chewing on my ass for something or other."

Mandey put her hand on his thigh. "I'm glad you're here today," she told him.

Shannon took her hand in his. "Me, too," he said. "Where's Marcia?"

"Getting ready. Michael's supposed to be here soon," Mandey said.

"Oh, yeah," Shannon said. "Tell me again what he's like?"

"He's nice. He was nice to me last summer when I worked as a file clerk at the law firm," Mandey said. "He's handsome, I guess. He definitely looks like an attorney. Marcia seems to like him a lot, or she wouldn't have invited him to dinner."

As if on cue, Michael knocked on the door. Mandey got up to let him in. Michael was about six feet tall with an average build, brown hair, and tortoiseshell rimmed glasses. He was wearing khaki pants with a woven brown belt and a faded denim-blue long-sleeved Polo shirt. In one arm was a bottle of wine.

"Happy Thanksgiving," he said as he entered.

"Happy Thanksgiving," Mandey replied. "Michael, this is Shannon Douglass. Shannon, this is Michael Bayer."

Shannon stood quickly to shake Michael's hand, then sat down again. Marcia came into the living room.

"Hi," she said to Michael, smiling.

"Hi," he replied, kissing her cheek. "I brought this to go with dinner."

Marcia took the bottle and glanced at the label. "Ooh, I love this wine," she said. "Why don't you have a seat? The game will be starting soon."

Michael sat down in the armchair. Mandey followed Marcia to the kitchen to continue with dinner preparations. Shannon looked after her, wishing she would stay in the living room with him. He didn't know how to make small talk with a lawyer. The only lawyer he had ever talked to was his public defender in his robbery case, and he had spent maybe forty-five minutes talking to Shannon one-on-one, basically to tell him to plead guilty, which he did. That was one topic he didn't want to bring up with Michael. Shannon was glad to have the football pre-game show to watch.

"Can I get you something to drink, Mike?" Marcia asked from the kitchen. "You want a beer?"

"Yes, thanks," Michael said.

"Shannon, you want one, too?" Marcia asked.

"Sure," Shannon replied.

Mandey brought them their beers, in brown glass bottles, along with a tray of green and black olives, celery stuffed with cream cheese, and crackers with spinach dip.

"This is the life, isn't it?" Michael said to Shannon. "Sitting in the living room watching football while two gorgeous women make us food and bring us beer."

"I heard that," Marcia said from the kitchen. "Next year Mandey and I are going to sit on our butts and you two will make the dinner."

"They'll probably make us a Charlie Brown Thanksgiving dinner," Mandey said. "Toast, popcorn, and jellybeans."

"No, no, no," Michael said. "I'm sure we could do better than that. I was thinking nachos and frozen pizza, right, Shannon?"

Shannon snapped to attention, startled to be addressed, then said, "Turkey nachos."

"Yeah, turkey nachos," Michael agreed.

"Mmm, I can't wait," Mandey said sarcastically, going back to the kitchen.

"Who are you betting on to win today? I'm going with Green Bay in the first game and Dallas in the second," Michael asked Shannon.

"I'm not betting on anyone," Shannon said. "I don't care who wins the Packers/Lions game, but I want the Patriots to beat Dallas."

"New England? You live in Texas. How can you root for the Patriots?"

"I root for the Patriots," Marcia said from the kitchen.

"I'm an Oilers fan," Shannon said. He almost added, "The Cowboys suck," but he held his tongue.

"The Oilers haven't given anyone much to cheer about this year," Michael said.

Shannon shrugged. "They're still my team."

"You are a true fan," Michael said, "but I'm rooting for the Cowboys all the way."

They got into a good-natured discussion about football, which relieved Shannon, because it was a fairly harmless subject. Before long, Mandey and Marcia came in to join them to watch the game.

At half time, Green Bay was ahead, 21-17, as they sat down to dinner. Shannon had never seen such a spread in his life. The huge turkey lay steaming, golden brown, on a platter. There was a basket of rolls, a bowl of potatoes, a boat of gravy, dishes of vegetables, a plate of cranberry sauce, and more.

"Wine for everyone?" Michael asked, opening the bottle.

"Just a little," Mandey said. She held up her can of Tab.

"You like the hard stuff," Michael said, teasing, pouring a small amount of wine into the glass Mandey held out to him.

Having wine with dinner was a new experience for Shannon, but he didn't remark on it. Wine was unfamiliar territory for him, period. The girls in the gang liked to get a bottle of Boone's Strawberry Hill or Tickle Pink once in a while. That was about as close as he ever got to wine. He tended to drink beer or the hard stuff, and that didn't mean Tab.

"Let's do a toast," Michael suggested. "To good food and the women who made it."

They all clinked their glasses together and took a sip of wine.

Shannon thought about his mother and sister as he filled his plate with food. They (along with Leon, but he didn't care about him) would be eating an overcooked turkey with canned sweet potatoes and cranberry sauce. He didn't let the feeling last long. His family didn't have an elaborate meal, but they seemed to be stocked up on cigarettes and beer, so they would be okay. He knew that may have seemed callous, but it was the truth.

The meal was delicious. The food at Mandey's house was spoiling him. He had always been overweight, partly due to genetics, and partly due to eating a lot of cheap junk food. Now he was eating so much good food, he thought he was going to end up weighing a ton.

After dinner, Shannon and Michael retreated to the living room to resume watching the game. Shannon's stomach was fuller than he ever remembered it being. He was grateful to sink down onto the comfortable couch.

"Ready for pie?" Mandey asked with a grin, sticking her head into the living room.

"No," Shannon groaned.

"Didn't think so," she said, and went back into the kitchen.

When the kitchen was cleaned up, Mandey and Marcia returned to the living room at the beginning of the fourth quarter. The score was 21 Green Bay, 24 Detroit.

"The Lions are making a comeback," Shannon said.

In the end, the final score was Green Bay 28, Detroit 31.

"Hey," Mandey suggested to Shannon, "why don't we watch the next game in my room?"

Shannon looked at her. He knew they might not see a lot of the Cowboys/Patriots. She looked like she knew it, too.

"Okay," he said.

It was his favorite place to be in the entire world—with Mandey in her bedroom. The time he was able to spend there with her, talking and laughing, kissing and holding her, made all the garbage in his life more tolerable.

The room was on its way to being decorated for Christmas. Mandey had put up strings of Christmas lights, and hanging from the ceiling they cast a cheery muted glow of colors. She turned the football game on, set the volume low, and they lay down on her bed.

She let him put his hand underneath her sweater. He touched her breasts through her bra. They were a very generous handful each, and the nipples were erect, as was a certain part of Shannon's own anatomy. Through his jeans, Mandey's hand was making it even more so.

Suddenly she pulled away, and Shannon knew she had decided that things had gone far enough. God, he was horny. It had been a long time since he had been that horny. His shirt was open, and Mandey was fingering the buttons, not looking him in the eyes. She didn't say anything.

"Are you okay?" Shannon asked her.

She was silent for a moment before she answered him. "I'm sorry, Shannon," she finally said. "I'm just not ready yet." There was a tremor in her voice.

"It's okay," he told her and held her closer.

He felt her body draw a deep breath, and she sighed. "I know you want to, Shannon, and I don't want to disappoint you, but I'm not ready."

"Am I complaining?"

"No," Mandey said, shaking her head. "But I know you were getting excited, and I don't think you wanted to stop." Tears welled up in her eyes, and she looked down at his chest again.

"Hey," Shannon said, putting a finger under her chin and tipping her face up to look at him.

"It's just—" she began. "I know you aren't a virgin, but I still am. I don't want to rush things and maybe regret it, but I don't want to disappoint you, either." She wiped her tears with the back of her hand.

"Don't cry," he told her, and kissed her forehead. "Mandey, I'm just happy to be with you. Yeah, I want to sleep with you, but you're not ready yet. Someday you will be, and when you are, I'll be here."

"But what if it's a long time?" she asked in a small voice.

Shannon paused a moment, then said, "I spent eight months in jail without it. I can do it again."

"But you don't want to."

"I want what you want, Mandey."

"What I want is to make you happy."

"You already do."

"But would you really be willing to wait for months because I'm not ready yet?" Mandey asked, tears threatening again.

"Don't cry," Shannon told her. "Yes, I would."

She smiled up at him, her eyes shimmering. "Then I'm a lucky girl."

"I'm the one who's lucky," he replied and kissed her.

After a few more kisses and caresses, Mandey said to Shannon, timidly, "I know this is a personal question, but how old were you your first time?"

"Sixteen," Shannon replied, not offended by the question, but it made him wonder where she was going from there.

"With that girl you were going with?"

Shannon paused a moment. "No," he said shortly.

Shannon waited for her to ask another question, but she didn't. He had told her he had only gone with one other girl, so Mandey naturally assumed it was her. They lay there together in silence until he couldn't stand it. He wanted to be truthful with her about everything, but it was difficult to tell her some of the things he knew he should. Too much had gone on in his life that could make her decide he wasn't good enough for her, and the idea of losing her was terrifying. But if she ever found out certain things about him secondhand, it would probably be worse.

"Mandey," he said in a strained voice, pulling his arms away from her, "if I tell you what I'm about to say, you might not want me around no more."

Mandey felt her insides turn into icy slush. "Well, if it's that serious, then I think you'd <u>better</u> tell me," she said, hoping her tone sounded light. She didn't like that he had pulled away from her and was afraid of what he was going to say.

He turned and laid on his back, folded his hands on his chest, and stared gravely at the ceiling. He didn't say anything, and Mandey wondered if he had decided not to tell her.

He closed his eyes and took a deep breath. "I never slept with my girlfriend, but I've been with a few different girls," he finally said.

"Okay," Mandey said, letting the information sink in. It didn't make sense to her. He had told her before she was only the second girl he knew who liked him. Now he was saying he had slept with "a few different girls"? She felt like she had been gut-punched.

"But it's worse than that," he added.

Really? How? Mandey wondered.

"All right, how many kids do you have?" she asked.

"What?" Shannon asked, startled. He turned to look at her. "None that I know of. I always used a rubber."

"Then what, Shannon? What's the worst part of it?"

He turned over on his side, took both of her hands in his, and looked directly into her eyes. "All right, here's the truth, Mandey. This will probably make you sick and make you hate me, but every woman I have ever gone to bed with has been a hooker. A prostitute."

Mandey looked nonplussed, then blinked slowly and quietly absorbed this information. She looked down, focusing her attention on his chest again, and remained silent.

Shannon squeezed her hands in his. "Mandey, say something, please," he begged.

She heard in his voice how badly he was hoping she wasn't too angry with him, but angry was not how she was feeling.

"Why, Shannon?" she asked, confused, looking up to see his anxious face. "Why in the world would you have to pay someone to sleep with you? Because your girlfriend wouldn't?" Mandey was worried that was the case.

"No! That had nothing to do with it! My girlfriend wanted to sleep with me, but then I decided I didn't want her."

"Well, explain it to me, Shannon. It doesn't make a whole lot of sense to me."

She moved closer to him. She wanted to understand, and she wanted him to know that she wanted to hear what she had to say.

"I don't know if I can explain it so you can understand," he said hopelessly.

"Try. Please try?"

He sighed and drew her into his arms. He was glad that she willingly accepted his embrace.

"I had a bad experience with my ex-girlfriend. I caught her screwing around with another guy. A friend of mine asked me if I had twenty bucks, and he set me up with a gal to try and make me feel better."

"When you were only sixteen?"

"Yeah, well, going on seventeen. After that, I just always went to one whenever I wanted some. There aren't a whole lot of girls around the neighborhood to pick from, and I ain't no Casanova, so it was always easier for me to get it from hookers. No personal stuff to get in the way."

Mandey took in this information. "But now—what we have is 'personal stuff'. Are you okay with going from being able to sleep with some h—someone whenever you want to a personal relationship with me?"

"Yes!" he exclaimed. "Mandey, I love you! I know I'm a nineteen-year-old guy, and all I'm supposed to care about is getting my rocks off, but I got feelings, too. Going to a hooker didn't used to seem like such a bad idea. I wasn't doing it all the time, just when the urge got too strong. But eventually...it wasn't what I wanted anymore. I'm at the point now that I'd rather jack off."

Mandey let out a nervous giggle.

"I'm serious," he said.

"Oh, Shannon," Mandey said, and hugged him.

He hugged her back tightly. "I thought you'd be more upset," he said.

"Well, it wasn't what I was expecting to hear, but I guess I'm more concerned with our future than with your past," she replied, letting him go. "I feel sad for you. The idea of you paying to have sex with someone, like nobody wanted you, makes me sad. I want you, Shannon." She slipped her hands underneath his shirt and ran them down his back. "Someday I'm going to show you exactly how much I want you."

She pressed her mouth against his and kissed him deeply. Despite Shannon's bizarre confession, or maybe because of it, she was turned on—oh, God, was she turned on. A part of her wanted to shed all self-restraint and go for it, to hell with the consequences. She wanted to prove to him that she could please him better than any of the women he had been with before, but her common sense was a little bit stronger than her lust.

Shannon was startled when Mandey kissed him so passionately, but it turned him on, that and the fact that she said she wanted him. He rolled on top of her and when their lips parted, he said, "You're doing a pretty good job of showing me right now."

"It's a preview of things to come," Mandey said with a saucy grin.

"Hey," Shannon said mischievously as a thought came into his head, "what do you think Marcia and Michael are doing? Do you think they're still in the living room, or do you think they're in her bedroom getting it on?"

Mandey looked at him with wide eyes and laughed. "I don't know."

"I bet they think we're in here getting it on," he said.

Mandey smiled. "Maybe. One of these days when they're thinking about what we're doing in here, they'll be exactly right."

"Mmm," Shannon said. "I like the sound of that." He gently laid down on top of her, keeping his weight on his elbows. "After what I just told you, I thought I might be out the door and on my way home now. I'm glad I'm not."

Mandey slid her hands inside his shirt again as they kissed. They spent the rest of the afternoon and evening watching television, listening to music, and messing up Mandey's bed, taking a break for pumpkin pie late in the afternoon and making open-face hot turkey sandwiches around seven.

"I told you the Cowboys were going to win," Michael said as they sat at the kitchen table, eating their sandwiches.

"They still suck," Shannon said, feeling braver. Michael laughed.

Michael left around nine, but it was midnight before Shannon went home.

Shannon and Mandey stood on the front steps in the dark. He held her close to ward off the chill of the night.

"For the first time in my life, I have something to be thankful for on Thanksgiving," he told her.

She smiled. "I have lots to be thankful for, but I'm especially thankful to have you," she said.

He kissed her. "I've got to go. I've got to be at work early," he said. "I'll call you when I get off."

"My government class project partner is coming over tomorrow afternoon, but you can come over whenever you want. You won't bother us," Mandey told him.

"I'll still call first," he said.

"Okay. Drive carefully."

"I will. Love you."

"Love you, too."

36

The Lovers Quarrel

Mandey studied her reflection in the mirror, surveying herself in her blue jeans and black short-sleeved blouse. She fastened a braided silver chain around her neck and a matching bracelet on her right wrist, then checked her make up. Shannon would be over sometime later. Right now, she was waiting for Danny to arrive to work on their government class project.

What do I care how I look in front of Danny? Mandey thought, irritated with herself.

She lounged on the sofa and watched MTV while she waited for him to arrive. The front door was open, so she could see through the screen door out to the driveway when Danny drove in, driving his mother's brown Buick.

Danny came up the steps carrying a VCR. Mandey held the door open for him.

"You did say your VCR is VHS format, right?" Danny asked, setting the machine down on the nearest chair.

"Yes, it is," Mandey replied.

"Good, because that's what I brought," Danny said. "I've got the tapes out in the car. If you'll go get them, I'll start hooking up the VCRs."

Jeez, a 'You look nice today' might have been too much to ask for, but 'Hello' would have been nice, she thought as she trudged out to the car.

She found the tapes in a grocery bag in the back seat and brought them into the house. Danny was already busy hooking up the recorders, screwing various wires into various ports.

"You do know what you're doing, don't you?" Mandey asked him, setting the bag of tapes down on the couch.

"Of course," Danny said.

"Just checking," Mandey said, sitting down on the couch to watch him.

"There," Danny said a few minutes later. "You have the blank tape?"

"On top of the TV."

"Give me one of the tapes in the bag," he said.

She obliged. He put it in one VCR and the blank tape in the other, then set the pre-recorded tape to "play" and the blank one to "record" and let them run for a minute. Then he rewound the blank tape to see if it had recorded from the other tape. He pressed "play." There was only snow on the tape.

"Wait," Danny said, confused, standing back and looking at the TV with his arms akimbo. "Now what went wrong here? Mandey, do you have an instruction manual for your VCR?"

"In the bottom left-hand drawer of the console, I think," Mandey said.

Fifteen minutes later, after much switching of wires and channels, the system worked.

"Told you I knew what I was doing. I haven't spent three years as a library aide for nothing," Danny said.

They had been screening videos for about an hour when the phone rang. Mandey answered it on the second ring.

"Hey, it's me," she heard Shannon say.

"Hey. What are you doing?"

"Just got in from work. What about you?"

Mandey glanced over at Danny, who was fast-forwarding through the tape they were viewing.

"Oh, my partner for my government class project is here, and we're trying to put together a videotape for it."

"Oh. How long is that going to take?"

"Another hour or so, maybe. Why don't you come over? Wait, Danny!"

"What?" Danny asked, stopping the tape.

"Rewind it a little. That part looked interesting."

"Danny?" Shannon asked her.

"Yeah," Mandey admitted. "My project partner is a male. Now don't go getting all jealous on me. If something was going on between Danny and me, I wouldn't be inviting you over here now."

"I'm not jealous," Shannon said, but Mandey thought his tone sounded strange. "But if you're working on your project, you don't need me around right now."

"Oh, come on," Mandey urged him. "You won't bother us."

"I'll probably sit there and ask dumb questions about what you're doing, and you'll think I'm a moron," he said.

"Don't be silly," Mandey said.

"No, really, I've got some things I've got to do. I'll be over later."

"Okay," Mandey said, relenting.

"I love you, Mandey," he told her.

"I love you, too," she replied.

When she hung up, Danny asked, "Boyfriend checking up on you?"

"No," Mandey said.

"Sounded like it to me."

"If he were that concerned, he could come over and check you out for himself."

"Maybe he will."

"No, he said he wasn't going to disturb us while we're working."

"That's what he told you. Maybe he'll surprise you and show up thirty minutes from now to make sure you're doing what you said."

Mandey rolled her eyes at him. "He's not that paranoid."

"You never know."

"Just roll the tape, Danny."

Shannon hung up the phone after talking to Mandey and stared off into space, thinking. Her partner for her school project was named Danny. Last week he had beaten up a guy named Danny who was a drug dealer, a member of the Alley Cats, and a senior at Rogers High School. There might be half a dozen Dannys in Mandey's class; the two didn't necessarily have to be one and the same, but Shannon had a sinking feeling that they were.

He clutched his hair in his hands. There was no way he was going near Mandey's house until this Danny guy was gone. He wondered how he could find out for sure if it was the same guy without making Mandey suspicious.

If it's the same guy, what the hell is Mandey doing hanging out with someone like that? Shannon wondered.

Then he laughed at the irony of it. Like he was some kind of saint.

Suddenly he thought of the photograph of him and Mandey that she had on her desk in her bedroom. What if Danny saw it and told Mandey that the guy in the picture was the same guy who had beaten him up? But Mandey wouldn't have that guy in her bedroom, would she?

Frantic but powerless, Shannon began to pace. The shit was very close to hitting the fan, and he couldn't do a thing about it. He had to get his mind off it somehow, and he picked up his car keys and headed out of the apartment.

He drove, thinking he was cruising aimlessly until he found himself parked in a motel parking lot, staring up at Room 12.

"What the hell am I doing?" he asked himself aloud, rubbing his eyes.

He used to get a quick roll in the hay occasionally to get his mind off things, but those days were over, or had better be, if he wanted to keep Mandey. He wasn't even horny. If he did go to Arlene's room, what had happened last time would most likely happen again.

"Shit," he muttered.

His stomach was in knots. This was the second time in less than a week that he had been on the verge of cheating on Mandey, and neither time had he even been in the mood for sex. What was going to happen someday when he was really horny? Would he give in to his weakness and go see some whore? Worse, would he try to force himself on Mandey? He had promised he never would, but what if he broke that promise?

He slammed the car into gear and peeled out into the street, the radio blaring as loud as he could stand it, trying to drown out all his thoughts.

It was close to five o'clock before Mandey and Danny finished with fifteen minutes of footage for their project.

"Damn, all this work has made me hungry," Danny said, turning off the television.

"We've still got tons of leftovers from yesterday," Mandey said.

"Oh, God, no," Danny said, grimacing. "No offense, but a little turkey goes a long way with me. Want to go grab a burger?"

Actually, Mandey felt the same way. She looked at the clock, wondering if Shannon was going to call soon.

"Oh, come on. It won't take long," Danny said.

"Okay," Mandey relented.

They made a quick trip to Wendy's in Danny's car, and he dropped her off at her house less than forty-five minutes after they left. Mandey had been home about five minutes when the phone rang. She picked up the phone on the first ring.

"Hello?"

"Are you done?"

"Yep."

"Is your friend gone?"

"Yes, he is."

"I'll be over in about five minutes."

"Where are you?"

"I'm up at the Circle K."

"Is something wrong, Shannon?"

"No. I'm on my way."

"Okay."

Mandey turned on the porch light and went outside to wait for him. She thought Shannon was acting awfully flaky today. She didn't believe him when he said nothing was wrong.

He pulled into the driveway in less than five minutes. When he came up onto the porch, he brought his hand out from behind his back and presented Mandey with a bouquet of pink and white carnations.

Mandey looked at him with a bemused smile as she took the flowers. "Thank you."

"You're welcome," Shannon replied, then hugged her fiercely.

When he finally let her go, Mandey asked, "Gee, what was that for?"

"I love you," he said simply.

"Are you okay?" she asked him.

Shannon frowned. "Yeah, I'm okay. Is there something wrong with telling my girlfriend I love her?"

"You just seem edgy," Mandey said. "Let's go in. It's chilly out here."

He silently followed her inside. Mandey was miffed at his snappish attitude and didn't say a word as she went into the kitchen to find a small vase for the flowers. She rummaged through a low cabinet, and when she stood up again, Shannon was behind her.

"Sorry," he said, and hugged her again, more gently this time.

She hugged him back. "I'm going to ask you again, Shannon. Are you okay?"

He nodded and let go of her so he could look at her. "I'm okay. I'm always okay when I'm with you."

She brushed her lips quickly against his and let go of him so she could put her flowers in the vase. "Are you hungry?" she asked as she filled the vase with water. "We've got tons of leftovers from yesterday."

"I am kind of hungry," Shannon admitted.

She got the food out of the refrigerator, put a helping of everything on a plate, covered it with plastic wrap and put it in the microwave. When it was done, she placed it in front of him on the kitchen table.

"You're not eating?" Shannon asked her.

"I already ate," Mandey replied, sitting down with a Dr Pepper for each of them. "Danny and I ran out for a burger."

"Oh," Shannon said, concentrating on his plate. "You go out to eat with other guys a lot when I'm not around?"

Mandey felt her stomach bunch up. She didn't want to fight with him. They hadn't fought yet and she didn't want to start now.

"Shannon, Danny's just a friend of mine."

"I thought I'd met all your friends, except for Georgia."

Mandey sighed impatiently. "Well, I gave you the opportunity to meet Danny this afternoon, but you didn't take it."

"I didn't want to disturb your <u>work</u>," Shannon said, sarcastically stressing the last word.

Mandey abruptly got up from the table. "I guess Danny wasn't so wrong after all," she said, and stalked into the living room.

"What's that supposed to mean?" Shannon called after her.

He got up and followed her into the living room. She was sprawled on the couch and had turned on *Wheel of Fortune*. He sat down on the edge of the couch next to her.

"Huh? I asked you what that last comment was supposed to mean."

She turned her gaze from the TV to him. "Danny was joking about you calling to check up on me or coming by after you said you weren't, just to make sure I was doing what I said. I told him you weren't that paranoid. I really thought you weren't, but I guess I was wrong."

Mandey looked back at the television screen, hoping that Shannon wouldn't notice the tears that burned her eyes.

"Well, Mandey, if the situation were reversed and I told you I was out with some other girl, how would you feel?"

Mandey paused a moment, "Probably jealous," she admitted, "but if you told me she was a friend and nothing more, I'd believe you. Maybe it's because I'm naïve, but I think it's because I love you and trust you and I don't think you'd cheat on me."

She was able to get all of that out before a sob escaped her.

"Aw, man," she heard Shannon say, and suddenly his arms were around her.

"I'm sorry," he said.

Mandey flung herself into his embrace and buried her face in his chest. She choked back her tears, not wanting to cry over this, then pulled back to look at Shannon.

"No, I'm sorry," she said. "Please believe me. Danny is just a school friend. We're working on a project together, and we went to get a hamburger, that's all. You're the one I'm in love with. I'm not your ex-girlfriend. I won't cheat on you."

They hugged each other. When they let go, Mandey said, "I guess that was our first fight."

Shannon nodded. "I guess so."

Mandey smiled slyly. "That means we need to do some making up, right?"

"That's how I've heard it works," Shannon said, "although it never did with my ex-girlfriend."

"Or with my ex-boyfriend," Mandey said. "Why don't you finish your supper? I'll join you for a piece of pie and then we'll—"

The phone in her bedroom rang. "Hold on," Mandey told Shannon, getting up to answer it.

Mandey's heart sank when she heard Angelina's voice. "Jesse wants us to go to Liaisons tomorrow night," she said.

"Tomorrow?" Mandey repeated. She wasn't happy, but at least Angie hadn't said Jesse wanted them to meet tonight.

"Ten o'clock at Safeway, as usual," Angelina said.

"Okay. Sounds good," Mandey said brightly. "See you tomorrow." She went back to the living room.

"Who was that?" Shannon asked.

Mandey couldn't let him get suspicious. She had to come up with a cover story quickly.

"Well, I hope you don't mind, but I'm going shopping tomorrow with a bunch of girls from school," Mandey said. "We'll probably shop until the stores close. It's a big sales weekend, and I didn't get to do any shopping today."

"Oh," Shannon said, sounding a little disappointed.

"I'll be out buying you Christmas presents," Mandey said, trying to cheer him up.

"Well, okay," Shannon said, "but you're all mine on Sunday."

"Of course," Mandey said. "We've got a date to watch the Oilers game."

"They're going to make it three in a row," Shannon said.

"Let's hope so."

Mandey sighed to herself as she followed Shannon back out to the kitchen. She had managed to wriggle out of that tight spot, but she wasn't happy about it. She put the planned activities of the following night out of her mind as they had pie together, then went to her bedroom to make up and make out. They stood in the middle of her room, kissing, and Mandey unbuttoned Shannon's brown plaid flannel shirt. He quickly slipped it off and tossed it on the floor. The T-shirt he wore underneath came off next, then he ran his hands up her back, inside her sweater. She surprised him by pulling it up over her head and dropping it onto the floor with his shirts. She stood before him in her jeans and a pale pink bra.

"Oh, Mandey," he said, almost moaning, and pulled her against him.

"Not a homerun, but you've definitely reached second base," she told him, before his mouth covered hers again.

She led him over to the bed and they laid down together. Shannon's hands found their way inside her bra. She closed her eyes, loving how he was touching her. He moved down and kissed the top of each breast, then up her chest and neck to her face and her lips again.

Keep control of yourself, Shannon thought. *Not a homerun, only second base, she said.*

It was better that way, for now, at least. He knew what the limits were, and he didn't have to feel any anxiety about moving past that. Not that he was anxious. He felt rather confident—a hell of a lot better than he did trying to get with Kerri. Mandey truly wanted him. With Kerri, getting a guy to sleep with her was her way of making herself feel validated.

"Sometimes I still can't believe this is real," Mandey said.

Shannon looked into her eyes. "I know what you mean," he said.

Eventually they took a break and came up for air, and Mandey got up to use the bathroom. Shannon watched her walk away, clad only in her jeans and bra, then turned to lay on his back and stared at the ceiling. Simon Le Bon of Duran Duran was staring back down at him. Shannon stuck out his tongue at the poster.

Ha, he thought. *All you can do is look down at her. I'm the lucky guy who gets to make out with her.*

He sat up and looked at her bookshelves. On the bottom shelf were three high school yearbooks. He picked out the most recent one, from the last school year, and turned to the index. He found a name, followed by several page numbers. He thumbed to the first one and found the junior class picture of Danny Sanchez. His heart sank. The Danny who was working on the class project with Mandey wasn't necessarily the same guy, but something in Shannon's gut told him it was.

He heard Mandey turn the doorknob, so he quickly put the book back in its place. When Mandey came in, he saw that she had washed the make-up off her face and was wearing a pair of colorful plaid flannel shortie pajamas. She looked younger, but still as beautiful.

"I had to take out my contact lenses; they were bothering my eyes," she said, and yawned. "Are you okay?"

"Yeah," Shannon replied, with a slight shake of his head.

She sat down next to him and put her arms around him. Shannon pushed Danny Sanchez out of his mind and put his arms around his girlfriend. Underneath the pajamas, the bra was gone. Her body felt good, so soft and warm.

They laid down together again, and Mandey pulled the patchwork quilt at the bottom of her bed up over them. Shannon fantasized about what it would be like to stay there with her all night and wake up next to her in the morning. The same thought was going through Mandey's mind. She was sure that it was going to happen, and probably sooner rather than later.

37

Watch 'Em Burn

It hadn't exactly been a lie she had told Shannon; she and Georgia had ended up going to the mall that afternoon, and Mandey had picked out a couple gifts she planned to give him for Christmas. But that night, Mandey was in her van at the Safeway parking lot, waiting for the rest of the Alley Cats to show up at ten P.M., as was becoming the custom. As usual, she was early, and sat with the van stereo blaring. Tonight, she was listening to *War Babies* by Daryl Hall and John Oates, hoping the music would get her in the mood for what she was supposed to be doing.

Danny and Jeremy were already there when Mandey arrived, canvassing the moviegoers and loiterers to find buyers for Danny's product. Danny stopped by his car before he and Jeremy came to get in the van. After they greeted each other, Mandey asked, "You left it all in your car, right?"

"Mandey, I know your rule about drugs in your van," Danny said impatiently.

"Thank you," Mandey said. "I appreciate you respecting it."

Danny was silent for a moment, then got out of the van and walked back over to his car. Mandey watched him, shaking her head.

"You're way too nice," Jeremy told her. "If I were you, I'd be like, 'Get your fucking dope out of my van.'"

Mandey shrugged.

When Danny returned, Mandey did not comment on his return trip to his car. Instead, she said, "I am beginning to agree with you about one thing, Danny. This gang business is starting to cramp my style."

"Oh, is it taking you away from time with your boyfriend?" Danny asked mockingly. "Poor thing. Like you told me, nobody's twisting your arm. You can quit whenever you like."

"Well, I'm certainly thinking about it," she replied. "I don't like lying to him about what I'm doing. I'm a bad liar and I hate doing it."

"Why don't you bring him along?" Jeremy asked. "I bet if you mentioned it to Jesse and Terry, they'd be glad to have another guy in the gang. Especially someone not from school, since we're trying to keep what we've been doing from spreading around."

"Shannon would freak out if he knew what I was doing," Mandey said. "He's got enough stuff going on in his life. Getting involved in all this would be the last thing he needs."

"You're not going to quit, are you?" Danny asked.

"I don't know," Mandey said. "My initial lust for revenge has died down, and so far I don't see that we've been very effective in doing what we set out to do."

"That's the learning curve," Danny said.

"Well, then we need to do this," Mandey said, making a steep, upward curving motion with her hand. "Let's see how tonight goes."

Shannon had mixed feelings about being apart from Mandey that night. If he'd had his druthers, he'd have chosen to be with her, but since that was not an option, he knew he had some business to take care of. The Devils were pissed because he had been working or ripping off cars while they had been tangling with these Alley Cats. The graffiti painting incident and running into that dope dealer Danny last week showed that things were escalating. That was unacceptable. Shannon didn't care about defending the gang's "turf" and proving themselves to be the biggest bunch of badasses around. What he wanted was a minimum of conflict, because the more conflict, the bigger the chance that he could end up in jail again. He needed to get a handle on these idiots and figure out the quickest, least troublesome way to get rid of them.

He called for a meeting, and now all the Devils were assembled at their base. They sat around the living room with a chilly breeze blowing through the spaces between the boards covering the broken windows that made the lit candles, their only source of light, flicker. Their shadows quivered violently on the walls.

"Okay," Shannon began, surveying the faces of the gang, which looked truly demonic in the shadowy candlelight. "Let's talk about this so-called gang that's being a pain in the ass."

"It's about fucking time," Raff said. "We've been dealing with this shit for the last couple weeks while you've been off playing with yourself."

Shannon's face flushed with anger. Raff was getting bolder all the time.

"Raff, shut the fuck up," Shannon told him. "Yeah, I know I haven't been around much, but I've got a job I got to keep, plus Grubbs has been hassling me to get more cars for his nephew. I've got a lot more on my plate than going to Liaisons and instigating shit."

"We ain't the ones instigating!" Curt objected. "It's those damn Alley Cats."

Shannon ignored him. "I was hoping this was a problem that would go away on its own, but I guess it's not gonna, so let's pool our information on them and see what we can do to get them off our backs. Who are they, how many are there?"

"I can name off a few," Raff said. "There's Danny the dope dealer and his little midget henchman, Jeremy. Then there's that little Spanish prick, Jesse, who thinks he's the leader, and his whore Angelina."

"And there are three guys who look like they've watched *Fast Times at Ridgemont High* a few too many times," John added. "I think one's named Brad. I'm not sure about the others."

"There's a big dumb redneck," Lenny said.

"And there's two more girls," Kerri said. "A short, fat Mexican bitch and a snotty white one. I don't know their names."

"Is that it?" Shannon asked.

No one spoke up to add anyone else to the list.

"Well, that's ten, just like us," Shannon said. "What I was thinking was that since they mostly hang out at Liaisons, that's where we should be."

To be honest, he didn't want to get anywhere near the place. Now that he knew for sure that Danny the dope dealer was a classmate of Mandey's, he wanted to keep his distance. He wasn't sure if that Danny was the one Mandey had over her house the day before. He hoped to God it wasn't, and if it was, that Danny never saw that photo of him and Mandey together. Shannon supposed that if that had happened, he would have gotten an earful from Mandey. Even if Danny had seen the picture, he might have been too messed up that night to remember what Shannon looked like.

What Trick looked like, Shannon silently corrected himself. Having that damn gang nickname was a blessing in this case.

He still didn't want to take any chances. If Mandey knew Danny, she probably knew some of the other people in the gang, too. But he knew he couldn't run and hide and leave the gang to run wild.

"The redneck's name is Terry," Kerri said. "His brother owns that impound lot you keep breaking into."

Shannon stared at her. "How do you know this?" he asked.

"I talked to him a couple weeks ago at the club," she replied. "I was after his wallet."

"Oh, he was your first choice for that stunt?" Shannon asked, disgusted. "What happened?"

"The snotty white girl," Kerri said. "She saw us and ratted me out to him."

"Hmm," Shannon said. "All right. Some of us will go check out the impound lot and see if they're going to come around looking for us. The rest will go to the club and see what's going on there."

"And do what?" Raff asked. "We need to take some real action, not just find them and stand there with our thumb up our butt."

Shannon thought. The gang had never had any real opposition before, so the whole situation was new.

"Confront them. Ask them what the hell they're doing in our territory acting like they own it. Let them know they're way over the limit. Tell them there will be hell to pay if they don't back down," Shannon said.

"I don't want to fucking talk to them!" Raff yelled, frustrated. "I want to bash their fucking heads in!"

"Well, you may get to see a little combat action, because I don't think they're going to take too kindly to what we have to say," Shannon said. "But you'd better be careful about it. I have a feeling that if you send anyone to the hospital, you're gonna have cops on your ass in a heartbeat."

"What if they can't ID me?" Raff asked slyly.

"It don't matter if you're covered head to toe, they'll know it was one of us. Even though the cops have been real slack about the stuff that's been going on around here, I don't think they'll be so quick to turn their heads from a murder or attempted murder. Plus, if I hear you've gone and pulled anything stupid, you'll be in some piss-poor shape before the cops ever get their hands on you," Shannon said.

"You're such a fucking pussy," Raff muttered.

Shannon went rigid. "What did you say?" he asked, although the remark had come through loud and clear.

Raff stood up straighter, his muscles tensing up in preparation to fight. "I said you're a fucking pussy."

"Come over here and tell me that to my face," Shannon said. "Now, damn it."

Raff crossed the floor and stood in front of Shannon. "You want to hear it again, you fucking pussy?" he asked, clenching his fists.

Shannon lunged at him and grabbed Raff by the throat. As he did, there was a flash of light and an explosion outside that blew open the door to the Den. Everyone hit the floor.

"What the hell?" Shannon exclaimed, letting go of Raff and getting back on his feet.

The Devils ran outside to find broken glass shattered on the ground and small pools of gasoline burning brightly. They did not see who was responsible but did hear squealing brakes down the street.

"Mother fucker!" Shannon swore. "John, Curt, 'Nette, and Checkmate, y'all are with me. Raff, you take the rest and go to the club. We're going to the impound lot."

The Devils stood watching the dying flames, stunned.

"Now!" Shannon roared.

They scrambled to the cars. Shannon made it out to the street first and headed in the direction he had heard the squealing brakes. He had driven a few blocks when he came to a line of cars waiting to get into Liaisons' parking lot. It was impossible to tell if one of those cars held the people who tossed the Molotov cocktail.

"Shit," Shannon growled. He made a three-point turn and went to take another route to the impound lot.

"Whoo-hoo!" Terry whooped gleefully as they zoomed away from the Northview Apartments. "Brad, you've got a hell of an arm!"

"Yeah. I just never figured to be using it to toss Molotov cocktails," Brad replied grimly. He looked back at the apartments and saw a faint orange glow in front of the boarded up building. "I hope it's not going to burn the place down."

"Nah," Terry said nonchalantly. "There ain't much left to catch fire anyways."

"It was just an attention-getter," Jim assured Brad.

"Whatever," Brad muttered.

"Thank God we don't have to go hang around that damn club tonight," Terry said. "I know you guys like it, but it ain't my style at all. People with purple hair look at me like I'm the freak. Anyways, I got us a deck of cards and a case of beer. We're all set."

"Shouldn't we be more concerned with keeping an eye out for the Devils than with playing cards?" Zack asked.

"We'll be keeping an eye out," Terry said. "We might as well enjoy ourselves while we're at it."

They pulled up to the impound lot. Terry got out of his truck and unlocked the gates. The Rottweilers, Starsky and Hutch, came running up to greet him. Terry patted their heads and pulled a couple dog biscuits out of his pocket.

"Git it!" he yelled, tossing the treats across the yard.

While the dogs ran to fetch their biscuits, Terry got back in and drove the truck inside, then got out again to re-latch the gate.

"Don't get out until I get them chained up," he warned the others.

Once the dogs were safely secured, Zack, Brad, and Jim got out. Terry got the case of beer out of the back of the truck, and they all went inside the office.

At Liaisons, Mandey and the rest of the Alley Cats had claimed a table on the second level at the back of the club. It provided a good view of the entire venue except for the area directly below. Since the entrance was on the opposite side of the club, no one could get to that area below without first crossing into the line of sight.

On the way in, Mandey had spotted Andie and Mart on the dance floor. She had ducked quickly into the crowd; she didn't want to explain to Andie what was going on. She felt relatively safe up here at this table; she could spot anyone coming her way.

Just sitting up there felt too much like doing nothing to the Alley Cats. While the others decided to split up and scout around the place, Mandey volunteered to stay and save the table and act as a lookout.

"What should I do if I spot any of the Devils?" she asked.

Jesse thought for a moment. "You don't have a lighter, do you?" he asked her.

Mandey stared at him. "No," she replied.

In fact, the only one at the table who did was Dina. "Give Mandey your lighter," Jesse told her. "Everyone should look up this way every so often. If Mandey sees something we need to know about, she'll flick the lighter."

"What about the rest of us?" Dina asked, handing Mandey her pink plastic Bic. "How do we signal if <u>we</u> see something?"

"Hmm," Jesse said, thinking some more. "Jeez, I wish we <u>all</u> had lighters."

"How about a hand signal?" Jeremy suggested.

"Good idea," Jesse said. "But what?"

"Well, we're cats," Mandey said. She held up her right hand with her thumb and ring finger forming a circle and the other three fingers extended. It was the U of H cougar paw.

"That's good," Jesse said, trying the signal himself.

They came up with a system. If Mandey saw any of the Devils show up, she would hold the lighter up showing a steady flame. If any of the Alley Cats got into any trouble with the Devils, they would raise their hand in the cat's paw to show they needed back up. Mandey would keep her eye out for cat's paw signals, and would start flicking her Bic on and off and point toward the trouble spot.

As the others left the table, Mandey wondered if it was going to be a long, lonely, dull night. She sat there, overlooking the packed dance floor. She would have liked to have been out there, but she couldn't risk being seen by Andrea and Martin. This was beginning to suck. She had to lie to Shannon about what she was doing, and she couldn't tell her friends, either. She thought back to last year's psych class and the unit on adolescent psychology. Gangs were generally made up of misfits and outcasts who didn't fit in anywhere else. Mandey wasn't exactly Miss Popularity, but she realized she didn't fit the profile of the average gang member. Gang life was supposed to be all-encompassing for the members. Mandey had too many outside relationships and interests to devote that much loyalty to this cause. It was easy for Terry because he was so concerned with protecting his precious auto impound. It was easy for Jesse and Angie because they were so wrapped up in each other, they didn't care what they were doing as long as they were doing it together. The same went for the Siamese triplets, Brad, Zack, and Jim, although Mandey thought the seeds of discontent might be sprouting there. They were involved in a lot of other activities being impinged upon by their involvement with the gang. She had no idea about Dina, but Danny had already expressed his own discontent, and she assumed Jeremy probably felt the same way. It didn't seem likely to Mandey that the Alley Cats could continue to exist in its present form for long.

She didn't have a lot of time to continue her reverie. She had been sitting alone there for about twenty minutes when she spotted a cluster of black satin jackets entering the club. With a groan that would have been audible if not for the loud music, she held up the lighter in a steady flame for about a minute. Jesse looked up from where he and Angelina were on the dance floor. He nodded at Mandey and looked toward where she was pointing at the entrance. Five Devils were heading toward the edge of the dance floor.

Now what do we do? Mandey wondered. If Jesse and Terry had come up with a plan to confront the rival gang that night, they hadn't shared it with any of the other Alley Cats.

The Alley Cats had made their presence known to the Devils. Now it was time to show them that they meant business. Mandey realized that they couldn't separate their original intent of being protectors from taking more aggressive steps. The Devils weren't going to back off because a bunch of kids in fancy jackets wanted them to. The Alley Cats were going to have to take more drastic measures to get the Devils to take them seriously. Mandey didn't think the middle of Liaisons was a good place to start taking those drastic measures. Causing a melee would get them all kicked out, or maybe banned, and someone innocent could get hurt in the process.

Down on the dance floor, the Devils worked their way through the crowd toward Jesse and Angelina. Mandey had the Bic up and flashing even before Angelina had her hand in the air to give the distress signal. A moment later she saw Dina, Danny, and Jeremy heading out there. Mandey debated whether she should stay put or go down to help. She decided to stay where she was for the time being in case any more Devils showed up.

She watched, worried, as Jesse and Raff had heated words with each other. Suddenly Raff shoved Jesse, and Mandey knew all hell was going to break loose. She bolted from the table and made her way downstairs. Fortunately, she did not run into anyone she knew well enough to speak to on the way.

As Mandey got down to the next level, she saw the cluster of black jackets, denim and satin, marching up the stairs off the dance floor toward the door. She didn't see Rent-a-Cop Rick anywhere, so somewhat cool heads must have prevailed to get them to take it outside. She hurried through the crowd to catch up.

Danny was lagging behind the others. Mandey caught up with him and asked him what was going on.

"Well, we've got their attention, that's for sure," Danny said. "They're pissed about the graffiti, Raff's pissed about his flat tires, and he's also raving about us tossing a Molotov cocktail at them earlier tonight."

"What?" Mandey asked, surprised. "But we didn't—" She cut herself off short, then said, "Terry."

"That's what I was thinking," Danny said, "but we're getting the blame."

"That's what being in a gang is all about," Mandey said. "'All for one and one for all.'"

"Yeah, but it's not good when the left hand doesn't know what the right hand is doing," Danny said.

Jeremy turned around. "Enough of the clichés already," he said, rolling his eyes.

Danny pushed him playfully as they trooped out the door and into the parking lot. They divided up into their groups.

"Let's take it out back," Jesse said.

"How do we know you don't have the rest of your gang out there waiting to ambush us?" Raff asked.

"How do we know that you don't?" Jesse replied.

Slowly, silently, the two groups shuffled around to the alley running in back of the club. It was dimly lit by one outdoor light by the service exit and bordered by the woods, which stretched about a hundred feet over to the next street.

The two groups faced each other, Mandey, Danny, Jeremy, Jesse, Angelina, and Dina staring at Raff, Juanita, Kerri, and two young-looking Latino boys.

"Didn't Trick tell Dopehead Dan to give all of you the message to stay away?" Raff asked.

"Aw, are you too scared of us to let us hang around here?" Jesse taunted.

"It ain't for our sakes, it's for yours," Raff said. "You know we ain't nice people."

"We know you ain't nice, but that don't mean you're tough," Jesse said.

"Tough?" Raff repeated. "You don't know the meaning of the word, but we can show you."

"Raff, remember what Trick said," said the shorter of the two younger boys.

"Trick ain't here right now, Marco," Raff snapped.

"Trick is your leader, right?" Jesse asked. "He don't seem to be around much."

"Don't you worry about him. He's taking care of business as we speak," Raff said.

"What exactly did your leader tell you?" Jesse asked.

"Like I said, he's not here now, so it don't matter," Raff said. "And exactly who is the leader of your outfit? I thought it was you, but you didn't seem to know nothing about the firebomb we got hit with."

"I share leadership with Terry," Jesse said evenly. "Does your leader know about every move you make?"

Raff smiled a smile that made Mandey shiver. "No."

"Raff, you're always bitching at Trick for being too much talk and not enough action," Kerri said. "Are we going to do something or what?"

"Shut up," Raff replied, "or I'll slap your fucking mouth off your face."

"Oh, that's a nice way to treat a woman," Angelina said indignantly.

"Hey, I'll slap the hell out of you, too," Raff said to her.

"Over my dead body," Jesse said fiercely, balling up his fists.

"Okay," Raff agreed, whipping out a long, shiny knife.

A collective gasp escaped from the Alley Cats.

"Shit," Danny muttered.

"You've got to be kidding," Jeremy said in a low voice.

"Kidding?" Raff asked, holding up the knife to make sure all the Alley Cats could see it. "Does this look like I'm kidding?"

"You could do it, but you couldn't get away with it," Mandey said.

"You sound like our fucking leader," Raff said disgustedly.

"It's true, though, isn't it?" Jesse said. "The cops ignore a lot of what goes on around here, but they won't ignore murder."

"True," Raff said reluctantly, and slid his knife back into his pocket. "As much as I want to, I can't just spill your sorry guts out on the ground without catching the heat. But don't let that make you think you're safe."

"Look," Jesse said impatiently, "All we care about is being left alone. We don't care what you do as long as you don't do it to us or our friends."

"You don't give us orders," Raff said. "This is our territory. We live here, and you ain't welcome."

"We want to talk to Trick," Jesse said.

"What for?" Raff asked.

"He's your leader. We need to settle this once and for all."

"Why do you think Trick will want to talk to you?" Raff asked.

"I don't know if he wants to or not, but I want to talk to him, leader to leader, to see if we can come to an agreement."

"When?"

"When?" Jesse repeated, caught off guard.

"When do you want to talk to him?" Raff said impatiently.

Jesse paused and thought. Mandey imagined he was mentally going through his appointment calendar. "Wednesday, six o'clock, here in the Liaisons parking lot."

"Okay," Raff said. "I'll give Trick the message, but I don't know if he'll show."

"Just tell him," Jesse said shortly, then turned to the other Alley Cats. "Come on, y'all, let's go."

They turned to leave when Raff said, "Where the hell are you going? I didn't say we were done with you."

The Alley Cats froze. Jesse turned to look at Raff. "I want to deal with your leader. Until then, we're through with you."

Mandey shrieked when Raff tackled Jesse. All she could think about was the long knife Raff had shown them. She didn't want to see it again.

"Jesse!" Angelina yelled, jumping on top of Raff. That brought Juanita into the scuffle, as she grabbed Angelina by the hair. Then Dina was attacking Juanita, and Jeremy and Danny sprang into action, getting a hold of Raff and yanking him to his feet. Marco and the other boy joined the fray, trying to overpower Danny and Jeremy to get them to let go of Jesse. That left Mandey looking nervously at Kerri, who was staring back at her with narrowed eyes.

"Don't even think about it," Mandey said.

"What did you say?" Kerri asked, pushing Mandey in the chest.

"I said don't even think about it!" Mandey replied, pushing back harder. "I busted your girlfriend's nose when she was trying to steal a car, and I can do the same to you."

"Try it, bitch," Kerri said, with her pretty face in an ugly snarl. She shoved Mandey again.

The service exit door opened. A redhead stepped outside and stopped short. Her companion bumped into her from behind. It was Rick, the security guard.

"God damn it!" he yelled. "Get out of here! Go! I'm gonna call the fucking cops!"

He didn't stick around to see what the response to that would be; he and the redhead disappeared inside.

"Let's go!" Jesse ordered.

Mandey didn't need to be told twice. She turned and ran, nearly running into Danny, who was already ahead of her.

"'Pussies!" Kerri screeched after them.

"Wednesday night," Jesse said, backing away. "We'll take care of this."

He turned and caught up with the others. "Back to the van."

"Are they coming after us?" Mandey asked anxiously.

Jesse glanced back quickly. "Don't think so."

"Good," Mandey said.

"Come on, let's get out of here and over to the impound lot," Jesse said.

Shannon slowly drove past the impound lot. There were lights on in the office and a pick-up parked out front. The two Rottweilers started barking at the car and strained to get off their chains. They had been loose last week, which was why he had to feed them raw hamburger mixed with ground up sleeping pills. Anyone else would have gotten a shotgun and shot them dead, but he couldn't do that. He had always wanted a dog, and he thought Rotties were cool. He thought he might have one of his own someday. They were good protection under most circumstances, too.

He sped up when the dogs began to bark; he knew someone would come to the window to look out. He circled around the block again.

"Are we going to go in circles all night? I'm getting dizzy," Annette complained.

"I want to make sure we have the right guy," Shannon said. "Kerri said this Terry guy works with his brother. I want to make sure it's Terry."

"What do you care?" Checkmate asked. "Let's just blow them all away and be rid of them." He flashed a pistol tucked into his waistband under his jacket.

"Jesus, Checkmate, put that away!" Shannon exclaimed. "We ain't blowing anybody away!"

"Man, you're no fun," Checkmate said, hiding it away again.

Shannon decided to stop making circles. They passed the front gate of the impound lot five more times, but passed from both directions at different intervals. On the last pass, Shannon spotted someone in an Alley Cats jacket getting something out of the pick-up truck.

"There's your proof," John said. "What are we going to do?"

Shannon had been thinking the entire time they had driven around. He wanted to do something that would scare the shit out of them, but wouldn't hurt them. He didn't think that Molotov cocktail had been meant to do much harm, but they couldn't let it pass, because next time the bottle might not explode harmlessly outside. Shannon couldn't take that chance.

He knew whoever was inside the office was watching and waiting for something to happen, so even with the watchdogs chained up, they couldn't get too close. Shannon thought the Alley Cats had the right idea using a firebomb, something they could throw from a distance and disappear.

A metal chain link fence stretched all the way around the impound lot, a fact that stuck in his mind. Shannon took a page out of Raff's playbook and came up with an idea that, if it worked, would be spectacular and scary, if not too dangerous.

Fifteen minutes later they were parked on the street on the back side of the impound lot where they were least likely to be spotted.

"You've got to be quick about it because the dogs will start to bark," Shannon said as John and Checkmate got out of the car, each armed with a gas can. "Run and get back here ASAP."

Shannon sat there, nervous, hoping that this wasn't going to get out of hand. He heard the Rottweilers take up their barking again. *Hurry,* he thought, gripping the steering wheel.

Checkmate made it back first.

"Everything okay?" Shannon asked him.

"A-okay," he said, sliding into the backseat with Annette and Curtis.

John was back thirty seconds later.

"Light it and let's go," Shannon said.

John tossed a lit match at the base of the fence. The gasoline ignited. As they drove off, the chain link fence surrounding the lot was burning brightly.

"Oh my God!" Mandey gasped as she drove the van up the street toward the impound lot.

The whole impound lot appeared to be on fire. Orange flames engulfed the entire fence. Mandey parked as close as she could and the Alley Cats rushed out of the van. A few other cars were stopped, as well, and a few people were standing in the street. The air reeked of gasoline. Then they noticed that the flames appeared to be confined to the fence alone and were burning themselves out.

Through the blaze they saw Terry, Brad, Jim, and Zack in the yard. Terry was spraying the fence with a hose, and the other three had a bucket brigade going. Even without their efforts, the fire was dying down. Sirens wailed in the distance. Someone had called the fire department.

"Terry, what in God's name happened?" Jesse yelled through the gate.

"Not sure," Terry said. "I think they poured gas all around the fence and set it afire."

The sirens grew closer, making Mandey nervous. She wasn't the only one.

"God damn it, we don't need the cops coming," Jesse said.

"Hey, why don't you get these guys and all get out of here?" Terry said, coming closer to the gate.

"Are you sure?" Jesse asked.

"Yeah. We don't need the cops seeing us all together, and I don't want them to see that I've been giving beer to minors."

"I didn't even know you were nineteen," Jesse said.

Terry just nodded, then turned to yell at Brad, Zack, and Jim. "Hey, y'all, go with the others and get out of here. I'll handle the cops when they get here."

They each came with a bucket of water to make sure the fire near the gate was extinguished and the gate was cool enough to open. As they came through, there was only one corner of the fence still left burning with any intensity, and it was fading fast.

"Terry, I set us up a meeting to talk to that Trick character at six o'clock on Wednesday. I told Raff we want to settle this once and for all," Jesse said.

"Good idea," Terry said. "Go on, now. Get out of here."

The sirens were drawing near. The rest of the Alley Cats got into the van. Mandey didn't want to appear like they were making a getaway of some sort, but she didn't waste any time getting out of there before the authorities showed up.

38

Burning Again

On Sunday, Shannon arrived at Mandey's house close to 11. Both were bleary-eyed and tired from the night before, but neither one questioned the other about it.

"Think the Oilers will make it three in a row today?" Mandey asked him, as they prepared their lunch and football-watching snacks.

"Yeah, they should have a pretty good chance against the Browns," Shannon said.

Mandey yawned. Shannon yawned, too.

The food was the highlight of the game, as the Oilers lost 27-10.

Marcia was sitting in the living room with them, reading while the game was on. When it ended, she said, "I taped *The Burning Bed* when it was on, but I haven't watched it yet. Want to watch it now?"

"Sure," Mandey said. "I heard it was good."

"Yeah, they said Farrah Fawcett did a great job. She's more than teeth and big hair," Marcia said, getting up to put the VHS tape into the VCR.

The three of them were largely silent during the movie, which was about a woman named Francine Hughes, played by Farrah Fawcett, who was abused by her husband, Mickey, played by Paul Le Mat. After years of abuse, she set his bed on fire when he was drunk and asleep and burned him to death. Mandey found the graphic violence disturbing and difficult to watch. Also, she liked Paul Le Mat as John Milner in *American Graffiti* (he was hot), and to see him playing such a violent character so convincingly was unnerving.

"Wow," Mandey said when it ended. Shannon had his hand on her knee and was squeezing it firmly. Her hand was doing the same to his knee. When her hand relaxed, she felt his relax, too.

"That was pretty heavy," Marcia said, stopping the tape.

"Yeah," Mandey said. "Very heavy."

Shannon didn't say anything. The movie had emotionally drained him. Some of it was too familiar, and it also brought back memories of the nightmare he had the week before.

"Let's go to my room and listen to music or watch something a little less serious," Mandey suggested.

She and Shannon got up and headed down the hall.

"Maybe we shouldn't have watched it," Mandey said, noticing the strained look on his face.

"No," Shannon replied. "People need to see stuff like that. Maybe it will help to stop it from happening to someone else."

She put some records on the turntable and turned it on. They laid down on Mandey's bed and started kissing, but Mandey could sense that Shannon wasn't feeling it. She pulled back and looked at him.

"What's wrong?" she asked.

"Nothing," Shannon said.

"Are you sure?" Mandey asked.

He was quiet for a moment then said, "Yeah, I'm okay."

"That movie really bothered you, didn't it?" Mandey asked. "It makes you wonder how a person could treat someone they supposedly love like that."

"Yeah," Shannon said, turning to lay on his back and look at the ceiling. He reached over and took Mandey's hand in his.

"Did that remind you of Leon?"

"In some ways," Shannon said. "Except that guy didn't beat on his kids. Not exactly the same, but still too close to home."

Mandey kissed his cheek. It was covered in a rough stubble because he hadn't shaved that morning. He turned to look at her.

"I don't want to think about it," he said.

"Let me help you get it out of your head," Mandey said, kissing his mouth.

She unbuttoned his shirt, then took his hands in hers and guided them toward her blouse, indicating she wanted him to unbutton hers. He did, then Shannon's hand ran up Mandey's back to her bra and fumbled with the hooks. Finally, she sat up and unfastened it, then laid down again. Shannon lifted it, freeing her breasts, allowing him to hold and caress them. Mandey closed her eyes, loving how he was touching her.

"Put the bad stuff out of your mind," she told him.

His tongue was in her mouth, then his mouth was on her neck, giving her a love bite. His stubble was rough on her skin, but she loved it. Their legs entwined, and Mandey's hand ran up Shannon's back, under his shirt. Her other hand rested on the crotch of his jeans.

Suddenly, he stopped. "I don't ever want to hurt you like that," he told her.

Mandey stopped and looked him in the face. "Are you afraid you might?"

"Yes!" Shannon said, more fiercely than Mandey expected to hear. "I can say, 'I'll never do that to you', but sometimes I get scared that Leon's rubbed off on me, and I'm gonna to do something I'll regret." He drew her close and held her tightly.

His admission scared Mandey a little, but she felt his despair as he clung to her so desperately.

"You won't," she assured him. "You're too afraid that it might happen. I hope there will never be a time where that would even cross your mind."

Shannon squeezed his eyes shut. "I won't," he said, suddenly feeling stubborn. "I can't. I've seen too much, I've been through too much, and I can't let it get to me. I'm not like Leon, and I'm not like Mickey Hughes."

"No, you are not," Mandey said, reassuringly.

"I've told myself over and over that I am not going to be like Leon. I'm not going to be the kind of guy that beats on women. I'm not," Shannon said, sounding like he was trying to convince himself.

"Shannon, I believe you. Now believe it yourself."

He took a deep breath and exhaled slowly. "I never want to hurt you," he said, then buried his face in her hair.

"I'm not worried about it, sweetie," Mandey said. "I know you love me, and now I know how determined you are not to do anything that would hurt me."

"I can't imagine ever doing anything like that to you," Shannon said. *Except that dream...*

"If you can't imagine it, then you won't," Mandey assured him.

As he felt her soft lips kissing his neck, he started to calm down. He had managed not to smack Kerri, and she had infuriated him countless times. If he could control himself around Kerri, it should never even be an issue where Mandey was concerned.

Eventually, his mind came back to the present situation. He was lying on a bed with his girlfriend, and she had taken her tits out for him. He needed to pay attention to that.

"I love you," he said, finally focusing on what they were doing. He brought her hand down to his crotch, which was now getting hard. After a few minutes of heavy petting, he reached down and unbuttoned and unzipped his jeans.

"Shannon," Mandey said. "I—"

"I know, Mandey," Shannon said. "Just feel it through my underwear."

He took her hand and led it to the bulge in his briefs.

"That's yours," he told her. "You tell me when, and it's all yours."

She had no frame of reference except for what she had read, but he felt huge to her.

Mine, she thought, a flicker of pleasure lighting inside of herself.

"Someday, I promise," she said, a bit breathlessly between kisses. "You will have all of me, I promise."

39

Just in Case

The Alley Cats met at Jack in the Box after school on that Monday after Thanksgiving. Terry recounted what had happened Saturday night when the fire department and police had shown up. The fire department had determined that someone had poured gasoline around the fence and set it ablaze. No damage was done except that the fence was blackened along with a few stray tufts of grass and weeds growing up through the asphalt. The cops asked him what he had seen, which was nothing. They asked what he had been doing, and Terry explained he had friends over playing cards, but they had left right after the fire because they were freaked out by it. He was quick to tell the police that none of his friends had seen anything suspicious, either.

"They did tell me that someone they talked to mentioned seeing a white car driving around the neighborhood, but he couldn't give a description or a plate number," Terry said. "The cops didn't hassle me too much, but somehow I don't think they're going to do much about it since no one got hurt and there wasn't no damage done."

"We've got to do something before things get way out of hand," Jesse said. "I told Raff I wanted us to meet with Trick on Wednesday at six."

Zack and Jim looked at each other. "We have band practice on Wednesday night," Zack said. "The other guys are pissed that we've been cutting out on them so much. We've got to show. We're rehearsing two new songs."

Mandey giggled. "You mean you know other songs besides 'Crazy Train' and 'I Am Ironman'?" she asked.

"Hey, we also know 'Paranoid' and 'Breaking the Law' and—" Jim said indignantly.

"We don't all have to go," Jesse said. "All we're going to do Wednesday is talk. Is there anyone else who can't make it?"

"I've got basketball practice until five-thirty, so I don't think I'll be able to make it," Brad broke in.

"I can't, either," Dina said, lighting a cigarette.

"You can't? Why?" Angelina asked.

"My cousin's wedding," Dina said. "We're getting fitted for our bridesmaid dresses Wednesday afternoon."

"I have an eye doctor appointment at five that day," Mandey said. "I won't be done with that in time to go." She was relieved to have an excuse not to be there.

"Well, that leaves five of us, anyway," Jesse said. "Do we have your okay to negotiate on your behalf?"

"Sure," Zack said. The rest of the Wednesday absentees nodded.

"Good," Jesse said. "Now we've got to decide what it is we want from them."

"We know what we want," Zack said. "We want them to leave the club people alone. And Terry's brother's business."

"But how do we do that?" Brad asked.

"That's why we're here. We have to come up with a plan. We know we can't just say, 'Leave us alone or else.' We've got to be able to back it up with something."

"I want to state right now that I want nothing to do with anything involving guns or knives or weapons of any sort," Mandey said.

"I agree," Danny said. "I'm sure they are a lot more experienced using those sorts of things than any of us, and I personally don't want to get maimed or killed."

"Well, I personally want to take a sawed-off shotgun and go after the lot of them," Terry said.

"You won't be so cocky if you've got them all pointing guns back at you," Jesse said. "I agree with Mandey and Danny. We want to stay in one piece and we don't want the cops involved."

"So what do we do?" Zack asked. "Ask for an old-fashioned skin-on-skin fistfight?"

"Actually, that's not a bad idea," Jesse said. "From what I can tell, we're pretty evenly matched up with them. We could challenge them to a fair fight. If we win, they leave us alone. If they win, we'll back off."

"Jesse, they'll mop the floor with us," Mandey said. "I'm sure they've got more experience fighting than we do. Than I do, anyway. I've never fought anyone before."

"You smacked that bitch in the face and made her leave you alone," Angelina reminded her.

"Yeah, have a little faith in yourself," Dina said.

"The idea just scares the heck out of me," Mandey said.

"Hey, don't worry," Jesse said. "If it gets too intense, just back off. The rest of us will take care of it. You'll probably just fight that same girl or that blonde bitch, anyway."

Zack, Jim, and Brad were having a conference, then Zack said, "We've scuffled with some of those guys before. If they play fair, I think we've got a pretty good chance."

"I wouldn't mind mixing it up with that Trick fella," Terry said. "He gave me a concussion. I'd like to return the favor."

"Let's take a vote," Jesse said. "Is this what we want to ask for?"

Almost everyone nodded.

"In favor, raise your hand," Jesse said.

Eight hands went up. Mandey's and Danny's stayed down. Then slowly Danny's made it nine.

Everyone looked at Mandey. "I abstain," she told them.

"Motion passes with nine votes," Jesse said. "Watch out, Devils, here we come."

After the vote, the meeting broke up quickly. Mandey grabbed her Pepsi and trudged out to the van.

Angelina caught up with her. "Mandey, are you with us?" she asked anxiously.

Mandey sighed. "Angie, this had gone a lot further than I thought it would. I don't know how to fight anybody. That one punch I landed on that girl was just luck."

"Well, if the Devils agree to the fight, Jesse wants to have a meeting to talk about strategy and fighting techniques," Angelina said.

"Okay," Mandey said, feeling defeated.

"Alley Cats kick ass!" Angelina said, showing the cat's paw sign. Mandey smiled weakly and returned it. She hoped Angelina was right.

Before heading home, Mandey had a stop to make. Trish's comment about the Mexican switchblade last week had stuck in her head. She knew Trish was making a joke; she was always asking what outrageous things she could bring back from Mexico for her classmates, but there was an underlying note of seriousness to it. On Tuesday, she had pulled Trish aside before English class and asked her if she really could bring a Mexican switchblade back across the border and how much would it cost.

"Yeah, we can do it. We have before. They're really ornate and cool-looking. Are you sure you want one?" Trish asked.

"It might make me feel safer," Mandey said. "If I get jumped again, I don't want to be defenseless."

Trish gave her a price, which was lower than Mandey expected. Mandey brought had her the money Wednesday, and today at school Trish told her to come by her house to get it

Trish answered the door. "Come on in," she said, and led Mandey to her bedroom.

She handed Mandey a small box. Mandey opened it to find a lovely turquoise and mother-of-pearl handled knife. Trish took it out and hit the button to release the blade, which was sharp, shiny, and three inches long.

"Wow, that's beautiful," Mandey said, taking it from Trish. She held it up to admire it.

"Isn't it? I thought you'd like it," Trish said. "But be careful with it—that thing can be lethal."

"I hope I don't have a reason to use it," Mandey said.

"Let me show you a couple things."

Trish showed her how to pull the knife smoothly from her pocket and hit the button so the blade was at the ready in a split second.

"How'd you learn to do that?" Mandey asked.

"I asked the seller to give me some pointers so I could pass them on to you," Trish said.

Mandey thought Trish handled the knife more expertly than someone who had gotten just a few "pointers", but she didn't force the issue. "Thanks."

"No problem. Just don't get hurt."

40

Rules of Engagement

Two cars, one black and one white, sat in the empty parking lot of Liaisons at 6 P.M. on a chilly Wednesday evening. Shannon sat in the driver's seat of the Oldsmobile, smoking and trying to stay calm. Next to him was John, puffing nonchalantly on a fragrant clove cigarette, tapping his ashes out of the half-open window. In the backseat, Checkmate, Annette, and Kerri were also smoking. Although all the windows were cracked, the car's interior was still blue with smoke. In the black '72 Eldorado parked next to them, Raff sat with the rest of the gang. All the Devils had insisted on showing up. Shannon had threatened them all with grave bodily harm if anyone said or did one thing without his okay. His main fear concerned what Raff might take upon himself to do.

Shannon wished to God it hadn't gotten this far, but those fool Alley Cats wouldn't leave anything alone. They kept showing up in their territory and pushing and pushing. Then they asked for this meeting, to "negotiate an understanding," as Raff said the little prick Jesse had put it.

A green '79 Nova pulled into the parking lot and parked facing the Devils' cars. After a moment, the passenger door opened and a tall, burly, sandy-haired redneck got out.

Shannon pulled on his ski mask and got out of the car. He wasn't about to go maskless in front of these people he had once gone to school with; too risky that one might recognize him. He signaled for the others to follow. Out of the Nova appeared four others. Shannon knew there were more than five Alley Cats, but where were they?

"What's with the mask? Too chicken to let us see your face?" Terry sneered.

"Is the rest of your gang on the way?" Shannon asked, ignoring Terry's remark.

Jesse shook his head. "We didn't think we needed everyone here just to talk. We have permission to negotiate on behalf of the whole gang."

Raff had made his way over to stand next to Shannon. "Trick, we've got them outnumbered two to one. Let's take them down now."

"Not a good idea," Terry said, who had overheard the remark, "unless you want to piss us off and make this escalate even more."

"Raff, we don't know if they're telling the truth. The others could be hiding, waiting to ambush us if something goes wrong," Shannon said in a low voice.

"'Trick', that's what they call you?" Terry asked. "Thanks for the fucking concussion you gave me when you robbed my brother's impound lot."

Shannon looked at Terry. He remembered that night, and how he'd smacked him up against the head with a chair. Hard-headed son-of-a-bitch.

"All of us have some beef or another with y'all. You didn't think we were like you, just doing this for jollies, did you?" Jesse asked.

"We're tired of all your bullshit," Angelina said.

"We're sick of you stealing from us, too," Danny said, looking first at Trick, then at Raff.

Shannon stared at Danny, still bemused by the idea that his girlfriend might be doing a class project with this guy. Then he shifted his attention to the short guy standing between Danny and Terry. Next to Terry, he looked like a dwarf.

Jesus, I think I had P.E. class with that kid. Jeremy Something? Thank God I put on my mask, he thought.

He snapped out of his worried thoughts. "This is our territory. If you don't like it, stay the hell up there where you came from," Shannon told them.

"How the hell do you know where we're from?" Terry demanded.

Shannon stared straight at Danny. "I saw Dickweed's school ID the other night," he said.

"Why, you stupid bast—" Danny began, making a lunge at Shannon.

Jesse and Jeremy caught him. "Calm down," Jeremy told him.

"Stay away from here and you'll have no problem with us," Shannon said.

"You don't own this part of town!" Angelina said angrily. "You don't have the right to tell anybody where they can go or what they can do!"

"All I'm saying is if you don't like the way things are around here, stay the fuck away," Shannon said.

"But that's just it," Terry said. "Some of us like to come down here. Some of us need to come down here. They like to go to the club and have a good time. Me, I work down here with my brother. My job is here. So, I'd say this makes this our territory, too. We don't go around messing with nobody, and all we want is for y'all to leave us the hell alone."

"Sorry," Shannon said. "You choose to come into our area, you play by our rules. We aren't changing what we do for a bunch of whiny kids from the suburbs."

"'Suburbs'?" Angelina asked indignantly. "You don't know nothing about our 'hood. You better not underestimate us."

I know more about it than you know, Shannon thought, and he had no intention of underestimating them.

"Don't tell us what we know or don't know!" Annette spat, stepping forward threateningly. "Trick said y'all go to Rogers. I went there, too. Bitches think they're better than anyone else! I fucked up a little bitch named Dina Diaz real good! If she still goes there, you go find her and ask her! We ain't people to you want to mess with!"

For a moment Angelina was taken aback by Annette's outburst, but then she stepped forward toward Annette like she was ready to take a swing at her. Jesse pulled her back.

"Shut up!" Shannon told his sister urgently. He wished he hadn't said anything about where the Alley Cats called home.

"If you don't change your mind, you're going to regret it," Jesse said. "Right now you're dealing with ten angry people, but it wouldn't take much to double or triple our numbers. Other people who go to Liaisons have figured out what it is we're trying to do, and they want to help us. They're as sick of being your victims as we are."

Oh, shit, Shannon thought. *This has got to be stopped, now.*

"How are you gonna make us stop?" he asked them. "You can't come in here and make a few threats and expect us just to say okay. You've got to earn it."

"We will earn it," Jesse said. "Every time you push us, we'll push back. Every time you do something we think is wrong, we'll be on you like white on rice. This is just the beginning. And like I said, just because there are only ten of us now, it doesn't mean that there might not be twenty-five of us coming after you next week."

"But I get the feeling that's not what you want," Shannon said. "I think you'd rather get this settled once and for all as soon as possible."

Jesse and Terry looked at each other. "Maybe," Terry said.

"Don't screw around with me," Shannon said, disgustedly. "What do you want?"

"Is this your entire group?" Jesse asked, looking over the Devils.

"Yeah."

"We have ten, too."

"So?"

"We want to meet your gang and fight it out. Us against y'all. If you win, we back off and you're free to terrorize the neighborhood again. But if we win, you stay away from Liaisons and everyone who goes there, and Terry's brother's storage lot."

"Oh, what a bunch of bullshit!" Raff exclaimed.

"Shut it, Raff," Shannon warned, then turned back to the Alley Cats. "And what if I say no, we don't want to?"

"Then things go on the way they have been," Terry said. "We'll fight against y'all every chance we can, as dirty as we can."

"We'll recruit more of our friends," Danny added. "We'll be after you constantly. You won't be able to get away from us."

Shannon didn't say anything for a moment. The idea of having a face-off in a gang-bang didn't appeal to him, but even worse was the prospect of continual fighting. He looked the five Alley Cats over. He knew the Devils could mop the floor with them. If he agreed to the fight, he had to make sure that the Devils wouldn't get carried away.

He motioned for the Devils to join him in a huddle.

"I think we should do this," he told them. "I know we're all sick of dealing with them and their nasty surprises, and this is our way of getting them out of our hair once and for all."

"I agree," Raff said. Shannon looked at him, surprised. "They're a bunch of wimps and pussies. The faster we can get rid of them, the better."

"One thing, though," Shannon said. "I'm going to insist on a fair fight."

"No way, man!" Raff objected. "They want to come into our neighborhood, they got to play like we play."

"It's going to be a fair fight or we ain't doing it," Shannon insisted. "No ifs, ands, or buts about it. We'd do more harm to them than they would to us, but someone might end up dead, and we'd get the cops on our ass and someone would end up in jail. You don't want that, believe me."

"Fuckin' bullshit," Raff muttered.

"Are you a fuckin' coward or what, Raff?" Shannon asked angrily. "Don't you think we can beat them fair and square?"

Raff mumbled something unintelligible under his breath.

"I swear to God, anyone goes against what I just said is going to be mighty sorry."

Shannon broke from the huddle and faced the Alley Cats once again.

"We'll agree to settle this with a fight, but we've got a few conditions," he told them.

"Let's hear them," Terry said.

"First, it's a fair fight—fists, no weapons," Shannon said. "I don't think it'll improve your chances of winning, but it will increase the odds that y'all'll live to see another day."

"Well, that's mighty nice of you," Terry said sourly.

"We were going to insist on that ourselves," Jesse said. "What else?"

"We set the time and place. Let's get this done ASAP. Friday night, ten-thirty, at the vacant lot next to the Northview Apartments."

Now it was the Alley Cats' turn to huddle. After a moment, Jesse faced the Devils. "We accept," he told them. "But let's make it clear. No weapons of any kind. Any weapons show up, the whole deal is null and void."

"Agreed," Shannon said. "If we retreat first, we'll stay away from Liaisons and the impound lot. You retreat first, then you cut all the shit and mind your own business. If no one retreats, the winner is the side with the last man standing."

"Okay," Jesse said.

"We've got seven men and three females," Shannon said. "I don't want any guys beating on our women."

"You reserve that right for yourselves, I suppose," Jeremy muttered.

"Come again?" Shannon said ominously. "I didn't catch that."

"He said not to worry. Just by coincidence, we've got the same numbers," Jesse said.

"Good," Shannon said shortly. "Friday night, ten-thirty." He turned to the rest of his gang. "Let's go."

Shannon and the Devils got into their cars. Shannon watched the Alley Cats get back into the Nova. He hoped to God Friday was going to be the end of it. One less thing to have to deal with when all he wanted to do is get the hell out of there and be done with this stuff once and for all.

41

Too Much All at Once

On Thursday afternoon, the Alley Cats met after school at the park. Mandey sat in silence at a picnic table as Jesse and Terry provided the details of last night's agreement. While she was glad that both sides had settled for an old-fashioned fistfight, she still found the whole idea disturbing. They didn't trust the Devils to stick to their end of the deal. How did they know that as soon as they showed up on Friday the Devils might not besiege them with guns and knives? She thought about her lovely turquoise and mother-of-pearl-handled Mexican switchblade. She had no intention of using it, but it would be with her Friday night, just in case.

As Angelina had said they would, Jesse and Terry provided some tips for how to handle oneself in a fistfight. Terry sounded like he was speaking from experience. Jesse, on the other hand, sounded like he had just skimmed through a few books on self-defense and martial arts. Between the two of them, it was kind of a mish-mash of techniques. The two of them sparred, and the rest of the Alley Cats stood and imitated the moves Jesse and Terry demonstrated. After a while, Jesse and Terry's sparring started to look a little less like demonstration and more like semi-serious combat.

"Hey, guys, cool it!" Zack said finally, getting between them, and he had to dodge a fist Terry swung at Jesse. "We've got to save our energy for the enemy!"

That evening, Mandey and Marcia sat at the kitchen table eating homemade meatball grinders with lots of onions, green peppers, and mozzarella cheese. Mandey was reading the Entertainment section of the *Chronicle* as she ate.

"Mandey, there's something I want to talk to you about," Marcia said suddenly.

Mandey's stomach did a flip. She always felt a little sick when someone said that to her because it was usually followed by something unpleasant.

"What?" she asked through a mouthful of meatball, then swallowed. She laid down the paper.

"I noticed that you and Shannon are getting very close," Marcia said.

I think the sex talk is coming, Mandey thought.

"Yes," Mandey said slowly, drawing the word out until it almost sounded like a question.

"How close are you getting?" Marcia asked.

"I don't think we've gotten as close as you think we have," Mandey said.

"So you aren't sleeping together yet."

"No," Mandey said flatly.

"But you're going to, right?"

"Eventually," Mandey said slowly.

"Have you two talked about it?"

"A little bit," Mandey said.

"Mandey, I'm just concerned," Marcia said. "I'm not going to try to tell you what to do. When I was your age, I was already having sex, and I was irresponsible about it, so I ended up getting pregnant at eighteen. I don't want you to make the same mistake I did."

Mandey raised her eyebrows and said nothing.

"I know that sounded bad," Marcia said. "You weren't a mistake, you were <u>unplanned</u>. I was a freshman in college, and I wasn't ready to take care of a baby, especially since your father disappeared when I told him I was pregnant. I had to drop out of college; it was too scandalous to have an unwed mother-to-be in the dorms. I was lucky to have Ma and Daddy to take care of me and to take care of you. In the end it all turned out okay, but to be honest, if I could do it all again, I'd do it differently."

Mandey remained silent. Although Marcia was basically saying that she wished Mandey had never been born, Mandey didn't resent her for feeling that way. She knew enough not to take it personally. After all, Mandey hadn't had any control over the situation, and what was done was done.

"Mandey, if you got pregnant and had the baby, you know that baby would be adored by everyone in this family, but your life would never be the same," Marcia said. "You want to make sure you don't get pregnant until you want to."

"Well, I know when the time comes we'll use some sort of birth control," Mandey said.

"You've got to make sure," Marcia insisted. "You might get carried away some day and you won't be prepared. I talked to Ma about this the other night, and she agreed that you should get on the Pill as soon as possible."

"You talked to Ma?" Mandey exclaimed, mortified, covering her face with her hands.

"What?" Marcia asked.

"It's embarrassing, that's all."

"She's concerned. She doesn't want you following in my footsteps," Marcia said. "I'm going to make you an appointment with my doctor."

"But we're not at that point yet," Mandey said. "I already told Shannon I want to wait awhile, and he's okay with that."

"Still, it's better to be safe than sorry," Marcia insisted. "I'm not telling you to get on the Pill and go have sex with him. I'm telling you to get on the Pill so when you decide the time is right, you won't have to worry."

Mandey was quiet a moment, then shrugged. "Okay. You're right."

"Anyway, you have to be on the Pill for one whole cycle before you're regulated and it begins to work."

"Okay," Mandey said again.

"I'll call tomorrow and make you an appointment for after school next week sometime, okay?"

"Okay," Mandey said for the third time.

Marcia stared at her for a moment. "You sure are a lot less difficult than I was at your age."

Mandey shrugged again.

"Will you be nervous? Do you want me to go with you?"

Mandey shook her head. "No."

"My doctor is a man, but I can get you an appointment with a female doctor if that will make you more comfortable," Marcia said.

"I don't think it makes a difference. I'm not nervous."

"You're just like Daddy that way. You're so calm and matter-of-fact about everything. I wish some of that had been passed on to me."

"Must have skipped a generation," Mandey said. "I'm the strong, silent type. That's good in a guy, but not so good in a woman."

"I think Shannon would disagree," Marcia said.

"Perhaps," Mandey said. "All I know is that I feel very lucky to have him."

"Well, he's damn lucky to have you, too," Marcia replied.

"That's what he tells me," Mandey said. "I wish I could find a way to help him more, though."

"What do you mean?" Marcia asked.

"He's frustrated over so many things in his life," Mandey said. "You know what I've told you about his stepdad and his job and all that. I wish I could do something more to make his life better."

"Are things getting worse at his house?" Marcia asked.

"I'm not sure they could get much worse," Mandey said. "He's so desperate to get out of there."

Marcia was quiet a moment, then said, "Well, if it gets where it's intolerable, we do have an extra bedroom."

Mandey's eyes widened. "You mean he could move in here?" she asked excitedly.

"If worse comes to worse, yes," Marcia said. "Which is all the more reason you need to get on the Pill. I hope they'll have appointments open next week."

Mandey ate the rest of her sandwich while thinking about the possibility of having Shannon living with her. She knew of at least one other couple at school who lived together. The girl's parents were divorced, she didn't get along with her mother, and her father had moved out of state, so she moved in with her boyfriend and his family. So if Shannon moved in with her, it wouldn't be unheard of.

She wasn't worried about what other people would think about it, anyhow. It would be good for Shannon to be away from all the turmoil in his life, plus it would be wonderful to see Shannon every day, every morning, and every night. Yes, if that happened, being on the Pill would be a wise idea. Mandey still wanted to wait, but if Shannon was living with her, that might be difficult. Even now it was sometimes hard to resist him, not that he ever pushed her. Mandey <u>wanted</u> him; a large part of her wanted to let down her defenses and do it <u>now</u>. So far, she had been able to keep that urge under control, but it got a little harder all the time.

Shannon called her around eight. Mandey was worried that he was going to want to get together the next evening. She didn't know what excuse she would give him for not seeing him. To her relief, Shannon said he had to work the evening shift the next night and instead wanted to go out on Saturday. She told him it was okay that they couldn't get together on Friday because she and some friends were going to get together to study for a chemistry exam they were having Monday. A flimsy story, she thought, but Shannon didn't question it.

Mandey went to bed with her head spinning. Too much was on her mind, fights and lies and birth control and live-in boyfriends. She watched TV to try to block it all out. Sometime after midnight the television succeeded in numbing her brain and she slept.

42

The Rumble

When Mandey got home from school Friday, there was a message on the machine from Marcia. She was going to dinner with Michael directly after she left work, so she wouldn't be home until late. Also, she had scheduled Mandey a 4:30 appointment with her gynecologist on the following Thursday.

Mandey sighed and reset the machine. She missed her parents. She missed coming home after school and telling her mother about her day. She missed knowing that dinner was going to be on the table around five-thirty. She missed coming home late after a night out and seeing a light on in the living room, indicating that her mother was waiting up to make sure she got in safely. However, on this night, it was good that there was no one around.

Mandey turned on the radio and got in the bathtub, hoping a nice, warm bubble bath might relax her a little bit. It didn't. Then she went to the kitchen to scrounge up something for supper. She looked in the refrigerator and through all the cupboards and decided to make a scrambled egg sandwich on wheat bread.

There was a multitude of things Mandey would have liked to do that Friday night. Being part of a gang-bang was not one of them. This had ceased to be fun. Maybe this fight would settle things, once and for all. That was its purpose, at least, but she doubted it would solve anything. It would keep on going and going, and eventually she would have no choice but to tell Shannon about it. She didn't want to do that, but she couldn't keep it a secret much longer.

After tonight I'll tell them I'm not interested in this anymore, she thought. *It's been fun and good luck in your future endeavors, but I'm out of here.*

She considered calling Angelina and telling her she wasn't going to show up tonight. She knew they would think she had chickened out, which was okay; it would only be the truth. Deal or no deal with the Devils, somebody could decide to play dirty, and somebody could end up dead.

But she was already committed. There were three girls in the Devils, too, and if she didn't show up to take on one of them, they would be sure to gang up on Angie or Dina, two-on-one. Mandey knew who she was going to end up fighting, too—that sulky, pouty, bitchy blonde girl, Kerri. Mandey wasn't scared of her; she was fairly confident she could take her out, but she didn't want to. Angie was feisty; she had been in a few fights in her time, and Dina thrived on this stuff. Mandey had never so much as said "boo" to anybody, and it seemed that, as she was a senior in high school, it was pretty late to start now.

She finished her sandwich and went to her room to get dressed. Even as she put on her black jeans and her Alley Cats T-shirt, she was going back and forth in her mind about whether to go ahead with this. For a while she played her favorite records, hoping that the music would calm her down, but she still hadn't totally convinced herself that this was a good idea by the time she showed up at Angelina's house to finish getting ready.

"How are you doing your make up, Angie?" Dina asked.

"Oh, I want to freak their minds," Angelina said.

She made bold strokes with her black eyeliner. Mandey and Dina followed suit. They were in Angelina's bedroom, which was furnished with a canopy bed with a frilly pink comforter and matching canopy, a white dresser, and a matching vanity table. It clashed with the orange shag carpeting and pale yellow walls, which were covered with posters of John Stamos and Michael Jackson. Fashion and teen magazines were strewn across the bed, piled in a corner of the room, and stacked on top of the dresser. Barbie dolls were perched on stands all over the room wearing various outfits, all designed and sewn by Angie herself. Her goal was to get into the Art Institute and become a fashion designer. Mandey had seen some of Angelina's sketches, and although Mandey was no expert, she was impressed.

Angelina didn't have a stereo system, but she did have a portable AM/FM radio cassette player, which was cranked up.

"Let's make sure we know what we're doing tonight," Angelina said, talking above the music and looking at the other two girls in the mirror. "I'm going after Juanita, and I'm going to beat the hell out of her, after I pull her hair out of her head. Teach her to go around scalping people!"

"That's right!" Dina agreed. "Snatch that bitch bald-headed!"

"Yeah!" Angelina said, turning around to give Dina a high-five, and then Mandey. "You're going to fight that bitch I told you about, aren't you, Dina? The one who said she messed you over once upon a time?"

"Yeah," Dina said. "Nervy bitch. If it's the same girl I'm thinking of, she didn't get the best of me. I was beating her when the fight got broke up."

This was news to Mandey. "Wait, someone in the Devils knows you?" Mandey asked Dina.

"Yeah, I guess so. She mentioned me by name."

Mandey started to question her further, but then Angelina asked her, "Mandey, you're taking that girl Kerri, right?"

"Yeah," Mandey said.

"Boy, you don't sound very excited," Dina said.

Mandey shrugged. "Be honest. Isn't there something else you'd rather do tonight besides go get in a fight?"

"Mmmm-hmmm," Angelina said, "but I think Jesse and I will find some time for that afterward."

"Lucky," Dina said enviously. "I'm going to be all revved up, and Eduardo's on the road. Damn."

"What about you and Shannon, Mandey? You going to see him later?" Angelina asked.

"Are you kidding? I told him I was studying for a chemistry exam with some other kids tonight. He'd have a fit if he knew what I was really doing."

The guys arrived at ten P.M. on the dot. The girls peeked out the window at them as they got out of Jesse's and Jeremy's cars.

"Oooh, don't they look sharp!" Dina exclaimed.

They were dressed in black jeans and black T-shirts, tucked in, with black belts and shoes and their black denim jackets.

"Look, they've got their hair gelled up like some sort of greasers," Mandey said. "Do you suppose they got ready together, too?"

"Looks like it," Angelina said. "Don't Jesse look good? God, I want to jump his bones right now!"

"Well, let's go show ourselves to them," Dina said.

The girls walked outside into the driveway. The guys stopped talking and stared. The girls certainly were an impressive sight. Dina's and Mandey's hair had been unmercifully teased and sprayed. Angelina had hers smoothed down and curled under, reminiscent of Cleopatra. Their eyes were made up in bold black and silver. Angelina and Dina's lips were covered in blood red lipstick; Mandey had opted for a dark gray she found on sale after Halloween. Their nails were painted black, green, gold, and silver. All three wore their black T-shirts with black jeans and shoes and had spiked wristbands. Mandey and Angelina both had studded leather belts. To top it all off were the black denim jackets trimmed in green, gold, and silver.

"Damn!" Jesse said. "What happened?"

"Chu like?" Angelina asked with a smile.

"Y'all look wild!" Danny said, laughing. "I love the Siouxsie look, Mandey."

"Y'all look like a bunch of freaks," Terry said with a derisive snort.

"Terry, your opinion don't count," Dina said. "If you had your way, we'd all look like the cast of *Hee-Haw*!"

Terry turned to Mandey. "And I suppose you're going to blast that shit you call music in your van again tonight?"

"Oh, Terry," Mandey said. "If the fight turns out good, I'll play KIKK on the radio on the way home."

"Let's get going," Jim said, bouncing up and down on his toes. "I'm ready to kick some ass!"

"Let's do it," Brad said, giving Jim a high five.

They all loaded into the van. Danny called shotgun and sat in front next to Mandey.

"You all look great tonight, Dan," Mandey told him.

"Thanks," he said. "We went for the Fifties style, though, and y'all went for the punk look."

Mandey noticed how red Danny's eyes were. He was definitely hopped up on something.

She slid a tape into the cassette player and cranked up the volume. She had made a special mix tape of songs geared toward building a good fighting attitude. It included "Another One Bites the Dust" and "We Will Rock You/We Are the Champions" by Queen, "Whip It" by Devo, "Rumble in Brighton" by the Stray Cats, "Gangs in the Street" by Loverboy, "Beat It" by Michael Jackson, and "Quintet" from *West Side Story*. The drama department had put on a production of the musical the previous spring. Jesse had played "Bernardo", Zack had been "Tony", and Angelina, Jeremy, and Jim had all had parts, too. Mandey had auditioned, but didn't get a part, so she and most of the gang were familiar with the song. They sang along with the tape, trying to get psyched up. Everyone, that is, except Terry.

Mandey parked the van in front of the Northview Apartments. A few of the Alley Cats took off their jackets, including Mandey, and left them in the van before they made their way into the vacant lot next to the apartments. It was rough, gravelly, and weedy. In the dark lot she could make out some vague forms that she knew were the Devils. They were waiting. Mandey's stomach churned. She hoped she wasn't going to throw up.

The Alley Cats put their arms around each other in a huddle.

"Remember, if you see a gun or a knife or any kind of weapon, run," Terry said. "We agreed to no weapons, but we can't trust those bastards to keep their word. If they pull anything, get away as fast as you can. We don't need for one of us to get killed."

"All right now, are we ready?" Jesse asked. He seemed tense and high-strung, but so did the rest of them. "We're going to kick their sorry asses, am I right?"

"Yeah!"

"Let's do it!"

They broke out of the huddle and made their way into the lot toward the Devils.

My God, Mandey thought, starting to panic. *What am I doing here? I've never been in a fight in my life, and now I'm <u>here</u>? This is unreal. This is nuts.*

She felt the pocket of her black corduroy jeans. She knew it was supposed to be a fair fight, but the Mexican switchblade was there, just in case.

"Where's Terry, that fucking bastard?" boomed a big, deep voice.

The Alley Cats stopped about thirty feet away. "Right here," Terry replied. "Are you blind or something?"

Terry was talking to the largest of the Devils. Mandey squinted to get a clearer look, but to no avail. She saw that he was wearing a ski mask, and she was almost sure it was the one who had been trying to steal the car that night at Liaisons. She figured this had to be the notorious Trick.

"No," Trick replied, "but I'd rather be blind than an ignorant hillbilly."

"Can we cut the shit and get down to business?" Raff exclaimed.

Trick turned to face Raff. "Hey, this is my goddamn outfit, and we're going to do things my goddamn way, okay?"

Then he faced Terry again. "Y'all are going to regret the day you decided to fuck with us. Y'all are going to leave here with your tails between your legs, and we don't never want to see your faces around here again."

"Like hell!" Dina and Angelina chorused.

Why does he sound so much like Shannon? Mandey asked herself. He was built like Shannon and he sounded like Shannon, but it was so dark and he had that mask on. She couldn't see well enough to tell if it was Shannon.

It can't be him, she tried to reassured herself. *That's silly.* Her heart was pounding.

"Look at that, will you?" Trick said laughing. "Check out those chicks. Where'd they come from, Mars?"

"I'd rather come from Mars than the sewers like you," Mandey blurted, and felt her face go hot.

There was a pause. "Oooh, you really hurt me there," Trick said. Mandey listened to his voice. Something in his tone had changed. Had he recognized her voice? Damn, Mandey hated this.

Mandey waited for the others in the Alley Cats to say something, but no one did. The conversation was hers and Trick's alone. "You're a malicious, uncivilized, sadistic cretin," she said, choosing her words carefully. If this was Shannon she was speaking to, he certainly would recognize both her voice and her vocabulary, wouldn't he?

There was another pause, this one a little longer than the first. "What the hell?" Trick exclaimed, looking around at his fellow gang members. "Did she just insult me? I couldn't understand a word she said."

He was mocking her, but there was something-- *No, it doesn't really sound like him,* she tried to convince herself. *This guy sounds like what he is, an asshole full of himself and a lot of bullshit.* But it didn't ring true.

There was a little light on one side of the lot from the lights at the apartments. Even though he wore a mask, Mandey wished Trick would go step under one so she could see him better. As the two gangs approached each other in the dimness, her attention moved from Trick to the other members of the gang. Her eyes focused on a female with long wavy brown hair. She had to be the girl she had fought with at Liaisons. She was not wearing a ski mask tonight, and as they got closer to each other, Mandey remembered what Angelina said to Dina about the "bitch" who was gunning for her. Suddenly it hit her—it was Shannon's sister, Annette.

There was no more time to think. Trick let out a yell and lunged at Terry. Everyone ran toward each other, swinging.

Mandey knew whom she was aiming for, but she didn't need to seek her out because Kerri jumped her first.

"You bitch!" Kerri cried, grabbing Mandey's throat. Mandey pushed back, hard, and broke her hold. Kerri lunged at Mandey and grabbed her by the hair. Mandey decided to get off the defensive and punched Kerri as hard as she could in the solar plexus. Kerri fell to the ground, but she pulled Mandey down with her. They slapped, punched, and clawed each other as they rolled on the hard, gravelly dirt. Mandey had a twenty-five-pound advantage over Kerri and after what seemed like forever (but was only a couple of minutes), she was finally able to pin her. She hit Kerri several times in the face until she went limp. As Mandey started to get to her feet, Kerri pulled a knife out of her jeans. For a second, Mandey froze. She knew she was supposed to run, but she was afraid she wouldn't be able to get away fast enough to avoid getting slashed. She remembered her own knife, in the pocket of her own jeans, but did not reach for it. Instead, she brought her knee down hard on Kerri's forearm. Kerri cried out in pain and let the knife loose. Mandey snatched it up and threw it as hard as she could into the darkness. She immediately regretted it, because now someone could possibly retrieve it. Mandey stood up. Kerri stayed on the ground, holding her arm.

"Fucking bitch!" Kerri screamed, kicking Mandey in the shin.

"Ouch!" Mandey cried, staggering. Then she got mad and quickly kicked Kerri back three times, twice in her upper thigh and once in her hip. Kerri began to scoot away backwards from Mandey, her face twisted in pain and rage.

She didn't want to waste more time on Kerri. Mandey took a moment to survey the action. Everyone else was still locked in combat. She searched the scene until she caught sight of Terry, who was on the ground and not moving. She watched as Trick kicked him in the stomach, then turned toward another Devil who was fighting with Jeremy. It was time to confront him.

With a piercing shriek, she ran up behind Trick and tackled him. Taken by surprise, he fell to the ground with Mandey on top of him.

"God damn it!" he bellowed, throwing her off himself.

He backhanded her across the face as he got up, then yanked her to her feet as well. She fought back wildly, kicking and clawing and punching as he dragged her over to the fence and slammed her up against it. Now they were close enough to the light for Mandey to see. Her heart froze and sank into her stomach as she looked into Trick's burning hazel eyes. He was still wearing the mask, but she knew.

"Shannon!" she cried.

"Mandey!" he gasped. "It <u>was</u> you!"

"Oh my God, Shannon—"

"Come on," he said, grabbing Mandey by the arm.

He pulled her through a hole in the fence into the alley behind his apartment building. His hand was clamped around Mandey's wrist like a vise so she couldn't bolt. He dragged her down the alley, opened a first-floor apartment window, and practically picked Mandey up and pushed her through it, into his bedroom. He climbed in after her.

Shannon peeled off the ski mask and they stood there, breathing hard, staring at each other in silence. Shannon dropped down onto his bed. Mandey slowly sat down on the other end.

"My God, Mandey, I didn't recognize you with all that make up," Shannon said. He looked shell-shocked. "I heard your voice and it freaked me out, but I thought my mind was playing tricks on me. You didn't recognize my voice?"

"I thought it was your voice; I <u>knew</u> it was your voice, but I tried to tell myself it wasn't. But you were wearing that mask…I didn't know what to do. Then everyone started fighting. . ."

She was trembling, and now she started to cry.

Shannon went to put his arms around her, but she pulled away. She made a lunge for the door, but Shannon grabbed her by the arm.

"Let go of me! Leave me alone!" Mandey yelled, trying to pull away from him.

Shannon yanked her back down onto the bed. "Mandey, I am not going to hurt you," he said, quietly, releasing his hold.

Mandey moved away from him, sobbing.

"Oh, God, Shannon, how could you do this?" she asked through her tears. "How could you do this?"

Shannon watched he shoulders heave as she cried. He wanted to touch her, but he didn't dare yet. "Oh, Mandey. God, I never meant to hurt you."

"You hypocrite!" she spat, her tears turning to anger. "Feeding me all that bullshit about wanting to turn your life around when you're out doing this shit?"

Shannon's temper flared. "What about you?" he asked her, grabbing her arms and jerking her toward him. "That was some 'chemistry study party'. You didn't tell me what you were doing, either, so you've got a <u>hell</u> of a lot of nerve bitching at me. You're as bad as I am!"

He was squeezing her arms tightly and it hurt like hell, but Mandey was not about to admit it. Instead, she wrenched violently in his grasp and said through clenched teeth, "Let go of me, <u>now</u>!"

Shannon let go, and Mandey rubbed her arms where he had held her.

"I didn't want to get you involved because you've got enough problems as it is. If you'd known, I figured you'd either want to be a part of it or you'd tell me to quit because it's dangerous. Anyway, all we were doing was trying to protect ourselves and our right to come into this part of town and not be victimized. We may have had a few skirmishes with you, but we don't run around robbing liquor stores and stealing from people! You've got no right to say I'm as bad as you are! I'm not a criminal like you!"

Shannon's face went scarlet. Mandey saw him raise his hand to slap her.

"Go ahead! Hit me! Do it, <u>Trick</u>! That's the kind of guy you are, isn't it?" Mandey taunted.

"DON'T CALL ME THAT!" he roared at the top of his lungs, his face going almost purple. "I HATE THAT FUCKING NAME!"

He lowered his hand shakily. Mandey turned away from him, her face buried in her hands.

He had almost done what he had feared most. Shannon had pictured bad scenes between Mandey and him if she found out what he was doing with the Devils, but this was worse than he had ever imagined. How could she ever believe in him again after this?

"Mandey, please?" he said, his voice breaking, and he reached out to her once more.

She didn't resist when he put his arms around her. She felt too weak and confused to fight with him. She wanted to know how things went wrong so fast and how to make them right again. She leaned back against Shannon and felt his hold tighten around her; this time he wasn't hurting her.

"Mandey, listen to me, please?" he said softly in her ear. "I know I'm no angel. I'm sorry. I wish I could be. Every word you said outside was true. I understood what you meant. I'm a criminal. I'm rotten and mean. You deserve someone better than me. I'm sorry I hurt you." He was on the verge of tears.

"I don't want anybody else!" Mandey sobbed, tearing out of his embrace to look him in the face.

"I love you, Mandey, but I've hurt you too much," Shannon said, a tear rolling down his cheek. "I don't want to hurt you anymore."

"Shannon, please," Mandey begged tearfully. "I just want things to be like they were before."

"How can they be, Mandey? How can they be now that you know the truth?" Shannon asked in frustration.

"Because despite of what just happened, I still love you!" Mandey said desperately. "I don't want to hear you say you're rotten and mean. I want to know that the Shannon I've been in love with for the past month is real. I want you to tell me that my faith in you wasn't misplaced. I want to know that you haven't been lying to me about everything!" She began sobbing again.

Shannon sighed, ran his hands through his hair, and wiped his eyes. "Mandey, I really have been trying to go straight. I didn't lie to you about that, but it's hard. I'm the leader of the Devils, and I don't know how to get away. I'm. . .I'm scared to leave. I don't know where to go. I'm scared to leave, but I'm scared to stay. I'm afraid they're going to turn on me, no matter what I do. That sounds so fucking pathetic, the fearless, badass gang leader who's afraid of his own gang." He stood up and began to pace, agitated. "Damn it, Mandey, I tried to keep them from doing anything too bad, but I had an image and a position to keep up, too. Yeah, I robbed stores and I stole cars and I mugged people, but I ain't never raped or killed nobody. I can't do that kind of thing. You've got to believe me, Mandey." Suddenly, he kicked his nightstand. Mandey jumped, startled.

"Aaargh, I hate it! I hate my whole fucking life! I hate always feeling so fucking scared of everything!" He kicked the nightstand violently three more times, cracking the bottom drawer.

He sank down onto the bed again. His outburst had stopped Mandey from crying. She moved closer to him and tentatively hugged him. He put his arms around her and buried his face in her shoulder.

"You were the only good thing I had going and now I've fucked that up, too," he said, his voice muffled.

"No," Mandey said softly. "No, you haven't."

"I'm sorry," he said. "I'm so sorry."

Mandey began crying again. "I'm sorry, too," she said. "I said some awful things to you, and I wasn't honest with you. I'm so sorry. So sorry."

Shannon squeezed her tightly, but not in anger. He didn't ever want to let her go. Then he looked at her and groaned. "My God, Mandey, what have I done to you?" he asked. "Let me clean you up."

He took her by the hand and led her into the bathroom. She looked at her reflection in the mirror and was shocked. Her make-up had smeared. Her nose had bled a lot, and a cut high on her forehead had, as well. Her left eye was turning purplish, and her face was scraped. Shannon looked even worse. Terry had given him a pair of black eyes, and his nose and lip had bled profusely on Shannon's ski mask, and it had smeared all over his face when he had taken it off.

"Oh, God, look at us," Mandey said, covering her mouth with her hand.

"It'll be better once we wash up," Shannon said, and made Mandey sit down on the toilet seat while he filled the sink with warm, soapy water.

"Oh, babe, look what I did to you," he cried softly as he knelt in front of her and began to wash away the make-up and blood.

"Kerri did some of it," Mandey said. "How much of that did I do to you?"

"I think you split my lip. I hope you plan to kiss it and make it all better," he said. Mandey managed a weak smile.

"There's my Mandey," Shannon said when her face was clean. He brought a bottle of hydrogen peroxide out from under the sink. "This'll sting some," he said as he applied it to the scrapes on Mandey's face. They bubbled up white. "There were warning signs I should have seen."

"I know," Mandey admitted. "Just tonight Angie said some girl in the Devils had fought with Dina before, but Angie didn't know her name. I didn't think a whole lot about it because Dina used to fight a lot. She's the one your mother came after that day. It didn't hit me until it was too late. Still, I didn't want to believe it." She ran her hand through his hair. "I love you," she said.

Shannon kissed her forehead. "I love you, too."

He tended to washing himself. Mandey stood behind him, wrapped her arms around his middle, and laid her head against his back.

"I've got to explain this to the Alley Cats," she sighed.

"You're going to quit, aren't you?" Shannon said, the question sounding more like a statement.

"Yes," she replied. "I was going to after tonight, anyway. Will you?"

He didn't say anything for a moment. "Yeah, but it ain't going to be easy."

Mandey ran her hands over his back. "I will help you in any way I can," she told him.

He finished washing up, turned around, and hugged her. "If we can overcome this, we can overcome anything," he said. "I don't ever want to lose you."

"You won't," Mandey said as they walked back into the bedroom. "It should all be over by now, shouldn't it? The others are going to be looking for me, especially since I've got to drive them all home." She paused. "God, I don't know how I'm going to tell them this."

"I know how you feel," Shannon told her. "I don't know what to do. The only thing I do know is that I don't want to do it tonight."

"And how am I supposed to explain this to Marcia? I look like I got hit by a Mack truck," Mandey said, more to herself than to Shannon.

"Tell her we nearly got mugged."

"What do you mean, nearly?" Mandey asked. "Well, with any luck at all, she'll either still be out, or she'll be in bed when I get home."

"Mandey, I don't think I can stay here tonight."

Mandey looked at him. "You want to come home with me?"

Shannon nodded. "Do you think Marcia would mind?"

"No, not at all," Mandey said.

"Then why don't I meet you at the Circle K by your house and I'll follow you home from there after you finish getting everyone home?"

"Okay," Mandey agreed. "We'll tell Marcia we were attacked, and I was so shaky you decided to follow me to make sure I got home okay."

Shannon got a paper bag out from under his bed, pulled out his nightstand drawer, and tossed some items from it into the bag. Next, he got some clothes from his closet and put those in, too. Then he went into the bathroom and came back with his toothbrush. Mandey was looking out his bedroom window

"I can't see anything but the fence, but I don't hear anything," Mandey said.

"The Devils must have gone back to the Den, but I think we'd better go out the window, then I think I should be able to sneak to my car."

They scrambled out the window, then he kissed her quickly. "Good luck," he told her.

"See you in a few," she said.

Mandey walked down the alley toward where her van was parked, wondering what to say to the rest of the gang. The only thing she knew for sure was that she was going to say as little as possible. She wasn't in the mood to do a lot of explaining.

"Damn it! That slime has Mandey and God knows what he's doing to her! If only I could have stopped her when I saw her going after him!" Mandey heard Danny saying as she approached the van.

"I still say we've got to go look for her!" Angelina said.

"And get attacked by those bastards again?" Jesse said. "It's probably a trick to get us to split up so they can come after us!"

"Well, damn it, Jesse, we've got to do something!" Jeremy said. "She was trying to help me. We have to help her!"

"I can't stand the thought of him doing anything to her!" Danny said.

"I know, I know," Jesse said, sounding distressed. "But before we can do anything we've got to come up with some sort of plan."

"Hey!" she heard someone shout.

Suddenly there was the sound of running footsteps. Mandey broke into a run herself, anxious to see what was happening.

"Look what we found sneaking around!" Jim said.

As she came out from the alleyway, she saw Jim, Zack, and Brad coming around the corner from the front of the building. Jim and Brad each had Shannon by an arm.

"You fucking bastard! Where is she?" Danny yelled, ramming his fist into Shannon's stomach. Shannon doubled over in pain.

"What's in the bag, Trick? Is that your bag of tricks, Trick?" Jim taunted, taking Shannon's paper sack and tossing it to Jesse.

Jesse opened the bag and pawed through it. "What's this? A change of clothes and a toothbrush? Going to a slumber party or something, Trick?"

"Leave him alone!" Mandey cried.

They all turned around to look at Mandey. Their bruised and bloodied faces were a mixture of worry and relief.

"Are you all right?" Jeremy asked.

"What did he do to you?" Danny demanded. "I swear to God, I'll kill that son-of-a-bitch!"

"I'm fine," she assured them. "Really, I'm fine. But I need you to listen to me."

"What?" asked Jesse, suspicious.

Mandey knew he was not going to be pleased by what she was about to tell them. None of them would be. She steeled herself for the unavoidable negative reaction.

"Let him go," she said, referring to Shannon.

"Like hell," Zack said vehemently. "We're going to grind this mother-fucker into hamburger!"

Mandey's nerves snapped. "I said let him go!" she shouted, and stomped over to where Jim and Brad were restraining Shannon and pulled their hands away from him.

"What the fuck is wrong with you?" Jim shouted.

"LET HIM GO!" she screamed, verging on hysterical.

"Okay, okay," Jim said, and he and Brad pushed Shannon away from themselves.

Mandey stood in front of Shannon, as if to protect him, and faced the Alley Cats. Shannon slowly backed up against the wall of the building. He was trying to stay calm, but he was terrified. He realized how the Devils' victims felt as the Alley Cats closed in on him.

"What the hell is going on?" Jesse asked Mandey.

Mandey saw the hostility on their faces and knew this was going to be a tough sell. "Just give me a chance to explain," she said.

"I wish you would," Jesse said to her, glaring at Shannon.

"This is Shannon," she announced.

"What the—" was all she heard before the shouting and cursing became incoherent. All she was aware of was a snarling, angry mob screaming and closing in on her with pointing fingers and shaking fists. Her insides turned cold, her whole body felt hot, and all she wanted to do was run away, but she took a step backward and felt Shannon behind her. She knew running away would be the worst thing she could do.

"Listen to me! LISTEN TO ME!" Mandey screamed back at them, so hard she was sure something inside her was going to rupture. She kept on, trying to drown out the angry accusations, until finally she was the only person left screaming.

"We're listening," said a groggy, battered Terry quietly. "Quit screeching and say what you've got to say."

"Okay," Mandey said, hoping she had a voice left to speak with.

She took a few deep breaths to calm herself down, then began. "Shannon and I met about four weeks ago in Galveston. I didn't know he was one of the Devils, and I never told him about what we were doing because I didn't want him involved. Tonight when we got here, he had that mask on, but I thought I recognized his voice, although I tried to convince myself I was wrong. Shannon thought he recognized my voice, too, but he couldn't recognize me with all the makeup I had on. When I went after him, our worst fears were confirmed. We had a huge fight, but in the end we realized we love each other too much, so we're quitting, right now. I'm through with the Alley Cats, and Shannon's done with the Devils."

For a second there was total silence, then there was chaos as everyone began talking at once.

"You don't know what the fuck you're saying!" Jesse said.

"Love?" Danny spat. "You <u>love</u> this piece of shit?"

"You're crazy!" Angelina exclaimed.

"Listen!" Mandey shouted. "I know what 'Trick' has done. I don't love that part of Shannon. I haven't seen that part of him, although he told me about what he's done. But he's trying to change. 'Trick' only exists within the context of the Devils, and he's quitting."

"It's a lie!" Jeremy said.

"It is not a lie!" Mandey insisted. "I <u>know</u> how much Shannon hates the way he's been living and I <u>know</u> how much he wants to change it!"

"You are fucking nuts," Terry said.

"Look, when you just found him, he was trying to leave here because he doesn't want to face the Devils tonight. He's got to have time to figure out how to let the Devils know he doesn't want anything to do with them anymore."

"It's some kind of a trick," Jim said. "He's making you say these things."

"No, I don't think it is," Brad said thoughtfully.

Everyone turned to look at him.

"I was trying to remember why he looked familiar to me. Now I know why. He was with Mandey at school the night of the Honor Society induction," Brad explained.

"Okay?" Mandey said. "This is not a trick."

"How do we know?" Jesse asked. "You may have been doing the double-agent thing all this time."

Mandey sighed impatiently. "If I had had any idea that Shannon was one of the

Devils, and if I was supposedly secretly in cahoots with them, would I have brought him with me to the Honor Society induction, knowing full well that Brad was going to be there?"

"I don't know," Angelina said, disgusted. "Who knows how your mind works anymore?"

"Look, I want to go home," Mandey said, ignoring the remark. "I'm getting nervous that the Devils might come back at us. Can we go now, please?"

She took Shannon by the hand and pulled him through the throng towards her van.

"You're taking him home with you?" Danny asked, incredulous.

"You've got to be kidding. We ain't going nowhere with him," Terry said.

"Mandey, I'd just as soon drive myself," Shannon said to her.

"No, man, I don't like that idea, either," Jesse said. "We might end up with a car full of Devils following us home. But I don't want to share a ride with this stinking piece of shit any more than anyone else does."

"Oh, come on," Mandey said, turning to face them. "You guys look terrible. Terry, you're in pretty bad shape."

"Yeah, I'm in pretty bad shape because of that <u>fuckhead</u> there," Terry said furiously. "I don't want nothing to do with him, and if you do, then I don't want nothing to do with you, either."

"We all feel the same way," Jesse said. The others nodded in agreement. "Here, take your fucking overnight bag," he said to Shannon, and threw the paper sack at him. Shannon caught it.

"Metro buses don't run out to where we live. How are you going to get home?" Mandey asked.

"We'll find a way," Terry said. "We'll walk to my brother's place and get a car from there."

"Fine," Mandey said flatly. "All you had to do was ride in the same vehicle with him. I didn't ask you to be best friends with him, or talk to him, or even acknowledge his presence, for that matter. But if you want to cut off your nose to spite your own face, go ahead. Pray the Devils don't find you before you get to where you're going."

Mandey let go of Shannon's hand and got in the van. Shannon, however, remained standing outside, facing the Alley Cats.

"I'm sorry about what I've done," she heard him say. "I did some rotten stuff to y'all, and I ain't proud of it. I didn't do it because I got a kick out of it so much as I did because I had an image to keep up. I know that ain't no excuse, but I want to let you know I'm through with this. I've been wanting to be through with this for a long time now, but I was too much of a coward." He looked directly at Jesse and Terry. "Now that I'm out of the picture, Raff is going to take over. Y'all got to watch out for him. With him as leader, I don't know what's gonna happen. Y'all thought I was bad, but Raff is going to be a lot worse.

"And I know you're all worried about Mandey. I know I don't deserve her, but I'm going to do my best so that I will be good enough for her. If you ever see her upset or crying because I hurt her or broke her heart, y'all might as well come and find me and beat the shit out of me, because she don't deserve to be hurt."

Shannon turned, walked around to the passenger side of the van, and got in. Mandey looked at him in amazement.

"Wow," was all she said. He shrugged and looked out his window.

The Alley Cats were huddled together, having a conference. Mandey started the van. When she looked out the window, she saw Terry and Danny walking away from the group with disgusted expressions on their faces. She was fiddling with the radio to find some decent music when someone knocked on her window. It was Zack.

She rolled it down. "Jim, Brad, and I are going to ride with you," he told her.

"Okay," she said, feeling better that they weren't all totally rejecting her.

The three guys got in the back. She watched the other six as they walked off into the night. She hoped they would get home safely.

"What made you change your minds?" she asked them as she shifted into drive.

"We'd rather take our chances with one Devil in the van than nine out on the street," Jim said.

"I wish the others felt the same," Mandey said, fretting. "If anything happens to them. . ."

"They couldn't be persuaded," Brad said. "I said they should at least let you give them a lift over to Owens Towing, but they wouldn't listen."

The ride home was quiet. Shannon didn't say a word; he stared listlessly out his window at the dark streets. The guys sat in the back, talking quietly among themselves. Mandey thought that part of the reason Zack, Brad, and Jim were there was to make sure she was safe. Mandey turned the radio on low and lost herself in the music. She dropped them off at a corner near Jim's house, where the three of them had met up that evening. She noticed they were cautious about Shannon finding out where one of them lived.

"Night, guys," Mandey said softly as they got out. Zack and Jim didn't acknowledge her, but Brad met her eyes with a questioning gaze. She nodded and gave him a small smile to indicate she was all right. He gave a small gesture with his hand, as if to say goodbye. It made her feel a little better. Then Mandey and Shannon quietly drove home to her house.

43

Reconciliation

Marcia had just gotten in from a date with Michael when Mandey got home. Any other time she wouldn't have been home yet, or she would already have been asleep.

"What in God's name happened?" she gasped when she saw their battered faces.

"Mandey came down to my apartment, and we got jumped outside when she was leaving," Shannon said.

"Are you okay?" Marcia asked.

"It looks worse than it is," Shannon said. "Mandey was shaky after it happened, and I didn't think it was a good idea for her to drive home alone, so I rode home with her."

"Have you called the police?" Marcia asked.

"No," Mandey said.

"Well, I'm calling them," Marcia said, heading toward the phone.

"It won't do any good," Mandey said quickly. "They were all dressed in dark colors, and it was too dark to identify them."

"You should still report it to the police," Marcia said stubbornly, her hand on the receiver.

"Mandey's right," Shannon said. "They had masks on, so there's no way we could I.D. them. Besides, the cops don't pay much mind to what goes on in my neighborhood. I don't think they care. But from now on I think it's a good idea for Mandey to stay away from there after dark."

"Shannon!" Mandey protested.

"Mandey, there's no need of it," Marcia said.

"I've got a car," Shannon said. "I can drive or leave my car here and you can drive, but it's too dangerous down there."

"Okay, okay," Mandey said. "Marcia, I'm going to get Shannon set up in the guest room."

"All right," Marcia said. "You're sure you're okay and you don't want to file a report?"

"We're okay," Mandey said. "Honestly, we're fine."

"No," Shannon said. "Please, Marcia, if I call the cops and someone from down there finds out I did that, I'll be a prime target to get busted up even worse."

"Shannon, I would say you need to think about moving out of there," Marcia said.

Shannon nodded in agreement. "I know," he said, grimly.

They took turns showering, and afterward they sat on the couch watching television and saying nothing for a long time. Shannon nursed a beer and smoked while Mandey sipped a soothing cup of hot tea. Mandey was trying to digest everything that had happened earlier. It was difficult for her to reconcile the fact that "Trick", the violent gang leader, and Shannon, her sweet, kind-of-insecure boyfriend, were the same person. He led an extremely screwed-up life when he wasn't with her.

"This was some night," Mandey said finally.

"You said it," Shannon agreed.

"It's almost unbelievable," Mandey said, still staring at the television. "After everything that's happened, here we are together."

Shannon was quiet for a moment, then said, "I didn't think you'd want to be with me no more once you found out. That's why I've been so desperate to get out of there. I mean, I was desperate before, but when you came along, I got even more desperate. I wanted to get away from the Devils before you ever found out I was still stuck in all that bullshit. Mandey, I've got to make sure you know that I never wanted to make trouble for nobody. I never wanted to be caught up in all this gang shit. I didn't have a choice."

Mandey didn't answer right away. "Everyone has choices, Shannon."

He looked at her. Her eyes were still focused absently on the television.

"Yeah, and mine was to join the Devils or get my ass killed."

Mandey closed her eyes and rolled her head and shoulders. She was achy and hurting; the Tylenol she had taken hadn't kicked in yet.

"All I know, Shannon," she said, opening her eyes and turning to look at him at last, "is that by all rights we should have broken up tonight, but we didn't. All I care about is making things right again, and making sure no more secrets come between us."

"That's all I want, too, Mandey," Shannon said earnestly, and reached over to take her hand in his. "I made a huge mistake, and I don't ever want to repeat it."

They set down their beverages and hugged each other tightly. "I hurt you, and I made you cry," he said, sounding like he was on the verge of tears. "That's killing me. Just a few days ago I said I'd never hurt you like that, and look what I did tonight."

"It's okay now," Mandey said softly. "The fight was a different situation, but when we were in your room and you were tempted to slap me, you stopped. I know you would never intentionally hurt me like that."

They let go of each other. "I just want to put this all behind us," Mandey said.

Shannon nodded silently. Mandey yawned.

"I don't know about you, but I'm ready to go to bed. I'm exhausted," Mandey said.

They got up from the couch. Mandey put her empty tea cup in the dishwasher, and Shannon poured out the last couple sips of beer into the sink and put the can in the trash. They walked down the hall toward the bedrooms. Shannon opened the door to the guest room.

"Shannon."

He stopped and looked at Mandey.

"Where are you going?" she asked him.

"To bed," he replied with a puzzled expression on his face.

"Do you really want to sleep all alone in the guest room?"

He stared at Mandey but didn't say anything.

"I'm not talking about having sex yet," Mandey said, suddenly feeling shy and lowering her eyes, "but I'd like to have you sleep in my bed with me. . .if you want to."

She bit her lip and looked back up to see Shannon looking back at her intently. "I usually sleep in nothing but my shorts," he warned her.

"That's fine."

They stepped into Mandey's room, and she shut the door behind them. With his face slightly flushed, he took off his T-shirt and jeans. He turner pinker as Mandey surveyed him in the almost-altogether. She found him <u>extremely</u> attractive. He was exactly what she liked. He had a nice amount of dark hair on his stomach, chest, and legs. She couldn't help but wonder a bit how he looked <u>without</u> his shorts.

He was turning redder by the moment as she scrutinized him.

"Hold on a minute," she told him.

She passed Shannon, went to her dresser, rummaged in a drawer, and disappeared into the bathroom.

He got into Mandey's bed and covered up. The white and green ivy-patterned sheets were soft and clean smelling, just like she was. He felt something stirring and hoped it wouldn't get out of hand. Mandey had already said she wasn't interested in having sex tonight.

A moment later the bathroom door opened and Mandey stepped back into the bedroom. A silky baby blue shorty pajama set had replaced the T-shirt and warm-up pants she had been wearing. He groaned inwardly with nearly equal parts of desire and frustration. There was no way to stop the erection he felt coming on as he anticipated the feeling of her body against his, clad in that soft, silky fabric.

He threw back the covers and stood up. Mandey's eyes grew wide as they were drawn down to the rapidly rising tent pole in his shorts, and it was her turn to blush. He walked over to her, and she smiled.

"Get back in bed this instant," she told him.

"Ooh, I like it when you get aggressive with me," Shannon said with a grin, and scooped her up into his arms. Mandey squealed with laughter.

He carried her over to the bed and laid her down, then he turned out the lights and joined her under the covers. In a moment they were wrapped in each other's arms, kissing.

"Mmm, you are so incredibly sexy," Mandey told him.

Shannon chuckled, embarrassed. "Not me," he said, and kissed her neck. "You're the sexy one, all curvy and soft and sexy."

Against her thigh Mandey felt Shannon's hardness through his cotton briefs. She wondered how fair she was being to him, snuggling up to him in her sexy little pajamas and getting him all excited when she had no intention of following through.

As if he could read her mind, Shannon kissed her all over her face and hugged her tightly, making her giggle.

"Here I am with a boner the size of a baseball bat, guaranteed a major case of blue nuts tonight, but I don't care. I'm just happy to be here with you," he told her.

It was exactly the right thing for him to say. Mandey cuddled closer and laid her head on his chest.

"I admire your restraint. I don't think many guys would spend a night in bed with a girl they even found remotely attractive without trying to screw her," Mandey said.

Shannon grinned. "Well, I'm trying to be restrained, but I'm not dead," he said, his hand slipping under her pajama top and coming to rest on her breast. "But I love you, and I don't want to do anything you don't want to do."

Mandey ducked her head down and kissed his left nipple, making him gasp.

"Girl, don't do that or I might lose my restraint," he warned her, only half in jest.

She smiled up at him, although in the dimness of the room, he likely couldn't see it. "Sorry," she said.

He wrapped his arms around her again and made thrusting movements with his pelvis against hers.

"One of these days," he said in her ear.

Mandey kissed him. "It'll be worth the wait."

"Oh, baby, I know that."

They settled down to sleep. Her head was still spinning over the night's events, but she couldn't think of a better way for it to have ended. The secrets that were plaguing them were not secrets anymore, and they were still together. She had a feeling that this was a turning point for Shannon. Now that everything was out in the open, he could leave it all behind and start making the life for himself that he wanted so desperately. Mandey was determined to be by his side, helping him any way she could, every step of the way.

44

Avoidance Strategy

When Mandey woke up the next morning with Shannon's arm draped over her. She turned to look at him. His mouth was slightly open. Despite the bruises and cuts on his face, he looked peaceful. Mandey pressed her lips to his. He stirred, and without opening his eyes he tightened his grip on her and kissed back.

"Good morning," he said, opening his coffee-with-cream eyes.

"Good morning to you," Mandey replied, putting her arms around him. She kissed the end of his nose and rubbed her head against his.

His hands moved up under her pajama top to her breasts. Her nipples got hard at his touch. He kissed her face and neck, then sighed.

"God, I love you," he told her as he nuzzled her neck. "You kept me nice and warm last night," he said.

"I woke up a couple times in the night. I loved feeling you next to me," Mandey said. She sat up and stretched. "Want to go to Champ's for breakfast?" she asked him.

"Sure," he said. "But right now I need another kiss."

He pulled her back down and kissed her passionately. Their bodies pressed against one another, and Mandey felt his hardness against her leg. His hands ran over her silky pajamas, touching her private places, arousing her. Her hands responded in kind, feeling his strong body, and touching his hard manhood through his briefs. Suddenly she tore away from him.

"What?" Shannon said, fearing she was angry. "I'm sorry."

Mandey smiled to reassure him. "Don't be sorry," she said. She moved toward him and kissed him again. "You're just too sexy. If we'd kept on going, I don't know if I could have stopped." She scrambled out of bed. "I'm going to take another shower and try to get the rest of this goo out of my hair."

She got some clothes out and went into the bathroom. She started the water running in the shower to get hot while she used the toilet. She turned on the radio in the corner of the bathroom (safely away from the tub and shower stall). She took off her silky pajamas, tested the water, and got in. She turned the massaging showerhead up full blast and relished the feeling of the hot water pounding her aching body. She poured shampoo into her hand and lathered up her hair, glad to get the rest of that hairspray and gel out of it. She wished she had Shannon there in the shower with her. The opportunity was there, for sure. It just wasn't the right time. Oh, but wouldn't it be nice to have him step into the shower with her, to have his big strong hands caressing her and washing her, and to wash his back and neck and his buns and...

She shook herself out of her reverie and rinsed her hair, then finished washing up. It was cold when she got out of the shower, so she dried off and dressed quickly. She left the bathroom wearing her favorite jeans, a red and brown plaid flannel shirt, and red slippers. Shannon had gotten out of bed and was in the middle of making it.

"Thank you," Mandey said, helping him finish.

"I think I'm going to take a quick shower, too," Shannon said, and disappeared into the bathroom.

Mandey sat down at her make-up mirror to try to camouflage her injuries. The black eye and the bruises would be easy enough to disguise with concealer, but the scrapes were going to be hard to hide. She didn't want to cover them in make-up.

When Shannon re-entered the room, Mandey had herself looking almost normal, but the scrapes were still obvious and the cut on her forehead was covered with a Band-Aid. Her bruised eye could only be detected if one looked at her closely.

"Don't we look great together?" Shannon asked, grinning.

Mandey turned to look at him. His black eyes were going to attract some attention. His mouth was swollen, too. She also noticed how he was dressed—he had brought with him jeans and a red plaid flannel shirt.

"We're a matching pair," she said, grinning back at him.

Champ's wasn't too crowded for a Saturday morning, and Mandey and Shannon were seated right away at a booth right next to the buffet table.

"Oh, good, they're putting out more bacon," Mandey said, putting down her purse and going over to pick up a plate.

"I am <u>starving</u>," Shannon said.

"I'd like coffee, please," Mandey said to the waitress who came by.

"I'd like a coffee and a chocolate milk," Shannon added, picking up his own plate.

He filled it with sausage, eggs, grits, hashbrowns, and a biscuit with sausage gravy. Mandey chose pancakes with berry topping and syrup, fruit, and bacon. When they sat down, coffees and milk were waiting for them.

"I don't want to stay home today," Mandey said, pouring cream into her coffee. "I guess I'm running away, but I don't want to be home if anyone calls or comes over. I don't know if I can deal with it yet."

"Why?" Shannon asked. "You got through last night just fine."

"I guess," Mandey said, "but they need time to get used to the idea, and I'm not in the mood for arguing today. After last night, I'm in the mood to be happy and have some fun."

"I want to go shopping," Shannon said abruptly.

Mandey stopped with her coffee cup halfway to her mouth.

"You want to go shopping?" she repeated.

"Yeah," he said. "I need some new clothes."

"Can I help?" Mandey asked, smiling with delight.

"I wish you would," Shannon said. "I need all the help I can get."

"What do you want to buy?"

"Shirts, pants, shoes. Everything," Shannon said.

"Cool. I love dressing a man," Mandey said.

"You've done this before?" Shannon asked her.

"I shopped with James a few times," she replied. "He could never make up his mind about anything, so he was kind of a pain to shop with."

"I'll try not to be a pain," Shannon said.

"You could never be a pain," Mandey said. "What kind of clothes are you looking for, exactly?"

"Everything, Mandey. I need stuff to wear when I'm out with you, so I don't look like a bum."

"You never look like a bum," Mandey told him.

"Well, I don't look as good as I should."

"Okay, but don't do this for me or because of me."

"I'm not," he said. "I'm doing this because I want to and need to. I need new clothes, new shoes, and a haircut."

"Wow," she said. "Trying to change your image?"

"Maybe."

"Just as long as you're doing it because you want to and not because you think it's what I want."

"I <u>am</u>, Mandey," Shannon said. He sopped up some gravy with his last bite of biscuit. "And I don't blame you for not wanting to face anyone today. I don't, either."

"We may be running away from nothing," Mandey said. "It's possible they may not even want to talk to me. I don't know. I just don't want a lot of time on my hands to dwell on it. I want to enjoy the day with you."

Shannon went over to the buffet table and got another biscuit and more gravy.

"How did you become leader of the Devils, anyway?" Mandey asked Shannon when he sat down again. "I mean, you don't seem to be the kind of person who would want that kind of power. You're kind of like me, actually—kind of quiet, who likes to be a part of things, but not the center of attention. You don't seem like the gang leader type."

"I'm not," he said. "I didn't really want to be the leader, but it seemed like I didn't have much choice."

"How's that?"

Shannon took a sip of his milk. "Well," he said, "when I first moved there, I tried to keep to myself. I didn't want to be there, and I was a little scared, too. Man, you know how your neighborhood is; they do stupid stuff like break windows out of that abandoned church and sometimes get into fights with each other, but that didn't prepare me for what I was getting into.

"Annette actually joined them first. That kind of stuff is right up her alley. I tried to avoid them, but that was impossible. One day all the guys in the gang—Victor, Raff, John, Checkmate, and Curtis, came up to me. Lenny and Marco weren't in the gang yet; they were too young. They let me know that if I didn't join them they would make my life a living hell. So I joined."

"Victor was leader at the time. He was Raff's cousin, Marco's big brother. He was nineteen and he was <u>bad</u>. He was tough and could be meaner than a snake, but he took a liking to me for some reason, and I got the feeling he was trying to prepare me to take his place someday, if something ever happened to him. I thought it was weird, considering Raff was his own flesh and blood. Raff knew it, too, and he was majorly pissed off, although he wasn't about to get into it with Victor. He just started to plan how he could get rid of me. That's how I ended up in jail."

"He framed you," Mandey said.

"No," Shannon said, drawing out the word, "not exactly. I did the crime and I did the time, but I wouldn't have had to do the time if it hadn't been for Raff."

"What happened?"

Shannon shoveled in a mouthful of eggs, chewed, and swallowed. "Raff and I were gonna knock over a liquor store, and Victor was driving the getaway car. Well, we get in there, and—oh, God, Mandey, I don't want to tell you this stuff. You're gonna hate me."

Mandey regarded his eyes, full of worry and fear of rejection.

"No, I won't," Mandey said. "You forget, I've already heard about 'Trick' and the stuff he's done."

"I know," Shannon said. "It's just that I've never told you anything in detail before."

"Well, if you aren't ready to tell me, just skip over that part for now," Mandey said.

Shannon thought about this for a moment. That would be easy. But if he didn't tell her now, would he ever? Or would he decide that he didn't need to tell her any of this, and keep everything a secret? Would that be right?

He sighed. "No," he said. "I should tell you. No secrets, right?"

"Right," Mandey said, "but you're not really keeping a secret. You've told me what you did; you just haven't provided any details. But that's no crime—oops. Sorry. Bad choice of words."

"To hell with it," Shannon said. "No secrets." He went on.

"Raff and I busted into the liquor store around 11:30 at night. There was only the clerk and one customer inside. I pulled a gun on the clerk, and Raff pulled one on the customer. We demanded money from them. Raff got the customer's wallet and grabbed a couple bottles of liquor. I told the clerk to open the register and give me the money. He started to, but then he made a weird move, like he was gonna pull a gun. I freaked out a little, so I pistol-whipped him. Thank God that was my first instinct and not shooting the guy. What I didn't notice was that Raff had already left the store. I came out of the store and there was no getaway car. I found out later that he told Victor that the clerk had knocked my gun out of my hand and had pulled his own gun on me, so they needed to haul ass out of there. Victor believed him, I guess, because they took off. I took off running as fast as I could, but I got caught."

"And you didn't tell the cops that Raff and Victor were involved."

"Hell, no. You don't do that. You don't squeal on the other guys in the gang. You're liable to get killed that way. They offered to reduce my sentence for information on Raff and Victor, but I didn't give them any. They questioned the other Devils, but didn't get anywhere with them. I took the heat alone and ended up in jail. The judge took mercy on me since it was my first offense and put me in that youthful offender program, but if I screw up again, I get shipped to Huntsville."

"What happened when you got back?"

"I was trying to figure out how the hell I was going to stay out of trouble and be in the gang at the same time. Then about three weeks after I got out, Victor got shot in an argument with some guys outside a pool hall. He was in a coma for a week or so before he died. He never regained consciousness. I knew that if Raff took over as leader, which is what looked like was gonna happen, he'd have me doing so much shit I'd probably wind up in jail again within a month, if I didn't end up dead. I decided if I was to have a snowball's chance in hell, I'd have to be the one to call the shots. So when time came for us to challenge to become the new leader, I went for it and won."

They had both cleaned their plates and returned to the buffet table for more.

"They've got good biscuits and gravy," Shannon said, helping himself to more. "You ought to get you some."

"I don't care for white gravy," Mandey said, putting more pancakes on her plate.

"You don't like white gravy?" Shannon asked, incredulous. "Why?"

"We never had it at our house. White gravy's a Southern thing, I guess."

"You don't like it or you haven't tried it?" Shannon asked.

"I've eaten white gravy before. On chicken fried steak in elementary school. It was gross."

"Well, that was school food. That was different."

"Actually, the food in the a la carte line at Rogers is pretty good," Mandey said.

"I never got to eat in that line. I ate free lunch, so I had to eat in the regular line. It wasn't too bad, I guess. Better than what I had at home a lot of the time." He heaped bacon onto a second plate along with a stack of four pancakes. "Try some of that gravy and don't be stubborn."

"Yes, sir," Mandey said, adding a biscuit to her plate and ladling on some gravy.

"Was it everything you thought it was going to be, being leader?" Mandey asked when they sat down again. She tasted her biscuit with the white sausage gravy and was pleasantly surprised. She dug in.

"Yeah, everything and worse," Shannon replied. "I hated it. The only good thing is that I did manage to keep us all out of too much trouble over the last few months. That wasn't easy. I tried to pick the easiest shit we could do to keep down the risk of being caught, but the gang started thinking I'd gone soft. Hell, I was never hard to begin with. I might have acted like it, but it was only because I was scared shitless most of the time and didn't want anyone to know it.

"So, I'm responsible for starting all the shit with the crowd at Liaisons. The gang had pulled some shit on people there even while I was gone, but I decided when I became leader that would be our focus. I knew security there was bad, and there ain't many cops patrolling that area, so that would be a pretty safe thing for us to do. I ain't never been back in the place since that night I saw you there, but probably lots of times you were there, I was creeping around the parking lot, looking for something to steal."

"What did you think when we decided we'd had enough and began to fight back?" Mandey asked.

"That's the last thing I wanted," Shannon said. "That meant having to get down on a personal level with the people we were messing with. I didn't want to know too much about who I was dealing with, and I sure as hell didn't want anyone to know me and tip off the cops. The idea of that fight scared me to death. Mandey, you don't know how scared I was last night that someone was going to get killed. I told my gang that if I caught any one of them pulling something funny, I'd fuck them over so bad they couldn't see straight."

"Kerri pulled a knife on me," Mandey said.

Shannon stared at Mandey in disbelief. "That bitch. If she had hurt you—"

"She didn't," Mandey said. "I got the knife away from her. It turned out okay."

"It might not have," Shannon said.

"But it did," Mandey said. "Anyway, I had a knife in my pocket, too."

"You did?" Shannon asked, surprised. "Well, so did I, but I didn't pull mine on anyone, did you?"

"No."

"And Kerri wonders why I don't like her."

"Why don't you tell me how you became an Alley Cat?" Shannon asked Mandey a while later, as they left the restaurant.

"Well, it's not quite so exciting a story as yours. You and Annette tried to steal that car that night, and she attacked me. Danny and Jeremy were there at the club, and they came up to me and we started talking about what happened. I guess they told Jesse, because on Monday morning in choir class Jesse said he'd heard about it, too, and he said we needed to do something."

"Choir class? Jesse is in choir?" Shannon asked, looking a bit amused.

"Yes," Mandey said. "A bunch of us met after school and decided to fight back by forming our own gang. Personally, I think Jesse's motivation behind asking me to join was because I have a van, and I could haul everyone around in it."

"Why did you join, though?" Shannon asked. "You're even less the type to get involved in this kind of shit than I am."

Mandey thought for a moment. "For one thing, I wanted revenge, and the whole idea was kind of exciting in a way. And, I guess I can admit this, it was nice to feel accepted by the others. Not that I was ever outright rejected by any of them, but it was good to fit in with a group besides the brains.

"And it felt good to be mad and wild and rebellious and tough, all of which I'm usually not. But I was scared, too. I'm too much of a square to want to get into any trouble. I almost backed out of the fight last night. In a way, though, I think what happened last night was the best thing that could have happened."

"Yeah," Shannon said. "If things had kept on, someone would have gotten seriously hurt or killed, and you and I would have eventually gotten into real trouble. It's a relief to be out of it."

They went to Willowbrook Mall to do Shannon's shopping. Going to Greenspoint wasn't a good idea, since Mandey would likely run into someone she knew, and that was the last thing she wanted. Shannon spent a fair amount of money outfitting himself. Mandey knew he didn't make that much at his gas station job and figured that the money was ill-gotten gain from the Devils' activities, but she didn't say anything. She had fun helping him pick out clothes and giving him her opinion when he tried them on. She was as happy as he was with his new wardrobe. His new haircut, while not a drastic change, made him look neater and more sophisticated.

When they returned home, the house was dark and locked. Mandey opened the door with her house key, and they went inside. The dumped the bags on the couch, and Mandey went to the kitchen and found a note from Marcia on the refrigerator. She had gone out with some friends and wasn't going to be home until late, and there was lasagna to warm up for supper.

"Okay," Mandey said, crumpling up the note and putting it in the trash. She glanced at the answering machine. No messages were waiting. Marcia had probably checked them. No one must have called for Mandey or it would have been on the note. Her phone in her bedroom had a separate line, but Marcia wouldn't have answered it, and with no answering machine, she couldn't tell if anyone called her number. The Alley Cats only had the number for her private line, not the main number.

"No messages," Mandey said.

"Huh?" Shannon said from the living room, where he was unloading the bags.

"No phone messages."

"Oh. I guess we stayed away all day for nothing."

"Not for nothing," Mandey said. "You got some nice clothes."

She turned on the oven to preheat, got the lasagna out of the refrigerator, and began setting the table. Shannon came out into the kitchen and sat down.

"Mandey," he said.

"Yeah?"

"I can't go back there."

Mandey sat down with him at the table.

"I can't stand living like that anymore, but I'm not going to be able to afford a place of my own right now," he said, his head in his hands. "What do I do, Mandey?"

She was silent for a moment. "You can move in here."

"Aw, Marcia would shit—"

"No, she wouldn't," Mandey said. "Under the circumstances, I know she wouldn't."

"I couldn't pay much in rent—"

"That's not a problem."

He sighed and ran his hands over his face. He looked weary.

"I've already mentioned the possibility to Marcia, anyway," Mandey said.

"And she agreed?" Shannon asked.

"She said that if it came down to that, the guest room is yours."

Shannon sighed again, this time in relief. "Thank you. I need it. I've got to get out of that place."

"I know you do. That's why I asked Marcia a while ago if you could move in."

"God, girl, I love you," Shannon said, reaching over to take her hand in his.

Mandey smiled and stood up. "The feeling is mutual," she told him, bending over to kiss his temple.

After supper Mandey put on her pajamas, and Shannon changed into a new gray warm-up suit he had bought that day. Mandey brought out a king-sized quilt and spread it out over the couch. She and Shannon sat down, cuddled close, and wrapped themselves up in the blanket to watch television with hot chocolate and peanut butter cookies.

Shannon let out a sigh of contentment. "I feel like I'm in heaven," he said.

Mandey smiled up at him, and he bent his head to kiss her.

"So do I," Mandey said.

"Oh, yeah?" Shannon said. "I mean, here I am in a warm house with a full stomach and a warm, soft bed to sleep in tonight with a beautiful girl. What are you getting out of this?"

Mandey smiled. "I've got a very sweet, handsome man who says he loves me, and I believe it."

"I do love you," Shannon said.

"I love you, too," Mandey said.

"I didn't think anyone would ever feel that way about me," Shannon said.

"I've been wondering the same thing about myself," Mandey said.

"Girl, what I want to know is how anybody could <u>not</u> want you."

"Well, I somehow got through seventeen and a half years without anybody wanting me. James was only pretending. I've never had anyone really want me until you came along." She smiled. "What makes it even better is that I wanted you, too."

Shannon kissed the top of Mandey's head. "I don't know," he said. "I have a feeling a lot of guys probably want you. They're probably too scared to admit it."

Mandey's ears pricked up. Danny had said the same thing the night of Jackie's party.

"Scared of what? What is there about me that is so scary?"

"<u>I</u> was scared of you," Shannon said. "I couldn't even approach you. I had to get Curtis to tell you. And that's not even true. I didn't even want him to do that. I was afraid of your reaction."

"Well, I should thank Curtis for that, because otherwise I wouldn't have known how you felt."

"Yeah. That's true. But what I'm trying to say is, you're pretty and you're smart and kind and funny and generous and sexy. I think a lot of guys think they're not good enough for you. And they're not. I'm not."

"You are so," Mandey said. "Let me be the judge of who's good enough for me." She paused and decided not to tell Shannon about her similar conversation with Danny. "I've always thought guys wouldn't ask me out because I wouldn't get drunk or take drugs or go to bed with them."

"Well, if that's all that's stopping them, they don't know what they're missing," Shannon said. "But that's okay with me."

"It's okay with me, too," Mandey said. "Now that I have you, none of those guys would ever do."

Shannon chuckled, embarrassed. "If you say so."

"I do," Mandey said, and kissed his cheek. "I'm so happy you're going to be here with me."

"If you're happy, think how I feel," Shannon said.

The phone in Mandey's room began to ring. She made no move to get up to go answer it. They sat, quiet, listening to it ring seven times, then it stopped.

Mandey leaned over and kissed him again, this time on the mouth.

"I love it when you do that," Shannon said. He reached out of the blanket to get a cookie. "And I love your cooking. I hope you'll still love me when I weigh 300 pounds."

"Of course, but I won't let you get that big."

"Oh, you won't?" Shannon asked. "You're not going to starve me, are you?"

"No," Mandey said. "I'll just make healthier stuff. Your size isn't important to me, but your health is."

Shannon put his arm around her and laid his head on her shoulder. "I don't deserve you."

"Yes, you do," Mandey said. "With the life you've had, you deserve all the happiness you can get. I want to spoil you."

He hugged her. "I'm going to do the same for you one of these days," he told her. "One day when I finally have enough money to give you what I want to give you."

"You already spoil me," Mandey said. "Just by being you, and being so sweet and considerate and attentive. Love me and don't take me for granted, that's all."

The other phone rang. They froze and looked at each other.

"Let the machine pick it up," Mandey said.

Marcia's voice came on. "Hi. Sorry we can't come to the phone right now. Please leave your name and a brief message, and we'll call you back."

The machine beeped.

"Hey, Mandey, it's me. I know you're there. I just went by and saw your van in the driveway."

Mandey got off the couch and picked up the phone. "I'm here, George."

"Girl, I've heard some things about you today."

Mandey looked at Shannon and rolled her eyes. "I can imagine. Like what?"

"That guy you're going with is in a gang?" Georgia asked.

"Well, not anymore," Mandey said. "Who'd you talk to?"

"Danny called me at eight o'clock this morning," Georgia said. "Eight o'clock on a Saturday morning, can you believe it? He couldn't shut up about it."

"Well, listen," Mandey said. "Why don't you come over and meet Shannon?"

"When?"

Shannon was shaking his head and mouthing, "No."

"Not tonight," he said in a loud whisper.

"How about tomorrow afternoon?" Mandey suggested to Georgia.

"He'll be there?"

"Oh, yeah."

"Is he there now?"

"Uh, yeah."

"Oh, I see. I'm interrupting," Georgia said in a knowing tone.

"No, but listen, George, I know Danny bad-mouthed him up one side and down the other, but you've got to meet him before you form an opinion. You'll like him."

"All right. I'm really curious to meet him now. I'll see you tomorrow."

"Okay. Bye."

When Mandey hung up the phone she turned to Shannon and asked him, "Why didn't you want to meet her tonight?"

"Not ready yet," he said. "I don't know that I'll be ready tomorrow, either."

"It'll be okay," Mandey assured him. "She's my best friend, and she's been wondering for weeks when she'd get the chance to meet my 'mystery man.' Georgia's also the most popular girl in our class and a tremendous gossip. When word gets around that she's met you and you seem okay to her, that is going to help a lot."

"What if she don't like me, though?" Shannon asked, worried. "That'll just make matters worse."

"She's going to like you," Mandey assured him. "You're the opposite of James, and she can't stand James."

Mandey returned to the couch and got under the blanket again. They cuddled and watched television, but as the evening wore on, Shannon enjoyed it less and less. He was thinking about the messed-up state of his life, and realized that even though he had left the Devils, he still had some problems.

"What's the matter?" Mandey asked, noticing the change in Shannon's demeanor.

"I have another problem I haven't told you about yet," Shannon said.

Mandey's eyes widened. "What?"

"This guy I was working for at the garage hasn't been helping my situation any. He's the reason there's been so many auto thefts at Liaisons."

Mandey stared at him blankly.

"Grubbs, my boss, is a partner in a chop shop owned by his nephew. He wanted to make sure the business got enough cars, so he had me stealing for him. He threatened to lie to my parole officer and say that I was stealing money from the garage if I said anything. Grubbs isn't going to be happy that I'm quitting on him, and now I'm afraid he's going to tell Holtz I've been stealing from him."

"And you can't explain this to your parole officer?" Mandey asked.

"He wouldn't believe me. Confessing that I've been stealing cars for any reason would be his excuse to send me back to jail."

"Shannon," Mandey said in despair, hugging him. "You've been stuck in worse trouble than I ever imagined."

"I know," Shannon said miserably. "Grubbs has this bogus file on me. He's fixed it to look like evidence that I've been stealing from him. If I could just get my hands on it…"

"How are you going to do that?" Mandey asked.

"I don't know. He keeps it in a locked file cabinet in his office. I've thought about picking the locks and stealing it, but even though I've had the chance to, I didn't dare. Grubbs ain't dumb; he'd know I did it, and I'd just be hanging myself."

"So, if you tell your parole officer what's been going on, you'll get busted for car theft. If you don't, Grubbs will nail you with false documents for stealing money from him. The third option is to steal the file and get rid of the evidence and probably get busted for stealing the file. Who knows about the file?"

"Just Grubbs and me, and now you, as far as I know," Shannon said, thoughtfully. "Maybe that's my best bet. He can still claim I stole from him, but he won't be able to back it up, unless he has a back-up file."

"Do you think he does?" Mandey asked.

"No, I doubt it," Shannon said, and sighed. "This sucks. I don't want to steal anything, but I've got to get that file."

Mandey said he could drive her van since his car was still back at the apartment complex. He felt nervous, using her van so he could commit a crime. He had to be extra careful not to be caught; he didn't want Mandey implicated in anything.

Shannon wanted to wait until after Marcia got home and was asleep before he left. They watched Houston Wrestling from 10 until 11:30. Mandey fell asleep against him before it was over. He woke her up when wrestling ended and they went to her room. He tucked Mandey into bed and turned on the television, the volume low. Mandey dozed off. Shannon laid down next to her and flipped through the channels, watching a few minutes of something before moving on to something else. About an hour later, he heard Marcia arrive home, and then suddenly he was waking up and the clock said 2:45 a.m.

"Shit," he said, jumping up.

"Mmmmm?" Mandey asked drowsily.

Shannon told Mandey that if anything went wrong, she should tell the police she thought he was going out for cigarettes.

"I don't want to tell them anything, so you be careful," she told him as he got ready to go.

He bent down to kiss her where she lay in bed. "I will be. Just covering all the bases. Love you," he said.

"Love you, too."

"Go back to sleep."

"I won't sleep a wink until you're back."

His heart was in his throat as he drove up to the service station. It was three-thirty in the morning, the place was deserted, and traffic on the street was minimal. Then he remembered he didn't have his mask or gloves with him.

"Shit," he muttered.

He had to have the gloves, at least. They were in his car. He had left the ski mask in his bedroom, but he was not about to into the apartment to fetch it. He pulled out and drove to the apartments. His car sat where he had left it. No one was around; all was quiet. He parked the van, quickly got out, grabbed his gloves out of the car, and left as fast as he could.

At the garage, he parked in the back where the van would be less conspicuous. With a sigh he put on his gloves. He had hoped he would never have to use them again. He took the flashlight Mandey kept in the emergency kit in her van and got out.

Grubbs had entrusted him with a key to the front door, so he entered the store unimpeded. He did not have a key to Grubbs' private office or to the locked file cabinet. The lock picking kit attached to his wallet chain would be his aid in getting him past those obstacles.

Shannon knelt down and set to work picking the lock on the office door. Every little noise made him jump, although there was almost no chance of being caught. The lock opened with a little click, and Shannon stepped into the office and shut the door behind him. Even though the room was windowless, Shannon wasn't brave enough to turn on the lights, and kept using the flashlight instead.

Surprisingly, the lock on the file cabinet proved to be harder to pick than the one on the door. Shannon panicked, swearing under his breath, fearing he wasn't going to be able to do it. Finally, it clicked and he slid the drawer open. He thumbed through the manila folders until he found the one with his name on the tab. He took it out and opened it up on Grubbs' desk.

"What the hell?" he asked out loud.

He leafed through all the papers in the folder, and all but a single one was blank. That one page, front and back, was a ledger of the cars he had stolen, along with the dates and some dollar amounts Shannon didn't understand. Where was all this falsified evidence to implicate that he had been stealing?

Shannon went back to the drawer and searched for another folder with his name on it, but he knew he had the right one. Shannon remembered the coffee ring stain on it from the day Grubbs had shown it to him. The file drawer contained no other folders with his name on them.

He opened the other two drawers in the cabinet and thumbed through those folders, also coming up empty. Shannon thought about going through all of the folders, but he wasn't exactly sure what it was he was looking for. He might come across lots of papers with figures on them, but he didn't think he could determine if they were supposed to be incriminating or not.

He looked through the stacks of papers on Grubbs' desk but saw nothing there, either.

He's been bluffing, Shannon thought. *All that blank paper in my file is there just to make it look like he had a ton of stuff to pin on me.*

That was the only explanation that made sense to him. Shannon hoped it was the <u>right</u> explanation.

He wasn't about to leave that ledger page there; it was the only incriminating document he found. He folded it up and stuck it in his shirt pocket, then went through his file folder one more time before filing it away, setting the office to rights, and heading back to Mandey's.

"It was the damnedest thing," he told Mandey as he stripped down to his briefs and got into bed with her. "I got in there, picked the locks without much problem, and got the file with my name on it. I opened it up, and all the sheets of paper were totally blank except one. Grubbs said the stuff was supposed to have altered figures on them to show I'd been skimming off the top, but it was all a bunch of blank paper. The only thing I found was a page listing the cars I stole the last couple months." He handed it to Mandey.

"What does that mean?" Mandey asked, looking at the paper and back to Shannon.

"Well, I think it means he's been bluffing all this time," Shannon said. "Maybe he's not so sure I wouldn't be believed if I ratted on him and said he's been blackmailing me."

"So now what?" Mandey asked.

"I guess I'm going to take my chances and quit and leave it at that," Shannon said. "For cryin' out loud, it's not like I was the only supplier. They've got other guys doing their dirty work for them. They can get along without me."

They settled down and Mandey fell asleep. Shannon's mind bounced around, thinking of different possibilities of what that blank file meant, but he was exhausted, and after a while, despite his troubled thoughts, he also slept.

45

Introductions

Shortly before 8:30 A.M., after only a couple hours of sleep, Shannon parked the van in the narrow alley behind the apartment, close to his bedroom window, where they were less likely to be seen. He doubted that any of the Devils were up this early, but it would be his rotten luck to come across one of them, upset and hungover and unpredictable, so he didn't want to take any chances.

He and Mandey gathered up the paper bags that they were going to use to pack up his belongings. He peered into the bedroom through the window. The curtain between his side of the room and Annette's was not drawn; Annette's bed was empty. He tried the window. It wasn't locked, so he opened it, then he and Mandey climbed into the room and tossed the bags onto his bed. Immediately, the memory of the fight he and Mandey had Friday night came to his mind. He quickly set the thought aside. Shannon opened the bedroom door and peered out into the hall and into the living room. No one was there. The door to the other bedroom was shut. Taking one bag with him, he walked out of the bedroom to the bathroom.

Mandey followed him with her nose wrinkled. She had been too distraught to notice it the other night, but the apartment smelled stale, with a bit of cheap cologne and a touch of pee. The apartment's appearance was just as bad. The living room had old, stained tan carpeting, an old couch that had gone out of style in 1971, a stuffed chair that was coming unstuffed, and a wooden coffee table that was scratched, nicked, and obviously glued together. In the kitchen was a dinette set that looked like it had been though a war, and from Shannon's descriptions of his family life, she figured it probably had been. The sink was full of dirty dishes that had been there for God-only-knew how long, and a window with an old crooked window shade pulled down to the sill, but no curtain. There was also a closed door, which Mandey supposed led to Shannon's mother and stepfather's room.

"This place is a lot more depressing in the daylight," Mandey said.

"I know," Shannon said, opening the bag he held.

He put all his toiletries into the bag and handed it to Mandey, then they went back to his room. They both opened bags, and Shannon began taking clothes out of his closet. Mandey took them off the hangers and stuffed them into the bags. He didn't have much to pack: three pairs of jeans, two pairs of corduroy pants, four T-shirts, four plaid flannel shirts, and one dress shirt, the beige one he had worn to Liaisons the night he had noticed Mandey. He took his black leather jacket, but left behind the black satin Devils jacket, the one he had stuffed in the back of the closet after Danny ruined it with green spray paint. He also left behind his two work uniforms.

He had two other pairs of shoes besides his Nikes—a pair of black desert boots and an old pair of brown, pointy-toed cowboy boots, the sight of which made Mandey giggle.

"I guess those can stay here, too," Shannon said. "I never wear them, anyway."

He pulled the bottom drawer of his nightstand, which contained his underwear and socks, out of the stand and dumped the contents into a bag. He put the desert boots on top. Mandey climbed back out of the window, and Shannon began handing her bags. While she was putting them in the van, Shannon continued packing. As put in the last bag she had and shut the van door, she heard a terrible racket coming from Shannon's apartment. She froze for a moment, then climbed as fast as she could back through the window. From the bedroom she could see Shannon in the living room, engaged in a wrestling match with a giant. Shannon was a shade under six feet tall and about 250 pounds, but this man made him look small. Mandey knew this had to be Leon, and she knew now why Shannon was afraid of him. Shannon was fighting valiantly, but Mandey could see that Leon was on the verge of overpowering him.

"STOP IT!" she screamed.

"Get out of here!" Shannon yelled at her. "GO!"

Leon slammed Shannon against the wall. The whole apartment shook. He put his hand to Shannon's throat and began to choke him.

Mandey's stomach felt as though an ice storm was raging through it and it was going to freeze her whole being. She wanted to run, but even more, she wanted to fight. She couldn't stand there and watch that animal do this.

She let out a scream as she took a flying leap and landed on Leon's back.

"Let him GO!" she shrieked, pulling hard on Leon's ears.

Leon let go of Shannon, who fell to his knees, and with one swift movement he threw Mandey to the floor. He turned, grabbed her by the shirt, and yanked her to her feet.

"Bitch!" he shouted, striking her across the face, and then he pushed her. She fell over the chair and banged her head on the coffee table.

Shannon got to his feet. The whole room had a red hazy look to it, but he wasn't sure if it was due to oxygen deprivation or rage or both. He was going to kill that bastard. Leon could beat him senseless a million times if he wanted, but there was no way in hell he was going to get away with beating on Mandey.

"YOU DON'T TOUCH HER!" Shannon shouted, and lunged at Leon with renewed energy.

As Leon turned to face him, Shannon swung his fist with all of his strength. There was a loud crack as Shannon's fist smashed into Leon's nose, breaking it. Blood poured. Leon's pale blue eyes filled with a crazy white light that Shannon had never seen before, and it scared the shit out of him.

Shannon grabbed one of the dinette chairs. Leon rushed forward and tried to wrest it from his grasp. With every drop of energy left in his body, Shannon jerked the chair away from Leon and slammed it up against his head. It hit slightly askance, so not with the full force of Shannon's strength, but it was hard enough. Leon slumped to the floor.

Mandey got to her feet, holding her head.

"He's not dead, is he?" she asked, her eyes big.

"No, he's still breathing," Shannon said solemnly, gazing down at him. "I <u>could</u> fix that, though." Then he shook his head as if coming out of a reverie.

"Come on, let's get the hell out of here before he wakes up," Shannon said, going over to her and taking her hand.

They ran to his bedroom and Shannon handed her another bag of his belongings. He took a box and some bags and they went out the window.

"I'm going to get my car. I'll meet you at the corner at Exxon," Shannon said, tossing the box and bags into the van and sprinting away.

Mandey threw her bag into the van and got in, locking her door behind her. She started the van and took off for the gas station. Shannon drove in behind her, and they parked off to one side. He got out of his car. Mandey rolled down her window.

"God, Mandey, are you okay?" he asked her.

She touched the back of her head, where a large knot had formed. "Yeah," she said. "I've got a nice bump on my head, but I'm all right. But, oh my God, Shannon, look what he did to you!"

Shannon peered into the van's side view mirror. "What?" he asked. "I can't get a good view in this little mirror, but from what I can tell, I've had worse done to me."

"Your face is turning black and blue, and your neck is, too," Mandey said. She handed him some tissue from her jacket pocket for his bloody nose.

Shannon took the tissue and wiped his nose. "Thanks for your help," he said.

"My help?"

"If you hadn't distracted him by jumping him, he'd have beaten me to a pulp. But he could have hurt you bad."

"I froze for a minute, but then the only thing I could think about was you, and all I wanted to do was beat the hell out of him."

"I swear, if he ever lays a hand on you again, I will kill him," Shannon said.

Mandey knew by the flat look on his face and the tone of his voice that he was serious.

"Well, honey, don't worry about that," she said lightly. "We aren't coming back here, so he won't get the chance."

"You're right. Fuck him. Fuck everyone in this goddamn neighborhood. Let's get out of here."

He got back in his car and followed Mandey back to her house—his house, too, now.

"Now what?" Marcia asked, aghast, when she saw Shannon's face, which was blacker and bluer than it had been before he left. His right eye was swollen almost shut, and his lips were swollen, too.

"It's nothing," Shannon said, shuffling his feet and looking at the floor.

"His stepfather did that to him!" Mandey said. "See why he had to get out of that place? It was horrible! I thought Leon was going to kill him!" Without warning, she burst into tears.

"It's okay, Mandey," Shannon said, hugging her.

"I wouldn't have taken her with me if I knew this was going to happen," Shannon said to Marcia. "But it's not going to happen again."

"I should hope not. Good God," Marcia said. "Let me go make you an ice pack."

"You don't have to do that," Shannon said. "I'd like to get unpacked first, anyway."

"I'll put it in the freezer so you can have it later," she said, and went into the kitchen.

Mandey and Shannon went to his room. They set his stuff down and sat on the bed.

"How does it feel to have your own room?" Mandey asked him.

"It hasn't quite sunk in yet," Shannon said. "I'll have to sleep in here a few times before it sinks in." He grinned. "Actually, sharing a room with you doesn't bother me at all."

She smiled. "What's in there?" she asked, pointing at the box.

"Records and tapes," Shannon said. "I haven't listened to the albums in a while. My record player was gone after I got out of jail."

Mandey opened the box and looked at what he had: The Eagles, Boston, Steve Miller, Van Halen, Def Leppard, Foreigner, Ozzy Osbourne, and many others, most of which Mandey liked, too.

It didn't take long for them to put away his things, considering how few he had. When they finished, they went out to the kitchen. Coffee was ready, and they each got themselves a cup. Mandey got the ice pack out of the freezer for Shannon, and he sat down at the kitchen table.

"Eggs and English muffins okay for breakfast?" Mandey asked him, getting the muffins out of the breadbox.

"Sounds great," Shannon replied.

"How do you want your eggs?"

"Over easy?"

"Coming up," Mandey said.

In a few minutes she brought over a plate of eggs and a buttered English muffin to him, along with a glass of chocolate milk.

"Hey," he said.

"What?"

"Could you stand getting kissed by this ugly mug?" he asked her.

Mandey regarded his beaten face. "You're as handsome to me as always," she told him, bending down to touch her lips to his.

"Thanks."

She refilled their coffee cups and then brought her own plate to the table and sat down. After they ate, they went into the living room to watch television. Both of them had gotten very little sleep the night before, especially Shannon, and soon they were slumped together on the couch, fast asleep.

"Hey," Mandey heard someone say.

She and Shannon opened their eyes. Marcia was standing over them. She was on her way out. Again.

"The Oilers game is starting. I didn't think you'd want to sleep through it," she said.

"No," Shannon said, reaching for the remote control on the coffee table. "Thanks."

"You want a Dr Pepper?" Mandey asked Shannon.

"Sure," he said.

She went to the kitchen and returned with the sodas to find him with the ice pack, now mostly melted, on his face again.

"Does it hurt a lot?" she asked him.

"A little," he admitted.

"Want some Tylenol?"

"Yeah, I think so."

Mandey went to the bathroom and brought back two pills.

"I'm going to need more than that," Shannon said.

"But the recommended dosage is two," Mandey said.

"That don't matter," Shannon said. "If I don't take at least four, they don't do me no good."

She went back and returned with the entire bottle. "You are kind of a big guy, so I suppose the regular dose might be too mild for you," she conceded, sitting down next to him.

"Is Georgia still coming by today?" he asked, opening the bottle and pouring out four more pills.

"As far as I know," Mandey said. "But that doesn't mean she will. I've learned not to pin her down to show up at a certain time for anything, if she shows up at all." She watched him wash down six Tylenol with a Dr Pepper chaser. "Boy, you are hurting, aren't you?"

"I've been through worse," Shannon said.

"Tough guy."

The much-anticipated Pittsburgh-Houston game had sold out several days in advance. Through the first half the game stayed close, to Shannon's delight, as the Oilers had lost to the Steelers 35-7 at their last meeting.

As the third quarter began, someone pounded on the front door.

"That's got to be Georgia," Mandey said, getting up to open the door.

"Hey," Georgia greeted her.

"Come on in," Mandey said, opening the door wide. "Shannon, this is Georgia Cornell. Georgia, this is Shannon Douglass."

"Hi," Georgia said to him. Her big, wide Southern belle smile faded when she saw his face.

"Hi," Shannon replied guardedly.

"Have a seat," Mandey told Georgia. "You want a Dr Pepper?"

"Sure," she said, regaining her composure.

Mandey went out to the kitchen and returned with three sodas and passed them out.

"Are you an Oilers fan?" Georgia asked Shannon. She pronounced the word *Awlers.*

"Yep. Just about the biggest," Shannon replied.

Mandey sat down on the couch next to him. "I know you're wondering about Shannon's face," she said to Georgia. "He's really a good-looking guy underneath all the swelling and bruises."

"I remember what a fine-looking specimen he was when you pointed him out to me at the dance club," Georgia said. She smiled at him.

Shannon looked embarrassed.

"He got kind of beat up the other night, then he and his stepdad got into it this morning and made it worse," Mandey said.

"You look like you got a little beat up yourself," Georgia remarked.

"Yeah, a little. But I'm okay," Mandey said. "Did you talk to Danny again?"

"No. but called me at <u>eight o'clock</u> in the morning yesterday and he raved on and on," Georgia said. "I didn't know about what was going on with all y'all. I had to get him to explain everything. He said I needed to go talk some sense into you because you were dating a vicious gang leader."

"He's a little beat up, but does he look vicious to you?" Mandey asked Georgia.

"Not exactly," Georgia said.

Shannon squirmed. "I <u>was</u> a gang leader," he said. "I don't think I was vicious, though. But I've quit. I ran off after that fight Friday night. If I go back to that neighborhood now, I'll be just as much of a target as anyone else."

"How did Danny seem on the phone?" Mandey asked.

"He was upset," Georgia said diplomatically.

"I hope he calms down. He doesn't have to worry. Shannon is not a threat to him now."

"He sounded more worried about you," Georgia said.

"Well, tell him he can stop worrying," Mandey said. "They've got it in their heads that Shannon's some kind of monster, but he's not."

"But Danny said you <u>mugged</u> him?" Georgia asked Shannon.

Shannon looked uncomfortable for a moment, then said defensively, "I caught him sneaking around where I lived. I just wanted to chase him off, but he sprayed me with a can of spray paint. Thank God his aim sucks and he hit me in the chest instead of the face." He paused. "And I know he's no angel. I'm sure whatever I took from him was drug money."

"That may be true," Georgia admitted. "Well, y'all, I can't stay. I'm on my way over to my sister's house to take my nieces to the movies. Shannon, I have to say, you don't seem like the big meanie Danny seems to think you are. But you better be good to Mandey, because I will hunt you down if you hurt her." She laughed like it was a joke, but her eyes told a different story.

"That's exactly what he said to the gang the other night, that they should hunt him down if they ever saw me crying over him," Mandey said.

"Good. Glad we think alike," Georgia said brightly. "It was good to meet you, Shannon. Gotta run. See you tomorrow, Mandey. We'll talk more then."

With that she was out the door on her way back to her car.

"What did you think?" Mandey asked Shannon.

"I'm not sure. She was in and out like a whirlwind," Shannon replied.

"Yeah, that's Georgia."

"I do know I better not screw up and ever make you unhappy. I have a feeling there's a ton of people ready to beat my ass if I do."

"Would it be different if there wasn't?"

"No," Shannon said. "I'm still not going to make you unhappy."

"Good. Let's concentrate on making each other happy, then."

46

Reckoning

Mandey woke up the Monday morning after the rumble dreading the day ahead at school. She knew it would be a crappy day. It would likely be a crappy week. She wished she could skip the next two weeks and stay home until school started again in January, after Christmas vacation. Maybe she could get mono and stay home for a month.

She got out of bed, turned on her stereo and was greeting by the strains of Stevie Wonder's "I Just Called to Say I Love You."

"Nooo," Mandey whined, changing the station. She spun the dial and found another station playing "Blue Jean" by David Bowie. This was a crappy morning, and Mandey wasn't about to make it any worse by listening to crappy music.

Upon opening her closet, she decided to dress on the conservative side. She chose a calf-length purple skirt and a long-sleeved white blouse. Over the blouse she put on a sleeveless pink sweater. She wore hose and gray, low-heeled pumps. A string of white and gray beads and pearl earrings completed the look.

She was doing her make-up when she heard Shannon in the bathroom. He had slept in his new room the night before, to see what it was like. A few minutes later he knocked on her door and peeked in.

"Can I come in?" he asked.

"Sure," Mandey said.

He walked in and surveyed Mandey in her outfit. "Well, good morning, Miss Rowan," he said, grinning.

"I know, I look like a total school girl today," Mandey said.

"I was going to say you look like a teacher," Shannon said.

"Even worse!" Mandey said. "You're up early."

"I figured I'd better get an early start. I've got phone calls to make and I've got to start looking for another job."

"Mandey! Mandey, come here!" they heard Marcia shout.

Mandey and Shannon ran out to the living room. Marcia was standing there, ready for work, staring out the window.

"What's wrong?" Mandey asked.

"Someone egged your van and Shannon's car," Marcia said.

"What?" Mandey gasped, and ran outside. Her van was covered with dried eggs. Shells littered the driveway.

"Shit," Shannon said, coming up behind her.

Shannon's car was worse. Not only was it egged, but it also had been keyed and there were obscenities written all over it in black shoe polish.

Mandey stared at the mess, despondent. So much for being upbeat.

"God damn it, they better not have put sugar in the tanks, so help me," Shannon said, storming back toward the house.

"Where are you going?" Mandey asked him.

"To get our keys. I'm going to start the cars up to make sure they're okay, and I'm getting something to wash that shit off."

Mandey sighed and walked around her van and Shannon's car. "Die, Devil motherfucker" was written across the driver's side of Shannon's car. It only got worse from there.

Marcia joined Mandey in the driveway. "Mandey, what is going on here? First you get beaten up and now this. Who is doing this?"

Mandey shook her head. "I don't think it was the same people," she said, which wasn't a lie.

"Shannon, do you know who did this?" Marcia asked, as he returned with a bucket of soapy water and two sponges, which he set down.

"No, I don't," he said abruptly, getting into his car and starting the ignition. It started and ran normally. He left it running, then went to Mandey's van and did the same. There was no problem with her van, either.

"I can only guess," Mandey said to Marcia, "that it was some guy from school. Somebody told me that there are a couple guys who wanted to ask me out after James and I broke up, but they found out I was dating someone new. Maybe they got drunk, came by here, saw Shannon's car and put two and two together..." That excuse sounded lame to Mandey's own ears.

"Men are scum," Marcia said. "Present company excluded."

Shannon grunted in acknowledgement of the comment. He was scrubbing dried egg off the van.

"I've got to go or I'm going to be late," Marcia said. "Look, I don't know who is doing this or why, but it's going to stop, or I'm calling the police."

She opened the garage, got in her car, and backed out, maneuvering past the van and car. Mandey picked up the second sponge and began helping Shannon.

"Crap," she said flatly.

"I agree," Shannon said. "Engines seem okay." He turned the van off, then his car. When he rejoined Mandey in cleaning off the van, he said, "I'm sorry."

"Sorry? For what?" Mandey asked him.

"This mess," he said.

"You didn't do this. We know who did," Mandey said.

"Yeah, but it's my fault for starting all this shit in the first place," Shannon said.

"No, it's not," Mandey said.

"You don't look like you want to go to school today," Shannon said.

"I didn't, but now I want to, just to show them they can't intimidate me."

"Are you gonna be okay?"

"Oh, believe me, I'm going to be just fine," Mandey said.

The grim look of determination on her face did not escape him.

"Mandey, I'll do this," he told her. "You don't need to get your clothes all wet. Go in the house and eat something before you have to go."

"I'm okay," she said, intently scrubbing a back window.

"Go inside," Shannon insisted, taking the sponge from her.

She looked at him. He expected to see tears in her green eyes, but they were dry.

"Okay," she relented.

He kissed her forehead.

Mandey left for school as soon as Shannon came in to announce her van was about as clean as he could get it. She picked up her purse and books and kissed him goodbye.

"Thanks for washing my van," she told him. "See you tonight."

She had to speed to make it to school on time. The cereal she had eaten for breakfast felt like it had congealed in her stomach then petrified. She arrived at school just as the first bell rang. She hurried inside and merged with the crowds, heading for her locker and then on to Spanish class.

"Hola," Andrea said to her as Mandey sat down in her seat next to her friend.

"Hola," Mandey replied, putting her books under her desk.

"No estas feliz hoy?" Andrea asked her.

"No. Estoy pissed off," Mandey said.

"What's wrong?" Andrea asked. "What happened to your face?"

"I'm sure you'll hear all about it during the course of the day. For one thing, I woke up this morning to find my van got egged last night."

"What?" Andrea asked. "Who did it?"

She looked up and saw Brad coming into class. She averted her eyes before she made eye contact with him. She didn't think he was going to come over to her and bring up the subject of Friday night; after all, he had been fairly cool about everything. Still, she was relieved when he sat down at his desk, which was second from the front in Andrea's row.

"What kind of stuff?" Andrea asked.

"I'll write you a note," Mandey said.

Class got underway. Mandey and Andrea wrote notes back and forth in class every day. Señora Reynolds never saw, or if she did, she paid no mind. They were both "A" students.

"No quiero estar aqui. Quiero ir a casa," Mandey wrote.

"Yo, también. ¿Pero, qué pasó?" Andrea replied.

Mandey dropped the Spanish. "It's a long story, but I'll try to make it short. You know how that gang was harassing everyone who goes to Liaisons? Well, a bunch of us who were victims got together and tried to do something about it. On Friday night we met up and got into a scuffle with them. But guess who I found out was the leader of this gang?" She passed the note to Andrea.

"You were in a fight? I have no idea who it was," Andrea wrote back.

"It was Shannon."

Andie got a shocked look on her face when she read that.

"What?!!!! What did you do?"

"I'll tell you the details after class. Everything's okay between Shannon and me now. We decided we didn't want anything to do with this stuff anymore. Shannon came home with me Friday night, and we announced that we were quitting to the others I was with. Some of them wouldn't ride home with me because of Shannon. Anyway, Shannon is at my house permanently now, although I don't want everyone to know. But I guess enough people know, because we woke up this morning to find our cars egged, and Shannon's had obscenities written all over it."

"Wow! I can hardly believe that! That is totally bizarre! Shannon seems like such a sweetheart—you had no idea he was in a gang?"

"No. I had no idea, and he had no idea about me. We both freaked out when we realized what was going on, but we decided we mean too much to each other to let it break us up."

"¡Ay, caramba! I have no idea what I would do in that situation."

"Who would ever expect to be in such a situation?"

Choir was next. Mandey expected that one to be the worst, since she had three people in there to contend with. She walked slowly because she didn't want to give them any time before class to harass her. The tardy bell rang as she walked through the door. She avoided the eyes of Jesse, Angelina, and Zack as she picked up her music folio and pointedly cut a wide swath on her way to her seat.

The class went more smoothly than she thought. Like Brad, Zack totally ignored her. Angelina occasionally shot her "drop dead" looks, and between songs, Jesse, sitting a few chairs down in the row behind her, muttered under his breath in Spanish. Mandey was not familiar with the words he was using, but they must have been very uncomplimentary because classmates who understood more Spanish than she did had shocked expressions on their faces.

When the bell rang, Mandey practically ran out the door, not even stopping to put back her music folder. She fled to the relative safety of English class.

"You look upset. What's wrong?" Gayla asked as Mandey took her seat across the aisle from her.

"It hasn't been a good day," Mandey said, opening her journal and putting the rest of her books under her desk.

"It's only third period and your day has gone to hell already?" Charlie asked, turning around in his desk to face her.

"My day went to hell at seven o'clock this morning," Mandey said. "I guess I ought to tell you about it before you start hearing the rumors."

"I've started hearing the rumors," Jackie said as she sat down in front of Gayla. "Danny Sanchez was not very happy in Latin class this morning."

"That overgrown gorilla you call your boyfriend is a gang leader?" James nearly shouted as he came into class and slammed his backpack down on his desk. The desk tipped forward and hit the floor with a loud bang.

"What is going on in here?" Mr. Crenshaw demanded, his ample form bustling into the room.

"Nothing," James replied, picking up his books and desk. "I'm carrying around so many books with me, they made my desk fall over. It's the consequences of trying to become valedictorian."

"If you're not careful, you're going to learn the consequences of being loud and obnoxious," Mr. Crenshaw said, going back to the doorway to monitor the hallway.

"Fuck you," James mouthed silently at Mr. Crenshaw's back. Charlie gave the teacher the finger, although he couldn't see it.

Mandey found herself surrounded by all nine of her classmates.

"That's what Danny said, that your boyfriend runs a gang," Jackie said.

"Are you out of your mind?" James asked. "Have you gone completely off the deep end?"

"James, will you shut up and let her talk?" Trish said impatiently.

The tardy bell rang, and Mr. Crenshaw came into the room, shutting the door behind him. The class was still gathered at Mandey's desk.

"What is this, a convention of the hopelessly nosy and distracted? Or perhaps of those trying to fail English and ruin their grade point averages?" Mr. Crenshaw said sarcastically as he went to his desk to check roll.

The class slowly took their seats. "You're no fun," Gayla complained.

"It's not in my contract," Mr. Crenshaw replied.

Mandey copied down the day's journal topic, but didn't begin writing about it. Instead, she got out a blank piece of paper and wrote a short statement.

"It is true that my boyfriend has had something of a checkered past, and certain people do have reason to dislike him. My boyfriend admits he has done some things he is not proud of. He has had a hard, troubled life and is in the process of turning it around. He is no longer involved in any type of suspect activity, and he is sorry for any pain he has caused anyone."

She read over the paragraph. She knew she shouldn't end a sentence with a preposition, but "he has done some things of which he is not proud" sounded too pretentious. She didn't like the word "suspect" and, after thinking a few moments, obliterated it and wrote "anti-social" above it. She did not sign her name to it. Then she folded the note into eighths and wrote on the front, "Read and pass it on."

There was a television on a tall TV cart with a Betamax at the front of the classroom. As Mr. Crenshaw had said the week before, they were going to watch the musical *Camelot* this week. He turned out the lights and started the tape.

Mandey furtively passed the note she had written forward to Charlie. She pretended to concentrate on the movie, but she was constantly aware of who had the note. When it came back to her ten minutes before the class ended, everyone in the class had added questions and comments. No one signed his or her name, but Mandey knew everyone's writing. For the most part the responses were just curious. The only exception was at the very bottom of the page, a one-word comment:

Bullshit!

which was written in James's delicate, Oriental-influenced hand.

Mandey quietly folded the note as small as she could and stuffed it in her purse. She didn't know what James's problem was, and she was positive she probably wouldn't be able to figure it out, either. Moreover, she wasn't particularly concerned about it. James was no longer an important part of her life. But deep inside, that one word he had written had sent pinpricks into her soul, and that angered her.

The dismissal bell rang. It was time for fourth period; time to face Danny.

The entire ten students in Mr. Crenshaw's third period class were also in Mrs. Silverman's fourth period, and Mandey found herself with an entourage accompanying her, the lone exception being James.

"So is Shannon in a gang?" Charlie asked.

"He was," Mandey said. "He quit."

"He didn't act like he was in a gang when we met him," Gayla remarked.

"He never wanted to be in a gang," Mandey said. "This is the condensed version of the story: He moved to a rough neighborhood and got coerced into joining a gang. The leader of this gang got killed, and it looked like this guy's cousin was going to take over. This cousin hated Shannon, and Shannon knew that if this guy became leader, he'd either get Shannon sent to prison or get him killed, so Shannon challenged him and took over as leader. It was a survival thing."

"And you and Danny and some others started a gang of your own to try to stop your boyfriend's gang," Jackie said. "That's what Danny said, anyway."

"Danny's got a big mouth," Mandey said.

"He is not a happy camper," Jackie said.

"Well, that's too damn bad."

Danny was not yet in Mrs. Silverman's classroom when Mandey arrived. Not that it mattered; she knew he would show up sooner or later, and there was no way to avoid him.

She took her seat and busied herself by getting out her notebook, textbook, and pen. She did not look up when James took his seat next to hers. When Danny walked past her down the aisle to his desk a few minutes later, she pretended to be engrossed in her notes. He paid no attention to her.

The class was uneventful, to Mandey's relief. Lunch was peaceful, as well. She had half-expected Danny to come over and cause a scene, but she saw him only once at lunch, walking through the snack bar. He was not sitting with Jackie and Thad and the rest of his crowd at the table across the aisle from Mandey's. She didn't see Georgia at lunch, either. She hadn't seen her at all that day, in fact. Mandey had hoped Georgia would tell Danny what she thought about Shannon. Danny would probably listen to Georgia.

After lunch, Mandey ended up walking back alone to Mrs. Silverman's class for study hall. She was the first one back from lunch, and she sat down in the back of the room where she usually sat with Gayla and Charlie. She heard someone else come into the room, and when she looked up, she saw Danny glaring down at her. Her face went hot, and her insides turned icy.

He sat down in the desk in front of her, but turned around to face her.

"I can't believe that you've been running around with that bastard for the last month and you had no idea who he was," Danny said.

"Well, I didn't," Mandey said, opening a notebook to a blank page.

"And after realizing this, you still say you love him. Knowing all the shit he's done, you're okay with that," Danny said bitterly.

"I know what he's done, and I don't like what he's done, and he's not proud of what he's done, either. If you'd had sense enough to listen to him Friday night, you'd know that."

"Yeah, Brad told me about that line of bullshit he fed them."

"Is that what Brad called it?"

"It doesn't matter what Brad called it. Bullshit is bullshit. Shit by any other name still stinks."

James was coming down the aisle, and he sat down in the desk to Mandey's left.

"What is wrong with you?" he demanded. "How can you be so brainless?"

"James, this is none of your business," Mandey said, annoyed.

"I care about you," he declared. "I don't want to see you do something stupid."

"The stupidest thing I ever did was get involved with you," she told him.

"Jesus!" James said. "Can you talk some sense into her, Danny? Please?"

Mandey stared at the blank page before her, but she could feel Danny's eyes boring a hole through her skull.

"How can you even bear for a piece of shit like him to touch you?" Danny asked her. "It makes me sick thinking of him kissing you and groping you. The idea of you sleeping with him makes me want to vomit."

"Is that true? You're sleeping with him?" James asked, his eyes almost bugging out of his head.

"It's none of your business, Danny," Mandey said. "Or yours, James."

"Yes, it is my business. It's my business because someone who was supposed to be helping to stop the problems caused by those bastards turned out to be dating their leader. It's my business because now they have a way of finding out stuff about me I'd rather they not know. You acted upset that night when Trick jumped me and beat me up. How will you feel when a bunch of them jump me or one of the others in our own front yard because your boyfriend found the address in your address book?"

"That's not going to happen, Danny," Mandey told him. "If they ever find out anything like that, it won't be through me."

"You're so naïve," Danny said, disgusted. "He's going to use you to get to us."

"Danny, he quit. He doesn't have anything to do with them anymore."

"Bullshit," Danny responded. "How do you know what he does when he's not with you? You don't, or you would have figured this thing out a long time ago."

"Look, if you guys want to keep this thing going, that's your business. But Shannon and I are no longer involved. Shannon's even moved out of that neighborhood to get away from the Devils."

"Yeah, I know," Danny said. "He's living with you now."

"He's living with you?" James asked, aghast.

"I'm not telling anyone where he's living now," Mandey said.

"You don't have to," Danny said flatly.

Mandey bit back the urge to accuse him of vandalizing the cars. She knew he did it, and he knew she knew he did it, so what was the point?

"You're living together?" James asked, his eyes wide.

"James, leave me alone!" Mandey said, exasperated.

"You betrayed us," Danny said.

"Oh, bullshit, Danny. You leave me alone, too."

Gayla and Charlie were coming over to take their seats. "What's going on?" Gayla asked.

Danny got up and moved to another seat without another word.

"They're giving me crap, and I wish they would stop," Mandey said pointedly to James.

"Fine," James said. "I'll talk to you later." He went to go sit next to Danny.

"Let's talk about something else," Mandey suggested to Gayla and Charlie. "Anything besides how crazy I am to be going out with a vicious gang-banger."

"Anything? Okay," Charlie said enthusiastically. "Let's talk about sex."

"Let's not," Gayla said.

The last two classes were chemistry and art. There were no Alley Cats in either class to spar with, only James. He strode into the chemistry classroom and sat down with Mandey, Gayla, and Charlie at their lab table. He had sat there with them until he broke up with Mandey, at which time he moved to a regular table all by himself. Now he was back.

"James, if you're here to bug Mandey some more, you'd better move right now," Gayla said.

"Yeah," Charlie said. "It's none of your business."

"But it's yours?" James asked.

"They aren't berating me like you are, James," Mandey said. "I don't care if you sit there as long as you keep your snide comments to yourself."

"Snide comments? Moi?" James asked innocently.

"Oh, please," Gayla said, rolling her eyes.

Mrs. Hynde started class, so it was time to pay attention and take notes. Fortunately, she had a lot to cover, and there wasn't time for idle chatter.

Art class was another matter. Mandey and James were the only seniors in the class, and Mandey had no one, such as Gayla, to intervene on her behalf. She couldn't even use the excuse of listening to the teacher, because Mr. Slater generally only talked for a few minutes, and the rest of the time the class was free to talk quietly as they worked on their pieces.

"Mandey, I really want to understand," James began, as he worked on his grid drawing of a bikini-clad sunbather on the beach, "but I can't."

"What's not to understand?" Mandey asked nonchalantly, sketching the contours of Cyndi Lauper's lips in her own grid drawing. "We're in love. It's that simple."

"How can you love someone like that?" he asked. "He's so far beneath you."

"That's just rude," Mandey said, offended.

"Well, it's true," James said.

"That's social class snobbery," Mandey said. "There are more important things in life besides that."

"He's not exactly Honor Society material, either," James remarked.

"So what? He's not book smart, but he's by no means stupid," Mandey said. "I've learned a few things from him."

"I'll bet you have," James said sourly.

"Don't you get all sour about that. You know I was willing and able last summer, but having sex with a brown-haired fat girl was too appalling for you," Mandey said, glancing at his drawing of the sexy beach babe. "It's just as well. I like things better the way they are now."

"And just how are things now?" James asked.

"James, you broke up with me a month ago. Who I see and what I do with him is not your concern. I don't know why you seem to think it is."

"I still care about you. You're still my friend," James said, "aren't you?"

Mandey gave a long sigh. "I suppose, but that doesn't mean you get to run my life. Being my friend means having to accept the fact that Shannon is a part of my life now. You don't have to like it, but you have to accept it."

"What if I can't?"

"Then we'd better steer clear of each other until you can."

With that, James picked up his pencil, his drawing, and the magazine picture he was using as his model and moved over to an empty seat at a table of freshmen.

Mandey sighed again and concentrated on her artwork. Mr. Slater let them listen to the radio during class. Mandey hummed quietly to herself. "No More Lonely Nights" by Paul McCartney came on.

"No more lonely nights…no more lonely nights," she sang softly, thinking of Shannon at home. The song and the thought cheered her up.

The final bell rang at three-fifteen. It had been a hell of a day, but it was finally over, and she had survived. Now came the good part—going home to Shannon.

He was in the living room with the Sunday edition of the *Houston Chronicle*, reading the classified ads when she walked in.

"How'd it go?" he asked her as she set her purse and books down on the chair.

"It's over," she said with a relieved sigh, sitting down on the couch next to him.

Shannon put the paper down on the coffee table, put his arm around Mandey and kissed her. "Was it as bad as you thought it was going to be?" he asked.

"It wasn't a picnic," Mandey said, "but I think I expected worse. Danny was the worst of them. He let me have it during study hall. Jesse cussed me out under his breath in Spanish during choir class. I'm not up on all the bad words, but I got the message. But I got through it, and now that I'm here with you, I'm fine. How was your day?"

Shannon drew a deep breath. "Not very good," he said.

"What happened?" Mandey asked him, her eyes wide with alarm.

"Aaagh," he said, agitated. "I called Holtz's office at nine o'clock, right away, to let him know what's up with me, my change of residence and that I quit my job. Well, I didn't even get a chance to tell him I've moved, which is a good thing, actually."

"What happened?" Mandey asked again.

Shannon ran his hair through his hair and sighed. "He went nuts as soon as I told him I was quitting my job at the garage. I mean, totally nuclear. I tried to explain that I would have a new job within two weeks, like I'm supposed to, but he started all this shit about how he was going to have me arrested for parole violation—"

"Oh, Shannon!" Mandey exclaimed, dismayed. "Can he do that?"

"Man, I don't know," Shannon said, distraught. "I don't think he can, legally. I'm supposed to have two weeks to find a new job. He could get my ass for not reporting my change of residence, but he can't get me arrested if he can't find me. I don't think I can get in much trouble since I haven't left the county, and as long as I turn up for my next appointment with a job and my new address and phone number, I think I'll be okay."

Mandey knew that every day at school she would be thinking about Shannon possibly getting picked up by the police. It wasn't fair; he was trying to do the right thing, and now his parole officer wanted to get him arrested on a technicality.

"When is your next appointment with him, anyway?" Mandey asked him.

"I've been switched to Mondays. Two o'clock on the seventeenth," Shannon said. "That's two weeks from today. I've got to find a job, pronto." He picked up the paper from the coffee table again.

Mandey sat there, her eyes full of anxiety. Shannon noticed how she was looking at him and put his arm around her again.

"I'm sorry I got you all upset, Mandey. Maybe I shouldn't have told you," he said.

"No, it's good you did," Mandey said. "If something does happen, it won't be a nasty shock."

"I don't think anything will happen, though, Mand," Shannon said, calming down a little. He didn't want to make Mandey worry. "Like I said, I never got a chance to tell him where I am now, so even if he does send someone out to pick me up, they won't find me."

Mandey sighed and laid her head on his shoulder. "It's always something, isn't it?"

"Yeah," Shannon said.

"What happened when you called the garage?"

"Nothing. Grubbs wasn't there. I left a message with Tommy to tell him I quit. I was disappointed. I wanted to tell him to shove a slim jim up his ass."

"It's probably better you didn't get the chance," Mandey said.

47

A Little Good News

Mandey was never so glad for a week to be over as she was that Friday. She wished it were already the next Friday, though. The fourteenth couldn't get there fast enough for her.

When she walked into the living room, Shannon was on the couch, flipping through the television channels. He broke into a smile when he saw her.

"Guess what?" he asked.

"You're smiling, so it must be good news," Mandey said.

"I found a job today."

"You did? Oh, that's wonderful!" she exclaimed. She dropped her books and purse on the chair, then sat down next to Shannon on the couch and hugged him. "Tell me about it."

"I'm going to be a trainee for a company that builds and remodels houses," Shannon said proudly. "It's a forty hour a week job and even some overtime, and it pays $5.75 an hour to start."

"That's almost twice what you made at the garage," Mandey said.

"More than twice, because I almost never got more than thirty hours a week there."

"When do you start?"

"Seven-thirty A.M. on Monday."

"That's great!" Mandey said, squeezing him again.

"My new boss seems like a fair guy. He listened to me explain about my criminal conviction and I told him how I was trying to start over fresh, and he thought that was worth giving me a chance. They usually require a high school diploma or a GED, but he said he would waive that as long as I get my GED this spring. I think I thanked him five times, I was so happy. I told him I won't let him down. I'm going to be at work every day on time and I'll work all the overtime I need to and I'll take the GED test as soon as I can. I'm going to be the best damn employee he's ever had."

Mandey laughed. "I've never heard you sound like this before."

"Like what?"

"So enthusiastic. So determined."

"Things have never been going this good for me before. I've finally got everything going my way. I've got a decent job, I'm out of the gang, I'm living with you, I'm going back to school—I don't intend to let anything screw this up." He reached down, picked up her hand in his, brought it to his mouth and kissed it. "Oh, and I called my parole officer to tell him."

"What did he say?"

"I had to leave a message on his machine. Told him all the information, gave him the phone number, and said I'd bring in the documentation on the seventeenth."

"Did you give him the change of address?"

"No, I'm going to wait to do that in person," Shannon said. "I want to tell that prick to shove his arrest warrants up his ass."

"Now, you're not actually going to say that," Mandey admonished him.

"No," Shannon admitted, "but I'd like to."

"A remodeling company, huh?" Mandey said.

"Yep."

"Cool."

"And someday I'll be able to take what I've learned and build you the house of your dreams," Shannon told her.

Mandey laughed and blushed. "Still planning on keeping me around that long?"

"Sure, if you'll have me."

"I'll have you, all right."

"This is such a load off my mind," Shannon said, totally missing Mandey's double-entendre.

"This is cause for celebration," Mandey declared. "I think we should go out for dinner tonight. Monterey House—my treat."

48

Christmas Concert

On the evening of the choir Christmas concert, Mandey, Shannon, and Marcia had dinner together, as they did a few times a week. After finishing up and putting the dishes in the dishwasher, Mandey went to get ready. First, she brushed her teeth, then sat at the vanity in her room to re-do her make-up a bit more dramatically, so as to be more noticeable from the stage. Then she put on her pantyhose, her long black choir dress, and a string of pearls and stepped into her black pumps.

She walked back into the living room where Shannon was watching *Wheel of Fortune*. He stood up when he saw her.

"Wow," he said.

She smiled. Marcia came into the living room from the kitchen.

"What time are we supposed to be there?" she asked Mandey.

"The junior high choirs will be on for about 45 minutes, so about 8:10," Mandey replied. She gave Shannon a quick kiss on the lips. "See you later."

A few minutes before eight, Shannon was riding with Marcia in her car, heading to the high school.

"Shannon, can I talk to you for a minute?" Marcia asked him, turning the radio volume down.

"Yes, ma'am?" he said, but his stomach fluttered a little as he wondered what Marcia was about to say to him.

"Shannon, I've told you, don't call me that," Marcia said, then, sensing his discomfort, "It's nothing bad. I just want to talk a little about you and Mandey."

"Okay," Shannon said slowly.

They were at the stop sign at the head of the street, waiting to turn left. Marcia took a cigarette out of her cigarette case and pulled the knob out of the cigarette lighter to light it. She offered it to him, and he took it from her. Then she pulled out another cigarette, lit it for herself, and made the left turn.

"I know you've had kind of a rough time, and I want you to know you are welcome living with us. When I was young, I had a couple girlfriends who lived with me and my parents for a while. We never had a boy living with us, although there was one who was around so much, it almost seemed like he was. So, this family has a history of taking in kids who need a place to stay. I know Mandey is thrilled, and I am glad you are getting your life straightened out."

"Thanks," Shannon said. He was waiting for the "But—"

"I also know that you aren't sleeping in your room most of the time." Shannon's face flushed, but Marcia couldn't see it in the dark car. She continued, "I'm okay with that. Mandey's seventeen. I couldn't expect you not to want to sleep together. I just don't want her to get hurt. Although she is pretty mature for her age, she's still kind of naïve and very trusting."

"I would never do anything to hurt her," Shannon said seriously. "That's good to know," Marcia said. "I just hope you're taking precautions. I don't want to see her end up pregnant at seventeen."

"I know she's not ready to get pregnant, and I'm not ready for that, either," Shannon said earnestly. "But if she did, I wouldn't leave her. I'd marry her and take care of her and our baby."

"I am sure you would," Marcia said, "but there is no reason you would have to get yourselves into that kind of situation right now. I hope you're using protection."

Shannon's mouth opened, and he shifted uncomfortably in his seat. He started to say that he and Mandey weren't having sex yet, but he didn't think she would believe him.

"I always use a condom," he said, which was true.

"Good. Not just to prevent pregnancy, but also STDs," Marcia said.

"STDs?" Shannon repeated.

"Sexually-transmitted diseases. Syphilis, gonorrhea, AIDS?"

Shannon nodded numbly.

"I don't know how much experience you've had with girls, but I can tell you, whatever it is, it's more than Mandey's experience with boys. If you truly don't want to hurt her, I would suggest you make an appointment with Planned Parenthood and get tested."

Shannon had always used a condom, both because he didn't want to accidentally knock up a prostitute, and also because he didn't know who else they were sleeping with. He didn't think he had ever caught anything from one of them. He certainly didn't have any symptoms. He also didn't want to take the chance of passing anything on to Mandey.

"Okay," he said. "I will."

"Good," Marcia replied. "Thank you for being a responsible adult. I'll look up the number and you can call tomorrow."

Shannon and Marcia walked in the front entrance to the school. Some junior high students were passing out programs at the doors to the auditorium. Shannon and Marcia each took one and entered quietly, as the last junior high choir was still onstage. Marcia wanted to sit close to the front. There weren't many open seats, but they could have gotten fairly close to the stage, which is what Shannon did not want.

"Mandey told me that the sound is better if you sit farther toward the back," he told Marcia, which was the truth, and Mandey had told him to say that if Marcia wanted to sit near the front.

They ended up sitting in the third row from the back, which made Shannon feel fairly comfortable. He had the program to stick in front of his face, if needed.

The house lights came up as the junior high choir finished. That made him a little nervous. Then the lights went back down and the high school treble choir proceeded onto the risers to sing four songs. Mandey's group, the a cappella choir, would perform last.

While the girls' choir was singing, he thought about the conversation he had had with Marcia. He knew she was right, but he was nervous about seeing a doctor. He hadn't been to one in a long time. He didn't think Marcia would let it slide, and he knew it was the smart thing to do. Still, he wasn't looking forward to what was going to be an uncomfortable conversation with a stranger.

His attention came back to the present as the a cappella choir took the stage. The girls were all dressed in identical long black gowns with strings of white pearls around their necks, and the guys all had black tuxedos and white shirts. Shannon unconsciously slid down in his seat as he saw Jesse, Zack, and Angelina walking onto the risers. Then he focused on Mandey, third row on the right.

He listened to the singing, and he thought how strange it was to be there when he was fighting tooth and nail with four of them less than two weeks ago. Not a one of them on the stage was a real gang member. Gang members didn't sing Christmas songs in Latin. Still, he had to admit the Alley Cats had been scrappy. They had not been the pushovers the Devils had taken them for.

The music, though unfamiliar and in a language he didn't understand, was still beautiful. The Devils would have mocked him for thinking that way, but he didn't care. He didn't care anything about them anymore.

Mandey scanned the audience as she took her place on the risers. She finally found Shannon and Marcia toward the back of the auditorium, where she had told him they should sit. Shannon had his face partly obscured by the program. She hoped Jesse, Zack, and Angie wouldn't notice him. He was trying to be as inconspicuous as possible, so they probably wouldn't.

The a cappella choir performance went off perfectly, and the concert ended with all of the combined choirs singing "We Wish You a Merry Christmas". Mandey and the a cappella choir exited the stage and headed back to the choir room. As she put away her music and gathered her coat and purse, she heard Marcia's voice. "Wow, that was wonderful!"

Panic rose in Mandey's stomach. Surely Shannon wasn't with her. Jesse, Angelina, and Zack were all in the room.

She saw Marcia standing by the door, but to her relief, she didn't see Shannon.

"That was beautiful," Marcia said, as Mandey came toward here. "I haven't seen you sing since you were in elementary school."

Mandey smiled. "The level of experience and skill has improved since then, I hope," she said. "Where's Shannon?"

Marcia looked around. "I thought he was right behind me," she said. "He said he wanted to ride home with you. Maybe he went to the bathroom."

Mandey thought that might be true. He was lying low somewhere, at least.

"I'll track him down," Mandey said.

"I heard some of the kids talking about going to Pizza Inn. Are you going with them?"

Mandey shook her head. "No, it's a school night."

"Why don't we stop over at Dairy Queen and get a banana split? I'll buy," Marcia said.

"Ummmm, okay," Mandey said, a bit hesitantly. "Shannon and I will meet you over there."

Mandey was afraid for a moment that Marcia said she was going to wait for them, but instead she said she was going to run into Eckerd's for some shampoo. Marcia made her way to leave, to Mandey's relief. No, they weren't going to Pizza Inn where Angie, Jesse, and Zack would likely be with the other choir members. The truth was, if Shannon wasn't in the picture and the Alley Cats had never existed, she still probably wouldn't have joined the group. She was hoping they would not run into anyone at Dairy Queen that would cause any trouble, either.

She had to go find Shannon. The crowds were thinning as everyone was leaving. She hoped she would find him before any of the Alley Cats did. She walked to the front entrance area of the school where the offices were on one side and the auditorium doors on the other. Mr. Tichner was there, talking to some of the students and parents. She tried to sneak by, hoping he wouldn't notice her.

"Mandey! Come here, Mandey," she heard him calling to her.

She winced inwardly and reluctantly walked toward him. He smiled broadly and put his arm around her shoulders. Mandey managed a strained smile.

"Mandey is one of my top students," he told the people around them. "And so talented, too! You did a fine job tonight. You all sounded marvelous!" He squeezed her shoulder.

"Thanks," she said. "I have to get going."

"You have a good night," he told her, loosening his grip on her.

She gratefully moved away. "You, too," she said faintly, glad to escape.

She found Shannon lurking in one of the entrances to the auditorium. He had seen her get stopped by the principal.

"He just loves you, doesn't he?" Shannon said, an amused smirk on his face.

Mandey grimaced.

Shannon pulled her into the doorway, out of sight of Mr. Tichner, and kissed her.

"You sounded really good," he told her.

"Thanks," she replied, giving him a genuine smile. "Let's wait here a couple minutes and let a few more people clear out. Then we're supposed to meet Marcia at DQ."

"You're not worried about running into anybody there, are you?" Shannon asked.

"No. Sounds like Pizza Inn is where everyone is going. We'll probably be okay. If we get there and see anyone we don't want to talk to, we'll pretend one of us is sick and we can leave."

After about five minutes they walked out the front doors and around to the student parking lot, figuring it was safer than walking down the hall past the choir room. The parking lot was getting empty, and they walked to where Mandey's van was sitting alone.

As she unlocked it, a car from the other side of the parking lot came speeding up. Mandey recognized it, and her heart sank.

The window on the driver's side rolled down and Jesse flipped the bird at Shannon as they roared past. Angelina was doing the same over the roof of the car from the other side. Thankfully, they did not stop.

"Merry Christmas to you, too, assholes," Shannon called after them.

Mandey sighed as they got into the van. It could have been much worse.

"At least that's all they did," Mandey said, starting the van.

"I can live with that," Shannon said. "Can you?"

"What choice do I have?" Mandey said. "They were never close friends, just people I know. It will be okay."

She still regretted the fact that people she liked now regarded her as their enemy. It wasn't how she thought this whole thing would turn out. But she would live, and she wasn't going to lose any sleep over it.

"To heck with them," she told Shannon. "Let's go get ice cream."

49

The Christmas Dance

Mandey left school at five-fifteen the day of the Christmas dance. She was on the decorations committee and had stayed after school to help decorate the cafeteria. She was pleased with their work. They had bought a lot of red and green balloons, which they filled with helium and let float to the ceiling. Red and green crepe streamers were wrapped around the posts and strung about. They had also invested in crepe honeycomb decorations shaped like bells, snowflakes, and Christmas trees and hung them from the ceiling. Silver confetti was scattered all over the dance floor to simulate snow. It was probably as nice as Mandey had ever seen the cafeteria decorated for a dance.

Shannon was already home when she came in. She tossed the books she had brought home down on the couch. *Homework over Christmas vacation sucks*, she thought as she went out to the kitchen to greet him.

"Hi, sweetie," she said. "You're cooking?"

"Making spaghetti," he said, stirring sauce simmering in a pot. He paused to kiss her.

She hugged him. "Let me help you."

Shannon was frying pepperoni slices in a small skillet. Mandey began setting the table.

"It's almost done. The spaghetti's got to cook a few more minutes," he said, scraping the pepperoni out to drain on a plate covered with paper towels.

"It smells wonderful," Mandey said.

"I hope it's okay," Shannon said, patting the grease off the pepperoni slices and adding them to the sauce. "Did you get the cafeteria decorated?"

"Yes, we did. It looks pretty good, too," Mandey said. "Don't let me forget to take those two two-liter Cokes tonight for the refreshment stand."

"I won't."

"You know," Mandey said, "I half-expected to come home and hear you tell me you'd changed your mind and decided to stay home."

"No," Shannon said. "I have to stand with you and face people. I have to show them that you and I have nothing to hide."

Mandey smiled. "I'm going to be proud to have you standing next to me. I'm excited about showing you off."

"There's not much to show," Shannon said, embarrassed. "Just an overgrown juvenile delinquent."

"Oh, stop," Mandey said. "I'm going to have to beat the girls off with a stick to keep them away from you."

"Yeah, right," Shannon said. He turned off the burner under the pot of boiling spaghetti then poured the contents into a colander in the sink to drain. When he set the empty pot down, Mandey came up behind him and pinched him through the seat of his black sweatpants.

"Hey!" he exclaimed, turning around to face Mandey, who was laughing at him.

He grabbed her before she could dodge away and pinched her twice on the bottom.

"Ouch! Stop!" Mandey cried, laughing.

"Oh, turnabout isn't fair play?" Shannon asked with a grin, spanked her twice, and then he pulled her close to him and kissed her. She put her arms around him and kissed back.

"Let's eat," he said. "I'm starving."

He had made a big batch of spaghetti, so after they ate, they cleaned up their mess and put the remainder of the spaghetti and sauce in the refrigerator. There would be plenty for Marcia to have when she got home.

Mandey took great care getting ready for the dance. She did her make-up to look as flawless as possible. She curled her hair with the curling iron, brushed it, curled it some more, styled it, and then sprayed it to keep it in place. She was pleased that it was cooperating with her wishes that evening. She also touched up a couple chips on her red-painted nails.

She put on sheer black hose and then slipped into her black velvet dress with the decorative rhinestone buttons down the front and the hem that fell about an inch above her knees. To complete the outfit, she wore rhinestone earrings and a rhinestone tennis bracelet, along with new black suede pumps with rhinestone shoe clips. To finish, she dabbed perfume behind her ears, at the base of her throat, on the inside of each wrist, and between her breasts. When she looked at her reflection in the mirror, she was pleased.

Someone knocked on the door to the hallway. "Are you decent?" she heard Shannon ask.

"Come in and see for yourself," Mandey said.

He opened the door and stepped into the room.

"Oh, don't you look handsome!" Mandey exclaimed.

Shannon was wearing a new pair of black pants, a white dress shirt, a skinny red and gray striped tie, and a charcoal gray sport coat, along with his new pair of Stacy Adams shoes. He wasn't used to being so dressed up, but he wanted to make sure he looked good if he was going to be with Mandey in front of all of her friends. When he saw her, he was glad that he had made the effort.

"You are the most beautiful thing I have ever seen!" Shannon exclaimed. He meant every word of it.

Mandey laughed, pleased. "Thank you," she said, walking over to him and planting a soft little kiss on his lips.

Not only did Shannon look wonderful, but he smelled just as good. Mandey had an urge to lead him over to her bed and forget about the Christmas dance.

"Could you finish zipping me up?" she asked him, turning around.

Shannon's fingers fumbled slightly, trying to grasp the dress's tiny zipper. He wondered what it would be like to unzip the dress and slip it off, to lay her down on the bed and...

He felt a part of himself stir and start to stiffen. He quickly zipped the zipper.

"Ready?" she asked him.

"As I'll ever be," he replied.

They pulled into the Rogers High School parking lot at 7:45. The lot was about a third full.

"Things never get lively until after eight," Mandey said, starting to open her car door.

Shannon didn't move. "Are you okay?" Mandey asked.

He sighed. "Yeah."

She reached over and took his hand. "If anyone tries to start something, we'll just leave."

"I hope they don't. I don't want to ruin your night."

"It'll be okay."

They walked through the patio area of the cafeteria, where a few underclass students, mostly boys, were hanging out. A table was set up at the entrance into the cafeteria from the patio where they paid their admission, and Shannon carried the two-liter bottles of soda over to the refreshment stand for Mandey. He and Mandey stood together, surveying the cafeteria, which was serving as the dance floor. The lights were off, but the light from the snack bar area kept it from being too dark. The deejay was set up along the far wall, the equipment including various colored lights and a fog machine. "Stars on the Water," by Rodney Crowell was playing, and two couples were out there two-stepping.

"It'll pick up a little later," Mandey said. "Most of the seniors should show up. After all, we're the sponsors of this dance, and the money raised goes toward our prom fund. We may be an apathetic bunch about a lot of things, but one thing we all want is a nice prom."

The prom, Shannon thought. Tuxedoes and formal gowns and limousines—it was an alien concept to him. He hadn't expected to be going to a prom someday, but then, he hadn't expected a lot of things that had happened to him lately.

Mandey turned to him and gave him an affectionate squeeze. "The prom," she said, smiling at him. "I can hardly wait. I'm going to have the handsomest date there, just like I have the handsomest date here tonight."

Shannon chuckled and hugged her back.

"Hey, y'all," Georgia said, coming up behind them. "Watch where you put those hands."

"Who, us?" Mandey asked innocently, but with a brazen look at her friend as she goosed her boyfriend.

"Whoa!" Shannon yelped with a start. Georgia burst into laughter. Mandey's face was bright red as she dissolved into giggles.

Shannon regained some of his composure. "You're a wicked woman," he admonished Mandey.

"And you love it," she replied.

"Don't y'all look spiffy tonight?" Georgia remarked. "Mandey, I love that dress."

"Thanks," Mandey said. "And you look dressed to kill."

Georgia was wearing a red skirt, barely long enough to be dress code-legal, and a shiny white high-necked blouse that had a diamond-shaped cutout neckline that showed a fair amount of décolletage. Her curly blonde hair was piled on her head, with a few sexy curls escaping to frame her face.

"I know. Got to give these boys a thrill or two," Georgia said with a grin. "The freshmen, especially."

"Well, where's Kirby?" Mandey asked.

"Oh, him," Georgia said with an airy wave of her hand. "History. On to bigger and better things."

Shannon wasn't listening to their girl talk. He was watching the entrance, where he saw James Huynh walking in with another guy. Shannon felt his heart sink, but he knew that, as long as he stayed with Mandey, he would encounter people who didn't like him. He was going to have to deal with it.

"Oh, jeez, here comes everyone's favorite person," Georgia said, rolling her eyes when she caught sight of James.

"Oh, my goodness, don't he and Mark think they are the coolest things on Earth?" Mandey said.

James was dressed in black pants, a black shirt with sleeves rolled up to the elbows, and a skinny silver tie. Mark had on a pair of skintight white parachute pants (the ones under which he allegedly never wore underwear) and a white shirt with deck shoes and no socks. He also had on a bright green Christmas tie. Both wore new wave shades with mirrored lenses, even though it was night.

"Corey Hart and his brother," Shannon muttered, and Mandey laughed.

The song changed to "Easy Lover" by Philip Bailey and Phil Collins.

"Oh, I like this song. Dance with me, please?" Mandey asked, taking Shannon by the hand and leading him toward the dance floor.

They were the only couple out there; it was still relatively early, and the song was new and Mandey supposed that not everyone had heard it before. Shannon looked uncomfortable.

"We're the only ones dancing," he said, shifting his weight back and forth from foot to foot.

"I know," Mandey replied. They had to raise their voices to be heard over the music. "Shannon, you can dance better than that."

"No, I can't."

"You dance better than that when we're at home fooling around together."

"I don't want to draw attention to myself with all my Fred Astaire moves."

Mandey laughed and took his hands in hers. "Whatever. I don't care if you just stand there, as long as you're with me."

"Now <u>that</u> would really look stupid."

A few more people joined them on the dance floor, two other couples and a group of three girls. Mandey noticed Shannon start to loosen up. He didn't enjoy being the focus of attention.

When the song ended, the deejay played another country tune, "Love in the First Degree" by Alabama. Mandey groaned to herself. She was afraid this was going to be one of those deejays who would forgo playing a streak of somewhat-consistently-styled songs that people could get into. Instead, he would try too hard to play a variety, which would result in a big turnover on the dance floor after each song.

She started to walk off, but Shannon caught her by the arm. "Do you want to two-step?"

She stared at him, surprised. "I barely know how. Do you?"

"Why, yes, I do. Nothing fancy, but I can shuffle along okay."

He took her in her arms and they began to dance to the song. Mandey felt awkward. "I'm not very good at this," she said.

"You're doing fine," Shannon told her.

They made their way around the dance floor, stumbling only a little, with Mandey giggling at each misstep she made.

"You keep surprising me," she told him as the song ended. It segued into a slow dance, Chicago's "You're the Inspiration."

Pressed up against each other almost head to toe, they swayed to the music.

"'You're the inspiration'," Mandey sang along.

"No, <u>you're</u> the inspiration," Shannon said in her ear, then repeated after the song, "No one needs you more than I need you."

Mandey was surprised by how much Shannon was willing to dance with her. As the dance floor became more crowded, he seemed to become less self-conscious. She didn't need to worry about the disjointed styles of music; they danced to the Rolling Stones, to George Strait, to Whodini, to Madonna, and whatever else the deejay played. His eyes were on her the whole time, watching how she moved, noting the joy on her face.

When the opening piano of "Open Arms" by Journey began, almost everyone found a partner and crowded onto the dance floor. Mandey and Shannon danced close, pressed together from their chests to their knees, arms wrapped around each other, her head against his shoulder. They kissed as the song ended, then the deejay put on the "Cotton-eyed Joe" and everyone was scrambling to find their friends and get into lines to dance and shout, "Bullshit!" along with the song. Mandey laughed, one arm around Shannon and one around Charlie as they made their way around the floor. As the song segued into "The Schottische", they kept dancing. Several girls dancing on the outside ends of the lines, including Georgia, did fancy pirouettes to the music.

After that, they sat down to take a break.

"I need something to drink," Mandey said, fanning herself with her hands.

"Me, too," Shannon said.

He reached into his pants pocket for his wallet, then remembered that he had some crumpled-up ones stuffed in his jacket pocket. He turned around, fumbled with his sport coat which was hung on the back of the chair, and reached into one of the pockets. His hand came upon something that wasn't dollar bills.

"What the hell?" he asked, pulling out his hand.

He and Mandey looked down at what he was holding.

"Holy shit!" he exclaimed.

It was a plastic bag containing some brightly colored capsules and some white powder.

"Where did that come from?" Mandey asked, panic rising from the pit of her stomach like it was on an express elevator.

"I have no idea," Shannon said, making a concerted effort to conceal the bag and remain calm.

It dawned on Mandey how the bag had gotten into Shannon's pocket. Her heart was pounding, but she said, "Give it to me."

"No! What if you get caught?"

"<u>Give</u> it to me. I'll get rid of it."

He furtively passed it to her. She crumpled it up into a small wad until she could almost totally conceal it in her fist. Shannon checked his jacket thoroughly, but found nothing more.

"Why don't you go get us something to drink?" Mandey told him. "I'll be right back."

"Mandey, are you sure—"

"Yes, Shannon. Go."

She and Shannon got up; he headed toward the refreshment stand while Mandey left the cafeteria and went to the restroom.

Mandey felt like she was going to start hyperventilating. That would be all she would need, to go into a panic attack, attracting all sorts of attention while holding a bag of illegal dope. She struggled to keep herself under control, walking as fast as she dared into the restroom. She prayed there would be a stall open when she got in there.

God was good to her; two stalls were unoccupied. She locked herself in the first one she came to, flushed the toilet, and dumped the contents of the bag into the toilet. She flushed again and threw the bag in. A great wave of relief swept over her as she saw the bag being sucked down into the sewers. She used the toilet herself and sat there for a few minutes, face in her hands, trying to regain her composure. When she came out, she checked herself in the mirror and tidied herself up.

She knew Danny was responsible, and she was furious. She couldn't believe he would sink that low. That kind of sabotage was unacceptable. She had to do something.

When she left the restroom, she was greeted by the sight of Shannon being escorted down the hall by a Harris County deputy sheriff who was serving as a security guard for the dance. With them were Mr. Tichner and an assistant principal, Mr. Carr. A curious crowd was being held back from following by another principal and two teachers. Mandey pushed through, anyway.

"You can't go back there," Mrs. Hibbert said, grabbing Mandey by the arm.

Mandey pulled away from her and ran down the hall.

Oh my God, that was close, Mandey thought, rushing up behind them.

"I'm telling you I don't have anything on me," Shannon was saying, handing his sport coat to Mr. Tichner. "Check my pockets. Check the jacket."

He pulled out his wallet and handed it over, and then pulled his pants pockets inside out.

"What is going on here?" Mandey demanded.

Mr. Tichner turned around to look at her. "We were informed that your friend was seen with a bag of drugs in the restroom," he said, handing the jacket to the deputy sheriff.

"Shannon doesn't do drugs. If he did, I wouldn't be with him," Mandey said. "Who gave you this information?"

"I can't tell you that," Mr. Tichner said.

"Why not?" Mandey asked, her voice rising. "It's a false accusation, and I want to know who made it."

"We'll see if it was a false accusation," the deputy said.

"Jesus!" Shannon exclaimed. "There ain't nothing on me, I'm tellin' you!"

"I want to know the names of the people who say they saw him with these drugs," Mandey insisted.

They reached the door to the principals' offices. Mr. Tichner walked in, followed by Shannon, Mandey, and the deputy. Mr. Carr remained outside the door.

"The informant didn't want his identity revealed," Mr. Tichner said. "He claimed to be afraid of retribution."

"Yes, because he lied, that's why," Mandey said.

The deputy searched Shannon's jacket thoroughly once they were in Mr. Tichner's office. "The jacket's clean. Empty all your pockets. Place your hands against the wall, feet apart," the deputy said to Shannon.

"This is humiliating and unfair!" Mandey said, stamping her foot. It made an unimpressive sound.

The deputy set the jacket down on a chair and began searching Shannon. Mandey stood there with her arms crossed, frustrated. Somehow, she was going to make Danny Sanchez very sorry.

"He's clean," the deputy finally said. "I want to search the car you came in."

"Why?" Mandey said. "He has nothing on him! That person was lying!"

"I want a description of your car and your license plate number," the deputy said, taking Shannon's keys from where he had laid them on the principal's desk.

"Don't you need a warrant for that?" Mandey asked.

Shannon gave him the information, and the deputy left.

Mr. Tichner picked up Shannon's jacket and handed it back to him. Shannon jerked it away and put it on.

"I don't care if you promised to keep this anonymous. I want to know who told you this," he said to Mr. Tichner, his eyes blazing. "I resent being treated like a criminal when I haven't done anything wrong!"

"He could sue that person for slander," Mandey said. "He might even be able to sue the school district for emotional distress."

"From what I have been hearing from students, you aren't exactly a blameless innocent," Mr. Tichner said to Shannon.

Mandey was infuriated by the remark, and she opened her mouth to defend her boyfriend, but Shannon held his own. "Maybe not, but I'm not a drug dealer or a dope fiend like some of your students," he said.

"Go ahead and have a seat until the deputy finishes his search," Mr. Tichner said, ignoring the remark. "Mandey, I'm surprised you're mixed up in something like this."

Mandey and Shannon remained standing. Mandey moved close to him, and he took her hand in his.

"I'm not mixed up in anything," she replied. "The deputy is going to come back here and say he didn't find anything in Shannon's car."

She turned to Shannon. "It's going to be okay," she said softly to him.

"I know," he said in a defiant tone. "I have nothing to hide."

Some minutes later, the deputy returned. "The car was clean, too," he said, handing the keys back to Shannon.

"Okay. Am I free to go now?" Shannon asked Mr. Tichner.

"Yes, you can go," Mr. Tichner said, sounding disappointed. "But I want to let you know that we will not tolerate any more incidents such as this here at this school."

Shannon looked at Mr. Tichner in disbelief. "I'm not the one you need to tell that to. You need to tell your informer to get his facts straight before he makes any accusations." He snatched his belongings off the desk and put them back in his pockets. "Let's go, Mandey."

He stalked out of the office. Mandey turned to follow Shannon.

"Amanda, we'll talk about this after Christmas," Mr. Tichner said.

It was Mandey's turn to give Mr. Tichner an unbelieving glare. "The only thing to talk about is the person who made this false accusation. Otherwise, I have nothing to say," she said, and walked out.

The deputy did not wait until she was out of earshot to say to the principals, "I should have checked to see if the girl had a purse with her."

She stalked down the hall, further infuriated by that last comment. She ran to catch up with Shannon. His face was dark. Her first instinct was to ask him if he was okay, but of course he wasn't. She was feeling shaky herself.

"I'm sorry," she said, laying her hand on his back.

He didn't say anything. He kept walking, staring a few feet ahead at the gray tile floor.

They walked in silence through the cafeteria. Shannon refused to lift his eyes from the floor. Mandey saw people staring at them.

Let them stare, she thought. *We're obviously leaving of our own volition, not in the company of a Harris County sheriff's deputy.*

Danny was sitting at the admissions table by the cafeteria door talking to Mark. Mandey noticed the odd look on his face as they passed by. She knew he had expected to see Shannon leaving in a pair of handcuffs. She wanted to scream at him, but Shannon was not in a good state of mind and starting any more commotion tonight was not going to help things. Instead, she had to be satisfied with giving Danny a drop-dead look, knowing that she would confront him and let him know exactly what she thought of him and his stupid stunt. She rushed Shannon through the door and into the parking lot before he could see Danny.

50

Shannon's Doubts

The ride home was quiet. Mandey would have preferred to hear Shannon rant and rave and bitch, as he was entitled to, after that humiliating experience. It would have been the natural response. Instead, there was no response at all.

She turned the radio on low. "Do They Know It's Christmas" was playing. She placed her hand on his knee to comfort him. Usually, he would place his hand on top of hers and squeeze if affectionately, but not tonight. The drive home was silent, save for the radio.

When they got home, Shannon went straight to his room without a word and shut the door behind him. Mandey stared at his door for a moment, then went to her room to undress. She had to find a way to get him to talk to her. She didn't want him to go to bed in such a bad frame of mind.

She undressed and slipped into a nightgown. After putting away her clothes, she went into the bathroom to finish getting ready for bed. She heard no sound from Shannon's room, and she wondered what he was doing in there. She took out her contacts, washed her face, brushed her teeth, and used the toilet. When she was done, she knocked softly on his door, then opened it a crack. The room was dark.

"Shannon?" she asked, her hand fumbling along the wall to turn on the light.

The light clicked on, and she saw Shannon lying on his back on his bed, his left arm across his eyes. He had changed into his gray warm-up pants and a T-shirt. His shirt, pants, jacket, and tie lay in a heap on the floor by his closet.

Mandey sat on the edge of the bed. "Shannon—" she began.

"I'm ruining your life," he said. His voice sounded stuffy, as though he had been crying.

"That's not true," Mandey said, placing her hand on his thigh.

"Yes, it is," he said. "You've got people coming at you from all directions giving you grief about me. I don't want to be responsible for it." He took his arm away from his eyes, which were red-rimmed.

"It doesn't matter," Mandey said.

"It does too matter, Mandey," Shannon said, getting up from the bed. He started picking up his clothes. "I'm not worth the trouble I'm putting you through. You need someone you can be proud of, someone as good as you, someone who can give you all the stuff I can't—"

"No, Shannon! What are you saying?" Mandey asked. "You don't want to be with me anymore? You want to break up?"

Shannon stopped what he was doing and stared at her. "You'll be better off without me."

Tears came to Mandey's eyes. "I don't want to be without you," she said. "You make me happy, Shannon."

"I make you happy when some guy plants drugs on me to try to get me arrested? I make you happy when people egg your car because you're with me? I make you happy when your ex-boyfriend harasses you constantly about me? I make you happy when I get you in trouble with your school principal?"

"I don't care about any of that!" Mandey shouted.

"Well, I do," Shannon said wearily. "You will, too, sooner or later. You'll get tired of it, and then you'll start to hate me, and I wouldn't be able to stand that."

"You think I'm that weak and superficial?" Mandey asked.

"You can do better than me," Shannon said, his face blank. "You'll start college next year, and you'll meet all kinds of guys who'll be able to do right by you. You'll be happy to be free of me then."

"No!" Mandey said. "Why would you think that?"

"I'm being realistic," Shannon said.

"You're being a coward!" Mandey shouted, and immediately regretted saying it when she saw Shannon flinch like she had slapped him.

He threw the clothes he had picked up against the wall. "If being a coward means getting out of a situation where people try to frame me to get me arrested, then yes, I'm a fucking coward! What good will I do you anyway when I'm serving seven-to-ten in the state pen?"

Mandey broke into tears. "I hate Danny Sanchez!" she cried, burying her face in her hands. "I hate him! This is just what he wanted! Damn it, I'm going to make him pay for this--"

"Oh, Jesus, Mandey, don't go doing something stupid—"

"What does it matter to you?" Mandey asked petulantly, looking up at him. "You just told me you don't want to be with me anymore."

"Mandey, it's not about me not wanting to be with you. It's about what's best for you,"

Shannon said.

"Why can't you let me decide what's best for me?" Mandey asked, still bitter. "I'll admit, the past couple of weeks haven't been easy, but I've had you to come home to every day, and that made it all worthwhile." She paused a moment to regain her composure. In a softer tone she said, "I'm sorry I called you a coward. You aren't. If you're scared by what happened tonight, I don't blame you. If it's scared you enough to make you want to break up, then I don't know what I can do to stop you." She pressed her lips together tightly, trying to keep the tears back.

Shannon sat down on the opposite side of the bed, elbows on his knees, his face in his hands.

"The main thing is, I don't want to be responsible for you getting hurt, by me or by anyone else because of me," he said in a muffled voice.

"People are responsible for their own actions, no matter what their motivation is," Mandey said, her voice trembling.

"Yeah, Mandey, that may be true, but it's going to be a lot easier to get people to leave you alone if they don't have any more motivation."

"You say you don't want to hurt me, but this is hurting me more than I've ever been hurt before."

"Don't you think that kills me?" Shannon asked, turning to look at her. "No matter what I do, you end up getting hurt somehow. It's a no-win situation."

"Shannon," she said, moving across the bed to sit next to him.

"I don't belong in your life," he said. "It was a mistake to think I could."

"Shannon, please," she begged, slipping her arm around him. The tears were escaping despite her best efforts. "I love you and I want you in my life."

"I love you, too, Mandey," he replied. "That's why I never want you to be hurt or sad because of me."

"But Shannon," she said, "if you leave me, it will hurt me so much. Those people at school don't hurt me. The things they say don't bother me. You're all that matters to me." She took a deep breath and gave him a squeeze. "Now, tonight, that was a different story, but there are ways to fix that besides breaking up with me."

"Mandey, I don't want you confronting anybody about this," Shannon said.

"Don't worry about me," she said stubbornly.

"But I do worry," he told her. "I worry about you all the time."

She hugged him and was relieved to feel him hug her back.

"Shannon," she said, holding him close, "you aren't hurting me by being with me. You have made me so happy ever since the day we met."

"I feel like I'm all wrong for you, like I'll never be the kind of man you deserve," he said. "I'm dumb, I'm poor, and I've got a police record. That's not what you deserve."

"Sweetie," she said in his ear. "Come on. Let's get in bed."

She got up, turned out the light, and slipped under the covers. Shannon remained sitting on the edge of the bed for a few moments, then stripped down to his briefs and joined her.

"Shannon, you aren't dumb," she said, cuddling close to him. "You've decided to go back to school, and I am so proud of you. You've got a better paying job than you had two weeks ago, and while you don't have a lot of money, what does it matter right now? It's not like we're married and trying to live on your income. And didn't you tell me that if you make it to 21 with no further convictions that felony will be erased?"

"Yeah," Shannon said slowly, "but—"

"But what? What are you worrying about?"

"I—" he began, then stopped.

"What, Shannon? You can tell me," she said, kissing his shoulder.

"Scared," he finally said.

"Scared of what?"

"I—" he began again, then paused. Mandey didn't prod him. She sensed he was trying to find the words to tell her how he felt, and she didn't want to rush him. Suddenly the words came tumbling out, rushing to escape.

"I'm so scared of losing you, Mandey. God, you were so beautiful tonight, and I couldn't believe I was lucky enough to be with you. I feel like I'm living someone else's life. I looked in the mirror at myself all dressed up and standing next to you, and I felt like an impostor or something. Things are going better for me now than they ever have, with me living here, having this new job, and going back to school. I'm trying my best to be the kind of man you deserve, Mandey, but sometimes I feel like I'm fooling myself. Something is gonna go wrong, and I'll wake up one day and find I don't have you anymore. I know I don't deserve you, but I don't want to lose you. All I know is I don't want to drag you down and get you to start hating me."

His voice cracked, and a tear rolled down his face. "I felt so bad tonight. You were so beautiful, and you should have had a great time at the dance, and I ruined it for you, just like I knew I would. I want you so much, I love you so much, but I can't give you half what you deserve. I don't even know how to make love to you. I don't ever want to lose you, but in my heart, I know you would be better off with someone else." He wiped his eyes impatiently. "Damn it. I hate this. I'm crying like some damn baby."

"It's okay," Mandey said, running her fingers through his hair. "I'm not going to let a bunch of stupid, petty people ruin what we have, and you'd better not, either. Shannon, I've known from the beginning that you're a high school dropout with a police record. I could have run in the other direction then, but I didn't, did I?"

She kissed his lips. He kissed back gently. "I just want you to be happy," he whispered.

"I am," she whispered back.

They kissed again, holding each other close. She loved the way he kissed her, the way his arms held her, how his hands caressed her.

"What did you mean, that you don't know how to make love to me?" she asked him.

Shannon sighed. "Oh, Mandey," he said, closing his eyes and rubbing his temples. "That's hard to talk about."

"Why? You already told me about…you know."

"I know, I know," Shannon said. "This is about something that started when I was seeing Kerri."

"What?" Mandey asked, alarmed by Shannon's tone of voice. She wondered what he was about to tell her.

He sensed that Mandey was alarmed, which made him more reluctant to tell her. He felt better when she cuddled closer to him and held him more tightly in her arms.

"Not too long after we moved there, I went with Kerri for a couple weeks," he began. "I was still a virgin, and I thought Kerri was the prettiest thing I'd seen in my life. I about died when I realized she was interested in me. We started messing around, and I finally got up the guts to ask her to go steady. I knew she had been around; the guys told me they'd all had her, and they warned me she wasn't cut out to stick to one guy, but I didn't care. All I knew is the prettiest girl I'd ever laid eyes on wanted me.

"She made it real clear from the beginning that she wanted to sleep with me. I was horny out of my mind for her, but I was scared to death, too. I mean, she'd been with all these guys, and I didn't have any experience at all, and so I was real clumsy and shy when we were alone together. I'd be so horny for her, then I'd make some dumb mistake, and she'd start cussing me out and making me feel like shit. She'd say she'd had virgins who were better than me. She didn't know I hadn't done it before, and I wasn't going to tell her. I suppose any other guy would have slapped her upside the head to shut her up and done it anyway, because I've seen guys do it. In fact, I think she expects it. But I didn't do that. She'd start yelling and cussing at me and I'd…lose it, you know. I couldn't do it. She didn't know that; all she knew was I wouldn't sleep with her. I finally got to the point that I wanted to do her just to say I'd done it, but I didn't care much for her one way or another anymore. Then one day I found her and Raff together doing it doggy-style, and when they saw me, they laughed at me and kept on going. And that was it for her and me."

"Oh, I'm sorry," Mandey said, hugging him. Inwardly, she was happy he hadn't slept with Kerri.

"She messed up my mind pretty bad. I hated her so much, but I was mad at myself, too, for screwing things up. It wasn't too long after that that John offered to set me up with a hooker. She wasn't nothing to look at, and I was so scared I was sick to my stomach, but she told me she didn't care nothing about what I look like or how I did it. All she wanted was my money. I got what I wanted, and she got what she wanted, and I didn't have to worry about someone cussing at me or making fun, so from then on, that's what I did whenever I wanted some. And that's what's bothering me now. I know you'd never cuss at me or be mean, but I'm still half-afraid that one day we're going to start to make love, and I'm going to freeze up on you."

He hugged her fiercely and buried his face in her hair. "Mandey, I want you so much, and I want to please you and make everything perfect for you. I've seen you look at me with so much love in your eyes I couldn't believe it. I don't think I could take it to see you looking at me with disappointment in your eyes."

"Oh, baby," Mandey said, kissing his neck. She held him close and ran her hands up and down his back slowly, trying to comfort him. "I love you, Shannon, for what you are, the way you are. That's not going to change." She loosened herself from his embrace to kiss him. "Don't worry about what's going to happen when we make love," she told him. "You have nothing to prove to me, and you don't have to impress me. I'm a virgin, Shannon. All I know about sex is what I've read. When we make love, I won't know if your 'performance' was good or not, but I know you're going to do fine. But…now you've got me wondering about whether I'll be able to please you. I'm not pretty like Kerri. If you do 'freeze up' on me, I'm going to feel like I haven't been able to make you feel secure, or maybe I'm not attractive enough."

"Mandey!" Shannon exclaimed, shocked, placing his hand on her cheek and turning her face up to look at him. "Don't ever compare yourself to Kerri. You're a hundred times more beautiful than her."

After a pause, she asked him, "Do you trust me?"

"Of course I do."

"Then trust me when I tell you that I know you'll never disappoint me when we make love," Mandey said. "Maybe this sounds naïve and hokey, but I don't think making love is just about orgasms. Making love is about making each other feel loved."

She pressed her lips to his again, and he kissed her back passionately, rolling on top of her.

"And you are definitely good at making me feel loved," she told him.

He kissed her again, and Mandey's legs parted. He lay between them as they kissed and caressed each other. Shannon was very aware of his erection and the way he was rubbing up against Mandey's silky pink panties. He didn't feel anywhere close to "freezing up."

Mandey was aware of his erection, too, and although she wasn't ready to make love with him, it made her happy. It meant he found her desirable.

Finally, he eased off her and lay next to her once again.

"How do you think our first time together will be?" he asked her, kissing her temple.

Mandey had thought about it a lot, daydreamed about it through a lot of boring classes, but suddenly she wasn't sure what to say.

"I'm not really sure," she told him.

"Well, how do you want it to be?" he asked.

"I hesitate to tell you because you might start feeling inadequate again," Mandey said, teasing.

"Oh, that really makes me feel good," Shannon said sarcastically.

Mandey kissed his cheek. "Honestly, it's going to be absolutely wonderful, I know that much," she said.

"Tell me about it," he insisted. "I need to know how you want it to be."

"Okay," Mandey relented.

She receded into her daydreams. "I've kind of imagined us being married or at least engaged, but maybe that's a little unrealistic. Anyway, I see us together in the bedroom, and we're both very turned on and a little bit nervous."

The bedroom was dark, but Shannon didn't need a light to know that Mandey was blushing and had an embarrassed little smile on her lips.

"Are you imagining it?" he asked.

"Mmm-hmm," she replied absently.

"What's it like?"

"We're both excited and nervous. It's a little awkward at first, but as we make love, we gain more confidence. You're strong and passionate, but at the same time you're sweet and gentle. It's my first time, so it's kind of uncomfortable for me, but I don't care. I love the feeling of your kisses and the way you touch me, and I love sharing such an intimate experience with you. It's very sweet and special, and there's a closeness between us we don't want to end."

"I hope it will be like that," Shannon said.

"I know it will be," Mandey said, and kissed his mouth softly.

She settled down close to him, and he rubbed her back as he held her, thinking. In a few minutes he realized that she had fallen asleep.

"Oh, Mandey," he whispered, and sighed. "Am I going to be able to give you everything I want to give you?"

He kissed the top of her head. *God, she really loves me*, he thought. *With all my faults, she loves me. I'll be damned if I know why. All I know is that I love her, and I've got to do my best to take care of her the right way.*

His thoughts turned to what she had said about making love with him. She had said something about wanting to be married or engaged. He got a funny feeling in his stomach.

She's thinking about marrying me, he thought, amazed. He had to fight to keep from laughing aloud with joy.

He calmed down and thought about marrying her, making her his wife. *My wife*, he thought. To have her by his side forever is what he wanted more than anything. He had a long way to go before he would be worthy of being her husband, but, somehow, he would do it. In his mind's eye he saw her coming down the aisle in a beautiful white gown in a church full of flowers. He saw the heart-shaped diamond he was slipping onto her beautiful, soft, white hand. He saw himself lifting the gauzy veil from her sweet face and kissing her full pink lips. Then he saw her lying in the middle of a king-sized bed, wearing a white negligee, looking beautiful.

Imagining her that way made him hard. He imagined himself, excited and nervous, like she had said, joining her on the bed. She was smiling at him, holding out her arms to take him. Once he was in her arms, all the nervousness faded away. Everything was fine as he slipped the nightie from her body, revealing her beautiful, curvy figure. She slipped her fingers into the waistband of his shorts and was sliding them down his thighs, then touching him in <u>that</u> place, setting him on fire. They were naked between real satin sheets, and he wasn't afraid at all. He was in heaven making love to this beautiful, young woman he loved more than life, and she was kissing and caressing and loving him back. When it was all over, they were lying there together, holding each other close. He felt so lucky and so loved and so happy.

The next thing he knew he was waking up. It was a little after six. The painting crew was putting in some overtime hours that day, trying to finish a job before the holidays. He turned off the alarm so it wouldn't go off and tried to get out of bed without waking Mandey.

It was no use. He saw that she was looking at him through sleepy eyes. "Get back here," she ordered him. "You don't have to be up for another ten minutes."

Shannon grinned and got back into bed with her. "Sorry I woke you," he apologized with a kiss.

Mandey replied with a yawn and said, "You're forgiven. Did you sleep okay?"

"Yup," Shannon said. "I always do when I have you next to me. In fact, I had a terrific dream."

"You did? About what?" Mandey asked.

A smile came to his face. "About making love to you for the very first time."

Mandey's face turned pink. "Was I good?" she asked him.

"Terrific," he told her, reaching over to run his hand through her hair.

"Do you think I will be good?"

Shannon's smile grew wide.

"Can I take that as a 'yes'?"

"Yeah," Shannon replied, still smiling, and then he chuckled devilishly.

"What was that evil laugh for?" Mandey asked him.

He kissed her and replied with a wicked grin on his face, "I was thinking about all the things I want to do to your body."

Mandey blushed again, but her gaze met his and she smiled back. Her hand found its way to his crotch. Through his shorts she could feel his stiff manhood and began to fondle him.

Shannon drew in his breath sharply. "Ohhh," he moaned softly.

He kissed Mandey again as she continued to rub him down below. His hands found their own ways to the soft, private parts of her body. One went up the front of her nightgown, and the other slid inside the waistband of her little pink panties and came to rest on one warm, soft buttock. Then they pulled apart, their faces both apologetic and full of longing.

"Excuse me," Shannon said abruptly, and got out of bed and went into the bathroom.

Mandey had an idea that he was not just urinating in there. The ache between her own legs was tempting, but she let it fade. She stretched some more and wished the day she and Shannon would make love would come soon.

51

Confrontation

After Shannon left for work, Mandey got up, showered, and dressed, then called Danny's house. His mother answered the phone and went to rouse him out of bed. When Danny came on the line, Mandey gave him a terse message to meet her at McDonald's and then she hung up. She didn't know if he would show up or not, but she had a good idea that he would.

Mandey was nursing a large coffee and reading the newspaper in a corner booth when Danny arrived. She saw him glance at her as he came in, but his eyes were cold. He went over to the counter, and in a few minutes, he joined her with a cup of coffee of his own.

"I've got better things to do on a Saturday morning than have coffee with a convicted felon's girlfriend, so say what you've got to say," he said as he sat down.

Mandey felt hot tears come to her eyes, and she stared down into her coffee. A giant lump filled her throat, and the words wouldn't come unless she wanted to spill out a lot of tears along with them. She tried to dissolve it with a sip of coffee, but it didn't help.

"Look, either talk to me or I'm out of here," Danny said impatiently.

Mandey burst into tears.

"Damn it!" she cried, pounding her open palm on the table. "I wasn't going to do this. Fuck!"

Danny was taken aback. He had never heard her use that word before.

Mandey forced herself to regain her composure. She was angry with herself; she had wanted to tell Danny off, not fall apart in front of him.

"I am so angry at you, Danny. I want to rip your head off," she said thickly through her tears, pointing her finger in his face. "It's taking all my strength not to slap you. Why the hell did you do that last night?"

"Do what?"

"Damn it, Danny, don't play games with me!" Mandey shouted, her fist coming down hard on the table. People turned to stare. She didn't really care, but she lowered her voice.

"I know you don't like Shannon," she told him. "That's okay; that's understandable. But do you hate me that much? I could have been arrested last night. You hate me that much that you would do that to me?"

"Mandey, it was a baggie full of baking powder and cornstarch and Dexatrim capsules."

"What?" she asked in disbelief.

"That's why they let him go, right?" Danny asked. "You didn't think I'd waste good drugs, did you?"

"No, that's not why they let him go," Mandey snapped. "They let him go because he didn't have anything on him. We found the bag and I flushed it down the toilet."

"You did?"

"Yes, I did. Fake drugs or not, I still can't believe you'd do such a thing."

She impatiently wiped her tears as Danny replied, "Mandey, what do you see in that bastard? Don't you remember how he beat me up? And Terry? He's nothing but a scumbag, and you're a goddamn hypocrite. Getting on my case all the time about my business, saying you were so nervous to be around me when you're fucking a goddamn felon."

"Danny," Mandey said, "I know he did things that were wrong. The things he did were really wrong and they sucked, but it was because he was feeling desperate and it was the only way he knew to get by. You have no shame about what you're doing, but Shannon does, and he is determined not to go back to that kind of life. But I know I can't change your mind about him, and there's no use wasting my breath trying."

"Then will you tell me why the hell you made me drag my ass out of bed to meet you here?" Danny asked, agitated. "What do you want?"

Mandey sipped her coffee and gained control of herself once more. "All I want is for everyone to leave Shannon and me alone, and I don't want you to hate me."

"What does it matter how I feel about you? You're shacking up with your thug boyfriend, and everyone knows it. It obviously doesn't matter to you what anyone thinks."

"I don't care about what you think, that's right. I care about what you feel. There's a difference, you know."

"Why do you care about what I feel?"

"Because if you hate me as much as it seems that you do, then I've got to prepare myself for more stupid stunts like you pulled last night. But if you care about me at all, then I am begging you to please let me have my chance to be happy with Shannon. Please don't try to ruin it, and please don't put me in any more dangerous situations."

"Mandey, I still don't understand what you want with him. No, let me talk," Danny said, seeing Mandey open her mouth to object. "He's caused a lot of people a lot of pain. He's mean and violent, and he's going to end up hurting you. On top of that, he's a goddamn liar.

The Devils didn't keep their word. They're worse than ever."

"Well, Danny, think about it. Shannon's the one who made the deal, right? He's not involved with them anymore, so of course they're not going to stick to the deal. There's no one there to make them stick to it."

"You really think that would make a difference?" Danny said, scoffing.

"Yes, I do," Mandey said, "and if you all are still fighting with the Devils, you have got to be careful. Shannon told me that the gang has wanted him gone for a long time so Raff could take over. Shannon tried to keep the violence down to a minimum. Raff won't. Raff won't agree to fistfights; he'll just shoot you. I don't want to see you go and get yourself killed."

They were quiet for a moment, and then Danny said, "I still would much rather see you back together with James than with him. How can you love somebody like that?"

"He loves me," Mandey said. "He's so good to me, Danny. You look at him and you see someone violent and mean, but I've looked into his eyes and I've seen a scared, abused little boy. He's had a hard life; his stepfather abused him, and his mother is ill. Shannon's true nature isn't violent. If it were, I wouldn't be with him."

"You put up with a lot of bullshit from James, Mandey. I don't want to see you do the same thing with this guy."

"It's not the same thing, Danny. When Shannon said that all of you should come beat the crap out of him if he ever hurt me, he meant it."

"Believe me, if he ever does, I will be the first one there, with a baseball bat," Danny said grimly.

There was a pause in the conversation, then Mandey said. "I am still so angry and hurt by what you did last night, Danny. Shannon was so upset about it that he told me I'd be better off if he broke up with me because he doesn't want to cause me any kind of trouble. We nearly broke up the night of the fight, but we managed to get through all that. But since then, Shannon's seen me catching hell from so many people over him, last night was the last straw. He was ready to pack up his stuff and leave, but I convinced him that I don't care what people say or do, I will keep on loving him. And I mean that. But I will not tolerate sabotage, Danny. I mean it. I won't."

Danny sat back and crossed his arms in front of him. "Is that a threat?"

"I'm not sure what it is," Mandey said wearily. "Call it what you want. So, now what? Do we spend the rest of our senior year sniping at each other? I hope not, because I can't stand the thought of you hating me."

"Why?" Danny asked.

"You know why, Danny. You know how I felt about you a few years ago. That night when you were drunk and you kissed me at Jackie's party—suddenly I was fourteen all over again, and for a second all those old feelings came back."

Danny picked up his coffee cup and took a sip. "I don't hate you, Mandey. I just don't want you to get hurt. The night of the fight, when I realized he had you somewhere, I was terrified about what I thought he was doing to you. When I saw him come around that corner, I wanted to kill him."

Mandey smiled wryly. "I appreciate the sentiment, that you don't want me getting hurt, but what do you think you've been doing to me for the last two weeks?"

Danny sighed. "All right, Mandey," he said. "I still don't think that son-of-a-bitch deserves you, but it's your life, and if it's what you want, who can stop you?"

"You've been trying your darnedest," Mandey said.

"Look, dammit, I'm trying to meet you halfway here. Don't give me a hard time," Danny said.

"Then does that mean I don't have to worry about you pulling any more crap like last night?"

Danny paused and said, "As long as he leaves me and my friends alone, I'll leave him alone."

"I'm going to hold you to that," Mandey said, sliding out of the booth and picking up her purse. "Danny, believe me, he doesn't care one iota about you or the Devils or the Alley Cats. He's got more important things on his mind than some stupid turf war."

"You're leaving?" Danny asked her.

"Yeah," Mandey said slowly. "Aren't you the one who has better things to do than drink coffee with a convicted felon's girlfriend?"

"Sit down," he sat, motioning for her to sit again. She did.

Danny sipped his coffee. "He's living with you?"

Mandey nodded.

"Then I assume you've slept with him," Danny said.

"Why do you keep asking me that?" Mandey asked.

Danny looked at her long and hard. "The night of Jackie's party, I was going to ask you to go for a drive with me later, but then Jesse came along. I wanted to get you alone somewhere, boyfriend or no boyfriend."

She blushed but brushed off the remark. "Goes to show you how alcohol warps your perception," she said.

"That's not how it was," Danny said. Then he added, "I envy him."

"Oh, jeez, don't envy him too much," Mandey said, and decided to give Danny a straight answer to his question. She didn't care who knew. "We haven't done that…yet."

"If you love him so much, why haven't you slept with him?"

"I'm not ready yet. One of the things I love about Shannon is that he hasn't tried to push me into it. He's told me it's all up to me. There aren't many guys who would do that."

"Huh," Danny said, taking a moment to absorb this information. "But why aren't you ready yet?"

"Danny, what if I started asking you all sorts of personal questions about your sex life?"

"Ask away."

Mandey sighed. "I'm not ready because Shannon and I have only been together six weeks, and I'd kind of like to wait until I turn eighteen."

Danny laughed. "Oh my God, you're afraid of becoming a statistic."

"What?"

"Never mind."

"That's it. No more discussion about me," Mandey said. "Now you tell me, how old were you when you lost your virginity?" She smiled slyly. "Or have you?"

"I was seven."

"Seriously, Danny."

"Why do you want to know?"

"I've got an inquiring mind, too."

"It was over the summer."

"So you were seventeen."

"Yeah. I was a late starter. Don't go telling people."

"Late starter?" Mandey repeated.

"Seventeen's late for a guy," Danny said.

"If you say so," Mandey said. "Was it someone from school?"

Danny shook his head. "I was visiting my sister in Fort Worth. It happened up there."

"Okay, we've got that settled. I'm a virgin; you're not," Mandey said. "What I want to know is what we're going to do about our government class project. It's due in three weeks and we've been in limbo about it for the last two. I'd rather we finish it together than scrap it and start from scratch and spend Christmas break writing a research paper."

"I agree," Danny said.

"Coming over to my house to work on it probably isn't a good idea," Mandey said. "I think it would be a <u>little</u> awkward."

"No, that's not a good idea at all," Danny said, "but my house is kind of out of the question until after New Year's. My sister is visiting with her four kids, and I can't get a moment's peace."

"Then we can meet at the library some day."

"Yeah," Danny said. "They should let us use the AV equipment if we need to."

"When do you want to meet?"

"Don't know. Any day better for you?"

"No, not really."

"Why don't I give you a call in a couple of days and we'll set it up?" Danny said.

"Sounds like a plan," Mandey said, and stood up. "I'm gonna get going. I'm glad we had this talk."

"Yeah, so am I."

Mandey put her hand on his shoulder and placed her mouth close to Danny's ear. "And I'm sorry if I've done anything to hurt you, too," she said softly, and walked away.

Mandey spent the afternoon reading the first third of *Dune*, on which she had to write a book report for English class. This time she was getting through it much easier than she had when she had read it at the age of thirteen. The movie was supposed to have been released, but it wasn't playing in Houston yet. It was okay, though—the movies were rarely as good as the books.

Normally Shannon wouldn't be working on Saturday, but the company had a remodeling job that they needed to finish before the next weekend, therefore, he was working overtime. He was elated about it, because that meant time-and-a-half. She was happy he had a job he was so enthusiastic about.

When he got home, Mandey was in the kitchen preparing to make burgers for supper. He came out to the kitchen to kiss her.

"Mmm, hamburgers," he said, watching her making the meat patties. "I'm starving. Seems like it's been days since lunch."

"I'll wait until you get out of the shower before I cook them up," Mandey said. "Did you have a good day?"

"Yep. Did a lot of painting today, can you tell?" he said, stepping back to show Mandey his paint spattered clothing.

"I was going to say it looks like you got more paint on yourself than the walls," Mandey said. "Get yourself in the shower and get those clothes in the washer."

He showered and changed clothes, then sat on the couch with a beer, watching television, as Mandey fried the burgers.

It's almost like being married, she thought.

When the food was ready, she called him to the table.

"Where's Marcia tonight?" he asked, sitting down.

"Out with Michael, as usual," Mandey said, joining him.

"Wow," Shannon said, eyeing the fixings Mandey had laid out for the burgers—lettuce, tomato slices, sliced onion, chopped peppers, sautéed mushrooms, pickles, ketchup, mustard, mayonnaise, barbecue sauce, horseradish, ranch dressing and three kinds of cheese.

"Almost like Fuddrucker's," she said.

"Mmmm," Shannon said, building his sandwich. "Even better."

"I owe you an apology," Mandey told him suddenly.

He looked at her uncomprehendingly. "Why do you owe me an apology?"

"I've been doing a lot of thinking today about last night. I realized it was selfish of me to beg you to stay with me."

"Why?" he asked, still not understanding.

"Shannon, you were talking about all the bad things that have been happening in the last couple weeks. I was being selfish; I was only thinking about how it affected me. I didn't give much thought at all to how scared you must feel."

"Well, it's not so much myself I'm scared for; it's you," Shannon said. "I'm used to shit like this, although I hope I don't have to deal with it much more. I just worry about how it could all affect you. But last night you made it clear that you weren't going to let it affect you. That convinced me to stick around."

Mandey smiled. "Well, I'm glad you're sticking around," she told him. "I guess I ought to tell you I had it out with Danny today."

"Oh, Mandey, what did you go and do?" Shannon asked worriedly.

"It's cool," she said. "I called him and asked him to meet me at McDonald's for coffee this morning. I wasn't even sure he'd show up, but he did."

"Mandey, that could have been dangerous," Shannon told her.

"It wasn't, Shannon, and it had to be done. I'm glad I went."

"Well, what happened?"

"I chewed him out for the stupid stunt he pulled last night. You know what he said? He said the stuff in the bag was baking powder and diet pills."

"No shit?" Shannon asked. "Well, it still could have gotten me arrested."

"I know. He was mad at me because he still thinks of you as a threat. He thinks the Devils will be able to find him and the others out here through you via me. I told him he doesn't have to worry about that. Anyway, we came to an agreement—you don't mess with him or the other Alley Cats, and he'll leave us alone."

"So, you're friends again?"

"Mmmm, that might not be the word for it. Not feuding, anyway."

"They're still fighting with the Devils?"

"It sounds that way."

"It's just going to escalate," Shannon said, shaking his head. "Raff won't make any deals. He's going to go at them full throttle, no holds barred."

"I know, I know," Mandey said. "I tried to make that clear to Danny, but I don't think he was listening."

"Well, we're out of it, and that's all that matters," Shannon said.

52

A Visit with the Parole Officer

Shannon only worked half a day on Monday since he had to report to his parole officer at two o'clock. It was the first day of Christmas vacation for Mandey. She had lunch ready when he got home; they ate ham sandwiches and potato chips, then Shannon went to take a shower and change clothes. After he got dressed, he surveyed himself in the mirror in Mandey's room. He did not look like the same person who had been making Friday afternoon visits to Kevin Holtz's office for the last several months. Instead of old jeans, a T-shirt and his leather jacket, today he was dressed in navy blue Dockers, a white Izod shirt, and a Members Only jacket.

"Damn, I'm not used to looking this respectable," he remarked. "If the Devils saw me now, they'd puke."

He looked at Mandey's reflection, as she was standing by his side. She was dressed in black slacks, a shiny turquoise blouse, and silver accessories. Shannon felt that putting on an alligator shirt was a lame attempt on his part to gain credibility, but Mandey was the picture of good taste and respectability. He hoped that a little of what she had might rub off on him.

Mandey smiled. "You look like a frat boy," she said, "but I'm glad you aren't."

"I'm glad you're home to go with me," Shannon said.

"Why?"

"I once told Holtz I had a girlfriend who's an honor student. He didn't believe me, but now I have proof."

"Well, I'm not exactly going to bring my report cards along to prove it."

"You don't have to. One look at you and he'll know."

Shortly before two, Shannon and Mandey walked into the small waiting area outside

Kevin Holtz's office. Two young men, one white and one black, were sitting on opposite sides of the room, eying each other warily. Shannon and Mandey sat in the two chairs closest to the door.

"You in the wrong place, I think," the black guy said to them. "This ain't the marriage license office."

Mandey laughed nervously.

"No, I'm here to see Ass Holtz at two," Shannon said.

"Yeah, well, I was supposed to see him at 1:30 and that guy was supposed to see him at 1:00. He's running way behind," the black guy said.

"Looks like we're going to be here awhile," Shannon told Mandey.

Mandey's eyes roamed around the windowless cramped waiting room, trying to avoid the eyes of the other two men, who were now staring at her and Shannon. The walls were painted an ugly industrial greenish-gray, and the wooden chairs were strictly utilitarian. There was a coffee table covered with back issues of *National Geographic*. The fluorescent lights, along with the color of the walls, made everything look sick and washed-out.

"This is pissing me off, man," the white guy said. He was dressed in faded jeans, a white T-shirt, and a faded denim jacket. "I want to get the fuck out of here."

"So do I," Mandey said softly.

"Huh?" Shannon said. He had been thinking about how he was going to handle Holtz.

"He said he wants to get out of here. I don't blame him. This place is awful. I feel like I'm in jail," Mandey whispered.

"Holtz says it's to make us felons feel at home," Shannon said.

"Nice," Mandey replied.

The door to Holtz's office opened, and a young black male in jeans and an LA Lakers jersey came out, shaking his head.

"Man, you ain't right," he said, turning his head to look back into the room he had just left. Seeing the others in the waiting room, he jerked his thumb toward Holtz's office and shook his head again.

"We know what you mean, brother," said the black guy who was still waiting.

Still shaking his head, the guy left. A few seconds after the outer door closed behind him, Holtz appeared at his inner office door, looking down at a file. He glanced up and saw Mandey sitting there.

"Can I help you?" he asked her.

"Oh, no, I'm here with Shannon," Mandey said, blushing.

Holtz looked at Shannon. Mandey guessed Holtz had not recognized him.

"Douglass," he said, his eyes narrowing. "Step into my office."

"Uh, these other guys are ahead of me," Shannon said.

"They can wait," Holtz said.

Shannon looked at Mandey. She gave his hand a squeeze, and he rose and followed Holtz into his tiny office.

"Oh, what a bunch of horse shit," the white guy said.

"Bitching about it ain't going to help any," said the other.

"Hey, I'll bitch if I feel like it."

In Holtz's office Shannon sat in the hot seat.

"Okay, mister, you've got a lot of explaining to do," Holtz said, sitting down behind his desk.

Shannon handed him the manila folder in his hand. "This is documentation of my new job and my new address."

"Why wasn't I notified about this?" Holtz asked, taking the folder from Shannon.

"I'm notifying you now. I called you the day I quit my job, and I left a message on your machine when I got my new job," Shannon told him.

"I didn't authorize you to quit."

"Look, a condition of my parole is to have a job. It doesn't say it has to be the job you approve," Shannon said.

"How do I even know this is legitimate?"

"The phone number is there. The business is listed in the Yellow Pages," Shannon said. "Call Bert. He's the owner. He'll confirm it."

"Ed Grubbs was very upset when you quit," Holtz said. "He called and said you'd left a nasty message on his machine."

Uh-oh, Shannon thought, *here it comes.*

Suddenly, Mandey burst through the door.

"They're fighting!" she exclaimed.

Holtz jumped up out of his chair, knocking a desk tray onto the floor in the process. Shannon followed Holtz out into the waiting area. The two men were slugging each other, upsetting the chairs and coffee table and scattering the magazines everywhere. Holtz grabbed the white guy by his denim jacket, while Shannon grabbed the black fellow.

"Get your hands off me!" the white guy said angrily.

"Man, that mother-fucker's crazy!" the black guy exclaimed.

"Bring him out here," Holtz said to Shannon as he opened the door to the hallway.

While Shannon and his parole officer took the two brawlers down the hall, Mandey picked up the papers that had fallen on the floor. She wasn't trying to read them, but one caught her attention because she glimpsed Shannon's name on it. It looked to be some sort of ledger page—there were cash amounts next to Shannon's name.

Mandey wasn't sure how quickly Shannon and Holtz would be returning, so she rapidly scanned a few more of the pages she picked up. Something about them wasn't right.

She remembered that Shannon had brought back something similar from Grubbs' office. She quickly folded up some of the sheets and stuffed them into her purse, left the rest of them on the floor, and retook her seat in the waiting room. A moment later they returned, sans the two brawlers.

"Let's finish this up," Holtz said to Shannon. He saw Mandey and motioned to her. "Would you join us, please?"

Mandey followed them into the office. She sat down while Shannon remained standing. Holz picked up the desk tray and papers off the floor and put them back on the corner of his desk.

"This is my girlfriend, Amanda Rowan," Shannon said.

"Good to meet you," Holtz said, extending his hand. Mandey shook it.

"Shannon mentioned that you are an honor student. At which school?" he asked her.

"Rogers High School]'," Mandey replied.

"Have you known Shannon long?"

"About six weeks."

"And he's told you about what he did to end up in jail?"

"Yes, he has."

"And your family has no qualms about that?"

"Why are you putting her through the third degree?" Shannon demanded.

"It's okay, sweetie," Mandey said. "Well, I guess not or he wouldn't be living at my house now."

"You're living with her?" Holtz asked.

"Yes, her and her mother, who works at a lawyer's office."

"Is your mother a lawyer?" Holtz asked, his eyebrows raised.

"No," Mandey said, quickly. "She's an accountant at a law firm."

"Which one?"

"Friedman, Leach, and Woods," Mandey replied.

"I see," Holtz said. "How old are you?"

Mandey blinked. "Seventeen. The age of consent, if that's what you're getting at."

"Look," Shannon said, irritated, "I'm trying to do all that stuff you kept telling me to do. I'm going to start taking GED classes in January, I'm out of that lousy neighborhood I was living in and away from all those bad influences, and I've got a full-time job with better pay. I've given you my job information and my new address and phone number. As far as I can tell, I'm meeting all the conditions of my parole. What beef can you have with me?"

Holtz silently scowled as he looked over Shannon's papers. "I guess you've got everything in order, but I still don't like your attitude," he said. "Your next appointment is January fourteenth, two o'clock."

"I'm free to go, then? No more worrying about arrest warrants?"

"Not unless you mess up. You can go."

As they walked out of the building, Mandey said to Shannon, "When we get to the car, I've got something to show you."

"What?" Shannon asked.

"I'm not sure. Some papers that got knocked off your parole officer's desk."

"You stole some papers?" Shannon asked, incredulous.

"Shhh," Mandey hushed him. "Wait until we get to the car."

In the parking lot they sat in Shannon's car as they looked over what Mandey had picked up.

"Holy shit!" Shannon exclaimed. "Do you know what this is?"

Mandey shook her head. "Not exactly, but it looked suspicious to me."

"Fucking Holtz knew all along I was stealing cars for Grubbs. He was getting kickbacks! And it looks like I'm not the only one who's been in that situation."

"What do we do?" Mandey asked. "Should we go to his supervisor?"

"No," Shannon said, still studying the papers.

"We've got to tell somebody," Mandey said.

"Yeah, and then I'll get busted for car theft," Shannon said.

"But you were being blackmailed, Shannon! Now you have proof. You have the names of others in the same situation. They'll vouch for your story."

"I don't know, Mandey."

"Don't you want to bust that weasel?"

Despite the seriousness of what they were talking about, Shannon laughed at Mandey's last comment.

"What's so funny?" Mandey demanded.

"You talking like that," he said. "Yeah, I want to bust him, but I don't want to get myself busted, too."

They continued to debate the best course of action on the drive home.

"We should have stayed downtown and gone over to see Michael," Mandey said. "I'm sure he could tell you what to do."

"I don't have money for a lawyer, Mandey," Shannon said. "And then he'd tell Marcia."

"Attorney-client privilege," Mandey reminded him.

"Yeah, but with no money I'm not a client."

Mandey sighed. "Well, what if we mail the copies of the documents to the head of the parole and probation department?"

"No. My name is on them. I'm going to get in trouble," Shannon said stubbornly.

"But Shannon—"

"Do you want me to go to jail?"

"Of course not."

"Then don't push it."

"Then please call Michael when we get home, just to see what he says. Please?"

Shannon sighed. "All right."

Michael wasn't available when Shannon called, but he returned the call at 4:30. Shannon kept the details of the situation as general as possible, since he couldn't rightfully claim attorney-client privilege.

"What was his advice?" Mandey asked when Shannon hung up the phone.

"I mentioned sending the documents anonymously to the department head. He said he thought that might be a good idea. He said it would probably spark a departmental investigation that they'll want to keep quiet. He said he doubted they'd press charges against anyone who was blackmailed as long as they cooperated with the investigation. He said he didn't think I'd need a lawyer, but he's there if I need him."

"Are you going to do it?"

"Don't know yet," Shannon said. "It'd pay them back for putting me through hell. What irks me most is Holtz. He was constantly chewing my ass about cleaning up my act, and turns out he's the big actor. Pisses me off. I've still got to think about it, though, 'cause if something goes wrong, I'm screwed."

53

Christmas Party

On the Saturday before Christmas, Marcia and Michael were going to their office Christmas party, and then Marcia was going to spend the night at Michael's, so Mandey and Shannon would have the house to themselves. Mandey told Marcia that she wanted to have a Christmas party.

"Nothing crazy. Just a few of us having some food, maybe playing some games. We're going to do a grab bag gift exchange."

"Who's coming to this shindig?" Marcia asked her.

"Georgia, Andrea, Martin, Gayla, Charlie, Charlene, and Phillip. Not a whole bunch of people."

"That sounds fine. I know you're responsible, and your friends aren't too wild, either—the ones I've met, anyway," Marcia said. "However, if there is any drinking going on, I don't want anyone driving home drunk."

"I don't think there's going to be much drinking going on—"

"But if there is, they need to spend the night here. You and Shannon can sleep in my room. Let the others take your rooms. And there's the sleeper sofa, too."

The night before, Mandey and Shannon went to the store to shop for the party, to buy food; paper Christmas plates, cups, napkins, and disposable cutlery; and gifts for the gift exchange.

"This is going to be so much fun," Mandey said happily, grabbing a shopping cart. She hadn't had a party since her 7th birthday. It wasn't going to be on the scale of any of Jackie Seymour's house parties, but Mandey was excited, nevertheless.

Except for those occasional gang blow-outs, Shannon hadn't been to any parties since he was a kid, either, and he had never given a party. The Devils wouldn't consider what he and Mandey were planning a party, that was for sure, but he didn't care. He smiled absently.

"What's that look for?" Mandey asked.

"I'm still having a hard time believing how much my life has changed in the past few weeks," Shannon said. "Living with my girlfriend and throwing a Christmas party with her? This isn't my life, is it?"

"It's different for me, too," Mandey said. "Maybe not as drastic a change as for you, but definitely different."

They browsed the aisles, gathering the ingredients for Mandey's chocolate chip cookies and Christmas sugar cookies. At the meat case, she picked up three pounds of ground beef.

"I'm going to make meatball grinders," she said, as she put the packages in the cart.

"Meatball what?" Shannon asked.

"Grinders. Subs. Meatball subs," Mandey replied.

Once they had gathered all the items for the buffet, they then had to find gifts for the exchange. They needed to find gifts that were appropriate for either a male or female and cost less than five dollars.

"How about I just wrap up a pack of cigarettes?" Shannon joked.

"No," Mandey said, smiling.

In the end, they decided upon a coffee mug that they would fill with a couple packages of hot cocoa mix and some Hershey kisses for one gift, and a 1985 desktop calendar for the other. Once back home, Mandey made the sugar cookie dough and put it in the refrigerator, as it had to set overnight.

The next morning, they cleaned the house and wrapped their gifts. After lunch, Mandey baked cookies, then Shannon helped her make the meatballs. Once those came out of the oven, Mandey put them into the Crock-Pot with spaghetti sauce she had taken out of the freezer and thawed on the stovetop.

"This is real Italian sauce. It's one of my aunt's recipes. Both my mother's brothers married Italian ladies, so you know the recipe is the real thing."

Then it was time for them to get themselves ready for the party. After she showered and washed her hair, Mandey opened her closet to decide what to wear. It was a Christmas party, and she wanted to wear something festive, but it was 70 degrees outside and most of her Christmas-wear was made for a day 20 degrees colder. She decided on a red velour blouse with three-quarter length sleeves and big, sparkly, white snowflakes on it, and black slacks. Snowflakes and 70 degrees.

She was sitting at her vanity doing her makeup when Shannon walked in after taking his shower. She turned to look at him.

"Well, don't you look nice?" she said, surveying him in his black corduroys and red and gray plaid, but not flannel, shirt.

"Thanks," he said with a grin. "And you look beautiful, too."

"Well, maybe not yet. I'm still doing my face and I've got to do my hair," Mandey said. "You know, I can't get used to it being 70 degrees three days before Christmas. Next year we should go up North for Christmas. Christmas in Connecticut, doesn't that sound romantic?

You might even see a white Christmas."

"That sounds cold," Shannon said.

"But you'll have me to keep you warm," Mandey said, grinning. "Seriously, you'll like it. I love it. I think you'll love it, too, once you see it."

"I'm good spending Christmas anywhere, as long as it's with you," Shannon told her.

He had never been outside of the state of Texas. He listened as Mandey went on about how much she loved New England and how it was living there until her father got transferred to Houston.

"There are times I wish we had never moved," she said, "but, if we hadn't, I wouldn't be here with you right now, so I'm happy that we did. I can put up with sweating on Christmas for that."

Mandey wanted so much to show Shannon the beauty of her home state, so he could see why she loved it so. Shannon found himself thinking about going there with her, meeting her extended family, and seeing all the places that were near and dear to her heart. To him, New England seemed like a foreign country, but it did sound nice. So that might be what was in store for next Christmas. Right now, there was a Houston Christmas to celebrate.

They were getting the kitchen ready for guests when Michael arrived at 6:30 to pick up Marcia. Mandey thought he looked sharp in his black suit, white shirt, and bright red Christmas tie.

"Marcia said y'all were having your own Christmas party. It looks and smells good to me," Michael told them.

"Thanks," Mandey said.

Marcia stepped out of her bedroom and into the kitchen. She had on a long black skirt with a very long slit in the side and a short-sleeved red sequined blouse. She had her chestnut hair piled on her head, and was wearing bright red lipstick, almost the same color as Mandey's. Mandey sometimes wished she looked more like Marcia, but she was two inches taller and about 20 pounds heavier. Mandey had been on the heavy side since about the age of five, courtesy of her birth father's genes.

"Wow," Shannon exclaimed. "You look great."

"Thanks," Marcia replied, doing a spin in the middle of the kitchen like it was a fashion show catwalk.

"You are stunning," Michael told her, taking her overnight bag from her and giving her a kiss. "Shall we go?"

Marcia took his arm. "Yes, sir," she said. "Mandey, remember what I said about anyone drinking."

"I will. I'll remind everyone when they get here."

"I'll be back tomorrow, but probably not until around six. Have fun tonight."

"You, too," Mandey replied.

Michael and Marcia left, walking out the door into the balmy evening to Michael's waiting Mercedes. Mandey turned her attention back to the task at hand. She plated the cookies, then put out rolls, sliced mozzarella, and sautéed onions and green peppers to go with the meatballs. They had also bought some cheese and crackers to serve, and Mandey poured a can of Planters mixed nuts into a small bowl. Shannon lined up the two-liter bottles of soda they had bought—2 Cokes, 2 Dr Peppers, a Sprite, and an Orange Crush—and put two stacks of Solo cups next to them on the counter.

"You've done an awesome job putting this together," Shannon told Mandey, putting his arm around her.

"Thank you," she replied, slipping her arm around his waist. "Thank you for all your help getting things ready."

"So, we're supposed to sleep in Marcia's room tonight?" Shannon asked.

"Yes, well, if anyone gets drunk, they're supposed to spend the night. They can take our rooms, and we'll take Marcia's," Mandey said. "I guess we could get our stuff and move it into Marcia's room for tonight, just in case."

They got together what they needed and transferred it into the master bedroom. Shannon sat down on the edge of the king-size bed.

"We get the big bed tonight, he said, grinning and bouncing up and down.

"Yeah, the grown-up bed," Mandey replied.

Shannon stood and took Mandey into his arms. "And I get to share it with the most gorgeous woman in the world," he said.

"Really?" Mandey said. "Who's that?"

"That would be you," he told her.

"Me?" Mandey said. "You really think so?"

"I know so," Shannon said, and bowed his head to kiss her.

Mandey wrapped her arms around him and kissed back. She was liking the idea of sleeping with Shannon in the master bedroom, as master and mistress of the house.

There was a knock at the door, and they let go of each other. Mandey looked at Shannon and reached up to wipe her red lipstick from his mouth.

"Guests are arriving," Mandey said excitedly and bounded out of the bedroom to answer the door.

Andrea and Martin were the first to arrive. They brought a vegetable tray with ranch dip to share. Mandey took those and made a place for them on the kitchen table. Shannon took their grab-bag gifts and added them to the big sack where his and Mandey's presents already were. Andie and Mart were helping themselves to something to drink when Gayla and Charlie arrived. Gayla brought tortilla chips and taco dip, while Charlie contributed cold shrimp and cocktail sauce.

"Shrimp cocktail!" Mandey exclaimed. "Wow, Charlie, that's getting fancy!"

"Nothing but the best for your little soiree, my dear," Charlie replied in his Thurston Howell the Third accent.

A half hour later, the six of them were sitting, chatting, and drinking sodas when Georgia walked up at the same time Phillip and Charlene pulled into the driveway.

"Woooo, let's get this party started!" Georgia cried as she came in the door. "I brought hors d'oeuvres!"

Charlene followed her, carrying a covered cake pan, and Phillip brought up the rear with two six packs of Budweiser.

"Beer is here!" Phillip bellowed. "And Charlene made Jell-o shots!"

Mandey looked at Shannon. "What's a Jell-o shot?" she asked him.

He had an idea, but wasn't sure. "Let's go in the kitchen and find out."

"Is there room in the fridge? I don't want the beer to get warm," Phillip said.

"Sure," Shannon said, helping him clear a place for the six-packs.

Charlene placed the cake pan on the table and took off the cover. The pan was filled with small plastic cups, some containing green Jell-o and some containing red Jell-o, each topped with a dollop of Cool Whip.

Georgia picked one up and looked at it. "What kind of alcohol did you use?"

"Vodka," Charlene said. "I tried one at home—so-o-o-o good. They go down <u>real smooth</u>."

Well, I guess there will be some drinking going on tonight, Mandey thought. *Or whatever you call what you do with a Jell-o shot.*

"Hey, everybody? Reminder, Marcia told me that if anyone gets blitzed, they've got to spend the night here, okay? No one driving home and getting into an accident. We've got extra beds, so don't worry about that."

"No one's gonna get blitzed on a couple shots or a couple beers, unless you've got some booze around you haven't told us about," Phillip said.

There was liquor in the house, but Mandey wasn't about to tell anyone where that could be found.

"Just the same, it's better to be safe than sorry," Mandey said.

Now that all the guests were present, everyone got a plate and loaded it up. They all sat in the living room, where the television tuned to MTV. Charlene, Phillip, Georgia took the couch, Andrea and Martin sat in the loveseat, Charlie and Gayla each sat in a kitchen chair. Shannon and Mandey quibbled over who was going to sit in the recliner and who was going to sit on the floor.

"Mandey, Shannon is being a gentleman. I suggest you listen to him and take the chair," Phillip said.

Shannon looked at her. "See?"

Mandey shrugged. "Okay. Thank you," she said to Shannon, and sat down. Shannon sat down on the floor next to her.

Mandey had a little bit of everything on her plate, plus a plastic cup of Dr Pepper and a Jell-o shot, both of which she set on the end table next to her. She wasn't a big fan of Jell-o, but she supposed she should try one.

"Let's save the Jell-o shots for last and do them together," Georgia suggested.

Once everyone had cleaned their plates, Georgia and Charlene held up their shots. Everyone followed suit except Martin, who was opting not to drink.

"One, two, three, go!" Georgia said.

They tilted their heads back, put the cups to their lips, and chugged them down. The more experienced drinkers let the Jell-o slide down their throats. Mandey sort of ate her way through hers, taking three swallows to get it down. It was raspberry Jell-o, not strawberry, and that made her happy. Gayla managed to get half of hers down, but the other half somehow slid out of her cup, tumbled down the front of her blouse, and fell on the carpet, making everyone laugh.

Charlene went to light a cigarette. Mandey was about to say something when Andrea spoke up.

"Could you please smoke outside? I'm allergic to cigarette smoke."

Charlene got an irritated look on her face and opened her mouth to say something when Phillip tapped her arm and said, "Come on, let's go outside."

Mandey was surprised that Charlene didn't say anything and got up with Phillip. Shannon stood, too. "I might as well go for a smoke, too."

The three of them went out and sat on the wide front steps. It was a nice night out, but Mandey was right—it didn't really feel like Christmas, at least not the kind of Christmas you always heard about or saw in movies or on television.

"You're a lucky dog, Shannon, shacking up here with your foxy girlfriend," Phillip said to him.

"Don't I know it?" Shannon said. "A damn lucky dog."

"She idolizes you," Phillip said. "You can see it in the way she looks at you. What the hell did you ever do to rate that?

Shannon shook his head. "I don't know," he admitted. "But I feel the same way about her."

"Jesus, Phillip, if you love Mandey so much, why don't you see if Shannon will share with you?" Charlene asked, disgusted.

"Seriously, Charlene?" Phillip said. "Shannon's got himself a good woman, and I'm happy for him."

"Whatever," Charlene said, rolling her eyes and taking a drag off her cigarette.

"Yea, I'm not sharing," Shannon said.

When they went inside after their cigarette break, it was time for the grab-bag gift exchange. They passed the bag around, each taking a gift that they did not put in the bag. After everyone took one, they opened them. Shannon got a $5.00 book of McDonald's gift certificates. Mandey opened hers to find a pack of cigarettes.

Shannon saw the crestfallen look on his girlfriend's face. He had suggested doing that, but not seriously. Whoever brought them for the gift exchange was pretty shitty. He had a good idea of who it was, too.

"Hey, I'll trade you," he said.

"We don't have to trade. You can have them," Mandey said, handing the cigarettes to him. She shrugged. "It's not about the presents."

When it came time to leave, Mart hadn't had anything to drink, so he was good to take himself and Andie home. Phillip had had a few beers plus a couple Jell-o shots, but was insistent that he was okay to drive.

"I'm not drunk, I'm of legal age, I brought my own booze, and I'm just driving up the street. Charlene's staying at my house tonight, so she's not driving. And I'll take Georgia home. She only lives six houses down from here."

"Okay," Mandey relented.

Charlie and Gayla decided to stay. Neither was really drunk, but they were a little buzzed, Gayla a bit more than Charlie. Mandey had told everyone when she called to invite them about Marcia wanting anyone who drank to stay the night, and Gayla and Charlie must have taken it seriously, because they each had brought along a small overnight bag. Once the others had left, and it was just the four of them, Charlie asked, "You want to watch a movie?"

"What movie?" Mandey asked.

"Just a video I brought along. You'll like it," he said, grinning and reaching into his bag.

Charlie went over to the VCR and popped the cassette in. He sat back down next to Gayla with an expectant smile on his face.

The movie started with four heavily-made up, scantily clad young women in a car being pulled over by a rural sheriff's deputy. He called for back-up and arrested them for some trumped-up reason, and another patrol car came and they hauled the girls off to the county jail. Then the girls began to use their powers of persuasion to be released.

"Charlie, you brought a porno?" Gayla asked, disgusted.

"Oh, come on, Gayla, loosen up," Charlie said. "It's just sex."

Mandey was gobsmacked by a close-up of a penis thrusting vigorously into a vagina. She looked at Shannon sitting next to her on the couch. He was staring at the television with his mouth slightly open, then he noticed Mandey looking at him.

"Have you ever seen a porno movie before?" he asked her.

She shook her head.

"Do you want him to turn it off?"

"No, it's okay," she said.

She wasn't a prude. When she was 15, on a visit back home at her grandmother's house, she had been rummaging in the attic and found two books that had belonged to one of her cousins. One was *Everything You Wanted to Know about Sex but Were Afraid to Ask* and the other was *The Happy Hooker* by Xaviera Hollander. She devoured the books during her two-week visit and learned a lot from them. She had also seen a few R-rated movies with nudity and sex, but they were nothing like this.

She watched the movie, with the four women having sex with the two men in various positions, sometimes handcuffed, sometimes not. Sometimes it was one-on-one. Sometimes it was two women with one man, other times two men on one woman. Sometimes it was even two women together.

Mandey felt the blood pounding between her legs. She stole a glance at Shannon, who was watching the action intently. He turned to look at her, then she felt his hot breath as he put his mouth against her ear.

"Are you getting horny?" he murmured.

Then he started to kiss her face passionately. She could smell the alcohol on his breath—he had had a few beers and more than two Jell-o shots. Shannon's hands began to roam to some personal places. Mandey took his hands and moved them to less-intimate spots. She wouldn't mind if they were alone, but Gayla and Charlie were sitting on the couch six feet away. No sooner would she move them away than they would find their way back to those personal places again. Between the movie and Shannon's passionate lips and hands, Mandey was getting extremely aroused.

Gayla, despite her initial disapproval, appeared to be engrossed in the movie. Charlie, of course, was enjoying it. Mandey had a pretty good idea why he had brought it. Gayla and Charlie had decided in advance that they would spend the night there. Charlie must have brought the movie to try to get Gayla in a sexy mood, and then she might be receptive to his advances.

The movie ended just in time. Gently, Mandey extricated herself from Shannon's grasp. "Want me to show you to your rooms?" she asked Gayla and Charlie.

"There's another one on the tape," Charlie said.

"You're welcome to stay up and watch it, but I think I'm ready for bed," Mandey said.

Charlie smirked at her, then turned to Gayla. "What about you? Are you ready for bed?" he asked her.

"After all that sex, I'm ready for some lovemaking," Gayla declared. "And no, that doesn't mean you, Charlie." She looked at Mandey. "You and Shannon need to go make love."

Shannon wrapped his arms around Mandey from behind and kissed her neck.

"Sounds good to me," he said in her ear.

Mandey reached up and tousled his hair. "We have to show them to their rooms," she said, again gently removing herself from Shannon's arms. "Let me show Gayla my room, and why don't you show Charlie to yours?"

Gayla grabbed her bag and followed Mandey. Charlie's crestfallen look didn't escape Mandey.

"Charlie's not happy," Mandey said to Gayla in a low voice as they went down the hall.

"I know," Gayla said. "That video was his way of trying to seduce me."

"How romantic," Mandey said dryly.

"I like your curtain and comforter," Gayla said. "Are they new?"

"I got them a few months ago. New since you were over last," Mandey said. "Hope it's comfortable in here for you. The door to the bathroom and the door to the hallway both have a lock, in case you think someone might try to bother you."

"Thanks. I don't think he will, though," Gayla said. "But I was serious out there—after all of that soulless, gratuitous sex we just watched, you and Shannon should go to bed and make mad, passionate love to each other."

Mandey laughed and blushed. "We'll see," she said.

"'We'll see'? What does that mean? You both were acting like you were ready to tear each other's clothes off."

Mandey blushed even more. Gayla had told her about losing her virginity over the summer (with a boyfriend she had broken up with a month later) but Mandey had not shared much with Gayla about the state of her own sex life.

"We haven't gotten to that point yet," Mandey said.

"Well, I bet you'll get to that point tonight," Gayla said with a knowing smile.

"We'll see," Mandey said again, enigmatically. "Sleep good."

54

Almost

Shannon slipped between the covers of the king-size bed with scenes from the video Charlie had brought over replaying vividly in his mind. He had gotten so hard while watching the movie and making out with Mandey, and he was half-hard yet. He had started to masturbate in the bathroom, but he stopped. It wasn't going to satisfy him tonight.

"Hi, sweetie," Mandey said to him as he settled down next to her.

"Hi, beautiful," he replied.

He took her in his arms, held her warm, soft body, clad in a short, silky nightie and skimpy panties, and kissed her passionately. His cock stood at full attention immediately.

"Mandey," he said breathlessly between kisses, "I know you're not ready to go all the way yet, but I want to see your body and feel your skin against mine. Please?" He began pulling at her gown.

"Shannon—"

"Please, Mandey? I promise I won't do anything you don't want me to do. I love you, Mandey. I won't hurt you. I promise. I'd never hurt you."

Mandey didn't resist as he lifted her gown.

"Oh, Mandey," Shannon sighed, caressing her breasts and kissing her neck.

Mandey feared things were going to get out of hand, but she succumbed to the wonderful feeling of Shannon's caresses. She ran her hands through his hair and over his back and chest.

Shannon's hands made their way down to her panties.

"Shannon—" Mandey began to object again, but only weakly.

"Oh, Mandey. Please?" he begged in a whisper, sliding his hand into the waistband of her panties.

"Shannon, I don't want things to go too far," Mandey said in a high, small voice.

"They won't. I promise," he said, his hand cupping her right buttock. "I need to feel you, Mandey. I need you to feel me."

He threw back the covers. "You're so beautiful," he told her.

His hand moved into the front of her panties to the wiry patch of hair between her legs, then his finger slid into that hot, wet spot. Mandey winced with pleasure when he pressed her gently down there. Then he pulled her into his arms again and kissed her, hard.

One of his hands took one of hers and led it to the waistband of his briefs. "Pull them down," he told her.

Mandey did, slowly. She saw how the dark hair below his navel blended into the dark curly mass of his pubic hair. Then, pulling them lower, she released his long, hard member.

He took her hand in his and led it to his manhood. She touched him, grasping his penis gently but firmly, touching his scrotum delicately, learning the shapes and textures of a man's private anatomy for the first time.

Shannon touched her arm. "Don't be afraid, Mandey. We're not going to do anything you don't want to. You can trust me. You should know that by now."

"I know," she whispered, and wrapped her arms around him. "Oh, Shannon."

She kissed him passionately with their bodies pressed tightly against each other. She was so aroused she could hardly stand it. She longed to feel his strong, solid body pressing down on top of hers, and to spread her legs wide to invite him in. The feeling of his skin, the heat of his body, and his musky sex smell were all almost too much to bear. She couldn't stop herself from letting Shannon's persistent hand find its way between her legs again.

Shannon's mind was moaning that this had been a mistake. His hormones were on the verge of taking over. He knew he had to stop; he had promised her he would, but he wanted to keep going.

My God, I can't believe I was afraid I wouldn't be able to get it up with her, he thought.

Her body was so soft; her breasts and buttocks were so full and warm, firm but yielding. Her mouth kissed his hard nipples, making him shudder.

"Oh, God," he gasped, tearing away and grabbing a small jar of petroleum jelly from where he had set it on the nightstand. He scooped a glob of it on his fingers and rubbed it on himself, then took Mandey's hand and placed it on his penis again.

"Mandey, help me," he whispered.

Mandey's hand fondled his cock, rubbing and squeezing it just right. Shannon wished he could spread her thighs wide apart and slide inside her hot wetness, and go in and out, in and out—

He hit overload. "Oh, Mandey! I'm coming!" he gasped, his hand clamping down on Mandey's to add more pressure.

He didn't even try to bite back his moans of pleasure as thick, white fluid spurted onto the sheets, their hands, and Mandey's stomach. Mandey wondered if Gayla and Charlie might be able to hear.

He sighed as the spasms subsided, then he lay there still, catching his breath. Mandey kissed his forehead. Shannon cuddled close to her and they held each other, lying in the wet spot he had made but not caring.

"Oh my God," he said, still a bit breathlessly as he buried his face in her hair. "You feel so good in my arms. You're so soft and warm and beautiful."

Mandey felt herself blushing. "You're so strong and handsome and sexy," she told him. "You drive me crazy."

She felt Shannon chuckle quietly.

"Are you okay?" he asked her.

"I'm fine," she replied, "except you got your release, and I'm still so horny I can hardly stand it."

Shannon laughed out loud this time.

"I'm sorry. I don't mean to laugh," he said. "I turned you on?"

"Yes, you did."

"You were real wet down there, but I thought the movie got you excited."

"It did, but you were what <u>really</u> got me excited."

"Good," Shannon said, and kissed her, softly this time.

They lay there together quietly for a while, and Mandey felt the throbbing between her legs slowly subside. Part of her wanted to grab Shannon's hand and put it back there again, but she didn't.

"I'm just afraid of doing it before I'm ready," Mandey said. "I'm seventeen, and I know that's the age of consent, but I'd at least like to be able to say I waited until I was legally an adult."

"You won't be eighteen for nearly five months," Shannon reminded her.

"I know," Mandey sighed.

"Do you think you can hold out that long?"

"I don't know. Can you?"

He kissed her forehead. "It's up to you, Mandey. I won't pressure you to make love to me. I vowed when I met you that I wouldn't do that. I won't even ask you to do what we did tonight again, if you don't want to. I just got so worked up by that movie, I couldn't stand it."

Mandey nodded but didn't say anything.

"I'm going to tell you something," Shannon said. "Now, don't go getting the wrong idea, but I bought box of condoms to have on hand. If some night things go past the point of no return, then you won't have to worry about getting pregnant. Is that okay with you?"

Mandey nodded again. She hadn't told him about going on the Pill because she hadn't started it yet. The doctor said to start it the Sunday after the first day of her next period, which was due any day now. "That's a good idea." An extra precaution.

"But like I told you all along, you call the shots, Mandey. If I ever start getting too carried away, tell me. Don't be afraid. I might get frustrated, but I'd rather face a little frustration than end up doing something that might hurt you or make me end up losing you."

"That's a very mature attitude," Mandey said, then was silent again.

"What's wrong, Mandey?" Shannon asked.

Mandey smiled wistfully. "I'm wishing it were five months from now," she said, giving him a squeeze. "I love you so much, Shannon. I want so much to make love to you. I want to make sure you know that."

"I know," Shannon said. "Don't worry about it. When the time is right, you'll know it."

Awhile later they settled down to sleep. Mandey stayed awake for some time. She was remembering what she had seen in the video, but mostly she was remembering what she and Shannon had done. It probably wasn't what Gayla meant by "mad, passionate love", but it was still something. She replayed Shannon's orgasm over and over in her mind—the sound of his voice gasping that he was about to come, how his hand squeezed hers to add pressure, the way his eyes shut so tightly, the loud sound of his moans of pleasure, the sticky feeling of his semen, how he had lain so weak and vulnerable in her arms afterward.

I did that, she thought. *I made him do that.*

She had never felt so sexy or so powerful. She liked that feeling, and although her body was still awaiting a release that wasn't to come that night, she fell asleep with a smile on her face.

The next morning, Mandey was the first one up. She washed up in the bathroom, got dressed, then went to the kitchen to start breakfast. She made coffee and mixed up a package of blueberry muffins and put them in the oven. There were eggs and bacon in the refrigerator to cook, once the others woke up.

She replayed what she and Shannon had done the night before over and over in her mind. She wanted more of that—more of the desire, the intensity. Even though she was still technically a virgin, she now felt she had at least some sort of experience, and she felt a certain degree of satisfaction about that. She wasn't sure Shannon was going to be able to wait another five months until she turned eighteen. Despite what she had told him last night, she was beginning to wonder if she wanted to wait that long, either.

She heard Shannon in the master bathroom, turning on the shower, and could hear someone in the other bathroom, too, although she didn't know if it was Gayla or Charlie. She went outside to pick up the Sunday paper from the driveway. It was heavy and full of last-minute Christmas shopping advertisements. She poured herself some coffee and read the paper, waiting for the others.

A while later, Shannon came out of the bedroom. "Good morning," he greeted her with a smile.

"Good morning," she replied, smiling back.

He fixed himself a cup of coffee and gave her a peck on the cheek before sitting down at the kitchen table next to her.

"Thank you for last night," he said to her.

"You're welcome," Mandey said.

"We've got to change the sheets before Marcia gets back."

Mandey chuckled. "Yes, definitely."

Gayla walked into the kitchen from the living room. "Morning," she said, still looking sleepy.

"Morning," they greeted her, then Mandey asked, "Did you sleep okay? No interruptions?"

"Um, no interruptions exactly, but I slept great! Your bed is so comfortable, Mandey."

A moment later Charlie came into the kitchen, carrying the sheets from Shannon's bed in a big ball in his arms. He looked a bit sullen, almost certainly because Gayla had shot him down once again last night.

"I stripped the bed for you," he said. "Where can I put these?"

Mandey showed him to the laundry room. The look on Shannon's face did not escape her, but she didn't remark on it.

The muffins came out of the oven, then Mandey got out a carton of eggs, butter, and shredded cheddar cheese to make a pan of cheesy scrambled eggs. Shannon got a frying pan out for her and a second one for himself.

"I'll cook the bacon," he offered.

Fifteen minutes later the four of them were enjoying breakfast. Charlie's mood improved as he ate.

"You ought to open a bed and breakfast," Charlie said, as he nearly licked his plate clean.

"Maybe that's what I should major in, hotel and restaurant management," Mandey joked.

"If you're going to U of H, why not?" Gayla said. "They've got the program for it."

"I'm not going to declare a major for a least the first year. I want to explore my options."

Gayla was planning on going into nursing, but she was going to start college at North Harris County. She was too nervous to jump right into a four-year university environment. Charlie had his heart set on pre-med. He was hoping to get into either the University of Texas or Baylor.

"You're most likely going to be valedictorian, so I don't think you have to worry about not getting into either one," Gayla told him.

"Still, I'd like to get the acceptance letters in my hot little hands soon."

"Do you have any plans to go back to school, Shannon?" Gayla asked him.

Shannon found it was getting a little easier to field these kinds of questions.

"I'm going to take the GED test soon, then I'm going to start taking some classes at North Harris. I'm like Mandey; I don't know exactly what I want to do with myself yet."

"You two will figure it out together, I'm sure," Gayla said.

Gayla and Charlie left around 11 o'clock. Mandey and Shannon cleaned up the kitchen, then changed the sheets on Marcia's bed. They took the sheets into the laundry room. Shannon looked at the wadded-up bedding on top of the washer.

"Mandey, do you think Charlie jacked off in my bed?" he asked.

Mandey burst into giggles. "Yeah, maybe," she said. "You wanna check?"

"God no, gross," Shannon said, grimacing.

"You jacked off in Marcia's bed. What's the difference?" Mandey asked, amused.

"No, I didn't. You jacked me off. There is a difference," Shannon said adamantly. "Besides, Marcia thinks we're already having sex, so if she told us to sleep in her room, she knows what to expect." He watched Mandey put his sheets in the washer. "Hot water, lots of detergent. I want to wash the blankets, too."

Mandey giggled as he left. She guessed she would have been a little freaked out if Charlie had jacked off in her bed, too.

When Shannon came back with the rest of his bedding Mandey said to him, "Don't take this the wrong way, but, um, considering your history, I'm a bit surprised you're reacting this way."

He dropped the bedspread and blanket on the floor. "What? You mean because I used to go to hookers?"

Mandey looked at him and shrugged.

"I guess I didn't let myself think about it. Plus, I was going to them, so, you know, I figured I had to accept it, if I wanted to get what I was there to get," Shannon said. "But this is my bed. The only people I want coming in it are me and you."

They started the laundry and then went to their bedrooms to put on new sheets on their beds. Mandey got another blanket for Shannon to put on his bed while all his bedding got washed. She spread it on his bed, then laid down on it.

"Come here," she told Shannon. "Come reclaim your bed."

He laid down next to her.

"We took a big step last night," Mandey said. "At least, I thought it was a big step."

Shannon smiled. "It was," he said. "It was awesome."

They moved closer together and laid facing each other.

"I want to make you happy," Mandey said.

"You do, sweetie," Shannon said. "And I want you to be happy, too."

"I am," she said.

Shannon's distaste for what Charlie might have done in his bed the night before began to dissipate, now that he and Mandey were there together. He felt a little sorry for Charlie. And, hell, how could he blame him for being horny? He had been horny, too. He was lucky enough to have a girlfriend to help him out with it. Charlie had to deal with the object of his desire sleeping in the next room, not interested in him.

After a leisurely make-out session, they went to the kitchen and made themselves meatball sandwiches for lunch, then Mandey began baking some more Christmas cookies with the other half of the cookie dough still in the refrigerator. Shannon laid on the couch and turned on the Giants and Rams wildcard playoff game. Phillip had called him a lucky dog last night. That was for sure. He looked at the Christmas tree that he and Mandey had decorated. She had turned the lights on. It was the most beautiful Christmas tree he had ever seen, and there were tons of presents underneath it. The cookies smelled good baking in the oven. He had a job he liked, and he was making a decent wage. He was away from all the shit that had plagued him for the last three years. And Mandey…he was still stunned that she chose him. He was a very lucky dog.

55

Christmas

On Christmas morning Mandey woke up as it was getting light in her bedroom. She turned over to look at Shannon, who was still asleep next to her in her bed. His face was peaceful, and he seemed so young and vulnerable.

She reached over to her nightstand, quietly opened the drawer, and brought out a hand towel and a jar of petroleum jelly. She decided she would wake Shannon up with her Christmas surprise for him.

With a glob of petroleum jelly on the fingers of one hand, she gently made her way with her other hand under the covers to Shannon's shorts. She found his penis already stiff. She smiled as she pulled it out of his briefs, applied the lubricant, and began to stroke it.

"Mmmm," Shannon murmured, then opened his eyes.

He looked at Mandey for a moment, not quite sure he was awake, and asked her, "What are you doing?"

"Merry Christmas," she said, still smiling as she continued to stroke him.

"Mmmm," Shannon said again, rolling from his side onto his back and pushing the covers off. He closed his eyes. If Mandey wanted to do this, he was going to lie back and enjoy it.

He had done his share of jacking off, but it felt so much better having someone do it to him. He imagined making love to her, and how it would feel to have her underneath him, naked and kissing and touching him. Then he found himself thinking of her taking him into her mouth.

That last thought helped send him into climax. "Oh, Mandey. Oh, God. Mandey, I'm coming!" he gasped.

He came hard, semen spewing onto Mandey's hand. She continued to stroke him until his orgasm totally subsided, then Mandey took the towel from the top of the nightstand and wiped her hands and his genitals.

Shannon reached up to stroke her hair. "Thank you."

"You're welcome," she told him, tossing the towel onto the floor and bending down to kiss him. She lay down next to him again. Shannon pulled up his drawers and they pulled the covers up over themselves.

Shannon wrapped his arms around Mandey and kissed her. "You didn't have to do that," he said.

"I know," Mandey said. "I wanted to. I want to make you happy in every way."

"You do," Shannon told her, kissing her forehead. "You have made me so happy ever since we met."

"I'm glad," Mandey said, and kissed his shoulder. "After the life you've had, you deserve a little happiness."

"But what can I do to make you happy?" Shannon asked.

"Just keep on doing what you've been doing. Keep on loving me," she replied.

"But tell me how I can show you that I love you. How can I prove it?"

"You prove it every day, Shannon," Mandey replied. "You prove it when I see you looking at me like I'm the most wonderful thing on Earth."

Shannon smiled. "That's because you are."

Mandey smiled back. "Every time you kiss me or touch me, I know how much you love me," she said.

Shannon pressed his lips to hers, then slowly eased on top of her, kissing her torridly. Mandey embraced him and kissed back. She wanted to make love to him but was determined to wait awhile yet. Maybe not all the way until her birthday, but a while. She didn't want to make a mistake. It didn't seem like it would be a mistake, but she wanted to be absolutely sure. Still with each day, the desire to have him completely grew stronger.

Shannon felt a stirring in his groin as he kissed Mandey, despite having expended himself. He wanted her more than he had ever wanted a girl, but he wasn't going to push her. He could wait until she was ready, especially if she repeated her surprise from this morning once in a while.

They stopped kissing, and Shannon saw Mandey smiling up at him.

"I love it when you kiss me that way," she told him.

"Like this?" he asked, and kissed her some more.

"Yes, like that," she said. "Are you ready to get up and see what Santa brought us?"

Shannon sighed dramatically. "I guess so, but I bet Santa didn't bring me nothin' but a lump of coal."

Mandey shook her head and smiled bigger. "I think Santa knows you're really a good boy. I'll bet he left something nice for you."

"I already got everything I want, anyway," Shannon said.

They took turns washing up, and fifteen minutes later they were in the living room with Marcia. The Christmas tree was lit and gifts were piled under and around it.

"Our dad always passed out the presents on Christmas morning," Marcia said. "Shannon, would you mind doing the honors?"

"Sure," he said, going over to the tree.

As he passed out the gifts, he was surprised each time he picked up a package that said "To Shannon" on it. After they were all distributed, he stared at the stack in front of him.

"I think I've got more presents now than I've gotten in all my Christmases put together," he said.

"Are you going to open them today, or are you saving them for next Christmas?" Marcia asked him, teasing.

"I just want to look at them awhile so I can remember this."

"I can take care of that," Mandey said, running to her bedroom and returning with her camera.

"Smile," she said to Shannon, and snapped a picture of him in the middle of the living room floor with his presents.

Shannon began unwrapping the gifts he had received. When he was finished, he had a shaving kit, cologne, a pair of jeans, two new shirts, aa maroon and gray pullover sweater, a music store gift certificate, an AM/FM radio and cassette player, a Swiss army knife key chain, a watch, a backpack for school, a comforter for his bed, and an ID bracelet with an engraved message from Mandey.

"Wow," he said when he was through. "Thanks!"

"You're welcome, sweetie," Mandey said, hugging him.

He felt bad because Mandey and Marcia had bought him most of those gifts, and he had only been able to buy them a couple little presents each. But he realized they had lots of presents from other people, so it didn't really matter. Still, he wished he could have bought Mandey more.

Mandey, however, was delighted with what he had gotten her: a heart-shaped pink crystal-studded pendant on a silver chain and a scarlet baby doll nightie with matching panties.

When she opened the nightie, she glanced at Shannon, her face almost as red as the gown. She wasn't about to take it out of the box in front of Marcia.

"What's that?" Marcia asked her.

"Uh," Mandey said hesitating, "it's a nightgown."

"Let's see it."

Mandey reluctantly held it up.

"Oh, isn't that cute? Shannon, did you give that to her?"

"Yeah, I did," he said proudly.

Mandey looked at him, embarrassed.

"Oh, don't look at him that way," Marcia said. "I'm the one who told him to get you something like that."

"You did?" Mandey asked.

"Do you like it?" Shannon asked her.

"I love it," Mandey said. "It's adorable."

Besides Shannon's gifts, Mandey received several new outfits, jewelry, record and book store gift certificates, make-up, perfume, candy, a typewriter, and an Atari video game system.

Shannon looked at all the presents and suddenly thought about his sister Annette. He felt a pang of sadness knowing that she would be lucky to get a pack of cigarettes for Christmas. His mind flashed back to the Christmas he was five, a couple years before his father died. The memory was brief and hazy, but he remembered getting one of those stick horses and a sheriff's outfit—a hat, a tin badge, a vest, and a belt with two play six-guns. He had played with that forever, it seemed. He remembered Annette, with her long curls in pigtails, screaming with joy when she saw the doll she had wanted for months. They hadn't gotten many other presents, but it had been a really happy holiday.

After they threw away all the torn Christmas wrapping and took their gifts to their rooms, Mandey, Shannon, and Marcia sat at the kitchen table drinking coffee and breakfasting on baklava and rugelach. The turkey was already in the oven and making the house smell good.

Shannon could not get Annette or his mother out of his mind. He was thankful he was here having this glorious holiday, but it was bittersweet. He hadn't expected to feel that way; he had thought that once he was out of that hellhole, he wouldn't have given them a second thought. He knew they probably weren't sitting there at home wishing he was there for the holiday.

After breakfast, as he and Mandey hooked up her new Atari system to her television, Mandey asked him, "What's bothering you?"

Shannon hadn't known Mandey had noticed. He almost replied, "Nothing," but he knew that Mandey knew him well enough to know better.

"I've been thinking about my mom and Annette," he said. "I was thinking how different our Christmas is compared to what they're probably doing."

"I guess Christmas at your house wasn't very merry," Mandy said.

"No," Shannon said. He was quiet for a minute. "Well, I wasn't there for Christmas last year. I was in jail. They let the families come visit and have Christmas dinner, but mine didn't show up. I know it's because Leon wouldn't drive Momma to see me. It wasn't fun being there all alone with nothin' on Christmas.

"The year before sucked, too," he continued. "It started out not too bad, but Leon began drinking around noon, and by the time it was time to eat, he was stinking mean drunk.

We had a turkey, and Momma was so happy, but we didn't get to eat it. Leon got mad at Momma for some stupid little thing I can't even remember now, and they started fighting, and he ended up taking the turkey and tossing it out the window. Momma started crying, and I got into it with Leon. He was too drunk to fight back too much, so that was one time I was able to get the better of him. He left swearing that he was never going to come back, and Momma kept on crying, and we had to eat lunchmeat with our mashed potatoes instead of turkey."

Mandey had big tears in her green eyes.

"Don't cry," he told her, and put his arms around her. She hugged him.

"Other Christmases weren't so bad," he said. "The two we had when Leon was in prison were pretty good. We could afford Christmas dinner, and we had presents."

Shannon fiddled with the wires of the video game system for a few more minutes, then said, "I feel like I should at least call Momma to wish her a merry Christmas and let her know I'm all right."

"Why don't you?" Mandey said. "It'll probably make you feel better, anyway."

"I should, shouldn't I?"

"I think so."

He picked up Mandey's phone and dialed the number. It rang eight times before someone answered.

"Hello?"

"Merry Christmas, Momma. It's Shannon."

"Shannon? Mijo, where have you been? Where are you?"

"I'm okay, Momma. I'm still in town. I couldn't stand living there with Leon no more."

"Well, he ain't here no more."

"He ain't? Where'd he go?"

"He left last week and said he was going to visit his sister, and he ain't never comin' back. I hope the son-of-a-bitch don't."

Shannon covered the mouthpiece with his hand. "Leon's gone," he said to Mandey. "Maybe for good this time, but he's said that plenty of times before."

"Why don't you—" Mandey began.

"Hold on a second, Momma," Shannon said into the phone, then covered the mouthpiece again. "What, Mandey?"

"Well, maybe it's too dangerous, but I was thinking maybe you could take her some Christmas dinner later. We have so much food here…"

Shannon thought about this for a moment and nodded. "Momma, is it okay if I stop by later to see you?" he asked.

"Of course," she said. "I want to see my son on Christmas."

"Is 'Nette home?"

"She's sleeping. Do you want to talk to her?"

"No," Shannon said. "I'll talk to her when I'm there. I'll probably be by around five, okay?"

"It is, but Shannon, I didn't make dinner. I couldn't afford it, and I didn't get to the food shelf this month."

"Don't worry, Momma," he said. "It's okay. And Momma? Don't tell Annette I'm coming over. I want it to be a surprise."

After he hung up, he looked at Mandey and said, "Do you think we'll have enough left over to feed Momma and Annette?"

"Of course," Mandey said. "She's at home, too?"

"Right now she is," Shannon said. "That don't mean she will be later. I told Momma not to tell her we're coming over because I don't want her to tell any of the Devils."

"You said 'we,'" Mandey said. "You want me to go with you?"

"Well, yeah," Shannon said. "I mean, you don't have to, but I promise I won't let anything happen to you. I wouldn't go myself, but I know Raff won't be there. Every year he and his family go to Monterrey for a week over Christmas, so he and Marco and Juanita will be gone. I can handle Annette and anyone else we come across, but we probably won't."

"Well, if you want me with you, I'll go," Mandey said, feeling a bit nervous.

"I always want you with me, and I wouldn't be taking you if I didn't think we'd be safe," Shannon said. "And...I kind of want my mom to meet you."

"Okay," Mandey said. She thought it was sweet that he wanted her to meet his mother.

They went back to working on the Atari system. Mandey was thinking about Annette and Shannon's mother, with no Christmas dinner, and probably no presents.

"You know, Shannon," she said, "if we go see your mom and Annette, we ought to have some kind of gift for each of them."

"They're lucky they're even getting dinner," Shannon said. "It's a nice thought, but we can't go out and get anything for them; everything's closed."

Mandey thought for a second. "Well, it may be a little tacky to recycle Christmas gifts, but you know that black and silver blouse Georgia gave me? Not only is it a size too small for me, but I already have one exactly like it. Do you think Annette might like it?"

Shannon shrugged. "Sure."

"Now what about your mom? What does she like?"

Shannon thought about this for several moments. "To be honest, I don't know too much about what she likes. I know she likes candy."

"And you're wrong about everything being closed. Kroger's is open today from eleven 'til four. We could run by there and get a box of candy. What else?"

Shannon shrugged again. "Maybe some perfume? She used to like it, but I don't think she's had any in a long time."

"Between Marcia and me, we got about four or five different bottles of perfume today. Maybe you can give her one of those, or we can check out the perfume counter at Kroger's. It might be all picked over, but they probably have something left."

"She used to like some kind—I forget the name. It had a pink box, and there was a woman on it," Shannon said.

Mandey thought for a moment. "White Shoulders?" It was her grandmother's favorite.

"I think that might be it," Shannon said. "I'll know it when I see it."

"Well, let's go down to Kroger's now and get the candy and see if they have any White Shoulders, then we can get everything wrapped and ready to go."

Kroger was crowded, considering it was Christmas Day. It looked as though some people had waited until that day to do shopping for their Christmas dinner. Others had cartloads of beer and snacks in anticipation of spending the day glued to their televisions watching sports. And, of course, there were the many people who either had forgotten something important, or who were trying to compensate for the unexpected, like Mandey and Shannon.

The Christmas candy aisle was full of empty shelves, but Shannon and Mandey managed to find two Whitman's chocolate samplers. At the perfume counter they found a bottle of White Shoulders cologne. It was the last one.

"This perfume is really popular with mothers and grandmothers," the woman at the perfume counter said as she rang up their purchase. "We sell a lot of it around Mother's Day, too."

Mandey was glad they could check out at the perfume counter because there was no line there. Only one regular checkout lane was open along with the express lane, and both were at least six deep with customers. Shannon took the bag; they bypassed the lines, and headed for the door.

"Excuse me, sir, but I need to check what you have in that bag," a voice said from behind them.

Shannon jumped, startled. Mandey froze in her tracks.

Shit, I didn't do anything, Shannon thought.

They quickly turned around to see Georgia standing there, laughing.

"God, Georgia, you scared us to death!" Mandey said, starting to laugh. "What are you doing here?"

Georgia was still laughing at her little joke. "Poor Shannon!" she said. "I thought you were going to jump right out of your skin!"

"Jesus, Georgia, it's not funny," he said, but sounded more relieved than angry.

"Well, you looked funny," she said, reaching over to give his arm an affectionate squeeze. "What are y'all doing?"

"We came to do some last-minute Christmas shopping," Mandey said. "We're taking

Christmas dinner over to Shannon's mom and sister later, and we came by to get them some candy and some perfume for his mom."

"Oh, that's nice," Georgia said. "I came to get stuff to make banana pudding. The whole family is coming over for dinner tonight. Hey, why don't you and Shannon come by? We're going to eat around seven."

Mandey looked at Shannon. He shrugged.

"We might come by," Mandey said. "We're supposed to go by his mom's around five."

"Well, come over if you want. We're having plenty of food," Georgia said. "And, yeah, thanks for the daily organizer. Lord knows I have enough in my life to organize."

"You're welcome, and thanks for the blouse," Mandey said.

"Oh, good. Did it fit?" Georgia asked. "I saw it at Weiner's and thought, 'That looks like Mandey,' so I bought it."

"Oh, yeah. It fit just right," Mandey said, looking at Shannon.

"I've got to run. I've got to get cornbread stuffing, too, and Mom's expecting it in a hurry. I'll see you tonight," Georgia said, wheeling her grocery cart around.

"Okay," Mandey said. "See you later."

She and Shannon continued on their way out. "Damn," Shannon said as they walked through the parking lot. "She scared the shit out of me. I don't know why. I knew I didn't do nothing."

"That was rather perverse, wasn't it?" Mandey remarked.

"You've got some weird friends, Mandey."

"I know."

At one-thirty Mandey, Shannon, and Marcia sat down to their Christmas dinner. Michael had visitation with his two children over Christmas, and they were having Christmas dinner with Michael's parents and extended family. Dinner was every bit as extensive as the Thanksgiving feast they had had. In addition to the monster turkey, there were mashed potatoes, stuffing, gravy, squash, broccoli and cheese, cucumber salad, celery with cream cheese, olives, hot rolls, and pumpkin pie for dessert. They all ate until they couldn't eat anymore, and still there were leftovers galore. None of them ate pie right away.

Mandey fixed up the plates to take to Shannon's mother and Annette. Shannon wasn't sure what they liked or didn't like, so Mandey gave them each something of everything. In aluminum pie plates she loaded sliced turkey, stuffing, potatoes, rolls, and vegetables. She filled a medium-sized plastic container with gravy. On a separate plate she placed some cucumber salad, celery, and olives, and on another she put two slices of pumpkin pie and Christmas sugar cookies. Then she wrapped everything in plastic wrap and tin foil and put it all in a shallow cardboard box.

At four-thirty they left in Shannon's car with the food and the wrapped presents. Mandey noticed Shannon smiling.

"You look happy," she said.

"Oh," he said, now conscious of his expression. "I am. It's good to be doing something nice for someone for a change."

"That's good," Mandey said. "When I met you, I got the impression that you hated your family."

Shannon thought for a moment. "I don't hate my mother and my sister. I hate some of the things they do, but I don't hate them," he said. "If I could have a Christmas wish, it would be that Leon would never come back."

Shannon parked the car in the alley behind the apartment building to be as unobtrusive as possible, and he and Mandey walked around to the front. He glanced over to the building where Raff lived with his aunt and uncle, Marco's parents. (They were Juanita's aunt and uncle, as well, but Raff was blood kin to his uncle and Juanita was blood kin to her aunt, so they weren't blood kin to each other at all.) The old blue pick-up truck with the camper on the back that belonged to Marco's father was gone. Shannon knew they must have loaded up and left for Mexico for the holidays.

They went upstairs, and Shannon knocked on the door to the apartment. He was about to turn the doorknob and go inside when the door opened.

"Mijo! Come in!" his mother greeted him.

Shannon's mother looked about the same as she had the time Mandey had seen her up at school three years ago. She was short and plump with frizzy bleached hair. She was dressed in a large gray sweatshirt, baby blue warm-up pants, and fuzzy pink slippers. She was far removed from the pretty woman in the wedding picture Shannon had shown her, but in the puffy, haggard face Mandey could still see evidence that they were the same person.

"Merry Christmas, Momma," Shannon said, and Mandey followed him inside.

The apartment hadn't changed much since they day Mandey had been there with Shannon, except in one corner of the living room there was now a short, sick-looking Christmas tree, nearly dead, with some tinsel and a few ornaments on it. It depressed Mandey more to see that sad effort to decorate for the holiday than seeing an apartment totally devoid of decoration.

Shannon took the box holding the two dinners to the kitchen and put it on the counter. Mandey put the presents under the little tree.

"What's this?" Shannon's mother asked.

"Christmas dinner for you and Annette," he said, showing her. "Turkey and dressing, potatoes, vegetables, pumpkin pie for dessert. You'll have to heat the plates in the oven and heat the gravy on the stove."

"Don't that look good?" his mother exclaimed, bustling over to preheat the oven. "You don't know how I've been thinking about a real Christmas dinner!"

"Well, now you got one," Shannon said. "We brought presents, too. Where are the presents, Mandey?"

"I put them under the tree," Mandey said.

"Shannon, you haven't introduced your friend to me," his mother admonished him. "I didn't know you were bringing company or I would have cleaned up the house."

Shannon went over to Mandey and put his arm around her. "Momma, this is Mandey, my girlfriend," he said, smiling down at Mandey. "Mandey, this is my mom."

"It's nice to meet you," Mandey said, holding her hand out to her.

Shannon's mother looked her over, looked at her son's beaming face, and back to Mandey again. "I'm Deborah. So, I see you've stolen my boy's heart," she said, taking Mandey's hand.

Mandey gave an embarrassed little laugh. "I guess I did, but I gave him mine in return," she said.

"Well, come and sit down," Deborah said to them.

She sat down in the armchair. Mandey sat on the couch, and Shannon went over to the tree and picked up the gifts for his mother.

"It's not much," he said, laying the two packages in her lap. "I wasn't planning on coming here today until you said that Leon was gone. We had to shop at the last minute."

"Oh, Shannon, I don't have presents for you!" she objected, picking up one of the gifts.

"It's okay, Momma," he said. "I had a good Christmas." He sat down on the sofa next to Mandey to watch his mother open her presents.

"Oh, my!" she exclaimed when she opened her perfume. "I haven't had a new bottle of perfume in years! Thank you!"

She immediately opened it and put some on. "I always loved this kind. I used to wear it when you were little-bitty. How did you remember?"

Shannon smiled. "I remembered it had a picture of a lady on it, and whenever you wore it, you smelled nice. Mandey knew what kind it was."

"Your father used to buy me perfume all the time—for Christmas, for birthdays, Valentine's Day, Mother's Day," his mother said. "You look so much like him, Shannon. You got your dark hair and dark eyes from me, but in all other ways, you are your father's son."

Mandey noticed the pleased expression on Shannon's face. She was glad his mother had told him that.

"I'm glad you like it, Momma," Shannon said. "Open the other one."

She tore the paper off the candy box. "Oh, my favorite chocolates! I'm gonna sit in front of the TV tonight and eat my candy, if I can keep Annette out of it."

"We brought her a box of her own, so don't you give her any of yours," Shannon said. "Where is she, anyway?"

"Off somewheres. She got up right after you called and left. Probably at Dewayne's."

"Well, she's got two presents under the tree and a plate of food waiting for her when she comes in," Shannon said.

"Where have you been?" his mother asked. "I know you and Leon had a terrible fight and all your things were gone, and I haven't heard from you in almost a month! Why didn't you call?"

"I'm sorry, Momma. I had to get out of here. I've moved in with Mandey and her mother. I know I should have called. I didn't mean to worry you."

His mother nodded. "I don't blame you for leaving. I'm glad for you. And it looks like you're getting along okay," she said, looking him over. "I almost didn't recognize you at the door, with that haircut and that fancy sweater."

Shannon grinned sheepishly. "Yeah, I'm getting along real good."

"Annette said you don't work at the gas station no more, either," his mother said.

"Nope," Shannon said. "I've got a new job, learning how to remodel houses. I'm getting full-time hours and making a lot more than I did at the gas station."

"Good," his mother said. "I'm glad you aren't working for that bastard's gas station anymore. He never paid you right or gave you good hours."

"I'm glad, too, Momma. I like this job a lot better," he said. "Next month I'm going back to school at night to get my G.E.D. Once I do that, I think I'm going to start taking some college classes."

"College?" his mother asked, surprised. "I never knew you wanted to go to college."

Shannon looked at Mandey. "Well, Momma, I didn't know, either. For a long time, I didn't know what I wanted to do with myself. I knew things couldn't go on the way they were. Mandey made me realize I had to at least finish high school, and she said I ought to take some college classes, too, to train for a career. She's going to start college in the fall, too."

"I can't believe it," his mother said, her hand going to her forehead as though she were going to manually force this information into her brain. "My son, my baby, going to college. I'm so proud of you!"

Shannon grinned sheepishly again. "Well, I haven't started yet, and I'm probably only going to go for a one-year certificate or a two-year degree."

"I am so happy," his mother said. "I'm so happy you found this girl you love, and I'm so glad you're going back to school. I hate to think what would have happened if you'd let that little blonde piece of trash sink her claws into you. She'd probably have two babies by now and you'd be handing over your scrawny paycheck from the garage to feed them."

"Momma, I went with her for two or three weeks over two years ago. It never got that serious," Shannon said, then said to Mandey, "She don't like Kerri, either."

"Anyway, Momma," Shannon went on, changing the subject, "how are you doing? Do you really think Leon's gone for good this time?"

"I hope so," Shannon's mother said. "I threw an ashtray at his head when he was leaving, but I missed, damn it. He ain't going to be back for a while."

Mandey looked at the heavy green glass ashtray on the coffee table. She realized it should have been round, but instead it had a flat, rough edge.

"Momma, if he does come back, I wish you wouldn't take him back. It don't matter to me anymore, but you don't need him. He's bad for you."

"What makes you think I'm going to take that low-life, lying son-of-a-bitch back?" Shannon's mother demanded.

"You always do, and he's made us all miserable. I'm begging you, don't do it this time. You don't need him."

"Shannon, I don't want to talk about this. I'm telling you, I ain't taking him back no more. I know I don't need the likes of him. I got on just fine without him when he was in jail, remember?"

"But you still took him back—"

"I said I don't want to talk about Leon! It's going to ruin Christmas."

"Okay," Shannon relented, but Mandey knew by the look in his eyes that the subject was far from closed.

"You don't say much, do you?" Shannon's mother said to Mandey.

Mandey smiled awkwardly. "I'm the quiet type, I guess."

"Shannon ain't the type to talk too much, either," his mother said. "It's a wonder you two ever got to know each other."

Shannon and Mandey smiled at each other. "It's a long story," Shannon said. "I'll tell you about it sometime, Momma."

"Well, I don't mean to be rude, but I'm about starved, so if you don't mind, I'm going to put my dinner in to heat," Deborah said.

"Go ahead, Momma," Shannon said. "We can only stay a few more minutes, anyway. We're going over to Mandey's friend's house a little later."

When they were going out the door, his mother hugged him. Mandey noticed how happy he looked as he returned the hug.

"Don't go another whole month without calling," his mother told him.

"I won't, Momma. I promise."

"It was good to meet you," Deborah said to Mandey, opening her arms to give her a hug.

"You, too," Mandey replied, hugging her back.

As they walked outside, Mandey said to Shannon, "That went well."

"Yeah, it did," Shannon said. "I'm glad we came."

They heard footsteps on the stairs coming down from the second floor, followed by two loud female voices.

"Oh, shit," Shannon said.

Coming down the stairs were Annette and Kerri.

Holy crap, Mandey thought.

The two girls stopped in their tracks, looking down at them. "What the hell happened to you?" Annette demanded of Shannon.

Kerri stared at Mandey in disbelief. "What the hell are you doing here?"

Annette turned her attention to Mandey and gave her a piercing stare. "You're the bitch who broke my nose!"

"Trick, what the fuck are you doing with her?" Kerri demanded.

"I don't fucking believe you," Annette said to Shannon, coming the rest of the way down the stairs and standing in front of him. Kerri followed. "You disappear after a gang-bang, which we lost thanks to you, and your stuff disappears a couple days later, and then you show up here with this bitch—"

"We just came by to wish Momma a merry Christmas," Shannon said. He took Mandey by the hand and tried to walk around Annette and Kerri.

"No!" Kerri screamed, and grabbed Mandey by the hair, causing Mandey to yelp in pain. "How could you choose this bitch over me? How could you?"

Shannon whirled around and smacked Kerri across the face with his open hand, making her let go of Mandey's hair. He had finally hit her, something he had been able to refrain from doing for over two years. Assaulting his girlfriend was something he couldn't ignore.

He grabbed Kerri by the arms, much the way he had in his car the day they had visited the jewelry store together, and pulled her close and looked her in the eyes.

"You don't touch her," he said in a deadly quiet voice.

"Let her go!" Annette cried, punching Shannon in the side. He didn't seem to notice.

Shannon gave Kerri a little shove and released her. "Go away, Kerri. I want to talk to my sister for a minute."

"I don't got to listen to you," Kerri said, pouting. "You ain't leader of the Devils no more. You ain't nothing no more."

"Fine. Whatever," Shannon said, and paid no further attention to her. He turned to his sister.

"You're a goddamn traitor," Annette spat at Shannon.

"Oh, get over it," Shannon said, disgusted. "Y'all didn't want me around no more, anyway, so what's the big deal?"

"I knew you was getting ready to quit, but I didn't think you'd be going over to the enemy's side," Annette said.

"I didn't go to the enemy's side!" Shannon insisted. "Mandey quit the Alley Cats the same night I disappeared. Whatever's going on between y'all and the Alley Cats now has nothin' to do with me or Mandey."

"Bullshit!" Kerri screeched. "We know you're one of them now! Look at you! You can't deny it!"

"You're all dressed up like some rich boy," Annette sneered. "You ain't nothing but poor white trash, Trick. No fancy sweater or fancy watch or fancy haircut can change that."

"Annette, I'm not going to fight with you. You're going to think what you want, anyway," Shannon said wearily. "We brought Momma some presents and some Christmas dinner to warm up. There's a plate of food for you, too, Annette, and two presents under the tree. Let's go, Mandey."

"Wait a second. You brought Christmas dinner and presents?" Annette asked.

"Yeah. Don't thank me. It was Mandey's idea. Merry Christmas."

"I don't need your fucking charity!" Annette called after them as they walked away.

"Fine. Do like Leon and toss it all out the window. I don't give a damn," Shannon said.

Shannon stalked to his car in silence with Mandey following a half step behind, watching him anxiously. After they got in the car and left the apartments, Shannon let out a long sigh.

"It was nice until Annette and Kerri showed up," he said.

"Yeah," Mandey agreed.

"Although it could have been worse. I think Annette's more jealous than anything."

"I suppose they'll tell the rest of the gang that they saw us together," Mandey said.

"Yeah," Shannon said. "I ain't too worried about it, though."

Shannon's spirits lifted as they got farther away from the apartments. However, Mandey found herself becoming more troubled. She wondered if the Devils wouldn't be able to track Shannon down if they wanted to. Mandey hoped that Annette and the rest of the gang would let the issue rest and leave Shannon alone, but part of her was convinced that the trouble was far from over.

Back at the Northview Apartments, Annette and Kerri went inside Annette's apartment. Deborah was sitting in the armchair, eating her Christmas dinner.

"'Nette, your brother was just here," she said between mouthfuls. "Look what he brought—a real Christmas dinner! There's two presents for you, too."

"Yeah, I just saw him," Annette said.

"Him and that bitch," Kerri added.

"Where do you get off calling my son's girlfriend a bitch?" Deborah asked through a mouthful of turkey.

"She's the bitch who broke my nose," Annette said.

"Her? That quiet little girl? Why did she do that?"

"Because she's a fucking bitch, that's why!" Annette said angrily.

"I don't understand," Deborah said. "What is Shannon doing with her, then?"

"I have no idea," Annette muttered. Her will was getting weak. The plate of food her mother had looked and smelled so good, and she hadn't eaten anything but a bag of potato chips all day.

"She's a snob and a stuck-up bitch, just like all the rest of them Alley Cats," Kerri said.

"She's one of them kids y'all have been fighting with?"

"Yeah. Now he's gone over to their side," Kerri said.

"Well, he looks good, and he's doing real good, from what he told me. He's even going to start college in the fall. Maybe you girls would do good to run off with some of those boys," Deborah said.

"College?" Annette said, remembering the conversation she had had with Shannon in Taco Bell. Of course, Mandey had been the "friend" who put that idea in his head.

"Yes, college. He's going to get his G.E.D. and then go to college."

Annette sat down on the floor and took the two presents out from under the Christmas tree.

"Are you going to open them?" Kerri asked her.

Annette stared at the brightly-colored wrapped packages. Tears came to her eyes, and she didn't know why. She didn't give Kerri a reply, and began to tear open the first package. It was a one-pound box of chocolates.

"Ooooh," Kerri said. "Candy."

Annette silently laid the box aside and opened the next. She held up the blouse for Kerri and her mother to see.

"I like that!" Kerri said. "If you don't want it, I'll take it." She was hoping Annette wouldn't want it. She wouldn't mind having the box of candy, either.

"That's real nice, Annette. It'll look real pretty on you," Deborah said.

Annette was quiet for a moment, then said. "Shannon said it was his girlfriend's idea to do all this. Why would she go out of her way to do anything for me? Why are they being so nice?"

"They're just trying to rub it in, to show that they've got everything you don't," Kerri said.

"That's not true," Deborah said. "Shannon's a good boy; he cares about his mother and sister."

"That's a bunch of bullshit," Kerri said. "Trick don't care about no one but himself."

"Will you quit calling him that name? I gave him a name, and that's not it," Deborah said.

"He earned it," Kerri said. "That's all he ever wanted to do, go be a trick for some whore somewhere, even when I wanted to be his girlfriend."

"I'd rather he go visit some whore than be stuck with a girl like you," Deborah said.

Kerri stood up. "I don't have to sit here and listen to you badmouth me!" she shouted. She stomped out of the apartment, slamming the door behind her.

"Good riddance!" Deborah shouted after her.

Annette sat there, oblivious to her mother and Kerri's exchange, looking at the box of chocolates and the blouse. Then she got up and went to the kitchen to heat up her dinner.

Later that evening, Shannon and Mandey celebrated Christmas with the Cornells. The house was jammed with Georgia's sisters, brothers, cousins, aunts, uncles, nieces, nephews, and other assorted relations. The feast was huge, as it had to be to feed that many people. Everyone grabbed a Chinet plate, served themselves, and sat down wherever they could find a spot. After dinner, although it was dark and getting chilly, a bonfire was lit, and Georgia's new volleyball net was set up in the front yard. The younger folks played in the beams from the porch light and outdoor security light. Then they turned out the lights and set off fireworks and lit up sparklers. Mandey's troubled thoughts had dissipated long ago, and Shannon had the time of his life.

56

Sick

The next morning, Mandey woke up sick.

"Ohhh," she groaned, burying her face in her pillow.

"Are you okay?" Shannon asked her. He was up and finishing dressing for work.

"Ionfeegud."

"What?"

Mandey lifted her head slightly. "I don't feel good," she repeated, and fell limp on the pillow again. "Ow."

"You sounded like you were getting sick last night. Playing volleyball out in that cold night air probably didn't do you any good, either," he said, sitting down on the edge of the bed.

"Don't come too close or you'll catch it," Mandey said, moving away from him.

Shannon rolled his eyes. "You were breathing on me all night, so I'm probably already infected," he told her.

"Hnng," Mandey said, turning over onto her back and laying her arm across her eyes.

"Where do you feel bad? Your head or your throat…?"

"All over," she replied. "My head aches and feels all stuffed up, my throat feels like I swallowed a cactus plant, I can't breathe through my nose, I ache all over from playing volleyball, and to top it all off, I'm having the worst menstrual cramps I've had in I-don't-know-when."

"In other words, you feel like shit," Shannon said.

Mandey managed a dry chuckle and took her arm from her eyes. "Yes. A big, steaming, stinky pile of it."

"Ewww, you're gross," Shannon said, but looked more amused than disgusted. "I hate to leave you alone when you're feeling so bad. I'd rather stay here and take care of you."

"I'll be okay," she murmured.

"Can I bring you home something from the store?" he asked.

She closed her eyes and thought for a moment. "Mmmmm, yeah. Some 7-Up, some orange-pineapple juice, and a bottle of Nyquil."

"Seven-Up, orange-pineapple juice, and Nyquil," Shannon repeated, committing the items to memory.

"And a couple cans of soup. Chicken noodle, chicken and rice, chicken and stars—any of those."

"Chicken soup. All the things to make you feel better."

"I hope," Mandey said. "My purse is over there. There should be a twenty-dollar bill in it."

"I'll buy it, Mand. Don't worry about it," Shannon said, standing up. "I'd better get a move on. Now, you stay in bed and rest, you hear?"

"Yes, sir," Mandey replied. "But before you go, could you do a couple things for me?"

"Sure. What?"

"Bring me the box of tissues from the bathroom, and the jar of Vicks, and a glass of water and put them here on the nightstand. And look in the bottom drawer of my bureau. There's supposed to be a heating pad in there."

Shannon brought her the items she requested, plus a bottle of Comtrex cold pills he found in the medicine cabinet.

"Take these," he told her.

Mandey grimaced. "I don't like them. They make me all spaced out," she said.

"Cold pills space you out?" Shannon asked in disbelief. "Damn, I hate to see what Nyquil's gonna do to you."

"I've never taken Nyquil before, so I don't know. I guess we'll find out," Mandey said. "Seriously, the last time I took Comtrex I laid on my bed for an hour and a half and stared at the ceiling. I couldn't fall asleep, but I couldn't get up the energy to do anything else, either. I hated it."

"Well, they're here if you change your mind," he said, setting them down on her stand.

He plugged in her heating pad and kissed the top of her head.

"Love you. I hope you feel better."

"Me, too. Love you, too."

It was the first time Mandey had ever been home all alone when she was sick; she had always had her mother there with her, taking her temperature, bringing her hot tea and soup in bed, keeping her comfortable. She lay there in bed, slathered with Vicks, heating pad on her abdomen, feeling sicker than she could ever remember being, and also feeling very lonely.

Her parents had called the day before to wish her a merry Christmas, but she had left with Shannon for his mother's. Mandey decided to call her mother to make up for the call she had missed and to get a little comfort and sympathy. As usual, her mother picked up the phone on the second ring.

"Hi, Ma, it's me," Mandey said.

"Mandey, what's wrong? You sound sick."

Mandey smiled to herself. Her mother hadn't changed.

"I don't feel too good. My head's all stuffed up and my throat hurts."

"Marcia didn't say anything about you being sick yesterday."

"I felt okay yesterday. Well, I started feeling a little bad last night, but when I woke up this morning, I didn't even want to move."

"Do you have a temperature?"

"I don't know. I don't think so."

"Well, if you don't feel better in a couple of days, you'd better go to the doctor. You don't want to let it go and turn into something serious."

"We'll see," Mandey hedged. She didn't mind going to the doctor, but she didn't like to go unless it was necessary. "I'm sure I'll start feeling better tomorrow."

"I don't like this," her mother said, sounding like she was starting to cry. "I should be taking care of you when you're sick."

"Oh, Ma, it's okay," Mandey said, hating that she had upset her mother. "Shannon's at work right now, but he's going to bring home some juice and 7-Up and cold medicine for me. He'll take care of me when he gets home this afternoon."

"I know, but you shouldn't be home all by yourself when you don't feel good," her mother said. "I don't like being so far away from you. I wish you were up here with us, Mandey."

"Well, I'll probably be there next Christmas," Mandey said. "I couldn't enjoy it much right now being sick, anyway. It probably wouldn't be good for Daddy if I was up there around him like this, either. How is he doing?"

"Pretty good. He still gets tired easily, but he's been getting restless. He shouldn't be out in the cold, so he's staying cooped up here in the house. He keeps talking about going back to work part-time."

"I wish he'd realize he's 66 now, and he's had a major heart attack, so it's okay for him to slow down."

"We moved up here thinking that the slower pace was what he needed, but now I'm wondering if being idle isn't harder on him than working."

They talked about ten minutes, but Mandey's throat was starting to hurt more from the effort.

"Well, thank you for the presents you sent to me and Shannon. We both loved them. And I love you, Ma, and tell Daddy I love him, too, and to take it easy," Mandey said, and sneezed.

"You take care of yourself, Mandey. We love you."

After getting off the phone with her mother, Mandey spent an hour watching *The Price Is Right*. At eleven when it was over, Mandey began trying to motivate herself to get out of bed to scrounge up some lunch. At eleven-fifteen, she finally managed to get herself out into the kitchen. Her head was heavy and pounding, and she could feel fluid moving thickly around in her sinuses. Her throat was sore, so whatever she ate had to go down easy.

Being ill usually had little effect on Mandey's appetite, but today it was hard to think of anything that sounded appealing. She eventually decided to make a scrambled egg sandwich on white bread, which wasn't exactly what she wanted, but it was close enough. With her sandwich and a tall glass of milk mixed with Hershey's chocolate syrup on a tray, she got back into bed and watched the end of *The Young and the Restless* while she ate her lunch. The chocolate milk tasted wonderful and made her throat feel better. She wished she had made an even bigger glass and considered going back to the kitchen to make more, but couldn't get up the gumption to make another trip out there.

The noon news came on, and Mandey decided to forego being informed in favor of playing with her new video game system. However, after about forty-five minutes, her eyes felt hot and she was getting tired. She set her VCR to tape *Guiding Light* at two and snuggled under the blankets to take a nap. She was awakened from a deep sleep at one-thirty by the phone ringing. It took several rings before her head was clear enough to pick it up.

"Hey, Mandey. It's Danny."

"Hey," she said.

"What's wrong?" he asked her.

"I'm sick," Mandey said.

"Oh," Danny said, sounding disappointed. "I was going to ask if you wanted to meet at the library again tomorrow and try to finish up our project. Maybe not."

"Not tomorrow, I don't think," Mandey said. "I don't remember when I've felt this lousy. I might feel better by Friday, though." She sneezed twice.

"Whatever you have, don't give it to me," Danny said. "I'll give you a call Friday morning and see how you're doing."

"Okay, Dan."

"Hope you feel better."

"Thanks."

She hung up the phone and settled down again. It wasn't long before she was asleep again, and this time she slept right through until she heard Shannon coming in the front door.

"Did you rest?" he asked her, sitting down on the edge of the bed.

"I only got up when it was absolutely necessary," Mandey said. "I slept for a few hours, too. I thought I would feel better after I woke up, but I was wrong."

"Want me to fix you a bowl of soup?" he asked her.

"That would be good."

"What kind? I got one of each kind you asked for."

"You got Chicken and Stars?"

"I sure did. Coming up."

A short time later, Shannon, now changed out of his work clothes, returned to the bedroom with a tray for Mandey. On it were a bowl of soup, six saltine crackers, a glass of 7-Up, a smaller glass of orange-pineapple juice, and a can of Snack-Pack chocolate fudge pudding.

"You must be psychic!" Mandey exclaimed, her face lighting up. "I've been thinking about chocolate pudding all day!"

"I'm good," Shannon said, grinning proudly. "I know just what my baby needs."

"You are good," Mandey agreed, raising a spoonful of soup to her mouth. "Mm, mm, good."

"I'm going to get a bowl for myself and eat with you," Shannon said.

He came back with his own meal on a tray, like Mandey's plus a turkey sandwich and minus the juice. He sat down at Mandey's desk to eat.

"How was work?" Mandey asked him.

"Good," he said. "This is a short job. We'll be done by Friday. It'll be a four-day weekend again like this week was."

"Not a lot of hours," Mandey said.

"No, but I did get that overtime before Christmas when we were rushing to get that job finished. It'll pick up again in a few weeks. I'm still doing better than I did working for Grubbs."

After they ate, Mandey took a long, hot bath and changed into clean pajamas. She felt much better. Marcia popped into the room where she and Shannon were spending the evening playing with the Atari to see how she was doing. When Mandey wanted to go to sleep, Shannon left her with a kiss the top of her head and went into his own room, so she could sleep more peacefully by herself, and maybe keep himself from catching her cold, if he hadn't already.

"Thanks for taking care of me, sweetie," she said to him as he left the room. "Love you."

"No sweat," he replied, and blew her a kiss. "Love you too."

57

New Year's Eve

By Friday Shannon had come down with Mandey's bug. He had made it through the work day, but spent Saturday and Sunday mostly in bed. Mandey was feeling somewhat better, and she nursed him through the weekend much the way he had done for her. By the time Monday arrived, they both agreed that neither one was feeling a hundred percent, so they decided that staying home on New Year's Eve would be the best thing to do.

"Are you sure you don't mind?" Shannon asked her when Mandey brought up the subject. "I know you like to get dressed up and go out—"

"Honey, as long as I can ring in the New Year with you, I don't care where we do it," she told him.

Marcia and Michael were going to celebrate at a party at Marcia's friend and colleague, Maxine's, house. Marcia said Mandey and Shannon were invited to come, as well, but Mandey declined.

"We're tired and don't feel like going anywhere," she told Marcia from where she and Shannon were listlessly sprawled on the couch, wrapped together in their big blanket.

Marcia stood in the doorway looking at them. "If you're like this now, I'd hate to see what you'd be like after being married awhile."

About an hour later, the phone rang in Mandey's room. She didn't bother to get up to answer it. After several rings, it stopped, but then the phone in the kitchen started ringing. Mandey slowly got up off the couch and went into the kitchen, but she didn't get to the phone before the machine picked up the call.

"Mandey, it's Georgia. Pick up if you're there."

Mandey put the receiver to her ear. "Hi, Georgia."

"Hey, girl. What are you doing?"

"Shannon and I are on the couch watching TV. What's up with you?"

"You know Jackie's having a party tonight. Are y'all going?"

"No, I don't think so."

"Why? Do y'all have a big date planned?"

"We sure do. We're going to sit on the couch with a big Domino's pizza and watch Dick Clark in Times Square."

"You're kidding, right?"

"No," Mandey said. "Shannon's still kind of sick with the cold I gave him, and I'm not 100% yet. We figured celebrating at home was probably the best."

"Uh-huh," Georgia said with a smirk in her voice. "I get it. You're going to stay home and have a <u>private</u> party."

"That's not what I meant," Mandey said, rolling her eyes and looking at Shannon.

"Well, okay. You two have fun. See you at school on Wednesday."

"Boy, we're a popular couple," Mandey said. "Georgia wanted us to go to Jackie's party, and Andrea called yesterday and wanted us to go with them to see her cousin's band play."

"Are you sure you're not disappointed about not going out?" Shannon asked her again.

"Positive," Mandey replied, getting back on the couch and under the blanket with him. "I'm having pizza with the man of my dreams. What more could a girl ask for?"

"Mandey."

"I'm serious," she said. "There's nothing wrong with watching the ball drop on TV as long as you've got the right person to watch it with you."

By the time Marcia was preparing to leave for Michael's, a fine, cold drizzle had settled over the city.

"Try not to fall asleep before midnight," Marcia said, looking at the two of them on the couch as she put on a clear plastic slicker.

"No guarantees," Shannon said with a yawn.

Mandey got up to look out the screen door as she left.

"I'm glad we don't have to go out in that," she said with her nose pressed against the glass. "Let the delivery guy bring us food so we can sit around in the warm house all night and eat."

"Among other things," Shannon added. He winked when Mandey turned to look at him.

"Are you starting to feel better?" she asked him.

"Not really, but I'm not dead yet," he said, grinning.

He held the quilt open and wrapped her back up as she sat down next to him again. Then he burst into a fit of coughing.

"Man, I feel lousy," he said weakly after the spasm subsided.

Ninety minutes later, they were still on the couch watching MTV with two medium Domino's pizzas, one pepperoni and sausage and one mushroom and onion, on the coffee table in front of them, along with a six-pack of Coke.

"Decadent self-indulgence," Mandey said. "Delivery pizza, mindless television, and thou."

"Huh?" Shannon asked, with cheese dripping down his chin.

They sat there, barely talking, hardly moving, staring at the television and drinking the six-pack of Coke. They both started to doze off. At 10:30 they roused themselves long enough for a bathroom break. Mandey changed the channel to ABC, to Dick Clark's *New Year's Rockin' Eve*. Shannon came staggering back to the living room from the bathroom.

"Man, I don't think I'm going to make it 'til midnight," he said.

Mandey yawned. "Me, neither. Well, we can watch the ball drop at eleven and know it's 1985 on the East Coast. That's good enough for me. I was born on the East Coast, so being here in the Central Time Zone, I'm an hour behind my age. At eleven, I'll be in 1985."

Shannon stared at her. "What?"

"Sorry. I babble when I get tired."

Shannon went to the kitchen and opened the refrigerator.

"Are you getting pie?" Mandey asked.

"No. Too tired to eat," Shannon replied. "That's a first, huh?"

She heard a loud pop and then Shannon re-entered the living room with a bottle of champagne and two plastic champagne glasses.

"Got to toast the New Year," he said.

He sat down on the couch next to her and set the bottle and glasses on the coffee table. They watched Scandal with Patty Smyth and John Waite perform, punctuated by over-enthusiastic chatter from the co-hosts Priscilla Barnes and Adrian Zmed. Then Shannon stood up again.

"I've got to stay awake. Let's dance," he said.

"What?" Mandey asked. "That cold medication must be affecting your brain."

Shannon grabbed her hand and pulled her up.

"A slow dance," he said.

They clung to each other and swayed sleepily, indifferent to the music Night Ranger was playing on TV.

"God, can you imagine if we'd gone out to celebrate tonight?" Mandey asked with a giggle.

"We wouldn't have made it," Shannon said.

"Next year we ought to try doing something livelier," Mandey said.

"We'll worry about that next year."

The countdown to the ball drop began. They sat down on the couch and Shannon poured the champagne.

Mandey chanted the countdown.

"Ten...nine...eight...seven...six...five...four...three...two...one...Happy New Year!"

Shannon kissed Mandey on the stroke of eleven.

"Happy New Year," he said, handing her a plastic champagne glass.

"Happy 1985," she replied.

He lifted his glass. "Let's make a toast," he said. "This year ended good. May next year be even better for both of us."

"Hear, hear," Mandey said, and they tapped their plastic glasses together and each took a sip.

Then it was bedtime. Shannon corked up the champagne and put it away; they threw out their garbage and turned off the TV.

"Mandey, don't be offended, but I'm going to sleep in my room again tonight," Shannon said as they walked down the hall. "I don't want to keep you up with my coughing."

"You're probably more comfortable sleeping by yourself when you're sick. I know I was," Mandey said. She reached up to kiss his cheek. "Happy New Year, sweetie."

58

Annette's Announcement

On the first Friday evening in January, Shannon decided to call his mother to check on how she was doing. He found out that Leon was still gone, thank God, and his mother needed a way to the bank and to do some grocery shopping.

"As long as Leon is gone, I'm going to go over and help my mom out," Shannon told Mandey when he got off the phone. "When Leon's around, he always takes the checks, so Momma has nothing to do with it, but whenever he's been gone and I've been there, I help her with the money. I'm going to take her to the bank to cash the checks and get money orders and I'll take her to the food shelf and the grocery store. Otherwise, she's got no one to take her."

"But what if you're seen?" Mandey asked, worried. She didn't want him getting hurt.

"I'm going early tomorrow morning, and I know how the gang is—they don't usually get going until afternoon. If I come across any of them, I'll just have to deal with it. No one else will take care of my mother."

"Not even your own sister?"

"Annette's too wrapped up in herself to care. She and Dewayne should borrow his mother's car and do errands, but do you think she'd think of doing something like that?" Shannon asked.

"You're a good son," Mandey told him.

"Not as good as I could have been," Shannon said, "but I'm trying."

He got out of bed the next morning at 6:45. He wanted to be at his mother's by eight. He showered and dressed and came back into the bedroom to get his wallet out of his other pants.

"You going now?" Mandey asked sleepily.

"Uh-huh," Shannon said.

"Be careful, sweetie," she said.

"I always am."

He called his mother before he left to make sure she was awake.

"I'll be ready," she assured him.

Shannon's mother greeted him at the door of the apartment looking more together than he had seen her in a long time. She had on navy blue pants, a button-down flowered blouse, and brown loafers. Her hair was combed and pulled back in a bun, and she had on lipstick.

"Got the checks?" he asked her.

"In my purse," she said, tapping her shoulder bag.

"Then let's go."

In the car, he asked her if she wanted to get something to eat. Naturally, the answer was yes. They stopped at McDonald's for coffee and Egg McMuffins and to smoke a cigarette. Then it was to the bank to cash the checks and to get money orders for the rent, phone, and lights. Next, they went to the food shelf, where his mother picked up the monthly staples of government rice and cheese along with some other items, and then Shannon took her to the grocery store to use her food stamps. He used his own money to buy her some extras, too. When they returned to the apartment, it took three trips to haul everything inside.

"What's all this?" Annette asked, standing in the middle of the living room in a T-shirt and sweat pants, rubbing her eyes. "What are you doing back here again?"

"I took Momma to run some errands," Shannon said as he helped his mother put away the groceries. "You and your boyfriend could do that once in a while, you know."

"Annette, are you going to tell your brother the news?" their mother asked.

"What news?" Shannon asked, suspicious.

"Oh, Momma, he don't care," Annette said.

"You're going to be an uncle, Shannon," their mother said.

"What?" he exclaimed, looking at Annette in surprise. "You're pregnant?"

"Yeah," Annette said. "About two months along."

"I thought you had an IUD."

"I did. I got it taken out."

"You what?" Shannon shouted. "Annette, what the hell were you thinking? Is Dewayne going to marry you?"

"Hell, no. Not right now, anyway," Annette said, walking out to join them in the kitchen. "Hey, did you get any Dr Pepper?"

"He had better do the right thing by you, I swear, or I'll—"

"I don't want to marry him right now."

"You want to have his baby, but not him?" Shannon asked.

"Listen, Shannon," Annette said, finding the two-liter bottle of Dr Pepper, putting some ice out of the freezer into a glass, and pouring soda into it. "You wanted to know what

I planned to do once my Social Security checks ran out. Well, this is it. Dewayne took me down to the welfare office, and I found out how much aid I could get by having a baby, but I don't get hardly nothing if I'm married to the baby's father."

"You did this on purpose so you could keep collecting welfare?" Shannon asked in disbelief.

"Oh, quit it. You act like I'm the first girl who ever got pregnant so she could have a roof over her head and food on the table," Annette said.

"There's other ways, Annette," Shannon said. "You could have gotten a job."

"Yeah, like you got so far ahead working for Ed Grubbs," Annette said.

"That was a bunch of bullshit. I've got a real job now, and I am starting to get ahead."

"And it helps to have a rich girlfriend, doesn't it?"

"She's not rich, Annette. Better off than we are, but not rich," Shannon said. "Okay, you're pregnant. You'll get aid for doctor's visits and the delivery, food stamps, WIC, whatever. Where are you going to live?

"Like I told you, me and Dewayne are going to get Section 8 housing."

"And he's going to supplement your income by stealing cars and knocking over liquor stores," Shannon said.

"Whatever it takes. Don't act so holier-than-thou. You did it yourself."

"But I wasn't ever happy about it. You're going to have a baby, Annette. Do you know what that means? You're going to be constantly responsible for another human being. Are you gonna go gang-banging with the baby in a piggy-back holster?"

"Momma said she'll babysit sometimes," Annette said.

"Jesus Christ," Shannon swore, then he heaved a sigh. "Okay, Annette. You seem to think you have it all figured out. Good luck."

All the way home Shannon thought about Annette and the baby she carried. That baby wasn't going to have a chance. It made him sick. When he got home, the expression on his face alarmed Mandey, who had gotten up to eat breakfast and was back in bed, reading.

"What's wrong? What happened?" she asked.

"My sister's pregnant," Shannon said, sinking down onto the edge of the bed.

"You're kidding," Mandey said.

"Nope," Shannon said.

"She's been getting in fights with people and she's carrying a baby? When did she find out?" Mandey asked.

"I don't exactly know," Shannon said, "but she's probably known all along. She got pregnant on purpose."

"What?" Mandey asked. "Why?"

"When my dad died, Annette and I started getting Social Security checks every month—"

"I know. I've been getting them, too, since my dad had his heart attack and couldn't work."

"Well, then you know you get them until you're eighteen, or if you're eighteen and still in high school, you get them until you leave school. Annette's not in school, and she turns eighteen on the eighteenth, so this month is her last check."

"Right."

"So, if she's an unwed mother with no income, she's entitled to all kinds of welfare benefits. Rather than get a job, she decided having a baby was the way to go."

"Seriously?" Mandey asked.

"I know," Shannon said. "Annette told me to quit acting so shocked, because lots of people do it."

"That doesn't mean it's a good thing," Mandey said.

"No, it doesn't," Shannon agreed. "Annette and Dewayne ain't even getting married. She'll get more money that way."

He gave a long sigh. "Our family got the Social Security checks and the food stamps, but basically, we fell through the cracks. We moved around a lot, and Leon always made sure our addresses were up to date, because he had to make sure the money would make it to us so he could have it. But Annette and I probably should have been taken away from our mother and put in foster care years ago. We slipped through, though, and it never happened." His face hardened. "That baby is not going to suffer the way we did."

"Oh my God," Mandey said, as a thought struck her. "I kicked Annette in the stomach that night I fought with her. Oh my God. What if I hurt the baby, Shannon?" Tears came to her eyes.

"Mandey, Annette said she's only a couple months along. I don't think she was pregnant enough for you to have done any harm."

"I hope not," Mandey said, worried.

"It might have been better if she'd lost it, though," Shannon muttered.

Mandey sat up and hugged him. "It will be okay," she told him.

"I hope you're right," he replied, kissing her hair.

"Why don't you get back in bed with me and rest for a little while?" Mandey suggested.

Shannon stood and stripped down to his T-shirt and briefs. "You're being lazy today," he remarked as he got in bed and flipped on the television.

"It's good to be lazy once in a while," Mandey replied. "It's even better to have someone to be lazy with."

In bed with Mandey, his troubled thoughts began to fade. He kept thinking about a baby, but not Annette's baby. Instead, his mind made pictures of Mandey, pregnant. The idea of her carrying his baby made him smile. The time for that was far in the future, but that was okay. He wondered what their baby would look like. Chubby, brown hair, green or hazel eyes. He visualized a bouncing, happy baby in a walker, toddling around the house they would have someday, with him and Mandey proudly looking on.

He made himself put the thought out of his mind before it overwhelmed him. More than anything, he wanted the kind of family life that he lost the day his father was murdered, but he feared if he thought about it too much, he might jinx it, and it would never come true.

59

A Visit to the Principal's Office

Mandey thought Mr. Tichner had forgotten about the incident at the dance and his promise that he would talk to her about it after the Christmas holiday. The first three days of school in January went by without her even seeing him, and she thought she was safe from having to go through that uncomfortable conversation. But on Monday morning in English class as she was writing in her journal, there was a knock at the door. Mr. Crenshaw answered it. Outside was Amy Murrill, Charlie's sophomore sister, who was an office aide that period.

"Mandey?" Mr. Crenshaw said, looking at the pass Amy held out to him.

Mandey's heart sank. She slowly stood up and walked over to Mr. Crenshaw and Amy.

"Mr. Tichner wants to see you," Mr. Crenshaw said.

She felt her classmates' eyes on her as she followed Amy out the door. Mandey walked behind Amy in silence down to the front office. Her heart was pounding. She dreaded this.

Once in the office, Mrs. Sutter, the secretary, told her to take a seat in one of the chairs in the hall that led to the principals' offices. She was the only one there. She sat there, her mind whirling, wondering what he was going to ask her. She wasn't sure what the point of this meeting even was. The security officer had found no drugs on Shannon's person or in his car and let him go. He hadn't done anything wrong, and the only thing Mandey was "guilty" of was bringing Shannon to the dance in the first place.

About five minutes later, the door to Mr. Tichner's office opened. "Mandey, come in," he beckoned her.

She stood and walked into the office. She had never been in Mr. Tichner's office except for the night of the Christmas dance, but then she hadn't paid much attention to the surroundings. Today, she noticed more of the details. It wasn't particularly remarkable, but one thing stood out to her—on the wall behind Mr. Tichner's desk hung a wooden paddle with holes drilled in it.

Mr. Tichner told her to sit down in the chair in front of his desk. He sat down in his chair on the other side. Her eyes still focused on the paddle. She figured it was strategically placed there; anyone in the hot seat in front of Mr. Tichner would not be able to avoid seeing that paddle there, just above the height of the principal's head while sitting. It didn't cause her too much concern, however. She couldn't imagine that she had done anything to be in that much trouble.

"I want to talk with you about what happened at the dance before Christmas," Mr. Tichner said.

Mandey took a silent but deep breath. "Okay."

"Is that boy you brought with you a drug dealer? Was he dealing drugs that night? Because two students said they saw him in the boys' restroom with drugs," Mr. Tichner said.

Mandey wasn't sure who the second student was, but figured it was probably Jeremy.

"No! Mr. Tichner, he never even went to the restroom until right before you dragged him down to the office. We had been together and dancing most of the night. He isn't a drug dealer. Like I said then, I wouldn't be with him if he was."

The principal's face showed he was skeptical of what she had told him.

"Then who is a drug dealer? Your boyfriend seemed to know of one here in the student body."

Crap, Mandey thought. She did not want to rat Danny out.

"And what's this rumor that I heard that your boyfriend is in a street gang?" Mr. Tichner continued. "I also heard that some of the students here at Rogers were participating in gang activity. What do you know about that?"

Oh, my God, too many questions at once, Mandey thought, her mind racing. She kept silent.

"I'm waiting for an answer, young lady."

Mandey was a terrible liar. Mr. Tichner didn't buy it when she told him that Shannon wasn't a drug dealer. If he didn't believe her when she was being truthful, he was going to see right through her if she told a lie.

"I think Shannon was generalizing about there being a drug dealer in the student body," Mandey finally said. "I mean, chances are good that someone in a school of twenty-five hundred students sells drugs."

"I think it's probably a very good possibility," Mr. Tichner said. "But maybe your boyfriend knows who the dealers are because they are in cahoots. Or competition."

"Mr. Tichner, Shannon is not a drug dealer!"

"Is he in a gang?" Mr. Tichner asked.

"No!" Mandey said emphatically. Not a lie. Mr. Tichner's question was present tense. Shannon's gang involvement was past tense.

"Mandey, don't lie to me," Mr. Tichner said, looking disappointed.

Mandey decided to keep her mouth shut. She had a feeling the principal was going to lay down a minefield of questions, and if she continued answering, her lousy ability to lie was going to make it all blow up in her face.

He began to lecture her about falling in with the wrong crowd and getting into trouble. How drugs and gang activity were both punishable by expulsion, and if she wasn't careful, she would be repeating her senior year. He occasionally threw in a question, but Mandey remained stony silent, her insides petrified. Unable to get her to talk, he ended his lecture with this:

"I regret to inform you, this is not a court of law. You do not have the right to remain silent, Mandey."

Mr. Tichner stood and walked over to the door to the office. He opened it and called over into the office kitty-corner across the hall. "Ms. Percival, could you come in here, please?"

A couple moments later, Ms. Percival, one of the assistant principals, walked into the office. Her hair was short and bleached blonde, and her face looked like she constantly smelled something slightly offensive. Mr. Tichner shut the door behind her, then closed the blinds of his office window.

Mandey had a sinking feeling, which was made worse when Mr. Tichner went back behind his desk and took the paddle off the wall and set it on the edge of his desk.

"I am very concerned about this path you seem to be headed down. Your conduct record has been spotless until now, and I want to nip this in the bud."

"But I don't understand what I've done," Mandey said, feeling honestly confused.

"You are being uncooperative and disrespectful—"

"I am not being disrespectful!" Mandey blurted, then realizing her mistake in protesting, said meekly, "Sir. Sorry."

"You're lying to me," Mr. Tichner said. "I know you know more than you're telling me. And if you're going to keep lying, there's going to be consequences. I could suspend you next week, or I could give you swats."

Mandey felt her jaw drop and her face get hot. Her mind raced. This couldn't be happening. She couldn't rat out Danny and the Alley Cats, but the alternatives were grim. Tichner knew what he was doing. If he suspended her next week during semester finals, her grade point average would take a hit because she would not be allowed to make up the tests. She wouldn't fail, but the zeroes would bring her A's down to B's or even C's, and her class ranking would suffer. She didn't want that, but she also did not want swats with that paddle. She had worn a matching maroon skirt and sweater set to school that day. The skirt was dress-code legal, but only by a half inch or so, and the material wasn't very heavy. It was going to be rather immodest if she had to bend over Mr. Tichner's desk, to add to the total indignity of it.

What would Georgia do? What would Georgia do? If Georgia were in this situation, she likely would have sweet-talked her way out of it and would be back in class already. Mandey, unfortunately, didn't have that silver-tongued Southern charm Georgia had. If Georgia couldn't talk her way out, the next step was crying. Georgia had a talent for crocodile tears, but in this case, Mandey didn't have to fake it.

"Mr. Tichner, please," she begged. "I don't know anything! All I know is my boyfriend is not a drug dealer, and he's not the horrible person people say he is! I don't know anything else! I don't use drugs, I don't buy drugs from anyone, I don't sell drugs to anyone, and I don't know why I'm in trouble! I didn't do anything, and Shannon didn't do anything!"

The tears must have worked, because she left the office with only a warning that he would be keeping an eye on her, and she that she needed to remember she was an Honor Society student and a role model, and should comport herself as such.

When she got back to English class, two-thirds of the way through the period, her eyes were still shiny, although she had stopped in the restroom to compose herself first.

"What happened?" Gayla mouthed at her from the next row, with a wide-eyed alarmed look on her face.

Mandey shook her head slightly and opened her notebook. She kept her head down and didn't make eye contact with anyone else until the bell rang. When it did, she quickly gathered her things and hurried out the door. She didn't want to talk to anyone. She ducked back into the restroom to check herself in the mirror again, hoping she didn't look like she had a breakdown less than 30 minutes ago. She brushed her hair and put on a little more lipstick and powder. She wished she had eye make-up with her so she could touch up her eyes, but she was not one of those girls who brought an entire make-up kit to school with her.

She timed it so that she slid into her seat in fourth period about ten seconds before the tardy bell rang. Half of the class was review for finals next week, and the other half was devoted to project presentations. Mandey was glad she and Danny weren't presenting today. They were scheduled for the last day, Wednesday. Gayla, Charlie, and Trish were the second of the two groups presenting that day. When he wasn't speaking, Charlie was looking at her with an almost bug-eyed expression on his face. She wasn't sure what his problem was.

On the way to lunch, she found out. Gayla and Charlie caught up to her as they walked to the cafeteria.

"Mandey, what happened in Tichner's office?" Gayla asked her.

"Nothing, really," Mandey said vaguely.

"I saw my sister after English class. She told me you got swats!" Charlie burst out.

Mandey felt her face burn. "I did not!"

"That's not what my sister said," Charlie said, not convinced.

"Seriously? You got swats? Why?" Gayla asked, concerned.

"I didn't get swats!" Mandey insisted.

"My sister said Mr. Tichner called Ms. Percival in his office with you and shut the blinds. That's what he does when he gives a girl swats. Then you came out of the office crying."

"That's what happened, but he didn't give me swats."

"Did Ms. Percival do it?" Charlie asked.

"No!"

While they were in the lunch line, Mandey tried to explain what had happened in the principal's office, but she wasn't sure either Gayla or Charlie totally believed her. They sat down at their usual table and started eating, when they were joined by James.

"Mandey!" James said in a loud voice, sitting down next to her. "Mr. Tichner gave you a spanking?"

Mandey cringed, then turned to him. "Will you be quiet!" she said and gave him a look that said "drop dead". It didn't faze James at all.

"Maybe it was just what you needed," James said smugly.

"Oh, my God, I did not get swats!" Mandey said, exasperated. "Who told you that?" She shot Charlie a black look.

"It wasn't me!" Charlie said, almost laughing.

"It's all over school," James said.

It was. The rumor had caught fire with amazing speed. Danny met her at the door at study hall after lunch and escorted her to the far corner of the room to talk.

"What the hell happened in Tichner's office this morning?" he asked her. "He gave you swats?"

Mandey was about to tell him the truth, but then she decided to play along with him. In a low voice she said, "It was all your fault, Danny. He wanted info on who's dealing drugs here at school, but I kept my mouth shut."

"Shit. Seriously? He wanted info about me?" Danny said.

"I told him I know nothing, but he didn't believe me."

"So he gave you swats? Jesus," Danny said. "I'm sorry."

He looked so guilt-stricken that Mandey felt sorry for him. "No, Danny, I didn't get swats, but I <u>almost</u> did. He threatened me with them, or suspension, if I wouldn't talk, but I started crying and neither one happened. And I didn't rat on you."

Danny gave a little sigh of relief but still looked at Mandey skeptically. "Are you sure?"

She didn't know if he meant sure she didn't get swats or sure she didn't rat him out. "Yes," she said, going to her seat as the bell rang.

Despite her telling everyone who asked the truth about what happened, more people seemed to want to believe the rumor. Mark Ruggeri smirked when he saw her in the hallway between fifth and sixth periods, then when he saw her looking at him, he mimed holding a paddle and giving a swat. Mandey rolled her eyes and moved on to class.

Even the teachers weren't immune. When she got to art class, Mr. Slater stopped her at the door and they stepped over to the side to talk.

"Mandey, what happened this morning?" Mr. Slater asked her, looking genuinely shocked and concerned.

Mandey liked Mr. Slater. He was about thirty, and had a blonde streak in the front of his brown hair. James said he was gay. Mandey didn't know for sure, but it didn't matter to her, anyway.

"Not what you probably heard," Mandey said, and proceeded to tell the story again.

As they were talking, the teacher next door, whose name Mandey didn't know, came over to them.

"That skirt looks awfully short," she said to Mandey, surveying her outfit. "I should send you to the office to have it checked."

Seriously? Mandey thought. *Sixth period and you want to send me to the office for a possible dress code violation now?*

"Mr. Tichner's already seen me today," Mandey replied curtly. She didn't want to make a return visit today or any other day.

The teacher looked at Mandey skeptically, but didn't say anything, then looked at Mr. Slater, who just shrugged. She walked back toward her classroom. Mandey looked back at Mr. Slater, who rolled his eyes. Mandey giggled.

"I think your outfit looks great. Anyway, I'm glad you're okay. I was worried about you when I started hearing the rumors," Mr. Slater said.

"Yeah, I'm okay, thanks," Mandey said, and smiled. And for the first time since third period, she believed it.

When she got home, there was a message on the answering machine. It was Mr. Tichner wanting to speak with her mother.

"Uh, nope," she said, deleting it.

Marcia didn't need to know about this. For that matter, neither did Shannon. He was worried enough already that his presence in her life was causing her more grief than he was worth. It absolutely wasn't true, though.

Would you feel the same if Mr. Tichner had paddled you? Or suspended you? Would Shannon still be worth it? a small voice asked in the depths of her mind.

"Yes," she said out loud. Given the choice of having Shannon in her life or having a sore butt for a few days, or graduating 14th instead of 4th, she would choose Shannon every time.

60

Mid-Term Tension

Mandey and Shannon fell into a domestic routine, getting up in the mornings, Mandey going to school and Shannon to work, making dinner when they got home, homework and television in the evening. They were becoming more familiar with each other's bodies, but they always stopped short of going all the way, although Mandey sometimes repeated her Christmas morning surprise for Shannon. It was clear to them both that soon that was not going to be enough. Shannon sometimes fretted to himself about the fact Mandey had said she would have considered sleeping with James when they were together, but she was putting off sleeping with him. She said she loved Shannon far more than she ever cared about James, but she didn't want to go all the way with him. After one very overheated make-out session and having to stop short again, Shannon said he thought it might be better if they slept apart.

"Mandey, you know I want you, and for whatever reason, you don't want me."

"I do want you, Shannon," she said tearfully. "Please don't think that I don't. I want you more than you could ever know."

"Then why are you denying me and denying yourself?" Shannon asked. He didn't wait for an answer. "I know, you want to wait 'til you're eighteen. And I'll wait for you, but I can't sleep with you in here tonight. It's too tempting. I'm going to my room." He threw off the covers and got out of bed.

Mandey burst into a fresh flood of tears. "Please don't go," she begged.

He sat back down on the bed next to her. "Don't cry," he said in a soothing voice. "I'm not breaking up with you. I'm just going to sleep in the next room tonight. I don't want to do something we both might regret. Understand?'

Mandey nodded. "I do. I'm sorry."

"Don't be sorry. I just need to cool off." He kissed her forehead. "See you in the morning."

The bed was so empty and cold without him next to her. She cried for a long time after he left. Even before that evening, she had been seriously re-considering her dedication to keeping her virginity until May. Danny was right; she was worrying about being a statistic instead of following what her heart and soul felt was right. She had already decided Valentine's Day would be a good time. It would be a very special present to give Shannon that night. It wasn't that far away, either. Eventually, Mandey began to think about all the things she could do to make it a very special day for them and fell asleep with a smile on her face.

Mandey and Danny managed to finish their project on the Cold War and presented it to the class. Their classmates found it interesting, and Mrs. Silverman awarded them each an A. Semester final exams were given the following week in January, and the results would cement their class rankings for graduation in May. The tension was palpable between Charlie and James. They barely spoke to each other, and when they did, they only snapped or argued. One day they almost got into a fistfight in their calculus class. Mandey was going to be glad when the end of the month came and they would know their rankings and that would be the end of it.

The rumor that Mr. Tichner had given her swats didn't die, but it began to fade as the month wore on. Mandey knew she would just have to live with it. Mark, whether he believed it happened or not, continued to torment her, miming giving her swats every time he saw her in the hallway, and blowing her a little kiss along with it. She ignored him. There were a few more messages on the answering machine from the principal, but Mandey managed to intercept and erase them before Marcia could listen to them.

Shannon registered to begin evening G.E.D. classes at the start of the spring semester. He was nervous about it, but he was also looking forward in a way to sitting with Mandey and doing homework together. Even though the weather was cold, he was still busy with his job, doing indoor projects like mudding and taping and painting. He enjoyed it, and sometimes he fantasized about working on a dream home for Mandey and himself one day.

The ledger pages Mandey picked up in his parole officer's office remained a source of worry for Shannon. He debated (to himself) about what to do. He thought about taking Michael's advice, but he was scared that it might backfire and end up landing him in jail again. Part of him wanted to take those papers to his next appointment, confront Holtz, and demand to know what the deal was, but again, he was afraid that if he did that, the cops wouldn't believe him and would side with Holtz against him.

What he ended up doing was making several Xerox copies of the pages from both Grubbs' and Holtz's offices. Mandey helped him write an anonymous letter, which she typed for him, and made several copies of it, as well. He blacked out his name on the copies of the pages. As an afterthought, he blacked out the names of the other probationers, as well. He didn't want to narc on them when they were in the same boat as he was, and if there were other similar documents still in Holtz's office, they might be able to figure out it was Shannon's name that was blacked out, and that would identify him as the whistleblower. On the Friday before his meeting with Holtz, he mailed out the copies of the ledger pages and the letter to Holtz's boss, Holtz's boss's boss, and the chief of police. He and Mandey had discussed the best time for him to do it, and they decided to send them before Shannon's January appointment, but late enough that Holtz wouldn't yet have any knowledge about it. There was the possibility that Holtz had noticed the papers missing after his last visit. He hoped not, but it was possible. If he did, and if he threatened Shannon during the appointment, the documents would already be in the pipeline and postmarked prior to the 14th.

Shannon practically held his breath during his meeting with Holtz, but there were no questions about the missing ledger pages. He probably thought he had mislaid them or misfiled them some place. Shannon hoped so, anyway. He left the office feeling like he had dodged a bullet and felt lighthearted as he drove back home.

Charlie suggested going out to celebrate the end of finals week and the semester by going to see "some grown men beating the shit out of each other." He and Shannon had found a common interest in Mid-South professional wrestling. Shannon was very psyched about going to see it in person instead of watching it on television. "Aw, that'll be cool!" he said excitedly when Mandey mentioned Charlie's idea.

Mandey had never watched wrestling before she and Shannon had gotten together, but she was learning who the wrestlers were and kind of enjoyed it, herself. (She had a little crush on the Handsome Half-Breed, Gorgeous Gino Hernandez, but didn't tell Shannon that.) She was enthusiastic about going to the Sam Houston Coliseum to see the matches. "I'll try anything once," she said. Well, maybe not <u>anything</u>, but lots of things.

Gayla was a different story. "I don't understand why people want to watch that kind of stuff," she said, but Charlie convinced her to go, and so the four of them went downtown to see the matches.

"Ted DiBiase versus Hacksaw Duggan in a Street Fight match!" Charlie exclaimed when he saw the bill.

The Rock-n-Roll Express, Chris Adams, Kevin von Erich, Kamala, and Butch Reed were slated to wrestle that night, too. Mandey was a little disappointed that Gino Hernandez wasn't going to be there.

When they entered the Coliseum, they went to the concession stand for drinks. Shannon had a beer, but Mandey, Gayla, and Charlie all got cokes. They found their seats, and Shannon and Charlie quickly became caught up in the action once it began, standing and hooting and hollering along with the rest of the crowd. Mandey watched it a little more clinically. She knew it was all choreographed and the outcomes planned, but she did admire the athleticism of the wrestlers. It wasn't all fake—you had to be in shape to do this kind of stuff.

Gayla, however, suddenly burst into tears about an hour into the show. "They're beating each other up!" she cried. "How can you sit there and enjoy watching them do that to each other!" She covered her face with her hands.

The other three looked at her, perplexed. "Gayla, they aren't really hurting each other," Charlie told her. "Seriously, Gayla."

Shannon and Mandey looked at each other. "Really, Gayla," Shannon said, "it looks worse than it is."

"I just can't stand them being so horrible to each other!" she wailed, and sat down.

"It's okay," Mandey said, sitting down next to her and putting her arm around her shoulders. "They practice this stuff all the time so they won't seriously hurt each other."

"I'm so tired of people being mean to each other!" Gayla sobbed.

Charlie and Shannon turned their attention back to the action while Mandey calmed Gayla down. After about fifteen minutes, she had regained her composure and stood to watch again.

"Are you okay now?" Charlie asked her. "If I'd known that was going to happen, I wouldn't have asked you to come."

That set Gayla off, and the two of them began to argue, then Gayla shouted, "Oh, fuck off!" and made her way past the other people in the row and stormed up the aisle toward the concessions.

"Women," Charlie said, shaking his head.

"Maybe we ought to go?" Shannon said to Charlie, although he didn't want to leave so soon.

"Nah, she'll get over it. She's over-emotional. I think she's on the rag," Charlie said.

Mandey gave him an elbow in the ribs and frowned at him. "Owwww!" he exclaimed, holding his side.

Gayla came back about twenty minutes later, markedly less agitated, and didn't say anything during the rest of the matches and almost nothing on the way home.

After Charlie dropped them off, Shannon said, "I had a good time, but next time let's leave Gayla home."

"I agree. Next time, let's just you and me go."

Tickets for the prom went on sale at the end of January, and Mandey bought hers and Shannon's the very first day. Two days later, tickets for the Daryl Hall and John Oates concert at the Summit also went on sale, and Mandey HAD to have those, too. Andie and Mart wanted to go to the concert, too, so Mandey and Andrea went to the Ticketmaster outlet at Foley's and got tickets together. It sucked that the concert was going to be on a Monday night, but still, it would be a lot of fun.

On the last day of January, the class rankings were released. Each of the students in the top fifteen percent of the class was called down to the counselor's office individually. When Mandey's turn came, she was told she was 4th in the class of nearly 500 students, as she had expected.

"I'm third?!" James cried indignantly as he came into English class. "That's bullshit!"

Gayla was second, and Charlie was first. He sat there looking at James with a big grin on his face, gloating.

"The only reason I'm not valedictorian is because they didn't weigh my credits from California the way they were supposed to," James said angrily. "My father is going to call the principal about this."

"Oh, get over it," Charlie said. "It's not going to do you any good. Mr. Tichner doesn't even like you."

"That's the problem!" James said flatly. He sat down at his desk for a moment, then had a change of heart. "I'm going to the counselor's office," he declared, picking up his backpack and stalking out of the room.

"Where are you going?" Mr. Crenshaw called after him as he took off.

"To deal with this bullshit!" James said, already halfway down the hall.

Mandey was good with 4th. No stupid speech to have to make. She could have ranked higher, but she had chosen some easier classes than the other three. She didn't have to have a certain class ranking to validate herself. She knew she was smart. She had already applied to several colleges and had already been accepted to the University of Houston, the University of Texas, and Bates College in Maine, pending her final grades. A few months ago, Bates was her first choice, but she knew now she was going to stay in Houston and become a commuter student at U of H. She didn't know yet what to choose as a major, but she wouldn't have to do that until her junior year. She had time to figure out what to do with herself.

61

The Unthinkable

When the Social Security checks were disbursed in February, Shannon made plans with his mother to go to the bank and grocery shopping again. Mandey didn't expect him home before 11 that Saturday morning, but he came in the door at 9 A.M. "You're back early," Mandey said when he walked in, then she saw his face. "What happened?"

"Leon's back," Shannon said, taking off his jacket and tossing it on the chair. He sat down heavily next to Mandey on the couch. "I guess he blew in last night. I should have realized something wasn't right when Momma didn't answer the phone this morning."

"You fought with him again. Oh, Shannon," Mandey said, dismayed.

"Why couldn't he have stayed in Arkansas? I really thought he was gone for good this time," Shannon asked. "His sister probably couldn't stand him and kicked his ass out."

"What did you fight about?" Mandey asked.

"Same old shit. Money. I told him I was helping Momma take care of her money, and he told me that since I'd moved out, it wasn't my business. I told him I could say the same to him—and you know the rest."

"Oh, man," Mandey said. "Why doesn't she get a restraining order against him?"

"She did once, but then she went and violated it herself. Didn't do a bit of good," Shannon said, and sighed. "They'll be out on the street in two months. The way Leon spends, they can't survive on Momma's SSI alone. Mother-fucker." He rubbed his face with his hands.

"Honey, I think you've done all you can for her," Mandey said.

"Augh, I just get so mad."

"I know. Why don't you go clean up? I'll get the ice pack ready. Jeez, I was hoping that was retired. And give me your shirt—your nose bled on it."

Shannon unbuttoned his blue plaid flannel shirt and handed it to Mandey. She sprayed stain remover on the bloody spots and set it on top of the washer.

"Guess I'm not going back there again. Leon made it clear I'm not welcome. Not that

I really care, except for my mom," Shannon said, getting up to go wash his face.

When he came back a few minutes later, he had washed off the blood and put on a fresh shirt. Mandey handed him the ice pack. He placed it on his left eye, which was starting to bruise.

"I wish I could do more," Shannon said. "I'm afraid that if they lose the apartment, Leon is going to move them somewhere else and won't tell me. He's going to cut me off, too, like he did to the rest of Momma's family. The only reason he didn't kick me out long ago was because of my social security checks, and then when I got back from doing my time for the attempted robbery, I got a job and had a paycheck coming in. The reason I stuck around so long was for my mom. But sometimes I hate her for marrying Leon and then always taking him back. I know she's sick, but that's no excuse…"

He sank into a stony silence. Mandey put her arm around him and laid her head on his shoulder. She didn't say anything, but hoped the closeness would be some comfort to him. He put his arm around her, and he began to feel calmer. It did help.

In the very early morning hours of Sunday, Mandey was awakened by an out-of-the-ordinary but not unfamiliar sound. Her bedroom window was closest to the road, and Mandey was accustomed to the sounds of the traffic that went by. This morning she heard cars outside, moving swiftly and quietly and then stopping.

Police cars? she thought, and peeked through the blinds. One Houston police cruiser was in the driveway, and two Harris County Sheriff patrol cars were in the street.

"What the heck?" she said out loud.

"What?" Shannon asked sleepily.

"Shannon, there are three police cars outside."

"What?" he said, and sat up, panicking. He knew it. They had figured out he was the one who had sent those ledger pages about the stolen cars, and now he was getting busted. "Shit!"

There was pounding on the front door. "Open up," said a voice on the other side.

Mandey leapt out of bed, threw on her robe, and ran to the door.

"Yes?" she said to the two officers at the door.

"Does Shannon Douglass live here?" one asked her.

"Why?"

Marcia had joined her at the door. "What is going on here?" she asked.

Shannon appeared behind Mandey, wearing a pair of sweatpants.

"Are you Shannon Douglass?" the officer asked, looking at Shannon.

"Yeah. Why?"

With one swift movement, the second cop had Shannon's hands cuffed behind him.

"We have a warrant. You're under arrest for the murder of Leon Pawlowski," the first officer said.

"What?" Shannon, Mandey, and Marcia chorused.

"You have the right to remain silent—" he began, and droned the Miranda warning as he followed the second officer and Shannon out to the police cruiser in the driveway.

Shannon turned around and looked back at Mandey. "I didn't do it, Mandey!" he shouted frantically.

Mandey's head spun. *Murder?* she thought dazedly.

"Shannon, don't say anything until you get a lawyer!" Marcia called after him.

"I don't know what you're talking about!" Shannon protested as the officer placed his hand on the back of his head and pushed him down into the back seat of the police car.

An officer from one of the other cars came up to the house. "Officer, are you sure you have the right person?" Marcia asked.

"We have witnesses who placed him at the murder scene," the officer said.

"Who?" Mandey demanded.

"Some of the neighbors."

"Who?" Mandey asked again. "What are their names?"

"I don't know. I didn't interview them. We do have a search warrant to search the premises."

"I'm calling Michael," Marcia said.

"Who's Michael?" the officer asked.

"An attorney," Marcia said, going to the phone. "I don't want you in here touching anything until he's here and checks out your warrant."

"We'd also like to get a statement from the both of you."

"All the more reason to call a lawyer," Marcia said, dialing.

"There's nothing to say!" Mandey burst out. "He didn't do anything, and whoever said they saw him do it are liars!"

"Mandey, calm down," Marcia said, with the phone to her ear. "Go get dressed. They're not doing anything and we're not saying anything until Michael gets here."

Mandey went to her room and got dressed, then sat on her bed, too stunned to cry.

It's not fair, she thought. *I knew things were going too smoothly for us.*

She went to the bathroom to brush her teeth, comb her hair, and splash water on her face. Then she busied herself making the bed and straightening up her room until Michael arrived. She didn't want to be out there with the police officers.

When Michael arrived, he perused the search warrant. "It looks to be in order," he said.

The three of them sat at the kitchen table, silent, as the three officers conducting the search went through Shannon's bedroom and the laundry room. Michael and Marcia drank coffee; Mandey was too upset to ingest anything.

The officers found the clothes Shannon had been wearing the day before in the dryer. They left with a small box of items of interest.

"We are impounding the suspect's car to be searched for evidence. A wrecker is on its way to tow it to the impound lot," said the officer who had spoken to them earlier. "And like I said before, we need the two of you to come down to the station and answer a few questions."

"We'll follow you downtown," Michael said.

"All right, what is going on here?" Michael asked as soon as he, Marcia, and Mandey got into his silver Mercedes.

Mandey explained it all, about Leon's abuse and money squandering and the fights he and Shannon had had. She also explained about the gang situation, something she had kept from Marcia.

"A gang, Mandey?" Marcia asked, dismayed.

"They were all turning against him," Mandey said. "His heart was never in it, but he was afraid if he wasn't recognized as their leader, the ones who didn't like him would get him arrested or killed. Since he left, he's been avoiding them, except for going down there to check on his mother. He's been afraid of what they might do if he ran into any of them. I think they're trying to frame him."

"Hmmm," Michael said. "Okay, I'm starting to understanding this now."

"Raff framed him—well, left him in a bad position holding the bag—once before," Mandey said, and told Michael and Marcia about how Shannon ended up going to jail.

"Mandey, why didn't you ever tell me any of this?" Marcia asked. "I knew he had a lot of problems, but I never knew he'd gotten into that much trouble."

"All he's cared about for months is turning his life around and getting to twenty-one without any more convictions so he can get his record erased," Mandey said. "I know he didn't do this. He wouldn't do anything to screw it up."

"But you said he's got a long violent history with his stepfather," Michael said, glancing at her in the rearview mirror. "Do you think it's possible he finally had enough and just snapped?"

"No," Mandey said shortly. "If Shannon was going to do something like that, he would have done it long ago."

Mandey lay back in the seat and shut her eyes. She wanted to go back to sleep and wake up in her bed with Shannon next to her and realize this was only a horrible nightmare.

At the station, the police questioned Marcia first. Michael went in with her. Mandey sat on a bench outside the interrogation room, watching people getting booked. Shannon was not among them. After ten minutes, they called Mandey in. Michael and Marcia sat in chairs against the wall. Mandey sat in a chair at a large table, facing two plainclothes detectives.

One introduced himself as Detective Bettis, and his partner was Detective Marquez.

Michael had told her that she didn't have to answer any of the questions the police asked her if she didn't want to. There were some questions she wanted to answer, because she wanted them to know that Shannon hadn't done it. When they began asking about Shannon's criminal involvement, she declined to answer. She didn't want to provide them with any extra ammunition for their case. She was more open when they wanted to know about Shannon's family life and his relationship with his stepfather. When they asked Mandey what she knew about what happened the morning Leon was murdered, she was more than willing to tell them.

"Shannon came home because he and Leon had a fistfight over Shannon's mother's SSI check. Leon had been gone since before Christmas. Shannon didn't know he was back or he wouldn't have gone over there to begin with. He wanted to take his mother to cash her check, pay bills, and do some shopping, but Leon got his hands on the check first. They fought and Shannon left. He got back home around nine, nine-ten, or something like that. He was upset because Leon was back, and he said he was afraid his mother would soon be out on the streets because of it."

"So, he spoke as if the victim were still alive," Detective Marquez said.

"Yes!" Mandey said. "He was frustrated, the same frustration about his family I've seen from him since I've known him. I know I've never come across someone who had just murdered somebody, but I think if I did, he'd be acting a lot more anxious and panicky than Shannon was."

"We have three witnesses who can place him at the murder scene. They said they saw him getting out of the victim's car," Detective Bettis said.

"Who?" Mandey asked.

"One of them is the suspect's sister."

"Annette?" Mandey said.

"She and Dewayne Robinson and Rafael Santos. There may be others; we're still interviewing people at the apartment complex."

"Raff Santos hates Shannon," Mandey said. "He would do or say anything to get Shannon into trouble."

"How do you know this?"

"Shannon has told me, many times."

"How do you explain the suspect's sister giving the same account?" asked Detective Marquez.

"I don't know. She and Shannon don't get along that well, either."

"Are you going to be the suspect's counsel?" Detective Marquez asked Michael.

"Well, I hadn't—"

"Please, Michael," Mandey begged. "Marcia, I'll talk to Ma and Daddy and get my college money to pay the retainer."

"Oh, no," Marcia said firmly. "Absolutely not."

"But he can't afford an attorney himself!" Mandey protested.

"That's okay. He'll be assigned a public defender," Detective Bettis told Mandey.

"I know that, but I want him to have a lawyer who'll actually care about proving his innocence!" Mandey said.

"Mandey, to be honest, I don't know that I can take on something as big as a murder case right now," Michael said. "Besides, I think I'm a little too close to the matter. If I represented Shannon and he still ended up being convicted, you would resent me, and it would make things between Marcia and me kind of awkward, as well."

"But he didn't do it!" Mandey said. "I don't want him stuck with some attorney who's only going to advise him to plea bargain."

"All right, look, I can't take the case, period," Michael said firmly. "But I do know there's another attorney in the firm who is doing some *pro bono* work. Let me give him a call. I think he'll take the case."

Michael left to use the telephone. When he came back, he announced that the attorney, Joe Figueroa, wasn't home, but he had left a message on his machine.

"We need to question the suspect, but he refuses to talk to us without an attorney present," Detective Bettis said to Michael. "Do you think you could sit in as his counsel long enough for us to get his statement?"

"If he's willing to do that, I will," Michael said.

"I'll have someone bring him up," Detective Marquez said.

Mandey and Marcia went to sit outside in the booking area. In a few minutes, an officer brought Shannon up, hands cuffed in front of him, still in his sweat pants, but they had given him a gray T-shirt and a pair of tan slip-on shoes for his bare feet. His eyes were large and dark with worry.

"Mandey," he said, veering toward her. The officer pulled him back.

Mandey started to get up and go to him, but before she could, he was ushered into the interrogation room and the door closed behind him. Mandey sat down, bent over with her elbows on her knees and her face in her hands.

"Mandey, I wish you'd told me everything about him. This is shocking," Marcia said.

"It was the past. I thought it was irrelevant. All he wanted to do was escape from all that crap," Mandey said, her words muffled. "I thought once he moved in with us, everything was going to be okay."

"Well, despite what I've just learned about him, I still can't say I believe he's a killer," Marcia said. "I don't think you would keep him around if he was that kind of person, either."

"Of course, I wouldn't," Mandey said. "It's got to be one of those three witnesses who did it. Raff is the one I think did it."

"How well do you know this Raff?" Marcia asked.

"Not well," Mandey said, not wanting to get into the Alley Cats' confrontations with Raff. "What I know is mostly what Shannon told me, and he's told me over and over again how much Raff hates him."

"Well, if he's one of the witnesses, the police are going to examine that story with a fine-tooth comb. If there are any cracks in it, they'll find them," Marcia said.

"If they want to," Mandey said glumly.

Almost an hour passed before the door opened and Shannon was brought back out. He looked toward Mandey but was dragged away without being able to talk to her. Michael came out shortly thereafter. Mandey looked up at him, anxious to hear what happened.

"His story meshed with what you told us," Michael said. "His was more detailed, but for the most part it was the same. They asked him a few tricky questions to try to trip him up, but they couldn't do it. He stuck to his version. I think he did really well, but the cops remain convinced that he's the perp."

"Why?" Mandey asked.

"The witnesses, mostly."

"Did Shannon try to explain about Raff?"

"Yes, but they weren't buying it. They expect suspects to try to blame someone else."

"Can I go see him?" Mandey asked.

Michael shook his head. "They haven't finished processing him, for one thing, and they only allow visitors during regular visiting hours. They're posted over there by the door." He pointed in the direction of the hallway where they had taken Shannon.

Mandey hurried over to look at the posting. It stated visiting hours were on Tuesday and Thursday evenings and Saturday afternoons. Dejectedly she walked back over to Marcia and Michael. The next forty-eight hours or so were going to drag by.

"I think we're done here," Michael said. "Why don't we go grab something to eat, then I'll get you two back home?"

They drove in Michael's Mercedes to Denny's. Mandey ordered a Grand Slam breakfast, but only picked at it. Her mind was whirling so fast, she couldn't stop it long enough to let any words out.

This has got to be some horrible nightmare, she told herself, even though she knew it wasn't true. She always knew when she was dreaming, and she knew that this was no dream.

Back at home, the day was bleak. Mandey was exhausted and tried to sleep, but she had a headache that wouldn't let up, despite the Tylenol. Around 2 P.M. the phone in the kitchen rang. Mandey got up and opened her bedroom door. Marcia answered the phone. Mandey listened to the one-sided conversation and knew it was her mother calling. Marcia was telling her what happened. Mandey wished she wouldn't, but she knew her parents would find out eventually.

Marcia called Mandey to the phone. Mandey reluctantly made her way to the kitchen and took the receiver from her. Her mother was very upset, not only about what had happened to Shannon, but about a letter that had been forwarded to her from Mr. Tichner, telling her he had left numerous phone messages that were never answered, so he decided to try contacting her through mail to discuss Mandey's visit to his office. Mandey burst into tears and thrust the receiver at Marcia and retreated to her room. She heard Marcia and their mother having a discussion, but she shut her bedroom door and turned on her stereo so she didn't have to hear it.

A while later, Marcia knocked on the door.

"Can I come in?" she asked.

"Sure," Mandey said.

Marcia entered and sat down on the end of Mandey's bed. Mandey sat up and turned down the stereo's volume.

"I told Ma to take it easy with you. I know this is a lot for you to handle. I wish I had known about all of this. And I didn't know about your visit to the principal. Did you delete all his messages?"

Mandey nodded.

"Did Shannon have drugs on him when you went to the dance?"

"No!" Mandey said. "Somebody said he did to try to get him in trouble! They searched him and his car and didn't find anything! I wouldn't be with Shannon if he was into drugs!"

"And now someone is trying to say he murdered his stepfather to get him in trouble?" Marcia asked.

"Yes!" Mandey cried. "I know, Shannon hasn't lived a perfect life, but he isn't a drug dealer, and he isn't a murderer!" Mandey wiped her eyes. "Ma has only talked to Shannon on the phone a few times. She doesn't know who he is. But he's been living here for two months, so you do. You don't think he's a drug dealer or a murderer, do you?"

"Well, I can't say I've seen any kind of behavior from him that would make me think that," Marcia admitted.

"Can you please tell that to Ma? He just started going down the wrong path, but he's been trying to turn himself around. He's not what she thinks he is."

"I'll talk to her," Marcia said.

"Thanks," Mandey replied.

"I really do hope this is straightened out soon and he can come back home," Marcia told Mandey, and gave her a hug.

"Me, too."

Shannon's arrest made the Sunday evening news—the 4th story into the broadcast on Channel 11. A small news story about the murder also appeared in the Sunday paper, but it was written before Shannon had been taken into custody. Houston averaged more than a murder a day, so unless it was something particularly sordid, it wasn't likely to be headline news. She was hoping the story might not have been seen by anyone she knew. No one called to ask her about it, so that was good.

For the most part, she wanted to turn inward and away from everybody, but another part of her longed to spill her agony to someone. She didn't feel she had anyone she was ready to turn to, though. Although she considered Georgia her best friend, Mandey feared once Georgia heard the news, it would only be a matter of time before the entire school knew. Heck, before people from other schools knew. Mandey recalled the time in ninth grade when she had made an F in algebra on progress reports right before Christmas. Georgia was the only one she had told. That night at the Christmas dance, Carlos Mendiola had asked Mandey to dance. While they were dancing, he remarked, "I heard you made an F in algebra. I can't believe it." Carlos wasn't even attending Rogers that year—he was going to a magnet school, and even he knew about it.

Mandey wasn't sure about telling Andrea. Everything about Andrea's life was so perfect, at least the way Andrea made it seem. Mandey didn't think she would understand this.

Gayla was the only one she might have been able to tell. She, too, had dated guys from troubled backgrounds. She had dated James, as well. Lately, though, Mandey hadn't been spending much time with Gayla, at least not time where they could talk privately. Mandey knew Gayla had some issues of her own that she was dealing with, too. So, for the time being, Mandey was going to have to carry the heartache inside.

62

A Waking Nightmare

On Monday morning, the clock radio went off at 6:00 blaring "Bang the Drum All Day" on the Q-Zoo station. Mandey woke up with a start, then laid there trying to focus. A fog of despair rolled over her as she remembered it hadn't been a bad dream—Shannon really was in jail on murder charges.

She staggered to the bathroom and looked at her reflection in the mirror. She was a mess. She hadn't fallen asleep until after three; her head pounded and her eyes were swollen from crying. After using the toilet, she washed her hands, splashed water on her face, and shuffled out to the kitchen. When Marcia came out of her bedroom dressed for work, she found Mandey at the kitchen table with her head in her arms. Mandey looked up when she heard Marcia enter.

"I don't want to go to school today," she said. "I only slept about three hours, and I'm not going to be able to concentrate on anything, anyway."

"I didn't think you would," Marcia said. "Want me to call in for you?"

"Please."

"This is your first absence this year, isn't it?"

"Yeah. So much for perfect attendance. I don't care."

"What's the number?"

Mandey recited the school phone number from memory, then went back to her room and crawled back into bed. She hoped she would be able to go back to sleep.

Marcia came in the room. "Are you still planning on coming down to talk to Shannon's attorney?"

"Yes," Mandey said. "Four o'clock, right?"

"That's what Michael said. If it changes, I'll call you."

"Okay."

After Marcia left, Mandey settled down under the covers. The only way she was going to get to sleep was to force herself not to think about Shannon. The words of the Todd Rundgren song went through her mind.

I want to bang on the drum all day.

She felt like banging, punching, hitting something, that was for sure. She took a deep breath, which turned into a yawn. Eventually, she fell asleep.

At four o'clock Mandey knocked on the door of Joe Figueroa's office.

"Come in," he said.

She opened the door. "Hello, Mr. Figueroa," she said, entering.

"Joe, please," he said, rising from his chair behind his desk. He was barely taller than Mandey, with short black hair, a round face, and a wide smile underneath a thick but well-groomed mustache. "Come in and have a seat."

She approached the chairs in front of his desk. He extended his hand to her. She shook it, then sat down. He sat down again, as well. He picked up a pen and positioned a yellow legal pad on the desk in front of himself.

"Okay, so, your boyfriend is in jail charged with murder," Joe said.

"Yes," Mandey said. "You haven't spoken with him yet?"

"No, not yet," Joe said. "He's making an initial appearance in court tomorrow afternoon. I will go to see him before that happens. Mike filled me in on the statement he made to the police, but why don't we talk and I'll see what more you can give me."

"Okay," Mandey said. "On Saturday morning he went over to see his mother. He was going to take her to the bank and the grocery store."

"She doesn't drive?" Joe asked.

"I'm not sure. She didn't have a car," Mandey said. "Her husband, Leon, took the car and went to Arkansas."

"Shannon was going to take his mother to do errands."

"Yes."

"What time did he leave to go do this?"

"Early. Around seven-thirty in the morning."

"Why so early?"

"Because there are people over there at the apartment complex where he used to live who don't like him. They're usually not up and around that early in the morning, so if he goes over there early, he avoids them. He was also going to take his mother to get something for breakfast."

"Okay. Why did he go over there at all if Leon was there? Couldn't he take his own wife to the bank?"

"As I said, he went to Arkansas before Christmas," Mandey said. "Shannon didn't know he was back."

"Why didn't his mother tell him?" Joe asked.

"Shannon spoke with her on Thursday night, and she didn't mention it. I assume

Leon was still gone at the time. Shannon called his mother again Saturday morning before he left to make sure she was up, but there was no answer. He assumed his mother was still sleeping."

"And what time did Shannon return home?"

"Around nine-fifteen. I was surprised he was home so soon."

"What was his explanation?"

"He said when he got there, Leon was there, and they got into an argument."

"About what?"

"Money," Mandey said. "Leon always takes Shannon's mother's money and squanders it before all the bills are paid."

"How does Shannon's mother earn this income?"

"She's on SSI."

"She has some sort of disability?"

"She has severe manic depression."

Joe gave a low whistle, scribbling busily on a notepad.

"What did the deceased—Leon—do for a living?"

"From what Shannon told me, not much," Mandey said. "Most of what he did do was illegal. He liked the set up with Shannon's family because Shannon and his sister were getting social security benefits after their father died, and their mother was getting SSI, so Leon was happy to mooch off their checks."

"I take it there was no love lost between Shannon and his stepfather."

"No."

"Was it just an argument, or was it more physical, this altercation that took place Saturday morning?"

"I wasn't there, but Shannon said it had escalated and punches were thrown by both of them," Mandey said. "That wasn't unusual."

"Is there evidence of their fight?" Joe asked.

"Yes," Mandey said. "Shannon had a bloody nose and his face was bruised and his hands were scuffed up. He had some blood on his shirt."

"A lot?"

"No."

"Let me ask you—do you think it's possible that your boyfriend killed his stepfather?"

"No," Mandey said vehemently, shaking her head. "Shannon and I have only known each other for a few months, but I think I know him well enough to know he didn't. When he came home, he seemed upset about his stepfather being back, but I know he would have been more agitated if he'd committed murder. In fact, if he had, I don't think he would have even come home. He would have been so freaked out by what he had done he'd have taken off. Besides, when he came home, he was still talking about Leon in the present tense, as though he were still alive."

"Was Leon physically abusive toward Shannon as a child?"

Mandey nodded. "Very, and towards all the family, not just Shannon."

"Did you ever meet Leon yourself?" Joe asked.

"Uh, sort of," Mandey said.

"Sort of?"

"I went with Shannon to help him get his things when he moved in with Marcia and me. Leon was sleeping off a drunk, I think, but he heard us and woke up. I took some stuff out to the van, and when I came back, Leon and Shannon were fighting."

"You witnessed one of these fights?"

"Yes," Mandey said. "Leon had gotten the better of Shannon and was holding him against the wall, choking him, so I jumped on Leon's back to get him to stop."

"You what?" Joe exclaimed in disbelief.

"I had to do something," Mandey said, shrugging.

"Then what happened?"

"Leon threw me off, then he hit me. I fell backwards over a chair. But it was long enough to distract him. Then Shannon knocked Leon out and we escaped."

"Shannon knocked him unconscious?"

"Yes, with a dinette chair," Mandey said. "If he'd wanted to kill Leon, he could have finished him off then and there, but he didn't."

"Hmmm," Joe said, opening a file on his desk. "I've got some info here from the police department. I see that Shannon Douglass has a previous record."

"Yes," Mandey admitted.

"Armed robbery?"

Mandey nodded.

"Did he tell you about it?" Joe asked.

"He wanted to be honest with me," Mandey said. "He also told me he's been trying to stay out of trouble because if he can make it to 21 with no more convictions, they'll seal his record."

Joe looked over the records. "It says here he was accompanied by a second person, but he refused to identify him. He was seventeen at the time, and got sentenced to twelve months in a youthful offender program because it was his first offense. With time served and time off for good behavior, he served eight months."

Mandey nodded again. "That's what he told me."

"Who was the guy with him? It says here that the cops suspected it was some sort of gang activity."

"He was part of a gang called the Devils," Mandey said. "The guy with him was named Rafael Santos."

"Rafael Santos," Joe said, shuffling through his files. "Wasn't he one of the eyewitnesses who claim to have seen Shannon exiting Leon's car that morning?"

"That's right," Mandey said. "Do you have his police statement? What exactly did he say?"

"No," Joe said. "I have some preliminary information, but the police haven't given me everything yet."

"Well, whatever Raff said, I'm sure he was lying," Mandey said.

"Why do you say that?" Joe asked.

"Because Raff hates Shannon. After Victor, the first leader of the Devils, died, Raff wanted to take over, but Shannon did instead. Shannon made sure that happened because he wanted to call the shots and keep himself out of trouble as much as he could. Raff has resented him ever since."

"But Shannon's own sister says the same thing, and so does another person, a Dewayne Robinson."

"Annette and Dewayne are a couple, and Annette's pregnant," Mandey said. "I don't think Dewayne cares much for Shannon, and Shannon and Annette haven't gotten along for a while."

Joe looked seriously at Mandey. "It sounds to me as if no one likes your boyfriend very much but you," he said.

Mandey raised her eyebrows. "It seems that way, but Shannon's really a good person. You'll find that out when you talk to him," she said. "Do you think you can discredit those three witnesses?"

"Maybe Rafael and Dewayne. Dewayne is in this gang, too?"

"Yes. So is Annette, for that matter."

"They have girls in the gang?"

"Yes. So di—," Mandey cut herself off. She didn't want to bring the Alley Cats into the conversation. "Yes. Three."

"Do you know all the people who are in this gang?" Joe asked.

"Well, I know their first names, but that's about it. They all live in the Northview Apartments or close by. Shannon can tell you their names."

"Why don't you give me what you know. I don't know how much time I'll have to talk to Shannon tomorrow, so the more you can tell me now, the better."

Mandey rattled off the names that she knew.

"Okay. I don't know how or if I'll use them, but they're good to have just in case. Now, what can you tell me about Shannon that will impress the judge?"

"Well," Mandey said, "he has a full-time job working for a house remodeling company. Bert Rappoport is his boss's name, and I know he'd be a good character witness for Shannon. Shannon also just started GED classes a couple weeks ago. He wanted to get that soon so he could start junior college in the fall."

"Good," Joe said. "And he's got Marcia and Mike for character witnesses too, if necessary."

"I guess I'm too close to the situation to be of any use that way, huh?" Mandey said.

"Well, any testimony you provide will be more than about his character," Joe said.

"I don't think I'm going to like going to court," Mandey said.

"Depending on what we decide to do, there's a possibility you may not have to," Joe said. "If Shannon decides to plead guilty, we won't have to go through a whole court trial."

"He's not going to plead guilty to something he didn't do," Mandey said.

"Regardless of whether or not he's guilty, if he goes through a court trial and is convicted of first-degree murder, he could get the death penalty."

Mandey felt sick to her stomach. "You've got to make sure that doesn't happen," she said desperately.

"I have to talk to Shannon and see what he wants to do," Joe said. "He might want to plea bargain. We could get the charge reduced to second degree and point out the history of abuse. He would only get fifteen to twenty."

"No," Mandey said, struggling to keep tears back. "He can't go to prison for something he didn't do."

"I'll do whatever I can to keep that from happening, but I've got to talk to Shannon and get this first court date over with before we decide how to proceed."

"Do that," Mandey said. "Shannon won't confess to something he didn't do."

"Okay," Joe said soothingly. "Don't get too upset. Have a little faith that the truth will come out and justice will be served."

Mandey swallowed hard and nodded. "I hope so."

"I'm going over to the jail tomorrow. Shannon's supposed to go in front of the judge during the afternoon session. He'll be formally charged and bail will be decided."

"How much do you think bail will be?" Mandey asked.

"For a murder charge?" Joe asked. "At least $250,000."

Mandey sighed, defeated. She didn't have $25,000 lying around to post his bond. Shannon was going to have to stay in jail.

"Okay," she said, standing. "Thank you for talking to me, and thank you again for taking this case."

"You're welcome," Joe said, coming from behind his desk to show her to the door.

Mandey drew a deep breath and let out a long sigh as she walked down the hallway. She stopped to see Marcia on her way out.

"How did it go?" Marcia asked her.

"I gave him all the basics, and he told me the possibilities of what could happen," Mandey said. "He's going to see Shannon before court tomorrow. Oh, I can hardly wait for visiting hours tomorrow night. I've got to know how he's doing."

"Joe's pretty new, but he knows his stuff," Marcia said. "He'll do right by Shannon."

"God, I hope so," Mandey said. "I'm off to fight rush hour traffic."

"I might not get out of here until six. I'll probably grab something to eat on the way home. Do you need any money?"

"No, I'm okay. I'll probably stop and get something too."

It took more than twice as long to make the trip up U.S. 59 as it did when it wasn't rush hour. As the van inched along, she had a feeling that until this situation with Shannon was resolved, life was going to seem like it was crawling along no faster than the traffic.

63

Jail

For a moment, when he woke up Monday morning, Shannon thought he had had a terrible nightmare. Then, as his eyes came into focus on the bottom of the bunk above where he lay, his heart sank into the pit of his stomach. How the hell could this have happened?

Guards were coming through, turning on lights, yelling at the prisoners to wake up for breakfast. Trays were being slid through the slots at the bottom of the doors. Breakfast was reconstituted powdered eggs and white bread, not toasted. Shannon took his tray and sat back down on his bunk. The evening before he had tried to pick up the trays and distribute them to his cellmates, but they had yelled at him and accused him of trying to steal their food. No, he had not been trying to steal it. It had been a bland, vaguely grayish chicken stew, also served with white bread. After eating it, he had wished he had let one of the others have it.

The cell had two sets of bunks, so it could hold four men. Right now, there were three. Only one had been in there when Shannon arrived; the other arrived later in the day on Sunday. Shannon was thankful he was able to get a bottom bunk. Not only did he have a fear of falling off, but he also felt more vulnerable on a top bunk. He wouldn't be able to move as fast, if he needed to.

The man who had been in the cell when Shannon arrived had blond hair that was short in front and long in back and a bunch of tattoos on his arms. Something about him vaguely reminded Shannon of Leon. This guy's name was Carl. He had asked Shannon's name and when Shannon replied, Carl had said, "Ain't that a girl's name?"

"No," he said shortly. Shannon had known two other boys through the years with the same name and only one girl.

"I think it's a girl's name," Carl said.

Shannon didn't reply. He wasn't going to argue with this guy. He laid down on his bunk and faced the wall. Carl didn't pursue the subject, and Shannon eventually somehow fell asleep. He woke up a couple hours later when the next prisoner arrived, a slim Hispanic fellow named Roberto. He was yelling in Spanish and looked like he was messed up on something. Shannon hoped he would come down or sober up fast, or it would be really unpleasant being in such close quarters with him.

"This is bullshit!" Roberto had yelled, switching to English when the cell door slammed shut. "The bitch deserved it!"

"Old lady getting out of hand?" Carl asked him casually.

"Bitch cheated on me!" Roberto said. "She started it! They need to arrest her, too!"

"Maybe when she's out of critical condition," the guard said dryly, "although I doubt it."

Carl, as it turned out, had also put someone in the hospital in critical condition. He had been arrested for his sixth DWI. That was bad enough, but he was carrying a loaded, unregistered gun, and he had hit a person on the freeway who was trying to fix a flat tire on the shoulder.

When they had asked Shannon what he was in for, he only said it was for something he didn't do.

"That's what they all say," Carl said.

Shannon knew they would eventually find out what he was charged with, but he didn't feel like talking about it.

Now, picking at his tasteless breakfast, he felt like crying. Of course, he couldn't let himself do that, not in front of anyone. He started to think about Mandey, but then quickly put her out of his mind. Thinking of everything he had lost, thinking of how she must be feeling—it was only going to make things worse. He had to concentrate on his current situation and how to get through it. He was not even thinking about speaking with a lawyer, or his court appearance tomorrow, or his eventual trial. He just needed to survive being in jail. This wasn't juvenile detention, and he wasn't going to be sent to "kiddie jail" this time. Now he was in with the big boys, and it was likely he was going to be sent to Huntsville before too long, and that would be one long nightmare. He would be a convicted murderer. Maybe that would give him a reputation as a tough guy, and that would help him survive, but if he was going to spend decades in prison, he wasn't sure that he would want to survive.

64

The News

Mandey forced herself to go to school Tuesday morning. As she knew it would be, the news was out. She was standing outside the school library before the first bell, waiting for her girlfriends from English class and wondering what she was going to say to them, when Danny approached her.

"Danny, what are you doing?" asked Jackie, who was a few steps behind him, as he roughly grabbed Mandey by the arm and pulled her over to the doors of the auditorium. He pushed the door open and shoved her in ahead of himself.

"Knock it off!" Mandey said crossly, jerking out of his grasp.

"We found out what happened to your boyfriend," Danny declared flatly. Mandey took the "we" to mean the Alley Cats. "Murder? He was arrested for murder? What kind of monster is he, Mandey?" Danny asked, his voice rising as he spoke.

"Shhhhh, keep your voice down," Mandey said.

"Why? It was on the news. It's not a secret."

"Danny, he didn't do it," Mandey said.

"That's what they all say."

"He didn't do it, Danny, and don't you go around saying he did!" Mandey exclaimed angrily. "He says he didn't do it, and I believe him. Period."

"Mandey—" Danny began.

"Don't 'Mandey' me," she said. "I don't want to hear it."

She turned and opened the auditorium door with a bang, then stomped down the hallway from Danny and away from where her friends were now gathered.

"You can't run away from it, Mandey," Danny called after her.

She wanted to be by herself to collect her thoughts before class. Actually, what she really wanted was to walk out the doors and go home, but she stopped in the hallway near the wing where her Spanish class was. The hall was too crowded for her to be alone, but she stood against the wall, surrounded by people she didn't know well, if at all.

Then she saw Patty Forbes lumbering up to her, scowling. "I just saw that little scene with Danny. You know, he seems to hang around you an awful lot. What's the deal? I thought you was going with Shannon," she said, standing in front of Mandey with her arms crossed.

Oh, just what I need, scorn from the deluded, Mandey thought.

"I am going with Shannon. Danny just doesn't like him very much," she said, opening her purse and bringing out a piece of notepaper and a pen. She scribbled her phone number on the paper and handed it to Patty. "Can you tell Phillip to call me? He should have the number, but here it is, if he doesn't."

"Why?" Patty asked, grabbing the paper.

Patty didn't seem to have heard the news. She would soon enough. "It's about Shannon," Mandey said.

The bell rang, mercifully, and Mandey headed to her locker. She got her books, went to Spanish class, and sat in her desk with an index card-sized piece of paper and some colored pencils making herself a sign during the morning announcements. In bright red capital letters, it said, "NO COMMENT." She decorated it with colored shapes all around the words, then pinned it to her shirt.

Andrea initiated the first note. "¿Qué es eso?" she wrote, referring to the message on Mandey's chest.

"Hay un problema del que no quiero hablar."

"¿Tienes un problema?"

"Actualmente, no. Shannon tiene un problema muy grande. I don't want to talk about it."

"So it's a very serious problem?"

"Sí. And I can't do much to help him. You'll hear about it, don't worry. I just can't deal with talking to anyone about it right now. I didn't want anyone to even know about it, but it was inevitable. Everyone will know by the end of the day."

"Ay, ay, ay."

"That sums it up. I might feel more like talking mañana. Today, I'd like to blend right in with the woodwork, if I could."

As she walked through the hall on her way to choir class, she saw people staring and whispering. She was always a bit paranoid about people talking about her behind her back, but she realized that being paranoid didn't mean it wasn't true. Suddenly, she didn't think she could deal with it today. She couldn't get in her van and leave now, because she would be busted for skipping school. Instead, she went to her counselor's office. She hadn't had much contact with her during her high school years, save for a couple times when she switched classes and when she was notified that she was a National Merit Scholar semi-finalist. Not like James, who was in her office a couple times a week (which might be a good thing, considering the episode from the summer before). Now Mandey was going to need a little support.

It was awkward, because she did not want to pour her heart out to Mrs. Williams, but she needed to get across to her that the situation was upsetting. She explained it as calmly as she could and avoided bringing the Alley Cats into it. She told the counselor that she was anxious about how some of her classmates might react to her dating someone (living with someone) who was charged in a murder case. Mrs. Williams was very sympathetic to Mandey's plight. She called Marcia, who gave permission for Mandey to leave school and go home for the rest of the day. She also sent her aide to Mandey's classes to get her assignments from her teachers.

"If you find you are being harassed about this, come to my office. If necessary, you can come here and do your work until things calm down," Mrs. Williams said.

When the aide came back, Mandey got a hall pass to go to her locker to get her books, then took a note from Mrs. Williams to the attendance office to check out for the day. As she was getting ready to leave, she saw Mr. Tichner outside the attendance office, talking to Mr. Carr. She paused and turned away from the glass and hoped Mr. Tichner would go away.

"Is something wrong?" asked Mrs. Carrizales, the attendance secretary.

"No," Mandey said quickly. "I'm trying to think if I'm forgetting something I need from my locker."

She paused a moment more, then saw Mr. Tichner walking back toward his office.

"No, I guess not. Thank you," Mandey said quickly, and hurried out the door.

She walked by the choir room as she headed out to the parking lot. Everyone was standing, practicing one of their songs for the U.I.L. concert and sight-reading contest coming up soon. She hoped she would be feeling braver tomorrow and back to rehearsing.

Mandey worked on her school assignments during the afternoon, then watched television for a little while before it was time to go see Shannon. At five, she turned on the Channel 11 news. The second story in was about Shannon. Now they had his mug shot, and he stared out of the screen at her, his face bruised, his eyes confused and haunted. The newscaster described the general details of Leon's murder, then announced that Shannon had been charged with first degree murder, and his bail set at a quarter of a million dollars.

Mandey sat there, her feelings matching that expression on Shannon's face. Two hundred and fifty thousand dollars. Even ten percent of that, $25,000, was going to be impossible to come up with to bail him out. And first-degree murder? With the history of abuse in the family, they still went with first-degree?

She wondered if Mr. Tichner would haul her into the office again. She hoped not, but at this point, it wasn't high on her list of worries. Getting through this nightmare was all she cared about.

Mandey felt a bit shaky as she walked into the waiting area of the Houston city jail. She had never dreamed she would ever have to visit anyone <u>in jail</u>. There was a short line at the sign-in desk, and after she signed her name on the list, she maneuvered through the crowd to find a seat. She was sure she stuck out like a sore thumb. At least a dozen children of assorted ages were running around, playing, oblivious to where they were.

She sat quietly in an orange vinyl-covered chair and tried to concentrate on *Madame Bovary*, which she was reading for English class. With the shrieking children and the cacophony of voices around her speaking English, Spanish, Vietnamese, and a couple languages she couldn't place, the environment was not conducive to reading, and she eventually gave up.

Finally, they called her name. She joined a group of six adults and a couple children in a line and filed down the hallway. They were ushered into a room where six chairs sat in front of six bulletproof glass windows, with a small partition between each. A telephone hung on the dividing wall at each station.

Mandey was directed to chair number four, and moments later Shannon was sitting in a chair on the other side of the glass, looking at her with haunted eyes. He put the receiver of the phone to his ear.

Mandey blinked back the tears that were threatening to fall before Shannon could see them. She picked up her phone. "Shannon."

"I am so glad to see you," Shannon blurted in a tinny, over-the-phone voice.

"I am, too," Mandey said, putting her palm up to the glass. Shannon held his palm up to hers from the other side. "I wish I could touch you."

"Me, too," Shannon said.

"How are you holding up?" Mandey asked him, setting her hand down again.

"I've been through this before, but I don't like it any more now than I did then," Shannon said. "I'm managing. What about you?"

"I'm okay," Mandey lied. "I'll be better when you're back home with me."

"That won't be for a while," Shannon said mournfully. "No way I'm getting out of here on bond. They charged me with first degree murder. Bail is set at $250,000."

Mandey winced, even though Joe had told her that and she had heard it on the news. "I know," Mandey said heavily. "It was on the news."

"Great," Shannon said. "The whole story?"

"Pretty much," Mandey said. "Shannon, if I had the money, I'd have you out of here in a second."

"I know, Mandey," Shannon said.

"Any word on a trial date?" Mandey asked.

Shannon shook his head. "All I know is Joe said it won't be for a couple months."

"What do you think of Joe?" Mandey asked.

Shannon shrugged. "He seems okay. I didn't see him for very long. He said he talked to you yesterday and you filled him in on a lot of stuff."

"Yeah. He said he might not be able to spend much time talking to you today," Mandey said. "I hope that changes."

"He did run down the different ways this could play out," Shannon said. "Everything from getting acquitted to getting the death penalty."

"I get sick to my stomach just thinking about that," Mandey said softly. "That can't happen, Shannon. We can't let that happen."

"He did say I could probably plea bargain. If I plead guilty to second degree, I'll get sent up for twenty. Which might just be karma paying me back."

"You don't want to do that, do you?" Mandey asked, alarmed.

"Jesus, no," Shannon said. "What I want is to walk out of here right now and go home with you. But I don't want to die, either."

"Shannon, I don't like thinking about it, but if you did get the death penalty, you'd get an automatic appeal. We'd appeal and appeal until the truth came out."

"Which might take fifteen or twenty years, and then I might run out of appeals and get executed anyway," he said flatly.

"Don't say that!" Mandey said. "Is that what Joe said to you?"

"Not in so many words, but I know how the system works," Shannon replied.

"I swear, Shannon, if he's not going to give you a proper defense, you petition the court for a new lawyer. I wish I had money to pay for a lawyer for you," Mandey said, frustrated.

"I think he's going to do all right by me, Mandey," he said. "He just told me like it is."

"I'm going to keep on him to make sure he is doing right by you," Mandey said.

"I still can't believe this," Shannon said. "One minute I was safe and warm in bed with you, and the next I was in a police car getting hauled down here."

"They told you that Raff, Dewayne, and Annette all say they saw you getting out of Leon's car, right?" Mandey asked.

"Yeah, and that's a bunch of bullshit," Shannon said angrily. "When I left there, Leon was still upstairs in the apartment."

"Why would Annette say such a thing?" Mandey asked.

"I don't know. I know we don't get along real well, but I don't think she'd lie just because of that," Shannon said.

"Do you think what I think, that Raff did it and is pinning the blame on you?" Mandey asked.

"That's what I'm thinking, but I don't know if I can get anyone else to believe it."

"Somehow, we'll get to the bottom of it," Mandey said. "Raff needs to pay for all the crap he's done. It's going to catch up with him, wait and see."

Visiting time only lasted fifteen minutes, and too soon a jailer came and announced it was over. On the other side of the glass, a jailer escorted Shannon and the other inmates back to their cells, and Mandey and the other visitors filed back out to the waiting area. Feeling numb, she left the building and walked to where her van was parked. Seeing Shannon so sad and defeated had shaken her to the core. She had to do everything in her power to get him out of there, but she didn't feel like she had the power to do anything at all.

She wanted to cry, but she held back the tears. *I have to 'let it turn',* she thought, thinking of a scene from *Red Dawn*, in which Tommy Howell's character was letting his sorrow turn to anger against the invaders who had killed his family. The character had kind of gone off the deep end after that.

"Maybe I shouldn't 'let it turn' that much," she said aloud, and chuckled in spite of herself. But the thought buoyed her spirits a little. Let the tears turn to anger, let the anger turn to action, and let the action get Shannon out of jail. Now she just had to figure out how…

Back home, Mandey sat at her desk to finish her homework, but she did it mechanically and unenthusiastically. With senioritis settling in and her concern for Shannon on top of that, it was a wonder it got done at all. When she finished with her Spanish and chemistry exercises, she began thinking about having to go to school the next day. She wished with all her heart that she didn't have to, but she knew that wasn't an option. She couldn't spend the rest of the school year in a self-imposed cocoon. Shannon was in jail charged with murder, and everyone knew it. She had to face it, and do it with her head held high.

The first thing she needed to do was give her friends the explanation she knew she owed them. The easiest way to do it was to write each one a note explaining everything, then fill in the details personally when they had questions. Her friends—Georgia and Gayla, in particular—were blessed with the gift of gab far more than Mandey could ever hope to be, so her version of what happened would spread quickly.

If I can't avoid the gossip mill, I might as well try to use it to my advantage, Mandey thought.

She drafted what turned out not to be a note but a two-page letter and copied it over twice, so she had one each for Georgia, Gayla, and Andrea. Putting the words on paper was cathartic; she hadn't even written about Shannon's arrest in her diary yet because she had been too upset to write.

When that was done, she took a shower and put on her pajamas. She was settling down to watch a little television before going to sleep when the phone rang. She didn't answer it immediately. Her mind flashed back to when she and Shannon were first dating and how thrilled she was every time she heard his voice on the phone. She wished she were going to pick up the receiver now and hear him on the other end of the line. Then she thought about talking to Shannon over the phone through the glass at the jail. She would just as soon never talk to Shannon on the phone again once he was back home.

She thought it might be Phillip. Instead, it was Danny. When she said hello, he responded by asking, "Are you going to talk to me or is your answer to everything still, 'NO COMMENT'?"

"Why should I talk to you?" Mandey asked, turning off the television. She set the phone on the edge of the bed and got under the covers. "Why should I tell you anything when I haven't even told any of my best friends?"

"Yeah, Georgia was freaked out when I talked to her. She didn't know," Danny said. "You haven't talked to anyone else about it yet?"

"No," Mandey said. "I will tomorrow. Today I wasn't ready to deal with it."

"Are you okay now?" Danny asked her.

"No, not really," she replied.

"I do care about you, Mandey. I want you to be all right."

"I know. Thanks."

"So do I have to wait until tomorrow to hear your version of the story?"

"You just want to have the scoop before anyone else," Mandey said, only half-teasing.

Danny's tone turned serious. "No, I want to know why the hell you're in love with a murderer."

Mandey sighed. "Danny, he's not a murderer."

"Then what the hell happened?" Danny asked.

Mandey gave him a brief account of the relationship between Shannon and his stepfather and of what had happened on Saturday when Shannon went to take his mother to run errands and on Sunday when the police came to arrest him.

"Well, how did the cops come to the conclusion Trick—Shannon—was responsible?" Danny asked.

Mandey frowned. "I personally don't think the evidence they have is as good as they think it is," she said.

"What is it? What do they have?"

"Well, that Shannon and Leon were fighting right before Leon got killed. The murder weapon is a knife that belongs to a set that Shannon's family owns. And three people allegedly saw Shannon getting out of the back seat of Leon's car around the time Leon was murdered in it."

"There are three witnesses and you don't believe it?" Danny asked incredulously.

"Danny, the witnesses are Raff, Dewayne, and Annette," Mandey said. "I trust them just as far as I can throw them."

"I see," Danny said, considering the information. "I can understand not trusting Raff or Dewayne, but Annette's his sister, right?"

"Yeah, but they haven't gotten along for a long time," Mandey said. "Maybe she doesn't care what happens to him, or maybe she's being coerced."

"Maybe," Danny said skeptically, "but why are you so eager to believe he's innocent?"

"Lots of reasons," Mandey said firmly. "One—if he had wanted to murder Leon, he likely would have done it long ago. Two—if he had done it, he probably would have fled rather than come home and act like nothing had happened. Three—he had been in a fistfight with Leon prior to his murder, so Shannon had some blood on his shirt, but not the amount you would expect if he had stabbed someone to death. Four—Shannon's been desperately trying to get his life on the right track. He's not about to do anything to screw that up. Five—"

"I get the picture," Danny said, interrupting. "So, what's going to happen now? When is he going to trial?"

"It hasn't been set yet," Mandey said. "His attorney estimates that it won't be until April at the earliest. But if he pleads guilty, he'll skip the trial and likely get sent to prison for twenty years."

"Is he going to plead guilty?" Danny asked.

"No," Mandey said stubbornly. "He can't plead guilty to something he didn't do."

"Well, yeah, he could—"

"I know he can, but he won't," Mandey said. "Here's the situation as I understand it. If he pleads guilty, they'll cut a deal, charge him with second-degree murder, and he'll go to prison for twenty years. If he pleads not guilty and the jury finds him guilty anyway, he could get life or possibly the death penalty. Or he could be found not guilty and go free."

"What seems most likely to happen?" Danny asked.

"I don't know," Mandey said. "The police seem to think it's an open-and-shut case. A fight between the two just minutes before, plus three eyewitnesses."

"What does Shannon's lawyer say?"

"I think he wants Shannon to plea bargain," Mandey said. "I realize he's acting as a public defender, so there's no money in it, but 'defender' is supposed to be the key word there."

"And what does Shannon want?"

"Obviously, he wants to come home to me," Mandey said. "He has said he's thought about pleading guilty. He said that even though he didn't kill Leon, he's done other stuff that he probably deserved to go to prison for. I told him he needed to make amends for those things, but not by admitting to something he didn't do. Then again, we're both terrified he could be sentenced to death."

There was a pause. "He's not my favorite person, but I don't think he deserves the death penalty," Danny said. "Not even if he did do it, if that man was the monster you say he was."

"He was. I know from personal experience," Mandey said, and related how Leon had hit her that day Shannon had moved out of the apartment.

"I'd have killed him right then and there," Danny declared.

Mandey doubted that, but didn't say so. "Shannon could have, too, but he didn't, which is another reason why I know he didn't kill Leon."

"Man," Danny said. "What a mess."

"A-yuh," Mandey said.

"If he didn't do it, who do you think did?" Danny asked.

"Raff. He hates Shannon. He set Shannon up to get arrested once when the two of them were robbing a liquor store. Shannon didn't rat on Raff even though it could have reduced his sentence. Raff hated Shannon when he was leader of the Devils, and he hated him more when he thought Shannon had defected to the Alley Cats," Mandey said. "I think he saw an opportunity to frame him, took full advantage of it, and got Dewayne and Annette to back up his story."

"Hmm," Danny said thoughtfully. "You might have something there. Want me to keep an ear out? I hear a lot of stuff, especially when I'm at Liaisons."

"Would you?" Mandey asked hopefully. "I would appreciate it so much."

"No problem. Well, I've got to go. Thanks for telling me what happened."

"You're welcome," Mandey said.

"See you tomorrow."

Mandey hung up, put the phone back on the desk, and got back into bed. Her mind was more at ease than it had been for several days. Writing it out had helped, and talking to Danny made her feel even better. She hadn't expected him to be so open-minded or understanding.

I bottle things up too much, she thought. *I try too much to do everything on my own. I'm always there for my friends. I need to realize they are there for me, too.*

65

Another Visit with the Parole Officer

On Tuesday, Shannon was surprised after he returned to his cell from his visit with Mandey to be informed that he had another visitor. He walked back to the visitation room and sat down at one of the booths. A moment later, Kevin Holtz appeared on the other side of the glass, glaring at him. Shannon reluctantly put the receiver to his ear.

"What kind of bullshit is this, you punk?" Holtz hissed. "You think you're gonna fuck me over? Well, I've got news for you—"

"What?" Shannon asked. "I'm already in jail. What else do you think you can do to me?"

"I will make sure you never see the light of day again," Holtz replied. "You fucked with the wrong guy, Douglass."

If Holtz thought he could intimidate Shannon, he was wrong. Once upon a time, Shannon had been cowed by him. He had never wanted Holtz to know that, hence the attitude he put on during most of their meetings. Things were different now. Sure, he was scared shitless at the prospect of going to prison, but he was not scared of this prick anymore.

"You made your own fucking mess, Holtz, and now it's all coming back to bite your ass," Shannon told him.

"I can make your life a living hell here in jail if I want to," Holtz told him.

Like it wasn't already.

"Look, I don't know what kind of trouble you're in, but if I tell my lawyer you've been threatening me—," Shannon said.

"You ruined your own life, so what? You figured you'd might as well ruin a few more?" Holtz said bitterly. Shannon thought the guy looked like he might start crying.

"I didn't ruin shit," Shannon said. "I didn't murder anybody, and I got framed for it. As for you, you deserve whatever you've got coming." He hung up the receiver and got up out of his chair.

"You're gonna pay, Douglass!" he heard Holtz shouting as he made his way out of the room.

    At least now Shannon knew that the letters he had sent were being read. Unfortunately, Holtz's visit showed they weren't as anonymous as he had thought they would be. Now that he was in jail, he wondered if he was going to regret spilling the beans.

66

Valentine's Day

Valentine's Day happened to fall on Thursday, a visiting day. Mandey wasn't sure how to approach the holiday. It was their first Valentine's Day as a couple, and they would only get to spend fifteen minutes in each other's presence, separated by bulletproof glass. It wasn't what Mandey had envisioned at all. Marcia and Michael were going out on a romantic date, so Mandey and Shannon would have had the house to themselves. What Mandey had hoped for was to have a romantic candlelit dinner at home together. Maybe cook a couple of steaks, have a little champagne, indulge in a rich, chocolaty dessert. Afterward, she would lead him to her bedroom, and he would assume they were going to make out like they usually did, and probably finish with a "happy ending" for him. They would make out, and it would be a happy ending for him, even happier than he expected because she was going to say yes. It was going to be too hard to wait until May. She wanted him too much. She wanted to enjoy the same sort of pleasure she was giving to him, and that he wanted to share with her, too. Valentine's Day would be the perfect time to let him know she was ready for him make her a woman.

Now that was not going to happen. In fact, there was a chance that it would never happen.

Why didn't I just do it Christmas morning? she asked herself despairingly. *Like Danny said, I was too damned afraid of becoming a statistic.*

She had cried every night since Shannon's arrest about not sleeping with him. Every night she forced herself to believe that justice would be served, Shannon would be freed, and they would be able to resume their lives together. She needed to focus on that because thinking about the alternative would kill her.

She was trying to figure out the best way to handle their fifteen-minute jailhouse date tonight. Dress up extra pretty for him? Show him the card she had bought for him through the glass? (He could receive mail, but it was personal and she didn't want jail staff reading it.) She wasn't sure she should even acknowledge that it was Valentine's Day; that might bring Shannon down even more. She decided to touch up her make-up a bit, but she wasn't going to make a big deal about the holiday.

As it was, she needn't have worried about it. When she arrived at the jail, she was informed that Shannon was not eligible to have any visitors that evening. When she asked why, the attendant did not have an answer, other than he was not on the list of being able to have visitors. After depositing some money into Shannon's commissary account (she was taking her lunch to school and saving her lunch money to do this), Mandey returned to her van, her mind whirling, wondering what might have happened. Was he sick? Had someone hurt him? Why wouldn't they let him have any visitors?

Shannon sat on the floor of the cold, dark room. There was a small, rectangular window at the top of the door that let in some weak light from the corridor, but it didn't help much. Not that there was anything to see. It was a tiny room with a lot of empty shelves and a drain in the center of the floor. He realized he was in a closet, probably a supply closet, emptied out and repurposed as a solitary cell.

He was freezing. He had been buck-naked for a few hours until finally someone had tossed a pair of drawers in for him, but nothing else. There had been no dinner. Shannon wasn't sure what time it was, but his stomach was rumbling. Even that gray stew would taste okay. And it was Thursday—visiting day, but he wouldn't get to see Mandey tonight.

He sat against the back wall, reflecting on how he got into this situation. He had been in the shower with three other guys. He knew those clichéd warnings about "Don't drop the soap" as well as anyone. The only thing is, he found out it wasn't a cliché. As he bent over to pick up the sliver of soap that had slid out of his hands, he suddenly felt a hand reach between his legs and grab his sack.

He shot upright, smacking his head on the cold-water handle on the way. Holding his head, he whirled around to see Carl with a shit-eating grin on his face. The next thing Shannon knew, his fist was smashing that stupid grin. The other three guys began egging him on, hooting and hollering as he punched Carl repeatedly. Blood splattered on the tile floor and washed down the drain. The guards rushed in, grabbed Shannon by the arms, and dragged him down the hallway. They threw him into the solitary cell, wet and naked, and slammed the door.

"What the fuck is this?" he shouted. "He grabbed my balls! You'd do the same fuckin' thing if someone grabbed yours!"

For about thirty minutes he yelled, asked questions, tried to bargain, and even begged. On the other side of the door, no one responded to anything he said.

"How long am I gonna be in here?"

No answer.

"Can I at least get some clothes?"

No answer.

Growing weary, he finally sat down against the wall. He pulled his knees up to his chin, but he still started to shiver. He had a headache. When he put his hand to his head, he found congealed blood where he had hit it on the lever. His right hand hurt, as well, from punching out that fucking homo Carl. What the fuck was he expecting? Shannon was going to spread his cheeks and say "Come on in"?

At least a few hours had passed since they threw him in here, but he didn't know what time it was. Mandey could be out there right now, wondering what the hell happened that he wasn't there for visiting hours. Like he wasn't giving her enough to worry about as it was. He wondered how long they were going to keep him in here. He slumped against the wall. This was bullshit. This was not his fault. Carl assaulted him first. His stupid pervert ass should be in here, not him.

His mind went back to his miserable childhood, and the times Leon had locked him in the closet after giving him a whooping for no real reason. Now he was locked in a closet again for something that wasn't really his fault. A sob escaped before he could stop it, and then his body shook as despair took over. He was alone where nobody could see him, and he let his grief pour out. Eventually, his sobs subsided, leaving him empty and exhausted, but it was a long time before he fell into a broken, restless sleep on the cold, hard floor.

67

Worried and Discouraged

Mandey wanted to relate the story of her non-visit with Shannon to Marcia, but there was a message on the machine when she got home. Marcia was spending the night at Michael's, but she would be home after work the next day. She thought about calling over to Michael's to talk to Marcia, but instead, she went to her room, finished the rest of her homework, then got ready for bed. Her mind was in a tizzy, playing out all the different scenarios of what she thought might have happened. Although she eventually slept, it wasn't a peaceful sleep.

She woke up the next morning with her mind still whirling and her stomach in a knot. That wasn't unusual, it had been her state almost constantly since Shannon had been arrested. Now something else awful had happened to him, and she didn't know what. The knot felt like it was being doubled up and pulled tighter.

She was quiet most of the day, not telling her friends about what had happened, or talking much about anything else, either. Almost everyone was preoccupied with the Sweetheart Dance to take place that evening. Mandey had figured she and Shannon would be going and having an evening with a much better ending than the Christmas dance. Instead, he was in jail for something he didn't do, and she was worried sick about him.

Before going to the cafeteria for lunch, Mandey stopped at the payphone by the front office to call Marcia. She wasn't at her desk, so she had to leave a message. She let her know what happened the night before. She hoped Marcia could bring her some news when she came home from work.

Marcia did come home with news. "Joe called the jail. Shannon got in a fight and was in solitary confinement yesterday."

"What?" Mandey asked, shocked, even though both a fight and solitary confinement had played into some of the scenarios she had imagined. "Why?"

"Something about a fight in the shower room. They didn't give him a lot of details. He's out now, and you should be able to visit him tomorrow."

At least now she knew, but she was upset. She worried about what might have set off the fight, and hoped that it wasn't going to be something that was going to repeat itself. Shannon being in lock-up was bad enough without fighting and solitary confinement on top of it.

The next day during visitation, Shannon shuffled into the room looking tired and sullen. His face brightened a bit when he saw Mandey waiting for him on the other side of the glass. He sat down and picked up the phone.

"Hi," he said.

"Hi," she replied. "What happened Thursday?"

Shannon told her about the fight with Carl and being thrown into solitary.

"Is that even legal?" Mandey asked, horrified, when Shannon told her about the conditions of the solitary cell he had been in.

Shannon shrugged. "Dunno. Anyway, they let me out the next morning and moved me to another cell away from him. Damn good thing, too, because I'd've ended right back up in solitary again."

Mandey was dismayed. "I hope you can steer clear of him from now on," she said.

"Oh, I am gonna be watching like a hawk for him, and anyone else who tries to get funny. But if they saw what I did to Carl, they should know to stay out of my way," Shannon said. "I'm sorry I missed your visit on Valentine's Day."

Mandey managed a half smile. "I wasn't sure you'd even realize what day it was."

"I did, and it sucked not being able to see you."

"Yeah, it did," Mandey agreed. "You can make it up to me next year."

"If I'm not in Huntsville."

"I can't think about that," Mandey said.

"Yeah, well, I think about it too much," Shannon said.

"You're going to get out of here," Mandey said.

"I hope so."

"I was going to tell you Thursday when I couldn't visit you that we got your car back from impound. Joe picked it up and Michael drove it back to the house," Mandey told him.

Shannon was silent. "I hope I'll get out of here to drive it again," he said finally.

"You will," Mandey said insistently.

After Mandey left, back in his cell with his three new cellmates, Shannon laid on his bunk (the top bunk, but maybe that wasn't such a bad thing after all). He prayed to God, silently, hoping He was listening, but afraid that He wasn't. Maybe this was His way of punishing him for all the bad things he had done, to give him something good (Mandey), to give him hope, and then yanking it all away. Shannon felt tears come to his eyes. God wouldn't be that cruel, would He?

68

The Truth Will Set You Free

The next Tuesday after Mandey's visit, Shannon thought about what he didn't tell her while she was there. Things had changed since Carl had pulled that stunt in the shower. The guards were being bigger assholes than they had been to begin with. They were restricting his access to the commissary, which meant no cigs, no snacks. Not being able to smoke was the worst. He had run out of cigarettes on Sunday, and now he was at the mercy of anyone he could manage to bum one from. He didn't think his promises to pay them back were going to work for too long. Besides that, when doing his assigned chores, which was a couple hours of mopping floors, the guards would kick his bucket over; if it was in a restroom, he watched them deliberately piss all over a floor he had just mopped so he would have to do it over again; when they brought him his meal tray, there was usually something missing from it (not a huge loss, but still); they jeered and harassed him verbally, and sometimes physically, though they always made it seem like an accident. A bump in the hallway that sent him sideways into the wall. A foot catching his, making him stumble. He even slipped once, onto the freshly mopped floor, and banged up his elbow and his knee.

He had heard a rumor that someone paid Carl in commissary credits in return for grabbing him in shower. He wondered if it was Holtz. His visit to Shannon the previous week made it apparent that some sort of investigation was underway, touched off by the letters Shannon had sent a few weeks before.

Holtz's supervisor had received the letter and had taken it immediately to her boss, the head of the Houston District Parole Office. However, he was unsurprised, as he had also gotten the letter. They started by quietly looking at Holtz's client files, without his knowledge. Some anomalies were found, and Holtz came to work one morning to find himself locked out of his office. After a heated exchange, he was put on unpaid leave and escorted from the premises. Next, they immediately went into damage control mode, sending a memo out informing employees of an unspecified "personnel issue", and instructing them to keep it confidential.

The anomalies they had found were these: Holtz and two other parole officers had been farming out their parolees to employers (like Ed Grubbs) who wanted to use them for illegal activities. They, in return, got kickbacks from the profits. In order to facilitate the crimes being committed (which went beyond the car thefts Shannon had been coerced into doing), Holtz and his cohorts greased the palms of some of the HPD patrol officers, encouraging them to take a "hands off" approach in the areas where the parolees were operating.

The police department had also received a copy of the letter. It had been Shannon's intention to let the police know what had happened in case the parole division tried to sweep the situation under the rug. Now it appeared that some members of the police force implicated in the scandal, and the police department was conducting its own internal investigation, also trying to keep it very hush-hush.

Although Shannon had sent the letters anonymously, it had not been that difficult to figure out he had been the one. Holtz had been named in the letter, so it was obviously one of his clients. Holtz himself knew it before anyone else. He had noticed his missing documents a few days after Shannon's appointment in December. He practically ransacked his office trying to find them, thinking he had misplaced them. Unlikely, because he was organized almost to the point of being obsessive-compulsive. As he thought harder about it, he remembered he had had them in the basket on his desk when the fight between Jenkins and Emerson had happened, and the basket had been knocked on the floor. He and Douglass had broken up the fight, leaving the girlfriend alone in the office. It was the end of the week before he noticed the ledger documents were gone. The girlfriend must have taken them. But why? How would she know what they were? At his January appointment with Shannon, Holtz had waited for him to bring up the subject. He had an excuse all ready, but Shannon didn't mention it. He had breathed a sigh of relief, but too soon, he found out.

Now that some members of the police force were coming under scrutiny for taking bribes to shirk their duties, they were telling the jailhouse guards that Shannon was a "narc". The guards needed no other motivation to make life miserable for a murder suspect with a case of diarrhea of the mouth.

On Wednesday morning, two guards appeared at the cell door right after breakfast. "Okay, Douglass," one of them said, opening the door. "Come with us."

Shannon reluctantly got down from his bunk, wondering what they had in store for him. Since being tossed into the solitary closet after beating up Carl, he was always wary that he might end up there again.

They shackled his hands and feet and marched him into an interrogation room. He sat down at the long table. The guards left and locked the door behind them. Shannon looked around the room. There was the mirror these rooms always had. He knew there were cops on the other side, looking through it at him. In a couple of minutes, two police detectives entered and began asking questions about Kevin Holtz, Ed Grubbs, and what his job duties were at the garage before he quit. They made it sound like it was in his best interest to tell them everything he knew, but Shannon wasn't so sure.

He answered the first few seemingly innocuous questions, but when they turned to asking about car thefts, Shannon said, "I want my lawyer," and refused to say another word. He could see they were getting pissed off at him, but Shannon was held his ground. They badgered him for what seemed like forever, oscillating between cajoling him and threatening him. It took a good bit of self-control on his part not to start mouthing off at them. He thought they would call his lawyer so they could continue their interrogation, but they didn't. Or maybe they couldn't get in touch with him. He wished they had, because he desperately wanted to talk to Joe again.

The next morning, he asked the guards if he could call his lawyer, and he was a bit surprised when he was allowed to call Joe (collect, of course). Shannon expected to have to leave a message, but the receptionist put him through to Joe and he was able to speak with him directly. Joe came down to the jail that afternoon at 3:30. Away from the ears of the guards, Shannon was able to explain the whole situation with Grubbs, Holtz, the chop shop, and the letters he had sent.

"They were wanting to question me because I guess they figured out I sent the letters. I told them I wouldn't talk without my lawyer," Shannon said.

"So, that's what they were trying to get in touch with me about," Joe said.

"They did call you yesterday?" Shannon asked.

"They did, but I was in court," Joe replied. "You were wise not telling them anything. If they want to talk to you again, tell them on the advice of your attorney, you have no comment. We're going to keep this to ourselves and see how it plays out. It may give us some leverage down the road."

"How?" Shannon asked.

"I guarantee you, TDCJ and the police are trying to cover this up. If any of the media try to question them, they are going to stonewall them. If you start talking to anyone, it's going to be harder to keep it under wraps. We may be able to use your silence on the matter as a bargaining chip during sentencing."

Shannon looked doubtful. "I hope I'm not going to get sentenced for anything," he said.

"I know you don't, but it's good to have some insurance."

"So, if I pleaded guilty, which I don't want to do, but if I did, you think they would cut me a better deal if I promised to keep my mouth shut about what I know?"

"Pretty sure."

Shannon was not overly impressed by the plan but didn't say so.

"Just keep quiet for now. I know they were giving you mixed signals about what they wanted you to tell them. That's what they do. I'll do some investigating of my own and see if I can figure out what they really want from you."

"Okay, but can you get the guards to quit harassing me? I don't know what they've heard about me, but they're making a bad situation worse, and I'm getting sick of their shit," Shannon said.

"I'll take care of it," Joe said. "Don't worry."

Well, that was a laugh. Don't worry? That's about all Shannon did now.

He asked Joe not to mention their conversation to Mandey. Shannon didn't want to upset her any more than she already was. He would tell her in his own time, when it seemed right.

Back in his cell again, he tried to take a nap, which was nearly impossible. He sat up some time later when he heard someone trying to get his attention.

"Son, would you like a Bible?" asked a man with graying hair and a graying mustache, wearing tan plaid suit. He held up a small, red, fake-leather bound book. It was a copy of the New Testament. Shannon vaguely remembered people coming to his school and passing those little Bibles out to the students at recess when he was in fifth grade. He didn't remember what had happened to his copy.

One of the other guys, Rodney, had also taken up the man on his offer. The other two were ignoring him. Shannon got down off his bunk and took the tome the man was holding out to him through the bars of the cell.

"Thanks," he mumbled.

"Read it, son, and repent," the man said. "The truth shall set you free. Maybe not in this life, but certainly in the next."

Shannon looked at him uncertainly. "Thanks," he said again. He hoped to God the truth was going to set him free—and soon.

69

Taking the Initiative

The days seemed to crawl by. Mandey felt like she was on autopilot, going through the motions, doing the things she needed to do, but doing them in a fog. She tried to get herself engrossed in her schoolwork; she wanted to be engrossed in it, so that her mind was not preoccupied with worry about Shannon. Occasionally, she did forget, for a little while, and that was a blessing, but it was never for long.

She pestered Marcia for news from Joe every evening. Every evening it was the same; nothing new. She asked Shannon during their visits on Tuesday and Thursday if he had been in contact with his attorney. He said Thursday that he had talked with Joe, but there wasn't anything new to report. What was Joe doing to get Shannon's defense ready? Nothing, at least nothing Mandey could see.

On Friday night, Mandey dressed up to go to Liaisons. She wished she were dressing up to go out with Shannon, but if things went right tonight, maybe she would be again before too long. Tonight, though, she was going alone. She thought about asking Georgia, or Andrea and Mart (but not Gayla, she didn't like nightclubs, so she said. They made her uncomfortable and nervous). Anyway, things might get weird, so it was better to go solo.

Although possessed of a mild case of the jitters, Mandey felt better about Shannon's situation than she had since the whole thing began. She wasn't going to sit on her butt any longer. No one else was taking any action, so it was time for her to get the ball rolling.

She wore black pants and ankle boots, a red and black vertically striped button-down shirt (untucked), her silver-studded black belt, and her black fedora. It was her "Durannie" look. As she looked in the mirror, she wondered if red was the best color to wear, then shrugged it off. The color had no meaning for her anymore.

As usual, Liaisons was crowded. She hadn't been there since November, and it surprised her to see the wooded lot on the west side of the club cleared out to expand the parking lot. More powerful security lights had been installed, as well. The owners were wising up.

Inside, the club hadn't changed. Lights flashed and music throbbed as the throng cavorted and danced. Mandey made her way to an unobtrusive spot at the end of the bar that gave her a good view of the whole club. She ordered a Pepsi and waited for the Devils to show up.

As the minutes ticked by, Mandey began to worry that none of the Devils would make an appearance. Maybe now that Liaisons had more security measures in place, the club was a less attractive target. Or maybe the Devils were worse than ever (like Danny said) thus the heightened security.

She was ordering a virgin piña colada when she spotted Danny entering the club. At the other end of the bar, he stopped and ordered a drink. He noticed Mandey and when he got his drink, he came over to sit next to her.

"What are you doing here?" he asked in a not-unfriendly tone.

"I need to talk to Shannon's sister," Mandey explained. "The phone has been disconnected, and I don't dare try to go over there, especially not alone. I don't think I'm likely to see her here, but I'm hoping I can persuade one of the other Devils to give her a message."

"Good luck," Danny said dryly.

"I haven't been here for a while. I see they finally expanded the parking lot and got some new lights," she said.

"They've hired another security guard, too," Danny said.

"Have things gotten worse around here?" Mandey asked.

"Mandey, maybe you were right. Once your boyfriend left the scene, all hell broke loose for a while. They won't let anyone in wearing a Devil or Alley Cat insignia anymore."

"I noticed you didn't have on your shirt or jacket," Mandey said. "Are you here doing business or are you an Alley Cat tonight?"

"I'm here to make money tonight," Danny said with a grin.

Mandey secretly hoped to hear him say he was no longer dealing, but she knew that was unlikely to happen.

"Do the Devils still come in here?" Mandey asked.

"Oh, yeah. Like I said, for a while all hell broke loose. We won that damn fight, but Raff declared himself leader and said all deals made with Trick were null and void. We were gunning for each other every weekend. Hey, did you know we recruited Keith Saunders and Mark Ruggeri?"

"No, I didn't," Mandey said.

"The Devils have been doing some recruiting of their own. Most of them look to be awfully young, not that that means anything."

"What have they been doing?" Mandey asked.

"Mostly fighting with us. One night we nearly started a riot in here. That's when they banned the gang insignias. And Raff, Jesse, and Terry are all banned for life."

"I didn't know that," Mandey said, eyebrows raised.

"I thought having Raff out of the picture would be good for me, but he lurks out in the parking lot and sells, and he has some of the new kids dealing for him in here," Danny said. "If you want to send a message, the new ones would be the ones to use, since they don't know you from Eve."

"That's a good idea," Mandey said. "Can you point one out to me?"

Danny stood up and scanned the crowd. "I don't see any of them right now. I'm going to go about my business. When I find one, I'll come show him to you."

"Thanks, Dan."

Mandey sat, eyes searching the crowd in vain for a familiar Devil face. About thirty minutes later, Danny returned.

"See the kid in the black jeans and the white T-shirt, with the long germ tail?" he asked, pointing through the crowd. "He's talking to the stoned-looking chick in purple."

Mandey nodded.

"His name is Noe. He's one of the new ones. Try him out," Danny said. "How much money do you have on you?"

"About thirty dollars. Why?"

"You'll probably have to give him an incentive to pass along your message," Danny told her.

"Oh. Of course," Mandey said. "Thanks again, Danny."

"No prob," he replied. "Talk to you later." He merged with the crowd again.

Mandey watched as people approached Noe, completed some sort of transaction, then left. Hesitantly, she made her way toward him.

Noe was skinny and short; he was not much taller than Jeremy was. In her boots, Mandey towered over him. She felt like a giant.

"What choo need? If I don't got what choo need, I can get it," he said. His monotone delivery indicated he repeated this dozens of times a night.

"None of the above," Mandey said. "Do you know Annette Douglass?"

"Who wants to know?" Noe asked, suspicious.

"I want to know," Mandey replied. "I'm from Annette's old neighborhood. I've lost touch with her, and somebody said you run with her new bunch of friends."

"Maybe," Noe said.

"I was hoping you could do me a favor," Mandey said, showing him a sealed, unmarked white envelope. "I need this delivered to Annette. I want no questions asked, I want the envelope delivered to her sealed, and I want you to keep quiet about it." She saw him start to speak, probably to tell her to get out of his face, but she flashed him a twenty-dollar bill. "This is for your trouble. Twenty dollars is pretty good for delivering one little letter, isn't it?

That's a hundred times what the post office charges. Or it was until they raised the rates this week."

Noe looked from the letter to the money and back to the envelope. He snatched both from her hands and they disappeared into the back pocket of his jeans. "I'll take care of it," he said.

"Do it like I asked and I may utilize your services again," Mandey said. "Thanks." That felt odd, speaking civilly to—and thanking—one of the Devils.

The music enticed her to dance, but she didn't follow its call. Now that she had connected with Noe, she didn't want to hang around and risk running into any of the Devils who knew her. Her heart wasn't into dancing, anyway. She wanted to have Shannon dancing with her.

It was time to go home and wait for a phone call.

70

Mandey and Annette

Mandey's mood grew progressively more dismal with each day that passed without a phone call from Annette. She was wondering if she was going to have to go back to Liaisons again to try to contact her when her phone rang Thursday evening. The call was terse; Mandey got the feeling Annette was trying not to be overheard. Annette told Mandey where and when to meet her the following evening, and so on Friday night Mandey was sitting in her van in the corner of a Stop-n-Go parking lot, waiting.

Out of the chilly night, Mandey saw a figure in black sweatpants and an old gray sweatshirt coming toward the van. Mandey motioned for her to get in. Annette opened the door and hopped into the passenger seat. Mandey's green eyes met Annette's brown ones.

Neither one said anything for a moment. "As you know, Shannon's in jail," Mandey said.

"Yeah. Tell me something I don't know," Annette said sarcastically.

"Actually, I need _you_ to tell _me_ something," Mandey said. "I don't care what you and your boyfriend and Raff say. I don't believe for a second that Shannon did it."

"Well, that's your problem," Annette said, looking out the passenger window.

"I think that Raff is framing Shannon, just like when he set him up to get arrested during that robbery," Mandey said.

"Think whatever you want," Annette said indifferently, still avoiding Mandey's eyes.

"Do you want your brother to go to prison for something he didn't do?" Mandey asked.

"What happened, happened," Annette said. "You coming over here asking all these questions ain't going to make the answers come out any different."

Mandey closed her eyes and sighed, then opened them again. "Annette, he needs your help," she pleaded. "I'm going to visit him in jail tomorrow. Will you come with me? Come talk to him, please?"

"No way," Annette said. "I'm out of here." She started to open the door.

Mandey panicked. "Annette, please, don't go!"

Annette stopped, maybe because of the urgent tone in Mandey's voice. She shut the door again. "What the hell do you want from me?" she asked.

"Did you see him do it?" Mandey asked. "Did you actually see Shannon stab Leon?"

"No," Annette admitted, "but he got out of the back of Leon's car, and then I found Leon in there bleeding all over the front seat."

"You saw him getting out of the car, right?" Mandey said.

"Of course I saw him getting out of the car!" Annette snapped.

"That's what you told the police, anyway," Mandey said.

"That's what happened," Annette said firmly.

"Or is that what Raff said happened?"

"It's what happened!" Annette insisted. "Jesus, you're worse than the cops. Face the facts—he killed Leon."

"I refuse to believe that," Mandey said. "If Shannon was going to kill Leon, he would have done it a long time ago. I was with him the day he moved out of the apartment, and he had a chance then to kill Leon, but he didn't do it. I doubt he would have done it now."

"I wish he had done it a long time ago," Annette said quietly.

"Did you hate Leon as much as Shannon did?" Mandey asked.

"I hope he's rotting in hell," Annette said in a soft voice, full of hate. "You're doing the same thing the cops did. I didn't do it. I don't know how many times I wanted to, but I didn't do it."

"Then who did, Annette?" Mandey asked. "You say you didn't do it, and I know in my heart that Shannon didn't do it, either, so who did?"

"You know--what the hell do you want with Tr—Shannon, anyway?" Annette asked, changing the subject. "Momma said he told her about how smart and nice and wonderful you are. What does somebody like you want with somebody like him?"

Mandey realized that the direct questioning method was getting her nowhere, so Mandey figured she would let Annette ask a few of her own and see where that might lead.

"Annette, I first laid eyes on your brother when I was in ninth grade. He sat across the aisle from me on the school bus. I had the biggest crush on him. I thought he was so good-looking."

Annette snorted with laughter. Mandey figured if she had a brother of her own that somebody gushed on about, she might laugh, too.

"He didn't know it, though, and I was too shy to talk to him. I was devastated when he stopped coming to school. Then a couple months later, you showed up, and I found out you were his sister. You sat with Theresa and me on the school bus for that whole—what, week? Week and a half? —that you were there. Then you got in that fight with Dina. I saw Shannon up there at school that day, and kids were bugging him, wanting to know what happened. He just stood there, not saying anything, staring straight ahead. I wanted to go up to him and say something to try to make him feel better, but I was too scared to. And then after a couple more months, you all moved away."

"Wait--I sat on the bus with you?" Annette asked, surprised.

"Yes," Mandey said. "You and Theresa had classes together, so she invited you to sit with us." She paused. "I don't think you and I ever said anything to each other, but I remember hearing you tell Theresa that you'd gotten on the wrong side of some girls and you were probably going to get in a fight with one of them. I felt a little intimidated by you, I guess."

"They were a bunch of bitches," Annette said, recalling the incident that started it all. "The first day I was there, they stood in front of my locker talking and they wouldn't move. I finally butted by them so I could get my stuff so I wouldn't be tardy, and that pissed them off. From there it got worse and worse."

"After you moved, I figured I'd never see Shannon again," Mandey continued. "Then I spotted him at Liaisons one night, right after it opened. I was still too shy to go talk to him, and I guess he was shy, too, but his friend came and told me that Shannon liked me. I went to go find him, but they left before I could talk to him, so I lost him a second time. I went back to Liaisons a lot, but I never saw him again until I went to Galveston one day back in November. That time I didn't let him get away."

"You haven't answered my question," Annette said. "Why do you want him so much? He's fat and gross and mean. Kerri always wanted him, and I don't know why, except that she wanted to sleep with him and he didn't want to and that made her mad."

"I don't think he's fat or gross or mean," Mandey said. "He's been nothing but wonderful to me."

"Did he tell you about all the horrible, nasty things he's done?" Annette asked with a malicious smirk on her face. "Did he tell you about all the whores he slept with? Did he tell you about all the places he robbed and all the cars he stole and all the times he got drunk and high and stupid and all the people he beat up?" The look on her face made it obvious that she took pleasure in rattling off Shannon's sins.

"I know he's not a saint," Mandey said. "I also know he took no joy in the things he did, either. He would never have done most of that stuff if he hadn't gotten involved with the Devils."

"You're right about that," Annette said. "He tried to act all big and bad, but he wasn't nothing but a big pussy."

"Just because his heart wasn't into fighting and stealing doesn't make him a pussy," Mandey said.

"Whatever," Annette muttered.

"I love your brother, Annette," Mandey said. "Despite his flaws and what anyone else thinks about him, I love him."

Annette didn't say anything.

"How have you been feeling?" Mandey asked.

"Huh?" Annette asked.

"Shannon told me that you're pregnant," Mandey said. "Is everything okay?"

"It's none of your business," Annette said.

"I was worried when he told me," Mandey continued, ignoring the remark. "I remember kicking you in the stomach. I was afraid I might have hurt the baby."

"I was barely pregnant then," Annette said. "And why do you care?"

"You may not believe this, but you are the sister of the man I love, and I don't wish you any harm," Mandey said.

"Is that why you broke my nose?" Annette asked sarcastically.

"That wasn't intentional. I didn't know at the time it was you and Shannon trying to steal that car," Mandey said. "I'm sorry, if that helps any. I just wanted to get you away from me. I didn't mean to do any serious damage."

"Well, just so you know, I'm fine, the baby's fine, and the Devils are all doing fine without Trick's traitorous ass," Annette declared.

Mandey growled in frustration. "I wish you'd realize that Shannon never had anything to do with the Alley Cats. They hate him and want absolutely nothing to do with him. They're glad that he's in jail."

"He still abandoned us," Annette said.

"You didn't want him around anyway!" Mandey exclaimed, throwing up her hands. "You just said he's a big pussy. Aren't you all happier without him? Isn't that what you wanted?"

Annette didn't reply.

"Are you sure you won't come talk to Shannon tomorrow?" Mandey asked.

"I can't," Annette said.

That was different from "I won't" or "I don't want to," Mandey noted to herself.

"Why can't you?"

"Raff and Dewayne don't want me talking to him," Annette said.

"Why not?"

"They just don't, that's all."

"I didn't think you were the type who liked letting anyone tell you what to do," Mandey remarked.

"I don't," Annette said. "I don't want to talk to him, either. He's a traitor to our gang."

Mandey sighed. Back to square one. "Well, could you tell me how your mother is doing? Shannon's worried about her."

Annette frowned. "My mother is out of her mind."

"I heard she couldn't give a statement to the police," Mandey said. "What happened?"

Annette paused before speaking, as though to collect her thoughts and make sure she said the right thing. "After I found Leon dead in his car, I went upstairs to call the cops; that's something I never thought I'd be doing. Momma was sitting in the living room. I told her what happened. It took me a few times explaining it before it sunk in. Then she started getting hysterical and locked herself in the bedroom.

"When the cops came, still was still in there. They coaxed her out, but when they tried to talk to her, she kept saying 'Oh my God, he's dead' over and over again. She couldn't answer any of their questions. I told them she's not right in the head and she's on medication. They wanted to take her to a doctor, but I told them no. But she's bad off. She don't get out of bed most of the time. I have to make her eat. So now it's just me and her. Dad's dead, Leon's dead, Shannon's in jail. It's just us."

"It sounds like she needs to be in the hospital, Annette."

"We're *fine*," Annette insisted. "She'll snap out of it."

Both girls were quiet. The meeting hadn't been a total loss; Mandey had information about Shannon's family that he would want to know, and she felt she had at least cracked the ice between herself and Annette.

"If you change your mind about going to see Shannon, he's being held in the Houston jail downtown. Visiting hours are five to nine P.M. on Tuesday and Thursday and one to six P.M. on Saturday," Mandey said.

Annette didn't respond.

"Want me to drop you home?" Mandey asked.

"I'll walk," Annette said. "It ain't far, and no one's going to mess with me unless they want the Devils on their ass."

"Thanks for meeting with me," Mandey said.

"Yeah," Annette grunted, and got out of the van.

Mandey watched her disappear back into the darkness, then she started the van. Despite the rocky start, the conversation had given her much to think about. For one thing, Mandey couldn't believe that Annette hadn't asked her how Shannon was doing. She couldn't imagine what Shannon could ever have done to warrant such hatred on her part.

The questions she had asked Annette hadn't yielded the answers she wanted, but Mandey was more certain than ever that someone was hiding the truth about Leon's murder. Annette had been so hostile in her insistence that Shannon was responsible. Maybe it was just hostility toward Mandey, but she thought there was more to it than that. If she hated Leon as much as she said she did, why did she seem so angry that Shannon had killed him?

And Raff and Dewayne don't want her talking to Shannon, Mandey thought. *They're afraid she'll say something she shouldn't.*

Another thought came to her. *She's got to be stressed out. She wants to act like she's too cool to care, but she's pregnant, her brother is in jail, and her mother has gone off the deep end. That's enough to get to anybody.*

Mandey took heart in that thought. Annette might not be able to stand the pressure. Maybe if she tried again in a couple of weeks, she might start to crack. She would have to keep trying.

71

SS, DD

The next day when she visited Shannon, Mandey told him that she had met with Annette. He was upset, as she knew he would be.

"Dammit, Mandey, why did you do that? It could have been an ambush! They could have hurt you!" Shannon exclaimed.

"But it wasn't," Mandey said. "Shannon, I've been feeling like this whole process is bogged down and no one is trying to get to the truth of the whole thing. I'm sure Annette knows a lot more than what she told the police."

Shannon was torn. He appreciated Mandey for wanting to get his name cleared, but he didn't want anything bad to happen to her. He listened as she recounted what Annette had told her, and he was disturbed when she got to the part about how his mother was doing.

"She needs to go to the hospital," Shannon said. "I don't know why Annette is fighting it. Shit!"

"She said it's because she's pregnant and wants her mother home with her," Mandey said.

"That don't even make any sense! If Momma's that far out of it, how does that help Annette?" Shannon asked.

"I don't know, but that's what she said," Mandey said. "Seems to me it would make things harder on her."

Shannon rubbed his forehead wearily.

"I'm sorry I'm not the bearer of better news, but I thought you'd want to know."

"Don't be sorry, I do want to know. I hate being in here," Shannon said.

"How is it going with you?" Mandey asked.

"Same shit, different day. Doesn't really change," Shannon said.

"No one's been harassing you anymore, have they?"

Shannon frowned. He didn't want to mention the asshole jailers. "Since I punched Carl's lights out, most of them leave me alone," he said. "I've got to go around acting like a tough guy all the time, though, and that sucks."

Mandey remembered Annette saying how Shannon's badass image was just an act. She knew that was the truth, but that didn't mean he was a "pussy", as Annette put it. It was survival mode. Mandey figured Shannon had been on it most of his life, but she knew the man underneath. Tears sprang to her eyes as she remembered what she had observed about him when she had that huge, unspoken crush on him. He hadn't been trying to be a badass when she watched him with admiring eyes from afar in ninth grade. He was just a rough-around-the-edges kid. Spitting on the bus (gross). Riding around on his bicycle with no shoes on, the soles of his feet pitch black. His wavy hair always slightly unkempt. The pair of brown polyester pants with the snag in the left leg. Seeing him wearing those pants, stepping off of a church bus with a bible clutched in his hand. Shannon goofing around with Verna in the schoolyard, and how jealous she had felt. How stony and miserable he looked when his mother and sister were being detained by the police in front of everyone at school.

"I know, because that's not who you are," she said.

"Sometimes I wonder," Shannon said. "Maybe it really is."

"You don't believe that," Mandey said. "I don't."

"I don't know," Shannon said. "Maybe I am just a mean, heartless bastard."

"Why are you saying that?" Mandey asked, alarmed. "You know that's not true, and from what you told me, none of the Devils thought that way, either. They thought you were soft." She didn't use Annette's word, "pussy".

He shrugged. "I don't know," he said. "I don't know anything anymore."

"Shannon, look at me," Mandey said.

He looked up at her and saw her green eyes slightly shimmering with tears, but giving him a piercing stare.

"I do," she said firmly. "I know the man you are. Don't lose your faith in yourself."

He managed a half smile. "Okay. As long as I have you to keep reminding me."

"I will, as long as I have to," Mandey said. "I love you."

It made things a little better when she said that. "I love you, too," he replied.

Back in his cell, Shannon's dark mood eventually overtook him again. He never went into details with Mandey about what life was like in jail. He didn't want to depress her more. The harassment from the guards had let up some, thanks to Joe's efforts, but not completely. They harassed all the inmates to some degree, and the more serious the offense, the worse it was. His commissary privileges had been restored, at least. He wasn't allowed to buy all the items available, as that was determined by what you were charged with, but as long as he could have cigarettes, chips, and a coke, he could manage.

The other inmates had left him mostly alone since he had beaten Carl's face. They all knew Shannon was there on murder charges, and they seemed content to give him a wide berth, at least as long as he didn't let his guard down. Most of them did, anyway. There was one guy who came in after the incident with Carl who seemed to be trying to take Carl's place in agitating him. Unfortunately, he was assigned to mopping floors, as was Shannon, and his work period was at the same time, so Shannon had to listen to his mouth every day. He was scrawny with greasy, limp dishwater-dull blond hair, a hook nose, and a full sleeve of tattoos. He would mop the floor almost violently as he repeated his tirade against Shannon.

"You think you're a tough guy? Just because you killed someone, that don't make you tough. You ain't tough. I could beat your ass in thirty seconds, if I wanted to. You ain't shit…"

Every single day, on repeat. At first Shannon had no idea what set this guy off. He told the guy over and over to shut up. When that didn't work, he asked the guards to make him shut up. They didn't; they seemed to enjoy watching Shannon get pissed off. Shannon realized the guards were agitating this guy, who seemed like he wasn't playing with a full deck to begin with, and they wanted Shannon to snap and hit the guy like he had hit Carl. Shannon wasn't going to hit anybody, not unless they hit him first. He didn't want to go back to solitary again. Enduring two hours of trash talk from this guy every day was still better than that. Still, he was afraid the situation was going to escalate, and he was going to end up in that closet-turned-cell again, even if he wasn't at fault, and it probably wouldn't be for a day this time.

72

Mandey and Annette, Part II

Nearly two weeks had passed since Mandey had talked to Annette, and she had not heard a word from her since. Mandey had tried calling her a couple of times, but the phone number was still disconnected. She resigned herself to the fact that she was going to have to go back to the club, see if she could find Noe again, and slip him another twenty to deliver another message to Annette. Mandey wasn't even sure it would be worth it. Annette had shown up the first time, probably out of curiosity, but there was no guarantee she would again. Obviously, she didn't want to talk to Mandey, or she would have used somebody's phone to call her.

She was doing her homework Wednesday evening when her phone rang. To her surprise, it was Annette.

"I've got to talk to you," Annette said, sounding upset.

"What's wrong?" Mandey asked.

"I need to see you face-to-face. I'm on a pay phone at Stop-n-Go right now. Dewayne will be coming out any minute. Meet me tomorrow at five at the Jack in the Box on North Shepherd."

The phone clicked in Mandey's ear. Mandey wondered vaguely if Dewayne was making a purchase or robbing the store. No matter. Annette wanted to talk, and that gave Mandey some encouragement.

Mandey arrived at Jack in the Box a little before five and sat in a plastic booth in one corner. There was no sign of Annette. As the minutes passed, Mandey wondered if she had been stood up, or if this was all part of some sinister plan. Although she didn't think she was being set up for an ambush, as she was in a public place during daylight hours, she began to feel uneasy. She had nearly decided to leave when she saw a Metro bus pull up to a stop outside and Annette stepped off.

"I was beginning to wonder if you were going to show," Mandey said as Annette slid into the seat across the table.

"The bus was running late," she replied.

"Are you hungry?" Mandey asked her.

"Yeah, but I don't have no money."

"That's okay. I'll buy."

A few minutes later they were seated again, eating. Annette tore into her food wolfishly; Mandey figured it might be because she had been barely eating for one when she should have been eating for two.

"Where did you come from on the bus?" Mandey asked. She knew the Northview Apartments were within walking distance of Jack in the Box. "If you don't mind me asking."

"Doctor appointment," Annette said with her mouth full.

"Is everything okay?" Mandey asked.

"Well, she told me I need to be under less stress, I need to gain more weight, and I need to quit smoking," Annette said. "Ain't none of that gonna happen."

She admits she's under a lot of stress, Mandey thought. *It's not me imagining that.*

"Have they given you a due date yet?" Mandey asked.

"July twenty-second. I'm over halfway there."

"Dewayne didn't want to go with you?"

Annette scowled. "If he had gone with me, I wouldn't be sitting here talking to you," she said.

"Okay, so what's going on? You sounded upset on the phone last night."

Annette reached into her pants' pocket and pulled out a folded piece of paper. "Me, Dewayne, and Raff all got these yesterday."

Mandey took the paper from her and unfolded it. It was a subpoena to appear in court on May sixth in the matter of the State of Texas vs. Shannon Edward Douglass.

"Yeah, so? I got one, too," Mandey said.

"I don't want to go to court," Annette said desperately.

"If you want to send Shannon to prison, you've got to appear in court and make the jury believe your story."

"Why can't he just plead guilty and make it easier on everybody?" Annette asked.

Mandey lost her patience. "He should just go along with your lies and throw away the next twenty years of his life?" she asked Annette angrily. "What is wrong with you?"

"What's wrong with me? What's wrong with you?" Annette countered, nearly yelling.

Mandey bit back the urge to yell back. Instead, she took a deep breath to regain her composure.

"You know what's wrong with me?" she asked Annette. "My boyfriend is in jail for a crime he didn't commit. I'm trying to uncover the truth, which you know, and you keep stonewalling me. As for what's wrong with you, I've got a good idea about that, too. You keep telling this phony story, and you're afraid of having to repeat it in court because you might screw it up. If you'd tell the truth, half your problems would up and disappear."

"You think you know it all, don't you?" Annette sneered. "You don't even know the half of it."

"I would if you'd tell me," Mandey said. "Look, why did you call me to meet you? Did you think you could talk me into persuading Shannon to plead guilty so you wouldn't have to go to court?"

"All this stress I'm under is bad for my baby; the doctor said so," Annette said. "I know Shannon wouldn't want nothing bad to happen to his niece or nephew on account of him."

Mandey boggled at her. *She's using the baby for blackmail*, she thought in disbelief.

"What about your mother?" Mandey shot back. "You said she's already in a bad way, but what if she learns that her son has gone to jail for twenty years? She'll never recover from that."

"I've been expecting her to go off the deep end for years," Annette said.

"This is going nowhere," Mandey said, picking up her purse and sliding out of the booth.

"Where are you going?" Annette asked.

"To visit Shannon," Mandey said. "If you want to try to persuade him to plead guilty, you're going to have to do it yourself, because I'm not doing it for you." She turned to walk away.

"Wait!" Annette said. "Are you going there now?"

"Yes," Mandey said. She waited a moment before she asked, "Do you want to go with me?"

"Yeah," Annette replied, getting up.

The radio kept the ride down to the jail from being totally silent. During the drive, Mandey tried to keep her hopes from getting too high, but she thought that Shannon might have a better chance of getting through to his sister than she had. She wondered why Annette had a change of heart about going to see him, though. Surely, she didn't think she could convince him to change his plea?

They signed in and sat down together. Annette maintained a stony silence, and Mandey did not try to break it. It was as if now that she was going to talk to her brother, Annette no longer had any use for Mandey.

The officer organizing the visitation groups called their names.

"Do you want to visit him together or separately?" she asked them.

"Separately," Annette said quickly.

"Who wants to go first?"

"She can," Annette said.

Mandey got in line to go see Shannon. Annette knew what she was doing, she realized. Mandey could see Shannon first and prepare him for Annette's visit, but Annette would have the last word tonight, and Mandey wouldn't be able to discuss with him what was said until

Saturday.

"What's wrong?" Shannon asked as soon as Mandey sat down.

Mandey gave him a half-smile. "Nothing is wrong, but you also have another visitor. Annette is going to be in next to see you."

Shannon's eyes grew wide. "She's here?" he asked, amazed.

"Yes, and she insisted I come in first. I assume she wants the last word with you tonight." Mandey related her conversation with Annette.

"So, she's here to try to get me to plead guilty?" Shannon asked.

"I think so. She hasn't said a word to me since we left Jack in the Box. I just wanted to prepare you."

They talked a few more minutes before Mandey had to go.

"Don't let her upset you, and I'll be back on Saturday. I love you."

She kissed her hand and placed it against the glass. Shannon placed his hand against it from the other side.

Mandey left the room. Annette was sitting on a bench outside, waiting for the next group to be allowed in. She didn't say a word as she walked past Mandey to go into the visitation room.

Mandey took Annette's place on the bench to wait for her, wondering what was being said. She doubted Annette would tell her anything, so she would have to wait until Saturday to find out.

Fifteen minutes later Annette filed out with the others. Her face was a mask; Mandey couldn't tell how she felt about her visit with her brother.

"He was surprised when I told him you had come to see him," Mandey said to her as they exited the building.

"Yeah, he was pretty damn shocked," Annette agreed.

Mandey wanted desperately to ask Annette what was said, but didn't think it was a good idea. As they drove home, Mandey pondered how to pose a non-intrusive question that might give her some inkling of what had gone on.

"Was your visit worth your while, or was it a waste of time?" Mandey finally asked her.

"It wasn't a waste of time," Annette replied, but she did not elaborate further.

"Where do you want me to drop you off?" Mandey asked.

"Back at Jack," Annette said.

Mandey pulled the van into the parking lot and idled in front.

"Are you sure you'll be safe walking home in the dark?"

Annette laughed. "The scary people in the 'hood are all my homies. They ain't going to hurt me," she said. "You're the one who should be scared, not me." She got out and slammed the door.

Mandey was about to shift back into drive to leave when she looked in the rearview mirror. A group of people had come out of the restaurant, and Annette was walking toward them. Mandey turned around to get a better look and saw Raff, Dewayne, Juanita, and Marco. Dewayne was talking to Annette, but with the windows rolled up, she couldn't hear what was being said. Then she saw Dewayne grab Annette's arm and slap her across the face. At the same time, she saw that Raff was staring back at her. He reached under his jacket into the waistband of his pants like he was reaching for a gun.

"Holy sh—" was all she could say as she hunched down as low as she could and still see over the steering wheel and peeled out of the parking lot.

She looked in the rearview, afraid of seeing Raff's long black car pulling out into traffic behind her, but saw no cars coming out of Jack in the Box. Her heart pounded, and she felt like a coward, driving off and leaving Annette there, but she wasn't about to stick around long enough to see if Raff was bold enough to shoot at her. Annette had said that these were her "homies" and that she wasn't scared of them, so Mandey wasn't going to worry too much about her. She did hope somebody in the restaurant had witnessed the scene in the parking lot and was calling the cops.

She resolved at once not to meet Annette in Devils' territory again. If talking to her over the phone wasn't sufficient, Annette could get on a bus and meet Mandey somewhere on her side of town. She had a feeling she might not be hearing from Annette again now that Raff and Dewayne knew she had been talking to her. That worried her. She and Annette would never be best friends, but she was Shannon's sister, and Mandey still hoped that she was okay.

73

Powerless

All week at school, people had been talking about their plans for spring break. A lot of kids were going to Galveston or South Padre Island. Georgia was going on a church retreat trip to Pensacola, Florida. Andrea and Martin were going to Washington, D.C. with the Close-Up program. Having fun in the sun meant nothing to Mandey. She spent her first day of spring break the same way she had spent the past several Saturdays, at the Houston jail. It was more crowded on Saturdays, so she arrived as soon as visiting hours began, and she was assigned to the second group to go in. As usual, she found Shannon behind the glass, his face almost as colorless as his jumpsuit. Every time Mandey saw him, he looked a little more haggard.

"How are you?" she asked him.

"Same as ever," he replied wearily.

"No one's done anything else to hurt you, have they?"

He shook his head. "I'm doing okay." Not the exactly the truth, but he didn't want to worry Mandey any more than she already was.

"I worry so much about you," Mandey said. "You look like you're losing weight."

"Probably. The food sucks. I guess it don't hurt me to get rid of some of this lard."

"I want you home, Shannon," Mandey said, tears springing to her eyes before she could stop them. "I have to believe you will be coming home soon, and…" The lump in her throat kept her from continuing.

"Don't cry," he told her.

"Sorry," she said, after a moment, after she regained her composure. She hated to cry in front of him. "I'm okay. I'm dying to know about your conversation with Annette."

"I think she basically told me the same stuff she told you," Shannon said. "We got a little loud and they almost cut us off short. She was telling me to confess, and I was calling her a liar, then she started calling me a traitor. She was complaining about having to testify against me and how it was my fault she was under so much stress, and all this stress is making her and the baby sick. Same shit you said she told you."

"Did she say anything about Raff or Dewayne?"

"Not exactly. She did say the gang is a lot different now than when I was in charge."

"Did she seem afraid?"

"Of them? No. Why?"

"She didn't seem scared to me, either," Mandey said, "but that might have changed after I dropped her off."

"Why do you say that?"

"When I dropped her off at Jack in the Box, Raff and Dewayne came out along with Juanita and Marco. I couldn't hear what was being said, but Dewayne grabbed Annette and slapped her."

"He what?" Shannon shouted. The guard nearest to him gave him a threatening look. Shannon caught it and lowered his voice. "God damn it! He never slapped her when I was around. He knew I'd stomp his ass. Then what happened?"

"I don't know," Mandey said sheepishly. "Raff noticed me in the van and I--" She stopped herself from telling Shannon that Raff had a gun. "I didn't stick around to find out what went on after that."

"Shit," Shannon said, half-stunned. "I knew it. I knew things were going to go to hell with me gone. What the hell was going on there? Was it supposed to be a trap or something?"

"I don't think so," Mandey said. "They seemed to notice me as an afterthought. I think maybe they wondered why Annette was late coming back from her appointment and they were waiting for her to get off the bus." She paused. "I felt bad leaving her there, but I didn't want them coming after me."

"You did the right thing by getting out of there," Shannon said.

"Now that they know she and I have been talking, I wonder what they'll do?"

"I'm sure Annette came up with a reason why she was talking to you. She probably told them most of the truth—that she was trying to get you to convince me to plead guilty."

"Do you think they're forcing her to claim you're the one who did it?" Mandey asked.

"Oh yeah, although she won't come out and say it," Shannon said. "I asked her point blank if anyone was threatening to hurt her if she didn't play along with them. I told her if she would tell the truth and get me out of here, I could protect her from them."

"What did she say to that?"

"She said I hadn't done a very good job of protecting her before, so why should she trust me now?" Shannon said. "She said I can do more good for her by confessing."

"Meaning?" Mandey prompted him.

"Meaning I think she resents me for not keeping Leon away from her more. I did what I could, Mandey. I got in the middle of Leon and Annette and Leon and Momma more times that I can count. But I wasn't always there. I guess she felt I should have done more."

"You couldn't do it alone," Mandey said. "I've often wondered where your extended family is--your grandparents, your aunts and uncles? Where have they been all these years?"

Shannon shook his head. "Once Momma hooked up with Leon, my dad's family didn't want nothing more to do with her. Then we moved around a lot and totally lost touch. It was pretty much the same thing with Momma's family. She had one sister, my aunt Connie, who tried to keep in contact, but Leon wanted to cut us off from everyone. Last time I saw her was when Leon was in jail. She tracked us down somehow. She helped us out a lot while he was gone, but we ain't seen or heard from her since Leon got back. I don't even know if she knows he's dead."

"Another thing I've wondered," Mandey said. "Did Leon ever…molest Annette?"

"I don't think so. I guess something could have happened while I was in jail before, but Annette never said nothing about it," Shannon said. "I think that would have been too risky for him. He wasn't too worried about people finding out he was whaling on us. Lots of kids get beat. But molesting his stepdaughter would be taking it too far."

"Beating you is horrible enough," Mandey said, frowning.

Shannon sighed. "This is so fucked up," he moaned. "You haven't heard from Annette since then, have you?"

"No," Mandey said, shaking her head.

"Don't you go down there to see her, do you hear me? Don't go anywhere near there. Please, Mandey," Shannon begged her.

"Don't worry," Mandey said. "If Annette wants to talk to me face-to-face, she can get on a bus and come out and meet me where I want to meet her."

"Even if you do that, be careful," Shannon said. "I have nightmares about bad things happening to you."

After Mandey left, Shannon returned to his cell, brooding. He was afraid for her, and what might happen if the Devils caught her talking to his sister again. He wasn't lying about having nightmares about her being in danger. Every night when he closed his eyes, hoping for sleep to escape his current situation, he was instead plagued with disturbing dreams involving himself or Mandey, or both. Knowing that his nightmares could come true, and he was powerless to stop it, felt like a knife in his guts.

74

Spring Break

Mandey was laying on her bed, eyes closed, listening to her stereo, absorbing the music. It made her feel a little more balanced, a little more connected to herself. Still, she felt very alone. It had been six weeks since Shannon was locked up in a jail cell for a crime he didn't do. She felt like she was locked up, too. Her mind was there with him most of the time, worrying about what was happening to him. When she went to the jail for visiting hours, it was stab in the heart every time, as she could see him getting more hopeless on each visit. The police were building their case against him, counting on the three eyewitnesses to testify that they saw Shannon getting out of the car where Leon was murdered. Mandey was psyching herself up to testify on that date in May. She <u>knew</u> Shannon didn't do it, but her testimony would be far more circumstantial than what the eyewitnesses would have to say. She could only hope that the jury would believe her over Annette, Raff, and Checkmate. She wished Joe, Shannon's attorney, was doing more to clear Shannon of the charges. There probably wasn't much he could do. He was due to meet with the prosecuting attorneys in the next week to see if he could cut a deal, but a deal would mean prison time, a lot of it, and that wasn't acceptable.

She was glad to be out of school for a week. She was managing to keep up with her schoolwork despite being so distracted. Luckily, none of her classes was too demanding, and graduation was now only ten weeks away. She was a little more isolated than she had been in the past. It seemed fewer people talked to her now, not that she had ever had a lot of people who socialized with her. Her core group of friends—Georgia, Andrea, Mart, Gayla, and Charlie, were all very supportive and said they would be happy to testify in court as to Shannon's character, if asked. Mandey doubted it would come to anything like that, and would likely not make a difference, but she appreciated their willingness to help.

She lay there, contemplating hiding like a hermit in her room for the week, except for her visits to see Shannon, when her telephone interrupted the reverie.

"Mandey, did you hear the news?" It was Danny, not even giving her a chance to say hello.

"What news?" she asked, alarmed.

"Turn on Channel 13, quick!"

She turned on her television and switched the channel to Eyewitness News. There was a story about a large fire that had destroyed a building.

"Liaisons burned down?" she gasped. "How? Was anyone hurt?"

They watched the news report together over the phone. Liaisons had burned down in the early hours of that morning, after closing time. There were no injuries. Investigators were still trying to determine the cause.

"Wow," Mandey said when the report was over, then turned down the volume.

"Well, that's the end of that, I guess," Danny said, "unless they rebuild. But I bet they won't. If anything, they might open it back up in a different location."

"Wow," Mandey said again, still disbelieving. "I wonder what caused it?"

"I think it was intentional," Danny said.

"You may be right," Mandey said. "I guess we'll find out."

There was a pause. "How are you doing?" Danny asked.

"I've been better," she replied.

"Is there anything new with Trick--I mean Shannon's case?"

She told him about her most recent contact with Annette, and how she was so determined to get Shannon to plead guilty. She left out the part about what happened when she dropped Annette off.

"That does seem weird," Danny admitted. "You think she's covering for someone?"

"I'm sure of it. I think Raff or Dewayne—Checkmate—did it, and they're forcing her to say Shannon did it. She seems to be under a lot of stress, but I don't think it's just because she got a subpoena."

"Do you think she'll talk? To you, or maybe spill the beans in court?"

"I'm hoping she'll tell somebody soon, because it's going to be hard to beat three supposed eyewitnesses in court." Mandey sighed. "I wish I had a better way to contact her. I don't have a phone number, and I am not about to go down there to the apartments searching for her. Now I can't even go to Liaisons and find someone to give her a message."

"I hope if she's lying that she'll start telling the truth soon, for your sake, Mandey." He sounded sincere.

"Thanks, Danny. I appreciate that," Mandey said. "I have to believe everything is going to turn out okay. I can't bear to think of the alternative."

After she hung up with Danny, she went out to the kitchen to get something for her supper. Marcia was spending every other weekend with Michael, and she wasn't home yet. Most of the time Mandey didn't mind, but sometimes the house seemed very empty with only her there. She had quickly gotten used to having Shannon being there, living like a grown-up couple, in most ways. She wanted that back again more than anything.

She thought about Liaisons burning down. She doubted that was an accident. The Devils were most likely responsible, although she wasn't quite sure what the motivation was. Liaisons attracted a crowd that they were able to prey on, or make money off, and now it was gone. The Alley Cats had been limping along despite losing members, but now the only one with any reason to be in that area of town was Terry. The Cats no longer had a purpose. She hoped that meant the fighting would end.

She got a package of Kraft macaroni and cheese out of the cupboard and set about making it. Fifteen minutes later while she was eating it on the couch, watching MTV, Marcia came in.

"Have fun?" Mandey asked her as Marcia took off her jacket and hung it in the closet.

"It was a nice weekend, as usual," Marcia said. "How was yours?"

Mandey shrugged. "Saw Shannon yesterday. He's hanging in there, but it's really getting to him. And I just found out Liaisons burned down early this morning, so I guess no one's going dancing there anymore."

"It burned down?" Marcia asked. "What happened?"

"I don't know. They're still investigating."

"What are you going to do all this week while you're out of school?" Marcia asked, walking into the kitchen.

"I think I am going to get a start on my research paper for English class. It's not due for over a month, but I just want to get it over with."

"Oh? What are you going to write about?"

Mandey started to respond, but stopped short. "I'm not quite sure yet. I have a couple of topics I'm thinking about, but I need to do some research to see which one I want to use."

She had written a paper for her psychology class last year on teen gangs, before she knew anything about a gang called the Devils, or dreamed of joining a gang herself. She had made an A on it, but the teacher made everyone pass their papers back in after seeing their grade to prevent them from sharing their papers with other students. She still had her notes, but she could do some additional research, plus now she had some first-hand experience with the subject. She had no intention of being specific enough to incriminate herself or anyone else, Devil or Alley Cat, but she figured she had a certain perspective now that would make it interesting to write and, she hoped, worth another A. That had been the plan. Now, after her encounter with Mr. Tichner in January, she thought that wouldn't be a good idea. If any word got back to him about the subject of her paper, she might end up in his office again.

"I'll probably spend a lot of time at the library this week. Gayla and Charlie and I are going to do something next weekend, but I'm not sure what yet," Mandey said. "Michael hasn't heard any news from Joe about Shannon's case, has he?"

"He didn't mention it," Marcia said. "Last I remember, I thought he said Joe was going to visit Shannon again sometime next week."

"Yes, that's the plan," Mandey said heavily. Suddenly, without warning, she broke out in a sob. "I'm just getting so discouraged."

"Joe's doing the best that he can," Marcia said.

"He's been on vacation all this week!" Mandey burst out. "I feel like there is more that could be done. I know he's leaning toward a plea deal, and I can't stand the thought of that."

"Well, give him a call tomorrow. He said you could call him anytime. I'm sure he'll be happy to let you know what's going on."

"Or light a fire under him," Mandey said, grumbling. She almost always had to leave a message and wait a day or two for a call back, but she figured it was time for a direct update from Joe himself. She wished she had some better information of her own to share, about Annette, but she supposed the little she had learned from her was better than nothing.

When she visited Shannon on Tuesday, she told him about Liaisons burning down.

"Do they know what caused it?" Shannon asked.

"They're still investigating, as far as I know," Mandey said.

Shannon didn't say anything, but Mandey noticed the expression on his face.

"What are you thinking?" she asked him.

"Nothing," Shannon said. "Well, not nothing. Just thinking."

"Do you know who did it?"

"No," Shannon said, "but I have a hunch."

"A group of people, starts with 'D'?"

"One in particular, that starts with 'R'."

Saturday morning there was a brief follow-up to the story about Liaisons burning down—the police had arrested 19-year-old Rafael Santos for allegedly setting the building on fire. Shannon had been right. Mandey shared the news with him when she visited that afternoon. He didn't look surprised.

"Kind of cutting off his nose to spite his face, isn't it?" Mandey asked.

"He's got a nasty temper and likes playing with fire. He probably got pissed at someone there and decided to burn the whole damn thing down."

"The paper said he was arrested yesterday. Did they bring him here? You haven't seen him, have you?"

"They better not bring him in here," Shannon said, his face growing dark.

"Shannon, you'd better not do anything if you see him," Mandey warned, worried.

"I know," he said, sighing, "but it'd be hard not to punch his lights out."

"Don't you dare," Mandey said. "They'll put you in solitary again, and it'll make it look like you're trying to intimidate a witness."

"I know, I know, Mandey," Shannon said impatiently. "I don't need to make my situation worse than it already is."

Later, back in his cell, he thought more about the fact that Raff was in custody now.

Mandey had told him that Annette, Checkmate, and Raff had all been unhappy when they received subpoenas to testify at his trial. Now that they had Raff on an unrelated charge, Shannon figured they would find a way to keep him in jail so he wouldn't be able to disappear before testifying. They would probably encourage him to be as cooperative as possible with the prosecution to get Shannon convicted, and they would cut Raff a deal in return. He prayed they would have sense enough to keep Raff as far away from him as possible, because he even though he told Mandey he would not do anything to Raff if he encountered him, he was not sure he would be able to keep that promise.

75

Girls Night In

On the last Saturday of March, Mandey had a depressing visit with Shannon. His appearance had become progressively more tired and haggard the last few weeks, but now he looked haunted.

"I'm never getting out of here, Mandey," he said hollowly, his tired, dark-ringed eyes gazing through the glass at her.

"Shannon, don't say that," she implored him. "The truth is going to come out. We have to believe that."

"They're going to send me to prison," he said. "I might as well take the plea deal. I'm ready. I hate this place. I'm only out of my cell a couple hours a day, stuck mopping floors, there's four of us to a cell, they won't let me work on my G.E.D., although I don't think even matters anymore. At least send me to Huntsville and I can get on a work detail and do something and get out in the rec yard…"

"Shannon, please," Mandey begged. "Don't start thinking like that."

"I'm being railroaded, Mandey. They don't care what the truth is. Raff is gonna tell them anything they want to hear to get me convicted, and then he'll get a slap on the wrist and waltz out of here," he said despairingly.

"No, Shannon, no, he won't—"

"Mandey, I love you, but I just can't…" Shannon said, and suddenly hung up the phone, got up, and asked the guard to let him go back to his cell.

She managed to hold the tears back until she got into the van, then she broke down and sobbed. Something—or someone—was going to have to break soon.

She wasn't sure she was up to having a girls' night at her house, but that was the whole point of why Georgia, Andrea, and Gayla were coming to spend the night—to lift her spirits and get her to forget her troubles for a few hours. As she made a batch of chocolate chip cookies, she tried not to think about her visit to the jail. The cookies were just out of the oven when Andrea arrived, bearing Trivial Pursuit and California Coolers. Gayla came a few minutes later with UNO and chips and dip. About a half hour late, Georgia cruised in with a bottle of Boone's Farm Strawberry Hill and a bottle of Tickle Pink. After she arrived, they ordered pizzas from Domino's, and sat down to play Mandey's favorite game, Scrabble, with their snacks and drinks. They talked, laughed, and got a little bit tipsy. None of her friends brought up Shannon's name, keeping the conversation lighthearted and far away from the dark cloud of Shannon's situation. It did Mandey good to tuck that darkness away for a night.

After they played a round of each game (Mandey won Scrabble and Trivial Pursuit, Andrea won UNO), they went into the living room and moved the coffee table and danced to the videos on MTV.

"Look," Georgia said, laughing, as she started making overexaggerated hip and arm movements. "This is how Thad dances."

The other girls dissolved into giggles, because it was true, and they began to imitate Georgia imitating Thad.

Mandey heard her phone ringing in her bedroom. She looked at her watch. It was nearly eleven. Usually, phone calls that late were wrong numbers or bad news. "I'll be right back," she told the others, and scurried down the hall to get it.

It was actually kind of good news—it was Annette. "I need to talk to you. Can you meet me tomorrow?" asked Mandey.

"Can't you talk to me on the phone?" Mandey asked.

"Please, I want to see you in person," Annette said, sounding a little desperate.

Mandey sighed. She really wanted to talk with Annette, especially if Annette might tell her something that would help Shannon, but so far, she hadn't been all that helpful.

"I have plans tomorrow. My girlfriends are over here, and we're going to brunch and a movie. If you want to talk, meet us at Dalt's at Greenspoint Mall at 10:30 tomorrow morning."

"Can't you come over here?" Annette pleaded.

"No," Mandey said flatly. "When I dropped you off last time, the last thing I saw in my mirror was Raff looking at me and going for a gun in the waistband of his pants. If you come out here, you can have brunch with us."

Annette was silent for a moment. "Okay, I think I can make it. Ten-thirty, you said?"

"Yes."

"All right."

Mandey hung up the phone and went back to the living room where the others were still dancing. "We are going to have a fifth join us for brunch tomorrow," she announced. "That was Shannon's sister on the phone."

Andrea grabbed the tv remote and turned down the volume. "She's coming to brunch with us?"

"So she said. She wanted me to go meet her near where she lives, but I told her no. I don't care if Raff is in jail, I just don't feel safe."

"What does she want to talk to you about?" Georgia asked.

"I don't know. She's never too eager to talk on the phone. I think she's afraid someone might overhear," Mandey said. "It frustrates the hell out of me, because I know she knows something. I just don't know how to get it out of her."

"I bet we can get it out of her tomorrow," Georgia said confidently. "You know I'm good at getting people to talk."

"I don't know about her, Georgia," Mandey said. "I think we should take it easy, though. I don't want to scare her off."

A couple hours later, they went to bed. Andrea slept in Mandey's room, Gayla in Shannon's, and Mandey and Georgia shared the king bed in the Marcia's room. The wine coolers and Boone's Farm did their magic, and Mandey fell asleep quickly.

76

Brunch and a Breakthrough

As expected, Georgia didn't get up when the rest of the girls did. Mandey, Andrea, and Gayla were up by 8:30, drinking coffee or orange juice and listening to "Breakfast with the Beatles" on the radio. At ten o'clock, they were showered, dressed, and ready to go. Georgia was in the shower.

"If you don't hurry, we're going to leave you," Andrea threatened Georgia through the door to Marcia's bathroom.

"I'm almost ready," Georgia replied.

"We should have planned for ten o'clock," Andrea said to Mandey and Gayla. "That way we would have made it for ten-thirty."

At ten-thirty, they were on their way, although Georgia was still putting on her make-up in the van. As Mandey parked, she spotted Annette standing on the sidewalk in front of the restaurant. It was almost ten-fifty.

Annette scowled as the four girls approached, but she said nothing.

"Annette, these are my friends Georgia, Gayla, and Andrea," Mandey introduced them.

"Hi," Mandey's friends chorused.

"Hi," Annette said sullenly.

"Sorry we're running a little late," Mandey said.

Annette didn't reply. She fell into step behind the girls as they entered Dalt's. There was a short wait for a non-smoking table. The five of them sat down on a bench. Annette began to light a cigarette.

"Uh, do you mind going outside?" Mandey asked Annette. "Andrea's allergic to cigarette smoke."

Andrea leaned past Mandey to look at Annette. "Smoking isn't good for your baby, anyway," she told her.

Annette silently stood up and stormed outside.

"A little testy, isn't she?" Andrea asked Mandey.

"It's an improvement. Not too long ago, I think she would have told you to eff-off and lit up anyway," Mandey said, craning her neck to look outside. "She's not leaving, is she?"

"No, she's still there," Georgia said.

A few minutes later they were called to be seated. Mandey went outside to get Annette, who was sitting on the edge of a concrete planter full of pansies.

"Our table is ready," Mandey told her.

"Go eat with your friends. I'll wait out here until you're done," Annette said.

"Come on and eat, Annette," Mandey said. "It's my treat."

"Are you sure I'm good enough to eat with your high-and-mighty friends?" Annette asked sarcastically.

"Whatever," Mandey said. "You're the one who wants to talk to me, so do what you want. I don't care." With that, she turned and went back inside and joined her friends at a circular corner booth. Annette followed a minute later, and Mandey slid over to make room for her.

The girls studied their menus for a few minutes before ordering. The waitress brought coffee and juice. Annette looked around the restaurant intently. Mandey supposed she wasn't accustomed to eating anywhere that wasn't Jack in the Box or Taco Bell.

"When is your baby due?" Gayla asked.

"End of July," Annette said, returning her attention to the table.

"Do you know what you're having?" Georgia asked.

"Doctor said it's a boy," Annette said.

"Do you have a name picked out?" Andrea asked.

Annette shook her head. "I'm going to wait until I see him."

"Are you excited?" Georgia asked.

"Yeah," Annette answered indifferently.

"That didn't sound very convincing," Gayla remarked.

Annette shrugged. "I'm excited," she said.

"I've been going to see Shannon every visiting day," Mandey told Annette. "He was pretty surprised when I told him Raff got arrested."

Annette's head snapped. "How do you know that?"

"It was in the paper and on the news," Mandey said. "Shannon was wondering how it was Raff got caught. He said he couldn't imagine him being sloppy enough to get nabbed."

"They figured it out somehow," Annette mumbled. "Has he seen Raff in jail?"

"No, and he doesn't want to see him," Mandey said, then paused. "You didn't have anything to do with Raff getting arrested, did you?"

"We were getting sick of him," Annette burst out. "He was on this power trip. He had us doing all this shit for him, and he wasn't taking any of the risks, but he was taking all the money."

"I guess he took a risk when he burned down Liaisons," Georgia said.

"Wasn't that kind of stupid?" Mandey asked. "You targeted that place for so long. I thought you guys made a lot of money ripping people off and selling drugs there."

"Yeah, we did for a while, but Raff got banned, and then they decided to add more security to the place, and we couldn't do nothing no more. Raff got pissed and decided to burn the whole damn place down."

"All by himself?" Mandey asked.

"He had some help, but he won't talk. He knows better."

"Yeah, but somebody must have snitched on him—"

"Nobody snitched on him," Annette said firmly. "He got too cocky. He filled a gas can without his gloves on. It turned up not far from the club, and the prints matched Raff's record."

"Busted!" Gayla exclaimed.

"Exactly," Annette said.

"So no one snitched, but basically someone made it easy for the cops to catch the culprit," Mandey said.

"Maybe it's time for him to get his," Annette said stonily. "He can sit there and rot for all I care."

"I agree wholeheartedly," Mandey said. "He hasn't made bail?"

"Uh-uh. His uncle is pissed. He's been getting tired of Raff's shit, too. He ain't gonna bail him out."

"Well, who's taken Raff's place in the gang?"

"As leader? Dewayne," Annette said. "Now I'm the number one bitch again, like I was when Shannon was leader. I was number one because he didn't have an old lady. Juanita's pissed. Now she's nothing, like Kerri. Kerri wanted Shannon so bad after he became leader, but he didn't want nothin' to do with her. I get along with her okay most of the time, but I was glad Shannon didn't want her as a girlfriend, 'cause she and I wouldn't have agreed on who was gonna be number one. Anyway, she's glad Raff's gone, too. He was getting tired of her mouth and told her she was gonna have to start contributing more than just bein' a mattress for all the guys in the gang. He wanted John to start pimping her out. Raff beat her up when she said she didn't want to do it."

"That's horrible!" Gayla exclaimed.

"Oh my God," Georgia breathed. "Annette, how do you stand living somewhere with that kind of stuff going on?"

"I've had shit like that all my life," Annette said. "You get used to it."

"What about your baby?" Andrea asked. "You don't want to bring up your baby like that, do you?"

"No," Annette said. "With Raff out of the picture, things will be better."

"Oh my God, I hope you're right," Gayla said.

"What about you, Annette?" Mandey asked. "You haven't been beaten on, have you?" She wondered what Annette's response would be.

"I've been okay," Annette said, maybe a little too quickly.

"Good. Shannon will be glad to hear that. You may not believe it, but he does worry about you," Mandey said.

"I believe it," Annette said quietly.

The waitress brought their food. Annette stared wide-eyed at the plate set in front of her, which was loaded with pancakes, eggs, sausage, and hash browns.

"Wow, they know how to feed a person here, don't they?" she said, picking up her fork.

"Yes, they do," Andrea said, pouring syrup on her massive Belgian waffle, already topped with strawberries and whipped cream.

Annette began shoveling her food as if she were afraid the waitress was going to come take the plate back before she finished.

"I hope they figure out who the real murderer is soon," Gayla said. "Your poor brother. I feel so sorry for him."

"I do, too. He's such a sweetheart," Andrea said.

"And I don't know what it is about him, but he's so funny sometimes, it just kills my soul," Georgia said.

"Are you talking about my brother?" Annette asked with her mouth full.

"Yes!" Georgia exclaimed. "We're all so jealous of Mandey. Shannon is the perfect guy for her."

Annette looked at Mandey. "Boy, has he got y'all fooled," she said.

"No, I think he had you and the Devils fooled," Mandey replied.

Annette shrugged. "Maybe you're right," she said. "Man, would he be embarrassed to hear a bunch of girls talking like this about him."

"That's true," Mandey agreed, and couldn't help but smile at the thought.

"One time he overheard my friend Denise saying she thought he was cute, and he was so embarrassed, he wouldn't talk to her for a week."

"Speaking of Denise, you know she's pregnant, right?" Mandey asked.

"How would I know that?"

"Shannon and I ran into her on his birthday. She was about five months along then. She's probably had the baby by now, I think."

"Where'd you see her?" Annette asked.

"At a pick-up football game in the neighborhood. She and her boyfriend had broken up, and she'd moved back home. She wanted Shannon to say hello to you and tell you to come out and visit, but I guess he never told you."

"Who's this?" Georgia asked.

"Denise Wharton," Mandey said.

"Doesn't ring a bell with me," Gayla said.

"Me, either," Andrea said.

"Denise Wharton," Georgia said. "Brown eyes, curly hair, kind of--?" She made a gesture indicating a large chest.

"That's her," Annette said. "You know, it would be nice to talk to her about babies."

After brunch, the girls walked through the mostly empty mall toward the movie theater. They were going to see *The Sure Thing*, starring John Cusack.

"All right, what is it that you wanted to see me about?" Mandey asked Annette, letting the other three girls walk ahead.

Annette was quiet for a moment. "The cops came and got my mother on Tuesday."

Mandey looked at her. "What do you mean, they 'came and got' her?"

"I wasn't home. Dewayne and I were out. The cops came by while we were gone. I guess they were trying to see if they could get her to talk to them. When I came home, she was gone. I wouldn't have known except Marco said he saw the cops there. And now I don't know where they took her," Annette said, sounding desperate.

"You could have called the police and asked," Mandey said.

Annette scowled. "I ain't talking to the police about nothing."

"Well, you're gonna have to if you want to find out what's happened to her."

"Can you call and find out?"

"Me? Why me? She's your mother. I don't even know if they would tell me anything."

"I need to find out where she is," Annette said urgently.

"Then call the police station!"

"I don't want to talk to them! I don't trust them!"

Mandey guessed she understood Annette's distrust of the police, but it still made no sense to her that she wouldn't call to see what had happened to her mother.

"Fine, I'll call the police, but after the movie, okay?"

Annette shrugged. "Okay, fine."

Mandey found it hard to concentrate on the movie, because she was thinking about what Annette had told her. Her mind was going in all directions, wondering where Shannon's mother was, why Annette was so reluctant to contact the police to find her, how Shannon was doing today after their visit he had cut short the day before...

When the movie ended and they exited the theater back into the mall, Mandey told the others that she and Annette had to make a phone call, and then she would drive them home. Georgia, Andrea, and Gayla went to the arcade to play video games while Mandey and Annette used the payphone at the nearest mall entrance.

"She's been admitted to Harris County MHMRA," Mandey said, after two transfers and a brief conversation, with some help from Annette, because Mandey realized she didn't even know Shannon and Annette's mother's name. It was Deborah Pawlowski.

"So, they think she's crazy," Annette said. Her tone sounded almost relieved.

"I don't know about that. They said they sent her over there for a 24-hour observation, and they recommended that she should be allowed to stay. That's all I know."

"Can you take me to see her?" Annette asked.

"Why don't you take the bus?" Mandey asked. "Or get your boyfriend to take you."

"I don't really remember where it is, but I know it would probably take me three hours to get there on the bus."

"What about Checkmate—er, Dewayne?"

"I don't want to have to hunt him down," Annette said. "I don't want him there when I'm trying to talk to Momma, anyway." Her lips set in a hard line.

In reality, Mandey wanted to go, to find out what was going on. "Okay. I've got to take the others home first. What's the address?"

They looked up the facility in the Yellow Pages chained to the phone. Mandey had a map in the glove box of her van, so they could find it.

"Where did you tell everyone you were going today?" Mandey asked Annette, once she had dropped the others back at her house to get their cars. "I know you didn't say you were coming out to meet me."

"I didn't tell anyone anything," Annette said, now sitting in the front seat, looking out the passenger window. "Raff's not around to keep tabs on anyone, and Dewayne's spending the weekend at his cousin's place. I can do what I damn well please."

"Must feel kinda good, doesn't it? Not having to answer to anybody?"

"Damn straight."

"You haven't seen or heard from your mother since they took her away that day?" Mandey asked. "She hasn't tried to get in touch with you?"

Annette shook her head. "I haven't been at the apartment much, and the phone's been disconnected, anyway. Did they say why they kept my mom and put her in there?"

"No, they didn't tell me anything, except where we can find her."

"I've got to get her out of there," Annette said.

Mandey looked over at her. "If she's as bad off as you say she's been, this may be where she needs to be."

"She don't need to be in there! She was getting better until the pigs showed up!" Annette said angrily. "I'm gonna have a baby, and I want my mother with me while I'm going through this."

"What about your boyfriend?" Mandey asked. "I thought you were getting a place together."

"Yeah, eventually," Annette said, in a tone that made Mandey think she didn't really believe it.

Twenty minutes later they arrived at their destination and walked through the glass doors into the reception area. Although the color scheme was like that of Shannon's parole officer's office, the furnishings and lighting were more soothing. Mandey hoped the rest of the facility was the same way. They signed in at the reception desk and sat down to wait for an attendant.

"I don't want you going in with me," Annette said.

Mandey wanted to see Mrs. Pawlowski so she could tell Shannon about it at her next visit with him. She had done Annette a favor bringing her down here, so it seemed to her she ought to be a little more flexible, but she didn't want to argue with her. She would probably feel the same way under the same circumstances. When their names were called, Mandey remained in the waiting room while Annette went through the security doors and down the hall with the orderly.

She paged through a well-worn copy of *People* magazine, not absorbing anything she read. She really wanted to know what was going on between Annette and her mother. What was her mental state like now? Was she showing signs of improvement?

Suddenly she heard a commotion behind the double doors. A security guard and the orderlies were physically escorting Annette out of the patient area.

"Let me go!" she shouted, struggling in their grasp. "Let GO!"

"Hey, hey, she's pregnant!" Mandey exclaimed, jumping to her feet.

"Out," the security guard said, as they maneuvered her out the door and into the parking lot.

"What happened?" she asked the orderlies as they came back through the waiting room.

"She was yelling and upsetting the patient and the patients in the other rooms were getting agitated. We can't have that," one said.

"Wait," Mandey said. "Can I go check on Mrs. Pawlowski?"

"Hold on," he said. "Let me see how she's doing."

The security guard had not returned. Mandey figured he was outside keeping Annette from coming back in. She didn't think she would have much time to talk to Shannon's mother before Annette started making a fuss because she wasn't coming outside, but this might be her only chance.

The orderly came back to the doors and motioned to Mandey. She quickly followed him into the corridor. Everything was white—the floors, the walls, the ceiling, the harsh lights. Down that hallway, then to the left, almost to the end. The door was open. The room had a twin bed, a side table, and one straight-backed chair. Mrs. Pawlowski was sitting up in the bed, wearing a pair of sweatpants and a T-shirt, her frizzy hair combed and tied back in a ponytail. She looked very calm, unlike her daughter looked a few minutes before.

"Hi," Mandey said shyly from the doorway. "Do you remember me? I'm Mandey, Shannon's girlfriend."

"Mija," she said, looking at Mandey. Mandey thought for a second that she was confusing her with Annette, but she wasn't. "Please come in. Please tell me how he's doing."

Mandey entered the room and pulled out the desk chair and sat down. "To be honest, not that good," Mandey said. "How are you?"

"I'm feeling better," Shannon's mother said. "Things were pretty bad for a while, but they're getting better now."

"How is it here in the hospital? Are they treating you well?"

"Yes, I can't complain. I've been in worse places," she said. "Is it true what Annette said? Shannon is in jail for killing Leon?"

"Yes," Mandey said. "You don't remember? Annette said you kind of went a little crazy when you found out that Shannon was arrested." She winced inwardly, wishing she hadn't used the word "crazy".

Shannon's mother didn't seem to notice. "I'm starting to remember. I blocked it from my mind for a while."

"What do you remember from that morning?" Mandey asked, a touch of desperation entering her voice. "I know Shannon didn't do it; he couldn't have done it. He's set to go to trial in May, and he's at the point he wants to give up and take a plea deal even though he's innocent! Annette, Raff, and Dewayne are all going to testify that they saw him getting out of the car after killing Leon, and I know they are lying, but I can't prove it!"

"Mandey, I know he didn't do it. Shannon, he might be rough around the edges, and I know he's made a few mistakes, but he ain't a killer. I know, because I'm the one who done it. I killed that son-of-a-bitch."

Mandey's mouth dropped open. "Whaaaaat?" she asked slowly, trying to get over the shock of what she thought she just heard.

"Annette is mad because I won't go along with her story," she continued. Her tone was matter-of-fact. "That morning Shannon came to get me to go grocery shopping, I never saw him. Leon came back from his sister's a couple days before. I would have told Shannon if he had called me again, but he didn't."

"He tried to that morning, but he didn't get an answer," Mandey said.

"Leon musta unplugged the phone or something, then, I don't know, 'cause I never heard the phone ring. Anyways, I was in the bedroom when I heard Shannon come into the apartment, and then I heard him and Leon gettin' into another one of their fights. Leon was yelling at him and telling him to get out of the house and never come back, and Shannon was yelling and telling him to do the same thing. I started yelling at them from the bedroom to stop, but they didn't. Finally, after a few minutes of the apartment getting wrecked, I heard the door slam and then Leon came back into the bedroom. He told me Shannon wasn't welcome at our house no more, and I told him that was bullshit. He ain't gonna ban my son from my house! We started fighting and he started slapping me around. Finally, he quit and he told me to get ready and he would take me to cash my check.

"He went in the bathroom. I was…I don't know, in a daze or somethin'. I got dressed and told him through the bathroom door that I was going down to the car to wait for him. I got the butcher knife and put it in my purse and went downstairs. I got in the car, but I got in the backseat behind the driver's side to wait. When he came down a few minutes later, he got in the car and started it and started fiddling with the radio and he asked me what the hell I was doing sitting in the backseat, he wasn't my goddam chauffeur, and I took that knife in both hands and plunged it right down into his neck. He screamed and he started jerking around. For a minute I thought he was gonna turn around and get me, but then he just went limp. I got up and went back to the apartment. Then things got a little fuzzy, but a while later Annette walked in and saw me sitting in the kitchen with blood all over my clothes. She made me take them off and get in the shower. Then I went back to bed until awhile later, when the police showed up and asked me where Shannon was and said he was wanted for murdering Leon—"

"Miss? Miss?" It was one of the security guards in the doorway, beckoning to Mandey. "Does that blue van belong to you? Your friend is getting a little out-of-control outside."

Mandey jumped up, then hesitated. She didn't want to run out on Shannon's mother after what she had just told her, but she didn't want Annette to trash her van, either.

"I am so sorry about what happened," Mandey said.

"Why? I'm not. I am sorry about what happened to Shannon," she replied.

"Can I send Shannon's lawyer over to talk to you?"

"Miss? You'd better get out there."

Mandey didn't wait for the reply from Shannon's mother. She ran down the hallway, through the reception area, and outside. Annette, despite being five months pregnant, was kicking Mandey's van with all her might. She had made some nasty dents in it. She was screaming at the top of her lungs.

"Get out here now or I'm gonna bust out your windows!"

"Damn it, what is wrong with you?" Mandey shouted. "Cut it out!"

She grabbed Annette by the arm and pulled her away from the van. Annette tried to kick her.

"Stop it! You're going to hurt your baby!" Mandey said.

Annette stopped kicking, but she was still fuming. "I want to go, NOW," she said.

"You're messing up my van! Why should I take you anywhere? I should leave you here and let you figure out how to get home!"

"What did my mother tell you?" Annette demanded.

"The truth!" Mandey said.

"My mother is fucking nuts! You can't believe anything she told you!"

"Then why are you freaking out like this?"

"She's nuts!" Annette insisted. "She doesn't know what she's saying!"

"I think she does, and I don't know why you are so afraid of what she has to say!"

"I'm trying to keep her from doing something stupid!" Annette said.

"If she's lying, then who did it? And don't say Shannon, because I know it wasn't him!"

"Can we go? Can you just take me home?" Annette said, becoming sullen.

She was shutting down, and Mandey knew it would be almost impossible to get anything else out of her, but it didn't matter. She had enough.

"Only if you promise you aren't going to do a freak-out on me on the way home," Mandey said.

"I won't," Annette said carelessly.

"I'm serious," Mandey said as she and Annette got into the van.

Mandey was nervous as they drove away from the hospital. She didn't know if Annette was going to blow up again. She braced herself for any kind of outburst and was ready to pull over, even on the freeway, if she needed to. As it was, Annette didn't open her head, and after a silent ride, Mandey dropped her off about two blocks from her street. Mandey refused to get any closer to the Devils' neighborhood, even if Raff was in jail. She was going to call Joe as soon as she got home and let him know what had transpired. For the first time, she truly felt that Shannon would be free and back in her arms again soon.

77

Patience for the Process

When Marcia got home Sunday, Mandey told her the whole story. Marcia called Michael, who then called Joe at home, and Joe called Mandey. She told him about her visit with Shannon's mother. Joe told her he would pay a visit to Mrs. Pawlowski the next day. Then she spent hours on the phone with Georgia, Andrea, and Gayla, to let them know what had transpired after she dropped them off.

Monday morning when she was getting ready for school, Mandey noticed her calendar on the wall. It was time to turn it over to another month.

"April Fool's Day," she said aloud.

Nope. Nope. No, no, no, she said to herself. She was not going to get into that mindset, that this development that could lead to Shannon's freedom was nothing but a cruel trick. It was just a stupid coincidence.

At school, some of Mandey's classmates accused her of pulling an April Fool's joke when she told them Shannon would be getting out of jail soon. She said, "Seriously? You think I'd make a joke about that?" more times than she imagined she would have to. She didn't mind, though. For the first time in almost two months, she didn't feel like a zombie wandering through a nightmare.

At home, Joe called just before 5 P.M. to talk to her. He had been able to visit Shannon's mother that afternoon and had a long talk with her and her physician.

"I absolutely believe she's telling the truth," Joe said. "Afterward, I asked her doctor if he thought she was being honest and if he thought she could be considered reliable. He said he thought so; he had heard her recount the story three times by then, and it was the same each time. When I asked him if it was possible the mental fugue she had been in had affected her memory, he said he didn't think so. But he's going to get some additional input on that."

"Okay, but what about Shannon?"

"I'm going to go see him tomorrow morning and let him know what's happening," Joe said.

"Do you think they will release him soon?" Mandey asked hopefully.

"I'm hoping so, but you're going to have to have some patience. It's not going to be tomorrow. I can't guarantee it will even be next week, but it should be soon."

The next day was visiting day at the jail. Mandey was there as soon as visiting hours began. As Shannon entered the visitation room, she could see a change in his demeanor. The defeated shuffle was replaced by a brisker step; the invisible veil that had somehow clouded his face had lifted. His eyes now held hope as well as consternation.

"Hi, Joe visited me this morning," he said immediately when he picked up the phone. "Is it true my mother confessed?"

"She did," Mandey said, and recounted what had happened over the weekend, culminating with his mother telling her how she had killed Leon.

"I almost can't believe it," Shannon said, shaking his head. "She really did it. After all this time…"

"It sounded like she finally had enough and just snapped," Mandey said. "Now we know why Annette was lying."

"I get it, but Jesus, I wish I had known," Shannon said. "You said my mother seemed okay when you talked to her?"

"Yeah," Mandey said. "She seemed perfectly rational to me."

"Joe said the same," Shannon said. "He said her doctor believes her, but they're going to have to get a second opinion, and a third opinion…" Doubt was creeping into his voice.

"You're going to be out of here soon," Mandey said firmly.

"I guess so, but at what cost?" Shannon asked. "Instead, my mom goes to jail? I dunno…had I known, maybe I would have confessed to protect her."

Mandey was silent for a moment. The fact that he might have done that and gotten himself sent to prison disturbed her on one level, but on another, she could understand. She would probably do the same for her parents, if they were in trouble.

"It wouldn't be right, though," she said.

"No," Shannon agreed. "Now I guess we just wait?"

"I guess so."

"I still don't want to get my hopes up too high," Shannon said.

Two days later, when Mandey got home from school, the light on the answering machine was blinking. The message was from Marcia, telling her to give Joe a call when she got home.

"I don't know why; he's never in when I call," Mandey muttered to herself.

But she did call, and as usual, she had to leave a message. Only this time, instead of having to wait for days for a response, she only had to wait fifteen minutes.

"I thought you might like to know the latest development in Shannon's case," Joe told her.

"Yes!" Mandey said, sitting down. "I hope it's something good!"

"It is," Joe said. "The other doctors who have observed Mrs. Pawlowski are vouching for her state of mind. They believe she is being totally honest in her confession to her husband's murder."

"That's awesome!" Mandey exclaimed. "What does this mean for Shannon? Can he get out soon?"

"Well, I don't know that. This isn't a 'Get out of jail free' card. The prosecution wants a doctor of their choosing to talk to her first and see if his opinion lines up. They may want additional psychological testing done. It might take a while," Joe said. "The trial is likely to get postponed, at least."

"Will the police go back to their 'witnesses' and have them recount their stories?" Mandey asked.

"I think they will, to see if the stories are the same or if they start to change because they can't remember what they said before."

"This is encouraging, though, isn't it? I'm feeling encouraged," Mandey said hopefully.

"We'll see," Joe sad, noncommittally. "The prosecution might go with the idea that she is trying to protect Shannon by taking the blame."

"Seriously? Even if the doctors think she's telling the truth?"

"That's why there is probably going to be more testing done."

Mandey sighed. "Well, even if this still goes to trial, this should be enough to put 'reasonable doubt' into the mind of jury, shouldn't it?"

"It should, it should," Joe said. "I do have a good feeling about this, but we have to be patient and let the process play out."

That night, when she visited Shannon, he still seemed hopeful but impatient. When Mandey returned on Saturday, hopeful but impatient had degraded to discouraged. Joe had been to visit him the day before and said that Raff had been questioned again, and he was still insistent that Shannon had been the one who killed Leon.

"He hates you that much?" Mandey asked.

"He just wants to fuck my life up as much as he can," Shannon said darkly. "And the cops are still trying to hunt down Annette and Checkmate to question them again, but they can't find them. If they can't get ahold of them and get a different story out of them, we're still going to trial."

"Your mother's confession should be enough to put reasonable doubt in the jury's minds," Mandey said.

"Maybe," Shannon said. "Unless, like Joe said, they think she's trying to protect me."

Mandey remained optimistic. She wished they would track down Annette and squeeze the truth out of her, but she was almost positive that even if they didn't, Shannon's trial would be brief and he would be free again before her graduation day. But sometimes at night, when she was lying alone in bed, the little bit of uncertainty would gnaw away at her and keep her awake long past when she should have been asleep.

On Friday the breakthrough Mandey had been praying for came—the police found Annette and Dewayne at a Whataburger in southwest Houston and took them into custody. They had been staying with Dewayne's cousin Charles. Upon questioning, Annette finally broke and changed her story. Everything she said corroborated her mother's account of what happened. Michael came home with Marcia that evening to give Mandey the news.

"Are you serious?" she asked Michael in disbelief.

"Absolutely," Michael said. "With his mother confessing and his sister now changing her story, Joe is petitioning the court to dismiss the charges against Shannon. I don't anticipate the prosecution objecting. They should release him in a few days."

Mandey was overwhelmed. Tears of joy bubbled up before she could stop them. "I can't believe it. I can't believe it," she said, crying, hugging Michael and Marcia at the same time.

"Yes, you can," Marcia said. "You were the one who always believed it."

On Monday, the 15th, Joe and the prosecuting attorney appeared before the judge that was going to hear Shannon's case. Joe was petitioning for the charges against Shannon to be dropped and for him to be released. His client's mother had confessed to the killing. The three so-called witnesses to the murder were no longer united in their account of the events that happened: one (Raff) still insisted Shannon had killed Leon, but his client's sister (Annette) had changed her story to match her mother's. The third witness (Dewayne) was now invoking his Fifth Amendment right not to testify. Joe also brought up the fact that the defendant had been discriminated against due to whistleblowing regarding the corruption within the parole department, but the judge told him that was a matter to be taken up later. The judge did agree that the State of Texas no longer had a case against Shannon Douglass, and the prosecution did not dispute it. Shannon would be released immediately.

Except that it was late in the day. There was paperwork to process. Shannon would have to spend one more night in jail.

78

Reunion

Finally, Shannon was coming home, after a long, eleven-week nightmare. Mandey paced in the waiting area. Marcia and Michael were with her, sitting calmly. They had come up to school and Marcia checked Mandey out for the remainder of the afternoon. Michael offered to drive so that Mandey would be able to relax and enjoy the ride home with Shannon, and to be there to run interference, if needed.

Let him out already, her mind begged.

A reporter with a badge identifying himself as being on staff at the *Houston Post* approached her.

"Are you here for Shannon Douglass's release?" he asked Mandey. "Can I ask you some questions?"

Michael jumped up and came over to where Mandey stood. "She's a minor, and I'm serving as her legal counsel, so you can address any questions to me."

Suddenly the door opened and slowly Shannon shuffled out, wearing the sweatpants he had been arrested in, along with the jail-issued T-shirt, socks, and shoes since he hadn't been wearing any when he was taken into custody.

"Shannon," Mandey said in nothing more than a whisper, standing frozen for a second.

The look on his face was a mixture of anguish, joy, and relief. She walked quickly over to meet him. He stared at her silently for a moment, then their arms wrapped around each other. They stood there in their tight embrace, saying nothing, feeling each other's heartbeat, feeling each other breathe, for more than a minute. At last, they loosened their hold enough to look each other in the eyes. Both pairs were shimmering with tears.

"Are you ready to go home?" Mandey asked him.

Shannon nodded in reply. They let go of each other and grasped hands. The *Post* reporter had been joined by two other members of the press. They began shouting questions at Shannon. Michael got between them and Shannon and Mandey as they hurried toward the exit.

"Mr. Douglass has no comment at this time," Michael said, ushering them and Marcia out.

Two minutes later they were in Michael's Mercedes, Shannon and Mandey sitting together in the back, heading out of the parking lot.

"Shannon, we're glad to have you back," Marcia said. "The last few months must have been hell for you."

"Thanks, I'm thankful to be out," he said, finally speaking. "It was definitely hell."

Mandey cuddled close to him and laid her head on his shoulder. He turned in the seat and put his arms around her, and she laid back against him, her head under his chin. He kissed the top of her head.

"I didn't think I was ever going to do this again," he said quietly to her.

"I wasn't sure it was going to happen, either," Mandey said, closing her eyes.

"What do you want for dinner, Shannon?" Marcia asked. "We can go out wherever you want to go."

He didn't answer immediately. "You okay?" Mandey asked.

"Yeah," Shannon replied. "I haven't had many decisions to make in the last few months." Then he turned his attention to Marcia. "I could go for some Mexican food."

"Okay," Michael said. "We'll go to the house so you can take a shower and change clothes, then how about we go to Pappasito's?

"Sure," Shannon said.

"You don't sound that enthusiastic," Marcia said.

"I am," Shannon assured her. "It's just a big change, going from a jail cell to a nice restaurant in a few hours."

Mandey entwined her hand with his and brought it up to her mouth to kiss it. "You can relax now, sweetie," she said. "You're free."

He squeezed her. "It's gonna take a little while for me to get used to it again."

"I'm sure it will," Mandey said, "but you can start by going out and having some fajitas and a couple beers."

He smiled, the first she had seen from him in a long time. "That does sound good," he said. "With the girl I love."

At home, Shannon walked in to find a colorful, big banner in his bedroom. "Welcome home, Shannon!" it said, with big hearts on it that said "I Love You" inside. It also had some smaller writing on it; Mandey's friends had written greetings for him. Otherwise, his room was the same. All his things were there, waiting for him, as though he had never left. He was still feeling strangely uneasy. He had thought he would be jumping for joy once he was free, but his joy was muted, and he wasn't totally sure why. He was glad, though, that Mandey seemed to understand.

"I know I was gone less than three months, but I think I had gotten my mind set that I was going to spend the rest of my life in prison," he said. "Now I've got to get myself to believe that I'm really free."

"I'm sure after a couple days waking up here at home, you'll be able to start believing it."

While Mandey went to her room to change clothes and touch up her makeup, Shannon went into the bathroom to shower--a private shower, no one else, no having to watch out for somebody trying to grab his balls. He stayed in longer than usual, enjoying the hot water, privacy, and decent soap and shampoo. When he got out, he dried off and looked at himself in the mirror. He hadn't seen himself in a real mirror since before his incarceration. He was surprised he hadn't scared Mandey. He thought he looked like an old man. He had lost about 20 pounds, which wasn't necessarily a bad thing, but it made his face seem haggard. Dark circles under his eyes, scraggly hair. Did he even look good enough to go out in public?

He combed his wet hair and shaved then went to his room to get dressed. He wasn't sure he had anything appropriate to wear. When he had gone clothes shopping with Mandey, it was winter. He hadn't bought anything for warm weather. He opened his closet and found three new short-sleeved button-down shirts hanging front and center. Mandey had been thinking ahead. He liked all three, but he chose one that was half white and half black and had a black pocket on the white side of the shirt. Jeans that were now loose, black belt, and his black desert boots.

There was a knock at the door. "Can I come in?" Mandey asked.

"Sure," he said.

She walked in, dressed in short lime-green skirt with a matching short-sleeved jacket and white satin shell blouse. As always, he thought she was the most beautiful thing he had ever seen. She came to him, and he reached out to embrace her. This time, their lips met, for the first time since February. They kissed, softly and sweetly, for a long time.

"Are you ready to go?" Mandey asked him

"Sure," he replied.

Thirty minutes later they were with Marcia and Michael, being escorted to a table at Pappasito's. Shannon looked around the bustling, loud restaurant, smelled the enticing aromas, and heard the sizzling plates of fajitas being delivered to tables. It was a far cry from where he had been that morning. He had spent less than three months in jail, but even so, being out free in public was disorienting. It hadn't been like this when he had been in jail before. Well, that had not been the same kind of experience as adult jail, and when he had been released, going home then did not give him any sense of freedom. But now, he had Mandey, he had a decent place to live, he didn't live in turmoil anymore. He hoped this weird feeling wouldn't last too long. He couldn't imagine what it must be like for people who got out after years in prison. No wonder some of them committed crimes to get sent back.

"It feels so weird," he said softly, squeezing Mandey's arm.

"What feels weird?" Mandey asked.

"Not being locked up," Shannon said. "I guess I don't believe it. I feel like someone's going to say there's been a mistake and they are going to come get me and take me back." His voice cracked.

"No," Mandey said, shaking her head. "Never again, Shannon."

Shortly after they were seated, a server took their drink orders, and soon Shannon was drinking a Corona and eating chips with salsa and queso. Michael had a Corona, as well, Marcia had a margarita, and Mandey had a Coke. No one brought up the subject of his time in jail, which relieved him. Instead, the conversation was all about summer, school, job prospects. The future was looking bright, the beer and the food were starting to work their magic, and he felt the strange veil of uncertainty begin to lift a little. When the server brought out their food, two orders of fajitas for two, one steak and one chicken, for all four to share, he could almost believe he was human again.

At the beginning of dinner, Mandey was worried. Shannon was acting strangely. The only word she could think of to describe it was "numb". His emotions seemed muted, like he wasn't totally there in the moment, like he was disconnected. He had been that way many of the times she had talked to him while he was in jail, especially toward the end. She had hoped it would change once he was out, but she guessed maybe it was something that couldn't be switched on and off. She was relieved to see some of that "numbness" starting to wear off a bit as dinner progressed. He was emptying his second Corona and ordered a third. She hoped it wasn't just the alcohol altering his mood.

She thought about what might happen later, back at the house. As soon as she knew he was going to be coming home, she had decided she would make herself available to him, whenever he wanted her. It seemed like a long time ago when they were first together, and she wanted to wait until she was eighteen. Her birthday was less than a month away now, but if he decided tonight that he wanted her, she would give herself more than willingly.

Michael dropped Marcia, Mandey, and Shannon back home around 8:30. It had been a long day, and Mandey and Shannon both felt like it was a lot later. Mandey took a quick shower and changed into the blue baby doll nightie Shannon liked. She put a little lip gloss on and then went into her bedroom. Shannon was in her bed, already asleep and lightly snoring.

Guess it won't be tonight, she thought, slipping between the sheets next to him. *Doesn't matter. It will be soon enough. I'm just glad to have him back.*

79

Adjusting to the New Normal

Mandey awoke the next morning to her clock radio playing "No More Lonely Nights". She smiled and paused a bit before turning it off. The music didn't rouse Shannon at all. She turned it off, then looked at him sleeping next to her. She was so thankful to have him back. God, or somebody, had listened to her silent prayers.

She didn't want to leave him, but it was a school day, and she had already missed quite a few days that semester. She got out of bed, got dressed quietly, then went to the kitchen to get something to eat for breakfast. She was having peanut butter and banana on toast and a cup of coffee when Marcia came out of her room and into the kitchen.

"How was last night?" Marcia asked her. Mandey wasn't sure if she was asking out of curiosity about how Shannon was, or if she thought they had had sex last night.

"Shannon was out like a light as soon as his head hit the pillow, and he slept through the alarm this morning. I think he's going to need a few days to catch up on his sleep."

"He seemed kind of down, or distant, yesterday, but he seemed better by the time we left the restaurant," Marcia said.

"Yeah, I noticed it, too. I hope it keeps getting better."

"I didn't think you'd want to go to school today. I'll report you sick if you want me to."

"No, I'm going to go. Not too much longer now. Only 28 more school days and high school is over forever," Mandey said. "I'm going to use the payphone at lunchtime to see how he's doing."

When Mandey went back to her room, she saw that Shannon had gotten up and was in the bathroom. She brushed her hair and put on her shoes while waiting for him to be finished. He came out a few moments later, dressed only in his shorts.

"Good morning," she said to him.

"Good morning," he replied, then he smiled. "When I woke up, I didn't know where I was for a minute."

"You're <u>home</u>," Mandey stressed. "Where you belong." She stood up and walked over to him. "I'm on my way to school, but Marcia said she would report me as sick if you want me to stay home."

"Of course, I want you home with me, but you should go to school. I think I'm going to spend most of my day in bed. I didn't have a decent night's sleep the entire time I was in there."

"Are you sure?" she asked.

"I'm sure," he replied, looking down at her sweet but skeptical face. "I'm okay, Mandey. I will admit, I feel weird. I feel a lot of emotions, but I also kinda don't feel anything at all. Like you said, it's gonna take time to get used to things again." He kissed her forehead. "I don't think it will take too long."

"Maybe it's too soon to ask this, but time is running short," Mandey said. "Prom is coming up in ten days. Do you think you will be up to going with me?"

Shannon's mouth opened in surprise. "I nearly forgot about that!" he exclaimed.

"I mean, I don't want to pressure you if you don't think you'll be ready—"

Shannon stopped her with a kiss, then said, "Mandey, how could I miss it? No, no, I'll be ready. I guess I have to go rent a tux and stuff, huh?"

"Yeah," Mandey said.

"Did you buy a dress?" he asked her.

"No," she said. "I thought for a while about going by myself, but I didn't really want to go without you. So, I've got to find a gown, pronto. Guess I know what I'm doing this weekend. Anyway, I've got to brush my teeth and get going. You go back to bed and I'll call you at lunch time to see how you're doing."

A few minutes later she kissed him goodbye. For the first time since February, she was on her way to school and her heart didn't feel like it was sitting in the pit of her stomach. Shannon was home. All the worry of the last several weeks was finally over.

At the house, Shannon put on a pair of sweatpants and a T-shirt and went out to the kitchen to find something to eat. Marcia had just left, but she had brought in the newspaper from the driveway and left it on the kitchen table. Shannon made himself three over-easy eggs and two pieces of toast, poured himself a cup of coffee, and sat down at the table. He opened the paper and found an article about his release in the metro section. There was a photo of him and Mandey embracing in the waiting area. The article talked about how he had been cleared because his mother had confessed to the murder, and now she was being held in the Houston jail awaiting trial. That was an upsetting revelation. He had thought they would keep her locked up in a psych unit somewhere, not put her in the same jail he had just gotten out of. His first instinct was to get into his car and go down to see her, but then he remembered it was morning and visiting hours weren't until evening, and it was Wednesday, so it wasn't even a day with visiting hours.

The article also mentioned that he had been the one to accuse the parole office of blackmailing parolees into doing illegal activities. Somehow the media had found out about the whole thing. Joe had warned him that there was likely to be a trial and Shannon would be called to testify. Even though Joe guaranteed he didn't have to be afraid of being arrested for those crimes, Shannon was still uneasy. He forced himself not to think about it as he shuffled through the newspaper and found the section with the want ads. In their conversation at Pappasito's the night before, both Marcia and Michael had told him to not worry about getting a job until he felt better adjusted, but he couldn't sit around and keep taking everyone's charity. He browsed the ads and circled a few that were interesting. He was also going to call his old boss, Bert. Bert seemed to have liked him. Mandey said he offered to be a character witness for him, if necessary. If Shannon was lucky, Bert would have an opening and could take him back.

Shannon finished his breakfast, folded up the newspaper, and went back to Mandey's bedroom. He stripped back down to his underwear and got back into that nice, comfortable bed with the soft sheets and Mandey's sweet scent all over them, so different from where he had woken up the morning before. He hadn't been joking when he had told Mandey he would probably stay in bed most of the day. He closed his eyes and thought happy thoughts about her, and soon he fell deeply asleep again.

The next day was a busy one. Shannon called his former boss, Bert, to thank him for offering to be a character witness for him if his case had gone to trial. He was nervous about asking if he might have his old job back, but Bert offered it to him even before Shannon got up the courage to ask about it. He could start back the following Monday. There was one thing off his mind. He might have been cleared of murdering Leon, but Shannon was still on probation for the robbery until he turned 21, and he was expected to have a job and keep his nose clean. He was supposed to meet with his new probation officer the next day. He was nervous about that, too. He wondered if the new one was going to be an asshole like Holtz, and whether they would hold a grudge against him for blowing the whistle on Holtz and his compadres.

It was a warm spring day. He went out to his car and rolled down the windows and cranked up the radio. He was grateful to Joe and Michael for getting the car out of impound. He owed them a lot.

He pulled out onto the street and headed toward the Northview Apartments. As he pulled into the parking lot, he momentarily thought he was in the wrong place. Then he realized what was different—the burned building, where the Devils had claimed the one relatively-undamaged apartment as their own, had been razed. A sense of finality grew inside him.

Shannon pulled into a parking spot in front of the apartment he had shared with his mother, Annette, and Leon. He got out of the car and stood in front of the door. A sheet of paper was nailed to it. He tore it off and glanced over it. The rent was overdue for March and April. Eviction proceedings were underway.

He put his key in the lock. It still worked. He opened the door to the empty apartment. It looked the same, but it felt different. It was a little dim, so he flicked on the light switch. Nothing came on. Light bill hadn't been paid, either. He went into the bedroom he had shared with Annette. The curtain that had separated their halves of the room had been taken down. Annette's belongings were still there, so it looked like she was still using the apartment at least part of the time. Then he turned and went into the bedroom his mother and Leon had shared. He opened the curtains covering the window to let some light in. Leon's things were still there, his clothes, his shoes. He would have liked to have taken them outside and set a match to them, but he didn't. He thought maybe Lizzie would have come down from Arkansas to take her brother's things, but maybe she didn't care about them (or Leon) that much.

Shannon began going through the bureau, nightstands, and closet, looking for his mother's personal belongings. He didn't trust Annette to take care of her things, especially with that eviction warning on the door. They could come in and empty the apartment and throw everything in the trash.

"What are you doing here?"

Shannon turned around to see Annette in the doorway to the bedroom. She had on gray sweatpants and a loose T-shirt and was noticeably pregnant now. He had thought he would be angry at her for what she had put him through by lying to the police, but he wasn't. She was only trying to protect their mother, and besides, he was tired of fighting with her. Joe had told him that obstruction of justice charges were pending against Annette, as well as Raff and Dewayne. Shannon wasn't sure if Annette knew that, but he didn't bring it up.

"Rounding up some of Momma's stuff for safekeeping," Shannon said.

"What, you don't trust me?" Annette asked.

"You've got other stuff on your mind right now," Shannon replied. He took the notice that had been on the front door from where he had placed it on the bureau and handed it to Annette. "They're going to evict you."

"I know," she said carelessly, tossing the paper aside. "I'm staying at Dewayne's most of the time, anyway."

"Well, what are you going to do with all this stuff?" Shannon asked.

"I don't know, and I don't care," Annette said. "Take whatever you want. I'll take care of my stuff and leave the rest."

"When is your due date?" Shannon asked her, changing the subject.

"July 22nd. Another three months. I'm ready for this to be over with," Annette replied.

"Mandey said you're having a boy?" Shannon asked.

"That's what the doctor said," she said.

Shannon opened a box and pulled out an old photo album. He hadn't seen it in years.

He thought maybe Leon had made his mother throw it away.

"Hey, look at this," he said to Annette.

She came over and they sat down on the bed, looking at the old pictures. Pictures of them when they were little, pictures of their parents, pictures of family members Shannon vaguely remembered.

"Look at you—what a dork!" Annette laughed, pointing at Shannon's 5th grade picture.

"Me? Look at you!" Shannon said, pointing to a picture of Annette after she had given herself bangs that were about an inch long.

There was a photo of the two of them with their mother in the middle, with an arm around each one of them. It was Christmas time and they were sitting on the floor in front of the Christmas tree with wrapping paper everywhere. Big smiles on all their faces. It was the last Christmas they had with their father alive. He was the one taking the picture.

"Good times," Annette whispered. "Before everything went to shit."

"Yeah," Shannon agreed. He wanted to tell her things were going to get better, but honestly, for her, he didn't know.

"I'm going to visit Momma later," Shannon said. "Do you want to go with me?"

Annette shook her head. "Maybe another time."

She helped him gather up their mother's things and carry them out to his car.

"You still have Mandey's phone number, right?" Shannon asked her.

"Yeah."

"You can call me if you need something," Shannon said.

"Sure," Annette said, nodding.

They hugged briefly, awkwardly. She waved at him as he drove away.

The feeling of finality grew more inside him as he left. It wasn't necessarily a sad feeling, but more of a sense of change, that life was overwhelmingly different now. Now and forever.

He went back home and took his mother's things into the house. He brought almost everything she had, including her clothes. He made himself a sandwich for lunch, then put it all away. He kept out the photo album. He wanted to show it to Mandey later.

Mandey had choir practice after school, so he left her a note that he was going to go visit his mother. His stomach was in knots as he drove downtown to the jail. He wanted to see his mother, but going back to the jail, even as a free man, made him nauseated. As he got closer, his heart started racing. He wasn't sure he was going to be able to do it.

He made himself ignore the stares from the guards as he sat and waited his turn. When he was able to go in to the visiting room, the guard he passed going through the door finally had a smartass comment.

"Did you miss us, Douglass?" he asked with a smirk.

Shannon pretended he didn't hear him. He was focused on his mother, sitting in a seat he had sat in so many times talking to Mandey.

"Mijo," she said, when he picked up the phone.

"Hi, Momma," he said softly. He had wanted to say so much to her, but at that moment, the words were all bottled up inside of him.

"I'm sorry about what you went through," she said.

"It's okay," he said, then shook his head. "No, it's not okay. You shouldn't be in here. You should still be at the hospital."

"Well, I guess they decided I'm in my right mind now, so they sent me here," his mother said. "It ain't that bad."

"Don't give me that. I just spent over two months here. I know it's bad."

Shannon told her about going to the apartment and getting her belongings and running into Annette.

"Shannon, whatever you do, will you please look out for your sister?" his mother asked. "I don't trust that boy to stand by her and the baby. It don't look like I'm going to be around to help her out, so can you promise me you'll help her and that baby, if they need it?"

Shannon nodded. "I will, if she needs it and she'll let me."

"Thank you, mijo. I know you tried all these years. You let Leon use you like a punching bag. You always tried to distract him when you saw he was being mean to me or Annette. I was wrong to keep taking him back every time, but he used to scare me. He'd tell me one day you and Annette would leave me, and he would be the only one left to take care of me. I know that was bullshit, but he always got to me when I was feeling depressed, or anxious, or scared."

"He wanted it that way," Shannon said. "That's why he pushed all our family away and moved us around so much. He didn't want us to have any connections or any sort of lifeline."

"I know. I know," his mother said. "But you found a lifeline. Your girlfriend?"

Shannon broke into a smile. "I have. I never knew things could be like this."

His mother smiled at him. "I love to see you with a smile on your face, Shannon. That is all a mother needs, to know her children are happy."

80

The Dress

Mandey and Georgia hit Deerbrook Mall shortly after it opened Saturday morning. Prom was a week away, and Mandey had to find a prom dress ASAP. She had her green flapper dress from Halloween to fall back on, but as much as she liked it, it wasn't what she had hoped to be wearing to the prom. She had seen a gown worn by the character Roxie Shayne on *Guiding Light* that was a lot like what she wanted—white with a form-fitting bodice and a full, floor-length skirt, sprinkled with light-catching silver sequins. The gown was strapless, and Roxie wore white three-quarter length gloves. She also had a tiara and large earrings that looked like branches with rhinestones on the numerous tips. That was what Mandey wanted, except maybe not strapless. Being able to find anything like that on short notice and on her budget was a different story. At this late date, there was not much left to choose from. By mid-afternoon, they had covered all the stores in Deerbrook Mall and Mandey had only found a couple dresses she liked, but were far too small, and a couple in her size that were marginally acceptable, but nothing like what she wanted. The next stop was the bridal shop, but none of their prom offerings captured her attention, either. They browsed the wedding gowns, too, but none of the gowns at the bridal shop were "un-bridal" enough for a prom.

Greenspoint Mall was the next destination, but Mandey wanted to stop somewhere else first, before it closed.

"Goodwill? Seriously?" Georgia asked as they pulled into the strip mall parking lot.

"Yes, I just want to check quick," Mandey said. "They get used formals all the time. I might find something. It won't take long, then we can hit Greenspoint."

They walked in and Mandey saw it almost immediately. It was hanging up on the wall above the rack that held the evening dresses. It wasn't that much like what Roxie wore, but it was white and silver, which is what she wanted.

She asked one of the clerks it she could see it, and they took it down off the wall for her. Mandey looked at the label and her face fell. Size ten, two sizes too small for her.

"Is that what you want?" Georgia asked.

"Yes, but it's a 10 and I'm a 14," Mandey said mournfully.

"Let me see," Georgia said, taking it from Mandey. She looked it over. "You know, Mom could alter this for you so it would fit."

"You think so?" Mandey asked hopefully. Georgia's mother had sewn Georgia's prom dress and had also done Mandey's choir dress two years before.

"Sure!" Georgia said. "Definitely."

Mandey walked over to a full-length mirror and held it up to her, to get an idea of what it would look like. It had short, off-the-shoulder sleeves. The sleeves and bodice were covered with silver lace, beads, and sequins. The skirt wasn't the full, tulle skirt with twinkly sequins like Roxie's dress, but was long, flowing, and white with fine silver pinstripes.

"Are you sure she can do it by next Saturday?" Mandey asked.

"Yes. You might have to buy some additional fabric, but yes," Georgia replied.

Mandey joyfully paid for the gown and they went back to Georgia's car with the dress in a plastic garment bag. "Let's go to Greenspoint now so I can look for accessories."

It didn't take long for her to find jewelry, stockings, and gloves to go with the new dress. Nothing that matched Roxie's, but silver rhinestone earrings and a matching necklace; fingerless elbow-length white gloves; pantyhose with a hint of opalescent shine (not that they would be seen under the long skirt, anyway). She decided not to go with a tiara like Roxie had; that might be overkill. The next challenge was finding shoes to fit her double-wide feet, but she did—a pair of silver pumps with two-inch heels at Montgomery Ward. She was going to make sure she wore them around the house a bit during the week to break them in. Then Mandey went back to Judy's, where she had gotten her jewelry and gloves, to find decorative shoe clips that were similar to the earrings she had bought. Lastly, they stopped at the JC Penney salon and asked about getting appointments to have manicures and their hair styled the next week, and miraculously, there were still a few openings left on Saturday.

From the mall, they went to Georgia's house and Mandey talked to her mother about alterations to the dress. Mrs. Cornell took her measurements and looked over the gown. She figured she might have to buy a couple yards of fabric. She would get white fabric and silver lace to match the dress as close as possible. Mandey asked her much she would charge. She told her she would do it for free.

"Honey, you've been through so much the last few months," Mrs. Cornell said. "I'm so glad you're going to get to go to your prom now."

Mandey went home feeling relieved that she was able to get her prom outfit off her plate. She figured she should get some new makeup, too, but she could stop at the drug store on the way home from school one day. She went into the house with her bag of accessories and the bag with her shoes and found Shannon in the living room watching television.

"Oh, no," he said when he saw her with the two small bags. "Didn't you find a dress?"

"Actually, I did," she said, setting the bags down on the armchair. "It didn't quite fit, so Georgia's mom is going to alter it for me."

"Did you get what you wanted?" Shannon asked.

"Yes," Mandey said. "It wasn't exactly what I was looking for, but I'm happy with it."

"You're going to be the most beautiful girl there, anyway," Shannon said.

"I don't know about that, but I'm going to be the happiest one there, now that you'll be with me."

81

Prom

Mandey woke up in Shannon's arms the morning of the prom. Each morning that she woke up with him next to her, she was thankful. It had been a long eleven weeks waiting and wondering and worrying if he would ever get out of jail and back to her, but the hell was over now. He lay safe in her bed, and she was safe with him.

Tonight, she thought. *Tonight, after the prom, I'm going to tell Shannon to make love to me.*

She had to get up to use the toilet, but then she came back and settled into bed next to her boyfriend again. He didn't stir. His time in jail had exhausted him, and his body was still trying to catch up on sleep.

It was early, and Mandey wanted to sleep a while longer herself. They would be up until the wee hours of the morning, and she wanted to be as rested as possible. She drifted off to sleep with dreams of the prom and what would happen afterward floating in her head.

She was awakened about two hours later by a pair of strong hands gently rubbing her back. She lazily rolled over to see Shannon's hazel eyes gazing at her lovingly.

"Good morning," she said to Shannon.

"Good morning, Prom Queen," he replied, grinning at her.

"We don't elect a prom queen at our school," Mandey told him.

"Well, you're my prom queen," Shannon said.

"Yeah, I'm sure I look like a prom queen right now," Mandey said, smiling back.

"You look like it to me," Shannon said, brushing his fingers across her cheek. "It's great waking up to your sweet face instead of the ugly mugs of my cellmates."

"Don't even talk about that," Mandey said, snuggling up to him and burying her face in his neck. "I don't like thinking about it."

There wasn't much time to stay in bed. After breakfast, Mandey and Shannon left on their respective errands. Shannon had to pick up his tuxedo and the prom flowers, along with making a visit to his mother. Mandey had to go to her salon appointment at Penney's. Although she and Georgia could have ridden to the mall together, Mandey opted to meet her there. She wanted to be on time for her appointment, and Georgia was chronically late.

As it was, Mandey arrived on time for her scheduled appointment, but it didn't matter. Saturdays are busy days at hair salons, and this day was no exception. Busier than usual, because it was prom season. Fifteen minutes after her appointment time had passed Mandey was still sitting in the waiting area when Georgia rushed in.

"Can you believe prom is finally here?" Georgia squealed when she saw Mandey.

"I can't believe it's here and that it may turn out the way I've been dreaming it would be," Mandey said.

"'May turn out'?" Georgia asked, taking a seat next to her friend.

"I'm too cynical to get my hopes up too much."

"Stop it. You should be excited."

"Actually," Mandey said, smiling, "I'm _too_ excited. I'm trying to temper it with a little dose of pessimism."

Georgia got called first and then Mandey about five minutes later. An hour later, their hair had been washed, cut, and styled. Georgia had her blonde hair blown out straight and upswept into a sleek French twist. Mandey had her hair coaxed into soft curls falling to her shoulders and framing her face. With their hair set, moussed, and sprayed into place, the girls sat side by side at the manicure table. Georgia had long false nails that she was having filled and polished a dangerous red to match her dress. Mandey had a simple manicure and chose a medium shade of frosted pink for her nails. She had considered doing it herself and painting them silver, but she found she liked that shade of pink and thought that maybe silver nails would be overkill.

"Where are you guys going to eat?" Mandey asked Georgia. She was going to the prom with Ronnie, a guy from her church who was twenty-five.

"Steak and Ale," Georgia said. "What about you? You're still going with Charlie and Gayla?"

"Yep," Mandey said. "We're going to Birraporetti's."

"That sounds good," Georgia said. "I get tired of Steak and Ale all the time. Seems like that's the only place guys ever want to take me. I want to tell them, 'Hey, Red Lobster's good, too, you know.'"

"Andie and Mart are going to Vargo's," Mandey said.

"Wow, that's expensive," Georgia said, then added sarcastically, "I wonder whose idea that was?"

"I didn't ask," Mandey said.

"Like you'd have to."

Mandey and Shannon returned home almost simultaneously. Shannon had the plastic bag with his tuxedo slung over one shoulder, and a small plastic bag in the other.

"Is that my corsage?" Mandey asked.

"And my boutonniere," Shannon said, holding the bag out to her. "I hope you like it."

Mandey pulled out a clear plastic box. The corsage was made of small pink rose buds, baby's breath, and silver ribbons.

"It's a wrist corsage," he said. "Marcia said you might like that better, so it won't hide your dress."

"Wow," Mandey said, delighted. "The roses match my fingernails almost perfectly." She stretched out one hand and splayed out her fingers to show Shannon her manicure.

"Well, I did good, then," Shannon said.

"Yes, you did," Mandey said, "but you always do."

In the house, Mandey took a long bath, careful not to get her hair wet. After she was through primping, Shannon took his shower. Mandey applied her make-up, being careful to make it perfect, then began to dress. When she was finished, she walked down the hallway, feeling like a bride on her wedding day.

Marcia and Shannon were in the living room waiting for her to make her appearance.

"You look like you stepped out of a fairytale," Marcia told her.

Shannon said nothing. He stared, speechless, at this amazing woman he still had trouble believing was his girlfriend. His eyes started at her feet in the silver high-heeled pumps with the rhinestone shoe clips peeking out from under the white skirt with the silver pinstripes. The bodice of the short-sleeved gown had a sweetheart neckline and short, off-the-shoulder sleeves and was adorned with silver lace, beads, and sequins. A glittering rhinestone necklace with matching earrings and white gloves topped off the outfit. She was more beautiful than ever, with her eyes shining and a smile lighting her whole face.

"Are you going to tell her she's beautiful, or has the cat got your tongue?" Marcia asked Shannon, teasing.

He didn't take his eyes off her. "You are a shining star," he told Mandey, reaching out to take her hand. He slid the corsage onto her left wrist. "You're absolutely gorgeous."

"You are, too," Mandey said, taking his hand in hers, surveying him in his dove gray tux with the matching tie and cummerbund.

He bent his head and brushed his lips against hers. Marcia was already snapping pictures, of them together and alone, using up a roll of film before Gayla and Charlie arrived. Gayla walked in wearing a slinky black gown, with her long chestnut hair gathered by a golden beaded band and flowing in a loose ponytail over her left shoulder. Charlie was dressed in the traditional black tuxedo with the matching tie and cummerbund and, like Shannon, had chosen a white shirt with a pleated front rather than a ruffled one.

Marcia took several more pictures of the four of them, then Shannon helped Mandey put on her sheer silver shawl, and the four of them trooped out to the limousine, a black Lincoln Town Car. Marcia followed, still shooting.

Gingerly, the four prom-goers got into the car, carefully sitting down to keep their clothes from wrinkling. There was an ice bucket with a bottle of champagne waiting for them.

"Fancy," Shannon said, glancing around the car. "This is crazy. Last week I was in jail, and now I'm wearing a tux, riding in a limo, and drinking champagne."

"Not that fancy," Charlie said, passing out the champagne glasses. "The glasses are plastic."

"Freaky, huh?" Gayla said. "What was jail like?"

"It sucks big time. I don't recommend it," Shannon said, as Charlie popped the cork on the champagne bottle and began pouring.

"You look like you lost some weight," Gayla said.

"I did," Shannon said. "The food was gross."

"Well, you'll gain some of it back tonight," Charlie said. "Birraporetti's is so good, and there's going to be a big spread at the prom, too."

"What's going to happen to your mother now?" Gayla asked.

"I don't know yet. Should know more about it next week sometime."

"God, I'm so sorry," Gayla said. "It's good that you're cleared, but not so good that your mother's in trouble."

"Thanks," Shannon said, touched by her sympathy.

They had time to kill, so Charlie told the driver to take them downtown.

"Since we're dressed up and riding around in a limo, let's drive through River Oaks and pretend like we belong there," Charlie said.

"The bad thing about limos is that the windows are tinted and no one outside can see you," Mandey said. "I guess if you're rich and famous, you want your privacy."

"We've got a moon roof. You can stand up through it so people can see you," Charlie suggested with a grin.

"I don't think so," Mandey said.

"That would be so gauche, Charlie," Gayla said, affecting a pretentious manner, then dropping it. "Although if I were drunk enough, I might do it."

"May I pour you another glass of the bubbly, dear?" Charlie asked Gayla in his Thurston Howell the Third accent.

"Certainly," she replied, holding out her glass, "but it'll take a lot more than a little champagne to get me that drunk."

The driver took the limousine to the area just west of downtown where there were many expensive homes and exclusive neighborhoods. From the car they admired the big, fancy houses, many surrounded by concrete walls and iron gates. Some of the neighborhoods were gated, as well, to keep out unwanted elements.

"They may be gated off for security reasons, but I don't think I'd want to live in a neighborhood that has gates to keep people out," Mandey said.

"They're afraid the unwashed masses might come and contaminate their way of living," Charlie added.

"It's so pretentious," Gayla said. "Kind of insulting, too."

Shannon remained quiet, thinking back to how the Devils used to think the suburban kids were such rich snobs.

After driving through the residential streets, the driver looped around to drive down Westheimer Road.

"It's a lot tamer down here during the day," Mandey said as they rode down Westheimer from downtown toward the Galleria.

"The freaks don't come out until night," Charlie said.

The lower stretch of Westheimer was the funkiest part of Houston, with lots of off-the-wall shops, nightclubs, strip joints, tattoo parlors, and gay bars. On Friday and Saturday nights, it was the main drag strip for the entire city, and the street would be jammed with cars and people, the colorful denizens of the area and a lot of suburban kids looking for a thrill. As the street ran away from downtown, the surroundings became more upscale until reaching the Galleria area, which was rife with stores full of merchandise with "if you have to ask, you can't afford it" prices.

Where Westheimer met the Galleria area was also where it met the 610 Loop, and the limo took a right turn and headed north to take them back to Birraporetti's by Greenspoint Mall.

The driver drove up to the door and opened the limousine door to let them out. The four of them stepped inside the dark wooden and glass doors into the restaurant, which smelled of garlic and rich sauces. The lights were turned down for the dinner hour; the tables near the front had daylight, but it became darker, lit only by candles on each table, as the hostess led them to a table in the back.

"I love the candles. It makes it so romantic," Gayla said.

"Me, too," Mandey said.

The candles reminded Shannon of Tandy's Ice House, but this was a far better place to take Mandey on a date.

As they perused their menus, Mandey recommended the crab-stuffed mushrooms for an appetizer. "They're wonderful," she said.

For an entrée, Mandey chose cannelloni, Gayla picked ravioli, Charlie ordered lasagna, and Shannon opted for spaghetti and meatballs. Because of the crowd in the restaurant, it took some time for the food to arrive, but when it did, it looked wonderful.

The server asked if they needed anything else.

"Some extra napkins, please," Gayla said.

"For me, too, please," Mandey said. It would be a disaster to get her white dress dirty.

"Would you like extra napkins, too?" the server asked Charlie and Shannon.

"No," Charlie said, grinning. "It's just the girls. They've got poor eye-hand coordination."

"Stop it," Gayla said, smacking Charlie on the shoulder.

"Ow," he said, holding his arm.

Dinner was delicious, and they finished up as the prom was getting underway. They paid their bill and returned outside to the limousine. The Greenhaven Hotel was less than five minutes away, on the other side of the mall. It had only opened six months before. The lobby and main foyer were decorated in green carpet and marble floors with two fountains and lush greenery all around. A pianist played a black grand piano at the far end of the lobby. Perhaps people down on that end could hear it, but on this end all that could be heard was the thumping beat of the music emanating from the ballroom where the Rogers High prom was being held.

"Man," Shannon said, looking around in awe as they got into line.

"Pretty impressive, huh?" Charlie said. "We came over here and checked out the place when we heard where the prom was going to be."

"I don't know how our class could afford this, what with Mr. Tichner dipping into our funds all the time," Mandey said.

"I heard Mr. Smith set up a bank account for our class that Tichner didn't know about," Charlie said. "I also heard we got some of our money from a couple people's not-so-legal extra-curricular activities."

Mandey looked at him blankly.

"Drug money," Charlie said.

"Oh, no way," Gayla scoffed. "Who told you that?"

"'I heard it through the grapevine,'" Charlie sang. "I don't know where it originated."

"That's ridiculous," Gayla said.

"How else could we afford this? The twenty-dollar ticket price covered a lot, I'm sure, but I don't think the proceeds from a few dances and candy sales could make up the rest," Charlie said.

"Well, if it's true, I don't want to know about it," Mandey said.

They gave their tickets to the ticket-takers and entered the ballroom. Large round tables covered with white linen tablecloths surrounded three sides of a large dance floor. A huge crystal chandelier hung from the ceiling, its light dimmed to a low glow. Against the back wall, the deejay was set up, with large speakers blasting and lights blinking and spinning. Along the right-hand wall were long tables covered with white tablecloths laden with chafing dishes and platters and flowers. In the middle sat a huge punch bowl along with a massive ice sculpture of the number 85.

Each round table was set up to seat eight people. They found one near the punch bowl and claimed it for their own.

"Check out the party favors," Gayla said.

For each person, there was a commemorative pilsner glass, a pen that said "Rogers Senior High School Best Alive—Class of '85," and a garter in the school colors.

There was also a card for each person that was printed to look like a ticket and included the prom menu.

"What's 'beef Madagascar'?" Mandey asked, examining the card.

"Look at the stuff they've got. Jeez, we didn't need to eat out first," Gayla said.

The dance floor was still deserted as couples continued to arrive. Trish Hinojosa and her boyfriend Guillermo from Monterey and Thad Hurley and his date, a junior named Christie, joined Mandey, Shannon, Gayla, and Charlie at their table. Then Georgia walked in with her date, followed by Jackie and her boyfriend Peter and Charlene and Phillip.

"Phil's here!" Shannon exclaimed excitedly.

The six were surveying the ballroom. Mandey waved at them. "They can sit at the table next to us," she said.

Georgia swept over in her blood-red gown with its plunging neckline and long see-through sleeves. When Mandey had seen the dress at Georgia's house the previous week, the neckline had a lace overlay, an alteration by her mother making it considerably more modest. Georgia apparently had cut it out. Tagging behind her was her date, who was tall, blond, and skinny with a slightly ratty-looking mustache. He wore a white tuxedo with a ruffled white shirt and red accessories.

"Hey, y'all," she said, addressing everyone at Mandey's table. "This is my date, Ronnie."

"Hi," they chorused.

"Sit at this next table," Mandey said, pointing to the table to her left.

"Okay," Georgia said, glancing around. "Man, can you believe this place? I mean, I'm a class officer, so I was over here checking stuff out and getting stuff ready, but now it's the real thing, and I'm still impressed."

"Amazing," Mandey said.

Ronnie pulled out a chair for Georgia so she could be seated. Jackie, Peter, and Charlene followed them over to the table. Phillip stopped to talk to Shannon.

"Look at you, all slicked up and trying to look respectable," Shannon said to his friend.

"Me? Look at you," Phillip said, grinning. "Prison stripes to tails in less than two weeks."

Charlene came over, cleared her throat, and took Phillip by the arm. "Let's be seated," she said pointedly.

Phillip walked her over to the table. Charlene wore a baby blue gown that matched her eyes. The short-sleeved bodice was puckered all over, and the skirt flowed freely from the waist. Phillip's powder blue tuxedo was almost a perfect match. Phillip pulled out a chair so Charlene could be seated, then took the seat next to hers. It happened to be the seat closest to Shannon's, so they could turn their chairs and talk. Mandey noticed that Charlene didn't look happy, probably due to the seating arrangement. Mandey was glad that Phillip was there. Shannon had been kind of quiet, likely feeling a little out of place since everyone was Mandey's friend. It was good that he had a friend there, too.

Mandey heard the first notes of Chicago's "You're the Inspiration".

Shannon was talking to Phillip. She tapped him on the shoulder. "They're playing our song," she said to him. "Do you want to dance?"

"Sure," he said, then turned back to Phillip. "The lady wants to dance."

"What the lady wants, the lady gets," Phillip said.

"Always," Shannon said.

Mandey and Shannon made their way through to the dance floor, which was still not crowded.

"How are you doing?" she asked him as they put their arms around each other and began swaying to the music.

"Good," Shannon said.

"Feeling more comfortable?"

"Yeah," he said, and smiled. "I'm glad to see Phil here."

"I'm glad, too. Charlene doesn't seem too happy, though," Mandey said. "I wish she'd get over it."

"I need to have a talk with that boy," Shannon said, shaking his head. "I don't know why he puts up with her. She must be really good in bed."

"Shannon!" Mandey said, shocked but laughing.

"Well, do you have a better explanation?" he asked. "I could have ended up like that. If I'd been dumb enough to sleep with Kerri, had my first time with her, I might have stayed with her just because of the sex."

"That's a scary thought," Mandey said, shuddering.

Shannon wrapped his arms tightly around Mandey. Her body pressed against his, from her chest down to her thighs. It felt as electric as it had back in November, maybe more so, because for so long they had been unsure if they would ever be together again. Mandey tightened her own grip on him. She never wanted to be separated from him again.

As the song ended, Shannon bent his head to kiss her, then they danced to "All She Wants to Do Is Dance" by Don Henley before sitting down again.

At the table, her attention bounced from the conversation at her own table, to talking to Georgia, to glancing at the door to see who was making an entrance. She saw Jesse and Angelina arrive and head for the opposite side of the room. A few minutes later, the Three

Musketeers arrived, all dressed in identical white tuxes with tails and Ray-Bans. Each had a date on his arm. They didn't seem to notice Mandey and Shannon as they walked by.

Ten minutes later, Jeremy came through the door with his new girlfriend, Melissa. Last of all to appear was Danny. He was wearing a gray tuxedo like Shannon's but without tails. He had no one with him, and Mandey thought he looked a little lost. He saw Mandey watching him and gave her a solemn little wave, but did not come over. He walked over to Georgia's table and began talking to them. Thad and his date moved over to the two empty spots at Georgia's table, and Danny divided his time between them and a table of his cronies, including Jeremy and Melissa, Mark and his date, and two other couples.

Around eight-thirty, James made his entrance, dressed to the hilt in a black tuxedo with tails, a plain white shirt, white tie and cummerbund, and a top hat and cane. On his arm was his mystery date, a petite Vietnamese girl with shoulder-length black hair wearing a long daffodil-colored off-the-shoulder sheath dress. They strolled up to Mandey's table.

"Are these seats taken?" he asked, referring to the chairs vacated by Thad and his date.

Mandey, Gayla, Charlie, and Trish all looked at each other. Mandey looked at Shannon. He shrugged indifferently. So did she.

"You can sit there if you promise to behave yourself," Gayla told James.

"Behave myself?" James asked, pulling out a chair for his date. "I always behave myself. This is Thuy. She goes to Memorial High School."

"Hi, Thuy," the others chorused.

"Hi," she replied softly, and smiled nervously.

James sat down in the chair next to Mandey's. Mandey mused about the fact that at the beginning of the school year, she had figured to be sitting next to James at the prom, but as his date. Things had changed drastically since then, but she had no regrets.

James did not talk much to the others at the table, focusing his attention on his date. They spent more time on the dance floor than at the table, anyway, and James introduced her around to others in the room.

Shannon had once told a woman at a honky-tonk that he only danced with his girlfriend. This night he proved himself a liar. He danced with Gayla while Mandey danced with Charlie, with Georgia while Mandey danced with Ronnie, even with Charlene as Mandey danced with Phillip. He noticed Charlene seemed distracted while he danced with her, keeping her eye on her boyfriend, as though she were worried about what Phillip was doing with Mandey. He thought about saying something to her about it, but decided he didn't want his head bitten off, so he kept his mouth shut.

Around nine-thirty Mandey and Shannon had their prom portrait taken out in the lobby, then went back inside the ballroom and stood behind James in the buffet line. "Lover Girl" by Teena Marie began playing. Mandey started to dance and sing along, not letting standing in line stop her. Shannon smiled, amused.

They picked up plates and silverware. "Look at all this food," Mandey raved.

Even though most people had already gone through the buffet line, a lot of food remained. They discovered that beef Madagascar was little medallions of beef with peppercorns in sauce. In addition, there was peel-and-eat shrimp, crab cakes, chicken ala king, au gratin potatoes, sliced ham, eggrolls, fried mushrooms, cocktail wieners in barbecue sauce, cheese, fresh sliced fruit, vegetable sticks, and more. Mandey began to think that what Charlie had said about the prom funding might be true. She put a little bit of everything that looked good on her plate, and Shannon followed suit.

James was ahead of them, filling a plate for himself and one for Thuy.

"Thuy seems nice," Mandey said to him, to make conversation. "How did you meet?"

"You don't want to know," James said shortly.

Mandey paused. "Okay," she said, and decided not to press the issue.

"My parents know her parents," he continued after a moment. "They arranged the date."

"I see," Mandey said.

"My parents import a lot of Asian foodstuffs, and Thuy's parents own three restaurants, so getting us together would be beneficial for both families." He finished filling the plates. "I'll send you a wedding invitation," he said and walked off.

The music was so loud that Shannon hadn't been able to hear the conversation. "What was that about?" he asked Mandey.

"James's and Thuy's parents arranged their date," Mandey explained. "I guess they might want to arrange a marriage, as well."

"An arranged marriage?" Shannon asked. "Do they still do that kind of thing?"

"In some cultures," Mandey said.

"Thank God we don't," Shannon said. "No one would have ever paired you up with me."

They walked back to their table, then Shannon went to get himself and Mandey each a cup of punch. He was grinning when he handed Mandey her cup.

"They're guarding it like hawks to make sure no one spikes it," he said as he sat down.

"Thank you," she said. "Yes, I noticed. I think everyone knew that would be the case and got liquored up before they got here."

"Like we did," Shannon said, teasing.

"Yeah, I got so drunk off a few sips of cheap champagne," Mandey said, laughing.

A while later they had cleaned their plates.

"You want dessert?" Shannon asked her.

Mandey paused for a moment, trying to decide if she did. "Yes, I do."

"What do you want?" he asked. "I'll get it for you."

"I'm not sure. Something with fruit, if they have it."

While Shannon was at the dessert table, Danny came over to Mandey.

"Hi," he said.

"Hi," she replied, suddenly feeling shy.

"Pretty fancy shindig we're having here, huh?" Danny remarked.

"Yep."

"You look really beautiful tonight," he told her.

"Thanks," she said. "You look nice, too."

"Thanks," he replied. "Are you having a good time?"

"The best," Mandey said, smiling. "You seem a little lost, though. You're here, then there."

"Yeah, well...," Danny said, shrugging.

Shannon returned to the table. Mandey thought Danny would make a quick retreat, but he didn't.

"Hi," he said to Shannon.

"Hi," Shannon replied warily, setting down the dessert plates he had brought.

"I was wondering if you'd mind if I had a dance with your date," Danny said.

Mandey looked from Shannon to Danny and back to Shannon again.

"That's up to Mandey," Shannon said.

Danny turned back to Mandey. "Will you dance with me?"

Mandey hesitated. "I'm not—" she began.

"If you want to dance with him, go ahead. I don't mind," Shannon told her, then said to Danny, "By the way, Mandey told me you helped her out when she was trying to find evidence to clear me. Thanks."

Shannon extended his hand to Danny. Danny slowly raised his hand to shake with him. "You're welcome," he replied.

Shannon sat down next to Mandey again. "Go dance. I really don't mind," he said, leaning over to give her a peck on the cheek.

"Okay," she said, giving his knee a squeeze under the table before she stood.

Danny escorted her to the dance floor as "Just Once" by James Ingram began playing.

"I remember dancing with you to this song at the Christmas dance when we were in ninth grade," Mandey said as he put his arm around her.

"You've got a memory like an elephant," Danny said.

Ah, yes, exactly what a woman wants to hear, a man comparing her to an elephant. No wonder he doesn't have a date, Mandey thought. *Well, it could have been worse. He could have said I dance like an elephant.*

"Why didn't you bring a date, Danny? I'm sure Patty Forbes would have come with you," she said, teasing.

Danny rolled his eyes. "She's got a boyfriend now, so I've got her off my back," he said. "There were a couple girls I thought about asking, but they had dates before I got around to it. I thought about asking you, but I figured you'd say no."

Mandey nodded. "I might have come by myself, but there was no way I was going to come with anyone else but Shannon."

"Who's that guy Georgia brought?" Danny asked.

"Some guy who goes to her church," Mandey said.

"He's <u>weird</u>. She was the first one I thought about asking, but she already had a date. What does she see in him?"

"I have no idea. I think she just liked the idea of bringing an older guy for her date," Mandey said.

"I think it's weird that a guy in his mid-twenties would want to go to a high school prom," Danny said.

"I only met him tonight. I danced with him once, but he didn't say much," Mandey said. "How is he 'weird'?"

"I don't know," Danny said. "He doesn't seem all that bright, and he's kind of goofy."

"Sounds like a lot of guys in our class," Mandey said with a chuckle.

"Yeah, well, if she wanted to date an older guy, I'd assume it's because she wanted something better than the guys in our class," Danny said.

"I think her mother may have had something to do with it, too," Mandey said.

"<u>That</u> I would understand," Danny said. "Her mother doesn't like me too much."

"I wonder why?" Mandey asked sarcastically. "You know, I heard a rumor that this prom was partially funded by drug money."

"Who's been saying that?" Danny asked.

"I don't know who started it. It's a rumor," Mandey said. "Is it true?"

"I wouldn't worry about it, if I were you," Danny said.

"It <u>is</u> true!"

"I didn't say that. All I said is don't worry about it. This is our night to have a great time with our friends. Everyone should just enjoy it."

Mandey looked at him skeptically. "Okay," she said. Danny's response convinced her that the rumor had to have a least a grain of truth to it. Although still curious, she thought that the less she knew, the better.

"I can't believe we're graduating in four weeks," Danny said, changing the subject. "Man, am I ready. Southwest Texas State, here I come. I can't believe you chose U of H. You could probably have gotten into any school you wanted."

"I almost chose Bates," Mandey said.

"Bates? Where the hell is Bates? What the hell is Bates, for that matter."

"Liberal arts college in Maine."

"Why the hell would you want to go there?"

"I'm a damn Yankee," Mandey said.

"Oh, yeah, I forgot about that," Danny replied.

"I thought about going up there to be closer to my parents. But Shannon doesn't want to leave Houston, not right now, anyway. His sister is going to have a baby this summer, and you know about his mother. He feels obligated to stick around for a while."

"And you didn't want to leave him," Danny said.

"No," Mandey said. "Especially when I wasn't sure how things were going to work out. U of H is fine. I was figuring on going there, anyway, and it's a lot less expensive. If I get the urge, I can always transfer."

The song ended, and Danny escorted Mandey back to her table. "Thanks," he told her, then turned to Shannon. "Thanks." He abruptly disappeared into the crowd.

As Mandey sat down next to Shannon, she noticed too late Mr. Tichner approaching the table. In all her excitement and relief at having Shannon back home, she hadn't given the principal a thought. Suddenly, she worried that he was going to say he did not want Shannon there and would tell them to leave. Much to her surprise, Mr. Tichner was all smiles.

"My top seniors all here together," he said. Charlie, Gayla, James, Mandey, and Trish were the top five in the class. "Four weeks from today you'll be walking across the stage in the Summit. I want to say I am proud of all of you."

After Mr. Tichnor moved on, James made an exaggerated expression of surprise at the others at the table. "Proud? Of me? He hates me," he said.

Gayla said, "I think he's been drinking."

"He's been at the punch bowl several times," Trish said. "Maybe someone managed to spike it."

"Or maybe a few swigs from his flask," Charlie said, miming it and grinning.

"He acted like he didn't even see me," Shannon said. "I hope it stays that way."

82

After the Prom

The Class of '85 senior prom ended with the entire class in a huge circle around the dance floor, arms around each other, swaying and singing the number one song in the country that week, "We Are the World." Then the lights came up, and the crowd began to disperse. Some people had booked rooms at the hotel for the night; others had made plans to go to Galveston right after the prom. Mandey wanted nothing more than to go home and get into bed with Shannon.

The limousine had only been rented to take them to the prom. Gayla had parked her car at the hotel earlier in the day so she could drive herself, Charlie, Mandey, and Shannon home. As she pulled out of the parking lot, Charlie put his arm along the back of the seat behind Gayla and began rubbing her shoulder.

"A special night like this should have a special ending, don't you think?" he asked Gayla, looking at her hopefully.

"Charlie, we came on this date as friends," Gayla reminded him. "We're ending the date as friends, too."

He sighed. "You can't blame me for trying, can you?" he asked, and turned to leer at Shannon and Mandey in the back seat. "I bet *you* two are going to do something special, aren't you? Huh?"

"Maybe, but I'm not going to tell *you* about it," Mandey said.

"Damn. I can't even get any from you vicariously," Charlie said, in semi-mock disappointment.

"You're such a pervert!" Gayla exclaimed. "Get your arm away from me!"

"That's okay," Shannon said to Charlie. "I haven't gotten any from her, either."

Mandey felt her cheeks flame. She gave Shannon a wide-eyed stricken look. Gayla was watching through the rearview mirror. Charlie guffawed.

"What? You're kidding," Charlie said, unbelieving. "You've been living together since

December! You mean since you got out of jail, right?"

"Uh-oh, Shannon, I think you just stuck your foot in your mouth," Gayla told him, looking at him in the rearview mirror.

"I'm not complaining," Shannon said to Mandey hastily.

Mandey was at a total loss for words. She couldn't believe he made a remark like that in front of people.

"If you haven't gotten any before, you're really not getting any now," Charlie said, smirking.

"I'm sorry," Shannon said earnestly. "It was a dumb joke. Please don't be mad." He took her hand in his.

She clasped it. "It's okay," she said.

"Don't believe it," Charlie said to Shannon. "That's one of those 'it's okays' that women use when it's really not okay."

"We'll talk when we get home," Mandey said.

"That means you're going to get your ass chewed when you get home," Charlie declared.

Gayla reached over and hit him on the arm. "Shut up, Charlie. When did you become an expert on women?"

Fortunately, the ride to Mandey and Shannon's house only took about fifteen minutes. Mandey and Shannon were quiet while Gayla and Charlie sparred, which, annoying as it was, was better than dead silence. When Gayla dropped them off, Mandey and Shannon walked without speaking up to the front door. Shannon took Mandey's hand in his to break the ice.

"I'm sorry," Shannon said again.

"It's okay," she assured him.

Shannon unlocked the door, and they walked into the dark house.

"And so the prince and princess return from the ball," Mandey said, turning on the hallway light.

"Are you sure you're okay?" Shannon asked her.

She gave him a small smile. "Let's get ready for bed and then we'll talk," she said. She swept down the hall to her bedroom and shut the door behind her.

As she maneuvered out of her gown, she thought about Shannon, who was probably in his room kicking himself for making that remark. She knew it was a joke, but it told her that he was getting frustrated and impatient. Maybe he had expected her to greet him with open legs the minute he got out of jail. Maybe he didn't understand why, after he was behind bars all those weeks, she didn't want to bed him right away.

The thing was, she <u>did</u> want to. If he had said he wanted to, she would have, but it seemed like he was still trying to get his bearings, and she didn't want to push him. She had thought tonight after the prom would be the perfect time for her to become a little more aggressive and let him know that she was ready for him.

When she finished undressing, she put on the little red negligee that Shannon had bought her for Christmas. She put back on her high-heeled silver shoes. She freshened up and brushed her teeth in the bathroom, then knocked on the door to Shannon's bedroom.

"I'm through in here," she said through the door. "When you're ready for bed, come in my room." She walked through the other door to her room and closed it behind her.

She applied some sexy red lipstick, lit some candles, and chose a couple albums to set the mood. She put them on the stereo turntable and turned it on. Next, she busied herself setting the clocks in her room ahead an hour from 2 A.M. to 3 A.M., for it was time to spring into Daylight Savings Time. Then she turned out the lights.

When Shannon entered the room a few minutes later in his Fruit-of-the-Looms, he found Mandey in the candlelight, reclining suggestively on her bed in her red lingerie and heels.

"Wh--?" Shannon began.

"Hello there," Mandey said. She sat up and swung her legs over the side of the bed, crossing them in what she hoped was a seductive manner.

"What is this?" Shannon asked, confused.

"This is the night we've been waiting for," Mandey said, standing and walking over to him. She took his hand and led him over to the bed.

"Wait," Shannon said, hesitating.

Mandey shook her head. "The waiting is over," she said, and kissed him. He kissed back, tongue meeting hers, his arms going around her in a tight embrace. She felt him hardening against her hip.

He broke the kiss first. "Mandey," he said.

"Shannon," she replied, going to kiss him again.

"Wait," he said, placing a hand between them to stop her. "You said we were going to talk."

Mandey looked at him curiously. "You'd rather talk?" she asked.

"Just a minute," he said, flustered. "Let's get in bed."

Mandey stepped out of her shoes and the two of them slipped between the sheets, nestling down together.

"Are you okay?" Mandey asked him.

"I'm fine, except I feel like an ass for that dumb comment I made," Shannon said.

"I didn't expect to hear you say something like that in front of anybody," Mandey said.

"I know, and I'm sorry if I hurt your feelings or embarrassed you," he said.

"I don't mind people knowing that we haven't done it, but..." she trailed off.

"But what?"

Mandey struggled with herself before telling him. "I felt like you said that to get at me, because it bothers you that we haven't."

Shannon thought about this for a moment. "Is that what this is about?" he asked. "You're offering to have sex with me because I made that comment?"

"No," Mandey said emphatically. "I made up my mind about this a few days ago, after you came home. I wanted to do like Charlie said, to end up prom night in a special way."

Shannon heaved a sigh. "And I ruined it," he said. "Good job, Shannon."

"No, you didn't," Mandey said.

"Yes, I did," he said heavily. "Look at this—the candles, the music, you looking all sexy and gorgeous—and with one stupid joke I messed it all up."

"But Shannon, I still want to make love to you," Mandey protested.

"And I want to make love to you, too," Shannon said. "I must be crazy to say no, but…no."

Tears welled up in Mandey's eyes and spilled down her cheeks.

"Don't cry," he said, holding her closer. She buried her head in his chest and let her warm tears spill onto his bare skin. He hugged her and kissed the top of her head.

"Mandey, like I said, I messed it up. If we do it now, it will be with that dumb joke I made hanging over it, even if it didn't mean anything."

She gently pulled away from him, wiped her eyes, and looked at him again. "You're right," she said. "It wouldn't feel quite right tonight." She chuckled at the rhyme she made.

Shannon hugged her again. "Oh, why do you love a stupid idiot like me?" he asked.

"You're not stupid," Mandey said. "Your mouth was just working against you."

"Yeah," he agreed. "It's a good thing I'm usually the quiet type or I'd be in a shitload of trouble."

Mandey giggled.

He rubbed her back. "You really were ready tonight?" he asked hesitantly.

"Uh-huh," she replied.

"I thought you wanted to wait until you were eighteen."

"It's only two weeks away. Close enough."

"I think we should wait 'til then," Shannon said.

"Why?"

"Like you said, it's only two weeks away," Shannon said. "You'll have your wish of being eighteen."

"That doesn't matter," she said. "I'm ready and I want you, Shannon."

"And I want you, too," he told her, "but I've been thinking about this for a long time, and I want to make your first time special."

"Just being with you will make it special," Mandey said.

Shannon rolled his eyes.

"Well, it will," Mandey insisted.

"Yeah, yeah," he said. "Ever since that night after the Christmas dance, when we first talked about how you wanted it to be, I've been determined that when you and I finally do it, it's going to be something we'll never forget."

"What are you saying? You've been making plans?" Mandey asked, smiling.

"Yeah," he said. "They got put on hold while I was in jail, but I'm back to planning now."

"And what are you planning?" Mandey asked.

"I can't tell you yet," he said. "But I'll tell you this much—you'll find out in two weeks."

Mandey smile grew bigger. "I can hardly wait," she said, happily.

"Well, I hope it will turn out the way I want it to. I'll hold my tongue when I think I have something cute to say so I won't screw it up."

"And I'll try not to be so thin-skinned when I know you're making a joke," Mandey said. "Two weeks, huh?"

"Two weeks," Shannon agreed. "I'll tell you more about it as it gets closer so you'll know what to pack."

"We're going somewhere?" Mandey asked, delighted.

"That's hint number one," Shannon said, grinning.

"I won't press you for details, because I like surprises," Mandey said. "Good ones, anyway."

She kissed him enthusiastically. He responded in kind. The silly remark was forgotten as she held him in her arms, so thankful to have him back, so happy to have him in her bed, no matter what they were doing or not doing.

"You know what?" she asked him between kisses.

"What?"

"You didn't mess anything up. Tonight turned out perfect after all."

"I'm glad you think so," Shannon said. "Although…"

"Although what?"

Shannon paused, then sighed. He said awkwardly, "Well, you are rubbing your body up against me in that sexy nightie…" He bit his lip.

Mandey raised her eyebrows. "I see," she said with a knowing smile.

Her hand slid down to his bulging briefs. He sighed again, this time in pleasure, as her hand made its way inside to touch him. While she caressed him down there, his hands roamed over her body, inside and outside her negligee. Without protest she allowed him to pull the nightie from her body and slide the panties off.

"Two weeks," she reminded him.

"I know," he said with his eyes shut. "Two weeks."

His hand coaxed her legs apart slightly, and his fingers touched her swollen clit, making the blood pound harder down there. He pressed her gently, making Mandey gasp in pleasure.

"Do you want me to try to—you know?" he asked.

Mandey shook her head, although a very big part of her wanted to say yes. She stopped fondling him and reached down to pull his hand away from her. "That's a very tempting offer, but no," she said, with a rueful smile. "In two weeks you can, though."

"Okay," he said.

"The Vaseline is still in the nightstand drawer," Mandey told him.

"You don't have to do this if you don't want to," Shannon told her.

"I want to," she told him. "Get the Vaseline."

He turned and reached over to get it, then he tossed the covers back, exposing their bodies to the candlelight. Together they eased Shannon's briefs off, releasing his stiff, swollen organ. He rubbed a glob of Vaseline on himself, then led Mandey's hand to it again. In her grasp it became rock-hard as she began to stroke it.

It didn't take long. Shannon squeezed his eyes shut and started moaning loudly.

"Oh Mandey, oh baby," he gasped, and then let out a series of loud, inarticulate bellows. Once the spasm subsided, Shannon lay there, weak and spent, breathing heavily.

"That was pretty intense," Mandey remarked.

"That was the first time—since before I was arrested," Shannon said. "Thank you."

"You're welcome," Mandey said, kissing his forehead.

"Do you want me to get up and get you a towel?" he asked her.

"No," she said. "Actually, I have to wash my face and take out my contacts." She got up and quickly ran into the bathroom, feeling a little self-conscious because she was naked. She wondered if Shannon was looking at her, then realized that was stupid—of course he was looking.

As she got ready for sleep, she was extremely horny, but happy. She shuddered with pleasure as she thought about the way Shannon had touched her. It would have been easy to say yes, but she wanted to have her first orgasm with him on that night when they would give themselves to each other with no holding back. She put on a raspberry-colored nightshirt that was hanging on the bathroom door. On her way back to bed, she blew out all the candles, turned off the stereo, and picked up the sheer red panties from the floor and slipped them on before she crawled into bed with Shannon.

"Ooh, I love those panties," Shannon said, running his hand over the backside of them as she got into bed. "I can't wait to get in them."

"Two more weeks," she said.

"I know," he said.

"Don't blame me. You're the one who said we should wait."

"It'll be worth the wait for both of us, trust me," he said, as they settled down with him spooning her. He made thrusting movements against her bottom. "In two weeks, I'm going to do all sorts of things to your body."

Mandey laughed and brought his hand up to her mouth to kiss it. "I love you, Shannon. Thank you for making my prom night wonderful."

"I love you," he replied, and kissed her neck. "Thank you for making my life wonderful."

83

Two Weeks

The two weeks between the prom and Mandey's birthday flew by. The Monday night after prom, Mandey, Shannon, Andrea, and Martin went out for dinner at Dalt's and then drove down to the Summit to see Daryl Hall and John Oates with 'Til Tuesday opening. Mandey bought a program and a T-shirt before they took their seats. The lights went down and 'Til Tuesday came onstage, and suddenly the air was filled with the distinct aroma of burning joints. A little after nine Daryl and John and the band took the stage. Mandey was thrilled. She knew every song by heart and sang along to each one. She was so happy to have Shannon there to share the experience with her.

She was still dancing and singing as they made their way back to the car with their ears ringing.

"That was a lot louder show than I thought it was going to be," Shannon said.

"If it's too loud, you're too old!" Mart exclaimed.

"They're actually known for being pretty loud in concert," Mandey said.

"Nah, it wasn't too loud. I just wasn't expecting it," Shannon said. He had only been to one other concert at the Summit. He and Phil had gone to see AC/DC's "For Those About to Rock" tour. That was loud, too, but he had been expecting it. Except when the cannon was supposed to fire during the title song but didn't.

There was also senior night at Astroworld, which they went to with Andie and Mart, as well. They rode rides during the day, including Excalibur, Warp 10, Thunder River, the Alpine Sleigh Ride, Greezed Lightnin', and the Texas Cyclone. The concert at Southern Star Amphitheater that night was Huey Lewis and the News. Despite Shannon's opinion that they sucked and Mandey's disappointment that they didn't have an edgier, new-wavier act, they ended up enjoying the show. Afterward, they went to the House of Pies for pie and breakfast at one A.M.

At school, the spring choir concert was the evening of Tuesday the 7th. Shannon and

Marcia both attended, and this time, Shannon did not try to hide. He surprised Mandey when he came into the choir room after the concert when everyone was getting ready to leave. She watched tensely as he walked up to Jesse. Jesse was eyeing him warily, but didn't appear hostile.

"I want to apologize again for all the shit that went down between the Devils and the Alley Cats," Shannon said to him. "Maybe you can't let it go, and if you can't, I don't blame you. I still wanted to say I'm sorry."

"That doesn't bring my car back," said Zack, coming over to stand next to Jesse.

"I know," Shannon said, heavily. "I'd give it back, if I could."

"I guess you were getting blackmailed into doing it," Zack said, grudgingly.

"Yeah, I was," Shannon said, "but that's no excuse for the rest of the crap I was doing. I was letting fear rule my life, and it led me into some dark places. But I'm done with that now. I've gotta stand up and be a man. I ain't going to ask y'all to forgive me. I just had to tell you that I'm sorry." He glanced beyond Jesse and Zack where Angelina was looking at him. "You, too, Angelina. I'm sorry."

With that, Shannon turned and went over to Mandey. She smiled at him and took his arm. There was no yelling, no jeering, no sarcastic comments following them as they walked out the door. They took that as a win.

84

Number 18

Mandey skipped school (with Marcia's blessing) on the Friday before her birthday. She had things to do—renewing her driver's license, getting her hair cut, packing her overnight bag. She also did a little shopping for herself with the birthday money her parents had sent to her. Now she was taking a leisurely bath and primping for the evening to come. Shannon had told her the night before that he had made a hotel reservation for them in Galveston.

She laid back in the tub and closed her eyes. *Tonight's the night*, Rod Stewart sang in her head. Six long months in the making, and came damned close to never happening at all. She had thought she might be nervous about losing her virginity. Once upon a time, maybe, but not now. She had been ready at Christmas but had resisted. By the time Valentine's Day was approaching, she was convinced the time had come, but then circumstances had put the kibosh on that. Now her birthday was here (or almost, at midnight it would be), and there was no reason to wait anymore. In a way, she wished she had never told Shannon about wanting to wait until she was eighteen, because waiting had quit being a big deal to her, but what she had said had stuck with Shannon. He could have had her already, but it was important to him to make her wish come true. To her, that was amazing.

She carefully did her makeup (new that she had bought that day) and her hair, then put on a short-sleeved, short-waisted white blouse and a short black skirt with a large hibiscus print on it (also new). She surveyed herself in the mirror and was pleased with what she saw. Now to wait for Shannon.

Shannon got home from work a bit early. He found Mandey sitting on the couch, watching "Jeopardy!" Her purse, overnight bag, and portable radio/cassette player were by her feet. Shannon noticed the neon-pink-painted nails of her toes and felt a little thrill go through him. Even after all these months, sometimes it still seemed unreal that this was his girl. Now tonight, on the eve of her 18th birthday, he was going to make love to her for the very first time. He felt the hairs on the back of his neck stand on end as he shivered again.

"You can't be cold, sweetie. It's ninety degrees out," Mandey said, teasingly.

He grinned at her, then bent over to give her a kiss. "You're so beautiful, I get thrills and chills just looking at you," he told her.

"Really?" Mandey asked, smiling. "Flattery will get you everywhere."

"That's what I'm hoping," Shannon replied. "It looks like you're all set. Let me take a shower and change, and I'll be ready."

As he went to his bedroom and to shower, Mandey got up and put his lunchbox away for the weekend. Her mind went back over their time together, and then before that, back to when she was a fourteen-year-old with a huge crush on the boy up the street. Had she known then that this day was coming, how happy she would have been. Tonight, she was going to make love with him. Even though they had already shared a good degree of intimacy, the idea of finally going all the way still gave her butterflies. She could hardly wait until they were alone together, and he saw her in the new sexy teddy she had bought during her shopping trip.

In the shower Shannon was preoccupied with what was going to be happening in the next few hours. However, instead of excitedly imagining what he and Mandey were going to do, his mind stubbornly replayed memories of his failed attempts to have sex with Kerri.

Why the hell am I thinking of that now? he thought. *I thought I got past this a long time ago.*

It took some effort to put those images out of his mind. They were replaced by visions of the hookers he had slept with, none of whom many anything to him, and to whom he meant nothing but twenty bucks. He felt sick to his stomach.

Shannon and Mandey had come close to making love several times, and he had never had a problem getting it up and keeping it up with her. Despite it all, Shannon had a few nagging doubts. They had waited for tonight for six months. Mandey was going to give up her virginity to him, and he had to do everything in his power to make sure that this night, the night of her First Time (he had come to think of it with capital letters), was nothing short of perfect.

Then there was the issue of the engagement ring. He knew Mandey would love the ring, but would she accept his proposal? Shannon knew they couldn't get married right away; he was in no position right now to make her his wife, but he would be someday. If she didn't accept the ring, the whole weekend would be ruined. He thought about waiting until the end of the weekend to propose, but that would be tacky, as though he had waited to see how good she was in bed before asking her to marry him.

He was still feeling slightly queasy when he got out of the shower and dressed in a pair of white shorts and an aquamarine blue Op shirt. He studied his reflection in the bathroom mirror as he blow-dried his hair.

Is that really the same guy Mandey picked up on the beach back in November? he asked himself.

His life had changed a lot since then. He had changed a lot.

A short while later he appeared in the living room with his own overnight bag in tow, along with a small cooler.

"Ready?" she asked him, picking up her purse and bag.

"Yep. Here, let me take that," he said, taking the bag. She picked up the radio, and they headed out the door.

They took Mandey's van for the trip, but she was content to let Shannon drive. Before heading for Galveston, he was taking her to dinner at Red Lobster. As they made their way through the Friday rush hour traffic, Mandey watched Shannon, admiring his profile, much the way she did when she sat across from him on the school bus, although from the left back then, rather than the right.

Shannon noticed Mandey watching him. "What?" he asked.

"What?" she repeated, grinning.

"What are you looking at me like that for?"

She smiled wider. "I'm admiring my sexy, good-looking hunk of a boyfriend. Is that okay?"

He rolled his eyes at her and grinned. "Whatever you say."

"This is very romantic, going back to Galveston where we first got together."

"That's me, Mr. Romantic," Shannon said. "I'm glad I'll be sleeping in a bed this time instead of my car. You know, when I was getting dressed a while ago, I started realizing how much things have changed since that day. It's kind of stupid, what made me think about it. It was while I was blow-drying my hair."

Mandey giggled.

"I know that sounds dumb, but six months ago the thought of using one of those things wouldn't have crossed my mind. It got me thinking about all the changes in my life since you came along."

"Is that a good thing or a bad thing?" Mandey asked.

"Good," Shannon said, glancing over at her. "Do you even have to ask?"

"I don't want you to feel like I forced you to change. I remember how bad I felt when I realized that James would never love me the way I am. I hope I never made you feel like my love for you was contingent upon you changing."

He reached over to take her hand in his.

"Mandey, you never made me feel that way. You've stuck with me through so much shit, I know you really love me," he said. "But you have changed me, and that's good. If it wasn't for you, I'd be in prison right now for sure, or I might even be dead. I owe you so much."

"I don't want you to feel like you owe me, Shannon," Mandey said. "I don't want your gratitude."

They arrived at the restaurant parking lot. "Honey," Shannon said, pulling into a parking space and shutting off the ignition, then turning to face her, "my feelings for you aren't about gratitude, but I do owe you a lot. I owe it to you to be the best person I can be and to never let you down. You mean so much to me, Mandey. You believed in me, and you made me start believing in myself. You loved me when I didn't think I was worth loving. I won't ever get over that."

Tears sprang to Mandey's eyes. Shannon saw them, and he hugged her.

"Oh, Shannon," Mandey said, a catch in her voice. She hugged him tightly. "I love you."

"I love you, too," Shannon replied. "Come on. Let's eat."

"Yes," Mandey agreed, as they let go of each other. "You've got to keep up your strength for tonight." She gave him a wicked smile, and they got out of the van.

The meal was enjoyable; Shannon had steak and fried shrimp, Mandey opted for grilled chicken and shrimp scampi, and they shared a piece of complementary celebratory cheesecake for dessert. Then they got back in the van for the drive to Galveston, riding with the windows cranked down and the radio cranked up.

They checked into their hotel and took the elevator to their room for the night. As they entered, Shannon felt the anxiety sweep over him again.

"This is lovely!" Mandey exclaimed, setting her belongings down on a sea-green chair in one corner. The décor was in soft greens, pinks, and corals—understatedly marine in theme. Mandey opened the sea-green drapes to a twilight view of the Gulf of Mexico. Shannon ducked into the bathroom to use the toilet, then came back into the room to see Mandey still gazing out the window.

"You like it?" he asked. It wasn't the Hotel Galvez, but Shannon had made sure it was a nice place. He wasn't about to make love to her for the first time in some dump.

"I love it," Mandey said, turning around. Shannon was right behind her, and she slipped her arms around him. "I love you," she said, and she quickly kissed his lips. "I'll be right back."

Shannon lay down on the king-sized bed, which was covered with a coral and green bedspread. He now had a minute or two to think about what to do next. He had been with Mandey for six months and he felt closer to her than he thought was possible to feel to someone. It didn't make sense to be nervous, yet his mind raced over avoidance strategies. He could suggest that they go for a walk on the beach or down to the pool for a swim or anything so that he wouldn't have to risk embarrassing himself.

As she entered the bathroom, Mandey thought about grabbing her overnight bag, but decided against it. She didn't want to change into her teddy yet. The hesitation wasn't from nerves; she just didn't want to rush it. Sure, this was the night that the waiting was over, but it didn't mean they had to jump in bed that moment. She used the toilet and fixed her hair, which had gotten wrecked by the ride with the van windows down, then went back into the room to join Shannon. He was lying on the bed, staring at the ceiling. Mandey got the impression that he might be a little nervous.

"Mmmmmm, comfy bed," she remarked, lying down next to him.

He turned to look at her. "Oh, yeah. Much better than when I was sleeping in the back of my car," he said.

"Hope you're going to want to do more than sleep," Mandey said, grinning saucily.

He grinned back as he moved closer and kissed her. She wrapped her arms around him, kissed him back, and felt his body relax slightly. It surprised her a little; she hadn't expected him to be nervous. She guessed maybe the reality of the situation was setting in. When they stopped kissing, she sighed and laid her head against his shoulder.

"How are you feeling?" he asked her, bringing her hand to his mouth and kissing it

Mandey smiled. "Happy. Deliriously happy."

The look of joy on her face bolstered Shannon's confidence and convinced him to take the next step. "Maybe I can make you a little more delirious," he said, getting up off the bed. He went to his overnight bag and pulled out a beautiful small blue foil-wrapped box with a silver bow.

"A present?" Mandey asked, pleased and a little surprised. "You took me out to dinner, checked us into a nice hotel, you're going to make love to me, and you still have another present for me?"

Shannon grinned. "Of course," he replied. "My beautiful birthday girl has to have at least one present that's wrapped up in a box." He held it out to her. "I have to warn you, though. I sort of bought the gift for myself, too."

"What's that supposed to mean?" Mandey asked, sitting up and taking the gift.

"Open it and find out."

Gingerly she did, trying not to tear the paper too much. The white box said "Zales" on the lid. She opened it and found a small jewelry box. Inside it was a dainty white gold ring with a small oval diamond and a tiny emerald on either side.

Shannon took it from her and slipped it onto her left ring finger, his hands trembling very slightly. "You once told me that you wanted to be married or at least engaged before you made love, but then you got to the point where you just wanted to be eighteen," he said, looking deep into her green eyes. "I wanted to make your first wish come true. I don't want to marry you until I can take care of you the right way, but I want you to know that I do intend on marrying you." He got down on his knees in front of her. "Amanda, will you marry me?"

"Oh, Shannon!" she gasped, tears coming to her eyes. She threw her arms around him. "Yes, I will!"

Shannon embraced her and squeezed his eyes shut to keep a couple of his own tears from escaping. "I'm going to spend my life trying my best to show you how much I love you," he told her.

Mandey pulled back to look at him. "And I'll do the same for you," she said, looking into his teary hazel eyes.

Shannon pressed his lips to hers and while kissing her he made his way up onto the bed next to her. They laid down together and kissed and caressed each other for several minutes, gently at first, but gradually more passionately. Mandey finally managed to pull away, and she sat up and admired her ring.

"The ring is perfect, Shannon. I love it," she said, holding it up to the light.

"I wish it could have been bigger," he said. "I had visions of giving you this huge heart-shaped diamond."

"No, it's perfect the way it is," Mandey told him, still staring at the ring. "I love it."

She kissed him quickly, then said, "I'll be right back." She got up off the bed, grabbed her overnight bag, and went into the bathroom.

She had accepted his proposal! She was going to be his, forever! A great weight had been lifted from his shoulders, but he still felt a little jittery, so he busied himself by plugging in the radio/cassette player and putting in the tape they had made for this occasion. Shannon had recorded all the songs he wanted Mandey to hear on one side, and Mandey put hers for him on the other. Although he was curious to hear what she was dedicating to him, he decided he wanted her to hear his side first.

Once that was done, he worried about what he was wearing. When Mandey came out, how should he be dressed? Underwear, he decided, and closed the drapes and stripped down to his briefs. Even though the room was on the third floor with strictly an ocean view, he didn't want to make love with the curtains open.

He was still nervous. Horny as hell, but nervous. He went over to the small cooler they had brought with them. He took out a can of Coke and then got a small bottle of rum out of his overnight bag. He took the wrappers off two of the plastic cups sitting on the table by the ice bucket, scooped a little ice into them from the bag in the cooler, and proceeded to make Mandey and himself each a rum and Coke. He started to set the bottle down, then put it up to his lips and took a healthy swig, just for good measure.

When Mandey went into the bathroom, she shut the door behind her and stood with her back against it for a moment, propping herself up. She extended her left arm, spread the fingers of her hand, and admired the shiny thing on her ring finger. Even in the lackluster hotel bathroom light, it sparkled. She did a little dance of excitement, then freshened up and changed into her new lingerie. She touched up her makeup and hair and took a long look at herself in the mirror.

Eat your heart out, boys, she thought. *You missed the boat, and it ain't coming back.*

She opened the bathroom door and stepped back out into the bedroom, wearing her brand new sheer white stretch lace teddy with a silky fabric flounce at the hip. It was low-cut and high-cut in all the right places. Shannon was standing between the bed and the television, a plastic cup to his lips. He slowly set it down as his eyes took her in. He could feel himself getting hard just looking at her. She smiled, and suddenly his jitters were gone.

"Like it?" Mandey asked, twirling slowly around a couple times so he could get a view from all angles.

Shannon picked up the plastic cup that was on the bureau holding the television. "A lot," he replied, offering her the drink.

"What's this?" she asked, taking it from him.

"Rum and Coke, your favorite," he replied. He raised his cup. "Here's to my beautiful fiancée on her eighteenth birthday."

Mandey raised her cup. "And to my handsome fiancé for making it the best birthday ever."

They tapped the plastic cups together and took a drink. Shannon went over to the cassette player and turned on the tape.

"One of my favorite songs," Mandey said, delighted, when she heard the opening guitar riff of the Raspberries' "Go All the Way." "A very appropriate one, too."

She danced for him in her sexy little outfit, sipping her rum and Coke and singing along. Then she put her half finished drink on her nightstand and sidled up to him. She put her arms around him and continued dancing, grinding herself up against him. Shannon felt himself getting harder by the second. It wasn't going to stay down until he had her more than once.

"Baby, please go all the way," Mandey sang, smiling up at him.

Shannon quickly downed his drink and scooped her into his arms, making Mandey squeal. He carried her over to the bed, kissing her neck.

"I've never wanted anyone the way I want you," he told her, setting her gently down and lying down beside her.

"I want you so much," she whispered in his ear. "I want you to have all of me."

Shannon pulled at the negligee and bared Mandey's ripe breasts. He caressed them, relishing the feeling of the stiff nipples, then brought his mouth down to gently suck one, then the other. Mandey uttered a little moan of pleasure. Quickly, he removed the teddy from her body and tossed it to the floor. He ran his hands over her, from her neck to her thighs. Mandey's hands went to his shorts, and he let her strip them from him. The briefs joined the teddy on the floor. For several minutes they went on, kissing, touching, and exploring each other freely and extensively, more than they ever had before.

Mandey held his throbbing organ in her hand while she spread her legs wide to invite him in. Shannon had full access to her most private spot for the first time, and he put his fingers down there to feel her hot wetness. His probing fingers made Mandey wince with pleasure. He extracted himself from her gentle grasp and lay down between her legs. He had never tried it before. He had not wanted to put his mouth somewhere that hundreds of men had been. This was different; Mandey was his, she was virginal, and no part of her was off limits to him.

She gasped, surprised, but then settled back to enjoy what he was doing. She ran her fingers through his hair. "That's so good," she said softly.

He was happy to know he was pleasing her, but his own need was growing too strong to ignore. A few moments later, he stopped and kissed his way up her body. She reached to touch his cock again. It was veiny and rock-hard. He loved her touch, but he had long yearned to feel her soft, wet mouth around it. He was not sure she would be willing to do that her very first time, but he asked her, anyway.

She smiled. It was something she had been wanting to try.

They switched places, with him lying on his back with his legs spread apart so she could lay between them. She smiled at him, then turned her attention to his penis. Mandey was a little unsure of how to start. First, she stroked it with her hand, then she touched the tip of it with her tongue. She explored more and more of it until she was taking most of it into her mouth.

"Less teeth, please," Shannon said once.

"Oops. Sorry," Mandy said.

Don't wanna do that, she thought, laughing to herself.

She tried to deep-throat it and succeeded in making herself gag a little, so she eased off a bit. Shannon's manhood was pretty big, so she thought she was doing well for a first-timer.

He lay there with his eyes closed, loving the feeling of what she was doing. He ran his fingers through her hair and sighed with pleasure. After a few minutes, he shifted position, a signal for her to stop. His need was growing stronger, and he wanted to be inside her.

She stopped what she was doing and he sat up. He put his arms around her, kissed her hard, and eased her onto her back. She spread her legs and he knelt between them. He leaned over and got the Vaseline off the nightstand and slathered a glob of it onto his cock. Then he kissed her again and began to guide himself inside of her. Involuntarily, Mandey felt herself grow tense. Shannon sensed it and stopped.

"I'll be as gentle as I can," he told her.

"I know," Mandey replied. She smiled, hoping it masked her nervousness. She hadn't thought she would feel that way. She didn't want to feel that way.

Shannon pushed his way into her carefully, then paused when he reached full penetration. He stopped before pulling back because he needed to keep control of himself.

He wanted this to last for a while.

It was done; they were one. Mandey was looking up at Shannon, her eyes wide.

"Does it hurt?" he asked her.

"No," she said, and that was the truth. "I guess this means I'm not a virgin anymore."

"Are you sure you're okay?"

She smiled. "Yeah...it's just a little weird."

He smiled back and kissed her. "Once you get used to it, it won't seem weird," he told her, and moved outward and inward again. Her hot wetness was heaven. "You don't know how good you feel." He closed his eyes and continued his slow, deliberate thrusting movements.

The initial shock of losing her virginity was fading, and she felt pleased with herself because Shannon was obviously enjoying it. She ran her hands over his shoulders, arms, back and down his sides. He opened his eyes to look down at her. She smiled up at him, but he didn't smile back. He couldn't—he was getting too close to coming. His expression was intense as he started thrusting harder and quicker. He thought he heard her wince and wondered if he was hurting her, but he couldn't stop now. She put her arms around him and bit him on the shoulder, where she knew he liked it, and wrapped her legs around him.

"Oh, God, Mandey, I'm coming! Ahh, I'm coming!" he cried.

With a final series of hard, deep thrusts, Shannon came with a loud, long moan, spewing his semen deep inside Mandey, then lay on top of her, still inside her, breathing hard, his heart beating rapidly. He'd never had sex that good, ever.

She held him in her arms and stroked his hair. She could still feel his penis throbbing slightly inside her.

"I love you, Shannon," she whispered, and kissed his ear.

"Unnh," he grunted in reply. Mandey giggled.

"Feel good?" she asked.

"Unnh."

He slowly rolled off her, then took her in his arms and kissed her. "I love you, too. Mmmm, you were good," he murmured.

"I was?" Mandey asked, pleased.

"Very," he said. "How was I?"

"Well, I have no frame of reference here, but very good, as far as I could tell."

"But it hurt, didn't it?"

"Not really. A little uncomfortable," she admitted, "but I expected that."

"I'm sorry." He kissed her cheek.

"Don't be. I still liked it. The experience part of it."

Shannon smiled into her hair. "Don't worry. You're going to get a lot of experience."

"Oh, Shannon," Mandey sighed, laying her head against his chest. "You make me feel wonderful."

Shannon laughed. "Ha! I know I didn't make you feel even half as wonderful as you made me feel."

She kissed his chest and smiled up at him. "Weren't we silly that we ever felt nervous about this?" she asked.

"Yes," Shannon said, kissing the top of her head.

They laid there together for a while, holding each other close. Mandey listened to Shannon's heart beating. She knew the act of making love would make them closer, but she hadn't known the depth of the impact on her. They had shared the most intimate of experiences. Nothing could break this bond. She was his now, forever.

Eventually, Mandey loosened herself from his embrace. "I need to tinkle," she said, getting up.

"You're bleeding!" Shannon exclaimed, putting his hand to his mouth.

"Oh?" Mandey said, looking down at the spot she had left on the sheet. "It's okay." She paused. "Are you okay?"

"Uh, yeah," Shannon said, and shook his head as though coming out of a trance.

"You're the first virgin I've ever been with. I know about what happens, but I guess it startled me, anyway."

"Let me go clean up and I'll be back."

Shannon stretched. He felt great, but not totally sated. He reached under the covers to feel his member. His erection had not totally collapsed. He had been right knowing it was going to take a while before he was satisfied.

In the bathroom, she sat on the toilet and wiped away the semen and a little blood. She finished her business and washed her hands. Again, she checked herself in the mirror. She grinned at her reflection.

Mandey returned, her confidence apparent as she walked through the room, naked and unashamed. A smile played around her lips. She felt proud of herself and her newly gained womanhood. When she reached the bed, she picked up her drink from the nightstand and quickly drank down the rest of it. She laid back down on the bed and Shannon rolled on top of her. She saw that his cock was hard again. Or maybe still hard. At any rate, it was obvious he wasn't done yet.

"Mandey, I'm so horny for you," he whispered in her ear, and kissed her neck.

She promptly opened her legs to him. "Well, we've been waiting for this for six months."

He slid into her, holding her tightly, stroking deep and hard. As he did, he repeated her name with every thrust, getting louder as he got closer to exploding.

"Oh, God, Amanda! Amanda!" he cried, rearing up on his knees and lifting her legs up over his shoulders, pounding her as he came for the second time. He shuddered with ecstasy, then let her legs drop, and he collapsed on top of Mandey, exhausted.

"You do know that once you're through with me, I won't be able to walk for three days, right?" Mandey said jokingly, and kissed his ear.

Shannon was breathing hard. "Sorry," he managed to say.

"Don't be sorry," she replied, laughing, putting her arms around him.

Shannon was not able to recover so quickly this time. He lay on top of her for a few minutes, loving the feeling of her fingers running through his hair and over his back. Then he rolled off and lay close to her.

Mandey suddenly started giggling again.

"What?" he asked her.

She didn't answer, but kept giggling. The song playing that he had added to his side of the mixtape was both appropriate and totally unexpected. He caught on to what was amusing her.

"'Like a virgin—hey!'" Shannon sang to her. The little squeal he did for emphasis on "hey!" made Mandey laugh even harder.

"Oh my God, Shannon," she said, trying to catch her breath. "You're crazy."

"About you," he said, kissing her temple. "You have made me so happy."

"I'm glad," Mandey said. "We've waited a long time for this."

"It's not just that," Shannon said. "I'm glad you accepted my proposal. I want to be with you forever."

"I had no idea you were going to ask me to marry you tonight," Mandey said, smiling radiantly. "You made me very happy, too."

"I haven't given you a whole lot of satisfaction so far," he said. "I want you to enjoy this, too."

Mandey kissed his lips. "We are going to have our entire lives to figure out how to turn each other on."

Shannon paused. "You know a lot about how to get me excited, but I don't know as much about what you like."

Mandey smiled and blushed. "Well…"

She tentatively took his hand and moved it between her legs. He slid his fingers into her hot, wet slit and found her clit. Then he slid down farther and found her hotter and wetter vagina. She couldn't wait for him to set her off like a rocket.

He had touched her there briefly several times before that night, but she had not wanted him to get her off. Tonight was different. All his previous sexual encounters had been solely for him to get his rocks off. Now he had to learn how to please someone else.

He pressed two of his fingers against her clit, then began to stroke it, slowly and rhythmically, then sliding down into her hot, wet opening and back to her clit again. As he gradually moved faster, she began to moan in pleasure. Soon her moans got louder and her hips were pumping.

"Oh, Shannon," she gasped. "Oh, please, just like that…"

He obliged, and she began to writhe in the throes of orgasm, moaning and crying his name loudly.

"Oh my God, Shannon," she said breathlessly when he stopped and moved to slide his stiff organ into her one more time.

She wrapped her arms around him as he pounded her almost as hard as he had before. Mandey's legs wrapped around his hips, and she strained to push herself against him. With each stroke, Mandey contracted her muscles down there, squeezing him. That quickly sent him over the top. He bellowed her name and thrust into her like a raging bull as he came for the third time in less than an hour.

He collapsed next to her with his face in his pillow. In a muffled voice he said, "Damn, I don't think I can walk now."

Mandey burst out laughing.

The tape clicked off, signaling the end of Shannon's side of the mix.

"Rest," he said, sitting up. He lit a cigarette and laid back down.

In the air conditioning of the room, they cooled off quickly and got under the covers. Together they lay there, close, basking in the afterglow.

Mandey kissed his shoulder. "You made me come," she whispered. "You were wonderful."

Shannon kissed the top of her head. "You were the wonderful one."

"Was it worth waiting six months for?"

"Oh, yeah," Shannon said. "I wouldn't have wanted it to be any other way. What about you?"

Mandey propped herself up on her elbow and gave Shannon a soft kiss on the mouth. "You made my first time perfect."

Mandey awoke the next morning to see Shannon smiling at her. "Happy birthday," he said.

They kissed good morning, and Shannon brought her hand down to feel his morning wood. She grasped it firmly in her hand. His hand made its way between her legs. He wanted to give her another orgasm the way he had the night before. He would eventually learn how to do it the other way, but in the meantime, this would do just fine. He had to make her feel good on this morning of her official birthday. She was receptive, spreading her legs to let him touch her, and it wasn't long before she was moaning as convulsions of pleasure overtook her. She was still holding onto him, and he grew even harder in her hand when she cried out his name. Then he rolled on top of her and they made love, less urgently than the night before. He lasted longer than he had any of the times the previous night before he came inside her, breathlessly calling her name.

Afterward, it was time to get up and begin the day. They showered together for the first time and then got dressed. Mandey opened the drapes to a brilliant, sunshiny day. To say she was happy would have been an understatement. She had been made love to by the man she loved, the man she was going to marry someday. It was her 18th birthday, and she was a woman today, not just legally.

They went hand-in-hand downstairs to have breakfast in the hotel restaurant. They sat outside on the terrace, enjoying the view of the Gulf of Mexico. As they were drinking coffee, waiting for their food, an elderly couple approached them on their way out.

"You two must be newlyweds," the gentleman said, stopping at their table. "My wife and I were watching you, and she said you must have just gotten married."

Mandey blushed and opened her mouth to say no, when Shannon jumped in.

"Why, yes, yes, we are," he said, looking at Mandey.

She looked at him, surprised, but smiled and didn't contradict him.

"I knew it," the lady said. "You look so happy."

"Clara and I have been married 53 years," the man said, looking adoringly at his wife. "Best decision I ever made."

"Congratulations," Mandey said.

"No, congratulations to you two," Clara said. "You have a nice day."

"Thanks. You, too," Shannon said, as the couple walked on to leave the restaurant.

Mandey giggled. "Well, I kind of feel like a newlywed. We did what newlyweds do last night."

Shannon reached across the table to take her hand. "I can hardly wait to make you my bride."

She squeezed his hand. "Me too."

After checking out of the hotel, they went to the place where Mandey had parked her van and found Shannon sitting on the beach. Today, they spread a beach blanket out and sat in the warm sun, surrounded by a crowd of others, listening to music and making out.

"Wow, I had no idea when I was sitting here by myself, looking out at the waves, that six months later I'd be back in the same spot, making out with my fiancée," Shannon said.

"Same here. I drove down here to forget about a boyfriend, and ended up picking up my future husband," Mandey said. "What luck."

"I think it was more than that," Shannon said. "I think God meant for us to find each other."

"Maybe," Mandey said. "It was a really weird coincidence that we both showed up here that day."

"He brought you to me," Shannon said firmly. "I believe that."

"I'm glad He did," Mandey said.

They went to McDonald's for lunch, just as they had the day they met. They wandered up and down the Strand for a bit, looking more than buying, and finally headed toward home around 6. As they approached the house, Mandey noticed balloons tied to the mailbox, then saw cars parked in the driveway and along the side of the yard.

"What's this?" she asked, seeing a table set up near the house, and a crowd of people in the yard.

"Surprised?" Shannon asked, noticing how her face had lit up.

"Yes!" Mandey said, delighted. "Now I know why you wanted to go away the night before my birthday instead of on the actual day." She leaned over and gave Shannon a big smack on the cheek. "You are amazing!"

"Well, I didn't put it all together, your friends did, but I did get you out of the way so they could set it up."

"Thank you!" Mandey said, looking at the partygoers, who were now looking at the van as Shannon parked it. "Oh, this is the greatest weekend ever!"

They got out and joined the throng of people. There was a birthday cake waiting for her on the table. Marcia and Michael were both there to chaperone, and for that, Mandey was thankful. This wasn't a party on the scale on any of Jackie's house parties, but she didn't want to have to be the one to manage things if anyone got a little out-of-control. Michael and Mart were manning the grill, cooking hamburgers and hotdogs. There were two large ice-filled coolers full of cans of soda ("cokes", as they were called in Texas, no matter what kind of soda it was). Bags of chips, buns, and condiments were on the table with the cake (in a closed box to keep the bugs away). Someone else had brought a boombox to play tunes on so everyone could dance.

Georgia summoned Mandey over, and Mandey ran to her and they hugged. "Did you put this together?" she asked Georgia.

"Shannon asked me if I'd do and it and I said 'Sure! Anything for my 'sis". Marcia, Andie, and I all put it together," Georgia said. "Are you surprised?"

"Yes!" Mandey said. "So excited!"

"How was your night down in Galveston?" Georgia asked with a knowing smile.

"Absolutely amazing! Shannon proposed!" Mandey said, thrusting her hand out so Georgia could see her ring.

"He did?" Georgia gasped, genuinely surprised, taking Mandey's hand to look at the engagement ring. "Oh, pretty! I know how much you like green."

"They're my birthstones," Mandey said. "He said he wished the diamond were bigger, but I like it just the way it is."

"Oh my gosh, Mandey, what a birthday! I'm so happy for you," Georgia said, hugging her again.

"Thanks," Mandey said. "Thanks so much for throwing this party!"

It had already been the best birthday ever, and the party was the cherry on top. The crowd began to thin around midnight. It was after one when Mandey and Shannon slipped into bed together, happy and exhausted.

"Goodnight, birthday girl," Shannon said to her.

She moved closer to him and kissed him sweetly. "Thank you so much, sweetie," she said to him. "Best birthday ever, thanks to you."

85

Meet the Parents

Mandey's parents, Neil and Marjorie Rowan, arrived on the 18th for Mandey's graduation, a week before the ceremony. Marcia went to pick them up from the airport. Mandey and Shannon watched television in the living room, waiting for them to get home. Mandey was excited; she hadn't seen them since the previous July. Although he had spoken briefly to them on the phone a few times and had pleasant conversations, Shannon was nervous.

"Mandey, you didn't tell them I asked you to marry me, did you?" Shannon asked.

"Not yet. Why?"

"Did Marcia?"

"I don't know. I don't think so. It's not her news to share. Why?"

"Should I have asked them first if it was okay to ask you?" he asked, a concerned expression on his face.

He had been so eager to pop the question for Mandey's birthday, he hadn't thought about it until afterward. Asking the bride's father was the tradition, wasn't it? To be honest, the thought of asking Mandey's parents for her hand in marriage terrified him. He knew they didn't know everything about his past, but they knew more than enough to justify answering him with a great big, "NO". He didn't think that would change things between him and Mandey, but it would make him feel like crap.

"I'm old enough to make my own decisions, Shannon," Mandey told him.

"I know," he said. "but I'm afraid they're going to try to talk you out of it."

"Why?"

"Mandey," Shannon said, his tone indicating she should realize the obvious. "I am not the guy they would pick for you."

"That doesn't matter. You're the guy I picked for myself."

"Are you going to tell them we're engaged?" Shannon asked.

"I think we should both tell them," Mandey said.

"When?"

"Why not tonight?" Mandey said.

That answer did not do much to calm his nerves, but he said, "Okay." Might as well get it over with.

"It's going to be okay," Mandey reassured him, squeezing his knee. "You and I have already agreed it's going to be a long engagement. They'll be glad to know we're being practical about it."

A few minutes later Marcia drove in the driveway. Mandey and Shannon went out to greet them and to help with their luggage. Mandey's mother was 57. She was the same height as Marcia, a bit shorter than Mandey. Her short hair was dyed dark brown, a shade darker than her eyes. Her father was about the same height as Shannon. He had blue eyes and glasses and mostly gray hair that had once been brown. He was 9 years older than his wife, but his heart attack had aged him beyond his 66 years. Marjorie was brisk; Neil had always been more laid-back than his wife, but since his illness, the difference was even more pronounced.

Mandey hugged her parents, then introduced Shannon. He shook hands with her dad; her mother came in for a hug, which startled him a little, but was not unwelcome. They helped them bring their bags into the house. Marcia was giving them back the master bedroom during their 10 day visit. Marcia would take Shannon's room. Shannon also wondered what the Rowans thought about him living there and sharing a bed with their daughter. Marcia and Mandey didn't act as though they thought their parents thought it was a big deal. He wasn't so sure, but maybe they would welcome the news that they were engaged and that he had honorable intentions toward Mandey.

They sat in the living room and chatted a little bit, then had cold meat sandwiches and potato salad for lunch, after which Marjorie and Neil went to their room to rest for a while. Later, they were all going to meet Michael for dinner at Gallagher's Steakhouse. Mandey went to her room to study for her final exams, which were coming up the next week. Shannon went outside and mowed the lawn. Phillip drove by and saw Shannon in the yard. He stopped to shoot the breeze for a bit before he had to head to work. They talked about their plans for the following weekend, after the graduation ceremony, to take Mandey and Charlene and some of their friends to the beach. Shannon asked Phillip what he thought about the fact that he had gotten engaged to Mandey without her parents knowing about it.

"Might have been nice to talk to them first, but you can't undo it now," Phillip said. "Me, I've got Charlene's dad asking me when I'm gonna make an honest woman of her. I think he wants to get her off his hands." Phillip grinned. "Hell, I ain't even twenty yet. I ain't ready to settle down for good."

"What do you think? Do you think I should have waited until we're a little older to ask her?" Shannon asked.

"Naw, man, you've got to do what's right for you. The two of you are great together. She's totally devoted to you, and you've straightened up and you're ready to do right by her."

"I'm gonna," Shannon said. "That's all I want to do."

"Then do it. If her parents have any doubts, they'll go away when they see how happy she is with you."

Shannon finished the lawn, then went inside to take a shower. Mandey was studying for her Economics final. He decided not to disturb her, so after he showered he went out to the living room. Neil was sitting in the easy chair, reading. Marjorie and Marcia were at the kitchen table, chatting. Shannon went to the refrigerator and got a glass of lemonade, then went back into the living room and sat on the couch. He didn't turn on the television because he didn't want to disturb Mandey's father.

"You can turn the T.V. on, if you want," Neil said after a few minutes. "It doesn't bother me."

"Thanks," Shannon said, picking up the remote. "I don't want to disturb Mandey while she's studying."

He flipped around and found a rerun of *Welcome Back, Kotter.* He began laughing at Epstein, trying to fool Mr. Kotter with another one of his notes signed "Epstein's Mother." Then he noticed Neil had looked up from his book and was looking at the television. Suddenly, Shannon became self-conscious. It was just a dumb sitcom, but the central characters, the Sweathogs, were a gang.

"Uh, I can change the channel," Shannon said.

"No, no, I like this one," Neil said. "'Up your nose with a rubber hose'."

Shannon let out a laugh, surprised. He felt a little more at ease as he and Neil sat there together, watching the show.

Mandey came out a while later to take a break from studying. She found Shannon and her father watching a rerun of *Barney Miller.* That was nice; they were bonding. She went into the kitchen with her sister and mother.

"What time are we going to dinner?" she asked.

"Six," Marcia said. "We'll leave here around twenty-of."

Mandey sat down at the table with them and, for the most part, listened to their conversation, until it was time to get ready. Shannon and her father were still in the living room, watching sitcom reruns together. Shannon wasn't much of a talker, and neither was her father, but they were both laughing at the program and seemed to be getting along fine.

At five, Mandey went in the living room and told Shannon they were leaving at 5:40, and she was going to get ready. When Shannon came into the bedroom to get dressed for dinner, Mandey had already changed her clothes and was putting on her jewelry. She turned to face him, and he was immediately struck by what she was wearing—white pants, white blouse, and the long, dangling earrings with the stars on the ends.

She saw by the look on his face that he recognized the outfit.

"It's a new pair of white pants, but the blouse, the jewelry, and the shoes are the same. One thing I have now that I didn't have that night, though," she said, waggling her left ring finger at him.

He smiled, held up his index finger, then opened the closet. He took two hangers out of the side where his clothes were currently residing while Mandey's parents were visiting. Mandey recognized them immediately—the corduroy pants and shirt he had been wearing the night they almost met at Liaisons. He stripped out of his shorts and T-shirt and changed into them.

They stood facing each other, taking in each other's appearance, both wondering how different things might have been if they had only spoken to each other that night. It was hard to say that if that had happened that they would still be here, together, now. They had to be grateful that they had at least seen each other at Liaisons, and felt that attraction to one another, or maybe their meeting in Galveston would have turned out differently. There was no way of knowing.

They met Michael at Gallagher's Old Irish Steakhouse just after six. Shannon and Mandey went in his car, and Marcia took her parents in hers. Neil and Marjorie were already acquainted with Michael, having met him the previous summer before they moved. It was his weekend to have his children, but his mother was baby-sitting for them that evening. They met at the hostess stand, then were led to a round table near the center of the restaurant.

As they started to peruse their menus, Marcia laughed and exclaimed, "Oh, look, they have Beef O'Shannon!"

To their amusement, sure enough, there was a menu item by that name.

"Mandey, have you ever had the Beef O'Shannon?" Michael asked her with smirk.

Mandey turned red. Marcia got the joke and started laughing. Neil and Marjorie didn't seem to hear it, or if they did, they didn't get it. Mandey looked at Shannon. His nose was stuck deep in his menu. She could see his left ear was red. He put the menu down and picked up his water glass to take a sip.

"Yes, I have. It's delicious," Mandey replied with a straight face.

Shannon choked and almost spat the water out. He set the glass down, and Mandey patted him on the back. Marcia and Michael began laughing even harder.

After they ordered (no one actually ordered the Beef O'Shannon) and were waiting for their food, Marjorie remarked, "Mandey, that's a cute ring on your left hand. Is that new?"

Mandey glanced at the ring, then at Shannon, who was looking back at her.

"Yes, I got it on my birthday," Mandey said. She wasn't sure she wanted to have this conversation in the middle of a restaurant.

"Shannon, did you give it to her?" Marjorie asked.

She was looking at him like she already knew the answer. "Uh, yes, ma'am," he replied.

There was an awkward silence, then Mandey said, "Shannon asked me to marry him."

There was another lengthy pause, then Neil said, "Well, congratulations, but you had better take good care of my baby, Shannon."

"Yes, sir," Shannon said quickly.

"We aren't setting a date for a while," Mandey said. "We already agreed it's going to be a long engagement."

"I don't want to marry Mandey until I can take care of her, like you said, Mr. Rowan."

"Neil."

"Uh, Neil. Um, I guess maybe I should have talked to you about it first, but I wanted to surprise Mandey on her birthday…"

"We're going to wait at least a couple of years," Mandey said, looking at her mother. "Shannon's planning on getting a vocational degree. We want to wait until he's finished with that, at least, so don't worry that we're rushing into something prematurely. Shannon just wanted me to know his intentions."

"Let me see the ring," Marjorie said.

Mandey reached over her father so her mother could take a better look at it.

"That's a sweet little ring," Marjorie remarked. Mandey let her father have a look at the ring as she pulled her hand back.

"I love it," Mandey said.

"Shannon, like her father said, you'd better take good care of his baby," Marjorie said, looking directly at him. The expression on her face was of good humor, but underneath it was also deadly serious.

"Yes, ma'am," Shannon said, feeling a little more nervous again. "I'm going to do my very best."

"What kind of vocational degree are you going to get?" Marjorie asked him.

Mandey saw him get a deer-in-the-headlights look on his face. He, like her, was still trying to decide what area of study to pursue. There was a long pause, and for a moment Mandey thought she might have to jump in to save him.

"I've been looking at a few different options," he finally said. "Automotive technician and construction supervision are a couple I'm thinking about."

Neil nodded in approval. "Is there one you like better than the other?" asked Marjorie.

"I like both. I'm working in construction right now, so that might be what I'll choose."

The conversation moved on from there, further from the subject of their engagement, much to Shannon's relief. Salads and bread were delivered to the table, and a bit later, the entrees. Mandey ordered beef tenderloin and O'Brien potatoes. Shannon had a ribeye and a loaded baked potato. He had never eaten such a good steak in his life. Mandey was enjoying her dinner, as well. It was hard to beat a properly-cooked medium-rare steak.

Shannon leaned over and whispered in her ear, "Leave some room for a big helping of Beef O'Shannon later on."

Mandey dissolved in a fit of giggles. "I always have room for that," she whispered back.

86

Graduation

Graduation day came up quickly. Mandey, like most of her friends, had mixed emotions. She was proud of her achievement and happy to be going to university in the fall, but she was sad to be leaving an environment she had, for most of her school years, loved so much. She hadn't enjoyed either her junior or senior year as much as she had hoped she would, so in a way, that made leaving high school easier. Now she had a fiancé and was going to start college in a few weeks, taking college algebra at North Harris to get it out of the way. Time to get on with the business of creating a life and future.

The soon-to-be graduates lined up in the corridor on the floor level of the Summit. She was fourth in line, after Charlie, Gayla, and James. Gayla was twisting the pages of her salutatorian speech in her hand. Mandey thought she was on the verge of hyperventilating.

"I don't know if I can do this," Gayla said in despair, shifting back and forth on her feet. "There's so many people out there, and they're all going to be looking at me."

"You're going to do fine," Charlie told her.

"I don't know," Gayla repeated, her eyes full of worry.

James snorted in disgust. "If you can't do it, you shouldn't have accepted being salutatorian in the first place. I could have had the position. I'm not afraid of making a speech."

"Oh, knock it off, James," Mandey said. "Gayla, Charlie's right, you're going to do fine. Don't think about the audience. Focus on one person and make your speech to that person. Pretend like when you were rehearsing it with me."

"Okay," Gayla said. "It's going to be fine. I'm going to be fine."

She was still muttering it to herself as they processed out on the floor of the Summit while the band played "Pomp and Circumstance". Charlie and Gayla took their seats onstage as valedictorian and salutatorian. James had the first seat in the first row on the floor.

Mandey and the other choir seniors joined the rest of the choir to sing the alma mater and another song. Mandey scanned the audience, but the venue was huge, and she could not see where Shannon was sitting with her parents and Marcia and Michael. Once the choir was finished singing, the choir seniors took their seats with the other graduates-to-be. Mandey made her way to the front row to sit next to James.

Despite her nerves and a slightly shaky start, Gayla's speech was heartfelt, even though she and Charlie both had complained about the constraints by the school's censors. Toward the end, she was nearly in tears, but thankfully it was due to the emotional nature of her speech, not nervousness. Mandey felt herself get a little teary, too, as Gayla's words made her realize that she would never again see most of these people in her class. After she sat down and the applause died down, it was time for the graduates to file across to receive their scrolls. They were just for the ceremony; the real diplomas would be available to pick up at the school the first week in June.

Shannon and the rest of Mandey's guests were seated toward the top of the first tier of seats, slightly behind where Mandey sat in the front row of the graduate seating. Mandey was fourth to receive her diploma. After that, there were another 400-plus students to go. Shannon scanned his program. He knew some of the people through Mandey and a few others through his own time there as a student. He hoped that in a couple of weeks he would pass the general equivalency test and get his diploma, too.

Charlie's valedictory address, also censor-approved, was more cynical and much less sentimental than Gayla's speech, although he tried to lighten it up a bit toward the end. The dark outlook of his speech could not diminish the exuberance of the class, however, and soon their mortar boards were flying high. Then there was the scramble to return the rented gowns and get on with the business of celebrating.

As Mandey was leaving the rental table, James caught up with her.

"Can I have a hug?" he asked her.

Mandey felt tears come to her eyes as they embraced.

"I wish you all the best in the future," he told her, still holding her tightly.

"You, too, James," Mandey replied. "You're going to do great at Baylor."

Then he was off with his parents and brothers and sisters. Mandey went to look for her family.

After the ceremony, Mandey and her family went out for pizza at the best pizza place they knew in the area. An actual Italian family ran the restaurant, and the pizza was very close to what the Rowans were used to getting back in Connecticut. Once back at the house, there was cake and ice cream, and Mandey opened her graduation gifts, mostly cards with cash or checks in them, from her aunts and uncles, grandmother, and a few family friends.

Around four o'clock, Shannon and Mandey began packing up her van. They were going down to the beach for the weekend. It was going to be a much different weekend than the one they had spent in Galveston for Mandey's birthday. This time, they were going with a group of friends, and they wouldn't be sleeping in a hotel. Mandey and Shannon had an air mattress to blow up and put in the back of the van, so they would be fairly comfortable.

Charlie, Gayla, and Gayla's newest boyfriend, Calvin, drove up at 4:30. They loaded a tent and sleeping bags into the van. Mandey wasn't too sure about Calvin; she thought Gayla could do better but figured she shouldn't judge, because she knew plenty of people who thought the same about her and Shannon. She hoped that this wasn't going to become an uncomfortable weekend among the three of them. It surprised her that Charlie was willing to go if this new guy was going, too.

About ten minutes later Phillip drove up in his father's Ford Bronco with the camper on the back. He had managed to get Memorial Day weekend off by promising to work the Fourth of July holiday. He had Charlene, Georgia, and Jackie, who had just broken up with her boyfriend the week before, with him.

"Lookit all my wimmins," he said jokingly as Shannon went over to greet him. Charlene scowled and backhanded him in the upper arm.

Georgia stuck her head out of the driver's side passenger window. "Woo-hoo! Y'all ready to part-ay?" she asked with a huge grin.

"Hell, yeah!" Charlie replied.

"Let's do it!" Shannon said.

A few minutes later they were on their way, Shannon driving Mandey's van, following Phillip in the Bronco down to Crystal Beach. They brought Mandey's boombox along, with fresh batteries, and plenty of cassette tapes, so there would be plenty of music in the van and once they reached the beach. On the drive they rolled the windows down and tuned the radio to 97 Rock and jammed to Journey, Bad Company, Seger, AC/DC, Springsteen, Foreigner, and more. Shannon was singing and drumming along on the steering wheel. He looked happier and more carefree than Mandey had ever seen him. She sat back, the wind wrecking her hair, contented. Good friends, good music, a couple days of fun at the beach ahead to close out high school and to make up for all the crap that had gone on was just what they needed.

Crystal Beach was crowded, as it was Memorial Day weekend, but they were able to find a place to set up camp where the sand was packed enough that their vehicles wouldn't get stuck, and not too far from public restrooms, which the girls insisted on. They set up the two tents, one of which was for Charlie, Gayla, and Calvin, and the other for Jackie and Georgia. In the square area in which the corners were marked by the two tents and the two vehicles, they set up their beach blankets and beach chairs, and in the middle, they guys got a firepit going. As the sun was going down, they were listening to REO Speedwagon's *Hi Infidelity* and eating hotdogs and toasted marshmallows. The guys were drinking beer out of cans. The girls had Boone's Tickled Pink in red Solo cups, except Mandey. She didn't want to get busted for underage drinking. Phillip tried to convince her that the cops weren't going to bother them unless someone got wild and rowdy, but she stuck to Diet Dr Pepper. Everyone was talking and laughing, moon and stars were shining, there was a light breeze, and the ocean was murmuring in the background.

It was after midnight when Mandey announced she was going to bed. Shannon followed suit, although the others were still up. The two of them got into the back of the van.

"Remember, if the van's rockin', don't come knockin'," Shannon said cheerfully to the others as he shut the rear doors. Mandey giggled, and the others laughed and catcalled.

The two of them laid down on the air mattress. Mandey sighed and closed her eyes.

"Tired?" Shannon asked her.

"Yeah," she replied.

"Me, too," he said.

She sat back up and got a container of wet wipes and her contact lens case out of her bag so she could take out her contact lenses. Then she maneuvered out of her bra without taking off her blouse. Shannon took off his T-shirt and they laid down again on the mattress, pulling a sheet over them. They kissed, then settled down to go to sleep. They had just drifted off when they were jarred awake by someone pounding on the van.

"Holy shit!" Shannon exclaimed, bolting upright.

"Hey, it ain't rockin'! Why ain't it rockin', Shannon?" Phillip boomed. They heard a chorus of laughter.

"Go to bed, you asshole," Shannon called back, good-naturedly.

"Goodnight," Phillip said, laughing.

Shannon woke up early the next morning with a full bladder from last night's beer. He walked down to the water and looked around furtively before relieving himself in the Gulf of Mexico. The sun was just coming up. He stood there watching the sunrise and the waves and the seabirds, enjoying the quiet.

He sensed someone behind him. Mandey was there, her hair frowzy, looking sleepy. He slipped his arm around her and they both stood there silently, looking out over the sea. Eventually, they walked back to the van and got back in. A while later, the van was rocking as they made love. After, they dozed off until they heard some of the others outside, then they went out to greet them and cook breakfast of bacon and eggs in cast iron skillets over the fire. It reminded Mandey of when she was a child and her family would go to the park on Sunday mornings and cook breakfast there. It tasted so much better that way.

It was a fun day. Charlene and Phillip weren't arguing, and Charlie was too busy trying to ingratiate himself with Jackie and Georgia to mind when Calvin and Gayla were lying on a beach towel, making out. The girls left the guys for a while to go walking and came back with take-out barbecue sandwiches for everyone's lunch. Later, they changed into their bathing suits and they all went swimming. Towards the evening, they started the fire up again and turned up the boombox. The girls danced. The guys sat back with their beers and watched appreciatively as the girls did their thing, until the girls began urging them to join them. Lubricated with a few beers, Shannon got up first to join Mandey, to her delight. Soon, the rest of the guys followed suit.

Everyone went to bed a bit earlier than the night before. Shannon and Mandey were making out in the back of the van, on the verge of making love, when they heard Gayla shouting.

"Get out! Get out, Charlie! Just go!"

"Fine! I'm sick of you two, anyway!" Charlie shouted back.

Mandey and Shannon stopped what they were doing to listen. Mandey had been afraid there would end up being tension between them, and she was right. She got up to peek out the window. Charlie was stalking off into the darkness.

She sat back down. "Charlie's running off somewhere," she said.

"Probably just going to cool down," Shannon said.

"I hope so," she said, lying down again.

She was worried about Charlie, but she tried to relax and let Shannon's kisses do their magic. It took a few minutes, but finally she was back in the mood.

There was a knock on the back door. "Mandey, is Charlie in there with you?" Gayla asked.

"No," Mandey said loudly.

They stopped again, as they heard Gayla go over to Jackie and Georgia's tent and ask if Charlie was there. Mandey rolled down the window.

"Gayla, he went off that way," she told her, pointing in the direction he had gone.

"Come on, baby, don't worry about him," Calvin said to Gayla, his head sticking out of their tent.

"But he gets in these moods," Gayla said, worried.

"He's gonna be okay, Gayla," Jackie reassured her, coming out of her tent.

"What's going on out here?" Phillip asked, sticking his head out of the back window of the Bronco.

"Charlie took off somewhere. We don't know where he went," Jackie said.

"He probably just went to the bathroom," Phillip said.

"He was upset! He's mad at me," Gayla said, distraught. "He was saying some weird things to me the other day..."

"Doesn't he always say weird things?" Charlene asked, annoyed, joining Phillip at the Bronco's window.

"Shut up, Charlene," Gayla snapped. "I'm seriously worried about him." She whirled around in a circle. "I've got to go find him." She began walking toward the ocean.

"Gayla, come on, babe, he's gonna come back," Calvin said, going after her.

"Calvin, stay here," Gayla said, sounding annoyed.

Mandey quickly got into her shorts, T-shirt, and sandals, burst out of the back of the van and trotted toward Gayla. "Gayla, he wasn't heading toward the water. He was walking up towards the highway," she said. "Let me go with you."

Shannon followed Mandey, pulling his T-shirt on over his head. "Come on, we'll take a drive up the road and see if we see him," he said.

"Georgia and I will take a walk by the water and see if we see him, just in case," Jackie said.

"I'll go with you," Calvin said to Jackie.

Mandey and Shannon got Gayla calmed down and the three of them got into the van. Shannon pulled out onto the road. They drove slowly, looking on either side to see if Charlie was there. There were a few people out, but none were him.

"He's just been really negative and down lately. He's scared of what's next, now that we've graduated," Gayla said. "And he doesn't like Calvin much, either."

"I was wondering if it was a good idea, the three of you coming together on this trip," Mandey said.

"Charlie insisted it was fine," Gayla said. "I guess it really wasn't. Calvin and I wanted to get romantic, and we asked Charlie to leave for a few minutes, but he refused, and that's how it all started."

"Charlie's got it bad for you," Shannon said.

"We've been friends since kindergarten, but I just don't feel that way about him," Gayla said, glumly. "I care a lot about him; he's one of my best friends, but I don't think of him like a boyfriend. And now he's freaked out about going to UT in the fall and starting pre-med..."

They kept driving slowly, until the lights of the strip were behind them and they were approaching the ferry.

"No way he had time to get this far on foot, not even if he was hauling ass," Shannon said. "Let's turn around and see if he went the other way."

They got to the point where they had turned onto Highway 87, then kept going about the same distance as they had driven in the other direction. They saw nothing.

"He could be on any of the side streets," Shannon said.

"Dammit, Charlie, you asshole, where are you?" Gayla cried in frustration.

"He's around here somewhere. We'll find him," Mandey reassured her.

Shannon did a three-point turn and they headed back in the other direction again.

"It's so dark," Mandey said. "They really don't believe in streetlights around here."

Shannon slammed on the brakes. Mandey and Gayla shrieked as Mandey hit the dashboard sideways, and Gayla hit the back of Mandey's seat.

"Are you okay?" Shannon asked, worried. "Sorry, a dog ran out in front of us."

"I'm okay," Mandey said, sitting up and putting her seat belt on. Her heart was racing. She rubbed her shoulder.

"Did you hit it?" Gayla asked.

"No, it got by," Shannon said.

"Whew," Gayla said.

They got back to the intersection with Crystal Beach Road and turned into the convenience store parking lot on the corner.

"What next?" Shannon asked the girls.

"Go back to the beach and see if he went back there?" Mandey suggested.

"What if he did go into the water?" Gayla asked, fretfully.

There was a knock on Shannon's window. "Hey, y'all. What are you doing here?"

There stood Charlie, sucking on a straw in an Icee cup.

"Charlie, get in here!" Gayla yelled, opening the door and practically dragging him into the van.

"Get out, get in. Can't you make up your mind?" Charlie asked, closing the door behind him.

They began to squabble. Mandey and Shannon looked at each other. Mandey shrugged. Shannon pulled the van out of the parking lot and drove back down to the beach.

Thirty minutes later, things were quiet again. Mandey and Shannon were once again in their bed in the back of the van, but the mood had evaporated.

"It's been fun, but I'm going to be glad to be back in our bed tomorrow night," Mandey said.

"Me, too," Shannon agreed. "A lot less interruptions."

87

The End of Their Beginning

The first Monday in June, Shannon took his general equivalency diploma examination. Now that he had a girlfriend who had graduated from high school with honors, he felt it was more necessary than ever to get his G.E.D. Even though Mandey helped him review all weekend, he wasn't sure he would pass. Once the test was over, he didn't think he had bombed out, but he wasn't confident that he had passed, either.

In the meantime, Joe had taken over as his mother's counsel. They were going to proceed with a "guilty but insane" plea. Shannon did not agree with it; he thought they should plead not guilty by reason of insanity and go through a trial. Joe said they were going to ask for seven years, and with time off for good behavior, she could be out in five. If she went through with a trial, she was likely to be found guilty and sent to prison for at least 15 years, rather than five-to-seven in a mental institution, where she could get therapy.

The second week of June was bittersweet. Shannon's mother's court date came, and he and Mandey sat there in the courtroom as the prosecution and defense presented their plea deal to the judge. Although Shannon had reached out to Annette and offered to come pick her up so she could attend, she declined. The judge sentenced Deborah Pawlowski to seven years in the state mental institution at Kerrville.

"I didn't even get a chance to say goodbye to her," he said as they drove home, silent tears streaming down his cheeks. He stared out the passenger window so Mandey couldn't see them.

Mandey reached over and squeezed his knee. "I know it's hard," she said. "I can't begin to know how you feel, but I know it's hard."

"I mean, I know she's not perfect, but she's still my mom."

"I know, sweetie. We'll drive out there to see her whenever we can."

Shannon nodded but didn't reply. Mandey turned on the radio with the volume low and let him be quiet.

The next day, the G.E.D. test results came in the mail. He saw the envelope laying on the bar when he got home from work. He tried to ignore it. He went into the bathroom and took a shower, trying to forget it was there. Finally, he figured it would be best to open it and get it over with.

He came into the bedroom where Mandey was doing her college algebra homework.

"Guess what?" he asked. "I passed!"

"Congratulations! I knew you could do it!" Mandey said, jumping up to hug him.

He unfolded his G.E.D. certificate and held it up.

"We can frame it and put it on the wall next to my diploma," Mandey told him, and kissed his cheek. "I am so proud of you."

"Jeez, what a relief," Shannon said. "Thanks so much for helping me."

"I helped you study a little, but you're the one who did it. It's your achievement," Mandey replied. "I think we should go to Monterey House for dinner to celebrate."

Shannon bent his head to kiss her, and she returned it, enthusiastically. He took her hand and brought it down low.

"Maybe we can celebrate a little right now?" he suggested.

Mandey smiled and they embraced. "Let the celebration begin," she said.

Printed in Great Britain
by Amazon